PLEASURE

VS

PAIN

Vol 2

LAKEISHA KING

Cover design by Rabia Amir

Illustration by Dwayne Jones

Layout by Daiana Morales

Disclaimer

Be advised this book contains violence, abuse, and explicit sexual content. Please read at your own discretion.

Table Of contents

Chapter 1

I woke up in the morning with no clothes on and lying in my bed with a slight headache. I sat up and felt something fall from my chest to the v- shape crevices between my thighs. I looked closely at the glimmering object and realized it was my gold chain Sénar had held captive. I could see Tyrell's name tangled in the chain-links as it lay on the top of my coochie. It was a horrifying reality that it would land on the very place that was supposed to be Tyrell's but had been ravished by Sénar. I felt a knot in my stomach as guilt came over me. I grabbed the chain holding it close to my heart and cried like a baby as I realized all the bad decisions I had made. I took my necklace and hid it under my mattress, where I thought it might be safe. My heart was racing, as my reality was starting to set in. *What was I going to tell Tyrell? How could I explain my necklace being broken? Was he going to believe me?* I was devastated as I badgered myself with questions; I did not know the answers to. My emotions were spinning in a whirlwind, and I felt like I was being flushed down the toilet. Feeling like I would drown, I quickly got up and grabbed some clothes to take a shower. In the shower, I tried to scrub off any lingering evidence of Sénar on my body. I scrubbed and scrubbed until I couldn't bear it anymore.

After I got out of the shower, I had to hold my head to keep from losing it; I felt like I would throw up. When the phone rang after not having heard it for weeks, my heart felt like it stopped beating. I ran downstairs, almost slipping from the momentum I accumulated as I ran down the steps.

I answered, "Hello?" Trying not to sound out of breath while my heart resumed beating and was now threatening to beat my chest open from suspense.

Tyrell responded, "Hey, Treasure."

I wanted to make sure I was not hallucinating by asking, "Tyrell?"

He quickly responded, "Who else would it be?"

I shook my head as I did not want the conversation to end up in an argument, so I tried to convince him by saying, "Nobody, Tyrell. I am just shocked to hear your voice, that's all." Feeling like I had already messed up, I tried to get the conversation back on a better note and asked, "How was your trip?"

He was quiet on the other end for a second before responding, "Come over, and I'll tell you all about it."

Sénar came down the stairs and glared at me when he saw me on the phone. I felt like a piece of crap, as I hung up the phone in a trance. Before I could even snap out of it, Sénar grabbed me. I closed my eyes as I literally felt like I would faint from being overwhelmed.

Sénar said, "You can do better than him."

I glared at him and instantly filled with rage when I asked, "Like who? You think you're better?" I pushed him off me and ran upstairs to grab my chain and put it in the pocket of my shorts. Sénar tried to stop me from going out the door, so that he could talk to me. I pushed him away and opened the front door to see Tyrell ready to knock. As I opened the door, Tyrell and Sénar locked eyes; I quickly tried to close the door to prevent an altercation. Tyrell looked different; he was taller, bigger, and had a look in his eyes that gave me chills. My eyes were all over him when I called his name, "Tyrell?"

He scanned my body before he spoke, "Hey Treasure. Are you busy?"

He acted like he didn't just call me. Both scared and confused, I responded, "No. I was on my way to your house."

Sénar snatched the door open, and mad dogged Tyrell before walking to his car. Tyrell appeared unbothered but still asked, "Your little boyfriend got a new car, huh?" His voice was deeper, and his speech was pressured. Before I could answer, he said, "Let's go!"

I followed behind him like a little puppy to his car while trying to gauge his emotions, but he avoided eye contact with me. We got in the car, and he pulled out of his driveway without saying a word. I was nervous but didn't want to show it, so I asked, "How was your trip?"

Trying to keep the conversation light. He responded, "It was cool." He stared at me to search my eyes then asked, "What did you do the whole time?"

I held my composure despite the tension in his voice and cautiously answered, "I went to summer school and the library a lot."

He gawked at me in a mocking way, "Oh yeah, is that right?"

I felt like he was being sarcastic, so I replied, "Yeah, that's right."

He sensed my agitation and then asked, "Why do you have an attitude?"

I didn't want to make him mad, so I let my attitude go and responded, "I don't have an attitude Tyrell, I just want you to be happy to see me like I am happy to see you." As if he was shocked, he asked, "You're happy to see me?"

I smiled at him genuinely, "Yes, I am happy to see you, looking all grown up and stuff," I said, blushing. He smiled for the first time since he came to my door to get me. I felt like I could relax a little bit.

Eyeing me as he scanned me up and down before he said, "Shoot, you lookin' kind of thick over there. What have you been eating?"

I was almost offended, then I thought about all the food I ate, and I guess I did put on a couple of pounds. I was feeling a little pressed in my shorts too. I laughed instead and replied, "Food. Sheesh, thanks, I guess."

We both laughed until he asked, "Is that it?" I felt uncomfortable again, and then I countered, "Damn, what else would it be? You put some weight on too. So, what have you been eating?"

He just sighed and ignored my question before he replied, "Anyway, speaking of food, do you want to get some tacos?"

My mood changed instantly. I eagerly answered, "Yeah, that sounds like a good idea." We pulled up to the taco truck, and we got out to order our food. Tyrell sarcastically asked, "What, you want six now?" I slapped his arm, immediately thinking how much bigger his arms were now. He looked at me, and our eyes filled with lust.

"How can I help you?" Our gaze interrupted by a rude Hispanic lady rushing us to take our order. Tyrell ordered twelve tacos instead of eleven, to be funny, but he ate the extra one. They were so good, that we didn't talk much while we ate.

We pulled up to the park and sat in the car for a minute before Tyrell asked, "You want to go for a walk?"

I thought about the extra pounds I had put on and shrugged my shoulders before answering, "Yeah, I guess I could use the exercise." We both laughed and got out. He came around to my side and grabbed me, pulling me close to him. I clung to him and waited for him to kiss me; in case he wasn't planning on it to avoid being rejected. He gazed deeply into my eyes and asked, "Do you still love me?"

I quickly answered, "Of course I do. I never stopped loving you, Tyrell." I thought this might be the time to bring up the necklace before he noticed it. I said, "Tyrell I wanted-" He kissed me and wrapped his arms around me. I melted in his arms, allowing him to caress me, not wanting him to let me go. He let me go to grab my hand and then we walked the path for runners while we held hands. I wrapped my other arm around his arm and listened to him tell me about his trip. He talked about the weather being so different from our sunny California weather and how it was overcast a lot, making him appreciate our hot summers.

He laughed and then said, "They love sandwiches, or should I say, submarine hoagies and hot dogs. Shit, I wanted some tacos or some Chinese food. It was not happening when I first got down there, but my cousin took me to some spots eventually."

I laughed because we both love our tacos. He talked about their accents and how they said he had one too, which had him chuckling to himself. I asked, "You didn't have a bunch of groupies out there, did you?"

He smirked at me, then he quickly responded, "Not like you do." I rolled my eyes and realized I set myself up for that comment. We found some tables under a gazebo, and I sat on one of the tables. I looked at him, wondering if he missed me like I missed him, despite my weeks of misery and passion. He looked like he was wondering the same thing as he stood in front of me. He softened up a bit and reassured me by saying, "There were a lot of girls, but none of them were as fine as you." He kissed me passionately and rubbed his hand down the side of my face and neck. He stopped kissing me, and I could see his facial expression change.

He asked, "Where's your chain?"

I looked down as I nervously pulled it out of my back pocket. I took a deep breath to prepare myself to be ridiculed for whatever lie I chose to tell, to explain the situation. Before I could say anything, he asked, "Why isn't it on your neck?"

I opened my hand slowly to reveal the broken chain links to my necklace and then said, "I broke it when you rejected me and didn't call me for weeks. I thought you didn't love me anymore. I was hurt and angry." I looked down as I unwillingly started to cry; the tears streamed down my face. I was ashamed of how it really broke and that I had to lie about it with a mixture of my real emotions. He was angry but remained calm, I continued to try and console him with my apologies, "I am so sorry Tyrell, I regretted break-"

He snatched the chain out of my hand and barked, "Look, baby girl, I love you. You are special to me, but I don't want my heart to end up like this damn chain!" I heard every word he said, but I still felt anger surpass my guilt.

I asked, "Well, does that mean you can just break mine whenever you want?"

Now we were both upset and just glared at one another until he answered, "No, but damn Treasure, I need to know you are mine. All mine. That nig-"

I grabbed him and kissed him. I wanted him to know that I loved him and missed him. He pushed me off of him, gently enough to not hurt me but hard enough to not let me continue to kiss him. Tyrell confessed, "Damn Treasure, you're driving me crazy! I just don't know what to do with your ass!"

He sat next to me on the table and put his face in his hands. He then looked at the chain in his hand and maneuvered the broken chain links that surrounded his name. I could tell his feelings were hurt. I grabbed his arm and laid my head on it, feeling sorry for the both of us as we were both so emotionally impaired at the moment; for different reasons. I said, "I am so sorry, Tyrell. I love you so much. It hurts me when you just give up on us and leave me hanging. I never know what you feel until you're already mad. Then you just shut me –"

He cut me off and yelled, "Don't make it seem like it's all me! Your ass is not innocent!"

I looked at him, debating if I wanted to argue my innocence at a time like this or salvage what was left of our relationship. I chose to salvage what was left and pleaded with him, "Tyrell look, we made it through this year, and it was crazy. Let's make next year the bomb! Let's not let anything break our bond or trust for each other. We need to be confident in each other. Please, I need you, Tyrell."

He dropped his head in silence and then spoke, "Look, I just got home. I need to square away a couple of things, but I wanted to come to see you first. I need to prepare myself for the next school year and think hard, but I think we will get through this." He stood up and took a deep breath, and I got up to hug him. He held me tight in his arms and kissed me on the forehead. "You're my Treasure, no matter what, and now I have more to love." He squeezed my booty and laughed as I playfully pushed him away. He joked, "Jump on my back, and I'll give you a piggyback ride."

I laughed at his smart-ass joke and then jumped on his back, kissing his face as he carried me to the car. We drove back to the house and pulled up to see Sénar and London outside of the house, arguing. Tyrell rolled his eyes and parked the car. Not wanting to return to my captivity, I asked, "Well, can we watch TV and chill for a while before I go back to my hell hole of a house?"

He looked at me and shook his head, rubbing his waves of hair forward in frustration before he answered, "My mom is really tripping right now, ever since that day I left for Jersey. I must square away some stuff first, but maybe tomorrow we will get together. I have to unpack and get situated; we will see."

I was disappointed; I asked, "Well, can I call you?"

He just looked at me then said, "If I can, I'll call you, but if not, we will talk tomorrow."

I was devastated, not only did I have to win Tyrell's heart back, I had to try to get back in good standing with his mom. She was not happy to see us arguing that day, especially after believing our lies the day I broke my arm. I was really lost, not knowing where things would end up, and all I could do was believe him that we would get through this. I got out of the car, and he met me on my side as I tried to hold back my tears. He hugged me and kissed me before going inside, and I reluctantly walked back across the street to my house. I avoided looking at Sénar as I know he was watching me and Tyrell as we hugged and kissed. I heard London refer to me as a bitch. I ignored them both as I went inside with no chain, no confidence, and not knowing if my relationship with Tyrell was broken like my chain.

I laid in my bed to cry as I felt the vacant area of where my chain once lay on my neck. I wondered if Tyrell would ever want to give me back something I had allowed to be destroyed. My guilt made me feel like I didn't even deserve it. I was lost; my heart barely felt like it had a heartbeat left. I wanted to write, but I couldn't stop crying. I smelled food, but I didn't bother to eat or see what was being cooked. I didn't even shower, I just stayed in my room and cried until the next morning.

Barely sleeping, I could hear Sénar moving around through my door. I wanted to tell him all of this was all his fault. I wanted to blame him for my relationship failing and for what he did to my chain, but what would that solve? I tried to go back to sleep but I was so preoccupied with my thoughts, I just lay there torturing myself with questions, which answers I didn't have. My door opened, I looked to see who it was and saw Sénar. I avoided looking awake and closed my eyes wishing him away. Desperately wondering: *why out of all homes did him and Ken have to come to ours? Was there no other single mother and daughter that deserved this more than we did? How? Why?* He just closed the door and left. I cried until I fell back asleep. I woke up to Cassidy throwing her stuff on the floor and jumping onto her bed. She was a little frazzled and didn't appear to be in a good mood, so I guess that made two of us.

She looked over at me to ask, "Treasure what's wrong with you?"

I looked back at her to say, "I was about to ask you the same thing."

Cassidy sighed then said, "Sabrina's ass is dumb as hell. That's my sister, but damn she is really dumb."

I stared at her as if to say, *"Duh"*. I then replied, "I already know that....so that's why you're mad?"

She looked at me with a funky attitude before she responded, "Never mind. Don't be so quick to judge. What's wrong with you?"

I was hesitant now that she was withholding her real reason why she was mad when I answered, "I just wish me, and Tyrell were doing better that's all."

She scanned me with her eyes to search for truthfulness before she asked, "Oh, is that why you don't have that pretty chain around your neck?"

I was quick to correct her, "No, that's not why. It just broke."

She quickly asked, "How?"

I regretted telling her instantly. I just shook my head and then lied, "I broke it Cassidy."

She laughed at me before responding, "Girl, please. How?"

I had to think quick before I answered, "I pulled it off my neck because I was mad."

She stared at me like I was trying to play her and then replied, "Yeah right! How did it really break?"

I jumped at the sound of Sénar's voice calling my name through the door. Annoyed, I answered, "What?"

She looked at me and sat up straight on her bed. Sénar said, "Come here really quick."

I went to the door to ask, "What do you want Sénar?"

He raised his eyebrow and smiled; I rolled my eyes impatiently at him. He asked, "You wanna smoke?"

Irritated already with my situation, I answered, "No, I don't want to smoke."

I said it as if I didn't do such things. Cassidy interrupted, "I heard smoke. Shoot, I want to smoke!"

I tried not to roll my eyes in the back of my head when Cassidy said, "Girl, stop acting brand new. I have smoked with your ass before."

We all went downstairs to the backyard. Sénar lit it, then passed it to Cassidy and then she passed it to me. I gave it back to Sénar to hit it and Cassidy asked, "What are you cooking Sénar?"

He started cheesing and then replied, "Pops and Carmel will be here in a little while, so I'm frying chicken. Yo' ass ain't getting none anyway."

She laughed and said, "Yeah right. What, it's just for you and Treasure?"

I sighed and rolled my eyes at her. Cassidy hit the blunt twice and passed it to me before responding, "Oh no! I don't wanna make you mad because Treasure, you're like the hulk when you are mad!"

She started laughing uncontrollably. I hit the marijuana filled cigar and hoped it would make me like her jokes more because at this point, I was getting irritated.

Sénar asked, "What the hell are you talking about Cassidy?"

She was still laughing when she answered, "This girl talking about, she broke her chain because she was mad."

Sénar laughed dryly while Cassidy laughed hysterically. I was so angry and embarrassed. With an attitude, I asked, "What's so funny about that?"

She tried to pull herself together when she saw that my mood had changed, but still she inquired, "Girl, now, you did not break that chain. Who really broke it?"

I wanted to punch Cassidy square in her mouth; she was really pushing it.

Sénar asked, "Why is your ass worried about it?"

Cassidy smacked her lips at Sénar and said, "I'm not talking to you, Sénar." She put her attention back on me, "Yeah, Treasure probably broke it just like she tripped and broke her arm, huh?"

I was furious with her and told her, "Well, you're just as dumb as you said your sister was." She rolled her eyes at me and Sénar tried to change the subject back to Sabrina.

He asked, "Well, what did you and your fast ass sister do the whole time?"

She looked at Sénar with an attitude of her own and replied, "Boy you got your nerves. It was wack, we couldn't do anything because her ass might be knocked up."

Sénar was irritated when he asked, "What! Pregnant by who?"

Cassidy shrugged her shoulders and answered, "I don't know. She wouldn't tell me, so we probably know him."

Sénar shook his head in disappointment and I kept my comments to myself. Cassidy assumed I was judging by not saying anything then accused, "Treasure, don't be judging. Your ass is not innocent!"

She was on my nerves and was the second person who informed me of my lack of innocence today. I quickly responded, "Wow, I didn't even say anything. You need to calm down."

Sénar chimed in, "Damn Cassidy, you are trippin'!"

Cassidy retorted, "Shut up Sénar!" She put her focus back on me to ask, "Your weird ass boyfriend Tyrell probably broke the chain, huh?"

Cassidy was still laughing at me when I responded, "My man is not weird, and he did not break it, so you need to shut your damn mouth!"

Sénar was annoyed with both of us and suggested, "Why don't y'all both shut the hell up?"

she replied, "Boy, you shut your ass up! Your crazy ass probably broke that shit!"

Sénar was now uneasy when he complained, "We are supposed to be chilling. Not arguing about stupid shit!"

Cassidy rudely ignored his complaint when she said, "Whatever, I'm hungry."

She then went inside the house leaving me and Sénar outside. Cassidy sat at the kitchen nook to wait for Sénar to go inside. I was beyond irritated and wanted to run to my room.

Sénar said, "Hell nah, y'all can both help instead of running your mouths."

Cassidy responded, "Boy please, I am here for moral support, y'all can do it, I'll just watch."

She had her hand under her chin and looking at us. I sighed out of irritation with her. Sénar responded, "Well then watch, and shut up while you do it because don't nobody want to hear all that other shit. You are acting like we are on the *Ricki Lake* show or something."

Cassidy replied, "Boy, shut up!"

Sénar ignored her and said, "Treasure, here's the potatoes."

She watched as he passed me a bowl with the potatoes in it. I washed them and cut them how he taught me. Cassidy smiled and sarcastically said, "Oh shiznit, this is the Chef Sénar and Treasure show! Oh, I ain't ever seen this show!"

I had enough of her mouth and replied, "Well, I guess we can watch your sister on the *Maury Povich* show next."

Sénar and Cassidy both gave me a look to insinuate I had went too far. Cassidy replied, "Sénar, you better get your girl Treasure. She -"

I cut her off to say, "I am not his girl, and you talk too damn much! Your mouth keeps running, I almost want to pop your ass in it!"

Sénar yelled, "Both of y'all need to shut the hell up!"

The front door opened as we all argued. Ken came in the kitchen and asked, "What the hell is going on in here?"

My mom came in behind him. Everyone was quietly mad dogging each other. Ken looked at all of us and again asked, "Oh, why are you guys quiet now? It sounded like the *Jerry Springer* show up in here a second ago. Y'all need to calm y'all asses down."

Sénar dropped the first piece of chicken in the fryer and continued to prepare the rest of the chicken for frying. Ken smirked when he saw me cutting potatoes, and my mom said hi to all of us before they went upstairs to get settled in. The aroma of chicken filled the air and loosened the tension a little bit.

Cassidy said, "I was just playing, dang. I'm about to go shower real quick, I'll be back."

I ignored her pathetic attempt to apologize and Sénar replied, "Whatever man. I'm not smoking with your ass no more, if you going to be acting like that. You messed my high up, shoot!"

She smacked her lips and went upstairs. She wasn't even up the stairs all the way when Sénar asked, "What did you tell Cassidy?"

I looked at him like he was stupid and asked, "Nothing. Why?"

He said, "Don't play dumb Treasure. Why was she pressing you so hard about the chain anyway?"

I was mad all over again when I replied, "None of your damn business. This is all your fault!"

He asked, "Where is it anyway?"

I felt like I would cry if I had to tell the truth. So, I lashed out at him instead, "That's really none of your business! I don't know why you care so much either!"

He smiled sadistically before he answered, "I don't know. So, if you fix it, I can break it the same way."

He reached out to touch my breast and I slapped is hand away before I tried to leave. He pulled me to him from behind and smelled my hair while he embraced me. He said, "Damn, you smell so good. Don't leave, the food is almost done. Oh, and you didn't finish the salad."

He released me to start his second batch of chicken while I reluctantly worked on the salad, leaving the tomatoes for him to cut. I said in a low voice, "Neither one of us will probably ever see that chain again."

Ken came down before my mom and Cassidy, he appeared to be in a good mood. He said, "Ooh wee, boy you got it smelling good up in here." He looked at me sideways and then asked, "Oh, I see you in there helping today, huh? I also see, you may have learned a little something." Sénar looked uncomfortable, and I was still agitated. Ken sat at the table and watched me as I prepared the salad. He got comfortable in his chair before he said, "Damn Treasure, you put a little bit of weight on. What have you been eating? Oh, I know ol' Sénar here been feeding you, huh?"

Sénar was nervous and pleaded, "Pops, come on man."

Ken responded, "Sénar shut your ass up, and hurry up with the food. I am not talking to you." Ken stared at me, while waiting on my response.

I wanted to snap at him, but I knew that was not a good idea. So, I just replied, "Yep, I like food. A lot." At least I didn't have to lie when I answered.

He laughed and then asked, "Is that right?" Sénar and I were both uncomfortable now.

Sénar pleaded, "Pops?"

Ken responded, "What? I'm just saying, she in here cutting up salad and looking thick ass fuck. She ain't just been eating no damn salad."

My mom and Cassidy came down at the same time. I was never so happy to see them because Ken was really on one tonight. Cassidy hugged her dad and asked him how his trip went.

Ken replied, "It was alright." He started laughing and looked at my mom playfully.

My mom purred, "Whatever Ken, you know we had a good time." She was smiling from ear to ear.

Ken said, "Yeah, and more bathroom trips than ever." They both laughed. Ken yelled, "Boy, y'all hurry up in there! Babe get me a beer and a plate."

My mom came in the kitchen and said, "Hey Treasure. You look nice today." She was smiling as she grabbed plates and a beer for Ken. She gave Ken his beer and came back in the kitchen to make their plates.

"Oh Sénar, the food looks great as always. Boy, you can really cook, huh?" My mom said this smiling at Sénar and marveling at the presentation of his food.

Sénar beamed a bright smile and replied, "Chef Sénar is at your service, madam."

He then bowed his head and led her to the chicken. My mom giggled before she made their plates. Sénar handed me a plate and I handed it to Cassidy quickly, making her flinch back. Sénar laughed while handing me another plate but Cassidy smacked her lips in embarrassment. Ken watched us all interact in the kitchen as my mom handed him his plate. We made our plates and then sat down at the table. My mom said a quick prayer to give thanks for the food and their safe travels.

Ken asked, "What did y'all do this whole time?"

Sénar looked uncomfortable because his dad was not done prying, but he answered anyway, "I worked a lot and went to the city to go school shopping; it was cool, I got to see Louie too."

Ken stared at Sénar and then smirked while eyeing me next, but still asked Cassidy, "What about you?"

She answered, "I went to visit Sabrina. We chilled and went school shopping. It was cool, daddy."

Ken put his attention on me, and his tone changed a bit when he asked, "Well, Treasure, what did you do?"

I finished chewing my food before I answered, since everyone was so attentive on my answer. "I went to summer school; wrote a play and I went to LA to school shop with Sénar." I kept it short, in hopes he would leave me alone after.

Ken responded, "Oh nice. I see you learned something in summer school and at home. With all that time alone y'all didn't play a little game of Sénar says?"

Ken drank his beer, and everyone responded differently to his question. My mom slapped his arm playfully, Cassidy chuckled while trying not to be too obvious, and Sénar almost choked on his food. I turned my fury into humor when I replied, "Oh yeah, we did."

I kept eating, Cassidy's mouth fell open, my mom looked at me like I was crazy, and Ken had a sadistic smile on his face. Sénar was blank with emotions and waiting on me to continue. I then said, "That's how he taught me how he likes……his fries cut." Sénar looked like he was holding his breath until I spoke again. I stuck a fry in my mouth and Sénar almost looked relieved with everyone else, until I added, "He just hasn't taught me how to make dessert yet." Sénar almost choked on his spit, then the phone rang. I nearly flipped the table over when I jumped up to run and answer the phone.

I answered it and it was Tyrell. He whispered, "Hey Treasure, can you come over?"

I whispered back when I replied, "I am having dinner, but I'll come over after. I just can't stay out that late." I hurried off the phone and went to finish my food.

When I sat down Ken asked, "Damn, you got two teachers?" I had enough. I slammed my fork down on my plate and asked, "Can I be excused?"

Sénar seemed to be nervous and more agitated now. My mom answered, "Treasure, he's just playing baby. Yeah, you can be excused but don't be out too late."

I looked at Ken and said, "Maybe, you should be more worried about Sabrina, instead of me."

I washed my plate and Ken asked Cassidy about Sabrina. Sénar got up to give me the coldest stare I ever seen him have. When I was done washing my plate, I ran across the street to Tyrell's house.

Tyrell answered the door with basketball shorts on and no shirt. I smiled instantly as it was nice to see him that way. He smiled back at me and led me to his room. When we got into his room, he kissed me and fondled my breast. I was so excited that he came around and was not still in his feelings. He laid me down on his bed and kissed me passionately.

He stared me in my eyes to ask, "Do you still love me?"

I wrapped my legs around him and kissed him on his lips before I answered, "Yes, I love you, Tyrell Clark."

He kissed me back even more passionately, then took his chain with my name on it off to put it on my neck, "You can wear this one for now. It's thicker, so you can't break this one." He must have added gold to it because it was now two tone with my name in gold.

He fastened it on my neck and walked me downstairs before his parents got back. We kissed each other goodnight, and I went home. When I got inside, Sénar was watching TV on the couch. I pretended like I didn't see him and ran up the stairs but Sénar damn near dragged me back down by my shirt.

I snatched my shirt back, "Stop! What do you want?"

He looked at me like I was stupid when he answered, "You already know what I want. What the hell is wrong with you? Why did you dry snitch on us like that?"

I looked at him in a confused state when I asked, "What are you talking about?"

He rolled his eyes as he appeared to be agitated that he had to explain, "Treasure, you basically told on Sabrina and me, without telling on us all the way."

I looked at him blankly and then replied, "I don't know what you are talking about. Do you want me to tell on you for real? If not, then leave me alone!"

I tried to run to my room, but he grabbed me by my shirt before I could reach it and then pulled me back to him. He turned me around and pushed my back against the wall.

He got really close to my face when he said, "Treasure, stop playing victim, you know you liked that shit too." His eyes darted to the chain on my chest with my name dangling from it, instead of Tyrell's name. He rubbed his hand over it, and I slapped his hand away. He smiled deviously before he said, "I like this one better. I won't break that one." He left me in the hallway with my heart beating like a drummer boy was playing inside of me. I went to my room, and Cassidy was yapping her gums on the phone. She rolled her eyes at me as I laid down. She called my name, but I ignored her and went to sleep.

The next morning, I called Tyrell, and he answered. I asked, "So, what are you doing today?"

Tyrell answered, "I have to go somewhere with my dad later, but you can come over for a bit if you want."

I smelled breakfast, so I told him, "I will be over right after I eat something." After we hung up, I went to the kitchen where Sénar was making breakfast. He had a sports tank top on and his basketball shorts.

He glanced at me and asked, "What do you want?" I rolled my eyes and looked in the pan to see eggs with ham, cheese, and green onion for breakfast burritos. I grabbed a burrito shell and warmed it up in the microwave, then put it out in front of him for him to serve me.

Sénar looked at me like I was crazy before he said, "No, grab a plate, Treasure." I was irritated, but I grabbed a plate anyway. He put the eggs in the shell for me and put extra cheese on it. I said thanks but wondered, *did he want to fatten me up, so I would be a butterball and then no one would want me?*

I was lost in my thoughts when Sénar asked, "What are you thinking about Treasure?"

I looked at him while he sat down with his plate and two cups of juice. I answered, "Nothing really.... but do you think I gained weight?"

Sénar laughed and answered, "Yeah, you put a few pounds on, but it's in all the right places."

I rolled my eyes at him and contemplated whether I should finish my burrito, but the thought didn't last long. I asked, "Are one of those juices for me?"

He answered, "Hell nah, go get your own."

He laughed but then handed me one. He was such a goof sometimes, and he really got on my nerves. I finished my juice, washed my dish, and ran out of the house to see Tyrell. When I got there, he wasn't dressed yet; I was secretly excited, hoping he would put on a show for me. I watched TV while he took a shower. It was my lucky day; Tyrell came out the shower in a towel wrapped around his waist and his chocolate skin glistening with droplets of water clinging to it. I was trying to keep myself calm as I wanted to jump on him and have my way with him. He cheesed like he was posing for a picture. He was picking out an outfit when I got up and hugged him from behind. He turned around and kissed me, and I melted in his arms. I could feel his member growing threw his towel. I wanted to rip his towel off when we heard footsteps.

Tyrell's mom knocked on his door and said, "Tyrell, your father called, and he's going to be here any minute, so be ready."

Tyrell replied, "Alright, mom."

She hesitated before asking, "Is someone here?"

He put his hand to his lips to shush me as he answered, "No mom, I'm just getting ready."

His mom responded, "Ok," before she went to her room.

Tyrell pushed me off him and grabbed an outfit to get dressed. He took his towel off, but his back was facing me, and I must say, I was so disappointed. He turned around to kiss me on the forehead and then said, "Treasure, I'll call you later or tomorrow."

I was beyond disappointed that it seemed like we were hiding when we never had to hide before. He snuck me out of the house quickly. I went home frustrated, horny, and confused. To make matters worse, I walked in to see Sénar was with London. They were laid up on the couch watching TV, which meant I could not even watch TV. I was super annoyed with the situation at Tyrell's house and didn't even want to entertain the idea of having to deal with Cassidy. So, I went into the living room anyways and sat on the couch as if London and Sénar were not there.

Sénar was so shocked, he asked, "What are you doing Treasure?"

I smacked my lips at him and countered, "What does it look like Sénar, I am watching TV."

London rolled her eyes and said, "Come on, let's go to your room Sénar."

I glared at Sénar before I suggested, "Yeah Sénar, go to your room." I also said it to mimic London.

She looked at me like I was crazy, and I laughed in her face. London was so mad, along with Sénar's shock filled face, I thought, *I should give them another reason to leave.* I snatched the remote controller off the table and laid back on the couch, flipping through the channels for something I wanted to watch. Sénar was still shocked and still had not said anything, but London, on the other hand, was pissed.

She whined, "Sénar? Sénar? Sénar?"

Until he finally answered, "What?"

She was now frazzled and begged, "Come on, babe."

He looked at her and said, "Go to my room. I'll be there."

It was a demand, not a suggestion. London looked like she wanted to argue, but Sénar glared at her, silencing her before she left. Sénar stood over me as I lied on the couch and again asked, "Treasure, what are you doing?"

I played dumb before responding, "What? I'm watching TV."

He smiled mischievously and asked, "Oh, yeah?"

I smirked at him and replied, "Yeah."

He responded, "Don't start no shit, won't be no shit."

I ignored him and kept watching TV. He probably wished we were here alone, so he could do whatever he was thinking. Sénar grabbed his man stick while laughing and then said, "You play too much." I rolled my eyes at him and continued to watch TV. He reluctantly left to go join his girlfriend in his room. Sénar and London must have been having fun because they were up there so long, I fell asleep watching TV until I heard Cassidy ask, "Where's Sénar? Shoot, I'm hungry." Trying to come to my own conclusions, after just waking up, we heard footsteps coming down the stairs. London and Sénar came down the steps with her giggling and holding on to Sénar's arm like she would lose him if she let go.

Cassidy waved hesitantly, and London replied, "What's up, Cassidy."

She kissed Sénar before leaving and he kissed her back, but never took his eyes off me. Sénar laughed and asked, "Y'all silly asses is starving, huh?"

Cassidy said, "Heck yeah, what are we eating?"

Sénar answered, "I don't know, something easy like tacos. I'm tryna watch some TV and maybe have some dessert."

Cassidy was irritated with Sénar when she said, "Boy, don't nobody care about no damn dessert. We are talking about dinner, so get to work!"

Sénar replied, "Man, shut up Cassidy."

He walked into the kitchen with Cassidy following him. I stayed on the couch until I smelled the food. On the way to the kitchen I saw my mom and Ken come down, since they also smelled food. We all piled into the kitchen as Sénar finished up the food. Sénar saw me come in last and made eye contact with me, but I avoided his stare. He handed me a plate. I made my three tacos with all the fixings and then sat down to eat. Ken studied me as I ate, and he also observed Sénar watch me eat. I was so uncomfortable, I asked Cassidy if she wanted to go to the mall with me to break the awkward silence.

Surprised, she asked, "For what, and how are we going to get there?"

I responded, "I just wanted to get a few things. We can take the bus, even though I never rode one before."

She looked at me like I was crazy and said, "Girl, I don't do public transportation. People are crazy. If you find a way for us to go, I'm down."

Sénar shook his head and didn't offer at first, until Ken said, "Chef Sénar can take y'all."

Sénar didn't want to seem eager or encourage his dad to continue his probing. So, Sénar replied, "If y'all need a ride, I'll check my schedule."

He finished eating and got up to clean up. I went in after him to clean my plate. Before my mom left, she told me I had a doctor's appointment the next day. Sénar took the plates from my mom and washed them. Before I could leave, he handed them to me to dry and put away.

Mad, I asked, "Why are you always trying to give me something to do? Make Cassidy do something too."

Cassidy got up to hand me her plate and said, "Because I'm the oldest, lil' girl."

She left laughing as I handed Sénar her plate, but he did not take it; he just stared at me. After Ken noticed the tension between Sénar and I, he shook his head and grabbed himself a beer, then left. I was there washing Cassidy's plate and drying it while Sénar watched my every move. I was timing him because I knew he was up to something. When I finished putting the plates up, Sénar grabbed me from behind and smelled my hair while he embraced me.

He whispered, "Yummy, you smell so good. You still want to watch TV?"

I pushed him off me and declined. He laughed and then bragged, "That could have been you up there. All you had to do was ask?"

I smirked at him and replied, "No thanks, Sénar, but I do have something for you, just in case you get bored with London."

Sénar stared at me, then asked, "What?"

I said, "I'll be right back."

I went upstairs and grabbed Leah's number that was written inside of a heart on the paper she gave to me, so I could give it to him. When I got back downstairs, I said, "You can call your buddy and hang out with her."

He was annoyed with me but took the number anyway. Sénar again bragged, "Well, Leah is freaky, she might even let me call her Treasure from the back."

After he said it, he chin upped me before leaving me downstairs. He was too much; I swear, I could not figure him out, but I quickly decided not to waste my energy because I was still trying to figure Tyrell out. Tyrell changed, and his mom seemed to be more concerned with who and what he was doing now. I didn't want to overthink anything, but I was really annoyed with today. I was so tired; I just went to bed.

With less than two weeks of school break to go, I was anxious to have my days filled with something other than eating and playing mind games in this little cul-de-sac of a life I had. I actually considered getting a job in the next school year to keep me busy because I felt like I was losing my mind. I called Tyrell in the morning, only to hear he would be busy again today. It didn't bother me because I had a doctor's appointment anyway, to get a shot in my ass to not end up like Sabrina. So, I got dressed and just watched TV to avoid Cassidy's nosey ass until it was time to go.

My mom came down the stairs and summoned me to come with her. I got up to follow her out to the car. Once in the car, I was hoping she would put her Christian music on and leave me be, but she wanted to actually talk to me. Feeling a slight attitude coming on, I closed my eyes to discourage her and to encourage myself to remain sweet little Treasure.

She started the conversation out with her best shot; she asked, "So, what was the play about that you wrote?"

I wanted to tell her none of her business, but I answered, "It was a play about a girl and a bully that went on a talk show."

She laughed and then replied, "Oh, well, that was creative. I wish I was here to see it."

I laughed sarcastically and said, "Yeah right, mom."

She looked a little offended when she asked, "Yeah, right? What do you mean, Treasure?"

I cleared my throat and thought wisely about my answer. Instead I asked, "Oh, you would have come?"

She also thought wisely before she answered, "Yes, I would have if you had told me. I would have been there."

I wanted to be honest with her, but I didn't want to hurt her feelings. So, I settled for, "Maybe next time, mom."

She asked, "Did Sénar or Cassidy go?"

I answered, "Not Cassidy, but Sénar came, unexpectedly."

She smiled and said, "Oh, well, you know Sénar was going to come, that boy is so catering to you. I don't know why you're so mean to him. He cooks, he cleans, and I don't know what I would do without all the things he does around the house."

My eyeballs almost fell out of my head when I tried to roll them; I wanted to shatter her perfect imagery of Sénar with just one of the many stories of their mini vacation they left me on. But instead, I asked, "When did you start to admire Sénar so much?"

She smiled and said, "I've noticed a lot of growth in him; he has come a long way. I think he is trying to get his act together, so Treasure, why don't you just give him a break." I laughed hysterically in my head and almost told her what a pervert he could be sometimes. She added, "Plus, Chino was a nice boy too, he was just lazy as hell and the other girls, ugh, I don't have anything nice to say. Sénar is the only one I really care for; at least he helps me and is respectful now. So, I can't complain, and that boy can really cook." I was done hearing about all her lovely compliments toward Sénar.

I jealously replied, "That's nice mom. I'm glad you are so fond of him. I hope you think that highly of me one day."

She laughed and said, "Oh, Treasure, don't be jealous. You are growing up to be a fine young lady as well, just stay out of trouble and don't let Tyrell get you into any more trouble. I think you've learned more from Sénar than Tyrell. I saw you in there cutting up potatoes and preparing salad when we got back."

I was officially done with our conversation; she was glorifying a crazy ass little boy, who was ruining my life from the day he arrived. I asked, "Can you put some music on momma?"

She laughed, then answered, "Yeah, but first, why did you bring up Sabrina? Is there something we should know?"

I remember what Sénar said last night and shook my head no, but I still said, "Nothing new. It's just that she is the one y'all should have been worried about, not me."

She shook her head and replied, "Well, knowing her fast little tale, she probably should be going with us. See, that's why I wasn't taking no chances with you. Talking about you are not having sex and had a boyfriend for I don't know how long........"

I tuned her out and thought about what else she had going on in that confused little mind of hers. She was clearly losing her mind if she thought Sénar was a better kid than Tyrell, and now she was really on my last nerve. She called my name, "Treasure? Are you ignoring me? I asked you a question." I stared blankly at my mom like I did Leah when she was just running her mouth. She snapped, "Treasure, answer me!"

I snapped back, "Answer you about what?"

Unable to hide my irritation any longer, she looked at me like her feelings were hurt and turned her music on. I didn't know what she asked me, so I started to feel bad for tuning her out, but she had already moved back into her Lala Land before I could care. We went inside, and the doctor asked me if I had any concerns. I shook my head no and continued to daydream about what it would be like to have things back to normal with me and Tyrell. My mom was done with her attempts to make conversation, and I was glad about it. Whenever she did open her mouth, the content was never forewarned. Tyrell's car was gone when we got back, so I didn't bother to call him. I just went to my room to face the possibility of having to see Cassidy's face just long enough to get my clothes to take a bath. My phone rang and made a loud buzzing noise. Cassidy looked at me like I was crazy.

Knowing it could only be Sénar, I answered, "What?"

Sénar was taken aback when he asked, "Damn, girl. What's wrong with you?"

I felt bad for a second and left the room so I could have some privacy, since Cassidy was so nosey. I replied, "Sorry, what is it?"

Sénar said, "It's cool. Can you do me a favor?"

Feeling my attitude coming back, I said, "Oh gosh Sénar, it depends on what it is."

He was quiet for a second before he said, "I'll be home in a bit. Can you cut some onion and bell pepper for me, please? So, I can whip up the fajitas quickly after I shower. I'm starving and tired. Please?"

I smiled a little before I answered, "Ok, yeah, but don't complain how I cut them either. Or you can do it yourself."

He happily replied, "Thank you! I'll see you later, ma."

I shook my head and laughed too myself for being in such a crazy reality. I hung up to see Cassidy staring at me as she stuck her head into the hallway to ask, "When did you get a phone? Who was that?"

I eyed her with an attitude and said, "Damn girl, mind your business."

She rolled her eyes and waited for me to come back to the room. To avoid Cassidy, I should just go downstairs to do what Sénar asked me to do. I was going to turn, *"mind your damn business,"* into a song I swear, if I had to say it one more time this week. I was ready to go back to school already, with one more week to go; it seemed like an eternity. Before I could go downstairs, my mom came out of her room. She appeared upset but didn't say anything to me. To avoid her as well, I went back to my room to grab some clothes to take a shower. I heard my mom call my name from downstairs. I quickly threw my clothes down and ran down the steps to see what she wanted. My mom was sitting at the table in the kitchen with a glass and a bottle of wine.

She asked, "Do you hate me, Treasure?"

I was shocked by her question. I looked around the kitchen to make sure we were by ourselves. I sat down, "No, momma, I don't hate you. Why would you ask me that?"

She cried, "I feel like you do. Shit, I even think Ken hates me too. Sometimes I think the people I love the most, hate me more than I hate myself. I didn't even think that was possible. Just don't be a dumb ass like me, ok?"

I wanted to hug her, but she wasn't exactly the mother I once knew. I was almost afraid to tell her how I really felt. I just said, "Ok, momma. Don't worry, everything will be fine. What's wrong anyway?"

She looked at me and said, "You wouldn't understand, darling."

I got a little offended and asked, "Is that why you ignore me because you think I'm too stupid to understand anything. So, you just leave me to figure it all out on my own and then tell me not to end up like you?"

She scowled at me like I cursed at her and snapped back, "Look, little girl, I gave my best years to you and your sorry ass father! Don't you dare speak to me that way! You're just an ungrateful brat! Prancing around everywhere like you're so cute! When really, you are just as screwed up as me. So, don't be so quick to judge!"

She was in my face and smelled like sangria with a touch of liquor. I quickly realized this was a set up to take her frustration out on me. So, I shrugged my shoulders and replied, "Well, I'm sorry to hear that momma, I'll be sure to remember that for future references."

I walked past her and went to the fridge to pull out the bell peppers and onions. She stood there glaring at me, but I had enough drama in my life and refused to take the bait. I figured the least I could do was give her a break because I wanted to destroy her belief of being there for me in the last couple of years.

Instead, I said something that would hopefully make her happy, "Well, at least we are still standing, screwed up and all."

She looked hopeful for a second and said, "That a girl."

She sat back down and drank her wine while I rinsed and cut the bell peppers. Sénar came in to see my mom at the table and me cutting the bell pepper. He looked a tad bit worried until my mom saw him and happily greeted him, "Hey Sénar," she said it with a smile. He smiled nervously when he said, "Hey, Carmel."

He looked at me to see my expression, but I just rolled my eyes at their fondness of one another. My mom said, "Treasure's in there trying to steal your other job Sénar."

He laughed before he said, "Nah, I'm the chef; she's the helper."

My mom just laughed at him. Sénar then said, "Hey, Treasure."

I reluctantly replied, "Hey," without looking up at him. He came in to see me cutting the bell pepper and onion while flashing my favorite smile, but I was too bothered by my mom's words to acknowledge it.

He couldn't help but ask, "Can you cut them a little bit thinner, please?" He chin upped me before saying, "Ok ladies, I'll be back to put on my show, I gotta shower and get changed." He left as quickly as he had come. My mom just sat there and drank her wine. I was cutting the onion when Ken walked in the door. My stomach felt a twinge of intuition when I saw the anger in his face at the sight of my mother.

He smirked at me as I cut the onions, and I braced myself for whatever was about to take place next. He threw his stuff on the floor and walked over to my mom. Ken demanded, "Get up, we need to talk! Now!"

I jumped at the tone of his voice. When he noticed the look on my face, he said, "Hey there, Treasure."

He was sarcastic with his greeting. I cut the last of the onions and tried to leave, but he stopped me. He then asked, "How was your doctor's appointment?"

I was reluctant to answer but said, "It was fine, Ken."

I tried to walk out, but he stood in front of me then asked, "Well aren't you lucky, your mom was smart enough to take precautions with you, while my little girl ends up knocked up!"

I pushed past him; I had a bad feeling of where this was going. Ken snatched me back by my arm and then demanded, "Where are you going?"

My mom got up and begged, "Leave her alone Ken! I made her do it; she didn't even want to. She is not a fast ass like Sabrina! So, don't take your anger out on her, please."

He was enraged and still hadn't let me go. I was starting to panic as my mom pleaded with Ken, "Let her go!" She tried to take my arm away from Ken, but he shoved us both to the ground. I got up and ran upstairs, almost knocking Sénar down on my way up.

Worried, Sénar asked, "Treasure, what's wrong?"

Ken was dragging my mom upstairs against her will. Sénar appeared to turn into a scared little boy. He whimpered when he saw his father enraged, but he still stood in front of me as I cowered behind him.

Ken said, "Move boy!" Sénar stood there and refused to move.

My mom yelled, "Leave them alone, Ken. Your problem is with me! Leave them alone, please. Ken!"

He picked her up and put her over his shoulder then left Sénar and I on the stairs like two scared little children.

Sénar appeared more afraid than me when he begged, "Treasure, just go to bed, please. I'll bring you something to eat if you're hungry."

I was in shock, and food was the last thing on my mind. Looking at Sénar, I didn't know whether to run away from him or to hug him. I was confused and scared, feeling alone in a world of chaos. I didn't say anything, I ran to my room and slammed the door behind me. I pressed my eyes closed and drifted into a place where I felt safe enough to rest.

Chapter 2

I woke up the next morning smelling breakfast and was instantly reminded by a growling stomach that I did not eat before going to bed. I was scared to even move after Ken's explosive episode of anger towards all of us last night.

I laid in bed until Cassidy woke up and asked, "Treasure what happened last night?"

I was quiet because I didn't want to re-live the moment and if she was so concerned, she would have come out of her safe haven to see for herself. Cassidy smacked her lips and confessed, "Ugh, I hate when you do that."

Irritated already with her, I asked, "You hate when I do what Cassidy?"

She got up to answer me, "When you act like you're asleep or like you don't hear me when I'm talking to you."

I was quiet again to avoid saying anything that would cause an argument. She smacked her lips and said, "I'll just ask Sénar, knowing your slick ass mouth, you probably deserved it!"

I got up swiftly to reply, "I didn't deserve that crap, you stupid bitch! I'm tired of your mouth and your psycho ass family! All of you are crazy, except for Chino but he's probably a serial killer or something too!"

Cassidy looked at me like I had slapped her. I was ready to slap her if her next comment warranted it. She said, "Damn that was really cold. I guess you and your mom are perfect, huh? And we just ruined your perfect little world? Well, I am so sorry we ruined your world and enhanced ours. This is an upgrade for us compared to our life prior, so I guess somebody has to suffer."

She laughed in my face before trying to leave, but I pulled her hair and slammed her onto the ground. Cassidy yelped, "Get off me!"

I was about to wear her ass out when Sénar came in and snatched me up. Cassidy ran out of the room and into the bathroom.

Sénar asked, "What are you doing Treasure? You know my dad is already tripping man."

I had fury in my eyes when I replied, "I don't care, I am tired of Cassidy's mouth and your dad's too, quite frankly."

He closed the door behind him and offered, "Well, you can take it out on me however you want to, but don't take it out on Cassidy, please, damn." He was both sincere and serious when he continued to reason with me, "Look, my dad is upset about Sabrina being pregnant. So, don't go running your mouth or go after Cassidy because it will just give him more reason to trip on you." He grabbed me as I was ignoring him, he looked me in my eyes before he said, "Treasure listen man, I don't want you to get hurt. Just chill ma, he won't be mad forever. Just stay out of his way for now, ok?"

I defiantly nodded my head in a yeah motion to agree, but I didn't speak. I tried to leave but Sénar blocked the door while he stared at me waiting for a response. I sighed and quickly agreed, "Ok, dang! Move out of my way!"

I tried to leave again, Sénar bit his bottom lip to suppress whatever he was thinking and let me pass him. I waited for Cassidy to come out with Sénar standing behind me as she came out cautiously. When Cassidy saw me, she almost closed the door back until she saw that Sénar was behind me and it was safe to come out. I 'iffed at her and when she flinched back, Sénar immediately said, "Stop playing, Treasure."

Cassidy yelled, "You are the crazy one! Don't put your hands on me again!"

She was feeling herself, since she had a bodyguard present, but I didn't care, I was going to let her know I wasn't scared of either of them. I walked towards her to ask, "Or what Cassidy?"

She smacked her lips and turned to leave down the steps. I wanted to jump on her back when Sénar pulled me into the bathroom with him. He put me on the counter and locked the door.

He asked, "Do you need an outlet, to let some of that frustration out?"

He rubbed my thighs while spreading my legs apart, forcing himself in between them. I squeezed my legs together and pushed him back then said, "Move, I have a boyfriend for that."

He laughed and said, "Oh well, he must not be doing a good job."

I pushed him off me but only because he let me. He looked out the door, when he saw it was clear he left me in the bathroom. I brushed my teeth and rinsed my face before going downstairs. I left my pajama pants and T-shirt on and went to see what was cooking. My mom was making her famous breakfast and appeared to be in a good mood. Me and Sénar were both confused when my mom asked, "Sénar, could you do me a favor?"

He looked at me before he answered her, "Yeah Carmel, what's that?"

She turned around to look at us, Cassidy was sitting on the other side of Sénar when my mom ignored her presence to ask, "Can you organize the garage for me? Treasure can help you clean it and sort stuff out. I could barely move around in there this morning."

Not only did she pretend like Ken didn't try to rip us to shreds last night, she volunteered my services that I did not agree to. I rolled my eyes and smacked my lips then said, "I might have something to do."

Ken came in unannounced and startled me when he opened his mouth to say, "You are going to do whatever your mom tells you to do."

Ken gave me instructions as he was feeling my mom up from behind and smelling her hair. He then said, "Hey suga."

She turned around and kissed him like they were on a movie screen. I was super uncomfortable, Sénar was quiet, and Cassidy just sat there waiting for him to acknowledge her. When he was done with my mom he turned to Cassidy and said, "Good morning Cassidy, tell Sabrina to call me."

She looked down and responded, "Ok daddy."

He looked at Sénar and asked, "Boy, what do you need to do the garage?"

Sénar respectfully responded, "I need the shelves to organize the boxes. Six will probably do."

Ken nodded his head and said, "Alright then, I'll get it later." Ken glared at me before he said, "I don't care what you have planned, you can help Sénar get the garage cleaned before you go anywhere."

My mom gave him his plate and he walked to the table without waiting for my response. My response never came as I sat there in silence to conceal my hatred for Ken. Sénar got up to make his plate as my mom left the kitchen to sit with Ken and drink her coffee at the table. Cassidy got up to make her plate while I sat in Lala Land, wondering if I would ever leave this house with my mind and body intact.

Sénar came back from making his plate and then tapped my thigh before saying, "Treasure, go make a plate."

I snapped out of my trance and reluctantly walked pass Ken and my mom. Ken was still glaring at me, I grabbed a plate and noticed Sénar was pleading with me with his eyes to remain calm. We all ate quietly, except the giggling coming from my mom and Ken. Cassidy was done first; she threw her plate in the sink and ran upstairs. I was so irritated with her; she didn't clean up after herself or have to do anything for herself. My mom took Ken's plate to the sink and they went back upstairs. Sénar got up and ran some dish water as I picked at my food. He raked the food out the pots and set them aside. He looked at me and smiled sadistically before he said, "If you let me see them pretty titties, I'll wash the dishes."

I looked at him like he was stupid and responded, "No, jackass!"

He laughed and left the kitchen, leaving me there to do the dishes. I wanted to scream and fall on the floor to throw a tantrum, but I used my energy to wash the dishes instead. After I cleaned the kitchen, I called Tyrell. He answered and I happily responded, "Hey babe!"

Tyrell responded, "What's up Treasure?"

I was eager to see him, so I asked, "What are you doing today?"

He replied, "I have some stuff to do, but I'll call you when I get back. So, what are you about to do?"

I answered, "My mom wants us to clean the garage."

Tyrell laughed and responded, "Ok, I guess, whatever. I'll hit you up later."

I said goodbye and went to change my clothes. It was hot and muggy outside, so I put some shorts and a T-shirt on then went to the garage. I took my phone with me as I intended to tell Tyrell that I had a phone eventually. Sénar had already started when I walked in, he asked, "You wanna smoke before they come back from the store real quick?"

I wanted to say no, but it was a long week and I had to spend the next couple of hours with Sénar in this muggy garage, so I said, "I guess." We walked to the backyard to smoke, purposely not telling Cassidy's dumb ass.

While smoking in the backyard, once I was high, I asked, "Sénar, are you going to be like your dad?"

Sénar looked down before he answered, "Hell nah, I don't want to be like him. I pray every day that I don't end up like that. I know I do some dumb ass shit, but I don't want to be anything like him." He put the blunt out and waited for me to go inside before coming in behind me. He said, "Come on, let's clean up this mess."

When we got to the garage, he put the music on while I looked for somewhere to secure my phone. I wanted to be able to call Tyrell later from my cellphone, so the whole house would not have to know when he called me. When I turned around Sénar was already putting in work, but he was always very strategic in whatever task he had before him. It was almost genius, how he meticulously planned everything that he did. He caught me staring at him while I was deep in my thoughts, he asked, "What? Are you going to just stand there and admire from afar?" He licked his lips and flexed for me. I rolled my eyes at him and put my phone down on one of the boxes.

I folded my arms and said, "I am not picking up any boxes."

He sighed before he said, "Ok, well, all this shit can't be important. So, go through the boxes, sort out the important stuff and we'll set it aside away from the stuff that can be given away or thrown away."

I was almost irritated because it was one of the smartest things, I ever heard him say. Annoyed that he gave me a rather important and necessary task, I smacked my lips with attitude then started on the labeled boxes. There was so much crap, I was already starting to feel overwhelmed. It was bad enough that I was high, but all of this just seemed too tedious for me. Sénar was smart, he put all the labeled stuff where I was. He then put all the unlabeled boxes on the other side of the garage. After the area was clear of boxes, he swept and cleaned the dusty areas. I was only on my second box when I looked at Sénar he was dripping in sweat. It was hot and humid in the garage, so he opened the garage door for air. He was listening to music and had his game plan already in action. I looked through all the stuff confused at how I was supposed to know what my mom wanted and what she didn't? I opened a box that had pictures written on it and pulled some pictures of my mom out when she was younger. There were so many pictures, I sat down and looked at some of them.

My mom and I looked so much a like when she was younger with a few variances. Her skin tone was lighter than mine and she had the same voluptuous shape, but she was shorter. I wanted to see more, so I got up and looked through the rest of the pictures. She looked so young, happy, and vibrant in most of them. There was a picture of a tall dark skin young man in a football uniform. He was handsome and had a smile that looked so familiar. I continued to look through the pictures and saw him and my mom together, in love, holding a baby. The more I looked through the pictures the more I realized he was more than just a man; he was my father. He was in all our pictures until I was about three or four years old. After that my mom appeared sad and lonely as he wasn't in those pictures anymore. One of them she was holding me and looked pregnant. The more pictures I saw the more they revealed. My mom was pregnant for sure after me and I wondered where the other baby was. Sénar came up from behind and embraced me. I felt his sweat on my skin as he smelled my hair and held me gently in his embrace. I pushed back and squirmed out of his arms; he let me go without a fight.

He asked, "What are you looking at?"

I shrugged my shoulders and said, "I don't know." I put the pictures back in the box, closing it up to ask, "I should probably go through the boxes that don't have labels, huh?" He looked like he wanted to clap at my success in thinking things through with a realistic plan.

He responded, "Duh!"

I slapped his arm for his sarcasm and went to work on the other side of the garage. Sénar slapped my ass so hard, I stumbled forward knocking my phone over behind all the boxes. The music was blasting and Sénar resumed his task effortlessly while I tried to grab my phone. I bent over all the boxes and tried to reach for my phone as it had slid in between the crevices of the boxes and the wall. I reached and reached for it as I was only an inch or so away from getting it. I tried to grab for it with all my might, lifting one leg to give the extra length I needed to grab it. As I braced myself to prevent losing my balance, I could hear the music go lower as I continued to reach for my phone. Once I finally grabbed my phone, I lost my balance. When I fell, I landed on my ass and screamed when I bounced off the ground. I looked up to see Tyrell, Ken, and Sénar looking at me like I was a piece of meat on the grill. A box was falling but Sénar ran and pulled me off the ground before it fell on the top of my head. Tyrell and Ken observed Sénar's instinct and concern.

Ken spoke, "Damn Sénar, you are on point with the garage."

Ken was laughing as he went in his pocket to pull out some bills and handed them to Sénar. I walked towards Tyrell to greet him when Ken gave me a one-hundred-dollar bill and said, "Here, this is for the inspiration!"

He was smiling from ear to ear when he handed me the money and went inside as my mom had already went in. Both Tyrell and Sénar looked irritated with our current situation. Tyrell grabbed my hand and demanded, "Come on, I want to take you to get some stuff."

I didn't want to just leave, so I said to Sénar, "I'll go through the boxes when I get back or tomorrow."

Sénar shrugged his shoulders and kept working, but Tyrell pulled at my hand to hurry me along. Tyrell asked, "Why did you feel the need to tell that nigga what you are or aren't going to do?"

I took a deep breath before responding as we both got in the car because I already felt embarrassed. I replied, "My mom told me I had to help him. Tyrell stop, you're acting like I was at some strange guy's house?"

He looked at me with disgust and conviction when he replied, "Well, that's exactly what it feels like. Man, get out and go work on your garage, since you were putting on a show and I just happened to interrupt it."

Shocked at his entire comment, I responded, "I was just trying to reach my phone after it fell behind all those boxes."

Tyrell looked at me and asked, "What phone? You have a cellphone?"

I nodded my head yeah and quickly responded, "I just got it, not that long ago."

He smirked at me and asked, "Who got that for you and who pays the bill?"

I didn't think he would want to know all that and hadn't really thought it through. I was annoyed and a little flustered, but I responded, "Tyrell I got it for emergency purposes. I wanted to give you my number so you could call me wherever I was. Don't you have a cellphone that I don't have the number to?"

He looked frustrated when he said, "This is not about me Treasure."

I folded my arms and acted like he never told me to get out. Tyrell was highly agitated when he said, "Whatever, let's go to the mall and get some clothes that fit that fat ass you got now."

I pouted as it did not sound like a compliment but a problem rather, giving me the feeling that I was in trouble. He appeared agitated with me and I just sat quietly and put my seatbelt on as he drove off aggressively. I could not look at either of them, I knew Sénar was watching and I could feel Tyrell staring a hole into me. I was miserable for a second, then I realized Tyrell was still staring at me.

He asked, "Do you like your big brother more than you like me?"

I stared at him like he was stupid and answered, "Sénar is not my brother, or boyfriend, or anything other than Ken's son. Why do you care so much about him? I don't want to be with him, I want to be with you."

He smirked at me in disbelief and replied, "Yeah right, that dude sure doesn't feel the same way. He over there playing super man and shit. He sure didn't let that box knock you upside your head."

I shook my head in frustration, knowing he had a point before I said, "Dang Tyrell, I can't be responsible for what Sénar does and feels, ok? I can only be responsible for what I do and feel. Besides I'm fat, remember? Nobody is even thinking about me. Sheesh, I can barely get you to pay attention to me."

He picked up speed when he confessed, "I'm tired of this shit man!"

I looked at him with an attitude and asked, "Tired of what?"

He shook his head, "Never-mind, come on."

He pulled into the parking lot and got out of the car. I got out reluctantly because I was super offended and annoyed with his jealousy. He took me to the Old Navy store and had me try on pants that didn't look too tight or revealing. He got me four pairs of jeans and a couple of T-shirts. He picked out a skirt that went to my ankles, but it was still cute and if he was trying to hide my butt it was not successful. We went to get something to eat in the food court and saw some of the kids from our school looking at us and talking. I tried to relax and forget about our conversation on the way over to the mall. He was becoming so mean and intolerant with me, especially with my situation at home.

I was in my thoughts when Tyrell asked, "What are you thinking about Treasure?"

I looked at him, careful not to say anything that would cause an argument. I hesitated before I replied, "I'm just thinking about why we have to hide all the time now and why we argue when we do get together. What happened?" He ignored my question.

He got up and said, "Let's go."

He then started to walk off without waiting for me and didn't even offer to help me with my bags. I held the bags and followed after him. He opened the door with his alarm fob. I put my stuff in the back and we drove back home. When we pulled up to the house, Tyrell said, "Call me tomorrow and give me your number."

Feeling like a little child who got in trouble, I ran home with my bags and went to my room. Cassidy was lying in her bed on the phone as always. I just ignored her existence. I went through my stuff putting my clothes away. I thought about, *why I put so much weight on and if it was really that much.* I was in my thoughts when I was startled by Sénar's voice, "Treasure, come here."

I sighed and put my pants in the drawer before opening the door and asked, "What, Sénar?"

I saw his face and he looked happy, instantly making me wonder why. He said, "Come here. Let me show you something." I smiled and followed him.

We went downstairs to the garage and he showed me the finished product of his work. I was impressed, it looked amazing. Everything seemed to sparkle, except for one corner. My facial expression changed when I asked, "What is all that?"

He smiled and said, "I'm glad you asked. Those are the unlabeled boxes."

I rolled my eyes and tried to leave but Sénar said, "I did all this work by myself, that's the least you could do, so I could finish."

I pouted because he was right, but I didn't want to. I whined, "I just got back. I can do it later."

Sénar was frustrated when he replied, "Man, I'll help you, but this is not my stuff or my pop's stuff. Plus, I don't want him tripping and the first thing he's going to ask about is this garage."

He was seriously trying to convince me without demanding me to do it. I rolled my eyes and started opening the boxes. I was scanning the contents and maneuvering things around when I thought, *a marker would be a great idea.* I looked up at Sénar and he was holding a sharpie marker in his hand, grinning at me. I rolled my eyes at him and went to get it from him cautiously, knowing he was always strategizing. I got to him and he gave it to me without doing anything dumb. Again, I was impressed until I felt a smack on my ass that literally sounded like a gun shot. I turned around to say something and he was already waiting for me laughing.

He makes me sick. Before I could say anything, he said, "Sorry. I won't do it again. I could not help myself. Come on, let's finish."

I wanted to slap the smile off his face, but I kept working instead. As I labeled them, he put them on the shelves he installed. Most of the stuff was art supplies my mom and I never used for the space we use to have. We were staying on task and almost done when Sénar asked, "Why do you like Tyrell?"

Feeling uncomfortable, I didn't want to answer, but I still replied, "It's none of your business. Why don't you like him?"

He shook his head and then answered, "I don't like him for a lot of reasons. But I'm not about to go into detail. I just don't like his grimy ass."

I folded my arms and replied, "Well, he's my boyfriend and that's something you should just except. I love him and want to be with him."

He shook his head again and said, "Well, whatever. Are you sure he feels the same way about you?"

I was offended and unsure for a moment, before replying, "Why are you worried about it anyway? Don't you have London to worry about? Why do you like her?"

He sighed and answered, "I don't like her, I am just with her because she's attractive, her dad gave me a job, and she gives good head. Hey, she keeps me out of trouble."

Appalled by his honesty, I answered, "That is so scandalous Sénar. Sheesh, I would hate to be London."

He smirked at me, making me think about Tyrell and wonder for a second. I quickly started going through the boxes again, ignoring my insecurities and Sénar. I continued labeling the boxes and Sénar put all the boxes up neatly with the labels showing. He looked at me and said, "Good job Treasure. You did all that work looking pretty."

I rolled my eyes and asked, "What are you going to do with this stuff?" I referred to the boxes on the ground that were filled with miscellaneous contents that were not worth labeling.

He shrugged his shoulders and said, "Let's throw it away."

I looked at him like he was crazy and went through the stuff again. He walked up to me then pulled me up and then said, "I know who I do like, what I like, and that's you, Treasure." I was uncomfortable but I tried not to show it.

I stared at him before I replied, "I can't do anything about that. I don't know why you like me. You should not, it's inapp-"

He kissed me and squeezed me. I pushed him off me, my heart was beating so hard, both in my chest and in between my legs, where it was now moist. I took a deep breath and said, "Sénar I told you, I have a boyfriend, and this is not normal!"

He laughed and said, "You are funny, that's one of the reasons why I like you."

He winked at me and opened the garage. He picked the boxes up to throw them away as I walked towards the opening of the garage to ask, "So, you're just going to throw the stuff away?"

He looked at me and then answered, "Yeah."

I crossed my arms and looked across the street to Tyrell's house. I noticed his car was not there and thought about where he could be. Sénar saw me in my thoughts and continued throwing away the rest of the stuff. When he was done, Sénar stood there with me and said, "He doesn't feel the way about you that I do. That's for sure." Sénar closed the garage door leaving me to ponder again in my thoughts.

I shrugged my shoulders and thought, *he could have gone to the store; his car not being there means nothing.* I glared at him while the feeling of irritation overcame me and I said, "You don't know that. You need to worry about your girlfriend and leave me alone, Sénar."

He put his hands up, "Fine."

We both came out of the garage irritated with one another, after doing all that work and having an unnecessary conversation. We came inside and Sénar washed his hands in the sink. He gave me a look as if I needed to do the same. I reluctantly got up and washed my hands.

Sénar said, "Now, you can sit pretty. Your job is already done in here."

He pulled out the veggies that I sliced for the fajitas we never had. He must have put them in zip lock bags last night. I sat on the counter and watched him prepare dinner until Ken came into the kitchen. He stood in front of me as I sat on the counter, making me nervous the closer he got to me.

Ken glared at me before asking, "I saw you leave with your little boyfriend. Did you finished helping in the garage like you were supposed to?"

I wanted to ignore him, but I knew he was looking for a reason to trip on me. I tried not to roll my eyes before answering, "Yeah, it's finished."

I had to scoot backwards on the counter to make more distance between Ken and I. Sénar shook his head as he cooked, and Ken went to the garage to check for himself. Sénar raised his eyebrow at me and said, "See, I told you." My mom came down and I jumped off the counter.

"Smells good in here," she said before going to the garage where Ken was. They came out smiling before my mom exclaimed, "Sénar and Treasure! You guys did an amazing job. Sénar, the organization of the shelves are impeccable." She was so impressed that Ken got a little jealous.

He said, "Alright, woman get me a plate and a beer."

Cassidy came down the stairs to eat, she spoke to Sénar and ignored me. Everyone ate without really talking because everyone seemed to be consumed by their own thoughts. Cassidy was the first one done, throwing her plate in the sink. My mom and Ken did the same as they dispersed, leaving us to clean up. I helped clean up and went to check out the window to see if Tyrell was back.

Sénar sat on the couch and said, "His ass ain't there."

I looked at him with an attitude and said, "Shut up!" I started to leave while Sénar started to watch TV.

He asked, "You don't want to watch some TV with me?"

I shook my head no and he replied, "Damn you cold. So, you rather kick it with Cassidy, than me?"

I thought about it and once again he was right. I turned around to sit on the couch and said, "Don't make me regret staying down here."

He smirked at me while rolling his eyes then said, "Shut your ass up."

I sat on the other couch and we watched *Fresh Prince Of Bel Air* until I got sleepy. Sénar watched me as I lied back on the couch to get more comfortable. When I started dozing off Sénar got up and pulled me off the couch to say, "Don't fall asleep down here when my pops is here." I rubbed my eyes sleepily and nodded my head at him to say ok. He was so intense sometimes. I went upstairs got in my bed and went to sleep.

The next week went by so quickly. Tyrell put a two-week notice in at the movie theatre when he got back from Jersey. He worked his last couple of shifts and did whatever else, but he barely called me during the week. He also never gave me his number or asked for mine. Even at home the week zoomed past with Sénar working so many hours. School was starting soon along with the football season, so neither of them would be able to work. I watched TV to avoid Cassidy and she spent time with Nevaeh when she was bored enough. I read every book in my room and wrote a lot in my diary to pass time to keep myself busy. I woke up Saturday morning excited about this being the last weekend before school started back and I couldn't wait. This had been the longest summer ever for me, I almost went down memory lane until I heard the phone ring downstairs. I ran down to answer the phone and it was Tyrell telling me to come over.

I quickly got myself together and ran to Tyrell's house. He opened the door in his night clothes. I smiled at him because he looked so cute in his pajamas. He hugged me and kissed me before leading me up to his room. When we got inside his room, he told me how much he missed me. He was being so sweet; I didn't get the chance to be mad at him for not calling me that much this week. He kissed me and fondled me as I lay there and let him touch me all over. He got up to take a shower, leaving me annoyed that he didn't go further. I just laid there and watched TV until he was done. He came out the shower with a towel around his waist looking all sexy and stuff. I smiled as I had some very naughty thoughts going through my mind. He went to his closet to pick something to wear.

He looked at me when he asked, "I'm going to a party later, do you want to go?"

I wasn't sure I wanted to go to a party, but I asked, "What kind of party?"

He looked at me like I was annoying him by asking him that. Tyrell sighed before he answered, "It's at my boy's house. We are about to party before school and football season starts."

I shrugged my shoulders, then said, "I don't know."

He smirked at me and then said, "Don't worry, your little boyfriend will probably be there too."

He ruined my mood by his last comment. I whined, "He's not my boyfriend, I don't know why you have to say stuff like that Tyrell."

He just ignored my claim and asked, "Are you going or not?"

I contemplated whether or not I wanted to because I didn't want to pass up an opportunity to spend time with Tyrell, so I replied, "Yeah, I'll go."

He smiled at me and said, "Cool. Wear something cute, like that skirt I bought you."

He smiled at me seductively, making me excited all over again. I jumped up and hugged him and his towel fell off. My eyes widened with surprise as I took in the image of his naked chocolate body standing before me. With all his muscles, including his man stick that was slowly growing while I looked at it and the birthmark above it that resembled a star. I was aroused times ten thousand. I grabbed him around his neck and started kissing him. He kissed me back taking one of my hands to place it on his member to feel it continue to grow in my hand, making me even more excited. He walked me back to his bed when his mom knocked on the door and said, "Tyrell, I need you to do something for me in the garage."

He looked agitated and replied, "Ok, mom."

He was frustrated but not as frustrated as I was. It was like his mom had radar or something. He reluctantly got dressed, leaving me standing there all hot and bothered. He just threw on some basketball shorts and a T-shirt on to walk me downstairs. When we got to the door, he said, "I'll call you later when I'm ready to go."

He sent me on my marry way across the street to go home, annoyed with him and his mom that I did not get a piece of the action I desired with Tyrell. I went inside and Sénar was on his phone talking about the party while he was making something to eat. I wanted to be nosey and see what he was eating but I decided not to and started to go up the steps. Sénar got off the phone and called out to me, "Treasure, come here."

I had a mini tantrum before I responded, "What?" I was horny, hungry, and frustrated.

He asked, "You want a sandwich?" I didn't want to deal with Sénar at the moment because I was irresponsible with my ability to say no to pleasure. I just wanted to take a bath to release my frustration.

I answered, "No thanks," my stomach started to growl in disagreement.

Sénar was laughing when he said, "Stop lying. Did that nigga feed you?"

I was ready to snap as I was thinking of both food and my sexual deprivation when I answered, "No, why?"

He was laughing when he said, "Girl, come get this sandwich." He smiled sadistically and I rolled my eyes as I went to get my sandwich. I thought to myself, *I am such a fat ass*, when he passed me my sandwich on a saucer with chips. He poured some juice for the both of us and sat down with his two sandwiches. He asked, "Are you going to the party?" I ate my sandwich and nodded my head in a yeah gesture as I enjoyed my chicken salad sandwich.

It was so good, and I was so horny that I said, "Damn, this is so good."

Sénar chuckled and said, "Yeah, that's what they all say." He winked at me and I rolled my eyes ignoring his humor. I ate and rinsed my plate. Sénar bit his lip and asked, "What else do you need?"

I ignored him and quickly left to my room. I didn't trust myself, let alone him, and especially in the state I was in. I looked for clothes to wear to the party. I found my skirt Tyrell bought me and a cute red shirt with sparkling lips on it. I pulled out a fresh pair of red white and blue Perry Elise's to wear with it. I just knew I was about to look super fly. For sure, Tyrell would not be able to resist me. I picked red panties with a matching bra to go with it. I was ready, I gathered my things and went to the bathroom. Before I could close the door Sénar slipped in behind me. Shocked, I asked, "Damn Sénar, what are you, Houdini's nephew? Get out!"

He smiled sadistically while he closed the door, locking it behind him. I had all my clothes in my hand, squeezing them close to me as he spoke, "Treasure, ma you look like you need some help."

I looked at him to ask, "Help with what Sénar?"

He smiled bashfully before he answered, "Let me help you out. It will be my pleasure."

I pushed him before I replied, "I'm fine. You are crazy! No Sénar, I will take care of it myself."

He sighed first, then asked, "Why do you be playing so much? You know your ass is horny. That fool is slippin', let me help you out and then I'll leave you alone."

I was irritated with him when I replied, "No I'm not. I am fine. You don't know what you're talking about!" I was lying, I was horny as hell and my coochie was pulsating as I tried to convince Sénar it was not.

Sénar chuckled before saying, "Treasure please, I know everything about your ass. The good and the bad. I like it all. So come on, stop playing, we are wasting time."

I actually for a moment, let my coochie think for me but I knew it would not be wise. So, I just used my favorite word, "No!"

Frustration arose in Sénar's face and then he shrugged his shoulders again before he said, "Fine." He started to leave, and I started to feel kind of bad. I put my clothes down on the sink, almost relieved, but he turned around to pick me up to put me on the counter and kissed my neck while he caressed my body.

I pushed him back and said, "Sénar I can't do this. What part of no, don't you understand?"

He laughed and then the doorbell rang. We both looked at each other confused before he went to get the door. I followed him, looking down from the top of the stairs and heard a bunch of laughter and commotion. Sénar was so excited when he came back with his cousins Travis and Louie, following him up the steps.

They saw me and in unison said, "Hey Treasure."

I smiled and replied, "Hey guys."

Totally forgetting Sénar was about to do something foolish. Sénar told them, "My room is straight ahead, I'll be there in a second."

He turned to face me as I headed back to the bathroom, he called my name, "Treasure?"

I kept walking but responded, "What?"

He smiled and asked, "You sure you don't need any help?"

I rolled my eyes and answered, "Go help your company."

He laughed and said, "Even when you give it up to that loser, he will never be able to please you like me." He smiled sadistically before he left me there in my feelings.

I was annoyed with the many realities that threatened the possibility of me having a normal life. I locked the door, ran the water, and undressed in front of the mirror. My chain on my neck said Treasure instead of Tyrell. I wasn't sure which one I liked better, out of the two chains. I was satisfied with the one I had for now; it was safe and the likely hood of me being able to keep it intact was far more realistic. I examined my body and saw the enhanced weight in areas it wasn't before, and thought, *it wasn't that bad, but I should probably do something about it before I ended up looking like a butterball.* I slipped in the tub and immediately grabbed the shower head. I closed my eyes and thought of Tyrell's naked body and how bad I wanted to jump on him. Light waves of ecstasy traveled through my body as the shower head messaged my little man in the boat and teased my opening with the heat of the water passing over it. I moaned quietly squeezing the shower head with my legs as the intensity of pleasure rose. Flashes of me kissing Tyrell pranced about in my mind as I felt my nipples harden as a result. Then suddenly, flashes of Tyrell were replaced with flashes of Sénar doing things to me that caused electric waves to surge through my body. I tried to put my focus back on Tyrell but Sénar's sadistic smile flashed in my mind. Images of Sénar licking me until I exploded took over my mind. I squeezed the shower head as I felt a volt of electricity shoot through my body. I yelped out in pleasure as my coochie pulsated from the stimulation of reaching its peak. I quickly turned the water off and instantly felt shame because I could not even get off without Sénar's face flashing in my mind, no matter how hard I tried to prevent thinking about him. I convinced myself that it was simply because I didn't have enough experience with Tyrell and that surely this would not be a problem once me and Tyrell finally had our own moments of pleasure together.

I washed up and got out to get dressed for the party. I felt a little better after I got some of my pent-up frustration out. I was ready to get dressed and stunt on everybody because my outfit had me feeling myself. I was dressed and my hair was in a high bun with a cute little bang that I twirled to perfection with my fingers. I put on my gold earrings to match my silver and gold-plated chain with my name sparkling in gold on my chest. My pearly whites were bright as I smiled at my image in the mirror. I was feeling great at the moment, despite hearing Cassidy's voice out in the hallway. I opened the door to see Cassidy hugging her cousins and introducing them to Nevaeh. I went to the room to finish getting ready. I had some fresh red socks to go with my Perry Ellis shoes and a cute ankle bracelet. I mixed lotion and coco butter together and put it all over my body to give my skin a shine. Cassidy and Nevaeh walked in as I was applying my concoction to my legs; I continued as if they never walked in.

Sénar poked his head in the room and smelled the air before he said, "Damn Treasure, it smells good in here. I'm about to make some tacos before we go to the party."

He looked at me and licked his lips before leaving. I just rolled my eyes and shook my head at his shenanigans.

Nevaeh smacked her lips and asked, "Sénar, you are cooking the tacos?"

He looked at her and replied, "That's right. And it's Chef Sénar."

He smiled at her then winked his eye at me. I looked away and finished doing what I was doing. Nevaeh said, "Damn, Cassidy. Your brother is fine, and he can cook?"

Cassidy rolled her eyes before she said, "Girl, I don't want to hear that shit." She grabbed a couple of things without saying a word to me and her and Nevaeh headed downstairs. Everyone was chattering and having a good time when I came down. Sénar's facial expression changed to awe, everyone looked toward me and grew silent.

The boys again, said in unison, "Hey Treasure."

I tried not to smile and replied, "Hey guys."

Cassidy and Nevaeh looked agitated and kept talking. Sénar's cousins were sitting at the table and Sénar took his shirt off, so he could cook. I grabbed a chair at the table and Sénar said, "You should grate the cheese and cut the lettuce for the tacos."

I smacked my lips before I answered, "No. I don't want to mess my outfit up."

Nevaeh rolled her eyes at me and said, "I'll grate the cheese, damn."

Sénar ignored her and gave me the shirt he took off. I snatched it from him, annoyed as I put it on over my clothes. It was baggy and covered me pass my behind. Sénar smiled and said, "You should go to the party like that."

Him and his cousins laughed, but Nevaeh was feeling some kind of way. Annoyed with them both I grabbed the things to do my part on the Chef Sénar show.

Nevaeh asked, "Don't you have a girlfriend Sénar?"

He looked at Nevaeh and tilted his head and asked, "Why you wanna know?"

She put her hand on her chin and answered, "Because you're acting like you like Treasure's raggedy ass."

He laughed and said, "It's Chef Sénar to you, and I'm not acting, so don't worry about it." He dismissed her and started the tacos.

I was grating the cheese and minding my business, trying to avoid her stupid attempt to insult me when she said, "Whatever, I'm waiting for Tyrell to stop acting like he's not tired of her ass, so I can snatch him."

Sénar without looking back responded, "Well, that makes two of us."

That was it, I threw the cheese grater at Nevaeh's face. When it hit her in her forehead, she jumped up and tried to grab me, but I took the opportunity to slap her in her mouth. Sénar snatched me up because I was trying to rip her face off when he carried me into the kitchen. Cassidy scurried to grab the cheese grater off the floor. For the first time ever, Cassidy grabbed the broom to sweep up the mess that fell from the cheese grater upon the impact with Nevaeh's face. Sénar held me against the fridge and placed his hand on my stomach while Nevaeh yelled at Louie, "Let me go! I'm about to fuck this bitch up!"

Sénar whispered in my ear, "See, all that frustration, you should have let me help you earlier." He laughed and I pushed him off of me as Ken walked in the door.

Ken came in the dining room, "What the hell is going on in here?" He asked Louie as he held Nevaeh trying to calm her down and Sénar had me hemmed up against the fridge.

Cassidy was flustered when Sénar whispered, "See. Your ass always getting me into some shit."

Sénar turned to his dad and said, "Nothing Pops, just horsin' around and making some tacos."

Cassidy was nervous as Louie chimed in, "Wassup Unc, how you doin'?"

Ken smiled before he gave Louie a hug and turned to hug Travis while Louie escorted Nevaeh back to her chair with her never taking her eyes off me. I was ready to jump on her again when Sénar whispered, "Treasure chill man. Let's just eat with no more drama."

I smacked my lips and walked around him to finish my task when Ken asked, "What's your problem girl?"

He looked at me in Sénar's T-shirt shaking his head and waiting for a response. I looked away and replied, "Nothing."

As I finished cutting the lettuce, I stared at Nevaeh and dared her to say anything that would give me a reason to slice her face off. My mom came down to say hi to everyone. Hugging the cousins and then asking how their mom was doing. After I finished with the lettuce, Sénar gave me my plate first and then handed out plates to everybody else. I made my plate and sat down at the table with my mom and Ken while the cousins made their plates. My mom was in a good mood when she said, "Hey, Treasure." I quickly replied, "Hi," and then ate my food. Cassidy and her dumb ass friend made their plates and ate at the counter. Everyone talked while I drifted away into my thoughts until the phone rang. I jumped up to answer the phone and it was Tyrell asking, "You ready?" I replied, "Yeah, I am ready." He was quiet for a second before he asked, "Damn, y'all having a party over there first?" I sighed before I answered, "No, Tyrell that's just Cassidy's dumb ass friend and her cousins in the background." He sounded like he was irritated when he said, "Well, come over here, I'm ready." I replied, "Ok." I hung up the phone and walked back to the table to grab my plate. I took Sénar's shirt off and threw it at him before grabbing my plate with a half a taco left on it from the three that I made. Sénar caught his shirt and scanned my body before he smelled his shirt. He smiled before he said, "Mmm, it smells like chocolate." Sénar laughed along with his cousins, agitating Ken even more as he watched Sénar look like my number one fan. Ken also scanned my body with his eyes before he asked, "Where the hell are you going Treasure, dressed all fancy?" I took my plate to the sink to rinse it and replied dryly, "I am going to a party." Before Ken could say anything, Sénar added, "We are all going to the same party Pops." My mom offered some help when she said, "Sénar, I'll clean up and you guys go get ready for the party." Sénar didn't pass the opportunity, he and his cousins got up to put their plates in the sink. I walked out of the front door happy to escape my mad house when I saw Tyrell come out his front door.

He smiled when he said, "Damn Treasure, you look fly as hell!" He unlocked his car and we got in. I replied, "Thanks babe."

He pulled out the driveway and asked, "You want to go get some tacos?"

I answered, "I just ate some tacos, but I didn't get to finish, so I'll take one."

Tyrell eyed me before he asked, "Who made tacos?"

I looked at him and asked, "Why?"

He was instantly frustrated when he asked, "Damn, that nigga Sénar makes tacos too?"

I ignored his question and he continued with his assumptions, "That's probably why your ass is so fat. That nigga been feeding you?"

I was tired of the conversation when I replied, "Tyrell, can we change the subject? Big deal, I ate tacos who cares? Dang."

He was angry with me as he pressed the gas petal, picking up speed as we drove to our destination. I felt a sense of fear that prompted me to grab his leg to say, "Well, you look nice babe."

I eyed him too, taking in his own flyness with his red Polo shirt, beige crisp Khakis, and fresh K Swiss. I noticed a blinging gold chain around his neck with his name hanging from thicker chain links. It was really nice but at that moment, I realized I would never get it back.

He saw me in my thoughts and said, "Thanks. You look good too Treasure. Man, I don't even want tacos no more. I want a drink."

He drove to the party instead of going to get tacos. I couldn't help but ask, "You got it fixed?"

He looked at me with a little irritation when he asked, "Got what fixed?"

I replied, "The chain on your neck Tyrell."

He smiled and said, "Yeah. It's nice huh?"

I replied, "Yeah, it's nice."

Feeling sad, now knowing he had no intentions of giving it back to me. He said, "Yours looks nice too."

I forced a smile to avoid a potential argument. We pulled up to his friend Triston's house. There were people outside in the front. His friend Triston ran up to Tyrell and they did their little handshake. Triston looked at me and said, "Hey Treasure." He said it as if he was shocked to see me at the party.

Triston led us inside his house where the rest of the people were. Tyrell asked, "My man, what you got to drink in here?"

Triston laughed and pointed to the spiked punch that had a smiley face on the bowl. I shook my head at Tyrell's eagerness and watched him make himself a drink.

Triston asked, "You want a drink Treasure?"

I shook my head no. I looked around scanning the crowds of people from school talking in groups and listening to music. Tyrell asked, "Who are you looking for?"

I shook my head and for a second, I regretted coming to this stupid party but didn't want Tyrell to regret bringing me. I had to wait until my attitude subsided before answering his stupid question. I replied, "Nobody. Tyrell I am just checking out the party that's all."

He shrugged his shoulders out of irritation. Tyrell decided to do his own scanning of the crowds and stopped at a group of girls from the cheerleading squad as they waved at him. I just watch Tyrell watch them and their little show. Leah walked through the front door breaking his attention away from the cheerleaders. I watched him as his eyes filled with lust, he smiled to himself. She spotted Tyrell, checking her out and then me.

She came over to greet me, "Hey, Treasure girl!"

Tyrell looked at her and then at me. I cleared my throat and said, "Hey."

She smiled at Tyrell and he smiled back at her. I was super uncomfortable as Leah introduced herself to Tyrell, "Hey, I'm Leah. You must be Tyrell?"

She smiled flirtatiously, Tyrell looked at me before he responded, "Yep, the one and only."

He smiled back at her flirtatiously. I smacked my lips, "Hello?" I said irritated with the both of them.

She noticed my irritation and asked, "Where is Sénar's fine ass at?"

Tyrell's smile evaporated. I responded to her question with an attitude, "I don't know, go find him."

As soon as I said that Sénar walked in the front door with his cousins. Leah watched Sénar's every move as Tyrell became more agitated. Cassidy and Nevaeh walked in behind them. Nevaeh spotted me and Tyrell rolling her eyes at the sight of us together. Leah was excited she grabbed my arm, "Ooh, I found his fine ass!"

Sénar walked up to Triston to say what's up and to do their little handshake. Leah watched Sénar's every move making Tyrell even more agitated. Triston told them about the spiked punch. Sénar declined as his cousins helped themselves to the spiked punch. Sénar spotted me when he came in and hadn't taken his eyes off of me except to mad dog Tyrell. Leah saw the tension between the two of them and smiled a sadistic smile of her own.

She walked over to the punch to make a drink and said, "Hi Sénar."

He replied, "What's up Leah," without taking his eyes off me.

Leah looked at me to ask, "Treasure are you going to have a drink?"

I was so irritated as I could feel the tension increase. I made my way to the punch bowl to make myself some spiked punch. Before I could even drink it, I felt a nudge in my back almost making me spill my drink all over myself. I turned around and Nevaeh said, "Move lil' bitch."

Leah put her cup down and asked, "Yo, who the hell is this broad?"

Nevaeh replied, "What bitch? Who are you talking to?"

Leah quickly got puffed up and wanted to get her when Sénar said, "Man Nevaeh, stop trippin'. Cassidy get your homegirl."

Tyrell made him another cup of punch and walked off. I followed behind him and Leah followed behind me with her cup in her hand. Tyrell appeared annoyed as he walked. I called his name to try and get him to slow down.

He responded, "What Treasure?"

I asked, "Where are you going?"

He looked back at me and impatiently answered, "It's a party. Man, go kick it with your home girl. I'm about to kick it with my homeboys for a minute."

He walked off and Leah asked, "Damn, what's wrong with him?"

I was annoyed with her already but didn't want to be left by myself, I answered, "I don't know. How did you find out about the party?"

She said, "Girl please, you know I'm nosey. Everybody that matters is here. I'm trying to get in where I fit in, so I will have a bomb ass school year."

I rolled my eyes and sipped my drink while she downed hers. Sénar and his cousins were still at the punch bowl when Leah made her way back over there. Cassidy and Nevaeh were talking with a group of girls off to the side as I made my way over to Leah just in case those lil' heifers tried some shady stuff.

Sénar asked, "Are you going to dance?"

Leah started cheesing and then said, "Hell yeah!"

She made her a drink and danced seductively. Sénar smiled along with his cousins while Tyrell watched from afar. I was annoyed with Leah's desperation as I put a little more spiked punch in my cup.

Sénar asked, "What about you Treasure?" He raised his eyebrow before clarifying, "Are you going to dance?"

I shook my head no and walked away with Sénar laughing in the background. I went to find somewhere to sit and sip my drink. Leah found me and sat down next to me. She asked, "I didn't know Sénar and Tyrell had beef. Over what?"

I wanted to tell her to mind her damn business, but I had enough enemies at the party and didn't need another one. I responded, "I don't know what you are talking about."

She shook her head and asked, "Why are you always trying to play me?" She had an attitude now.

Before I could snap back at her, I saw London and Nevaeh talking while looking at us. When they started to approach us, I took a nice sip from my cup and then nudged Leah. She looked in the direction where London was and we both stood up to prepare ourselves. Leah said, "Damn girl, I didn't come here to fight. I want to have some fun!"

I took another sip from my drink and said, "Me too."

I sighed as London walked up to us to say, "You, little bitch!" Pointing her finger at Leah, "Stay away from my man," London looked me up and down then said, "and you, Treasure," she said it like she needed to read my chain to know my name, before she threatened, "worry about your own man and leave mine alone or else."

Tired of fighting and arguing with bitches, I replied, "Deal."

I then smiled in London's face and Leah responded, "No deal for me sweetie." Looking at London, Leah continued, "I do what I want, when I want, and right now, that's dance!"

We walked off laughing and found a clear spot to dance to the music playing. Leah swiveled her hips and danced on me. She had all the guys in the party watching when she said, "Come on Treasure, let's dance. Move those hips!" She placed her hands on my hips and moved them for me. I giggled as she was being more silly than seductive.

I told her, "I might need another drink to move like that."

She laughed and said, "Come on, let's go get a drink."

Tyrell was making himself a drink when we got to the punch. He smiled and said, "Nice little show y'all put on out there."

We giggled as we made our drinks. I was starting to get a buzz and I was finally starting to have a good time. Sénar stared at me while his cousins came to make a drink. Leah said, "Damn Treasure, you are looking super thick in that skirt girl." Sénar and Tyrell smiled, I'm sure for different reasons.

I responded, "Girl shut up, that is the last thing I want to hear, but you look really cute tonight. Mission accomplished."

She laughed before she said, "I'm not saying you're fat, I'm saying your ass is nice and fat." She tapped my ass flirtatiously, and I almost blushed. Tyrell grabbed me, kissed me, and started squeezing my butt cheeks. Sénar instantly had fire in his eyes. When Leah saw Sénar she said, "Yikes!" Tyrell released me and Leah dragged me on the floor to dance. Leah danced while she observed the expressions on both Tyrell and Sénar's face.

She said, "I think I know why they are beefing."

Sénar and his cousins watched us along with all the guys in the party. I was starting to loosen up, I danced with Leah ignoring her comment until Tyrell came and got me. Tyrell whispered in my ear, "Damn Treasure, y'all got everyone up in here looking at you."

He didn't seem mad; he was just more aroused than usual. He grabbed me and kissed me again, while Leah watched. Then he said, "Let's go."

Leah came to us to ask, "Can you guys take me home?"

Before I could answer no, Tyrell replied, "Fo' sho, let's go."

Leah waved by to Sénar and his cousins. I could barely look at them, so I just left holding Tyrell's hand with Leah following behind us. We dropped Leah off while listening to all her plans she had for the upcoming school year. I was so happy when she was finally out of the car.

When we pulled up to Tyrell's house, he said, "My mom isn't home yet, so you want to come upstairs?"

I looked in his eyes and saw the lust present in his eyes. I bit my bottom lip with anticipation before answering, "Sure."

We went inside and he led me upstairs. Once we were in his room, he pinned me against the door kissing me passionately and fumbling with my clothes. He was drunk and was stumbling all over the place. He smiled at me deviously and kissed me deeply. I kissed him back, already feverishly waiting for him to have his way with my body, since earlier today. His eyes filled with fiery lust as he grabbed me to lay me down on his bed, fumbling to take my shirt off. He was groping me and kissing my neck as I removed my bra, he then kissed me all over my breast. He started pulling at my skirt as he was having difficulty. I helped him accomplish his task by removing my skirt. His hands traveled up my legs until he felt my warm, anticipating honey pot of pent up sexual desires. It was wet and juicy as I was turned on by his excitement and participation. He quickly removed his pants and boxers. It was dark but I knew this was the moment I have been waiting for. He entered me with urgency as if his opportunity might expire. The moment he entered my warm and silky insides, there was a slight twinge of pain before I entered a world of ecstasy. I held on to him tightly, not wanting him to stop this time, I was ready for this moment that I had fantasized about. I moved my body with his eager pumps of lust and moaned quietly in his ear. We clung to each other as he plunged himself in and out of me, while kissing me all over my face. We both were panting for air as we smothered each other with our bodies until I felt a hot explosion take place inside of me.

Tyrell whimpered like a puppy and collapsed on top of me. I almost panicked for a second, until he told me he loved me, with him now out of breath. Before I knew it, he was sleeping like a baby on top of me. I whispered his name to wake him, with an idea of what just took place. He woke up just long enough to roll off me. I got up to gather my clothes and went to his bathroom to clean myself up. I had a slight smile on my face knowing that the hot explosion that took place was Tyrell pouring me a cup of his man juice. I used tissue to soak up his juices that were seeping out of me. I thought about my mom's statement and couldn't be happier knowing I was not going to have to worry about getting pregnant. I quietly left Tyrell asleep, peacefully. I crossed the street and tip toed my way back inside my house. I crawled into my bed with a smile on my face, feeling loved as I fell asleep, blissfully.

Chapter 3

The next morning, I woke up smiling from ear to ear. I had sweet dreams of Tyrell finally taking my body to a level of ecstasy that I fantasized about constantly; It felt like a dream come true. I couldn't wait to see him again and explore each other's bodies. I got up and found something enticing to wear under my clothes and quickly went to the bathroom to shower. The door was locked, so I went back to my room and tried to stay focused. I did not want to spend any time with myself that I could be spending with Tyrell. When I finished getting dressed, I went downstairs to call Tyrell, his phone just rang and rang. After last night, he was probably trying to sleep off some of the alcohol he drank. Our first time wasn't what I expected but it was definitely still rememberable. I wanted more and all I could think about was what the next time would be like.

After Tyrell didn't answer, I was a little annoyed, but it was still early. I figured he would call me later when he woke up. Sénar and his cousins came downstairs as I was hanging up the phone. Sénar was not happy but he did not say anything; his cousins hesitated but still spoke. I felt kind of bad because I knew they weren't expecting to see me with Tyrell, but it's not my fault what Sénar may have told them. I didn't want to sit in their faces when Sénar was probably mad at me, so I just sat in the living room. I didn't want to go upstairs and have to deal with Cassidy or Nevaeh. Sénar and Travis went to the store, while Louie stayed to take a shower and get dressed. Louie came down to ask me where Sénar and his brother went.

I answered, "They went to the store, I think."

He was getting ready to go back up the steps but then he turned around to ask, "Aye Treasure, why you do my cousin Sénar like that?"

I stared at him and tried to not have an attitude, "Like what?"

He shook his head and thought about whether he should say anything before he said, "You know how he feels about you, right?"

I shrugged my shoulders and replied, "I don't know Louie. I try not to think about it; it's complicated."

He went upstairs to wait on them to come back. Shortly after Louie left upstairs, Sénar and Travis came back. Travis went upstairs and Sénar came in the living room to ask, "Did you have fun last night?"

I was a little bashful, knowing he was implying both at, and after the party. I looked down and answered, "It was cool. Did you have fun?"

"It was cool," he walked away after he replied.

He went back upstairs, and I got up to look across the street to see if I saw Tyrell's car. When I saw his car there, I decided to call him again. The phone just rang and rang. Frustrated, I hung up and went to my room. I noticed Nevaeh wasn't in the room and asked, "Where's your stupid ass friend Cassidy?"

She smacked her lips and answered, "Where do you think?"

I looked at her and rolled my eyes at her. I guess Nevaeh was in Sénar's room. I felt a bit of jealousy and wondered who she was in there for. I shook that feeling and grabbed my stuff to take a shower, but someone else was in the bathroom again. So, I went back downstairs to watch TV until the bathroom was free. Louie and Nevaeh came down first, then headed to the kitchen. I wondered what they were up to since they appeared extra friendly with one another. Travis came down after having showered then Cassidy. Everyone was in the kitchen and Sénar was cooking while everybody chattered. I felt some remorse and did not want to go in there with Sénar being mad at me, but he called my name from the kitchen. When I came into the kitchen, everyone just stared at me. It was an awkward silence that made me feel like I was in trouble.

Sénar glared at me before he said, "Come help me."

Louie smirked a little when Sénar asked me for help. I didn't talk back or ask why, I just humbly asked, "What do you want me to do?"

Sénar smiled then answered, "There's a lot of things I want you to do, but for now just crack the eggs and grate the cheese."

Nevaeh squirmed a bit in her chair, prompting Louie to chime in to say, "With no extra tricks and shit."

Sénar laughed while I grabbed what I needed to do as he asked. Travis suggested, "We should have just smoked first." Sénar rolled his eyes and said, "That shit wouldn't even have worked." Cassidy rolled her eyes at Sénar's comment.

Louie asked, "Aye Sénar, you gonna make some of that fire ass chicken before we leave?"

He was cheesing when he answered, "Yeah, I got chu my nigg!"

Sénar made grits, scrambled eggs, and bacon for breakfast. Louie rolled two blunts while he talked to Nevaeh, and she was much quieter today than she was yesterday. She didn't even speak to me. She also didn't talk to Sénar or talk about Tyrell at all. Sénar was watching me watch them. He handed me my plate first and then handed everyone else their plates. I made my plate then sat at the table with Sénar and Louie. I ate my food while Sénar watched me eat. It was making me uncomfortable but at the same time, it made me wonder what he was thinking about. Louie got up to wash his plate along with Travis. Nevaeh and Cassidy threw their plates in the sink giggling as they walked out.

Cassidy turned around to say, "Call us when y'all are about to smoke."

Travis and Louie left to the living room, leaving me and Sénar in the kitchen. Sénar got up to run the dishwater. I debated if I should volunteer to do the dishes, but I really wanted to shower. I swear it was as if he could read my thoughts, Sénar said, "Keep the shower on for me."

I left quietly and quickly to take a shower. My heart was racing, I didn't know what to expect with Sénar because he was so crazy. He didn't seem mad or upset with me, he just acted like he was unbothered. Once in the shower, I couldn't' help but think about me and Tyrell's night. I thought about how awesome it was to have an experience like that finally and tried to think about it as the water messaged my hot spot. No matter how hard I tried to concentrate on Tyrell, Sénar kept popping up as flashes of pleasure that I could not shake. I stopped as guilt had stricken me, and I did not want to take too long in the shower. I got out leaving the shower on. I put on some shorts and a tank top. Sénar came out of his room as I was coming out of the bathroom with the stuff for his shower. He walked pass me without a word.

I couldn't help but ask, "Sénar, are you mad at me?"

He looked at me like I asked him a dumb question and then replied, "For what?" He closed the door in my face. Leaving me confused and wondering why I even cared if he was mad at me. I just went downstairs to call Tyrell, just to listen to the phone ring again. I looked outside to see if I could see his car parked in the driveway, but it was gone. I was instantly irritated and did not want anyone to notice, so I just went back upstairs.

Sénar was coming downstairs as I was going up and asked, "Where are you going? Aren't you going to smoke?"

I just stared at him before I replied, "I guess but I really don't want any drama."

He smiled before he said, "Don't react to it then." I rolled my eyes and followed him to the backyard. He told everyone as we were on our way to smoke that we were about to light the blunt in the backyard.

When Sénar and I got outside he asked, "Are you ready to start school tomorrow?"

I took a deep breath before answering, "Yeah, I'm ready. I guess."

Sénar said, "Your little friend is ready." He said it seductively and I rolled my eyes. Louie came out and I passed him the blunt after I hit it twice. Louie hit the blunt as Sénar continued to pry, "I didn't know you could dance like that Treasure. Shit, here I thought I knew everything about you."

He laughed and Louie passed him the blunt to hit. I was a little uncomfortable with where the conversation was going, so I said, "Well, Leah did most of the dancing."

Sénar hit the blunt and blew an O before responding, "Yeah, but I was watching you, and ya' boy was watching her."

He passed me the blunt and I hit it before responding, hoping it would make his statement less true or maybe even funny. I was embarrassed but I had a quick comeback, "Well, I couldn't tell, she's not who he was with last night."

Louie put his head down and Sénar smirked as he filled with jealousy when he said, "Well, I guess neither of us got what we wanted." I hit the blunt again and almost turned to leave but Louie said, "Nah, don't leave Treasure. We about to bounce in a little while and I don't know when I'm going to make this trip to kick it with y'all again."

Travis, Cassidy and Nevaeh came out to hit the blunt. Louie passed the blunt to Travis. I stayed quiet while everyone talked about the party. Sénar didn't say anything else about the party, he just glared at me. I was tired of being scrutinized, so I went inside to call Tyrell. His car was still gone when I looked out the window as Sénar came in shaking his head.

He sat on the couch and pushed play for the movie *Next Friday* then said, "Treasure, sit down and watch some TV, instead of watching the window."

Now mad, I asked, "Sénar, why are you always in my business? Don't you have your own relationship to worry about?"

He just laughed at me and ignored my question. I sat down upset, I was totally in my feelings. I was high, so I was thinking extra hard as everyone came in to watch the movie. We were all high and laughing at the movie. For a moment, I forgot about checking out the window for Tyrell. The phone rang and I quickly jumped up to go answer it. I didn't bother looking out the window, since I knew it was Tyrell.

I answered, "Hello?" Leah responded, "Hey girl, what's poppin'? You ready for school tomorrow?"

I was shocked and replied, "Um yeah, but how did you get my number?"

She instantly got an attitude when she asked, "Damn, why does it matter?" She continued to go on as if I asked her the same, "Ooh, I can't wait. What are you wearing?"

I replied, "I don't know."

I was waiting on her to ask for Sénar, but instead she said, "Ok, well I'll see you tomorrow."

She hung up quickly and I ran to the window to see Tyrell pull up. I ran outside to meet him as he pulled into his driveway. I waited for him to get out of his car.

He stared at me before asking, "What, Treasure?"

He acted as if I was bothering him. I folded my arms and asked, "Why haven't you called me?"

He gawked at me with his irritation level full blown, he asked "You came across the street to ask me that?"

I was furious with his nonchalant attitude. I asked, "Where are you coming from Tyrell?"

He snapped at me, "Mind your damn business! My momma don't even ask me that shit anymore?"

He looked at me carefully when he asked, "Why are your eyes like that?" He couldn't tell that I was high as the tears filled my eyes and flowed onto my face.

He said, "Man, you are tripping. Go home and get ready for school tomorrow. I'll see you in the morning."

I was hurt and confused, "Why can't I come inside with you?"

He sighed before he quickly answered, "My mom is home. I'll see you tomorrow."

I was enraged, I felt like he didn't even care as he grabbed me and kissed me on the forehead. He went inside, leaving me outside without mentioning last night, why he didn't call me, or where he had been. I ran back across the street and slammed the door before running to my room. I cried so hard when I got to my room, I couldn't even control myself. I didn't even stop when I heard my door open or turn back to see who it was. I just buried my face into my pillow when I heard the door close back. I stayed in my bed and cried, until I heard a knock at the door.

I asked, "Who is it?"

He answered, "It's me, Travis."

I replied, "It's open."

He cracked the door open to stick his head in and said, "Sénar wants you to come downstairs."

I snapped, "Tell him, no!"

Travis pleaded with me, "Treasure, he wants your help in the kitchen."

I had an attitude when I replied, "Tell him to ask Nevaeh or Cassidy to help him."

Travis chuckled before he said, "Nevaeh is kinda busy, and you know damn well Cassidy's ass ain't doing that shit."

I didn't care, I said, "Tell him, I said no."

Travis gave up when he closed the door and I just debated if I should go down or not. It wasn't long before Sénar came up next, calling my name, "Treasure?"

I snapped at him too, "What!"

He asked, "What's your problem, Treasure?"

I had a mini tantrum when I said, "I don't wanna help!"

He noticed that I had been crying and his face softened because he was just about to get angry when he asked, "What are you crying for?"

I lied, "I'm not crying, I'm not hungry, I'm not anything right now!"

He laughed and said, "Ok, whatever ma. Get yourself together and come help me, Treasure. We have school tomorrow and I'm not trying to be cooking all night."

Cassidy slipped in on the other side of Sénar. She looked at me and then at Sénar before she asked, "What's wrong with you now Treasure?"

I smacked my lips as I got up and yelled, "Nothing!" Cassidy stared at me like I was crazy.

Sénar put his hands up before he said, "It wasn't me."

I went to the bathroom to wash my face and splash cold water in my eyes. I followed Sénar to the kitchen to avoid Cassidy's nosey ass. I did not want Nevaeh to see me in my weakened state, so I pulled myself together before I reached the kitchen. Sénar had some basketball shorts and a sports tank top on as he started to prepare the chicken. Travis was watching TV on the couch, but Nevaeh and Louie were nowhere in sight and Cassidy was still upstairs. Sénar watched me as I grabbed all the ingredients that I needed for the salad in addition to the things I needed to cut and clean the potatoes.

He said, "Treasure, I don't know why you act like I didn't warn your ass."

I ignored his comment and cut the potatoes. I didn't want to give him any unnecessary information. I just kept my mouth shut because I was practicing not reacting to everything. He fried the chicken while my mom and Ken came in with a bunch of groceries and of course, beer for Ken and wine for my mom. Ken sat the bags on the table and walked upstairs. My mom came in and said hello to me and Sénar then sat some small bags on the table. Sénar grabbed the bags and put everything away while I cut the potatoes for fries. Sénar came up from behind me and smelled my hair while he held me in a delicate embrace.

He whispered in my ear, "I don't know what's wrong with him, but you are my inspiration."

He let me go before I could push him off of me. I wanted to be Tyrell's inspiration and I wondered what Sénar saw in me that Tyrell didn't. I knew I shouldn't dwell on it because I was going to see Tyrell tomorrow and did not want to mess that up too. So, I just didn't say anything at all. I noticed Louie and Nevaeh had come downstairs smiling and giggling. Sénar and I looked at each other and smiled as I finished up the fries to start on the salad. I was glad Nevaeh had someone else to focus on instead of Tyrell. I was feeling a little salty when I thought about Tyrell and how we should be like that. instead of him sending me home with no answers. I was agitated and started on the salad. I was thinking really hard when I noticed Sénar looking at me, shaking his head.

I took a deep breath and asked, "What?"

He laughed before he said, "Damn ma, take it easy with the knife, and don't touch the tomatoes."

I rolled my eyes at him and continued to prepare the salad. Cassidy came down with my mom and Ken. Louie and Nevaeh moved to the counter to watch me and Sénar finish preparing everything. Nevaeh and Louie looked at us and smiled at each other the same way we did when we saw them in their love connection earlier.

Cassidy rolled her eyes, "Oh gosh! Is the Chef Sénar and Treasure show almost over?"

I looked at Cassidy and Sénar gave me a plate to discourage my response. Ken asked, "Hell, why does Treasure always get her plate first?" Everybody laughed, even me because I wanted to know too. I made my plate and Sénar passed out plates to everyone else.

Sénar answered, "Because she helps."

Ken shook his head and said, "Yeah right, ok."

My mom made his plate and he continued, "I can't wait til y'all asses go back to school. Then we can actually come out of our room." He laughed and my mom giggled as she served him his plate, then made one for herself.

We were eating dinner when Louie said, "Speaking of school Unc, we are about to head out in a minute back to the city. We just wanted some of Sénar's chicken. Shoot, if y'all ever get tired of his ass, send him back with us because we miss his cooking."

Sénar shook his head and Ken replied, "This lil' dude can't even keep his ass out of trouble out here. I definitely ain't sending his ass back to the city. Please, he is going to keep his ass right here to play sports, stay out of trouble, and spend less time in this damn kitchen."

Sénar rolled his eyes in irritation but ate in silence. Ken looked at Sénar then asked, "Right Sénar?"

Sénar looked at him before answering, "Yes sir."

He got up to wash his plate and run dish water. Louie and Travis hugged Ken before Sénar walked them outside. My mom put her and Ken's plates in the sink. She routinely made sure to grab her wine and beer for Ken. Before she left, she said, "Goodnight Treasure. You have been a really good helper."

She kissed me on the cheek and went upstairs. Nevaeh put her plate in the sink with Cassidy and walked outside with the boys to get a ride home. Ken sat at the table drinking his beer. I got up to put the dishes in the sink and wished Sénar would hurry up back.

Ken said, "Treasure, get me a beer." I looked at him like he was stupid.

Ken snapped, "Girl, I ain't asking!"

His tone alarmed me as I quickly went to get him a beer from the fridge. As I bent down to get him a beer, I could hear the front door open and close. When I brought Ken his beer, he snatched it from me and handed me his empty bottle to throw away without asking me. I took a deep breath to keep from saying anything and continued washing the dishes while Sénar put the rest of the food in containers.

Ken was buzzing when he asked, "Hey Sénar, you remember Daisy? Is she still fine?"

I could see that Sénar was super uncomfortable before he answered, "Yeah Pops, she cool."

Ken chuckled then said, "Yeah, we taught your ass everything you know about-"

Sénar cut him off, "Pops, come on."

I ignored Ken and kept washing the dishes. Ken smirked at Sénar and said, "Shut up boy. Treasure, you met Daisy?"

I took a deep breath and replied, "Yeah, I met her Ken."

He laughed as he got up and sang, "Oh Miss Daisy," before going up the stairs. Sénar was now agitated.

I asked, "Sénar what is he talking about?"

Sénar shook his head then answered, "Man, I don't want to talk about that shit." He was upset and flustered when he spoke, "Man look, next time just go upstairs! Try to avoid being alone with him. I will finish this up, just go to bed."

I stopped washing dishes to run upstairs and tried not to cry because I felt like I did something wrong. I held back my tears to avoid Cassidy's questions and picked something to wear before going to bed. I had a feeling tomorrow was not going to be a good day.

I woke up after a terrible night's sleep to brush my teeth, wash my face, and get dressed. I called Tyrell, he answered, "Yeah, come on over."

I hurried across the street and tried to forget about yesterday. He was still in his nightclothes when he opened the door. I smiled and hugged him before he led me upstairs. Once we were in his room, we kissed and fondled each other. I didn't want to bring up yesterday and mess up the mood. I just wanted him to have his way with my body and talk later. He got me all hot and bothered then stopped to take a shower. I wanted to do more, but I just watched TV and waited for him to get out of the shower. He came out in his towel and looked for an outfit.

He looked at me, looking at him then asked, "So what did you do yesterday?"

I carefully answered his question, "Well, I called you several times and waited for you to come home."

He sighed before he said, "Whatever."

He continued getting dressed and ignored me in the process. When we got to school, we went our separate ways. At lunchtime, I got a pizza and sat at one of the tables. I watched all the people that were at the party talk in different groups, and a lot of people were staring at me. Tyrell was talking in a group of his friends from the basketball team. I was just about to eat when Leah came and sat next to me with her food. She was excited to see me.

She said, "What's up, girl?"

I said, "Hi, Leah."

She was smiling when she said, "Girl, so many guys tried to get at me today, it's crazy. But I don't want any of their asses. I want Sénar's fine ass."

She said as she searched the cafeteria for him. Sénar was sitting at a table with a group of his football buddies talking and laughing. He was already looking at me when I spotted him. Leah finally saw him too and then fanned herself.

Irritated with her antics I said, "Go talk to him."

She smacked her lips, "Girl, I am not trying to beat his girlfriend's ass on the first day of school. I'll get his ass."

She sounded like Nevaeh. I rolled my eyes and started to eat as Tyrell made his way over to our table. He sat next to me and took a piece of my pizza when he sat down. Leah smiled flirtatiously when she said, "Hey Tyrell."

Tyrell said, "What's up, Leah?"

She ate her food, and Tyrell turned to me to say, "I have practice after school."

Tyrell got up to kiss me on the cheek before he left. Leah ate her food while waving bye to Tyrell. She asked, "So, have you and Tyrell fucked yet?"

I looked at her anticipating my answer and saw Sénar was watching us.

I asked, "Why?"

She innocently replied, "I don't know; I am just curious."

I ignored her question because it was none of her business. When lunch was over, I went to my next class. I was so glad Leah wasn't in any of my first three classes. She really got on my nerves. It was just my luck that she was in my next class. She sat next to me and asked, "Tyrell is so tall, does he have a big dick?" I was blown away by her questions.

I asked, "Leah, why do you want to know?"

She smirked and said, "I guess it wouldn't be that hard to find out."

She stopped talking to me and left me in my thoughts.

She then asked, "Well, since you don't want to talk about Tyrell, then what about Sénar?"

I stared at her before I breathed in deeply to refrain from cussing her out and asked, "What about Sénar?"

She smiled before she inquired, "Well, does he have a big dick?"

I quickly responded, "How am I supposed to know that?"

She replied, "I see the way he looks at you. I know you have seen that shit at least once."

I rolled my eyes at her and lied, "I don't know what you are talking about."

She smirked before replying, "You never do."

I wanted the class to be over already. She was not in my next class and I thanked God for not torturing me further. However, she was in my last class. The good thing was we had assigned seats, so because my last name was Lee and hers was Banks, I didn't have to sit next to her. As if it couldn't be any better, it required more reading than talking as it was a history class. I hated history class in every grade, so the least it could do was give me a break with Leah. I was very pleased with the break. After class, she walked up to me and asked, "What are you about to do?"

I hesitated before responding, "I am going to Tyrell's practice."

She volunteered to go with me. I sat at Tyrell's practice and listened to Leah run her mouth while I watched Tyrell. The cheerleaders huddled together and noticed us sitting on the bleachers. All the players noticed too because they were all watching us on the bleachers during practice. Leah just smiled and enjoyed watching all the boys run with their muscular bodies. After practice, Tyrell said something to the cheerleaders and went to grab his stuff. He made his way over to me and Leah on the bleachers. I got up to meet him, and Leah followed us. I noticed London waiting for Sénar while we walked with Tyrell to his car.

Tyrell asked Leah if she needed a ride. She said, "Hell yeah!" He didn't even need directions to get to her house when it was dark the first time that we took her home, and he was drunk. I was in my thoughts and folded my arms out of irritation on the way back.

Tyrell asked, "How did you meet Leah?"

I smacked my lips before I answered, "Summer school, Tyrell."

He asked, "What's the attitude for?"

When he pulled into his driveway, I asked, "Why are you so worried about Leah?" He laughed and shrugged his shoulders as if to say, he didn't know.

I looked at him and said, "Well, she likes Sénar."

He smirked at me then asked, "Oh? So, what, he doesn't like you anymore?"

I shook my head before I answered, "I don't know Tyrell, but all I do know is who I do like, and there is no room for Leah or Sénar."

Tyrell smirked before he asked, "Well, does Sénar like Leah?"

He waited with anticipation for my answer. I snapped, "Tyrell, I don't know!"

He got out of the car and said, "Damn girl, calm your ass down."

He looked agitated by our conversation as I followed him to the door and waited for him to invite me in. He hesitated until he saw Sénar pull up.

He said, "Man, come on, but I don't want to talk."

I frowned my eyebrows when I asked, "What is that supposed to mean?"

Once we were inside his room, he said, "Take your pants off."

I folded my arms in defiance. I didn't exactly want to have sex, but I felt like I was slowly losing him as I sat down on his bed.

I asked, "Tyrell, why are you being so cold?"

He rolled his eyes, "I said I didn't want to talk." He pulled me to him and kissed me. He squeezed my booty before he said, "I want to do this, not talk."

I let him kiss me and take my pants off as he laid me on his bed. He pulled out his eager member to put the tip in and moved it around until he felt the moisture that he needed to slide inside of me. I laid back as he filled me up, it felt good, but it was hard to relax. I had so many thoughts running through my mind. By the time I was actually starting to enjoy it, Tyrell pulled out before he exploded and then grabbed a towel. He tossed it at me when he was done with it. I wiped myself off a little disappointed that I did not reach the level of pleasure that I wanted to reach.

He said, "My mom will be here soon. I'll call you later."

I felt used and was starting to regret ever having sex with Tyrell. I just dismissed my thoughts and tried to ensure myself it will get better once we have more experience. I went home after getting dressed, with no hug, no kiss, just a walk to the door. I walked across the street and immediately went to my room in a trance to grab my things to take a shower. Cassidy was on the phone and did not even acknowledge me when I walked in. I felt invisible to everyone except Sénar. On the way to the bathroom to take a shower Sénar was coming out of his room. When he saw me, he said, "What's up ma."

He smiled his special smile for me. I looked down when I said, "Hey Sénar."

I couldn't even look him in his eyes. He stopped to ask, "What's wrong, Treasure?"

On the verge of tears, I answered, "Nothing. I'm fine."

He shook his head and said, "Ok, well, I am making dinner in a minute, are you going to help me?"

Without looking at him, I replied, "Yeah, I'll help."

Sénar was excited when he said, "Ok, cool."

I took a shower and cried because I felt so vacant inside. I was in a house full of people and had a boyfriend that lived across the street, but somehow, I still felt alone. I showered and put some pajama pants on and a T-shirt to go help Sénar with dinner downstairs. He was in a good mood.

"Hey, Treasure," Sénar said, smiling at me when he gave me the vegetables I needed to cut. I rolled my eyes at his happiness. I washed the vegetables and set them up to cut them. I sighed before I called his name, "Sénar?"

He was gazing at me when he asked, "What's up ma?"

I asked, "What are you making? How do you want me to cut them?"

He answered, "I am making beef and broccoli, so you have to mince the vegetables, instead of slicing them." He came toward me and showed me how. Then he went back to cutting and seasoning the beef. I really wanted to ask him what he saw in me that Tyrell didn't, but I didn't have the courage. I just did what I was told and kept my mouth closed.

Sénar made conversation, "Tomorrow I find out what position I play. I can't wait! I want to smash fools all season! I hope I get a good position and a lot of playtime." He was full of excitement when he asked, "How was your day?"

I shrugged my shoulders, "It was ok."

Sénar smirked, "Well, it doesn't look like it."

Sénar's phone rung, he answered, "I am doing something, I'll call you back when I'm done." Whoever it was must have said something to irritate him. He repeated himself, "I told you, I would call you back when I'm done." He hung up the phone and looked at the vegetables I cut, then decided to mince them smaller before he put them in with the beef.

Sénar continued, "Find something to do Treasure. Don't waste your time in the bleachers all day and maybe you will have a better school year."

I just ignored him as Ken came downstairs and complained, "Damn, y'all act like y'all own the damn place."

Sénar laughed and greeted his dad, "What's up pops?"

Ken sat down at the table and said, "Treasure, get me a beer."

Sénar finished up the food and tried not to look bothered. I reluctantly got up and went to the fridge to open it for Ken's beer but didn't see any.

"They are way in the back, you're going to have to put your back into it to reach them."

He laughed, and I smacked my lips then bent over to get his stupid beer way from the back of the fridge. Before grabbing one, I rearranged some things to bring them to the front and grabbed one to bring to him. When I was done, Sénar and his dad were staring at me. I walked toward Ken to give him his beer, "Damn, it took you long enough," Ken complained.

I gave Ken his beer and went to sit back down at the kitchen nook to avoid sitting with Ken at the table. My mom didn't come down, so when Sénar handed me a plate, Ken said, "Treasure, make me a plate and bring me another beer."

Sénar appeared agitated with Ken's rude requests. I made Ken a plate, grabbed him a beer, and set it on the table. He waited for me to have an attitude, but I just went back to the kitchen to make my own plate. Sénar scanned me for emotions, but I was drained from my thoughts, I couldn't even read them. I just made my plate and ate my food silently. Sénar sat down with me and watched me without a word. Ken got up and threw his plate in the sink and grabbed his own beer before going back upstairs. I didn't look at either of them, I just got up to wash my plate as Cassidy came down to put a little food in a bowl before turning back to go upstairs. Sénar put the food up and cleaned as I washed my plate. When I was done, I went to my room and went to sleep.

Every morning, I went to Tyrell's house to make out. Sometimes having sex before we went to school and sometimes after practice, if his mom wasn't home. Every time we had sex It was always quick or rushed. The first two weeks of school were pretty hectic. Tyrell and I were having sex regularly, but he only worried about his own pleasure, he didn't even bother to make sure I was satisfied. It was Friday and tonight was the first game of the school year. That was all Tyrell talked about this week, with the exception of Leah. I went to his house before school and wanted to have sex, so I came on to him.

He pushed me off of him and said, "Girl, I need my energy for the game, maybe afterwards."

I smacked my lips and pouted, and he asked, "Is your girl Leah going?"

I was annoyed with his fascination with Leah and answered, "I don't know. Why?"

He ignored my question, then said, "Call her and see if she wants a ride."

I rolled my eyes out of frustration and asked, "Why do you care so much? Sheesh let her find her own way."

Tyrell looked at me with an attitude and asked, "Why you hatin' on her so hard like that?"

Laughing, I said, "Tyrell, you sound silly."

He smirked, "What, you don't like competition?"

I looked at him with my own attitude brewing before I answered, "I didn't know we were in a competition."

He laughed then said, "Whatever, let's go."

I was so irritated with Tyrell and Leah because they were way too familiar. Leah was always calling the house asking me stupid questions about me and Tyrell or me and Sénar. When me and Tyrell got to school, we went our separate ways without saying a word to each other. I thought long and hard about Tyrell's stupid comments this morning. I was going to ask Leah some damn questions of my own today. At lunch time Leah came to sit with me at the table where I ate my lunch every day.

She sat down and said, "Damn, that bitch London don't give Sénar no breathing room." I just stared at her and ate my food. She looked at me then said, "That's how you need to be with Tyrell's ass."

She laughed and I looked for Tyrell to see him talking with one of the cheerleaders and some of his boys. The cheerleader wrapped her arm around Tyrell, and I wanted to rip them off. Leah said, "Damn girl, are you going to let her disrespect you like that?"

I sighed and replied, "Girl please, I am not worried about her."

Leah said, "Oh, I see."

Tyrell came to the table to talk to me and Leah. He was smiling and greeted us both, "Hey ladies."

Leah smiled back, I rolled my eyes and got up. Tyrell asked, "You need a ride to the game later, Leah?"

She answered, "Hell yeah!"

Tyrell then offered, "Me and Treasure will pick you up before the game."

Before Leah walked off, she replied, "Cool."

Tyrell saw my irritation and asked, "What?"

I threw my trash away before I walked off. I noticed Sénar watching us as London tightly held on to him. Tyrell came after me, grabbing my arm, "Aye, don't walk away from me like that!"

I snatched my arm away from him. Angry now, I replied, "Don't grab me like that!"

I had fury in my eyes and my breathing increased. Tyrell looked at me like I was crazy. Sénar had his own lustful fury in his eyes as he bit his lip and watched from afar. Everyone was watching and I did not want to make a scene. "Tyrell, I am going to class now, ok? I will see you later," when I said it, my speech was pressured, and I felt like I was going to snap. Tyrell pulled me to him smiling flirtatiously when he demanded, "Give me a kiss first."

I hesitantly tried to kiss him quickly, but he pulled me forward by the back of my neck and forced his tongue in my mouth. I was so embarrassed, I pushed him off me with him laughing. I left the lunchroom infuriated. I needed to pull myself together before my next class with Leah. I was trying to look busy when Leah hurried over to me to ask, "Treasure, did you and Tyrell get into it?"

I looked at her with an attitude, "Why and how do you know?"

Shocked, she replied, "Damn everybody is talking about it. Why do you sound like you are mad at me?"

I snapped, "Well, why are you so friendly with Tyrell?"

She rolled her eyes, "Girl, every girl flirts with Tyrell and you are worried about me? I guess I will take that as a compliment."

She smirked then smiled at me, which instantly made me think about punching her right in her smile. My fury started to come back when she laughed.

"Damn girl, you are pressed," she said before she turned to do her work. She dismissed me before I could dismiss her, which further agitated me. I went to my next class and avoided eye contact with everyone; I was ready to explode. In our last class, I tried not to stare a hole in the back of Leah's head as I thought of all her stupid comments and questions. She got up leaving the class without waiting for me. After school, Leah made her way over to Tyrell and was just chatting away while they waited for me. I saw Sénar and London walking to

London's car. I was so mad, I wanted to rip Leah to shreds but instead I walked to the passenger side of Tyrell's car without saying a word. I got in the car first, then Leah and Tyrell got in the car at the same time. It was only quiet for a moment because Leah did not speak to me, but she did speak to Tyrell the whole ride to her house. When we pulled up to Leah's house, Tyrell told Leah we would be back to pick her up for the game. I had an attitude but didn't say anything. Tyrell said, "Treasure you need to stop tripping. That shit is a turn off." I opened my mouth so wide from shock, I quickly closed it back to trap in the many cuss words that would have fallen out of it. I knew how crazy Tyrell drives when he is mad, and I didn't want to experience Tyrell driving like a madman. I folded my arms and successfully kept my words in my mouth as we pulled into Tyrell's driveway. When he parked, I jumped out of the car to cross the street, but Tyrell came from behind me. He grabbed me, forcing me to turn around to face him to say, "Treasure be ready by five thirty. Oh, and get rid of the attitude." He let me go as soon as he saw Sénar pulling up. I quickly ran inside to my room to see Cassidy getting her things ready for a shower. Before she left, she asked, "Why were you and Tyrell arguing?"

My eyes were red, and my irritation level was still high. I lashed out at her, "None of your damn business!"

She smirked, "Whatever!" She said as she hurried out of the room to take a shower. As she left Sénar came in, "See there you go, taking your frustration out on Cassidy. What's on your mind Treasure?"

I felt hurt, angry, and betrayed but I denied it. I replied, "Nothing, Sénar I am fine."

"Well, Tyrell needs to calm his ass down. I wanted to put hands on him. Yo' man, leave his ass alone Treasure."

I was frustrated when I replied, "Leave me alone Sénar! Aren't you doing the same thing to London?"

He got offended, "I don't put my hands on her."

Now offended as well, I responded, "Oh well, what about what you do to me?"

He rolled his eyes when he said, "That's different, Treasure."

I asked, "Oh, is it Sénar?"

He was agitated when he responded, "Look, I don't want to talk about that shit. I just don't want to see you get hurt."

"Don't worry about me. I am fine!"

He glared at me before he said, "Whatever, I have to get ready for my game."

He left and prepared himself for the game. I found a cute outfit; the skirt I wore for the play, a royal blue shirt, with my blue and white Sauconys. I felt cute and the Royal blue was popping. I came out and Sénar's eyes widened when he said, "Damn Treasure." He bit his bottom lip and just gazed at me for a moment. I rolled my eyes and went to the bathroom to brush my teeth and wash my face again. I stared at myself in the mirror while fixing my hair when Sénar poked his head into the bathroom.

I sighed before I asked, "What is it Sénar?"

He mimicked me before he said, "Shut your ass up. Here, take these, it will make the blue pop even more." He handed me a pair of silver hoop earrings with crystal rhinestones on them. I was astonished at how beautiful they were, with them being the perfect size, not too small not too big. I could where them every day if I wanted to.

"Wow, these are nice. Where did you get them from?" When I asked Sénar rolled his eyes before he answered, "Damn you nosey. I got them when we were in the city. I just never gave them to you because you were so worried about that punk ass chain." He smirked at me.

I had an attitude now, so I said, "Shut up Sénar!"

He just rolled his eyes again before saying, "Just put the damn earrings on! Damn. Your mouth is way too slick sometimes." He had a serious face now as he waited for me to put them on. I took my gold earrings off and put the ones that he gave me on. Wow, they were beautiful, and he was right it made the blue stand out even more.

Forget the shirt they went so well with my chocolate complexion. I smiled when I looked in the mirror, I was popping tonight. When I looked at Sénar he was smiling my favorite smile. I was a tad bit aroused and bit my bottom lip before I said, "Move!"

Sénar looked at me appalled when he asked, "Is that all you have to say?"

I smiled as I walked out of the bathroom. Then in a sweet voice, I said, "Thank you Sénar."

He smiled sadistically when he exclaimed, "You look perfect!"

As I turned to walk away, he slapped my ass so hard that I turned around and socked him in his arm. He was laughing as I said, "Ouch! See, that's why I said to move."

Ken came up the stairs as we were tussling, "Damn, Treasure. You are going to the game like that? Shit, what, are you trying to get pregnant too?"

Sénar straightened up when Ken continued, "Boy, get cho' ass ready for the game!"

Sénar turned around to finish getting prepared for the game. I ignored Ken's comment and went downstairs to make me a chicken salad sandwich. I took a bite of my sandwich as Sénar was coming in to get something to drink before leaving. I was chewing on my sandwich and I could feel him behind me.

Sénar said, "Damn Treasure." He smelled my hair and rubbed his hand down my face. When he let me go, I turned around and gave him my sandwich. He winked at me, "Thanks, ma."

The phone rung and I ran to get it and it was Tyrell saying, "Come on. You are ready, right?"

I answered, "Yeah, I'm ready."

I hung up the phone and quickly made me a half of a sandwich before I left out the door. Tyrell was coming out with his football pants and cleats on. He was so tall and so dang fine, I grinned at him.

When Tyrell saw me, he said, "Damn girl." Tyrell's eyes were all over me as he took in my assemble. I was still chewing on the last bite of my sandwich when he said, "Damn you like fine as hell, but what the hell are you eating? I was going ask if you ate but let me guess, you have already."

I looked at him with my feelings hurt and answered, "Damn Tyrell, it was just a half of sandwich."

He shook his head in disgust. I wanted him to have a good game, so I didn't say anything else. I also kept my mouth closed to prevent an argument before picking Leah's dumb ass up because I didn't want her to see us arguing. We picked Leah up and she talked the whole time about cheerleading tryouts that were coming up in the next few weeks. Leah pumped herself up when she said, "I'll run circles around all them hoes."

Tyrell listened attentively before he said, "You can dance too. Yeah, you'll make it." I was silent as I listened to the two of them run their mouths. Leah noticed and asked, "Treasure, do you want to try out with me?"

Before I could say anything, Tyrell replied, "Treasure can't dance." He was laughing when he said it. Offended, I replied, "I am a fast learner and you don't know what I can do."

Tyrell smacked his lips, "Girl, you ain't said shit this whole time. Keep it that way, if you are going to have an attitude."

Without an attitude, I replied, "Leah, I'll think about it."

She exclaimed, "Hell yeah!"

We pulled into the school parking lot to see so many people waiting to get in and it was still early. Since we were with Tyrell, we bypassed all the people in line and went in. Tyrell went to the locker room with the rest of the guys and we found some good seats in the front. Leah and I waited in the bleachers for the game to start as people were starting to pile in. Cassidy and London arrived shortly after us and sat further down from us in the front. I saw Tyrell's parents they waved but the mom was not looking my way, I couldn't tell who she was waving too. I didn't think too much of it because my mom and

Ken walked in right after. I started not to wave but my mom waved at me, so I had to.

Leah waved too and asked, "Damn who is that?"

When I looked at her, she was staring at them. Ugh, I sighed before I answered, "That's my mom and Ken."

Leah smiled, then said, "Damn, your mom is pretty like you, and damn Ken is fine as hell. Ooh, I can see where Sénar gets that shit from."

I rolled my eyes and paid attention to the game as they were ready to introduce the players. Tyrell was a wide receiver, number 11 and Sénar was a running back, number 22. They introduced all the players from our team and then the opponent's team. The game started off explosive with an aggressive running back from the other team who was all over the place with eagerness for the ball. He scored a touchdown early in the game and was dancing on the other side of the goal line. Tyrell and Sénar had words on the field after the other team scored. Tyrell seemed to be talking to Sénar when he walked back to his position as running back. The ball was in our team's possession and the opponent's place kicker kicked the ball down to the field. Tyrell and Sénar ran down the field with Sénar catching the ball. Sénar aggressively ran through the field with Tyrell running behind him. Sénar got cracked hard when he was tackled right before he got to the goal line. He was down for a second but jumped back up and got ready for the next play.

London yelled, "Get 'em, baby!"

The next play Tyrell caught the ball in the end zone for the touchdown and we got the extra point from the field goal too. The game was 7 to 7 at half time. When they came back from half time the boys were hungry for action. Everyone was playing fast and hard. The advantages were obvious as the other team had the size and we had the speed. The opponent's team tried to run the same play as earlier to gain a quick touch down as the player ran down the middle of the field. Sénar caught up to him stopping him with a massive tackle. There was no way Sénar would let him pass again. The next play the quarterback threw the ball to one of his bigger players knowing Sénar would have difficulty stopping him. Sénar caught up to him, hitting him hard but the dude was huge and was able to keep running. Tyrell smashed him right before he reached the goal line. The quarter back from the other team knew he could not get through both Tyrell and Sénar, so they opted out for a 3 point-field goal.

The score was now 7 to 10 with our team down by three. The football was in our team's possession, Tyrell and Sénar ran the middle of the field. Tyrell caught the ball, going for a long touchdown with Sénar ahead of him stopping whoever tried to get in Tyrell's way. Tyrell scored a touchdown! Me and Leah screamed and rooted for them both. The other team faked a pass to the player who cracked Sénar earlier in the game. Sénar was quick to stop him dead in his tracks, tackling him by grabbing his feet. Sénar wasn't letting anybody get passed him. The away team were still down by 3 points the team couldn't get a touchdown and took a field goal for 3 points. Now we were tied with only three minutes left in the game. The ball in our possession the quarter back threw it to Tyrell in hopes of a touchdown, without Sénar in the vicinity he got cracked immediately. The quarter back threw the ball to Tyrell again and ran as far as he could before he was pummeled. After that play, they were all over Tyrell. With only two minutes left in the game, our team's quarterback faked the throw to Tyrell and handed it to Sénar. With the ball in his hand, Sénar took off running toward the goal line with speed and agility that no one could stop. Anyone who came close got schooled with his quick moves. He was approaching the bigger players guarding the end zone and his two boys, linebacker Jerry and defensive guard Rodger made a way by taking the dudes out in the way. He made it to the goal line for a touch down! We missed the field goal for the extra point. With only seconds left, the team went into formation anyway and the clock ran down with the score 19 to 13 with us giving us the win by 6 points. Everyone cheered on our side and went nuts running out to the field. Leah and I walked onto the field to meet Tyrell. He grabbed me and kissed me on the forehead, then put his arm around me and Leah to leave. Before we turned to leave, I could see Sénar watching as he and London kissed on the field. Everybody was congratulating Tyrell and Sénar for their hard work. We met up at Round tables pizza after the game. Our local Round Tables happily fed the football players and their girlfriends to show their appreciation.

Tyrell, Leah and I sat at the table with all his boys from the team and ate pizza. I wasn't the biggest fan of pizza at the moment, with all the commotion and discomfort of having Leah getting the same royalties as myself. Leah had like three different types of pizza on her plate as I had a slice of pepperoni.

Tyrell noticed and said, "Damn Treasure, don't be scared to eat food now, half a sandwich my ass man."

London and Sénar sat at a different table with some of the cheerleaders and Sénar's boys, Jerry and Rodger. After we ate, we headed to the parking lot to hang out before calling it a night. Leah was having a blast talking about the game and drinking beers with Tyrell and his boys. Tyrell gave me a beer; I tasted it and almost gagged because it tasted horrible. I just held it in my hand as I noticed Sénar and London approaching us.

Leah saw Sénar and said, "Hey, Sénar."

He looked at her and said, 'What's up Leah."

Tyrell stopped talking to his boys to hear what Sénar had to say. Sénar turned his attention to me and said, "Aye, don't be out too late, man, I'm not trying to hear my pop's mouth."

Tyrell responded before I could, "Man, get cho' weak ass outta here, Sénar! You ain't her daddy, and neither is that nigga!"

I saw the fire in Sénar's eyes, and so did Leah as she watched Sénar like a hawk. London tightened her grip on Sénar's arm and whined, "Come on babe, let's go; just let her ass get in trouble."

I didn't want to say anything to her and make the situation worse, so I ignored her comment, since Sénar ignored Tyrell's. I looked at him and said, "I heard you, Sénar."

Leah said, "Damn Sénar, have a drink and chill."

London quickly checked her, "Look, little girl, focus on what you got going on over there."

London put her hand up to include Tyrell and me in her hand motion of a triangle. Sénar watched Tyrell as he continued to drink and said, "Yo ass weak nigga, drinking like that knowing you have to drive."

Tyrell snatched the beer out of my hand and downed it in front of Sénar. He handed Leah the empty bottle to put in a bag that was next to her. Tyrell said, "My business and my girl."

Tyrell grabbed me from behind to pull me near to him, kissing me on my neck and rubbing his hands all over my body in front of everyone. Sénar smiled, but his eyes filled with fire and fury as London grabbed his arm to beg, "Babe, let's go!" Tyrell turned me around to face him and squeezed my ass, lifting my skirt, almost revealing my butt cheeks, then stuck his tongue in my mouth. I resisted a little but felt his grip tighten on my ass, then he released me when he saw Sénar move.

Tyrell miffed at him and challenged him, "What lil' nigga, what are you going to do?"

Some of their teammates came over to get between Sénar and Tyrell. I tried to calm Tyrell, and London tried to calm Sénar. Leah just watched everything unfold and didn't say another word. Sénar was enraged along with Tyrell. Sénar and London left, and we drove Leah home. On the way home, Leah didn't say much until right before we got to her house.

She asked, "Treasure those are some dope ass earrings, where did you get them from?" I could tell by the way she asked; she was trying to start some shit. I ignored her attempt to further sabotage the night.

Tyrell asked, "Didn't you hear her ask you a question? What's your problem? Answer her damn question!"

He demanded me to answer, and I reluctantly answered, "From the city."

She quickly said, "Yeah, girl, they are popping! I ain't ever seen those before."

Tyrell thought for a second before he asked, "From the city? When did you go to the city?"

I answered, "In the summer."

He looked at me, angrily and asked, "With who?"

I hung my head low and hesitated to answer. He got even more upset and again asked, "With who, Treasure?"

I yelled, "With Sénar!"

Leah was probably smiling in the back seat because she knew exactly what she was doing. We pulled up to her house, and Tyrell said, "Goodnight, Leah," in a regular tone. When she got out, Tyrell drove off in a rage.

He looked at me with rage and asked, "What the hell, Treasure, you went to the city and shit with that nigga?"

I tried to console him by saying, "We went to go school shopping for the school year. Tyrell that was it! It was no big deal! Please slow down, Tyrell!"

I begged him because I was so scared of him being both angry and drunk. My heart was racing from the fear of us possibly wrecking the car with his unstable driving. We pulled up to Tyrell's house, tires screeching and all. I saw Sénar stand to attention as before he was relaxing on his car while London kissed all over him. Sénar and Tyrell locked eyes when we got out of the car. I quickly ran around the back of the car to meet Tyrell.

I begged, "Please don't make a scene. Tyrell, please."

He glared at me, "Take the earrings off."

I stared at him before I asked, "What? Why?"

He got infuriated and demanded loud enough, so Sénar could hear him when he said, "Take the earrings off!"

I didn't have to look back to know that Sénar was furious; I could feel his anguish. When I didn't move fast enough, he tried to snatch them out, and I could hear London begging Sénar to chill. I folded under pressure, "Ok, Tyrell, I'll take them off."

I took them out of my ear and tried to put them in my pocket, but he snatched them from me. Before I could turn around to go home, he grabbed me to say, "Nah, let's go upstairs."

I hesitated but said, "Ok, Tyrell, but please calm down first."

He replied, "Give me a kiss."

I held on to him tightly and kissed him passionately. He squeezed my ass and led me into his house. Once upstairs, he threw his football gear off and then threw my earrings on the floor.

He asked, "Do you love me, Treasure?"

I kissed him and answered, "Yes Tyrell, I love you."

I kissed him again, and he kissed me back, rubbing me all over. He pulled my skirt up and pulled my panties off. He laid me down on the bed, entering me with passion and lust rippling through him. He thrusted his self in and out of me deeply. He grabbed my neck from behind, biting and sucking on my neck so hard, it aroused me. I started to get excited and moved with his thrust as he plunged himself in and out faster until he quickly jumped up. I felt his hot juices splash on my thighs and some parts of my legs.

I asked, "Why did you stop?"

He looked at me like I was stupid when he said, "Why are you playing dumb? I just nutted all over the damn place, shit!"

He grabbed a towel to wipe himself off and then threw it at me to wipe myself off. I went to his bathroom to clean myself up and put my panties back on. When I came out of the bathroom, despite our crazy night, I told him, "Well, next time I want to nut too."

Once again, he looked at me like I was stupid before he said, "Girls don't nut. Wow. I think you need some sleep."

He laughed at me which prompted me to be clearer when I spoke, "Well then, I want to cum."

He laughed again, "What the hell are you talking about, Treasure?"

Now nervous, I replied, "I read about it in a book."

He responded as if he was irritated, "Treasure, my mom is about to be home. Maybe we can work on that in the future." I tried to grab my earrings, but he stopped me to say, "Hell no! You'll get them back when you cum." He laughed and said, "Come on."

I was upset, I was leaving without my earrings and without cumming. *Sheesh, what else was I leaving without?* He walked me downstairs and opened the door to see Sénar and London. He became instantly agitated. He slapped my ass and without giving me a kiss, he said, "Goodnight, Treasure." He closed the door, and I walked across the street.

Sénar got out of his car to say, "Wait up, Treasure."

I smacked my lips and dismissed his request with my hand as I walked in the front door of the house. Ken bellowed, "Why the hell are you coming in this late?"

I couldn't see him, but I heard his voice from the kitchen where he must have been sitting in the dark. He scared the living daylights out of me. I answered him cautiously, "We went to get pizza and stuff after the-"

He cut me off to ask, "Where is Sénar at?"

Sénar came in the door. Ken was silent, while Sénar went up the stairs. He quickly turned around and motioned me to come up the steps. Sénar whispered, "Man, go to bed Treasure."

He went to his room, and I went to mine. Cassidy was in the bed sleeping, so I quietly looked for nightclothes. I know Sénar told me to go to bed, but I wanted to take a shower. I grabbed my things and took a quick shower. On my way out of the bathroom, Ken was walking down the hall and smelling the air before he went to his room. I ran to my room and jumped in the bed thanking God Ken didn't do anything but smell the air.

Chapter 4

I woke up the next morning still feeling tired because I didn't sleep very well. I went to the bathroom to brush my teeth and wash my face, but the door was locked. Cassidy was probably in there since she wasn't in the room when I woke up. I went downstairs because I was starving. I barely ate last night after getting chewed out over a half a sandwich and not wanting that greasy pizza everyone else was happy to eat. Meanwhile, Leah had three slices of pizza and Tyrell didn't say anything to her. Ugh, I was at my wit's end with Tyrell, but I loved him and wanted to believe he meant well. Also, I wasn't worried about Leah, she was just as desperate as all the other girls. I looked on top of the refrigerator to see a box of Captain Crunch cereal that was looking like a full course meal to me right now. I grabbed it down and got a bowl, eager to eat something to keep my stomach from eating me. I didn't care, I had on pajama pants, a spaghetti strap shirt, with no socks or shoes on. Last night was so crazy that it really drained me.

Cassidy came down as I was pouring some cereal to ask, "Where were you last night, Treasure?"

I snapped at her, "Why do you want to know?"

Cassidy smacked her lips then said, "My daddy was looking for you. Your ass love trouble, huh?"

I poured milk into my cereal while Cassidy ran her mouth sitting at the counter. Sénar came down and saw me about to eat cereal. He pretended to be shocked and hurt before he said, "Oh, you couldn't wait for Chef Sénar?"

He was laughing until he saw Cassidy's facial expression change to shock for real, when Cassidy exclaimed, "Oh shit! What the hell is that on your neck?"

I almost forgot that Tyrell bit and sucked so hard on my neck last night that it hurt. Sénar grabbed my face to turn it so he could see what Cassidy was seeing. His eyes filled with hurt, and he was not playing this time.

Cassidy asked, "Has my daddy seen that yet?" Sénar didn't say anything but all his emotions were in his eyes. Cassidy said, "Ooh, you are going to get in trouble."

I smacked my lips, "Shut up Cassidy, I am not scared of him. It's not that big of a deal."

Ken came in and asked, "Scared of who? Treasure?" Everyone got quiet, especially Sénar. I just turned away and tried to eat my cereal when Ken said, "Treasure, get me a beer."

I put my spoon down with an attitude because I didn't even get a damn spoon of food before he came down with orders, and it was too damn early to be drinking. I bent over to get his stupid beer, way from the back of the refrigerator and pulled the rest to the front. I grabbed it and gave it to him as Cassidy and Sénar looked like two worried little kids. Ken snatched the beer from me. I tried to turn back to my bowl of cereal when he snatched me back by my arm and grabbed me by the face like Sénar did before he came in. Sénar got super uncomfortable and Cassidy squirmed in her seat when Ken roared, "What the fuck is that on your damn neck?"

I was scared and mad at the same time. I tried to snatch my face away from him unsuccessfully. He flung me across the kitchen as Cassidy got up to run upstairs. Sénar wanted to help me but he didn't move until Ken snatched him up by his shirt to say, "I know you didn't do that shit boy! I taught you better than that. Right?"

Sénar shook his head no to his first statement and to his question Sénar answered, "Yes sir, you did."

Ken looked at me as I was getting up off the floor with my now stronger arm that broke my fall against the floor. He was talking to both of us, "Y'all let that little nigga do this shit?"

I glared at him and stayed silent to prevent from snapping on him. He took the opportunity to go in on Sénar when he said, "Damn Sénar, I guess both your games are weak, huh? You let that lil' nigga do that shit to her?"

I was pissed off; he was talking about me as if I wasn't there. I felt bad for Sénar because Tyrell called him weak earlier and I could tell his dad calling him that hurt his feelings, on top of his reaction to my neck. I tried to stick up for him when I said, "It's not Sénar's fault, so don't blame him or try to demean him. I'm a big girl, so it was nothing he could do to stop me. And little nigga is not his name, it's Tyrell and he's my boyfriend. What's the big deal? It could be worse."

I folded my arms while Sénar put his head down in disappointment. Ken exploded, "What the fuck did you just say to me? You got a slick ass mouth! Your ass is on punishment until the fuck I say so! You better not leave this damn house unless me or Sénar know where your ass is at!"

My mouth dropped open out of shock and I yelled, "What? You can't do that you're not my daddy!"

Ken slapped the glass bowl of cereal I poured and never got to eat onto the floor, sending milk and glass shards throughout the kitchen floor. I stood in place as Ken got into my face and said, "Damn right I'm not your daddy and that nigga ain't here either, so you are going to respect me! If it wasn't for Sénar's ass, I would be your daddy, alright!"

Ken grabbed Sénar by his shirt, slamming him against the cabinet, "You heard what I said? Sénar you watch her motherfuckin' ass like a hawk for the next few weeks!"

I was fuming and ready to snap at Ken's bizarre punishment when my mom came in and asked, "Ken what's going on?" Ken was furious while he still held Sénar by his shirt giving him demands and making him feel like it was his fault as well. I wanted to start yelling out how crazy and inappropriate Ken was acting lately and how good Sénar fucked me when they were on their little mini vacation, but I knew she wouldn't listen because she was asking Ken, instead of me what was going on.

Ken glared at me before he answered, "Treasure was being the little fast ass that you swore she wasn't!"

He snatched me by my face to show my mom the hickey on my neck. Sénar winced when he had to see it again. I snatched my face out of Ken's hand. My mom appeared to be hurt when she focused on Sénar in a questioning manner, but Ken said, "He didn't do that shit, he ain't dumb enough to do that bullshit to her. That little nigga across the street did that shit to her!"

My mother's hurt changed to rage as she yelled, "You lied to me! Out there being a whore like your daddy!"

She slapped me and fury filled my eyes, along with flaming hot tears. I wanted to rip her to shreds and make her feel the pain I felt. Sénar became alarmed when he saw my anger increase. I yelled, "You lied to me too! All you care about is Ken! You said you would be here for-"

My mom cut me off, "Treasure, don't you dare try to make this about me. Have some respect for yourself! You are the one putting your business out there! Now everybody knows what your ass was doing last night! So now you have to pay the consequences! Ugh, you make me sick!"

She yelled at me, making me wish I could hit her but instead, I used my words, "No, it's probably the vodka, the wine or Ke-"

I couldn't even finish my sentence before she back handed me in my mouth and continued to hit me until I snapped. I pushed her off of me, almost hitting her afterward but Sénar grabbed me and said, "Treasure! What the hell, don't put your hands on your mom."

My mom pushed Sénar out of the way, almost slipping on the milk to get to me. She tried to maul me when Ken snatched her up and Sénar snatched me up having to slam me against the fridge to keep me from going after her. I couldn't feel a thing, I was numb with anger. I wanted to kill every single one of them in the house with me. Sénar pleaded, "Treasure? Man, you are tripping. Chill out, please!"

Ken grabbed Sénar with his other hand while holding my mom while she was still trying to get to me. Ken dared me to approach them as tears were streaming down my face and red flashes plagued my mind.

Ken said, "Y'all heard what the fuck I said!" He let Sénar go before he glared at me and pointed his finger in my face to threaten, "If you ever put your hands on your mom again, I will see to it that you never do it again." I glared back at him as I was ready for whatever. I was so furious that whoever came for me next, I was going to unleash all the pent-up frustration that I had brewing in my soul. Sénar could see that I was beyond my threshold and had a look of worry on his face.

My mom said, "I am so disappointed in you! You, disrespectful little bit-" Ken shook my mom and roared, "Enough!" He released her and she ran upstairs crying. He looked at Sénar and said, "You heard what the fuck I said, right?" Sénar answered, "Yes sir!" Ken looked at me and smirked before he said, "Let's see how much he likes your ass when he can't get to that pretty neck and that tight little pussy of yours." He looked back at Sénar to ask, "How that little nigga get two Treasures?"

He laughed at Sénar before he said, "Sénar, y'all clean this shit up."

There was milk mixed with blood and shattered pieces of glass all over the floor. Ken left upstairs while Sénar glared at me and said, "What the fuck Treasure! Was it worth it at least? Did you even cum?"

Still angry and embarrassed, I answered, "I don't know, but it felt good."

He laughed and said, "Oh, so you let him mark you up like territory and he can't even make you cum?"

I stared at him because I was passed angry with his stupid questions. I replied, "Why are you so worried about it? It's none of your business!"

He was so quick to come to me, I thought he used the milk to glide across the kitchen. He explained, "It is my business because you be about to get me and you murked in here! You disrespected your mom and you put your hands on her!" He yelled at me. I panicked when he moved so close to me and lowered his face to mine.

He whispered, "And you had the balls to talk back to my pops, when you know his ass is crazy! You're going to get us both killed if you don't watch that slick ass mouth of yours! And all over some grimy ass nigga that can't even make you cum!"

He was infuriated with me, I whimpered as the fury slowly left my body. Sénar's speech was pressured when he said, "Maybe if he knew what he was doing, your attitude wouldn't be so damn bad!" When Sénar snatched me up into the air, fear gripped me as he slammed me down onto the counter onto my ass. Then he said, "You probably just need to be fucked right, to get some act right!"

I was so scared, I braced myself for what was next. He bent down, I held my breath as he grabbed my foot and lifted it up. Confused, scared, and belittled as I waited to be further abused when pain surpassed all my current emotions. I just put my head back, bit my bottom lip and closed my eyes until the pain stopped. I opened my eyes and looked down to see Sénar staring at me with his sadistic smile. He said, "Ooh, yo ass is nuts!" He checked both of my feet with a perplexed look on his face. He asked, "You didn't feel all this glass in your foot?"

It was blood everywhere when I looked around the kitchen and it was all coming from my feet. The fury that pumped through my blood this entire time continued to subside as Sénar's face appeared concerned. He got up and said, "Man, stay right here. I'll be right back." He left me sitting on the counter in my thoughts while he went upstairs for something. Cassidy came back downstairs and gasped when walked into the kitchen.

She asked, "What the hell happened in here?" She looked mortified at all the blood, milk, and glass on the floor. Then looked at me patiently waiting for Sénar as I ignored her question. Cassidy hated when I ignored her, so she flashed, "You're such a bitch! I know you heard me!"

I jumped off the counter and the pain in my foot dropped me to the floor. I wanted to scream but instead I moaned until I was able to force out a response, "You are the bitch! It's none of your fuc-"

Sénar cut me off, "Treasure!"

I stopped talking as Sénar put all the stuff in his hand down and snatched me off the floor, then slammed me back down on the counter where he told me to stay. Sénar reprimanded me, "Damn, I told your ass to sit here!" Cassidy looked at both of us like we were crazy.

She was emotional when she asked, "Sénar, what happened?"

He organized all the stuff he brought down, grabbing the first aid kit then answered, "Cassidy, if you wanted to know then you would have stayed. You did the right thing, trust me."

She smacked her lips then said, "Whatever, with Treasure's smart-ass mouth, I am sure she got whatever she deserved!"

I tried to jump off the counter again to get to Cassidy and Sénar was quick to rush to slam me back down. Sénar demanded, "Treasure sit your ass still man and calm your ass down, so I can get this damn glass out of your foot!" He stood in between my legs with his hand on my chest as we both had fury in our eyes. Sénar broke our stare and glared at Cassidy before saying, "Go! I will come get you when I clean this mess up and make something to eat!" She quickly left and ran up the stairs without another word. Sénar still had his hand on my chest, so I slapped it away. He glared at me then said, "Dang, your ass is fucking crazy!"

He pulled a chair up in front of me and snatched my right foot to hold it up to carefully examine it. He let it down gently and checked the left foot but didn't need to spend as much time to examine it. He got up to wash his hands and prepared a bowl of water to clean my foot. He grabbed a towel and dipped it into the bowl to clean the left foot. He said, "Hold still this won't take long, it's not as bad as the other foot." He took the pieces of glass out with a pair of tweezers and wiped it clean with alcohol. He squeezed it and asked, "Do you feel any glass or pain still?" I shook my head no. He put Neosporin on my foot, wrapped it with gauze, and put a sock on it. I just watched Sénar swiftly doctor up my wounds like an expert. He got up to pour the water out of the bowl to make a fresh batch and grabbed another towel. He washed his hands again and returned to sit down to work on my right foot. When he grabbed it, I winced in pain as it was extremely sore.

He smiled before he said, "I'm going to get the smaller pieces out first. This is going to hurt but knowing your kinky ass, you might like this shit!"

He bit his bottom lip and smiled his famous sadistic smile. I closed my eyes then put my head back as the intense pain pierced my conscience and cleared my mind. I groaned and bit my lip until the pained decreased. When I opened my eyes, Ken and Sénar were gawking at me. Instantly alarmed, I straightened up when Ken spoke, "Damn Sénar, now you're her doctor too?"

Ken laughed and Sénar just shook his head. He probably was thinking Ken was nuts just like I was thinking. Ken looked at me sadistically and then looked at Sénar to say, "Sénar hurry up and clean this shit up. It looks like a murder scene up in here." Sénar winced at his words then replied, "Yes sir." I glared at Ken and he glared back at me until my mom came down and attempted to come into the kitchen.

My mom asked, "What's wrong now?" Seeing all three of us in awkward positions. Ken stopped her from coming any further as if he was preventing her from seeing the mess in the kitchen.

Ken said, "Nothing angel baby, Sénar got it!"

My mom and Ken headed out the door with my mom yelling back at me, "Treasure we need to talk when I get back!"

Ken rushed her out the door and I rolled my eyes. Sénar smirked at me then said, "Damn, you are really trippin', Treasure."

I looked at him and said, "Shut up Sénar, damn!"

I snatched my foot from him and tried to get up and he grabbed my waist to sit me down, without even getting up. He roared, "Sit cho' ass down, man!" He snatched my foot back and squeezed it making me moan as he smiled at me deviously.

I sighed before I said, "Sénar, stop playing."

He laughed and then got serious when he said, "This last piece of glass needs to be taken out, but it is deep." He tried not being inappropriate when he said deep, but my legs were wide open, and he was already aroused by my reactions. He said, "Damn Treasure, I wish I could get you to open up like this when I am having dessert."

He winked at me and snatched the glass out of my foot. I tilted my head back and screamed as the pain arched my back from the intensity surging through my body. I moaned while Sénar squeezed my foot to apply pressure to stop the bleeding. When the throbbing pain subsided, I opened my eyes and Sénar was looking at me intently while holding my foot. He grabbed a brown liquid and put it on my foot instead of alcohol.

I asked, "What's that brown stuff Sénar?"

He answered, "It's a type of iodine to sterilize the area to help prevent infection because it was so deep. Let me wrap it tight. I am almost done, ma." He checked the other areas of my foot to ensure all the glass was out before he wrapped it up and put a sock on it. He stood up and squeezed my thighs pulling me closer to him then said, "There, all better."

I looked down to avoid eye contact as I reluctantly said, "Thank you, Sénar."

I looked at the mess in the kitchen as my reality started to settle back in. I tried to hold onto my anger to keep from crying. Sénar chin upped me and started to clean up after putting a pair of his Nike flip flops on me which were too big but really comfortable.

I started to feel bad as he started to clean, so I asked, "You want me to help you?"

He looked at me when he answered, "Yeah."

I started to get up, but he stopped me by gently pushing me back down. He said, "Just behave, work on your attitude, and sit pretty." He winked at me then continued, "Besides Treasure, you will be lucky if you can even walk in the morning, the cut is pretty bad."

He didn't say anything else as he cleaned the kitchen, organizing everything and putting everything back like it was before the chaos took place. He had a method and plan in everything he did. I watched him perform a miracle in less than ten minutes. The kitchen was spotless all the way down to every crevice and corner. He put everything back that he brought down to treat my foot and washed his hands before he started breakfast.

He then said, "Wallah! Chef Sénar is here."

I allowed myself to laugh at his goofiness amid a traumatic experience as if nothing ever happened. I drifted into my thoughts of wondering how he so effortlessly doctored me up and then cleaned everything up methodically to appear as if it was a normal Saturday morning. "Treasure?" Sénar called my name startling me back to my current reality when he asked, "Treasure what are you over there thinking about?"

I shook my head and almost didn't say anything, but I gained the courage to ask, "How did you learn to do everything so fast?"

He grew weary when he answered, "Treasure, you really don't want to know that ma. Trust me."

He continued cooking and made me a plate before he called Cassidy downstairs to eat. Cassidy came down cautiously, sitting at the kitchen nook to peak over it to ensure the scene was cleared before walking in to make a plate. After she made her plate, Cassidy returned to sit at the kitchen nook to eat. Sénar made a plate and sat at the table, while I sat on the counter in the kitchen. I was afraid the floor would consume the rest of me if I got down. Ken and my mom came in after I finished eating with bags and of course their drinks of choice.

My mom still agitated with me, said, "Treasure get down off my counter."

She glared at me and I glared back with anger fueling my urgency to get down. Everything went from calm to chaotic as my foot hit the floor after forgetting about the massive gash in my foot as I yelped in anguish. Sénar jumped to assist me as I fell to the floor.

I pushed him off me and said, "I'm a big girl, I can handle it."

I still used him to stand up before I limped off, hopping away until I used my anger to fuel my tolerance to the pain. I heard my mom ask Sénar what was wrong with me. Sénar explained my injuries to her to the best of his ability. I could hear my mom apologizing to Sénar for pushing him which further agitated me. How could she apologize to him when I am the one, she hurt? I crossed my arms and was fuming inside. I hated her and wished I could limp away, since running was not an option, but I had nowhere to limp to. I hated all of them at the moment. Sénar was almost an exception, although I didn't know why, except maybe that he helped me so much; even though I hated to admit it. Somehow once again, I was being held hostage. I couldn't believe Ken wanted to punish me and was going to use Sénar to enforce it. I thought, *what kind of sick stuff was that?* My mom was crazy and didn't seem to care about me anymore, so she could care less how I was being punished. She barely spoke to me, unless she was demeaning me or asking dumb ass questions. Sénar finished cleaning and came to sit with me in the living room to watch TV. He looked at me and shook his head in disappointment.

Still agitated, I asked, "What are you shaking your head for Sénar?"

He looked back in the kitchen to ensure no one was coming and said, "You need some act right." He grabbed his man stick and added, "From me, somebody who knows how to handle that ass."

I rolled my eyes at him, ignoring his comment and we watched TV. The doorbell rang and my mom answered the door. It was London at the door and my mom was hospitable as she invited her in.

Sénar looked at me then said, "You can get it instead of her, if you stop playing so much."

London walked into the living room with us and kissed Sénar in his mouth like she was looking for something in there with her tongue. My mom returned to the kitchen where Ken was. I was so annoyed with everyone, even London. She was so clingy and insecure, which I could not understand. She was pretty and popular, but she was so sprung on Sénar that it was pathetic. I remembered what Sénar said about her and laughed to myself as I turned the channel to my favorite show *Girlfriends*. Sénar watched me as if he knew what I was thinking and smirked at me while London touched all over his body.

"Babe chill," Sénar said because she was all over him.

She smacked her lips and glared at me. Sénar asked, "Treasure, what is this crap you are watching? Put something else on."

I had my own attitude when I responded, "No!"

Cassidy happened to walk pass and give me a dirty look before going upstairs. London chimed in with her usual request, "Come on babe, let's go to your room."

Sénar was annoyed with her already, "London, I will take care of you, ok? Just relax, you just got here, damn."

She pouted and quietly sat next to him, never taking her hands off of him. I was annoyed that Sénar could do whatever he wanted with his sex life. Hell, even Sabrina and Cassidy did whatever they wanted at one time. Why was Ken so worried about me? I was in my thoughts feeling a little salty when I looked at Sénar, he had his famous sadistic smile as if he could read my thoughts.

I rolled my eyes at him and London asked, "What's her problem?"

Sénar and I both ignored her and continued to watched TV. She couldn't keep her hands off of him and I was getting annoyed. I turned the TV up, so I didn't have to hear her desperation. Ken walked into the living room and asked, "Why is the damn TV so loud?"

He saw London all over Sénar and smirked at me before he said, "Turn that shit down."

I turned it down and Ken went upstairs with my mom following behind him like a puppy. London kept begging Sénar to go to his room. He finally got up and snatched her ass off the couch and then slapped her on her ass. Not as hard as he slaps mine; it was more like a tap.

She still got excited though. Sénar said, "Go upstairs, I'll be there in a minute." London got even more excited and ran upstairs. I rolled my eyes at Sénar before he said, "You are something else. Do you need anything before I go upstairs?"

I shook my head no and ignored him. He laughed, leaving me there on the couch and went upstairs to perform his other duties. The house was so quiet, I took a nap on the couch. Sénar and London came back down after a couple of hours. She was smiling and happy as he kissed her goodbye. I felt a little jealousy when I saw how happy she was when she left and Sénar noticed.

He said, "Hey, I told you that could be you. Let me know when you ready for an attitude adjustment."

I looked at him and said, "Shut up Sénar."

He laughed and walked away. I tried to get up and fell to the floor when the piercing pain shot through my right foot.

Sénar turned around and asked, "Where do you want to go ma?"

I sighed before reluctantly answering, "To the bathroom."

He picked me up off the floor and took me upstairs. I told him he could put me down. I hopped into the bathroom and dropped to the floor to crawl to the toilet, to prevent walking. When I was done, I crawled to the door to open it from the floor to see Sénar waiting for me. I was embarrassed, I thought he went back downstairs.

He snatched me up off the floor and said, "Umph, I should take you to my room."

I panicked and said, "No! Sénar, stop playing."

Ken came out and rolled his eyes as he walked past us. Sénar straightened up and followed Ken down the stairs with me in his arms. He smelled my hair and I pushed his head back as he carried me to the kitchen nook. Sénar knew I didn't want to sit at the table with Ken. He just glared at me as Sénar got stuff ready for Tacos. I swear, we never got tired of tacos or fried chicken.

He gave me the cheese grater and said, "Well, there's nothing wrong with your hands, so you could at least grate the cheese." He ran the water and came around to the side of me. He said, "Get on your knees in the chair when I pick you up."

I looked at him like he was crazy and asked, "Why?" Sénar sighed before he answered, "So you can wash your dang hands."

I did as I was told and hovered over the nook to let him put soap on my hands. He rinsed them under water then he dried them. He was going to come around and help me, but I sat back down by myself. He handed me the cheese grater and when I looked at Ken his stare made me so nervous, if my feet worked, I would have walked out.

While Sénar cooked, Ken gave Sénar pointers on his game, "You need to get your weight up and don't get so easily distracted on the field…"

Sénar listened attentively as his dad gave him instructions on how to improve his performance. I was quiet as I grated the cheese and watched Sénar and Ken in their father and son bonding moment. My mom and Cassidy came down to eat and both of them ignored me after making their plates. Grating the cheese was much more of a task tonight as I was sore and unaware of it. After I ate, Sénar saw that I was miserable and tired. He asked, "Do you want to go upstairs?"

Everyone stopped talking and waited for my answer. I just looked down and said, "No."

He shook his head and said, "Ok, well, if you need help, just let me know Treasure." He went back to cleaning the kitchen. I wanted everyone to leave, so I could say yes to him helping me, but everyone just kept talking. I handed Sénar my plate and he asked, "You ready?"

I nodded my head in a yeah motion. I tried to get up, but I had a lot of difficulty. I hopped to the steps on my left foot with Sénar's help. I'm sure everyone was watching when we got to the stairs, he picked me up and took me to my bed. I didn't say anything as he turned around to go back downstairs quickly. I was asleep before I knew it.

Sunday morning, I felt like I got hit by a damn truck. My whole body ached all the way down to my feet. I could barely move, so I just laid there. I listened for breathing to verify if Cassidy was in the room with me or not. No need to listen for breathing, she said, "I know you are awake. So, don't even try to play sleep." I ignored her, so she snapped at me when she said, "Whatever Treasure, you are such a bitch. I swear you get in trouble just to get attention."

I tried to ignore her, but she was completely idiotic to think I wanted all this extra drama or people in my life, currently. I snapped back, "The only time you speak to me is when you are being nosey and then you use the information against me. So, how about you leave me the hell alone and you won't have to worry about being ignored you little bit-"

Sénar came in interrupting me and Cassidy's conversation by asking, "Treasure, how are you feeling ma?"

I just stopped talking and played dead. Cassidy said, "Ugh, she is so stupid!"

I sighed and warned, "If I could get up and whip your ass, Cassidy, I would have done it already! So please, leave me alone. Damn!"

I tried not to cry but I just wanted to be left alone. I held my breath to keep from exploding. Sénar waited for Cassidy to leave before he came in and said, "You never answered me Treasure. How are you feeling?"

I didn't answer him. I just laid there. I was in a lot of pain and I felt emotionally drained. I asked, "Why Sénar?"

He sighed and said, "Damn, I want to know. That's why."

I had an attitude and replied, "I'm fine!" I couldn't see his facial expression, but I assumed he was agitated.

He snapped at me then said, "I'm not the one who got you in trouble, so I don't know why you are acting like that. I know you're in a lot of pain, so I was just checking on you to see if you needed anything."

I was on the verge of tears; I was hurting in so many different ways. I didn't want to speak, and then him hear the pain in my voice. I was quiet but as if he knew I was crying, he left and came back with tissue. He turned me over to face him and he wiped my tears. I didn't stop him as he dried my face. He removed my blanket off of me and I asked, "What are you doing Sénar?"

He opened the door and answered, "I am going to take your crazy ass to the bathroom."

I was confused at first, until my full bladder reminded me why I needed to go to the bathroom, which made me even more nervous. He came and scooped me up off my bed and I held on to him as he carried me to the bathroom. Once in the bathroom, I wanted him to put me down and leave, so I said, "Ok thanks, but just put me down now."

Careful not to agitate him when asking. He did as I asked him, and I swear I almost passed out when my feet touched the ground. I yelped in pain, he picked me back up swiftly and placed me on the counter. I put my forehead on his chest for a second, to gather the strength I needed to speak.

I said, "Damn, that was crucial." We both started laughing and I almost cried when I thought about what was next. I whined, "Oh gosh, what's next Sénar?"

He laughed and said, "Well, you're such a meany pants, you should start with taking those off."

He smiled sadistically in anticipation of me removing my pants.

I pouted, "Sénar no! That's dumb!"

He laughed and asked, "Well, how are you going to use the bathroom dumb ass?"

I popped him on his shoulder while he laughed. After laughing he became serious when he spoke, "You need to take your pants off and I'll put you on the toilet. Then when you're done, get naked."

I looked at him like he was crazy and asked, "Sénar have you lost your mind? You are crazy! No!"

He sighed, then he asked, "Look, you want my help or not?"

I was frustrated when I asked, "Why do I have to get naked?"

He smiled nicely and answered, "Because, I'm going to put you in the bathtub with Epsom salt, to help the soreness of your lovely body. When you get out, I'm going to rub you down with some stuff and take your chocolate ass downstairs to feed you."

I looked at him like he was crazy again. I then saw the bath water ran with bubbles and towels for a bath next to it. Hell, the only thing he didn't have was an outfit picked out. I was in my thoughts when Sénar called my name, "Treasure?"

I snapped at him, "What?"

He looked at me impatiently when he said, "Hurry your ass up man. I'm trying to do this before Cassidy's nosey ass comes up here cuz she hungry and shit!"

I snapped at him back and said, "Well, I didn't exactly expect this Dr. Sénar!"

He rolled his eyes and said, "Hurry up."

Irritated, I responded, "Well, don't do anything stupid."

He was also agitated when he retorted, "I could have left your ass in there to suffer, but I'm trying to help your mean ass. I had fun last night too. I just wasn't dumb enough to have no bullshit like that shit on your neck to prove it. Now take your damn clothes off!"

I was annoyed with him, no matter how much he was helping me; I had too much pride. I said, "Fine, just close your eyes or put me on the floor. I don't know, sheesh, I can do it myself!"

He was so annoyed when he said, "Treasure, I have seen every part of your body even the inside, so stop acting brand new and let me help you, so I can do what I have to do."

I reluctantly wiggled out of my pants but cautiously as he helped me. I shielded my private area and he shook his head as he scooped me off the counter to put me on the toilet. I clenched up and asked, "So, you're going to watch me pee too?"

He answered, "Yeah, hurry up Treasure. Take the rest of your clothes off."

I reluctantly peed. Even though it was extremely awkward, I took my shirt off but hesitated to take my bra off. He smiled sadistically before he said, "Nah, I'm going to see them pretty titties before I leave, to make it worth it."

He winked at me and I snapped at him, "Turn around, so I can wipe myself!"

He rolled his eyes and turned around. I wiped myself and quickly took my bra off but held my breasts in my own embrace. Sénar scooped me off the toilet and placed me in the tub. Innately, I braced myself with an arm on each side of the tub when he lowered me, letting my breasts go, to see Sénar's eyes widen with delight. I quickly covered myself, he again rolled his eyes at me before he said, "You are hilarious!"

He grabbed my feet to unwrap them and placed them in the hot water. It stung a bit, but it still felt good. I sunk into the water letting the water engulf my body. Sénar gazed at me and asked, "Nice, huh?"

I closed my eyes and responded, "It's cool."

He laughed then said, "Don't try no dumb shit. I'm going to come back to get you out and you can dress yourself. Then I'll take you downstairs."

As he opened the door, Cassidy was calling him from downstairs. Sénar looked back and winked at me before he left to tend to Cassidy. Sénar was something else, he really had his whole task planned out or he just really wanted to see me naked. I don't know but at least this bath was giving me life back and everything was starting to feel better. I closed my eyes and my thoughts drifted into how things were going to end up. Knowing Sénar, he probably had something crazy planned. I started to think about all the things he has done to my body, despite my rebuttals and I still got aroused. My hands were all over my body at the thoughts of being handled by Sénar and all the sensations I felt when he did. I was touching myself and moaning softly when Sénar opened the door.

I quickly straightened myself up before I said, "Dang Sénar, you could have knocked first."

He laughed then replied, "My bad ma, but you don't have to stop." He grinned and came in with some clothes for me to put on. I rolled my eyes when he said, "I can help you with that too."

I sighed, "Sénar, don't make this more awkward then it already is."

He laughed and complained, "Damn, your ass is mean."

He closed the door behind him and sat the clothes down on the counter. He pulled a tube of something out of his pocket and sat it down next to the clothes. He came to the bathtub and pulled the plug out then said, "Sit up and when the water comes out, dry yourself off. Unless you want me to do it."

I quickly said, "I can do it myself, thanks."

Sénar smirked before responding, "Whatever, just hurry up."

We were both getting annoyed with each other. The water was almost out, I dried myself off while he laid a towel on the floor. I looked at him after wrapping myself with the towel to ask, "What are you doing Sénar?"

He tried to be patient with me and explained, "I am laying this towel down, so you can sit on it and get dressed Treasure. I also have some stuff I want to rub on your back and shoulders. Then I'll take you to your room and we will finish there."

I was glad he informed me of his next moves, but it didn't make me any less nervous, and what did we need to go back to the room for? He picked me up and sat me on the floor then handed me my clothes. He gave me instructions, "Get dressed but leave your shirt off."

I looked at him before I said, "Well turn around, so I can get dressed."

Sénar was losing his patience. He complained, "Damn, I don't know why you make shit so difficult."

I smacked my lips and waited for him to turn around. I put my underwear and shorts over my feet carefully and then I laid down to pull them up. Then I put my bra on that matched my blue panties. Sénar turned around just in time to see me adjusting my bra. He smiled before he said, "Damn Treasure, you look so damn good in blue…. hell, you look good in everything." He bent down to pick me up off the ground, inhaling deeply as he smelled my hair and then sat me down on the counter. I stared at him confused and asked, "Why are you doing all of this Sénar?"

He stared at me blankly and grabbed the cream he took out of his pocket. He answered, "Because I like you most of the time."

He smirked at me while he applied the cream to my shoulders, upper back and down my arms. He handed me my shirt and said, "Come on let's go. Hop on my back but don't hurt me."

He laughed and turned around for me to hop on his back. I wanted to slap him but refrained from doing so, and reluctantly, got on his back for him to carry me to my bed. There was gauzes and first aid supplies on my bed with a pair of new Nike slip on sandals that were my size. He sat me down on my bed and left to wash his hands. He came back and sat on the floor to examine my feet. He applied Neosporin and wrapped them carefully.

Cassidy came in to ask, "What the heck are you doing Sénar?"

He was annoyed with her question, he asked, "What does it look like, Cassidy?"

She smacked her lips before she rudely suggested, "I don't know but you should let her ass suffer, she did that shit to herself."

I tried to take my foot from Sénar, and he snatched it back. Sénar instructed, "Treasure, stop! Learn not to react to everything. Man, just ignore her ass!" He told Cassidy, "Leave her alone and stop being so damn nosey."

She folded her arms and watched Sénar finish wrapping my foot. He put some socks on me and then put the shoes he bought for me on. Sénar got up and told me to stand up really quickly to see if my feet felt any better. My legs vibrated as the pain registered to my brain, but it wasn't as bad as it was before the bath. I sat back down quickly to stop the pain. He then bent down in front of me and slapped my leg insinuating for me to jump on his back. I glared at Cassidy as I reluctantly got on Sénar's back.

He carried me out as Cassidy said, "I don't know why you are babying her ass; she is such a little bitch."

I held on to Sénar tightly with my legs and left arm because I used the right arm to hold my hand up, to flip Cassidy off with my middle finger. Then I held on to Sénar with both arms as we went down the stairs. My mom had come out too late, or she would have been the other person who deserved my middle finger display. She said, "Good morning Sénar." He turned to acknowledge her when he said, "Good morning Carmel"

He hurried down the stairs with my mom behind us as she finally spoke to me, "Treasure, we need to talk."

I sighed before I asked, "About what mom?"

Sénar squeezed my less injured foot and I changed my response to, "Ok momma." Sénar brought me to the kitchen table and let me down on one of the chairs. He proceeded to warm up a breakfast burrito he made earlier while my mom sat at the table with me. She asked, "Treasure, what has gotten into you lately?"

I took a deep breath and tried not to be a snob and answered, "Momma, I don't know what you are talking about."

I tried not to roll my eyes as Sénar was pleading with me not to be a brat with his eyes. She was a bit agitated as Sénar got a plate to put my burrito on, she said, "You are so mean and hot tempered lately. Then you had the nerve to come with that damn tramp stamp on your neck! Then disrespecting me and Ken and even Sénar. What is wrong with you?"

I was appalled that she added the way I treated Sénar to her complaints. It took all my might to not rip everyone's world a part, since my world was being shredded daily. I looked down to hide my rage before answering, "I don't know, momma. Maybe you should send me away too."

Sénar brought me my food then told my mom that her and Ken's food was in the microwave before he left us there to talk. I didn't want to talk, I wanted to eat and forget that yesterday ever happened, even though I had to be treated like a paraplegic this morning. My mom said, "That's not an option, you are my daughter and my responsibility. We are going to get through this, but you have to work on your attitude and stop letting Tyrell get you into trouble. He should not be putting marks on you! First it was a rock, then a broken arm, and now this? You totally ignored me when I asked you if you were having sex. And now that your lies are surfacing, you have the nerve to disrespect everyone, including yourself, by running your mouth! So, Ken said you were on punishment, I wasn't here for the details, but I support it 100% and if there are any problems, he can extend it for as long as he wants. Besides, you two need a break anyway, and you need to focus on something other than boys."

I was speechless, although she was correct with some of her points, she was completely one sided and already ruined her chances of me responding with remorse after she completely ignored her role in any of my behavior. I looked at her blankly as she waited for my response.

She became impatient, "Ok, you want to play like your deaf now? You know you're really good at that, maybe you should do the same with your mouth more often to keep your ass out of trouble. You are lucky you have Sénar to help you because no one else wants to deal with your attitude. Hell, I don't know why he does either."

She dismissed me by saying, "I don't want any more problems out of you Treasure." What was supposed to be a conversation, turned into a lecture with me just taking in her words and her feelings. Mine were snipped and stuffed back into me. I ate my burrito by myself and forced my tears to stay where they were, so I could remain energetic because I was feeling better before her stupid lecture. I started to think about Tyrell and realized he had not called me all day yesterday or this morning. I was annoyed that I had got into all this trouble and Tyrell hadn't even called me. I hopped to the sink to put my plate away and then I hopped to the phone. Not wanting to ask Sénar to help me call Tyrell, I sat down on the steps to call him. It rang a couple of times before I hung up. I hopped over to the living room where Sénar was lying down watching TV. I couldn't help but look out the window to see if Tyrell's car was there. When I saw that it was there, I was a little relieved. Sénar just rolled his eyes at me as I ignored him. I hopped to the nearest spot on the couch on the opposite side of him, since it was closest, but he stopped me.

Sénar said, "Nuh uh, sit on the other couch." I was shocked and deliberately sat down anyway. He sighed, "Don't be crying when your ass gets snatched up. I might not let you go."

He flashed his sadistic smile and bit his bottom lip. I quickly got up to hop over to the other couch because I knew he was serious, and I didn't have the energy to fight him off. He relaxed a bit when I moved to the other couch and we watched TV as I drifted off into my thoughts. I thought, *how was I going to be able to go to school, why Tyrell didn't call me, why my mom hated me, and why Sénar was so obsessed with me?* I was exhausted by just thinking about it all.

Sénar asked, "What are you thinking about ma?"

I shrugged my shoulders to insinuate that I didn't know. He laughed before he spoke, "Ok, well you can't go to school like that. Tyrell is only with you to get to me. Your mom wants you to stay out of trouble and work on your smart-ass mouth. And me, I love me some Treasure. Whether you're angry, mad, happy, sad, whole, broken, crippled…. Hell, whatever state you are in, I want to touch you, feel you, breathe you, eat you, fuck you, lov-"

I cut him off, "Ok Sénar. Damn, you're freaking me out. Sheesh, I don't know how you do that."

He asked, "Do what?"

I shrugged my shoulders again but this time in agitation, annoyed with him for answering every question I asked myself. I felt my heartbeat increase when he said, "Come here."

I shook my head no, in a defiant manner. He laughed then continued to watch TV as I watched him, and his member grow through his basketball shorts. He raised his eyebrow and flicked his tongue at me. I quickly put my attention on the TV while Sénar chuckled, I could feel my coochie pulsating. I closed my eyes to try to ignore it, feeling my heartbeat increase both in my chest and in between my legs. I was on the verge of panicking, so I breathed in deeply, held my breath for a second and then let it go. I could feel myself calm down a little when Sénar called my name, "Treasure?"

I quickly responded, "What?"

He chuckled a bit first and then he asked, "What are you thinking about?"

I snapped at him, "Nothing, damn! Mind your business!"

I kept my eyes closed to try and block out all the naughty thoughts that crossed my mind. I licked my lips and pressed my eyelids together until I felt Sénar's lips on mine, along with his hand in between my legs. I tried to push him back and say his name when he stuck his tongue in my mouth. I shivered as he rubbed my pulsating coochie outside of my shorts.

When I caught my breath, I said, "Sénar, stop!" My heart was racing and my coochie was pulsating rapidly. I could feel the moisture in my panties as I tried to calm myself again. Sénar laughed at me when I yelled, "It's not funny Sénar! You are crazy!"

He laughed then said, "Yeah crazy about y-"

I cut him off again, "Shut up! Damn, take me to the bathroom!"

He bit his bottom lip before saying, "Yes ma'am."

He picked me up and took me to the bathroom. I got down once we reached the bathroom and closed the door in his face, locking it at the same time. He is crazy! My body was going nuts as I hopped to the toilet and sat down to pee. When I was done, I had to wipe myself several times to clean up the unwarranted excitement. I washed my hands and opened the door to see Sénar patiently waiting for me. I rolled my eyes at him, "You get on my nerves!" I said as I put my arms around him to carry me back downstairs.

Sénar taunted, "Yeah right, that's why you had to wipe yo' kitty cat so many times, huh?"

He squeezed my ass and smelled my hair. I pushed his head back, "Stop it!" He laughed and sat me down at the kitchen nook. He made tuna sandwiches and I turned my nose up at them. Sénar was surprised when he asked, "What? How dare you turn your nose up at Chef Sénar."

He was really appalled as I rolled my eyes and made my request known, "Can you put some pickles and onions in it?"

He looked at me like I was crazy before he answered, "Hell no! Ewe, that's gross!"

I started to pout, he then sighed before saying, "Fine, but what are you going to do for me?"

I had a quick come back, "You have to serve the crippled for free, remember?"

I bit my bottom lip and smirked at him because he knew that was a good come back. He laughed then chopped up the pickles and onions to add to the tuna. When he was done stirring it, I made another request, "Sénar, can you add some mustard to it?"

He snapped back, "Hell no, man!"

I batted my eyelashes at him and begged, "Please Sénar," I said in my sweetest voice, he sighed as he gave in, "You need to let me get some with all these damn requests."

I smacked my lips and asked, "Damn Sénar, is that all you think about? Dang."

His face was serious when he answered, "Yeah, it's a pretty large part of what I think about."

I was starting to get uncomfortable again. Sénar smirked at me before he said, "Well, you asked."

I ignored his response and made one more request, "Can you toast my bread?"

He rolled his eyes at me before complaining, "Dang, you with your toasted bread."

He toasted my bread then made our sandwiches and added chips to our plates. He poured us some water and got some canned Hawaiian punches for us to drink. I couldn't help thinking about how good he was at serving, and quite frankly, many other things as well. The tuna came out really good, so I asked, "Do you like the tuna like this?"

He smiled before he answered, "It's cool." We laughed together and then went to watch TV for a while. The sandwiches were so good we ate them for dinner too and then went to bed early.

Chapter 5

Monday morning, I should have been getting ready for school, instead of lying in bed watching Cassidy get ready. I grabbed my cellphone when she left to call Tyrell, since going downstairs was a task that I would face later without Sénar.

He picked up, "Hello."

I said, "Hey."

Tyrell was quiet for a second before asking, "Why aren't you here yet?"

I took a deep breath before explaining some of the details, "I got in trouble Tyrell, so I can-,"

He cut me off to ask, "What does that have to do with why you are not here so we could go to school?"

I almost had an attitude when I said, "You didn't let me finish. I can't go over there or ride with you until I get off punishment. They saw-"

He cut me off again to ask, "Who is they?"

I sighed, "Tyrell let me finish a sentence, sheesh."

He sighed as well and gave me permission, "Alright, go on."

Finally having the chance to speak, I said, "Anyways, my mom and Ken saw the hickey you put on my neck and flipped out. Everything turned into chaos. I cut both of my feet on all the glass that was broken on the floor. So, then they put me on punishment for like a long time, I don't even know how long."

He was quiet on the other end, I called out to him, "Tyrell?"

He sighed before he spoke, "Yeah whatever, man I'm about to get ready for school."

I was instantly mad when I asked, "Tyrell, are you serious? That's all you have to say?"

He got mad back, then countered, "Well, what the hell am I supposed to say?"

I started to cry, "I don't know, something else like am I ok or I'm sorry or-"

He snapped, "Sorry? Sorry, for what? You liked that shit, so don't blame all this on me."

That line was a gut punch for me because me liking things, makes it ok, I guess. I was angry when Sénar walked in. He rolled his eyes when he saw that I was on the phone but still came in. He bent down at my bedside while Tyrell vented, "Treasure that is some bullshit that I am not about to deal with, so I don't know what else to tell you."

I was cautious with my next line, for so many reasons. While Sénar checked my foot, I said, "Tyrell fine. I just wanted to let you know, so you wouldn't think it was because of me that I can't see you."

I avoided looking at Sénar as I laid back and put my hands over my face when Tyrell responded, "Whatever, I don't care. Man, I have to go!"

Click, just like that, he hung up in my face. I was livid! I called Tyrell back and Sénar shook his head, but I just rolled my eyes at him.

When Tyrell answered he said, "What, Treasure?"

I turned from Sénar and replied, "Tyrell, why are you mad at me? I… ouch!"

Tyrell asked, "What are you doing?"

I took my foot from Sénar and he snatched it back as I explained, "Nothing, my foot is just sore."

He was quiet for a second before he responded, "Well, how you getting to school then?"

I answered and tried not to make it obvious that Sénar was checking and re-bandaging my foot.

I answered, "I am probably not going to school. Tyrell, it's pretty bad."

He sounded annoyed and asked, "Well, what that nigga Sénar say?"

I was annoyed now too and answered, "Tyrell nothing really, it was mostly my mom and Ken."

He said, "Yeah right. Where is that nigga at now?"

I got mad and replied, "I don't know. Ouch! Tyrell, I am not his keeper. Where is Leah?"

I snatched my foot from Sénar, and he pulled me towards him while Tyrell flashed and asked, "Why do you keep saying ouch?"

I looked at Sénar with my eyes cut at him and answered, "Because I am trying to walk, and it hurts."

Tyrell snapped back, "Yeah, ok. You be playing games. If your foot so messed up, then who is going to bring you to school and home?"

I looked down before I reluctantly answered, "Sénar."

Tyrell blew up on the other end of the phone, he yelled, "That is some damn bullshit! Wow! That moth-"

I cut him off as Sénar snatched me off the bed. I quickly said, "I have to go to the bathroom, I'll call you back."

I hung up in a hurry as Sénar put me over his shoulder. Frustrated, I asked, "Damn Sénar, can I have some privacy next time I'm on the phone?"

He laughed and replied, "Whatever, hurry up, he shouldn't be asking about me anyway."

I cut my eyes at him before I said, "Both of you are crazy."

He laughed then said, "Nah, you the crazy one."

I just wanted to use it quickly, so I could call Tyrell back. I peed while Sénar just stood there, I was going to ask him to turn around, but he did it before I asked. I wiped myself and flushed the toilet, but I stood up on my left foot despite the pain, hopping to the sink to wash my hands.

I looked at Sénar before I said, "I'm good, I have to hop around all day, so I will be fine!" I hopped back to my room, almost losing my balance before closing my door and falling onto my bed. I quickly called Tyrell back, but no one answered. Ugh, I was so pissed off because everything was falling apart again. Sénar and Cassidy left for school, while I just sat on my bed and thought about how crazy my life was. I laid back and drifted into my own Lala Land. I was falling back asleep to be awaken by my mom and Ken giggling in the hallway. I got up to the rolling of my eyes and looking for something to wear. I hopped to the bathroom to brush my teeth and wash my face. All the hopping around had my left foot and leg over worked. So, I sat on the steps and scooted down them. I could still hear my mom and Ken giggling, so I took a deep breath before hopping over to the kitchen. I almost lost my balance when I saw Ken and my mom butt naked. Ken was standing by the fridge drinking a beer and my mom was cooking with something tied around her neck. Ken's body being exposed was devastating because he had an extremely large member that was at attention, and he was pretty fit for an older dude.

While he smiled sadistically, my mother quickly moved to stand in front of his nakedness, shielding him with her own. My mom being fully naked except for some leash or apparatus hanging from her neck, asked, "Treasure, what are you doing here?"

I was stuttering when I answered, "Um… um…. my foot…"

I quickly turned around to hop my behind back to the stairs before taking in, Ken's big ass smile. When I reached the stairs, I crawled up the steps with urgency and hobbled to the safety of my room. I just laid down and tried to unsee what I had seen in the kitchen until my mom came in.

She asked, "Treasure, are you ok?"

I looked at her and answered, "I'm fine momma. I am going to school tomorrow; I will figure something out."

She looked like my mom, instead of some Playboy bunny model or porn star in the middle of a scene. She smiled and replied, "That sounds like a good idea sweetie. Do you need anything? You want me to bring you something?"

I smiled and took advantage of the moment to ask, "Is there anymore tuna?"

My mom came back with a sandwich and some juice for me, I took a nap to avoid thinking about the scene I saw when I came into the kitchen this morning. When I woke up, I listened for voices before hopping to the bathroom to avoid another unsightly scene. When I was done, I scooted downstairs to watch TV. Sénar and Cassidy came home at the same time.

I looked at Sénar before I asked, "Why are you home so early?"

He quickly answered, "Damn, nosey, I asked my coach if I could come home early, so I can take care of your chocolate ass."

I sighed in irritation when I said, "You did not have to do that, I told you I was fine."

He went to get something he left by the door. He had crutches in his hand and asked, "Do you know how to use these?"

I shook my head no and Sénar demonstrated how to properly use them. He handed them to me to try. I was nervous but I tried. I knew I had no choice but to practice if I wanted to go to school tomorrow. Sénar went to the kitchen to grab something to drink and gave me a frozen spoon to put on my neck, saying, "Here, put this on your neck. I don't know why I didn't think of that before." He sat down to watch TV and asked, "How was your day ma?"

I shook my head and shrugged my shoulders before answering, "Besides this morning shenanigans with you and Tyrell I just happen to see my mom and Ken butt naked in the kitchen. My mom had some kind of, I don't know, thing tied around her neck." I was still traumatized at the thought of what it was and what it was being used for. I shook my head in disbelief and said, "Not cool."

Sénar laughed at me and said, "Damn, Carmel is a freak. I wish I would have seen that umph." He snickered and I smacked my lips at Sénar. He looked at me and asked, "What? Carmel is fine and I knew she was a freak to keep my dad here this long." He was grinning from ear to ear and then added, "Shit you and Carmel is fine as hell and y'all both some freaks." He bit his bottom lip and flashed his famous smile. I was annoyed with him already; I swear he was such a pervert sometimes. He laughed at me and said, "Come on let's go to the store. You need some practice on those crutches."

Ken came down the steps with proper clothing on. He smirked when he saw Sénar on the couch and asked, "Boy, what is your ass doing here?"

Sénar jumped up and answered his dad, "I am going to make up practice on Wednesday."

Sénar walked up to Ken and Ken put his arm around Sénar and said something. They both laughed hysterically, making me instantly uncomfortable. Sénar called my name from the kitchen and I snapped at him, "What?" Sénar and Ken stared at me from the kitchen table.

I was super uncomfortable when Sénar responded, "Come here girl. Why do you got an attitude, dang?"

Ken smirked at me, making me hesitate before I decided to hobble over there, remembering to grab the crutches to assist me. It was so awkward, I felt like it took me forever to get there. When I finally got there, Sénar was making the last of the tuna and laughed before saying, "I see you made your way to the tuna."

I blushed and replied, "My momma made me one earlier."

Ken cut in, "Well, your ass is going to school tomorrow or we are going to have to charge your ass for the show." Him and Sénar both laughed hysterically making me want to slap both of them.

Sénar asked, "Aye pops, we about to go to the store, let me use your truck?"

As Sénar handed his dad the sandwich Ken handed him the keys after glaring at me. I tried not to roll my eyes. Ken looked at the sandwich after he bit into it and asked, "What the hell, is this pickles and onions in this shit?"

Sénar laughed before he said, "Aye, that was Treasure's idea." Ken still ate it as we headed for the door. Sénar patiently waited for me, prompting him to say, "Yeah, you need some practice anyway ma."

He helped me into the car and put the crutches in the back. We went to an outdoor swap meet and walked around until we found a spot that had everything Sénar needed for his work out station. He grabbed a weight bench, the bar with assorted weights, a floor mat, some dumbbells and even a cute pink pair of 5lb dumb bells. He smiled at me and said, "Just in case you want to work out." He saw that I was tired and flustered, so he said, "Don't worry, I am almost done."

The Mexican guy that was eyeing me the whole time while selling his merchandise, offered me a seat as him and Sénar finished their transaction. Sénar went to get the truck to load all the equipment in the back while I sat and waited for him to return. The Mexican man asked, "Ayee my friend, you want to be ready mi amigo?"

Sénar looked at him as he was finishing loading up his purchase and laughed before he replied, "Ready for what man?"

The Mexican man looked at me and smiled then replied, "To fight for your pretty lady. I give you a deal for fifty dollars my friend," As he showed Sénar a punching bag with a pair of red and a pair of blue gloves to go with it. Sénar had a dark look in his eyes when he smiled before replying, "Forty dollars and we got a deal."

I rolled my eyes at both of them as Sénar finished loading the truck. Sénar walked up to me after he opened my door to say, "Come on ma, let's go." I got up and positioned myself on the crutches but Sénar took them from me, propping them up against the chair and picked me up to carry me to the truck. He went back to get the crutches and shook the Mexican dude's hand before we left. We stopped at Tastey Goody to get some Chinese food before going back home. When we pulled up, I noticed Tyrell wasn't home yet. I became instantly irritated, knowing we would normally be back by now from practice.

Sénar opened the garage to unload his stuff and I used it to go inside. Sénar stopped what he was doing to get the door for me. I went inside and sat at the kitchen nook and waited for Sénar to bring our food in. Sénar came in to sit the food down and pour us something to drink. As we sat down and ate our food, the phone rang. Sénar didn't move but I jumped up and used my crutches to get me over to the phone as quick as possible.

I answered it and it was Leah. She happily said, "Hey girl."

I dryly replied, "Hey Leah."

I was disappointed that it wasn't Tyrell. She said, "I didn't see you at school today. Are you good?"

I answered, "Yeah, I'm good."

She then said, "Cool. Well, are you coming tomorrow?"

I answered, "Yeah, I'll be there."

"Alright then I'll see you tomorrow," Leah said before she quickly hung up.

I hung up the phone and used the crutches to get to the window to see Tyrell pulling up. I took a deep breath before I went to sit down. Sénar asked, "What are you about to do?"

I shrugged my shoulders then answered, "I don't know, probably watch TV."

He asked, "You want to keep me company while I set up my workout station?"

I shook my head no but said, "But I want to see it when it's done."

He was disappointed but didn't complain then his phone rung. He answered his phone and I could hear him say, "Calm down, I had something to do."

As he walked into the garage. I got up and called Tyrell, but he didn't answer his phone. I watched TV until Sénar came and got me. I almost regretted telling him I wanted to see it when he was done because I was dreading the process of getting over there. He held the door open for me as I made my way in, with him following behind me to show me his new workout station. He used a section of the garage to set up his bench, weights, punching bag and hung the gloves on the wall. I couldn't help but smile as it looked great and I was impressed.

I minimized my response, "It's cool."

We both laughed, knowing it was better than just cool. Sénar was excited when he said, "I can't wait, I am about to be smashing fools!" He flexed and I rolled my eyes as I turned to leave. He rushed to open the door for me and said, "Your girl Leah asked about you today."

I looked at him and then dryly responded, "Oh, that's nice." I used my crutches to get me back to the living room.

Sénar followed me to say, "She mentioned you guys were trying out for the cheerleading team. Is that right?"

He was cheesing as he waited for me to respond. I sat down to ask, "Wait, so y'all had a whole conversation?"

He laughed before he said, "Yeah, until y'all boyfriend came and broke it up."

I was instantly irritated and took some calculated deep breaths. Sénar asked, "What are you doing Treasure?"

I calmly answered, "I am using a deep breathing technique to help me with my attitude and calm me down."

He shook his head, "Ok…. well, are you going to try out?"

I sighed before I answered, "I don't know Sénar. I really don't want to be around all those girls. They don't even like me."

Sénar responded, "So, who cares. You're either going to try out or not. It shouldn't matter who does or doesn't like you."

I looked at him to genuinely ask, "Do you think I can make it?"

He thought for a minute before giving me his honest opinion, "Yeah, you are a fast learner. If you practice and get in shape, you can make it. I hope your foot heals in time."

I smiled at Sénar and thought about how Tyrell said I couldn't dance. I was probably going to try out just to prove Tyrell wrong. I ate the rest of my Chinese food and went to bed early.

The next morning, I called Tyrell on my cellphone, and no one answered the phone. I was frustrated when his car was already gone, so I just waited for Sénar on the couch to take me to school. Cassidy did not want to ride with us, so we left without her and rode to school listening to music. When we pulled up to school, Sénar turned to me and gave me a lecture, "Treasure, hear me, my dad is not playing with either of us. So, don't put me in any crazy situations. Do what you have to do to get off punishment and don't do the shit again. Don't leave with Tyrell or go to his house. I'm not saying you can't talk to him, but don't let him put no marks on you and don't let him get out of line with all that touching he be doing."

I had a whole response prepared, but the look in his eyes knocked my attitude down several notches and minimized my response to one word, "Whatever."

He got out to get my crutches out the back seat as London was approaching us. I secured my backpack and took off to class with my crutches to help me. I could hear Sénar telling London to calm down before she even said anything. I made it through the first three classes smoothly because I was a professional at ignoring whispers and stares from nosey people that I cared nothing about. I went to the cafeteria to sit at my favorite table and put my crutches to the side.

Leah came up to me to ask, "Damn, girl, what happened to you?"

I ignored her question to ask, "Are you going to the line?"

She responded, "Yeah, why?"

I went into my bag for money and then asked, "Can you get me a sandwich, a bag of chips, and a soda?"

She looked at me like I was crazy when she asked, "Well, damn, how am I supposed to hold my own stuff?" I rolled my eyes at her and started to get up when Sénar came to the table with a sandwich, some chips, a soda, and some mayonnaise and mustard packets.

Leah saw Sénar bring me my food and said, "Hey, Sénar."

He replied, "What's up, Leah."

He put his attention back on me and said, "Treasure, I'll see you later at practice." He walked off to meet up with London. Leah looked at me strangely before she got up to get her food. I just ate my food until Tyrell came up and sat next to me.

My mouth was full when he walked up to me to ask, "Your favorite sport, huh, eating?" He laughed and moved the crutches out the way. He sat down with his legs open and gave me a hug.

Tyrell asked, "You still love me?"

I rolled my eyes playfully and answered, "Yes, I still love you."

Leah came back with her food and sat down. She looked at Tyrell and said, "Hey Tyrell," and he replied, "Hey, Leah."

I could feel the tension between the two, but I ignored it and ate my food. Tyrell kissed me on the cheek before he left to kick it with his homeboys. Leah just stared at me and ate her food. I finished eating and gathered my things carefully, making sure I could keep my balance. Leah or Tyrell didn't even bother to help. When I got to my next class, Leah found her way to sit next to me.

She asked, "So, you never told me what happened to you?"

I wanted her to leave me alone, but I dryly answered, "I cut my foot on some glass."

She smirked at me, then with an attitude she asked, "Oh, so that's why you are riding with Sénar and not Tyrell?"

I cut my eyes at her before I asked, "Did you still ride with Tyrell even though I was not here?"

She laughed before she replied, "Girl, please, I ain't turning down no ride for nobody."

She stared at me, "So, you're just not going to answer my question?"

I was annoyed with her, but I answered, "I got in trouble, and I have to ride with Sénar."

She sarcastically said, "Oh, some punishment. Yikes!" I looked at her like I wanted to slap her, and she continued her prying, "Well, you don't mind if I still ride with Tyrell, right?"

I glared at her, "Would it really matter, Leah?"

She laughed before she said, "You're right," she then turned around to do her work. I stared at the back of Leah's head with sinister thoughts running through my mind; she was really on my last nerve. Hell, she was passing the level of Sabrina, which I thought no human could do.

I went to practice and found a spot on the bleachers that was close to the front, so I didn't have to travel to far up or down the steps. Leah came to sit next to me. She asked, "Are we still trying out for cheerleading?"

I answered without looking at her, "I don't know; I'll let you know."

I was reading when London came and kicked my crutches over. She looked at me with a nasty attitude when she asked, "Why are you riding with my man and not with your boyfriend and his new girlfriend?"

She and all her little groupies laughed at me. Before I could respond, Leah replied, "Ooh, but I want Sénar so much more."

London called her bluff by pretending she was going to hit her, thinking she would flinch, but Leah didn't budge. I moved out of their way, ignored everyone, and said, "London, you should probably ask Sénar."

I continued to read, after rolling my eyes at all of them, causing London to go back to wherever she came from when she realized I was not entertaining her nonsense. Leah continued to run her mouth, "Ugh, I can't stand her insecure ass; she is so lame…….."

I totally ignored her until Tyrell called my name to rescue me from Leah's mouth. I looked up to see Tyrell with his fine self, carrying his football equipment in his hands. I put all my stuff away, grabbed my crutches off the ground, and scooted down to get to him. I stood up to hug and kiss him. He asked, "How long is your foot going to be like that?"

I answered, "I don't know, sheesh, it's kind of hard to get around."

He grabbed me and kissed me, purposely grabbing my behind as Sénar walked towards us. Sénar said, "Come on, Treasure, let's go."

Tyrell laughed then asked, "What, you her babysitter now, nigga?"

Sénar smirked before he answered, "Yup."

Amused, Leah watched the drama between Sénar and Tyrell. Sénar took my backpack from me, so I could position myself on my crutches. Me, Sénar, and London walked to his car, and Tyrell and Leah walked to Tyrell's car. Sénar opened the door for me and put my crutches in the back seat, then closed my door. London was like a shadow to Sénar's every move. She whined and pouted while Tyrell and Leah got in Tyrell's car to drive off.

Sénar appeared agitated when he said, "Damn Treasure, your ass is always getting me into some stuff, man."

We drove to Walmart before we went home to pick up some groceries. I bought some containers to make my lunch, so I would not be in the same position I was in earlier today. Sénar bought stuff to meal prep for his weight gaining goals. I wanted to lose weight, so Sénar bought extra vegetables. We pulled up to the house, and I noticed Tyrell was still not home yet. I was annoyed that he was still giving Leah a ride, and that he came home later than usual the last two days. The whole week went that way. By Friday, everyone was annoyed with each other for different reasons. I didn't go to the game because I did not want to have to maneuver around all those people with crutches, so I stayed home by myself. Over the weekend, Tyrell and I spoke briefly but barely even spoke to each other, unless we were at school. Sénar and I meal prepped over the weekend. While Sénar tried to keep himself busy working out, London blew his phone up.

Sunday afternoon, Sénar and I were on the couch watching TV when London popped up without calling. She was so angry with Sénar that they headed straight to his room for what Sénar called, *"an attitude adjustment"*. She was much calmer and happier when she came back downstairs, asking Sénar if she could stay. He politely told her no and sent her on her merry way. Sénar and I organized our lunches for the week and went to bed early. Monday, my first three classes went smoothly as normal. At lunch, Tyrell and Leah sat down next to me. Tyrell said, "Damn, your lunch is looking all fancy."

Leah chimed in with her agreement, "Yeah, it is fancy. Dang, Sénar be hooking it up like that?"

I ignored her, so Tyrell asked, "Damn, that's how you feel?"

I asked, "What are you talking about, Tyrell?"

He said, "Leah asked you a question."

I rolled my eyes before I lied, "All Sénar did was cut the tomatoes."

He also cooked the chicken too, but they didn't need to know that. Leah said, "Damn, it must be nice to be you."

Tyrell was agitated with her comment. I ignored both of them, and we all dispersed to our destinations. Leah again sat next to me in class to ask, "So, you never told me why you got in trouble or how long?"

I looked at her with an extremely high dislike for her and answered, "I don't even know how long and as far as to why, you and Tyrell are much better friends than we are, so why don't you ask him?" She did not hide her guilt before turning around to busy herself with her work.

At practice, Leah sat next to the cheerleaders to learn the moves for the upcoming tryouts. I went to their practice and ignored everyone until Sénar was ready to go. Sénar grabbed my backpack, and we walked to the car. When we reached Sénar's car, Tyrell pulled up with Leah in the passenger seat. He got out and walked up to me to kiss me.

He then asked, "What's up with you and Leah?"

I looked in the passenger seat of his car, and Leah had an attitude. I rolled my eyes and responded, "Nothing, that I am aware of. Tyrell, why don't you just ask her?"

He looked at me with an attitude, "Well, she won't tell me that is why I am asking you."

I was confused, *why did he care so much?* I said, "Tyrell, I don't know, you guys can talk about it on the way home."

I noticed Sénar was getting impatient, so I said, "I have to go."

I opened the door to Sénar's car and got in before London could reach us. Sénar drove off as if London was not coming towards us; he was frustrated with her and wanted to avoid her. I was annoyed too with my own situation, so I could care less about his. When we got home, Sénar went straight to the garage to work out. I was annoyed and wrote in my diary until I fell asleep. The next day was Tuesday, September the 11th, and it appeared to be a normal day; however, it was not. The first classes went smoothly as usual until lunchtime was different. I ate my lunch, and Tyrell and Leah were nowhere around. I, of course, felt some kind of way, but I ignored the thoughts running through my mind. The next class Leah didn't say anything to me, but I could care less. The teacher walked in with a look on his face like he had seen a ghost. He announced the tragedy in New York with the twin towers falling. The class was silent in mourning, and everyone was lost for words. My next two classes, people were really sad, and it was miserable. When school was over, every after-school activity was canceled.

As I walked to meet Sénar, Tyrell caught up to me to ask, "You don't be calling me no more, what you got a new boyfriend?"

I rolled my eyes before I asked, "Where's your girlfriend?"

He looked at me like I was stupid before he said, "Oh, so you are not my girlfriend anymore?"

I had an attitude, "I don't know Tyrell, it looks like Leah is my substitute?"

Tyrell was agitated with my response and asked, "So what, are we done? I need to know because I have options."

I was agitated now too, so I replied, "Well, it probably never stopped you before, so no big deal, right?"

He smirked at me as Leah walked up, he asked, "You ready to go Leah?"

She smiled before she said, "Hell yeah!"

I rolled my eyes and saw Sénar walking up with an attitude of his own. London was following him and yelling at him from afar. Sénar walked up to me and said, "Let's go!" He opened his door to get in.

Tyrell laughed before he said, "You heard him, well, I'll see you later."

He pulled me to him and tried to kiss me, but I pushed him off. He grabbed me forcefully, "Oh, so it's like that?"

Sénar got out to say, "I don't have time for this shit; let's go."

Tyrell said, "Aye man, shut the hell up; this doesn't have nothing to do with you."

Sénar got out and slammed his door then walked to my side of the door. He looked me in my eyes, then said, "Get in the car, Treasure."

Tyrell laughed as I rolled my eyes at him and got in the car. Tyrell said, "Oh, so you going to listen to your babysitter, over me?"

Sénar slammed my door. I saw Leah smiling from the passenger side of Tyrell's car at the drama unfolding before us. Sénar ignored Tyrell and got back in the car with an attitude, driving off in a rage. I didn't say anything because Sénar seemed to be frustrated and highly agitated. When we got home, he did not say a word to me. He went straight to the garage to work out. I watched the news to witness the turmoil across the nation at the tragedy that took place in New York with the twin towers. All the lives lost, and many assumptions people had. Sénar came in from working out to shower. He came down to start on dinner and didn't bother asking me for help. He made chicken Alfredo for the first time, and it was delicious. Sénar wasn't in a good mood, Ken noticed and asked, "Boy, what's wrong with you?"

He answered, "Nothing, I'm good."

Ken glared at me and then asked, "Treasure ain't giving you no problems with her punishment, right?"

Sénar shook his head and replied, "No," and then finished cleaning up.

Ken got up and walked over to me to say, "Treasure, I hope he is telling the truth because if he can't handle you, I'll take over." He said it in a threatening matter of fact tone.

I ignored him and waited until Ken left to ask, "Sénar, what's wrong?"

He cut his eyes at me before he answered, "Didn't you hear me when I said nothing?"

He had a tone with me that I hadn't heard in a while. I winced at his tone and snapped back, "Well, I hope it has nothing to do with me!"

He looked at me and responded with agitation in his voice, "Not everything is about you, Treasure! There are other people you should worry about besides yourself!"

He went upstairs, leaving me in the kitchen to think about what he said. My feelings were almost hurt, but I ripped them up in my mind, so no one else could. The day was crappy, and I just wanted it to be over already. I grabbed my stuff, hopping all over the place, and went to take a bath. When in the bathroom, I unwrapped my foot and looked at my wound for the first time. It was big and healing into a scar. It was still painful, but not nearly as painful as it was in the beginning. I poured Epsom salt in my bathwater and relaxed for a bit, then carefully got out. I took all my stuff with me, careful not to touch the floor with my right foot. I sat down to rest before I had to go back to grab the stuff to wrap my foot.

Sénar knocked before he entered with the stuff to wrap my foot. I rolled my eyes and said, "You don't have to do this Sénar; I can do it myself!"

He ignored my attitude and proceeded to wrap my foot but examined the healing first. I was still mad about his little outburst in the kitchen. I asked, "Why don't you save your energy for London since I am so selfish?"

He laughed before her responded, "Treasure, please, you are really something else."

I smirked at him before I countered, "Yeah, well, you are too."

He stared at me when he replied, "Whatever, London is straight. I take care of her needs; I give her money if she needs it or buy her what she wants. I straighten her back and adjust her attitude when it needs to be. I give her the attention she needs when she is not on my last nerve, and I'm only dealing with her for the most part."

I rolled my eyes, "Yeah, right, you are a coochie bandit!"

He chuckled and then said, "You're cute. Hahahahaha coochie, you're funny. You mean, pussy bandit?"

He licked his lips and flickered his tongue at me, making me squirm a bit as I sat on my bed with him wrapping my foot. He saw my reaction and snickered before he continued, "Anyway, you are the only girl she has to worry about, and she knows that. She does the job I need her to do, since you don't. That's why she can't stand your ass or this punishment you got yourself on."

I smacked my lips before I said, "Well, how does she know that Sénar?"

He looked at me like I was stupid and responded, "I don't know any human on this planet, that knows me and does not know how I feel about you. Including, Tyrell's punk ass."

He got agitated again, thinking about Tyrell. I was irritated too when I asked, "Sénar, what's your problem? You act like this feeling you have for me is normal."

He smiled and answered, "It's not, most people never feel this way that I feel about you and Tyrell's punk ass knew that! We used to be cool, until he found out how I felt about you. He wasn't even interested in you. He is only with you to hurt me."

He got up, and I asked, "Wait, where are you going?"

He was flustered and answered, "To my room, why?"

I thought for a second before I asked, "Wait, you don't think Tyrell feels that way about me?"

He smirked and said, "He definitely does not. Now Leah, maybe, but I doubt he feels the way about her that I do about you."

Disappointed, I asked, "Why?"

He was agitated again when he replied, "Girl, I don't know, and I don't care."

I corrected my question, "No, I mean, why do you feel that way about me?"

He gazed at me for a second, then smacked his lips before he said, "Man, I don't want to talk about this shit. None of your business. Unless you are going to let me show you." He smiled sadistically at me, I crossed my arms before I said, "Fine, then Get out!"

He laughed, "Goodnight, Treasure."

Cassidy came in and put her stuff on the floor, ignoring me and grabbed stuff to shower. I went to bed thinking about me and Sénar's conversation and was out like a light before Cassidy returned.

The next morning, I waited for Sénar in the living room and decided not to call Tyrell because he was really way too comfortable with my punishment. Tyrell appeared unbothered because he had Leah and many other girls willing to keep him company. I decided to get even with everybody, I was tired of being the only one who was suffering all the time. I was deep in thought when Sénar came down and asked, "Treasure, what you over there scheming about?"

I smacked my lips in irritation, then said, "None of your business!"

I was tired of him always trying to read my mind. He laughed before he said, "Come on ma, let's go."

When we got to school London was waiting for him like the stalker that she was. He pulled into a parking space and got out to give her a kiss as I got my crutches out the back seat. I saw Tyrell and Leah pull up and I was really feeling some kind of way when I came to the realization that he was now picking her up in the morning too. Feeling salty, I rolled my eyes and headed to class. My first three classes went by quickly. Lunch time was the only thing I was looking forward to because of my chicken salad sandwich and chips. I ate by myself as Tyrell and Leah were nowhere to be found. I saw Sénar watching me from afar while London smirked at me. I didn't care, I just finished my food and went to my next class. Leah came in and sat next to me but didn't speak.

I ignored her existence until she turned around and asked, "What's your problem?"

I looked at her like I wanted to slap her, then replied, "Why are you asking me like you care?"

She shrugged her shoulders and turned around, so I could stare a hole in the back of her head. I was furious with her and the nerve of her to even speak to me. Let alone, ask me what my problem was when her and Tyrell magically disappeared during lunchtime. I dismissed her and Tyrell's disappearance earlier, to get through the rest of my classes without snapping. I looked for Sénar after my last class.

When I found him, he smiled when he saw me. I smiled back, then said, "I'm going to the library Sénar and I'll go to practice after."

He said, "Ok, but we have to stay a little later today ma to make mondays' practice up."

I nodded my head in agreement and he chin upped me before he walked off. Leah, Tyrell and London watched Sénar and I interact which produced a very strange tension as I headed for the library. I grabbed some random books and even a couple of magazines to check out before I left the library. On the way to Sénar and Tyrell's practice I noticed Leah sitting with the cheerleaders watching them do their routine. London noticed me coming and whispered something to one of the girls holding a cup in her hand. I was having difficulty with my backpack, being so heavy now with all the extra books in it. The girl walked past me and acted like she tripped, spilling ice-cold water all over me. She quickly ran, prompting me to throw one of my crutches at her with instinct as I rubbed water out of my eyes, I could still see the crutch hit her in her back as I intended it to. I was infuriated and if my foot wasn't injured, I would have whipped her and London's ass. I could see Sénar and Tyrell witness the commotion, having their own tension on the field. When Leah turned to observe the situation, my shirt was soaked and plastered to my body, exposing my white bra beneath it. I covered myself in embarrassment and gave London a death threat with my eyes. Leah smiled and I gave her the same look I gave London. All the girls laughed, including Leah making me even more angry. I instantly turned my emotions off and hopped over with my one crutch to retrieve my other crutch as London approached me.

I snapped at her and threatened, "Look, do not say anything to me!"

I was ready to fight, regardless of my foot. When London saw my rage, she backed off because she saw Sénar watching us from the field. She laughed at my soaked shirt and with disgust said, "Ugh, you're so fat and black, I don't know what anyone sees in you."

I smirked at her and thought about me and Sénar's conversation last night. I smiled a sadistic smile of my own and suggested, "Oh well, maybe you should ask Sénar. You know, he loves chocolate!"

I laughed in her face as Leah listened intently. London was pissed off and got her feelings hurt, knowing I was telling the truth. She turned around and walked off in her feelings as I sat back down with my crutches and waited for Sénar. I had to wait an extra hour as Sénar ran extra laps and talked with his coach. He came and sat next to me and laid back, he looked so tired.

He said, "Damn Treasure, when you going to give me some?"

He had his eyes closed as he laid back waiting for my response. London came up, grabbing his man stick and hovered over him. He got excited, thinking I had given in, only to open his eyes to see London hovering over him. He played it off by pulling her to him and kissing her. I was annoyed with them both; London, for being a sprung bitch, who wouldn't leave me alone and Sénar, for being so persistent. He got up and grabbed my backpack to head to his car as London clung to him like she was attached at the hip. When we got to the car, she stuck her tongue in Sénar's mouth so desperately, I thought she would jump in his lap when he got into the car with me. He said bye to her, and we headed home in silence. When we pulled up, I noticed Tyrell's car was not back yet and Ken's truck was not there. I went inside as Sénar carried my backpack in, I hobbled up the steps to knock on my mom's door. I was hoping she would answer so I could ask her how much longer I was on punishment for. There was no answer, so I quickly hopped to my empty room as Cassidy was not back yet either. I almost panicked as I contemplated my next move when I looked up and saw Sénar holding my backpack.

He sat it down and gazed at me in a way that made me ask, "Sénar, what are you thinking?"

He smiled, "I would rather show you."

I was uncomfortable when I said, "No Sénar, I am tired, and I don't want to be bothered."

He laughed as he came in any way. I tensed up quickly, "Sénar no, call London, she is ready. I am not."

He laughed before he said, "You take it better than her anyways. Plus, I want you to do the work."

I blushed a little but still responded, "Sénar, no. None of this is supposed to be happening. Go to bed!"

He laughed again but still closed the door. He took his shirt off before he said, "Come on, let's work out!"

I got up and tried to limp pass him but he blocked the door. Although, I was sexually frustrated, after not having had any for a while, and Sénar looked so damn good to me at the moment, I still said, "Sénar no, call London, Leah or jack-,"

He kissed me and I pushed him off. He said, "I'm tired too but I want this." He grabbed my coochie and said, "I'll do the work then. You want A for ass down or B for bent over?"

I looked at him like he was crazy and laughed before saying, "Sénar, you are nuts!"

He laughed and pleaded with me, "Come on, take your clothes off." I had an attitude now, despite his patience and said, "No!" He got agitated and left without saying anything else. I argued with my coochie and told it to shut up as it pulsated in anticipation of Sénar. Then Treasure number two knocked on my mental door. I said, *"Whose there?"* An audible voice in my head said, *"Treasure number two."* I spoke out loud and asked, *"Treasure number two who?"*

Sénar opened the door to ask, "Who are you talking to?"

Embarrassed and confused, I quickly answered, "No one."

He looked at me for a second before he asked, "You good, ma?"

I thought about it for a second and responded, "Yeah, I'm fine," when clearly, I was not. He looked at me with a perplexed look on his face and closed the door. I was so confused, my mental compacity was a mess. I wanted to be with Tyrell, but my body wanted to experience sexual pleasures with Sénar. He was so much more advanced in that area and for the life of me, I wish I did not know that. I felt like I was losing my scruples and had to argue with myself at times, but this is the first time a voice was that audible. It scared me just like my nightmares and cold sweats. I was tired of everyone, so my temper was on the edge. I snapped at everyone and couldn't help but be mean. I literally hated everyone, even myself.

Cassidy came in the room and saw me sitting on the edge of my bed and asked with a nasty attitude, "What are you doing?"

I was so deep in thought, I snapped at her when I asked, "Why? Mind your damn business!"

She looked at me and instantly tensed up before replying, "Because your ass is over there looking crazy." She said it with such malice, I jumped up and asked, "Do you want me to show you crazy?"

Cassidy ran for the door, but I snatched her back before she could get out and slammed her onto the floor. She yelled, "Get off of me!"

I slapped her in her mouth and was going to punch her when I felt arms around me. Sénar held me as I wanted to rip her into pieces because I was tired of her mouth. He yelled at Cassidy, "Get out!"

She ran downstairs crying. Sénar said, "Take your clothes off!" He smiled sadistically and asked, "You like it ruff, huh? I'm about to help you with your attitude."

He winked at me and took his shirt off. I took a better look this time, he had put some weight on to indicate that his results were showing from him working out so much. I became even more enraged as my heartbeat increased and my coochie pulsated at the sight of his body. I pushed him out of frustration, but he pulled me to him and removed my shirt as we tussled a bit in the process. He smiled at me before he threw me on the bed and removed my shorts. He looked at me and bit his bottom lip while pulling me off the bed. Without bothering to take off my panties, he bent me over, sliding them to the side and entered me with a deep thrust. I was so moist from anticipation,

Sénar was excited when he asked, "Ooh, you been waiting on this, huh?"

I was quiet, I was in a state of ecstasy as my rage turned into passion, I moved against his thrust and started to moan. Sénar whispered, "Grab the pillow." I grabbed the pillow and put my face into it to muffle my moans as he gyrated and wiggled side to side. Sénar smacked my ass so hard, it felt like a shot of electricity went through me. I screamed into the pillow and shivered as my body released an unknown fluid all over him.

He said, "Ooh weee, jackpot!" He exploded inside me and I could feel his hot fluid release inside, mixing with my own. He shivered and said, "Oh my, Treasure, that was the best work out I had all week!" I laid down to catch my breath and looked at Sénar to see he was sweating profusely. He put his shirt over his shoulder and pulled himself together. Before leaving, he said, "I'll leave the shower on for you."

He left me there shivering from our explosive session. I couldn't even think my mind was blank. I laid down for a second before realizing I needed to get dressed in case Cassidy came back. I grabbed my clothes off the floor and got nightclothes and the stuff I needed for a shower. I came out of my room as Sénar came out of the shower leaving it on for me. He bit his bottom lip and then shook his head before he said, "Damn Treasure." I looked down, not wanting to look at him. He whispered, "Now, be nice Treasure." He laughed and went to his room and closed the door.

I took a shower with my mind still blank. I didn't think about anything as my body felt so relaxed and had a sense of relief. I heard a knock at the door. I asked in a nice voice, "Who is it?"

Cassidy said, "Hurry up, I have to use the bathroom."

I quickly got out and got dressed. When I opened the door, she looked at me with an attitude and said, "Move! I'm tired of you putting your hands on me!"

With the little base she had in her voice, I was sure Sénar was around. I smiled at her before I said, "I'm sorry, Cassidy. Just leave me alone, ok?"

She looked at me like I was crazy, and I politely, let her brush pass me while I went to put my things away. I wrote in my diary until I smelled food. I came down to the kitchen to see Cassidy and Sénar talking as they made their plates. Sénar handed me a plate and Cassidy rolled her eyes at me as my mom and Ken piled into the kitchen to eat. I just ignored Cassidy's attitude, made my plate, and sat down to eat. Ken sat down and waited for my mom to bring his food.

He studied Sénar before he said, "Sénar, aye man, you over there looking kind of swole" Sénar flexed and then grinned at me. Ken said, "Treasure, I know you didn't get to go to the last game, but your little boyfriend looks like he got a replacement."

My mom slapped Ken's arm before he said, "What? She over here acting crazy over that dude and it ain't been two whole weeks and he got another one." Cassidy giggled, Sénar shook his head, my mom just stared at me to gauge my emotions, and I got up to clean my plate. I was actually in a much better mood than I was normally in and I wasn't going to let any of them mess it up. I went to the living room to watch TV and Sénar followed. While I watched TV, Sénar watched me until I asked, "What are you looking at Sénar?"

He responded, "You."

I rolled my eyes and watched *Girlfriends* until the doorbell rang. Sénar answered it and it was London. She walked in and kissed Sénar. Ken watched my attitude creep back into me. He smirked at me as he and my mom went upstairs. Cassidy came to the living room to watch TV as London and Sénar came to sit down in the living room too.

Cassidy said, "Dang Treasure, you always hogging the TV!"

I responded in a friendly voice, "Just let me finish watching the show and you can watch whatever you want after."

Cassidy was shocked at my tone as I lay back and watched my show without saying another word. London, as always, was all over Sénar to the point where even Cassidy was annoyed. I handed the controller to Cassidy when *Girlfriends* went off, she handed it to Sénar, and he put a movie on. We all watched the movie until London eventually got Sénar to take her upstairs. They weren't up there as long as they normally were, but she was still smiling as she waved bye to Cassidy. My smile was bigger than hers as I waved bye to her too. Sénar saw me waving bye to London as I smiled in her face, Sénar flashed his famous smile. She pulled Sénar to her and kissed him before leaving. I rolled my eyes at Sénar and Cassidy rolled her eyes at me before going upstairs to talk on the phone.

Sénar came back to sit on the couch. He asked, "So, are you trying out for cheerleading?"

I smiled at him before I answered, "Yeah."

He smiled back at me and said, "Cool."

We watched TV and went to bed. The next day at school I was in a good mood still and patiently waited for Sénar on the couch. He smiled at me, "Good morning, Treasure." He said it flirtatiously, I rolled my eyes at him and we left for school. His number one fan was there waiting for him to arrive. Sénar brought my crutches out but I told him I would rather not use them; I would rather just limp a bit.

He asked, "Are you sure?"

I assured him, "Yeah, I have to walk eventually."

London rushed Sénar as he questioned me about the crutches. He watched me limp off as London tugged on him. I made it to my class without falling or having too much difficulty. It was painful but I was tired of the crutches. My next class, I tried to limp less by taking the pain and using it for strength. By the time I made it through my third class and to the lunchroom, I was exhausted and regretted not bringing the crutches. I just ate my lunch in hopes to gain some energy to make it through the rest of the day. I spotted Sénar walking through the cafeteria with my crutches, and I must say, I was very happy to see them both.

He brought me the crutches, "You are going to need these for the rest of the day. See you later, ma."

Leah came to sit down with Tyrell following behind her. They had pizzas and a soda while I ate my chicken salad sandwich and chips. Tyrell kissed me on the cheek before he started on his lunch. I just smiled at him and smiled at Leah but still ignored her. I ate my food and even smiled at London when she walked pass our table to get to Sénar. She scowled at me like she hated my guts, rightfully so. I finished my food, then got up to kiss Tyrell before leaving with my crutches.

As I was leaving, Leah said, "Damn Treasure, I haven't seen you smile like that since summer school." I smiled at her again and went to class, ignoring her attempt to be messy. In our next class Leah did her best to ignore me but she could not resist the urge to ask, "So, what do you and Sénar do all the time you guys spend together?"

I smiled at her and answered, "Normal stuff Leah. Why, what do you and Tyrell do with all the time you guys spend together?"

I knew damn well my life at home was far from normal. She smiled and answered,

"Nothing, we just chill sometimes but I don't ever smile like that or see you smile like that when you're with Tyrell."

I was annoyed but at the same time knowing she had a point, I said, "I am having a good day, crutches and all, and minding my business. You should try it sometimes."

I smiled genuinely at her and did my work. She instantly had an attitude while I was still smiling. She tried to take me there, but I didn't fall for it, I did my work and got through the rest of my classes then went to practice. I sat watching the cheerleading routine and waited until they were done. It was a short practice because they had a game the next day. So, I didn't have to wait long before Tyrell came up to me with Leah not far behind him to ask, "How long you on punishment for?"

I gazed at him and truthfully answered, "I don't know, they didn't tell me."

He looked at me like I was lying before he said, "That's dumb. How don't you know how long you are on punishment for?"

I smacked my lips and replied, "Tyrell I don't know, they didn't tell me."

Leah looked at me sideways as I tried to convince Tyrell I didn't know how long my punishment was for. He was frustrated, "You keep saying they, but my mom and dad is a "*they*", I don't know what your mom and Ken is."

He laughed then continued, "Ken ain't your daddy, so he shouldn't have a say in how long you are on punishment for. Damn, you sound as dumb as you make your mom out to be."

Leah laughed as Tyrell totally tried to humiliate and belittle both me and my mom in front of Leah. What he didn't know is that Sénar and London were behind him the whole time that he was putting on a show. My feelings were hurt, and I couldn't respond without crying, so I just remained silent. I was really starting to wonder how long my punishment was going to be for because I felt like it was just an excuse for Tyrell to get closer to Leah but further from me. I was startled when Sénar called my name, the sound of his voice kept me from drifting into my thoughts. I looked up at all their faces and they all seemed to be laughing at me except Sénar. I got my things ready while Sénar grabbed my backpack with London never letting him go in the process. I felt like I was going to cry but I refused to let them see me in a weakened state. I walked on my injured foot with the crutches there as support but allowed the pain from my foot to keep my tears trapped inside of me because it gave me something else to feel. When we got to the car London begged Sénar to come over while Tyrell Kissed me. I didn't refuse, I just kissed him and got in the car with Sénar as Leah and Tyrell walked to his car. Sénar knew I got my feelings hurt because he heard everything Tyrell said.

On the way home we didn't say anything, but I could tell Sénar was bothered too by what he said. I definitely needed a moment to gather my emotions, I was overwhelmed. I was tired both physically and mentally. When we got inside, I put my crutches by the door and was ready to crawl up the stairs to my room, so I can finally cry. Sénar picked me up and smelled my hair before he said, "Treasure, your value is greater when you know it too."

He placed me on my bed and left me there to drift away, wherever my mind decided to take me. I cried as I thought about all of them laughing at me, how Tyrell was starting to be a part of the problem instead of a solution to my problems, and how my plan for Leah backfired in my face. I was miserable when I heard a knock at the door, I asked, "Who is it?"

Sénar answered, "Sénar."

I was being a brat and asked, "Sénar who?"

He answered, "The one who wants you."

I rolled my eyes and almost laughed.

He smiled my favorite smile, then said, "Come on, let me take you to the bathroom."

I looked at him like he was crazy when I said, "No, I can take myself!"

He sighed, "Fine, then come on."

I didn't argue, I was convinced it would be worth it. I got up and walked to the bathroom despite the residual pain. I saw candles and a bubble bath. I smiled and pushed him, "You are too much, Sénar."

He laughed and picked me up to sit me on the counter to remove my shoes. He didn't close the door, so I wasn't uncomfortable. He removed the bandages on my right foot, then pulled out his handy cream and some Vaseline.

I asked, "What are you doing Sénar?"

He smiled, "I'm going to rub your stinky feet, so you can go to the game tomorrow without crutches."

I smiled back but said, "My feet do not stink."

He laughed, "I know but I wouldn't care if they did."

He was so weird. I let him rub my feet and enjoyed the mixture of pain and pleasure as he rubbed my sore feet. I put my head back and closed my eyes until I heard Ken's voice ask, "Boy, what are you doing?"

Sénar laughed and replied, "I am just removing the bandages and checking her foot, so she can go to the game tomorrow." Sénar said it as if it was normal and Ken rolled his eyes, then asked, "Oh, so you her Masseuse now too?" Ken was irritated and went to his room.

Sénar finished and said, "Now relax but hurry up before Cassidy gets home and start complaining."

He brought me a change of clothes and locked the door. With my foot rub and a bath, I felt like a million bucks as I went downstairs to watch TV. Cassidy and London came in and saw me on the couch. They both stared at me like I was an unwanted guess when London really fit the description better than me. Sénar was working out when they got there. They both came to sit down in the living room with me.

London laughed at me and said, "Maybe that's why Tyrell thinks you are so dumb. All you do is watch TV."

I ignored her until Cassidy said, "Oh, she really is dumb, trust me."

Before I could say anything, Sénar came in, looking super fine with his shirt off and body glistening with sweat. He looked at my anger change to awe and smiled before he asked London, "What are you doing here?"

London quickly responded, "I dropped Cassidy off and I wanted to see you. Ooh you look so good baby."

She tried to grab his man stick but Sénar stopped her and said, "Nuh uh, let me take a shower. I'll be back."

London saw the look in both our eyes and instantly got irritated while Cassidy just observed the situation. Sénar went upstairs to shower and I rolled my eyes at London as she looked at me like I said something, but I didn't say a word. I smirked at her and watched TV until London said, "I can't wait until he comes back, umph he was looking so damn good. I love me some Sénar."

Cassidy rolled her eyes at the both of us. London was getting impatient and decided to pick on me to pass time, she said, "I don't know why you so worried about Sénar when you should be worried about your own man and Leah?"

I laughed at her and replied, "I am not worried about them because I can't do anything about it while I am on punishment. Maybe you should focus on your man's focus instead of what I'm focused on." I giggled as she got all puffed up. I couldn't help but add, "Oh, I guess that's only a fat black girls' problem."

She jumped up and I didn't even budge as I saw Sénar grabbing her from behind. Cassidy just braced herself for the violence that almost took place. Sénar picked London up and sat her down on his lap and whispered in her ear as he stared at me. Cassidy was overwhelmed and fidgeted in her seat as I had a twinge of jealousy creep inside of me. Sénar sat her to the side and grabbed the controller to flip through the channels while London felt all over him.

Sénar was a little agitated and said, "London, you are not even supposed to be here, and you were tripping when I got down here. So, chill, ok?"

She pouted and asked to go upstairs. He ignored her and almost gave in until I complained, "I'm hungry," and Cassidy added, "Me too." I smiled at Sénar, he laughed at me and then at Cassidy.

London responded, "Treasure, your ass is always hungry from what I hear." She laughed as she rubbed all over Sénar.

He was agitated with her at this point and said, "I am hungry too, so London, I'll see you tomorrow. I need to figure out what we are going to eat and get ready for the game tomorrow."

London was shocked, "Wait, well I can stay. I'm not in a rush."

Sénar said, "I am tired, and I need my energy for my game tomorrow, plus you keep running your mouth."

She was mad now when she exclaimed, "Sénar, I am sorry she just gets on my nerve!"

He sighed before he said, "Yeah, but I already told you about that and you don't listen. I'm too tired to deal with It, so come on."

He got up and walked her to the door. She pouted as she got up, "Why are you acting like that? She was running her mouth too." Sénar kissed her before he said, "Goodnight."

He closed the door as she walked out before she could say anything. His phone was ringing five minutes later and would not stop as he started dinner. I followed him to the kitchen and Cassidy watched as I went to the kitchen. Sénar was looking at me like he knew I was up to something. I asked, "What?"

He looked at me and said, "You play too much."

I laughed because he heard what I told London and even though it was true, he knew I was only bragging in my own way. I played dumb and waited to watch the Chef Sénar show. Before he started, he again asked, "Treasure you are still trying out right?"

I hesitated, but I answered, "Yeah."

He smiled before he said, "Cool, but you gonna need to tighten up a bit if you want to make the team. You know, like eat protein and veggies, you can't be eating all this pasta like me."

He laughed at his own little joke and I listened attentively as he broke down a complete plan, "Ok, the cheerleaders' performance for try outs is a little over four minutes of high energy moves, so you have to have stamina if you want to finish strong. So, you need to start working out at least thirty minutes to an hour a day and eat lean to build muscle and burn fat."

I looked at him as I almost wanted to change my mind but saw that he was super excited and animated when explaining how I needed to achieve my goal. Plus, I wanted to prove Tyrell wrong and make it because he basically said I couldn't, and Leah could. I laughed at Sénar because he is always observing everything. He was smiling when he asked, "So, do you want me to help you?"

I hesitated again but replied, "Yeah, I guess."

He smiled again then said, "This should be fun."

I was skeptical as I thought about what kind of fun he was talking about. I had less than two weeks to get prepared and I was not looking forward to exercising but I knew I needed to.

Sénar asked, "Any special request before I snatch all your carbs?"

I looked at him like he was crazy when I asked, "What are you talking about Sénar?"

He smiled and replied, "You'll see."

I shook my head but gave my request any way, "I want some chicken Alfredo."

I watched the chef Sénar show as he made my special request. I laughed at his goofy behind until Ken came and messed everything up with his attitude.

Ken snapped at Sénar, "I hope you put as much effort on the field tomorrow as you put into this damn kitchen."

Ken glared at me as if to insinuate I was the kitchen when he said, "Get me a beer Treasure!"

I jumped at the tone in his voice and went to the refrigerator to grab a beer way from the back of the fridge. Sénar responded to Ken's remark, "Oh don't worry, I got chu pops!" In hopes of getting him to calm down and not focus on me. I rearranged things so they would be in the front and Ken roared, "Girl, hurry your ass up!" I quickly brought him his beer. He snatched it from me and then barked, "Now, put them back where you got them from."

Sénar was uncomfortable but he didn't say anything as I went back to the fridge to put the beers back where I got them from. I hurried back to the kitchen nook and sat down trying to avoid Ken's glare. My mom and Cassidy came down at the same time. My mom didn't say anything and looked like she had been crying. She grabbed Ken a beer and made him a plate. She ate a little in silence and went back upstairs. Cassidy didn't speak to me but spoke to Ken and Sénar. She ate and left her dish in the sink and went back upstairs. I washed my plate and ran upstairs before Ken could bark anymore demands at me. I went to sleep wondering why Ken was acting that way toward me lately.

The next day at school, I was still in a good mood despite Ken's attempt to ruin it. I had something to look forward to for the next couple of weeks because I would be preparing for the cheerleading tryouts. My first three classes flew by, and I was excited about my lunch as I had brought leftover Alfredo to warm up. I didn't have my crutches today as I was willing to deal with the pain instead of having to carry crutches around. The entire cafeteria smelled like our kitchen as I warmed my food up. Everyone could smell the aroma of my food as I sat down to eat happily.

I was about to eat when Sénar walked up to me and said, "You better enjoy those carbs ma because this is your last day to enjoy them."

He smirked at me as Tyrell and Leah came in with Jack n' the Box. They came to sit down next to me. Tyrell kissed me and looked at my food. Leah sat on the other side of Tyrell and ate her food.

Tyrell asked, "Damn, that's you that has the whole cafeteria smelling like Alfredo?"

I ate my food happily and nodded, yeah. Leah smirked before she said, "Damn, somebody is still in a good mood."

I ignored her and ate my food. When I was done, I kissed Tyrell and told him I would be at the game later. Leah and I both ignored each other in class, and I could not be happier. The rest of the school day was a breeze. I met Sénar at his car and watched London as she clung to Sénar for dear life. We went home, and Sénar got ready for his game. My mom probably was not going, and I didn't want to take the chances of riding with Ken by myself, so I asked Sénar if I could ride with him because it was at a school in Rancho Cucamonga.

He answered, "Of course ma. Let's go."

We drove to the game listening to music. The game was great! We won by 13 points, and the home team that lost was highly upset. Tyrell and Sénar both had a good game. They both scored two touchdowns each and had numerous plays that kept the lead in their favor. Sénar and I went home after the game instead of hanging out with the team afterward. Ken was up when we got there, and I could hear him tell Sénar he was proud of him for stepping his game up. I am sure Sénar went to sleep pleased with his dad's approval.

Chapter 6

I woke up and recapped last night over and over in my head. Lately, anything I can't deal with at the moment, I just found somewhere to stuff into a mental compartment to deal with later. Sometimes I deal with it, and sometimes I don't. Often, if I dealt with it out of my impulse, based on my emotions, it could turn violent or end up in me giving into my sexual desires. I remember seeing Leah beat me to Tyrell last night after the game and Tyrell's mother speaking to her in a friendly manner. However, when Tyrell hugged and kissed me, she looked upset, which made me remember the first game when she waved at her and not at me. I also thought about the tension on the field between Sénar and Tyrell as they had words a few times during the game. Tyrell appeared to be the aggressor as Sénar kept walking away from him. I thought about everything and how everything was either coming together or completely unraveling. I could not differentiate between the two lately. I got up and washed my face and brushed my teeth. I went downstairs and saw Cassidy and Sénar talking in the kitchen. They sure talked a lot more lately. I just sat down, I didn't say anything, and Cassidy told Sénar she would be back after a shower. Sénar looked at me and asked what I wanted to eat; I shrugged my shoulders.

He said, "Good because you probably can't eat it anyway."

He had my breakfast prepared already; it was two boiled eggs, bacon, and half of an avocado.

I looked at the plate and asked, "Where's the bread?"

Sénar laughed, "Treasure, breads are carbs, short for carbohydrates. They turn into glucose in the body and often store themselves as fat if not burned off. The whole purpose is to cut them out to burn the fat that the body already has stored."

I looked at him and literally wanted to quit, and it was my first meal, but I took a deep breath and stared at my food. I took a piece of everything and tried to piece it together to eat it. Since it was bland, I got up to grab salt and pepper. I grabbed Morton's Salt with the girl in the rain holding an umbrella, and the pepper.

Sénar said, "Put that salt back and grab the sea salt."

He was serious; I was getting annoyed now and said, "Sénar it's salt, damn."

He put it back and gave me the sea salt. I stared at it before I picked it up and tried to pour it. When nothing came out, he showed me how to grind it. The black pepper was the same. They were both really good as opposed to the original ones I was used to. He laughed and schooled me, "That Morton's salt is poison and causes fluid retention and high blood pressure. That's why she is holding the umbrella to block all the poison they put in it to infuse the iodine."

He laughed, and I just looked at him lost for a second. He said, "Just eat the food for energy, don't worry about how it tastes. You're eating for a purpose."

I was getting more annoyed by the minute and informed Sénar, "I am hungry, ok, and I want food. So, leave me alone."

I ate the food and did not care about the blandness; I was just hungry. He laughed at me and ate French toast, eggs, and bacon. I was a little jealous, but he was already fit, and his goal was to gain weight, not to lose it.

He ate and then said, "I'll see you later, ma. I have to get out of this house. I'm not on punishment, and it is starting to feel like it. Your lunch is in there; I know you like chicken salad sandwiches but don't use bread. There is celery or cucumber that you can eat with it.

Oh, and a half of an avocado if you want. If you use salt, use the sea salt." I rolled my eyes and agreed reluctantly. He went upstairs to get dressed, and I just watched TV as Nevaeh and Cassidy left to the mall. Sénar came down after getting dressed to say, "See you later, ma."

Great, I was home with my mom and Ken. I was sitting on the couch when they came down; I was hoping they had clothes on. They looked like they were in a good mood, so I thought this would be the perfect time to ask when I would be off punishment. I took a deep breath before I entered the kitchen to approach my mom as she seemed to be looking for something.

She asked, "Treasure, have you seen the salt?" I thought about me and Sénar's conversation, and before I could answer Ken said, "She doesn't know, her ass don't cook. Ask Sénar."

I wanted to snap at him, but instead, I just said, "Sénar is not here momma, and it's in there. Sénar probably put it way in the back because he said we shouldn't use it."

She laughed, "What? That boy is something else."

I showed her the sea salt he told me to use, and she was happy with that. Ken just stared at my mom and I, making me uncomfortable to ask her about my punishment, so I just grabbed what Sénar left for my lunch. I wanted a sandwich so bad, I thought about cheating, but it was the first day, so I wanted to try it at least. I ate my chicken salad with celery, and it was actually decent. My mom looked at my food, and asked, "What do you have there, Treasure?"

I smiled at her and said, "Some healthy stuff that Sénar made momma."

She smiled back at me and replied, "Oh, ok, that's nice."

I was going to take the opportunity to ask my mom how much longer I had to be on punishment, but Ken glared at me. It was as if he could sense my next question when he said, "Oh, and don't think about bringing up your punishment because you got some ways to go. All you gonna do is run across the street, and that ain't happening no time soon, so bye Felicia."

I was instantly upset and lost my appetite after only eating a few bites of my food. Ken laughed, and my mom just shook her head, then said, "Ken is right, sweetie. You need a break from him, so find something productive to do with your free time."

I smacked my lips and sighed at her remark. Ken said, "Oh, that's the Treasure we know. The sweet little one you were a second ago was the one that needed to stay."

He laughed and told my mom to bring him a beer. I put the rest of my food away and went upstairs to take a nap. I woke up and smelled dinner cooking but almost just stayed in bed as I was not looking forward to seeing Ken again. My room was quiet until Cassidy barged in on her phone as always. I laid there until I heard my phone vibrate. I grabbed it and answered, "Hello?"

Sénar asked, "What are you doing ma?"

I answered, "Nothing, why are you calling me?"

He laughed and said, "Just wanted to hear your voice."

I laughed and responded, "You're so weird."

I almost said his name, but Cassidy was all in my business. I asked, "Well, what do you want?"

He quickly answered, "You."

I rolled my eyes and said, "Ok, well, I can't do anything about that, sooo....."

He laughed and replied, "Yeah, you can."

I was getting irritated when I said, "Well, I have to go; the food should be almost done."

He joked, "Don't cheat on the carbs."

I replied, "Bye," and hung up.

Cassidy asked, "Who was that?"

I ignored her and went downstairs. My mom and Ken were at the table having a drink. I went to the living room instead to watch TV. Sénar walked in the door and went upstairs before going into the kitchen. His hair was wild, but he had a hat on. I went to the kitchen as Cassidy was coming down. Ken got up and whispered something to Sénar, and Sénar's facial expression changed to a serious look. I wondered what he said because Sénar was irritated a little after. I looked in the pots, and my mom had made some beef with gravy, broccoli, and mashed potatoes. My mom was bringing Ken his food as he sat back down.

My mom said, "You get a break tonight Sénar because I'm the Chef."

Sénar laughed as he handed me a plate and grabbed one for himself. I made my plate as Cassidy said hi to everyone except me before she grabbed a plate. I could not be happier that she did not say anything to me. I put beef, broccoli, and mashed potatoes on my plate when Sénar said, "Put more meat and potatoes."

I looked at him and then asked, "Why?"

He just stared at me, so I put more meat and potatoes. Sénar took the plate I made and gave me his empty plate.

He said, "Now put meat and broccoli."

Again, I asked, "Why?"

Now I was irritated. He answered, "No potatoes, Treasure it's carbs."

I rolled my eyes as I put meat and broccoli on my plate. Cassidy got impatient, "What the heck are y'all doing? Hurry up; I am hungry!"

I was mad because I wanted some of my mom's mashed potatoes, and Cassidy needed to be slapped in her mouth. Sénar laughed as he sat down at the table. I reluctantly sat down with just meat and broccoli on my plate. My mom looked confused because she knew how much I loved her mashed potatoes and asked, "Treasure, why didn't you get potatoes?" Ken looked at me in anticipation of my answer too.

I answered, "Um, I guess it's carbs." Ken smirked at Sénar, and my mom just ate her food while Cassidy stared at me.

Sénar explained, "She is trying out for the cheerleading team, and she needs to get in shape." Cassidy giggled, making me want to slap her. I didn't say anything, I just ate my meat and veggies and then went to sleep.

Sunday, Sénar made me breakfast again. A boiled egg, smoke sausage, and some avocado. I ate it without any complaints as he ate whatever he wanted along with Cassidy. Cassidy giggled when she saw my food compared to her and Sénar's food. They had smoke sausage, scrambled eggs, and potatoes with toast. I hurried and ate my food and helped Sénar clean up.

I was going to watch TV when Sénar said, "Come on, Treasure, let's go."

I looked at him and asked, "Go where?"

He smiled and said, "Let's work out."

I was annoyed with his plan, and it was only day two. He had me stretch before he had me run in place, and it was uncomfortable as I felt everything jiggle while Sénar smiled sadistically. I closed my eyes, so I didn't have to see him be a little pervert. When I felt my heart rate increase and beads of sweat on my forehead, I almost stopped, but he said, "Uh uh, don't stop only five more minutes, and then you can do something else."

I felt a slight cramp in my stomach, and he saw me slow down but didn't say anything. When the five minutes were up, he said, "Ok, now do 20 jumping jacks."

I was uncomfortable again because I knew my breast would flop all over the place. It was as if he could read my mind and said, "Don't worry, I'm going to take you to the store after this, so you can get some work out stuff."

He smiled in anticipation of me doing jumping jacks. I did ten and then stopped because I was out of breath. Sénar edged me on, "Come on, Treasure, just ten more."

I used every ounce of energy to finish the other ten, almost giving up at 17, but made it to 20 and I wanted to collapse.

Sénar clapped and said, "Good job, Treasure, you did all of that looking, oh so pretty."

He smiled and squeezed me, smelling my hair. I pushed him off of me. I was sweaty and tired. I was a little shocked at how difficult it was for me and hoped I would build up my tolerance quickly. He slapped my butt and then said, "Now go take a shower."

I popped him before I ran upstairs to take a shower. As Ken was coming down, he noticed how sweaty I was and started to say something but just kept walking. I went to my room to grab stuff for a shower. Cassidy looked at me like I was stupid when she saw me sweating. I just ignored her and left to take a shower. Once I showered, Sénar told Ken we were going to the store, and Ken waved him off as to insinuate he did not care. As we were leaving, Tyrell was pulling off. We caught eye contact before he drove off. Sénar was unbothered, but I knew Tyrell would ask me about it tomorrow at school. Since he didn't bother calling me and never answered his phone anymore. He never gave me his cell phone number and still hasn't asked for mine.

I was really in my thoughts when Sénar called my name, "Treasure?"

I looked at him with an attitude and responded, "What?"

He laughed and said, "Damn meany, stop being so mean. You want me to help you out?"

I had an attitude when I said, "I think you are helping enough Sénar."

He laughed and pulled up to the mall. We went into Sears, and I asked, "Why did we come here, and not Walmart?"

He laughed and answered, "When it comes to work out clothes, Walmart is not the best quality, and with them big ass titties, you need a good sports bra."

It was an awkward moment, but I knew he was right. We went to the women's section and looked at the bras he asked, "What size are you?"

I looked at him, annoyed, and said, "Sénar mind your business, I can find one myself, thanks."

He smirked at me before he said, "Well, whatever size, try one size smaller, so you will have the support you need."

He watched me as I looked for my size, I found a 38c and went to try it on it was tight, but it did help keep them in place. He picked a blue one in the same size with some workout leggings and some sports tops for me already picked out when I came out. We went to purchase the stuff and went to a Nike store next. We found some good running shoes on sale in my size and grabbed them.

On the way home, Sénar said, "Tomorrow, while I practice, walk the track. I'll give you my Walkman, so you can have music to listen to while you walk. If you walk, it will help you get your stamina up faster and tighten your leg muscles; you will need them for cheerleading."

Sénar was serious, he wasn't even being inappropriate when talking about my legs, and *gluteus maximus,* was the word he used for my butt. I laughed at him and his intensity; he looked at me, raising his eyebrow.

He asked, "Are you listening Treasure?"

I stared at him because he was so intense but nurturing at the same time. I rolled my eyes and replied, "Yes, Coach Sénar."

He blushed and said, "Damn right! Umph, say that again!"

I smiled and said, "Yes, Coach Sénar."

He blushed as we pulled up to the house. I got out as he got my bags out to carry them in. I waited for him to come in before closing the door all the way. Ken was at the table, staring at me when I came in, prompting me to look outside to see what was taking Sénar so long. When I looked out to see London pull up and jump out of her car, all mad at Sénar. He walked into the house with London on his heels to give me my bags. London glared at me, so knowing Ken was watching, I was really friendly when I greeted her, "Hey London."

I took my bags and headed up the stairs before she could say anything. They followed me up the stairs; I could hear her ask, "Why are you going to the mall with her?"

He sighed and asked, "Man, London, do you want to go home?"

London was now quiet as I made my way to my room and they went to his. I put all my stuff away and ignored Cassidy's nosey ass.

She asked, "Who bought you that stuff? I thought you were on punishment?" I ignored her, but my patience was running thin. She continued, "Oh, so you are just going to play dumb like you always do?"

Ken was downstairs, and London and Sénar were in his room. Cassidy was testing me, and she knew I would get in trouble if I beat her ass like I did the other day, being that Ken was here. She smirked and said, "Yeah, you know better, bitch!"

I swear I heard a voice say, "Get her", but I shook my head because it was just her and me in the room. She looked at me and smiled her own Sadistic smile and said, "I wish you would."

I dropped my stuff and left the room quickly, but she followed me out. I grabbed my head as it felt like it was going to explode when she said, "That's what I thought!"

I snatched her by her hair, dragging her back into the room. She fought me back this time, but when she tried to scream, I put my hand over her mouth, and she bit me. I popped her in the forehead, and she yelled, "Get off me!" I let her go and moved back, hoping no one heard her. Sénar rushed into the room and closed the door with no shirt on and adjusting his pants.

He was breathing hard when he asked, "What are you guys doing?"

Cassidy yelled, "Treasure is trippin' again!"

Sénar begged Cassidy, "Stop yelling, damn. My pops been down there all day, and that is not a good sign, dang. Y'all about to have him come here tri-" The door opened.

Ken was at the door, and Sénar glared at the both of us when Ken asked, "What the hell is going on up here?"

Everyone was silent, but Cassidy had her arms folded with an attitude. I hid my hand that she bit and spoke first, "I am fine."

I tried to sound calm, but my heart was banging on my chest and I was trying to ignore the fact that I was almost vibrating with fury. I wanted to rip Cassidy to shreds for starting this purposely to get me in trouble. Ken looked at Cassidy and waited for her response. Sénar pleaded with her with his eyes when she answered, "Nothing daddy, we were just talking."

She glared at me, and Ken said, "Well, y'all talking too damn loud, so I better not have to come up here again."

Ken glared at me before he left, and Sénar looked a little relieved when Ken walked out. Sénar looked at me and then at Cassidy, closing the door before he scolded, "Y'all, both need to chill. My pops is not in a good space right now, so please stop!"

I smacked my lips and said, "Fine, tell her to leave me alone."

Sénar looked at me and replied, "Treasure, walk away sometimes."

I was going to tell him she followed me, but I didn't want to tell on her to Sénar since she didn't tell on me to Ken. I walked out and started to go downstairs but hesitated, knowing Ken was down there. Sénar grabbed my hand, and I snatched it back. He gave me stern instructions, "Wait here." He was going to walk away but stopped when he saw me hiding my hand behind my back. He looked at his hand to see that he had blood on it. He tried to grab my hand to observe it and felt me shaking as he urged me to let him see it.

He pulled me into the bathroom and said, "Open your hand, Treasure."

I was defiant and snatched it back from him and lied, "I am fine."

He pleaded with me, "Let me see it, Treasure."

He took it back and waited for me to open my hand, so he could see why it was bleeding. He turned the water on and ran water over it. When the water hit my fingers, I winced in pain as it really stung badly. He saw the teeth marks that ripped the skin on two of my fingers, the middle finger and wedding finger were pierced by her teeth. He washed it with soap and water, then grabbed some brown liquid to apply to the area and was bandaging it as London opened the door to say, "Sénar?" When she saw him tending to my wound, she grew angry instantly and asked, "Sénar, what are you doing?"

She was being loud and annoying when Sénar said, "Lower your voice and go back to the room; I'll be there."

She glared at me as she followed his instructions. He wrapped it with the gauze and told me to wait for him before I went downstairs. He put a shirt on and had London follow us. She was livid with anger as we walked down the stairs. Ken watched as we came down, and he noticed how upset London was. Sénar was agitated but did not want Ken to see him sweat, so he whispered in London's ear something, and she straightened up and appeared to be calm. We all walked in the living room, and I laid on the couch, turning away from them. Ken called Sénar into the kitchen, so he left London and I in the living room.

London said under her breath, "You need to stay away from my man."

I ignored her because I could not, even if I wanted to. She wouldn't understand if I told her because I couldn't even understand it. Sénar talked to Ken and came back to the living room; he looked upset but didn't say anything.

He watched TV for a while then told London, "Aye babe, I'll see you tomorrow. I'll call you after I eat and shower."

London pouted, but Sénar was really sincere, she got up and let him walk her to the door. She kissed him goodnight, and he went to the kitchen to start dinner. I could see Ken talking to Sénar while he prepared the food. I couldn't hear what he was saying, but I could imagine it was not good the way Ken was glaring at me. Ken appeared to be agitated with me. I looked away and found something to watch until Cassidy came downstairs. She went into the kitchen area with Ken and Sénar, but I wanted to wait for my mom. When I saw Cassidy eating, I made my way into the kitchen slowly. Ken gave me an evil stare before telling me to make him a plate. Cassidy sneered at me as I made his plate. I even waited to see if he would ask for a beer, but he didn't, so, when Sénar gave me a plate that is when Ken asked for one. I put my plate down and got him a beer way from the back and brought it to him. I grabbed my plate and put the chicken stir fry on my plate without the rice and ate my food in silence. I washed my plate because I finished before everyone else and then went upstairs. I wanted to write, but I was numb to all my emotions. I just laid in bed until I felt safe enough to sleep.

In the morning I waited for Sénar on the couch after packing my lunch that Sénar had prepared. I also had an extra bag with my shoes and workout clothes in it. Sénar was serious about this and asked, "You ready? I like that." He smiled and then winked at me. He asked, "What did you eat?"

I smiled at him and replied, "Some toast."

The face he made, had me laughing so hard, while still ensuring him I was just playing. He snatched me off the couch cheesing before he said, "You play too much."

He gazed at me for a second before letting me go. Cassidy came down and rolled her eyes at us as Sénar said, "Let's go." We rode to school together, Cassidy sat in the front and I sat in the back behind Sénar because it was not a good idea for me to sit behind Cassidy. She would not have been very smart to let me either.

Sénar looked in his rear-view mirror at me to ask, "What did you eat fa' reals?"

I smiled before I confidently answered, "Two boiled eggs and half of an avocado Sénar."

He smiled and said, "Cool."

Cassidy smacked her lips and Sénar asked, "Cassidy why are you acting like that?"

She rolled her eyes at him and ignored his question. Sénar looked at her sideways before he put music on and drove us to school. We parked and I swear, London damn near jumped in the car when we pulled up, but she needed to move so I could get out. She glared at me as I left my gym bag in the back and grabbed my backpack. Sénar grabbed my backpack and moved the seat up, so I could get out. London became impatient, "Girl, hurry up."

Sénar said, "Chill out, babe." He grabbed and kissed her before he said, "Calm down and let her get out."

I side eyed them both before I grabbed my backpack and left on my marry way. I could hear her complain about me as I walked away. London was on my last nerve too and the more she irked me, the more I wanted to brag about Sénar's obsession with me. She was already insecure, so it was easy to get to her without much effort. All her dark fat girl jokes have been used for years by Cassidy and Sabrina, so they didn't really bother me. It was London that bothered me. I loved being dark skinned and I never wanted to be skinny, I just didn't want to be fat. I went to my first class and it was different today because we had to engage in groups of four to talk about the social issues in America. I was quiet but listened to everyone's opinions, it was quite interesting to hear what people had to say. My next couple of classes were the same and they went as quick as they came. It was lunch time, so I was looking forward to seeing Tyrell. I pulled my water bottle and salad out of my backpack. I looked at the dressing and was disappointed it wasn't ranch. The salad even had walnuts and cranberries in it. I almost wanted to close it back and get a sandwich but Sénar came up to me to say, "You will like it, trust me ma." He laughed before he said, "I'll see you after school, so you can grab your gym bag."

I nodded my head to say ok and poured the dressing onto the salad. I didn't see Tyrell and Leah, so I just took a bite of salad in hoped Sénar was right. I took all the toppings on my salad; chicken, walnuts, cranberries, salad dressing and put it into my mouth and was in food heaven. I closed my eyes and savored the taste of the fusion of flavors together. When I was done chewing, I opened my eyes and Tyrell was walking up to me with Leah behind him. They both had Taco Bell cups but no food. I was so impressed with my salad; I took another bite before I said hi to them.

Tyrell stared at me and asked, "What's up Treasure?"

I smiled back and replied, "Hey Tyrell."

He observed me intently before he continued, "I thought you were on punishment, but I saw you leaving with Sénar."

I quickly answered, "We just went to the store Tyrell."

He smirked at me and asked, "Well, what's up with all these fancy ass salads?"

I laughed before I replied, "I'm trying to eat healthy and get fit."

He just looked at me like I was stupid and said, "Oh, all of a sudden?"

I just stared at him blankly because I did not want to disclose any more details. Leah laughed as she sipped on her soda and listened to our conversation. I felt a little uneasy now because he was just staring at me but not saying anything. I finished my salad and put the container in my bag and got up to leave. He grabbed my hand and I snatched it back to protect my two fingers that were wrapped in brown gauzes individually.

He asked, "What happened to your fingers?"

I quickly answered, "I cut them making my salad."

I was so shocked when I said it because my little black lie slid out of my mouth so smoothly. Leah said, "Oh, I thought Sénar was the chef?"

Tyrell snapped at Leah when he asked, "How do you know?"

She laughed and replied, "I just heard he could cook, that's all."

Tyrell was irritated when he said, "Whatever, something always happening to your ass."

He eyed me suspiciously as I stared blankly at him again. I felt the need to change the subject, so I said, "Well, you are always talking about my weight, so I thought you would be happy about me trying to lose weight."

He laughed before he said, "You ain't about to lose no weight, just because you are eating salad."

I rolled my eyes at him and walked away. He grabbed my shoulder and asked, "Why are you walking away from me?"

I took a deep breath and answered, "I am not walking away from you Tyrell, I'm going to my class."

He had an attitude when he let me go and glared at me like he couldn't stand me. I wanted to cry, he was being so mean lately and it was really hurting my feelings, but I didn't want to lose him to Leah or because of this stupid punishment. His true feelings were starting to show as he started to be to Leah what he used to be to me, nice. Tyrell never showed interest in what interested me, my goals, or talents. He only talked about himself. He was always pushing Leah to try stuff and was supportive when he found out she was trying out for cheerleading. I started to drift into my thoughts about what Sénar said about Tyrell and how he felt about me.

As Leah sat down, she looked at me drifting away into my thoughts and said, "Either you are clumsy as hell or a damn good liar."

I did her like I did Cassidy and completely ignored her. She laughed before she said, "I wish Sénar was my chef."

It was bad enough she got Tyrell's attention and she still wanted Sénar's too. I swear if I didn't know any better, I would think she wanted to be me. I couldn't help but snap at her, "Well, wishful thinking never hurt anybody."

I did my work and dismissed her to avoid slapping her in the mouth while she just stared at me in an evil way. I didn't care, I was trying to stay out of trouble because I could not afford a fight before I could even try out for cheerleading. I got through the rest of the school day and met up with Sénar after school. He handed me his keys and told me to lock it back.

Before he could leave, I asked, "Sénar, do I have to wear the workout clothes?"

Feeling a little self-conscious after talking with Tyrell at lunch, I didn't want to put the workout clothes on and have to worry about people laughing at me. He smiled sadistically and said, "Nah, you can wear them at home for me ma. You're just walking the track, so you don't have to wear them. Just make sure to still stretch first though."

He said before running to practice to avoid getting in trouble. I walked to the car to get the Walkman as I didn't want to put the work out stuff on anymore to avoid any unnecessary altercations. Before I could walk back to the field, London walked up to me to say, "I don't know why you always need Sénar's help. You are so needy. Ugh, I can't stand your ass. I don't even need my real brother as much as you act like you need Sénar."

Her and her friends laughed at me. I was so annoyed with her and her audience, I smacked my lips and tried not to react by walking off. She laughed before she spat, "Your fat ass can eat as many salads as you want, you will never have a body like mine." She presented herself as if it was a standard for me to reach.

I turned around to say, "Awe, sweetheart, I am sorry, you will always be a little too pale and skinny for Sénar. So, keep up the good work with your mouth."

London looked as if I had slapped her, which was how I intended for her to feel as I walked away. I walked to the track and contemplated on if I should listen to the radio or the mixed Cd Sénar had in his portable CD player. I put the earphones on my ears and listened to the mixed Cd that he had in there already. I listened while I walked the track the whole time Sénar and Tyrell practiced. It was awesome, I felt like I was in a different world as I walked and listened to music. He had some really good songs on there and I loved the song with Nelly and Kelly *"Dilemma"*. I sang along with the song lyrics, *"No matter what I do, all I think about is you."* It was a dope song; I was walking back around when I saw Sénar holding my backpack with London holding on to his other arm.

Sénar smiled as he saw me approaching them, he said, "Dang, you weren't playing. Look at them shoes."

I looked down at my shoes and they were covered in red dust. London laughed at me as I was unaware at how dusty my shoes were or how many times I actually went around the track.

Sénar ignored her laughter and said, "You did good Treasure. Like I said you're a fast learner."

He winked his eye at me, and we walked to his car with London whining about having to leave early yesterday and not finishing what they started. Tyrell caught up to me with Leah behind him.

Tyrell asked, "What's up with all the dust on your shoes?"

Either he was really that dumb or he hadn't noticed me on the track walking earlier. I answered trying to hide my irritation when I replied, "I walked the track Tyrell, while you practiced."

He sighed and asked, "For what?"

I was irritated and snapped at him, "To work out! Why? Do you ask Leah why she is eating this or why she is doing that too?"

Leah raised her eyebrow when she heard her name being mentioned and London turned around to be nosey. I kept walking as I felt my anger increasing, Tyrell grabbed my right hand to pull me back to him.

I yelped, "Ouch! Let my hand go!"

I tried to snatch it from him, but he squeezed harder, I saw Sénar turn around, so I kept my pain in my fingers to myself.

Tyrell whispered in my ear, "Don't be trying to show off in front of your little boyfriend."

He let me go and then answered my question, "No I don't ask her all that, I guess because she doesn't need to do all that extra stuff."

Leah laughed along with London and I turned around to keep walking. I could tell Tyrell was mad and wanted to hurt me, just to make himself feel better. I was so upset but I just wanted to go home and take a shower, so I could cry in the privacy of the bathroom. That way no one would see how humiliated I felt having to explain to everyone I was trying to get fit for a team Tyrell said I couldn't make and eating healthy to help burn extra fat off my body for a team of skinny heifers who all hated me. I knew Sénar was agitated too because he didn't want to be bothered with London. She was asking why he was mad, and he told her to leave him alone. She was pouting as Sénar unlocked the car for me. I got in and did not say another word.

Sénar was upset when he asked, "Treasure, what do you see in him? He pretty much is dissing you in so many ways." I was still silent and ignored him, which made him more pissed off when he said, "Well, if you aren't going to say anything, then I will."

I snapped at him, "Why don't you just worry about London's stupid ass? She is worse than Tyrell!"

He yelled at me, "I already told you why she hates your ass! But Tyrell is supposed to be your boyfriend."

He said it mockingly, as I quickly retorted, "Oh, now you want to acknowledge that?"

We pulled up to the house enraged with each other. He got out and slammed his door and I slammed mine. I ran inside and took my shoes off at the door, since they were filled with dirt. I carried my own backpack up the steps and ignored Ken as he was sitting at the table. Sénar went straight to the garage to work out. I was so glad Cassidy wasn't home, but it wasn't but fifteen minutes before she walked in with an attitude.

I almost lost my mind when she said, "Why are you trying to mess with London? Just because Tyrell has a new girlfriend doesn't mean you can be hating on her for still having one." She smirked at me.

I had it with her, my fingers were bleeding because Tyrell squeezed the crap out of them and humiliated me for, I don't even know the count of the times. I pinched my fingers on the way out, hoping the pain would distract me from my anger. I was fed up and ran out the room to go downstairs with Cassidy on my heels and Sénar and London on their way up the steps. My eyes burned with fury as it felt like my tears were boiling them. With Cassidy on my nerves, London and Sénar in front of me, and Ken now behind them, I closed my eyes and felt like I was going to faint. Sénar grabbed me and yelled, "Treasure!"

I grabbed my head and sat down. I breathed in deeply to slow down my rapid breathing. I felt like the walls were collapsing on me and I couldn't breathe as I tried to gasp for air. Sénar grabbed me and shook me as he called my name, "Treasure?" I could hear a million voices laughing and calling me names. Finally, one voice that I knew, touched my last button when Cassidy said, "I told you she was crazy!"

I snapped and I yelled at the top of my lungs, "I'm fine!"

Everyone looked at me like I had three heads. I heard my mom run out of her room calling my name, "Treasure?"

I snapped at her, "What?"

In a worried tone she asked, "What's wrong, Treasure?"

I closed my eyes and replied, "I'm fine. I'm fine. I'm fine!" Until I believed it.

I could feel everyone staring at me as my breathing started to increase again, I could hear Ken tell my mom, "Let Sénar handle that shit, I got something I need you to do."

Cassidy said, "Her ass is nuts!"

Sénar scooped me up off the stairs to keep me from flashing and beating Cassidy until she couldn't speak any more. Sénar carried me downstairs and sat me on the chair at the kitchen nook. He then walked to the freezer to get something out.

He said, "Damn Treasure." Sénar gave me an Ice Cream Snicker and said, "You just need to be fed, ma." He smiled sadistically as he grabbed my thigh and rubbed my hair. London walked in to see me calmly eating my ice cream snicker and saw Sénar caressing my hair.

I moaned, "Hmm, this is so good."

Sénar was aroused when he said, "I bet," in a seductive voice. London said Sénar's name and he turned around but tried to hide his agitation with her. Before she could say anything else, he pulled her to him to say, "If you are going to use your mouth, use it for something I like."

She didn't say anything and just patiently waited for him. He instructed, "Treasure stay calm and out of trouble. Don't eat no more junk either."

I happily ate my ice Cream Snicker, he looked at me and shook his head at my happy dance as I ate my ice cream. I could see the hate in London's eyes, which made me enjoy it even more as she followed Sénar to his room. I went to watch TV and contemplated what would have happened if Sénar wasn't there to be the referee and get me to calm down. Sénar and London came down after only about twenty minutes. He kissed her and told her he would call her later. She glared at me before she left.

Sénar took a deep breath before he approached me to ask, "Treasure, you good ma?"

I laid on the couch, knowing damn well I was on the verge of losing my mind and I said, "I'm fine Sénar."

He stared at me like I was lying to him. Sénar tried to be sincere but couldn't help but be honest when he said, "You are fine when it comes to looks, but emotionally you are not. You need more than just carbs."

He smiled sadistically and offered, "I can feed you what you really need."

He smiled at me and was sincere with his offer. I knew I would feel better if I gave in to his offer, but I just couldn't, even though I knew he was right. I just laid there, and in my mind, I allowed him to have his way with me. Until I felt him touching me. I moaned and bit my bottom lip in anticipation of him doing whatever he wanted. Until I realized, it wasn't just in my mind, he was actually rubbing my body and kissed me to reinforce the reality of him doing as he pleased with my body.

He waited until I opened my eyes and said, "Damn, you are so beautiful, even when your ass is acting crazy."

Sénar snatched me off the couch and held me in his arms. He smelled my hair before he said, "I know Wednesday is our usual hump day, but you couldn't even make it until then, so let's adjust that attitude of yours."

I was offended and replied, "I am not the one who was tripping Sénar."

I wiggled out of his embrace and thought about how he should have just done whatever he was going to do and not have said a word. I, in my mind had given him consent before he had to mess it up. I was angry now because I really did want to feel the relief I felt when Sénar handled me, but now it was not chaotic enough for me to give in. So, I brushed him off and tried to go back upstairs.

He snatched me back and said, "Nuh uh, your ass don't need to go up there. If you want an outlet take it out on me, however you want."

I pushed him back and said, "Move Sénar, I won't do anything to her."

He smirked and then said, "Yeah right, you know you want this dick!"

He started laughing as I frowned my eyebrows at him.

I replied, "Shut up Sénar. I want food, not your, whatever you call it."

He snickered before he asked, "What? You act so brand new sometimes, come get this shit. You don't have to beat Cassidy up to get it."

He laughed and headed to the garage but said, "Come on girl, let's go in here and work out some of that frustration you have built up."

I was annoyed with his confidence, so I said, "No Sénar, your body is not the answer to all my problems, thank you very much."

I said body to refrain from using his choice word and rolled my eyes at him. He smirked at me and then said, "Ok."

He was being sarcastic and sat back down. He had the controller now and I knew I could not go up there if I didn't want to beat Cassidy to death. Sénar laid back and flipped through the channels and tried to ignore me as I stood in front of him. I wanted to slap him silly, I felt like he had some invisible cord to me that he tugged on whenever he wanted.

I was still standing up when he said, "Move Treasure, you are kind of in my way."

He seemed to be trying to dismiss me, without actually dismissing me. I grabbed the controller off his stomach grazing his abdomen with my fingers and he jumped up. I couldn't fight the urge to figure out why he jumped up so quickly, so I tickled him to see what would happen. He laughed, or should I say, giggled.

He grabbed my hands, "Stop. Unless you wanna wake up the beast."

He smiled his sadistic smile and let me go. I didn't care I have never seen Sénar that vulnerable, so I tried to tickle him again and he pulled me on top of him, smelling my hair while grabbing my behind. I felt his man stick harden as he whispered in my ear, "Look what you did, I might not let you go now."

I hurried to get off of him as my heartbeat increased and my coochie pulsated with anticipation. I sat on the other couch and tried not to indicate that I wanted him too. I sat down, bringing my knees up to my chest and embraced them while trying to stay focused on the TV. Sénar shook his head and watched highlights of the NFL football season. Ken came down and appeared to be in a rush when he came down. He left without saying anything. Sénar got up to go to the kitchen to pull out the stuff he needed to start dinner and I followed him.

He smirked at me before he asked, "What do you want Treasure? The food isn't even started yet." He then smiled at me, but he was being sarcastic. I ignored his sarcasm to ask, "Well, you don't want me to help?" I was being seductive. He blushed before he answered, "Treasure, I always want your help, but you play too much."

He shook his head and continued to get everything he needed. I asked, "What are you making?"

He gazed at me and then rolled his eyes before answering, "I am making us spaghetti and you something else."

I frowned and then he laughed at me before he said, "Carb withdrawals and dick withdrawals don't go well together, so you gonna have to get this." He said as he grabbed his man stick and bit his bottom lip.

I squirmed in my chair as he laughed. I was annoyed with him now. "Weren't you just with London?" I asked with a bit of an attitude.

He raised his eyebrow when he asked, "Why?"

I shrugged my shoulders, "I don't know."

He rolled his eyes, "I didn't feed her because I was trying to feed you. I just let her have some dessert," he said and then winked at me.

I was a little jealous when I said, "I thought you said you didn't do that for her."

He laughed before he replied, "You are too cute! I don't do that for her. I said, I let her have dessert."

He laughed because he saw that I was still lost, so he clarified what he meant when he said, "I let her give me some head Treasure, damn. You want to watch next time, so you can learn how to do it? She is really good at it."

He was still laughing when my jealousy was replaced with irritation. I rolled my eyes at him as he shook his head and finished getting the stuff prepared for dinner. He said, "Since you are being so nosey, why don't you cut up some of the vegetables. You need to practice on mincing anyways, amongst other things."

He smiled; I was really getting irritated with his sarcasm. He sensed my frustration, so he eased up a bit on his insinuating techniques and just focused on dinner. He was really swift with his preparation as it appeared, he was making his spaghetti sauce from scratch. He gave me a variety of vegetables and showed me how to mince them to his liking. I did my best to follow instructions without cutting my finger for real. When Sénar noticed my fingers, his facial expression changed to a serious one.

He said, "Oh yeah, you're fired. Even though you aren't actually touching the vegetables with your injured fingers, it's still unsanitary, so just sit pretty."

He re-rinsed the vegetables, even the cut ones and minced them so quickly, I wondered why he even asked for my help. He put everything where it needed to be and cut a purple vegetable that I had never seen before.

I asked, "What is that Sénar?"

He looked at me and smiled before he answered, "It's an eggplant. I am using this for your dinner as a replacement for pasta."

He smiled and proceeded to place them in a pan and put foil on them. After everything was on the stove and the meat was cooked, he turned it off and let his home-made spaghetti sauce simmer on low heat.

He said, "We got like forty minutes to burn."

He then said, "Come here."

I was skeptical, but I followed him anyway. We went upstairs, he took me to the bathroom to doctor up my fingers.

Then whispered, "Let me get some dessert? I'll feed you tomorrow because by then I know you will be ready."

I looked at him blankly as he opened the door and grabbed my hand leading me to his room. Once we were in there, he locked his door. He said, "Take your pants off, we don't have that much time."

I started to decline but I was really horny and since he said we weren't going to do it; I just took my pants off.

He smiled sadistically. "Good girl."

I smacked my lips. "Shush Sénar."

He agreed, "Ok." He pulled me to him and kissed me. I could not help but push him back. He laughed before he said, "You're so cute when you lie." He playfully shoved me onto Chino's old bed. He got on top of me to kiss me and fondle my breast. He lifted my shirt just to under my breast, to access my stomach. He licked all over it, causing me to squirm as it tickled, he then slid my panties off. Eager with anticipation, I allowed him to spread my legs. He licked and kissed all over my coochie until I moaned, loud enough for him to stop to get me a pillow. I held on to the pillow as he swirled his tongue around rapidly and then he slid his fingers inside of me. I put the pillow over my face as I braced myself for pleasure to consume me. Sénar put his hand down in the center of my stomach, over my belly button and then pressed downward as he slipped one of his fingers into my butthole. I sprang up, even though, I almost knew it was coming. He pushed down to gently guide me back down.

He stopped to tell me, "Get ready ma."

I put the pillow over my face as he licked, sucked, and twirled his tongue against my coochie while pressing down on my belly button. He used his two-finger hole stunt to take me over the top as I screamed into the pillow. My body spasmed and convulsed with pleasure shooting throughout my body. It was like a California earthquake, I trembled with aftershocks while he gently nibbled on, my now throbbing little man in the boat. I laid there for a second to regather my thoughts and rationalize why I once again was in this position. I quickly closed my legs just in case Sénar was having second thoughts of now partaking in the next level of ecstasy. When I removed the pillow, he was grinning at me. I was so embarrassed because he was waiting for me to remove the pillow.

He said, "Are you good ma?"

I blushed before I replied, "I'm good."

Sénar said, "Good. Now get out of here before you get me in trouble."

He laughed as he got up to look out his room to check if the coast was clear. He then instructed, "Get dressed ma."

I quickly grabbed my panties and pants to put them back on. I got up and waited for instructions.

Sénar grabbed me and whispered, "When you leave go to the bathroom first and then to your room."

I stared at him because he was so intense as he checked to make sure it was clear again. He kissed me and I wiped my mouth off, "Eew, stop that's gross."

He laughed, then said, "You're funny."

Sénar laughed again before slapping my butt and said, "Go!"

I quickly ran out to the bathroom but before I could reach the door, I heard Ken's voice from downstairs, "Aye, Sénar?"

Sénar responded, "What's up Pops?"

Ken said, "Come here real quick."

I quickly used the bathroom and washed my hands after. I opened the door to see Sénar was there to go in after me. I just heard the water running as I went into my room. Cassidy was sleeping, so I laid down to think about what just took place, until I drifted to sleep. Sénar came up stairs to get me and Cassidy for dinner. We both woke up and stared at each other, probably wondering how we both ended up asleep at the same time. She got up and left before me. My mom and Ken were already at the table eating when I came down. Everyone gawked at me like I was rising from the dead. I walked into the kitchen and saw everyone eating spaghetti and salad. I was hungry, so I was looking forward to dinner. Sénar handed me a plate and pointed to my dish. I sighed as I fixed a plate of his special prepared dish for me. I added salad and sat down. Sénar got some of both of the dishes with a salad. My mom saw my plate and then looked at Sénar to ask, "What's the dish Treasure has?"

Ken smirked at him and waited for his answer. Sénar proudly answered, "It's low carb eggplant lasagna. Do you want to try it, Carmel?"

My mom was excited when she answered, "Yeah, let me see what you have going on over there, Chef Sénar."

Ken looked at my mom like he wanted to slap her. Ken said, "Angel baby, don't get Sénar fucked up."

Sénar laughed as he made my mom a sample and then made one for everyone, including Cassidy. He gave my mom hers first, then Ken, then Cassidy. I ate my food and was pleasantly stunned at the amazing flavors in my mouth. Also, to my surprise, the consistency, to me, by far was better than pasta. I was so happy; I didn't realize everyone was staring at me. I rolled my eyes and kept eating as if they were not there.

My mom tasted her food, "Wow Sénar! You could make a fortune off of this! It's so good!"

Ken was irritated when he took a bite of my special dish. The facial expression Ken made had Sénar laughing. Ken asked, "Boy, why does Treasure get the fancy shit? This tastes better than the spaghetti!"

Everybody laughed but Cassidy was salty when she said, "I don't want that."

My mom quickly said, "Well, hand it over here Cassidy." Me and Cassidy were both shocked at how quick my mom snatched it. My mom took it and ate hers and Cassidy's with her salad, leaving the spaghetti on her plate. Ken was jealous but didn't say anything and Sénar just ate his food.

I was so happy with my food, I said, "Thanks Sénar, that was the bomb."

Sénar smiled and replied, "I know."

My mom laughed, Ken shook his head and Cassidy rolled her eyes at me as she finished her food. When Cassidy was done, I told her, "Let me take your plate to the sink and I'll start the dishes."

Cassidy looked at me as if I had flashed her. I took her plate, along with everyone else's and set them to the side. I ran the dish water as Sénar put the food in containers. Ken got up, my mom got their drinks and then followed behind Ken.

Sénar said, "Awe, you're so sweet when you want to be."

I rolled my eyes and said, "Sénar shush."

He laughed, grabbing me from behind to smell my hair. I pushed him off of me to say, "Stop it." He rolled his eyes at me and finished putting the food away. We went to bed shortly after, since today was a rather long day.

Cassidy refused to ride with us, so I waited for Sénar as Cassidy walked out the door. Sénar came down in a good mood, smiling when he saw me. I smiled back, and we left for school. Before pulling up to the school, Sénar said, "Don't let anyone take you to the point of anger that you can't control yourself. I know you are probably having carb withdrawals too, along with other frustrations."

I just stared at him for a second, almost annoyed because he thought he knew everything about me, but he did not.

He laughed before he continued, "Anyway, you will get used to meat and veggies, it's not so bad. Plus, if you had the right kind of meat in your diet, you wouldn't be so moody." Sénar laughed, as I stared at him blankly and confused.

Then I thought about what he said before I replied, "Sénar hush, ok, I am fine. I know how to take care of that myself."

He laughed, then asked, "Oh, really?"

I ignored him, and he still offered, "You can borrow my meat, since it makes you so sweet."

While he laughed, I said, "No thanks, Sénar, I don't think London would be happy with me borrowing her meat."

Through his laughter he still tried to convince me, "Well, let me worry about that. You need it more than her, and I want to give it to you more than her."

He winked at me as he reasoned with me, "Look, when you are sexually frustrated, you are mean and violent. Hell, you are already mean as it is sometimes. I can help alleviate some of your frustration, and you will burn some calories while having fun." He smiled at me as he was sincere in his reasoning.

I looked at him like he was crazy but still said, "No, Sénar, things are crazy enough."

Sénar sighed before he replied, "Because you make stuff difficult, trust me, you will need it. Every Wednesday, I have to clear my schedule for you anyway to feed your ass. I'll give you a meat voucher or dessert if you need an extra service added." Sénar laughed, but he was serious.

I ignored him but actually took his offer into consideration. It made sense, but I shook my head at the idea because it was difficult to admit. We got to the school, and I dodged Sénar's stalker's glare before she could open her mouth. I was out of the car and on my way to class before she knew it. When lunchtime came, Leah and Tyrell were already sitting at my favorite table as I went to warm up leftovers from my special Lasagna. I was excited to eat it again. My mom raved about it as if it was made with her in mind. Once again, the cafeteria smelled like our kitchen as my special lasagna's aroma filled the cafeteria. Everyone looked around as if to search for a culprit with award-winning food.

Leah couldn't help but ask, "What is that Treasure, it smells good." Even though we weren't really speaking at the moment, I still answered her to avoid Tyrell snapping at me.

I answered, "It's Lasagna."

Tyrell smirked at me before he asked, "What happen to your little diet? You can't be eating pasta, talking about trying to lose weight."

I laughed at him and he became irritated instantly. He asked, "What are you laughing at?"

I smiled before answering, "It's not pasta; it's eggplant."

Leah got up to go get something when she came back quickly with two forks, one for her and one for Tyrell. I looked at Leah like she was crazy and asked, "What are those forks for?"

She giggled before saying, "I want to try it."

I was going to deny her the pleasure until Tyrell said, "Don't be greedy Treasure, damn, she just wants to try it."

I wanted to slap both of them, but I knew it wasn't worth an altercation, so I let them try it before I could even get a fork of it myself. Leah went first, her eyes widened when she tasted it, and she closed her eyes as she chewed. Tyrell smiled when he saw how much she was enjoying it. I couldn't help but wonder what else she was trying and enjoying when it came to Tyrell. Then Tyrell tasted it next and rolled his eyes before he said, "It's alright, but I don't like the texture; just give me pasta."

I took my container and ate my food while Leah looked tempted to grab another fork of it, but my glare warned her not to even think about it. She stared at me before she said, "That was bomb Treasure. Dang, Sénar made that?"

I sighed, then asked, "Why?"

I just wanted to eat in peace. I saw Sénar watching us at the table while London held on to him for dear life. I was annoyed with everyone when I answered, "Yeah," and that was it.

Tyrell looked agitated with my answer when he said, "Oh, so he's your personal chef now too?"

I sighed again before answering, "Tyrell no, he just knows I can't eat pasta, so he made an alternative."

Leah said, "Damn, when can I go to your house, Treasure? I want some of Sénar's cooking."

Tyrell was pissed he got up and left the table, and I waited for Leah to leave too, but when she didn't, I was even more upset. I ate my food and ignored her as she watched me eat. When I finished, I put away my stuff and went to class. I chose a different chair to sit in to avoid Leah, which didn't work.

She still sat next to me to say, "Your punishment seems to be pretty beneficial, Treasure. Damn, I would love to be punished by Sénar and Ken."

The fact that she added Ken into the equation was disturbing and disgusting. I was feeling cocky when I said, "Oh, so you are already bored with Tyrell?"

She stared at me again and laughed before she answered, "It seems to me you have the real star as your babysitter."

I snapped at her, "Leah, you are really on my last nerve. So, I would suggest you keep your comments to yourself. You may be benefiting from my punishment as well, but not for long. When I get off, you are going to wish you were me."

I smiled my own sadistic smile at her and dismissed her by doing my work and paying attention to the teacher. I had it with her I was ready to beat her ass like I had to do Cassidy so many times. I couldn't afford trouble; it would only prolong my punishment. I just got through the rest of the day and tried to avoid anyone who didn't mean well, to avoid snapping. I met up with Sénar and grabbed his keys. I went to the bathroom to change into my work out clothes and shoes. The pants were tight, and the shirt was tightly fitted with my sports bra holding my breast in place. I felt great and looked like I meant business. I walked out of the locker room and straight to the track. I walked while I listened to music until my mind drifted to Leah and Tyrell. I thought about how they are always together and how Leah just hinted with remarks in regard to Tyrell's birthmark, right above his man stick. I was getting upset, so I picked up my pace in walking. I thought about Cassidy, my mom, Ken, and London. Before I knew it, I was running around the track and at a really fast pace. I could feel the sweat dripping down my face as I ran faster than I had ever ran in my life.

"Treasure!", Sénar called my name.

I slowed down until I could stop. I kneeled down to catch my breath before responding, "Yes, Sénar?"

I was sweating profusely and out of breath when he clapped. "Good job, Treasure!" He was smiling from ear to ear when he asked, "How did it feel, ma?"

I smiled before I replied, "It felt great!" He laughed, and I realized Tyrell, Leah, and London were standing behind Sénar, totally shocked as Sénar and I interacted. He had my backpack and gym bag, along with his stuff. London grabbed Sénar's arm, and we all walked toward the parking lot.

Tyrell caught up to me to ask, "What was that? Oh, so you are running now? Wow, what else are you doing? You act like you don't even miss me!"

He was pissed off, but I was still feeling great when I said, "I miss you, Tyrell. I just can't do anything about it. Call me sometime."

I patted him on his shoulder, and he lost it. He grabbed me by my pants, which took a lot of effort as they were really tight.

He pulled me to him, then said, "Don't play with me, Treasure. You be playing games. Are you my girl or not because you don't seem to be missing me at all?"

I could see Leah smiling as she observed the situation; I answered, "Tyrell, are you my man, or is Leah borrowing you until I am off punishment?"

He gaped at me like I was crazy when he demanded, "Treasure, answer my question."

I answered, "I am your girl, Tyrell, and I do miss you."

He smiled and then kissed me. He grabbed my ass before he said, "Umph, I can't wait till you are off of punishment."

I got excited at the idea as well and hugged him before I walked away to get in the car with Sénar. I could tell Sénar was annoyed, but I couldn't tell with who. I opened the door and heard Sénar telling London that he was busy on Wednesdays and listened to her whine before Sénar got in the car. We drove home and finished our conversation from the morning.

I asked, "Sénar, if it's a loan, how will I pay you back?"

He laughed then answered, "Give me the keys to your heart?"

For a minute, I thought he was serious, but he never indicated that he was not. As if this could not get any more awkward, I couldn't do what he asked. So, I had a better suggestion, "I'll let you tutor me on how to serve dessert." Sénar blushed but quickly agreed. We started our loan process as soon as we got home.

Chapter 7

The next week and a half flew by so quickly. I was working out every day after school and practicing the cheerleading moves in my room or the garage. I was in a better mood most of the time, since I didn't have all my frustration pent up. I was even nice to Cassidy when she wasn't running her mouth. Tyrell started to call me all the time. He all of a sudden, had my cellphone number, even though I never gave it to him. On Wednesday, he called me right before Sénar and I was supposed to start our second bartering session. I received my first official loan from Sénar last week, and I was ready for another one as I could feel my attitude creeping back.

Tyrell asked, "So, what made you want to be all athletic, all of a sudden?"

He was so jealous of the fact that I was working out and eating healthy. I actually had results and felt great most of the time when Leah, London, or Cassidy wasn't on my last nerve. Even Sénar and I were getting along as we were always doing something towards one of our goals. The tryouts were this Friday, and I was nervous, but I couldn't keep it a secret anymore.

I answered, "I am trying out for the cheerleading team."

He laughed before he taunted, "Oh, so you think because you ate healthily and worked out a week or two, you can make the cheerleading team?"

I sighed when Sénar came to the door to check if I was still on the phone. I was feeling self-conscious when I thought about what would happen if I didn't make it.

I sighed before answering, "I don't know, Tyrell, that is why I didn't tell you. I knew you would say something like that. Well, that is why it's called tryouts."

Tyrell was agitated with me and responded, "Don't get smart, Treasure. What, Sénar, be pumping your head up, making you think you can make the team?"

I said, "Yeah, you know, how you be pumping Leah's head up."

He got an attitude and demanded, "Man, shut up about Leah. I am tired of hearing it."

I snapped back, "Well, I have to go."

He asked, "Where are you going?"

I answered, "Nowhere."

He asked, "Then why do you have to go?"

Sénar was standing at the door waiting on me to get off the phone. I rolled my eyes and answered, "Because I have to practice and work out."

He was even madder when he asked, "With who?"

I was aggravated with his interrogation but answered, "By myself."

He said, "Yeah, right," and then hung up in my face. I was mad because I had wanted to hang up in his face a long time ago. I got up, and Sénar was irritated now too.

I asked, "Sénar, what's wrong with you?"

He sighed and replied, "You took so long-running your mouth on the phone with his chump ass, you are cutting into our time."

I almost felt bad, but then he smiled sadistically before he said, "Well, I guess I'll just tutor you on how to give dessert then."

I had an attitude now for a few reasons. I almost regretted suggesting my payment method, I rather be the one receiving dessert instead of learning how to serve it. I actually wanted to be "*fed*" as Sénar called it lately, but I wasted precious time on the phone just to hear Tyrell doubt that I could accomplish my goal. I pouted while Sénar laughed and said, "Well, at least we will be even. If you do a good job, I'll throw in a quickie voucher, no charge."

He winked at me before dragging me to his room. I complained, "What if Cassidy comes or Ken?"

He smacked his lips then answered, "Just let me worry about that; come on."

He grabbed my hand and led me downstairs to the garage. I was so nervous; my heartbeat was already speeding up as we snuck in the garage. He quickly gave me instructions, "You ever had a Big Stick ice cream?"

I giggled; it had been a while, but they were some pretty big ice creams. He smiled, "Well, act like you're eating one of those, and no teeth, ma."

I asked, "Well, how can I guarantee that?"

He asked with his eyebrow raised, "Did you let the ice cream touch your teeth?"

I thought about it for a second, "I don't know, geesh, let's get this over with."

He smiled when he pulled out his man stick. My eyes widened when I saw that it was bigger than the last time I was in this position. He laughed and winked before saying, "I know."

I smacked my lips and closed my eyes as I put my mouth on it, careful not to let it touch my teeth. It was difficult because it was not ice cream, and I didn't want to hurt him. I tried my best, and he seemed to like it. As soon as I was getting the hang of it, he stopped me to say, "Ok, that's way better than the first time. Now, bend over."

I tried not to show my excitement for the *"quickie"* as he called it because it was free of charge, so I didn't owe him any favors. He was quick, but it was effective, and I still got my rocks off. He was extra excited when he pressed down on my butthole, without penetrating it, and it felt like he pushed a release button. I moaned but not loud enough to need a pillow. Sénar released his fluids all over my behind and cleaned it all up just in time before we heard the front door open and close. I put my work out pants back on and quickly left the garage.

Sénar stayed in there as I went up the steps. London was knocking on Sénar's door before she entered, as I walked in my room to see Cassidy settling in. London came into the room where Cassidy and I were shortly after leaving Sénar's room.

I tried to stop her by saying, "Don't come in, Sénar is not in here."

London looked at me with an attitude and replied, "Girl, shut the hell up!"

She came in anyway, and Cassidy said, "This is not just your room, blacky!"

I laughed at her joke and told London, "Stay on her side then."

I ignored Cassidy's insult as London looked at my side of the room with disgust. London said, "I don't know why anybody would want to be next to your weird crazy ass anyway."

She then rolled her eyes at me as Sénar passed, he saw me with my arms folded and poked his head in our room. When he saw London in my room with Cassidy, he was almost annoyed when he asked, "What are you doing here London?"

She quickly answered, "Cassidy needed a ride home, so I gave her a ride."

He was quiet when he looked at Cassidy with inquisitive eyes. Cassidy asked, "What?"

I remembered he told London Wednesday was off-limits because he was busy on those days, but she found a way to still come over through Cassidy. I felt like putting her on blast, so I rolled my eyes before I said, "She is lying, she just came out of your room."

London's face looked like she was about to get in trouble when Sénar asked, "You were in my room?"

London quickly answered, "Yeah, but only for a second, I was looking for you."

He shook his head and nicely told her, "Babe, don't go in my room unless I tell you too, ok?"

He kissed her and led her out of our room. I rolled my eyes, making sure to include everyone in my eye-rolling techniques as I got my stuff ready to take a shower. When I came out of the bathroom, Sénar was waiting and ready for his shower. He winked at me before entering the bathroom, and I ignored him as I went into my room. I grabbed my phone and saw Tyrell had called like ten times. I saw eleven missed calls, the eleventh call was a number I had never seen before, so I called it back.

Tyrell answered, "Hello!"

I answered back, "Hello?"

Tyrell was in a rush when he replied, "I hope you had fun because now I am busy, don't call this number anymore. I'll see you at school tomorrow."

He hung up in my face prompting me to run downstairs to see if Tyrell was even at home, but his car was gone. I was so angry, I almost called him back when I turned around to see Sénar staring at me. I was embarrassed, and my feelings were hurt but I didn't want him to notice. He shook his head and sat down on the couch. I was even more annoyed when London came and sat down next to Sénar because she was not supposed to be here. My relationship was continuing to fall apart while Sénar's was still intact. I took some deep breaths. I tried not to make it obvious, but I was starting to get upset. I thought about how before talking to Tyrell, I was fine, so I just tried to relax again. Cassidy came down to ask, "Let me guess, Treasure has the controller?"

I gave it to her and continued to ignore reality. She just handed the controller to Sénar, and we all watched a movie. London went home before Sénar made tacos for everyone and a taco salad for me and my mom.

Thursday, instead of walking, I sat and watched the cheerleader's routine to get ready for tomorrow. I was nervous but confident. I would just be sure to avoid Tyrell before the tryouts tomorrow. My first classes were quick as always, and it was lunchtime before I knew it. Leah and Tyrell were already sitting at my favorite table. When I sat down, Leah and Tyrell both just stared at me. I pulled my taco salad out of my backpack and ate my food while I just stared back at them. They didn't say anything, so I didn't say anything either. When I was done eating, I got up to leave. Tyrell followed me, even though I kept walking. I stopped walking to turn around to face him, "What is it, Tyrell?" I asked while tying my best not to have an attitude.

He seemed as if his feelings were hurt when he replied, "So, you seem to be cool with how things are right now."

I didn't want to argue, so I replied, "Tyrell look, I don't know when I am going to get off punishment. I'm trying to stay out of trouble and be productive. Why can't you be supportive of that at least? You seem more concerned with Leah than me anyways. How can I compete with that?"

He was irritated when he answered, "Easy, you live with a dude who I cannot stand, and he's basically, obsessed with you! And you want me to believe there is nothing going on between the two of you?"

I saw Leah creep up and tune in to our conversation from afar. I answered him to the best of my ability, "I don't know what you are talking about. I don't know what you want me to do or say, Tyrell."

The bell rung as Leah walked pass Tyrell and I to get to class. Tyrell glared at me like he hated me before I left to class, and he walked away without saying another word. Leah was already sitting down. I thought that gave me the opportunity to sit somewhere else, but when I looked around, there weren't any other seats available. I reluctantly sat down next to Leah and put my attention on the teacher. He gave us the assignment to work in groups and make a message in a puzzle on graph paper with mathematical points. Be it that it may, Leah was my partner. We both had different reactions. I rolled my eyes, and Leah said, "Hell yeah!"

When we were done with our puzzles, we traded with each other. Her puzzle points created the star shape when I completed it. She was smiling at me when I looked at her. When she finished my puzzle, it spelled: U wish. My smile was bigger when her smile quickly faded. She became irritated, rolling her eyes at me. I ignored her attempt to insinuate her, and Tyrell was messing around by constantly mentioning or exaggerating the word star. I get it; she was trying to make me jealous, but it just made me feel less guilty about me and Sénar's arrangement. Since it was Thursday, the practice was short, and we listened to the instructions for cheerleading tryouts for tomorrow. Sénar came to find me, he took my backpack, and we walked to his car, of course with London attached to him.

Tyrell walked up to me with Leah close behind and asked, "Are you ready for tomorrow?"

I smiled at him before I replied, "Yeah, I guess."

He laughed and sarcastically asked, "You really think you are going to make it, huh?"

I answered, "As long as you aren't the judge, you already said I can't dance."

He laughed while Leah chimed in, "Well, I know I'm going to make it. I hope you make it too, Treasure."

She smiled genuinely as I responded, "Good for you, Leah and thanks."

I smiled back at her but thought about how much I couldn't stand her. London added, "You ain't gonna make shit!"

She laughed along with Leah and Tyrell. Sénar checked her when he said, "Aye, chill London."

Tyrell gave me a quick kiss, "See ya tomorrow."

Tyrell and Leah left, and Sénar told London he would call her later. She pouted and asked to come over, Sénar told her, "You talk too much, and I don't want any drama before my game so, no." She pouted again before she kissed him goodbye.

On the drive home, Sénar asked, "Do you want to work out?"

I looked at him like he was crazy and asked, "What kind of work out Sénar?"

He laughed and bit his bottom lip, "Whatever kind of work out you want."

I rolled my eyes and answered, "No."

He laughed before he said, "Well, I have an idea; you might like it."

I rolled my eyes but still followed him to the garage. He grabbed the boxing gloves and gave me the red pair, and he took the blue pair. He put mine on and put his on himself. He stared at me for a quick second before giving instructions, "Hit the punching bag, not me."

He laughed nervously as I wildly started to swing my fists. I quickly found out that it kind of hurt to hit the punching bag. Sénar showed me how to swing and hit it so it wouldn't hurt me. I tried it and loved it. I hit it so hard that it felt good. I eyed Sénar before I asked, "Let me hit you?"

He laughed and put his gloves up, "What chu wanna do?"

I swung on him, and he dodged it, but I got him with a two-punch combo. He tapped me on my side, and I hit him in the forehead. He looked at me like I was crazy before he warned, "There you go with the forehead punches. Don't start no shit won't be no shit, Treasure."

I swung on him again, and he squeezed me, so I couldn't hit him. I pushed him off of me and asked, "What, you scurred Sénar?"

He laughed while he let me give my best shots as he dodged and avoided them. Sénar tapped me on the side every so often to work me up, until I was tired and sweaty. He took the mats people used for yoga out and laid them down. I was skeptical but didn't say anything. He laid down and said, "Let's stretch and do sit ups."

I pouted and complained, "What? No, I need to rest first."

He laughed and then agreed, "Fine."

I laid down next to him but kept my gloves on. I laid there and thought about all the drama that we were constantly going through. Deep in thought, I asked, "Sénar, why do you and Tyrell hate each other so much?"

He stared at me as if I was playing dumb when he answered, "Treasure, Tyrell is a buster. He is only with you to hurt me. I tried to tell your ass that, but you are so dang hardheaded. I already had my own dirt, so I didn't want to destroy his chances completely, but your dumb ass fell for him anyway. Now he is probably feeding your girl the meat, he supposed to be giving you, but now I have to supply it on demand."

He smirked at me and then added, "Plus, I know he doesn't have more skills than me. Trust me, I know."

I couldn't argue that and asked, "Well, how did you get so good at it?"

He smiled my special smile, and I bit my bottom lip as I thought about how much pleasure I've experienced with him. Sénar shivered and asked, "Did you just say I was good at it?"

I blushed and punched him in the arm. I said, "You know what I mean."

He smiled his sadistic smile before he answered, "Ma, it's not exactly anything to be proud about when it was because of circumstances."

I looked at him like he was stupid; he laughed and answered, "Man, I was young Treasure; my dad is crazy. I saw and took on a lot of abuse, so my siblings would be left alone. That's why they are so spoiled, and I am so fucked up."

I felt bad for him for a second until he said, "But I don't regret the time I spent with you. I just wish it was under different circumstances."

I was overwhelmed; I didn't know how to feel. I wanted to pry and ask him more, but Cassidy came into the garage to ask, "What are y'all doing?"

Sénar sat up, "Cassidy, do you want to see Treasure in the gloves?"

Smiling at the idea of beating her ass, I challenged, "Yeah, Cassidy let's go?"

Cassidy rolled her eyes, "Um no. Sénar, what are we eating?"

He sighed, "Damn, must I do everything?"

She waited for him to get up before closing the door. He removed his gloves and helped me remove mine. Before we left, he said, "I want the keys to your heart. Your body is lovely, but I want you to be mine."

I was lost for words when he kissed me and smelled my hair before letting me go. He said, "I'm going to take a shower, and I'll make us something to eat."

He left me there in my thoughts, wondering what he saw and what he had been through. I remembered Cassidy's little speech she gave about how their lives were improved while me and my mom had to suffer. I didn't want to think about what she meant now. I guess everyone has a story. I went inside and saw Ken when I came in, he was talking to Cassidy at the table. They both glared at me as I hurried to my room. I wrote in my diary and took a bath after Sénar got out of the shower. I used the shower head and allowed my mind the freedom to do as it pleased until I reached the point of pleasure. I ate a fajita salad while everyone else had fajitas. I went to bed thinking about me and Sénar's conversation.

Today was the big day, I was super nervous as I waited for Sénar on the couch. Sénar came down, grinning, and said, "You ready Treasure, I like that."

I smiled and said, "Hell yeah!"

We both laughed as he knew I was mocking Leah. We drove to school, and I could not help but roll my eyes at London as she was waiting for us to park. I breathed in deeply and went on with the day. At lunchtime, I went to find a new place to sit outside and ate my lunch by myself. I watched Sénar come out to search for me with London attached to him like an accessory. When he spotted me, he relaxed a bit but did not come over to where I was. I made sure to get to my next class early, so I could avoid sitting next to Leah. I felt relieved that I was successful at finding a chair away from her. I didn't want to be self-conscious or have any doubts, so I stayed away from all negativity and got through the day as quickly as possible. The moment finally arrived; I was standing around trying to stay focused after having changed into one of my workout outfits. The music was playing, and all kinds of people came to watch the tryouts. The boys from football and basketball watched intently, knowing it was the opportunity to see what new options they would have to pick from after the tryouts. I tried not to let my nerves get the best of me when I saw Leah and Tyrell talking. I closed my eyes and heard Sénar's voice tell me all the things I needed to hear. I felt a hand on my shoulder; I looked up to see Tyrell and Leah.

Tyrell asked, "What are you doing, praying?"

I looked at him and answered, "No, but it's not a bad idea."

He laughed before he joked, "Yeah, you gonna need it."

They both laughed at me, and then before walking away, Tyrell said, "Good luck, ladies!"

Leah sat next to me, and I was not happy about it. I started to feel like they were purposely trying to sabotage me prior to my tryout. I ignored Leah and tried not to let my nerves get the best of me, but it was hard when I thought about how Leah had Tyrell's support, and I didn't. I put my head down and said a small prayer for comfort. I tried to think of something else when I felt another hand on my shoulder and felt warmth on my back. When I looked up, I saw Sénar standing over me.

He knelt down and whispered, "You got this ma. Why don't you stretch and ease your mind? I can't wait to see you perform."

He smiled his sadistic smile and winked at me. Leah said, "Hey, Sénar."

He acknowledged her, "What's up, Leah," before he walked away.

She asked, "What did he say to you?"

I smiled at her and then replied, "None of your business."

I started to stretch to help ease my mind and loosen my muscles. I must say, it was very effective and helped me calm down enough to focus. I watched all the girls try their hardest to make the team. Some fell, some got cramps, some gave up. Hell, anything that could happen happened. While several people judged and watched, whether they were judges or not. I was last, and not that I needed any more pressure, Leah performed before me. She did a good job and didn't hesitate to add extras at the end to get the guys all riled up. This was my moment, I said another small prayer and asked for strength to get through it, whether I made it or not.

I felt a shift in my mood when I heard my name being called, "Treasure Lee to the floor."

I heard everyone's chatter pick up and even heard some boos from, of course, London and all her groupies and a few other haters out there. I used it for fuel to enhance my drive as I felt Treasure number Two takeover; she was much more confident than me and had no shame in her game. I closed my eyes and waited for the music to start. I let my body move to the rhythm and allowed my photographic memory to play the dance moves as I reenacted them. In the end, I gyrated my hips, jumped high into the air, and then landed doing the splits to perfection. I even bounced using the strength in my legs to lift me up midway before I plopped back down. The crowd went crazy, and all the guys were going nuts. I got up and sat back down next to Leah to marvel at the shock in her face. We all waited for the results, when I heard my name, I was so happy. Leah made the team as well and was very excited. She ran to Tyrell, and I ran to Sénar to give him a high five, even though I wanted to hug him for all his support.

Sénar clapped his hands, "I knew you would make it, but damn, I didn't expect the splits."

Sénar stuck his tongue out, I slapped his arm as everyone closed in on us. London grabbed Sénar's arm, and Tyrell tapped me on the shoulder while Leah just observed everyone. Tyrell grabbed me from behind and whispered, "Damn Treasure, when you learn to move like that?"

He kissed my neck, and I turned around to face him. I answered, "I don't know when because I'm a fast learner. So, all I do know is that I made it!"

He kissed me before he said, "Congratulations. I'll see you on the field later."

I was underwhelmed by his response but smiled at him anyway. As I waited for Sénar, we could barely hide our excitement as London fidgeted with discomfort, similar to what I did when I was around Leah and Tyrell. Sénar noticed and grabbed her, giving her a kiss. She loosened up a bit but grew more upset when he told her he would see her after the game. We drove off with her standing, watching us with her arms folded in frustration. When we got home, Sénar went to the garage, and I went upstairs to get ready for the game. Since it was a home game, I just rode with my mom and Ken and listened to them talk about Ken wanting his own big rig truck. My mom complained because she didn't want him on the road; I just sat in the back quietly. When we got to the game, I walked my mom and Ken to the front of the line. The security guard let us in with no questions asked.

Ken smirked at me in disbelief and complained, "Well, I'll be damned, we been waiting in line this whole time."

My mom laughed as Ken acted like he was really shocked that we didn't have to wait in line. I sat in front of my mom and Ken when Leah spotted me; she came to sit next to me.

She said, "Hey, Treasure."

I tried not to have an attitude and responded, "Hey, Leah."

I am sure my mom sensed my tone because she stopped mid-sentence to listen to our conversation. Leah smiled at me before she asked, "Who are you rooting for, Tyrell or Sénar?"

I stared at her before I answered, "Same as you. I guess both."

She said, "Hell yeah!"

She turned to my mom and Ken and introduced herself, "You must be Treasure's mom, she is so pretty just like you."

My mom tried to be cordial, but I could tell she was annoyed with her presence when she replied, "Thanks, you're right on, darling."

Leah put her attention on Ken, "Ooh, you must be Sénar's daddy," she then giggled, leaving no need for her to finish her sentence. Ken raised his eyebrow, and my mom gave one of our signature stares to her.

She quickly said, "I'm Leah, Treasure's friend. Nice to meet you both."

She turned her attention back to me to ask, "Are you and Sénar going to chill after the game?"

I looked at her like she was stupid and answered, "No, Leah, I am going home after the game. So, can you have fun for me?"

She answered, "Hell Yeah!"

She laughed then said, "I'll see you on the field, Treasure!"

When she got up to leave, I thought about how I really could not stand her; she was so bold. My mom was annoyed after she left, and Ken told her to calm down. I watched the game and rooted for Tyrell and Sénar. I got pretty upset when Sénar got cracked hard by one of the players. Tyrell and Sénar played awkwardly as there was a lot of tension between them. They had words on the field and even on the sidelines. To the point where the coach was yelling at them both. They still won the game, but it was more difficult with all the extra tension. They were still going at it after the game; I could see London pulling on Sénar and Tyrell walking with Leah.

I wanted to go on the field, but Ken said, "Hell no, I ain't waiting for your ass. Let's go."

I left without seeing Tyrell and didn't dare argue back with Ken. When we got in the car, my mom asked, "How did you meet that fast ass little girl, Treasure?"

Ken responded before I could, when he asked, "Why she gotta be fast, but Treasure ass is not?"

I ignored Ken's question and responded, "Momma, I met Leah in summer school."

My mom ignored Ken's question too when she said, "I don't like her."

I wanted to say neither did I, but then Ken cut in to ask, "Isn't she who Tyrell be with after the games?"

He waited on my answer, but I hesitated before I replied, "Yeah, but she likes Sénar."

Ken laughed before he said, "Shiddd, London ain't having that shit!"

My mom laughed too but then said, "That Leah is a little snake."

Ken was quick to say, "Damn Angel baby, why are you sweating a little girl? Shit, if Treasure's ass wasn't on punishment, she would have been right where Leah is."

My mom agreed with Ken and didn't say another word. I hated it when Ken talked about me like I wasn't there. When we got home, I went straight to my room, but Cassidy was on her phone, and the look in her eyes made me leave. I did not want to take my anger out on her, so I went to watch TV to avoid an altercation. I watched the *Fresh Prince of Bel-Air* and laughed until Sénar came in shortly after. He was upset, but he didn't say anything, he just went upstairs. I got away with missing the drama this time by going home with my mom and Ken. Which made me think about the cheerleading team because, as of next week, I would be on the field with Leah and a lot of other girls who love drama. I quickly went upstairs to go to bed just in case Sénar was mad enough to tell me why. I didn't care about Cassidy; I still went upstairs to put night clothes on and go to sleep.

Saturday morning, I woke up and laid in bed thinking of what happened last night on the field between Tyrell and Sénar. I also thought about Leah and her stupid questions. In the middle of my thinking session, I heard Cassidy say, "I can't wait to get away from your ass. I can't stand being in here with you."

I was annoyed with her and I had just woken up. I acted like I didn't hear her, so she got up and left, slamming the door behind her. Sénar came in and made sure I wasn't beating Cassidy to death. I observed the relief in his eyes when he saw me lying down. He closed the door and I got up to brush my teeth and wash my face. Sénar and Cassidy were already downstairs when I came down. They were talking as

Sénar made breakfast. Cassidy did not hide her disappointment when she seen me. Sénar looked like he was in a somewhat better mood. He still said good morning and finished making breakfast. He still provided me with a low carb breakfast while him and Cassidy ate whatever he made them. I just stopped looking because it was torture sometimes. Ken came down and sat at the table.

Sénar asked, "Aye pops, can Treasure go with me and Cassidy to the city?"

I was not expecting him to ask that when Ken wave his hand in the air and answered, "As long as that lil' nigga Tyrell ain't going, I don't care."

Sénar laughed as we finished breakfast. He looked over at me to ask, "You want to go, right?"

I sighed and answered, "I guess."

It was the only way for me to get out of the house. We stopped to pick Nevaeh up before we went. I sat in the front with Sénar as Cassidy and Nevaeh sat in the back. We listened to music and when Nelly and Kelly song came on Sénar smiled at me, causing me to roll my eyes. When we got to Louie's house, I saw the excitement in Nevaeh's eyes. Sénar and Louie hugged each other and did their little handshake before Louie grabbed Nevaeh to kiss her. Cassidy rolled her eyes and went in to say hi to her cousins. Everybody was shocked to see Cassidy as she hugged them all.

Sénar's aunt said, "Hey stranger," to Cassidy before hugging her and asking about Sabrina. She grabbed me and hugged me too, "Tell your momma I said hi child," she said then smiled at me.

I nodded my head in agreement to do so. We went to the back with the rest of his cousins. It was so many of them, I could not keep up with all their names. Sénar had a girl cousin named Latosha and she was the only girl cousin who was nice to me. As the other ones were siding with Cassidy and Nevaeh. She talked to me and kept me company while the boys kicked it playing video games. She was braiding her little sister's hair and showed me how to braid. I practiced one on her sister's hair and then I noticed Sénar's hair looking all wild.

Latosha said, "You can practice on Sénar, I am sure he won't mind."

She said it while laughing, prompting Sénar to turn around to raise his eyebrow at her suggestion. Nevaeh and Cassidy stared at me with funky attitudes when I asked Sénar to practice on his hair. Sénar didn't even hesitate to sit in between my legs to let me practice on his hair. He was so comfortable there anyways it wasn't even awkward. I did six braids, technically seven as I went back to the first one to redo it. It was nice and neat when I finished just in time for Daisy to see him with his new look.

She said, "Ooh I like it Sénar, you look so fine."

She was all over him. He was doing his best to ward her off, but she was very aggressive and Sénar looked flustered. Especially, when Daisy asked, "What's up with Ken? Y'all gonna do her like y'all did me?"

She giggled and Sénar flashed, "Daisy, stop running your mouth!"

She saw that he was serious, so she replied, "Damn, my bad Sénar. Well, show me what else you learned."

She said smiling flirtatiously, he rolled his eyes and walked away. I went inside and she followed me. She eyed me before she sat next to me to ask, "Do you and Sénar be fucking?"

I ignored her question as Cassidy and Nevaeh waited to hear my answer. She laughed before she said, "Oh, I guess you must be something special. He never turns me down."

She got up and left back outside, leaving both Nevaeh and Cassidy staring at me. I ignored them staring at me until I couldn't help but ask Nevaeh, "What are you looking at?"

She smacked her lips before she inquired, "Well, are you and-" Louie cut her off, "Come here Nevaeh," before she could finish her question. Cassidy shook her head in disgust and I just rolled my eyes at her. One of Louie's friends tried to talk to me, and Louie told him

I was off limits. I was upset because he was actually kind of cute. We smoked some weed and played a game of dominoes.

When I won, Sénar was mad when he asked, "Where you learn to play dominoes like that?" Irritated that he had lost. I smiled at him before I replied, "Don't worry about it."

Sénar smirked at me and noticed the way Louie's homeboy Cedric was staring at me. I knew better but I smiled at him anyway. Sénar smiled sadistically but didn't say anything.

Louie asked, "Aye Sénar, you brought them gloves?"

Sénar laughed before he answered, "You know I got chu my nigg!"

Sénar swiftly jumped up to get the gloves from the trunk of his car.

Louie said, "It's just for fun Cedrick, but I'm not sure you want to go toe to toe with Sénar first. You might want to warm up first."

Sénar came back with Daisy following behind him. She had bags of drinks in her hand. Sénar gave Louie the gloves, so him and Cedrick sparred while Sénar grabbed drinks for us. He gave me a Boones farm sangria and it was so good. I drank it and watched them spar but when Sénar and Cedrick sparred it quickly turned into more, so Louie had to break it up.

Daisy asked, "Let me spar with your precious Treasure, Sénar?"

I looked at her like she was crazy. Cassidy and Nevaeh giggled as Sénar took his gloves off before responding, "Nah, I don't think that's a good idea."

Daisy asked, "Why? Is she fragile?"

Sénar laughed, then replied, "Nah, she can take it. I'm worried about you?"

Daisy snatched the gloves from Sénar. She glared at me, "You ready Treasure?"

I put my drink down, "Yeah, why not?"

Sénar smiled a dark smile and Cassidy wasn't the least bit shocked that I said yeah. Nevaeh was the only one who looked like she was waiting to see Daisy beat my ass. Sénar got the gloves from Cedrick and put them on me.

While putting them on Sénar said, "Sparring is not fighting. There should not be any hard blows, just taps."

He smiled at me and raised his eyebrow when he asked, "Are you listening Treasure? Daisy is probably going to spar dirty. So, if she hits you and it hurts, protect yourself."

I was buzzed but I understood him perfectly clear. I needed to beat her ass if she tried to spar dirty. Sénar had a similar talk with Daisy. She waved him off and came straight at me, we tussled a little as I was blocking her hits. I pushed her off and said, "Those are not taps!"

She said, "Stop crying, lil' bitch!"

She punched me hard in my chest, I flashed and bombed on her two or three times in her face before Sénar snatched me off of her. Daisy tried to come back and Louie grabbed Daisy. Nevaeh was jealous instantly when she saw Louie grab Daisy like he did her when we almost fought.

Sénar bragged, "Treasure! Ooh, you got chunkums! Yo' ass is nuts! Anyway, just sip on your drink and chill. I'll handle Daisy, ma."

Sénar went to Daisy and told her she started it and if she kept starting stuff then she would have to leave.

Louie agreed but said, "Or you can bounce now too."

She rolled her eyes at Louie and mad dogged me before she went to sit down. Sénar and I played dominoes one on one, but I still beat him, so we played until he won. When nobody was around, he snatched me into one of the rooms and kissed me. He smelled my hair and squeezed my ass.

I pushed him off me, "Stop, sheesh. Cassidy and Nevaeh are already looking at me funny."

He said, "I don't care." I pushed him off and tried to leave but he pulled on the back of my pants, "Give me a kiss and I might let you leave."

I was going to kiss him on the cheek, but he grabbed me and kissed me passionately. I kissed him back. He knew I was buzzing and horny as hell. Everyone else was doing their own thing.

He requested, "Let me get some dessert?"

With no hesitation, I let him go down on me to fulfill his request for dessert. I wanted to scream it felt so good. After I reached a climax, I wanted more. I tried to get him to do it to me. He got excited but still declined. I almost forced him until we heard voices in the hallway.

He urged, "Hurry up and get dressed."

I quickly put my panties and shorts back on just in time. He opened the door to make sure the hallway was cleared, "Come on, let's go."

I was still horny, so Sénar laughed at me and then said, "Ooh wee, wait til we get home." He smiled his sadistic smile and we joined everyone else. We all slept in the living room. I woke up to Sénar laughing at his lil' baby cousin sleeping on my breast and sucking his thumb. Sénar's cousin Latosha who taught me to braid came to get her son off me, "He is too much girl."

She didn't even look 18 yet as she grabbed her son and went back to her room. We left in the afternoon after Sénar's aunt cooked for us. We dropped Nevaeh off, and we went home. Tyrell's car was gone when we got back. I was instantly irritated, knowing he was probably with Leah. When we walked in the door, Cassidy ran upstairs and Sénar drug me to the garage. He closed the door, "Let's finish where we left off."

I looked at him like he was crazy because I was sober and Treasure number two was asleep. I answered, "No!"

He laughed but replied, "Wow, for real?"

I had an attitude, "No Sénar! Damn, we aren't even supposed to be doing this," I said it with my hand on my hip.

He laughed and then backed off, "You wasn't saying that last night."

I was offended and snapped back, "I was buzzing, and I wasn't in my right mind."

He laughed before he said, "You're so cute when you lie."

He rubbed his hand on my coochie and I jumped back, "Stop, ugh you get on my nerves."

Of course, my coochie was pulsating and now moist but I just ignored it. Sénar let me leave, so I went to my room and Cassidy was lying in her bed on the phone. I heard her say, "I know, let me call you back girl." She stared at me, but I ignored her, which made her even more agitated.

She asked, "What's up with you and Sénar?"

I got my stuff ready to take a bath. I took a deep breath because the last thing I needed was Cassidy running her mouth and having to use my hand to stop it.

I answered without looking at her, "Nothing Cassidy."

She smacked her lips before she assumed, "Yeah right!"

I snapped at her, "Then why did you ask?"

She studied me and stood up when she saw the look in my eye before she usually ends up on the floor. She yelled, "Don't touch me, you crazy bitch!"

Sénar opened the door before I could get to her. He saw the fury in my eyes and came in, closing the door behind him.

Cassidy screamed, "This bitch is crazy, Sénar!"

He looked at Cassidy and said, "You might be right, but you need to leave her alone man."

I was about to snap when Sénar turned to me and said, "Treasure calm down, ma. Get your stuff and go take a bath."

I held on to my tears and grabbed my stuff while Sénar waited for me. I waited until I closed the door to cry. Sénar knocked on the door and I opened it because I still had my clothes on but I turned away, so he wouldn't see me crying. I wiped my eyes and with my back turned, I asked, "What, you came in here to adjust my attitude?"

Sénar chuckled and answered, "Not unless... you want me to?"

I thought long and hard before I answered, "No, I would rather beat Cassidy's ass first."

He laughed and replied, "Nah, you don't have to do that just let me know and I got chu!" Sénar winked at me and added, "You have plenty of dick, I mean meat vouchers if you need them."

I smacked my lips and ignored his comment. He then asked, "You want to use one now?"

I rolled my eyes at him before I replied, "But I don't have a pillow."

He smiled so big, that we both laughed. I said, "Sénar, just go, I am fine."

He looked at me like I was crazy, and I changed my answer, "For real, I am good." He smiled at me before he left. I took a bath and avoided both Cassidy and Sénar by going to my room to read. Things were really starting to get crazy. I wanted everything to go back to normal, but nothing was normal, and I had trouble differentiating which way was better. The smell of food brought me back to reality. I went downstairs, to of course, see Sénar cooking. My mom and Ken were sitting at the table talking. Sénar smiled at me and continued to cook.

My mom noticed me, "Hey Treasure, how are you honey?"

I answered her as Ken stared at me, "I'm good momma, how are you?"

She waved her hand, "Oh girl I'm fine, I don't do much. What have you been doing lately?"

I sat down and stared blankly at her to see if I could try to figure out what she was really asking and why. I answered, "I work out and eat healthy. I read and write a lot. I don't know."

Sénar chimed in, "Carmel, Treasure made the cheerleading team at tryouts this Friday."

Sénar smiled so big when he added, "She even did the splits at the end of her performance." Sénar tried to hide his excitement when Ken and my mom glanced at him.

My mom smiled at me before she asked, "Really Treasure? That's great! Congratulations!"

Ken smirked, "You accomplish more on punishment," he said it sarcastically.

My mom laughed before saying, "I agree Treasure, I know it's been a while, but you might need a couple of more weeks then we will see how things go. So far you have been staying out of trouble and I like it this way. I am proud of you too. You have been doing much better with your attitude as well. Just keep it up and you will be off punishment before you know it. Then hopefully you will make better choices."

Sénar was listening but tried to seem like he wasn't. Ken agreed with her and made it clear that it was really a break from Tyrell. He didn't care if I went somewhere with Sénar, he just didn't want me with Tyrell. Well, technically him or Sénar wanted me with Tyrell for their own reasons. My mom was no help because she always disliked Tyrell and she warned me about him prior to all this drama. I wondered if they would feel the same way about Sénar if they knew what kind of deal we had going on. I started to feel like there were wicked forces keeping me and Tyrell apart. "Treasure?" My mom called my name as I drifted off into my thoughts.

I shook my head, "What?"

My mom and Ken stared at me when she threatened, "Treasure, do not play with me. I will smack the taste out of your mouth!"

I tensed up in my chair and straightened up before looking over at Sénar as he shook his head. "I heard you momma," I replied dryly.

My mom glared at me before saying, "Maybe I spoke too soon about the attitude."

I got up swiftly, making both my mom and Ken glance at me questionably. I walked into the kitchen, dismissing them both and peaked into the pot to see what Sénar was cooking. I regretted not letting Sénar finish where we left off, maybe my attitude would have been better. I went to the fridge to get something to drink and realized my mom and Ken were still glaring at me.

I looked at Ken when I asked, "Ken you want a beer?"

My mom looked at me like I was stupid, but Ken smiled and replied, "Yup!" I bent over to get it way from the back. I grabbed my mom her bottle of wine and a glass to go with it and set them both on the table.

I said, "Cheers," in a sarcastic but almost sweet way. I walked back to the fridge to get some water as Sénar watched me and finish cooking. My mom and Ken drank and talked while Sénar finished up. My mom made her and Ken's food and got his next beer before they ate. Cassidy came down as I was about to make my bowl and complained, "Nuh uh, let me go first, y'all be taking too long."

I moved out of her way and let her make her bowl first. Sénar saw me avoid confrontation and said, "You can eat some potatoes but just don't go crazy with it."

I smiled and put as many as he let me until he said, "Ok, that's enough."

I laughed because I was going to keep going until he said stop. I took my soup to the table and happily sat down to eat. I was so pleased with my potatoes, I almost forgot about the punishment lecture. The beef and tomato soup was so delicious with the potatoes. Sénar added spinach to ours and my mom's soup. My mom raved about the soup and the eggplant lasagna until Ken was irritated with her. I helped Sénar clean up the kitchen. After everyone went upstairs Sénar turned to me to say, "You be trippin' Treasure. Don't play with my dad like that, I told your ass he is crazy."

I was shocked at his comment and defended myself when I said, "What, I just asked if he wanted a beer to avoid having an attitude when he asked."

Sénar shook his head as if he was getting impatient with me before he replied, "You be playing like you are dumb sometimes. My pops is a control freak, he has to be in control at all times. The minute he is not things can get really crazy, so stop challenging him."

I rolled my eyes at him because he was probably right. I asked, "Sénar what is it with Daisy? Why does he ask about her and her about him?"

He got agitated when I asked him, but he laughed and answered, "Treasure, you don't want to know that, trust me."

I was irritated because I did want to know. I stared at him defiantly and replied, "Yes I do want to know Sénar."

He was getting more impatient with me, but I didn't care. He finished up the kitchen and ignored my question. It was only seven in the afternoon, so it was still early when he said, "Let's burn off some of those calories you ate with all those potatoes."

I followed him to the garage as he totally was avoiding my question. He got the gloves down off the wall and helped me put them on. He put his own on but before he could finish, I punched him hard in his chest. I demanded, "Answer my question Sénar!"

He was so mad he yelled, "We fucked the shit out of her! Dayuum!"

I was shocked at what he said and how he said it. He was flustered and couldn't even finish fixing his gloves. He sat down on the ground and put his head down. He looked at me with pain in his eyes and confided in me, "My pops is crazy, he used to date her mom too, but daisy was something else, who knows how many dudes her mom Rose brought around before my pops. My dad and her used to mess around when Rose was at work and she worked a lot. He taught me everything I know about women on Daisy. Even before then, my dad likes control, so every woman he was with, he dominated them and if they had kids, which most of them didn't, he would take all their time because he demands so much attention. What he wants he gets. He used to do a lot of things and I was like his apprentice or wing man to keep him from involving the rest of them. That's how I learned to cook and clean so well trying to keep everything as stable as possible, amidst all types of chaos. When we moved in with Daisy and her mom, her mom hated all of us. She just wanted my dad but not us. All his women were like that. They wouldn't do anything for me and my siblings, so I had to do it. That's only one of the reasons why they are all so spoiled and I'm so fucked up. My dad used to come get me, I was only like ten. He would strap Daisy down and teach me to pleasure her until she orgasmed, no matter how long it took. My dad is obsessed with controlling women and making them cum. This is the most normal our lives have ever been. I thank Carmel for that because she is nothing like the women my dad dated before. She is not violent, for the most part, or smart at the mouth. She is submissive and most importantly, she is a freak. My pops is nuts, if she can keep him occupied this long, she must be something special. Like you are to me. With Daisy's mom Rose, she was always yelling at us and demanding things from me. She was mean to Daisy too because she was jealous of her own daughter. When Rose found out about Daisy and my pops, she got even by making me do things for her sexually when my dad wasn't around. I was miserable but I never told him because I knew he would kill her. To make matters worse, Daisy was older than me and bigger than me, so she would do the same thing whenever she wanted to get off and my dad wasn't around. Until this day, I wonder what happened to Rose because she left my dad and left Daisy with her sister. I never seen her again. They argued all the time, and everything was always chaos when they were around each other. I cleaned up enough scenes to last a lifetime within my childhood."

Sénar sighed before he stopped talking, he looked like a little kid trying to get himself together. Ken opened the garage door and saw Sénar sitting on the ground with his head down, he asked, "Damn Sénar, you let Treasure beat you up?"

Sénar chuckled and answered, "Nah pops, I was just fixing my gloves."

Ken appeared agitated as he observed Sénar's weakened state, he asked, "What are y'all doing?"

He came in and closed the door behind him. My heart started beating, I was so nervous now. Sénar also appeared uneasy as Ken walked in to check out his work out area. He smirked and said, "Nice set up you got here."

Sénar quickly said, "Thanks pops."

Ken glared at me before saying, "Let me guess, you are his inspiration."

Ken was really close to me and I could hear him smelling the air when he said, "Let me see what you got."

I stepped back when Ken looked at Sénar to say, "Let me see y'all spar."

Sénar was cautious but obedient, he jumped up, "Come on Treasure show him you got chunkems."

I was even more skeptical when Sénar said, "Let's work out!"

We swung at each other until Ken said, "Ok, that's enough. Give me the gloves." When Ken helped me take my gloves off, Sénar became tensed. I quickly gave Ken the gloves and turned to leave. As Ken put his gloves on, he said, "Don't leave Treasure, let's have some fun."

I froze in my tracks and reluctantly turned around. Once Ken put his gloves on, he was all over Sénar. Ken had no mercy, Sénar fought back but Ken overpowered him. He took it like a champ until my mom came in. She walked in the garage and looked around. She noticed Sénar's work out station and asked, "What you got going on over here Sénar?"

He was out of breath after experiencing a pretty devastating beatdown from Ken. My mom became excited when she saw Ken all worked up and sweaty. She was all over him. Sénar was overwhelmed, he took his gloves off and hung them on the wall. Ken threw his gloves at Sénar, then put my mom over his shoulder and left us in the garage.

Sénar shook his head before saying, "I should not have told you anything, but you asked. That's not even the half of it." He led me out of the garage, and we went upstairs to our rooms. I took a quick shower and tried to sleep.

Chapter 8

This was my first official week as a cheerleader. Monday was the hardest day so far because Sénar and I had a devastating night before after we returned from his aunt's house. I went through the day as quickly as possible, trying to avoid everyone; even Sénar to a certain extent. I went to practice and focused the best I could. Sénar and I went home after practice but barely spoke to one another. He made dinner that night, and we went to bed early. Tuesday was a little better, as we made it to Wednesday, without any issues. I avoided Sénar, Tyrell, Cassidy, Leah, London, my mom, and Ken as much as possible. I even avoided bringing up the conversation that I had with Sénar this past Sunday, even though, I had so many questions. Only because I knew it bothered him. He seemed to fall apart every time I, his dad, or Daisy brought it up. On Wednesday things started to drift back to the possibility of drama as Leah and Tyrell were both getting on my nerves again. Leah was really feeling herself, now that me and Tyrell barely spoke this week. After Tyrell and Leah played hide n seek at lunchtime, I was extremely agitated by the time I got to practice.

Leah and her inquisitive nature asked, "Are you and Tyrell going to be boyfriend and girlfriend when you get off punishment?"

I looked at her before I responded, "I didn't know we weren't boyfriend and girlfriend now."

She stared at me like I was playing her when she said, "You know what I mean."

I asked, "Why? Is he going to be your boyfriend instead?"

She laughed and then answered, "I don't want a boyfriend. I want to do what I want, when I want, and with who I want."

I looked at her like she was stupid and replied, "Oh, well, I wish you the best with that."

I got up and got my stuff ready as she followed me, she said, "I want Sénar. I think you are trying to keep him for yourself. For reals now."

Tyrell walked up to ask, "You ready to go, Leah?"

She dismissed me and then answered, "Hell yeah."

She grabbed her things before I could respond to her accusations. Tyrell stared at me blankly before he asked, "Damn, can I get a hug, a hello, or something?"

I hugged him and waited to see what he was going to do next to avoid rejection. He quickly kissed me on the lips before turning away to leave with Leah. He looked back and said, "I'll call you."

As they were walking away, Sénar and London walked up behind me. Sénar grabbed my bags, and we walked to his car. London whined; when we got to the car, she asked, "Dang, Sénar, how much longer is she going to be on punishment? I feel I am the one being punished."

Sénar sighed as if it bothered him too and then answered, "I don't know, just be patient."

I was offended at both of their remarks and folded my arms with an attitude. Sénar kissed London but sensed my irritation. On the way home, he asked, "What's wrong, ma?"

I looked at him with an attitude and replied, "Don't worry about it."

Sénar acknowledged my attitude before he said, "Well, it's hump day!"

He smiled at me and continued, "Just in time to adjust that little attitude of yours. It's a buffet today; you can have all the meat you want."

He winked his eye at me. I rolled my eyes at him and thought to myself; *I was going to give him an attitude adjustment one day too.* Just not today, I was too tired. I was going to let him do all the work. When we got home, Cassidy wasn't home yet, and my mom and Ken were gone. He had barely put my bag down before he snatched me into his room.

He said, "Take your clothes off, ma."

I was defiant and folded my arms to say, "I just want a quickie, free of charge."

He was not happy but performed perfectly and then let me go. I was satisfied with no complaints and Sénar didn't complain either, but he was not happy. I kissed him on the cheek and said, "Thanks for the meat."

I smiled at him and tried to walk out of his room. He snatched me back to whisper, "I should have let you practice serving me dessert, since you are in such a rush."

I rolled my eyes at him and replied, "Let London do it. You still have the rest of the day. Why punish her?"

He slammed the door in my face as I giggled before going to my room. I got the stuff I needed to take a shower. As I was showering, Sénar came in to get in with me. I started to decline, but my eyes were so happy with the sight of his wet naked body that we went for another round. I even practiced serving dessert. When I got out, Cassidy was in our room on the phone. I just had a towel on with my clothes in my hands.

I kept the towel on to conceal some of myself, but she still gawked at my half naked body before she asked, "Treasure eewe, why don't you have clothes on?"

I rolled my eyes at her and dropped my towel, so she could see a full view of all that she was lacking. Her eyes grew big, and she yelled, "Oh my gosh! You are so gross!"

Sénar rushed in as I was standing there naked, getting ready to get dressed. He bit his bottom lip before closing the door. Cassidy was in pure shock as I did not move fast enough for her to hide from Sénar.

In a disgusted tone, she said, "Eew, you are probably nasty like Daisy!"

I jumped on her naked and all, but she screamed, "Help!" I let her go quickly to put on my undergarments, right before Sénar ran back into the room with Ken behind him. I quickly grabbed the towel to hide from Ken when he asked, "What's the problem?"

Cassidy answered, "Treasure's being nasty! I don't want to see her naked!"

Sénar chuckled, but Ken stared at me as if he wouldn't mind. Ken rolled his eyes at our dilemma before he walked away.

Sénar said, "Get dressed, Treasure, and then bring your ass downstairs."

He closed the door behind him. I told Cassidy, "You are such a little crybaby. You know you like what you saw. And you and Sabrina are the ones who like to screw guys of all ages."

Cassidy was quiet because she knew I was right. I got dressed and went downstairs to sit on the couch. Sénar asked, "Can you braid my hair tomorrow?"

I shrugged my shoulders and answered, "Yeah, I guess."

He smiled and flipped through the channels until he came across my show *Girlfriends*. He watched the episode with me on the couch. He said, "Damn, the chocolate one is fine like you." He bit his bottom lip and laid back to watch TV comfortably. After the show went off, Sénar made tacos for everyone, and I made a taco salad. I didn't say much at dinner and went to sleep right after.

Today was Thursday, and I was glad the day flew by at school. Before I knew it, it was time for cheerleading practice. The boys didn't have much practice, being that their game was tomorrow. Sénar waited for me while London felt all over him. Tyrell didn't want to wait for Leah, so she asked, "Do you think Sénar will give me a ride?"

Tyrell got super angry and changed his mind, "Hell no! I'll wait."

Leah shrugged her shoulders, and we started practicing our cheerleading routine for the game. I totally ignored both of them. After practice, we all walked to our destinations quietly as there was a lot of tension between all of us. Mainly between Sénar and Tyrell, but London was also not happy with me or Leah's connection to Sénar. When we got home, Sénar went straight to the garage to work out. When he came out, he had no shirt on and was dripping with sweat. Dang, he looked so damn good. I wanted to jump on him, but instead, I just rolled my eyes.

He walked up to me to ask, "You want to take a shower?"

I answered, "No." I said it without looking at him to avoid being persuaded to change my answer. He sat down on the floor and asked me to take his hair down. I took his hair down for him, and he went to shower. He came back down; showered and hair washed. He had a comb and some grease as he sat down on the floor in between my legs. I proceeded to braid his hair when Cassidy walked in the door and saw me braiding Sénar's hair; she rolled her eyes at me. As if that wasn't bad enough, Ken came downstairs to see me braiding Sénar's hair and shook his head before he went to sit at the table. Sénar didn't care; he comfortably laid his head on my thigh and let me finish braiding his hair before he went to talk with Ken. After talking with Ken, he looked agitated and went to the garage to work out while Ken just glared at me from the kitchen table. I was so uncomfortable; I went to my room until I smelled food. I came down to see Sénar in the kitchen, and Ken still sitting at the table.

Sénar said, "Dang, I am glad you came down. Cool, you can cut the potatoes."

I grabbed all the stuff to cut the potatoes without complaining. Once I had everything I needed, before I could start, Ken said, "Get me a beer, Treasure."

I stopped what I was doing and went to get him a beer, way from the back of the fridge. I handed him his beer and went back to what

I was doing. I could feel him staring at me, even though my back was to him.

Ken said, "Sénar tomorrow, don't get distracted on the field. With Treasure on the field and your little arch enemy playing with you, you need to stay focused. I don't want to see the shit I saw last week."

I just cut the potatoes in silence as Sénar answered, "Yes, sir."

Cassidy came down to say, "Hi daddy, how are you?" Ken answered, "Hey Cassidy. I am fine sweetheart. How are you?"

She replied, "I am ok, daddy. Um, can I have a car?"

Ken almost spat his beer out before he asked, "Well damn Cassidy, you are going to graduate, right?"

She smiled, "Yeah, I think so," she then giggled after she said it. Ken replied, "Well, I think I'll wait until you know for sure."

She sighed then agreed, "Ok, daddy."

I wanted to laugh because Cassidy was dumb as a doorknob. She didn't clean after herself; she didn't think for herself. Hell, she didn't even change the channel to the TV on her own. She was just a naïve, mean little brat. Ugh, I couldn't stand her, even her voice made me want to punch her. We ate our food, and I was going to help Sénar clean up, but he motioned for me to go upstairs. "I got this," he said before I quickly ran upstairs to avoid Ken's glare.

Sénar and Ken's little secret made me uncomfortable when they were together talking in private. I was even uncomfortable when Ken and Cassidy were talking. I felt like it was always about me. The closer me and Sénar became, the meaner Ken got towards me. It was to the point that even Sénar mentioned it on the way to school the next morning, "Treasure, please be careful around my pops, he has really been focused on you lately. Don't fight with Cassidy, don't get smart with your mom, and don't do anything extra for my pops."

I was annoyed now. Sénar meant well but he acted like he could tell me what to do and I was not having it.

I replied, "Ken is not my daddy. He needs to stop worrying about me."

Sénar shook his head and then said, "I told you he was a control freak. Your ass is difficult to control, and he knows that. So, he is waiting on the opportunity to dominate you, like he does everything he is around. Trust me, Treasure."

I smacked my lips and rolled my eyes until Sénar just ignored my attitude and continued his warning, "Treasure, I know I told you some crazy stuff, but you have no idea, man. Please take heed to the warning. You are hardheaded, and I have warned you about several things, and you don't listen! This here that I am telling you, is something you need to hear."

Usually, when he is telling me something, and he is serious but not mad, he raises his eyebrow; but this time he wasn't even looking at me. He was looking straight forward and speaking to me in a trance-like state.

I called his name, "Sénar?"

He snapped, "What?"

I took a deep breath before responding as his tone was frightening. I cautiously said, "I am listening Sénar, but are you ok?"

Sénar sighed, then replied, "I'm fine, Treasure." He was quiet after that. I wish he would have said *I'm good,* instead. We pulled into the parking lot to see the one and only London; what a surprise. She was talking with some of her friends at least, so she didn't look as much like a stalker. When me and Sénar got out, I glanced at him, and he was not in a good mood.

London said, "Treasure you are like on the longest punishment ever. I think you are starting to like it." Before Sénar could say anything, I cut him off to reply, "I think you're right, London." I blew a kiss at her, even though Sénar was upset, I saw him laugh a little before he said, "London, please don't start it's too early for the drama, and I am not in the space to deal with it."

She hurried to his side and then agreed, "Ok, babe."

I rolled my eyes as I walked away. I heard her ask, "Babe, who braided your hair? It's so nice. I like it."

I smirked at her friends on my way to class. The morning started off kind of stressful, but the rest of the day was cool all up until lunchtime. I was eating a salad and doodling my name in a note pad when Tyrell and Leah came to sit down; one on each side of me.

Tyrell asked, "Oh, so you a writer now too?"

Leah laughed; she knew I was a great writer, but if Tyrell didn't know, then he didn't need to. I answered, "I am just scribbling my name, Tyrell."

I sighed and then asked, "Leah, what's the special occasion? Why aren't you sitting on the other side of Tyrell?"

I asked her without an attitude; I was curious. She smirked at me before she answered, "Because I can sit anywhere, I want, when I want."

I laughed at her before responding, "I bet."

I ate my food, and Tyrell got up as if he was annoyed with both me and Leah. I could see Sénar's face as London looked to be complaining. He looked really frustrated with her and saw me staring at them. Sénar shook his head, and I could hear Tyrell say, "What did you do, Treasure?"

I looked at Tyrell as I put my container in my bag; I knew it was time to leave. I asked, "Tyrell, what are you talking about?"

He got mad at me then snarled, "Don't play stupid!"

Leah giggled as I tried to leave, Tyrell stopped me and asked, "Why is London trippin' like that?"

I snapped, "I don't know Tyrell, that's none of yours or my business!"

I lowered my voice and said, "Leave me alone, Tyrell."

I could feel my irritation level go sky high when Leah said, "Damn, Sénar is looking fine as hell with his fresh ass braids. That's probably why she is trippin'. Treasure, did you do that?"

That was it, I asked, "Leah, why don't you shut your nosey ass up sometime?"

I tried to walk off, but Tyrell grabbed me and pulled me back to him.

He whispered, "We need to talk now."

He squeezed my arm, and I agreed to go to not make a scene, but I asked him nicely not to squeeze me so hard. He took me to a corner in the hallway to ask, "Did you braid Sénar's hair?"

I looked at him and answered cautiously, "Yes, Tyrell; it's just brai-"

He grabbed me by my shirt before he said, "I can't wait till you get off punishment."

He released me, walking away infuriated with me. I almost cried but remembered I was at school, so I straightened my shirt and went to the bathroom. I had to check to make sure I looked presentable to go to the next class, knowing Leah would be there. I looked at my chest where my name lay on it as it dangled from the chain there was a scratch on my chest. I was so upset I was hoping Sénar didn't see it or anyone for that matter. I wiped the fresh blood with water and a paper towel then patted it dry. I fought back the tears that wanted to push themselves off the edge of my eyelids. Any tears that escaped, I washed them away with a splash of cold water. Sénar was waiting for me when I came out.

He asked, "You good, Treasure?"

He looked highly upset when he asked, so I cautiously lied, "I'm good."

As if he knew I was lying, he said, "Well, don't respond to London, just ignore her. I already told her not to start no drama, but she is really tripping. So anyway, I saw Tyrell trippin' too. Don't let him put his hands on you."

I nodded my head ok and walked away, avoiding eye contact with him and everyone who might be looking. I went to class, and Leah was waiting for me to sit down. She turned to face me to ask, "Damn, what can I do to get Sénar to focus on me like he focuses on you?"

I wanted to punch her in the mouth, but instead, I truthfully answered, "I don't know Leah, but maybe try whatever you did with Tyrell."

She smirked, "I guess you're right; I'm not worried about London, it's you that's in the way. No wonder you never let me come over to your house." After she spoke, Leah looked like she had a light bulb come on in her head. I wish I could have turned it off because I had enough problems with her as it is. Today was a big day for the both of us performing on the field for the first time. That was all I wanted to think about, along with me cheering for a winning team. Leah eyed me the whole time and saw how into the game I was.

She asked, "Oh, so you really like football now?"

I answered, "Hell yeah!"

I cheered for Sénar as he made a touchdown. It was my first night on the field as an official cheerleader. I would have never thought I would make it on a team full of people who hated me; cheering alongside them for my so-called boyfriend, Tyrell, and I didn't even know what to call Sénar. It was so exhilarating to see them up close with their facial expressions and body movements. There was so much excitement; I could not shake the fact that Sénar was my secret lover. He was so visible amongst everyone else; he even outshined Tyrell tonight. Whether or not anyone else noticed, I knew that I was his inspiration. He caught eye contact with me every second of his plays and was sure to let me know I was his inspiration. Tyrell was highly agitated as a result, and Leah was envious of the obvious focus of Sénar. I rolled my eyes at Leah as I cheered for Sénar and Tyrell. After the game, Leah ran to hug Tyrell as I walked to him to give him a hug. We just stared at each other for a second before him and Leah walked off together.

Sénar walked towards me with London on his heels to ask, "Did you have fun?"

I smiled at him before I said, "Hell yeah!"

He laughed, and London smirked at me. She was so jealous; she said, "Babe, let's drop her off and celebrate with the team."

Sénar declined her idea, and the waterworks began. Sénar was annoyed when he agreed, "Fine, damn, but you are gonna drive."

She smiled and humbly replied, "Ok," with tears in her eyes. Sénar and I pulled up to the house. He pleaded, "Treasure, just go upstairs and go to bed, please."

I looked at him like he was crazy before I asked, "What? Why do I have to go to bed, Sénar?"

He sighed when he saw London pulling up behind us. He asked, "Well, what are you about to do?"

London was already jumping out of her car to retrieve her man. I answered, "I don't know Sénar, I don't want to go to bed. I'll probably take a bath."

Sénar was serious when he asked, "Then what?"

I smacked my lips, "Then go to bed, I guess."

Sénar smiled before saying, "Ok. Goodnight, Treasure." I got out of the car feeling like a little kid that had been told to go to bed. I took a bath and used the shower head to please myself and then went to sleep.

I was getting tired of being on punishment. I brushed my teeth and washed my face and headed downstairs. My mom and Ken were already downstairs talking. Sénar had not come down yet, so I went inside the refrigerator to grab some water. I said, "Good morning," in my sweetest voice to my mom before I walked out. I was trying to be nice, I needed to get off of punishment.

My mom replied, "Good morning."

She then went back upstairs, and Ken stayed at the kitchen table. When I saw Sénar come down I followed him into the kitchen. He made scrambled eggs, sausage and potatoes.

Ken asked, "Sénar, what are you gonna do when I let Treasure off of punishment?" Sénar smirked but not where Ken could see him. He answered, "Same thing I am doin now pops, nothing." Ken laughed, "Yeah right." He glared at me before he called, "Treasure?" I answered, "Yes Ken," in the sweetest voice I could, making Sénar cut his eyes at me. Ken softened his glare a little before responding, "This may be your last week of punishment, if you can manage to stay out of trouble."

My mom walked in in the middle of Ken's speech; she saw me sitting down at the kitchen nook attentively listening to Ken as he spoke in regard to my punishment. She immediately tuned in to what Ken was saying.

Ken asked, "You probably just going to run back to Tyrell's ass huh?"

My mom looked at Ken and said, "Well, that's exactly why she can stay on punishment. She doesn't need to get off. She has been doing so well, I just think-"

Ken cut my mom off mid-sentence and said, "I didn't ask what you think." My mom stopped talking and made herself some coffee. Ken continued, "Well, Sénar has other things to do, besides babysit your ass Treasure. Plus, London looks like she is about to have a meltdown. Stay your ass out of trouble, so Sénar can move on with his business."

My mom pouted and Sénar was quiet. Hell, everyone was quiet when Cassidy walked in the kitchen. Sénar handed me my breakfast when Ken wasn't looking, and we sat at the kitchen nook to eat. My mom tried to sweet talk Ken into changing his mind, but Ken was not having it. She got so upset, Ken glared at her and my mom instantly stopped talking. Ken was agitated when he looked at Sénar and said, "Y'all get out of here! Go to the city, I don't care shit, I need to spend some time with Treasure's mother."

My mom left and went upstairs crying. I started to say something but Sénar put his fingers to his lips. He was stoic for a second until Ken spoke again, "Did y'all hear me?"

He stood up to pull his wallet out and both Cassidy and Sénar flinched in fear. I was quiet and stiff as a board. Ken threw some bills on the table and gave Cassidy her own money and went upstairs. I was going to say something when Cassidy and Sénar headed for the door. I was still sitting there trying to figure out what the hell was going on when Sénar came back to grab me and the money off the table while rushing toward the front door. I could hear Ken and my mom yelling. I tried to go upstairs and get my phone but Sénar drug me out the door.

Sénar said, "Get in the car Treasure."

I wanted to go back and get my phone, so I smacked my lips and told him, "I need to-"

He cut me off and roared, "Get in the god damn car!"

Tyrell was coming out and could hear Sénar yell at me from across the street. I ran to the car without even looking at Tyrell to see his facial expression. Cassidy was already in the car and moved the seat up without Sénar having to tell her to let me in the back seat. Sénar jumped in the car and took off.

He told Cassidy, "Call Nevaeh and tell her we are going to the city, to see if she wants to go."

Sénar's face was so serious; Cassidy did as she was told. Cassidy called Nevaeh to see if she wanted to go, I was pretty sure she would not decline going to see Louie. I was irritated I wasn't able to grab my phone or anything else for that matter. Sénar stopped at the mall to get us something to wear for the weekend. We were still in our night clothes for the most part. We looked crazy out and about in the clothes we went to bed in. Sénar was fine he had basketball shorts and a shirt on but me and Cassidy had on pajama pants with a T-shirt on. We picked some outfits and was ready to pay when Cassidy complained about having to spend her money, so Sénar paid for both of our stuff. She was so spoiled; I could not stand her ass. Nevaeh was very quiet and didn't say, I almost forgot she was with us. Even Sénar asked Nevaeh if she was feeling ok. When we got to Louie's house we went inside and Sénar's aunt was shocked to see us.

She asked, "Hey babies, what's the occasion two weeks in a row?"

She saw Cassidy and Sénar's faces and looked at what me and Cassidy had on then said, "Never mind, I'm glad to see y'all."

She eyed me to gauge my emotions as I obviously was unaware of the obvious to them all. I happily greeted her, she smiled and said, "Hey Treasure baby."

She didn't mention my mom. After we greeted his aunt, we headed straight to the back with his cousins. Daisy was there sitting on the couch and lit up when she seen Sénar walk in, her smile quickly faded when I walked in behind him. I smiled when I waved at her and she responded with rolling her eyes more dramatized than I rolled my eyes. I giggled and Sénar looked at me, I asked, "What?"

He just shook his head and greeted Louie with a hug and their special handshake. Louie and Nevaeh left the room together while Sénar said hi to the rest of his cousins. Cassidy was happy to see her cousins as they ran to hug her. She was actually being nice and didn't have a mean demeanor. She softened up around her cousins as they appeared to look up to her. All her little girl cousins just stared at me and all the boy cousins said hi to me. Latosha's little boy Lil' James ran up to me and reached for me to pick him up. I picked him up and squeezed him as he laughed in my arms. I put him back down and he jumped in Sénar's arms next. Sénar held him and sat down grabbing the video game controller to play with his cousins. I watched everyone and started to drift into my thoughts wondering why we left in a hurry.

Sénar saw me drifting away and said, "Treasure?"

I snapped, "What?"

He replied, "Come here."

Cassidy and her cousins stared at us while I took my time getting over there and sat next to him on the couch to see what he wanted. Lil' James crawled into my lap and laid his head on my chest putting his thumb in his mouth. Sénar chuckled a bit before he said, "Stay present ma, we will talk about what happened later."

Louie and Nevaeh came back in the den where we were and looked distant. Nevaeh stared at me and Sénar sitting next to each other on the couch sitting so close together. I watched Sénar play video games until it was time to smoke. We passed a blunt around along with another and smoked until everyone was high even the people who didn't smoke. Louie and Sénar called it contact. Louie took the blunt when his brother tried to pass it to Nevaeh. Lil' James was chilling in between me and Sénar. Latosha came to grab Lil' James and he started to cry.

Sénar said, "Leave him alone, he was chilling."

Latosha said, "Sénar shut up, have your own little boy, I have to deal with him all day. He is about to eat and go to bed."

Sénar passed the controller to one of his little cousins and got up to whisper something to Daisy while handing her some money. Sénar and Louie went outside to talk. I sat and watched Sénar's little boy cousins play video games. Cassidy giggled while all her little girl cousins looked at me with disgust. I rolled my eyes at them and saw Cedrick walk in the den. He smiled when he spotted me and came to sit next to me, I smiled back but went back to watching them play video games. Cedrick tried to make conversation and asked, "What's up Treasure?"

Before I could respond Sénar and Louie came back in and saw Cedrick sitting next to me. Sénar called my name, "Treasure? Come here."

Louie was more irritated than Sénar as I got up without responding to Cedrick. Louie looked irritated but I couldn't tell with who. He didn't mention Cedrick he just said, "When Daisy gets back, we will talk but don't ask a billion questions."

I smacked my lips and asked, "Why do we have to wait for Daisy? And I will ask a trillion questions if I want to."

Sénar grabbed me and I tried to push him off me. Daisy walked up with a bag in her hand and said, "Damn Sénar, if she doesn't want it, I'll take it. I want to experience the grown Sénar."

He never let go of me, he smelled my hair and squeezed me before letting me go. Daisy handed the bag to Sénar and walked off reluctantly. She turned and asked, "You want your change?"

Sénar rolled his eyes at her and she kept walking. He handed me a Sangria Boones Farm and he got out his Orange Jubilee Mad Dog 20/20. He called Louie to come get the rest of the drinks to give to whoever wanted to drink. Sénar drank his Mad Dog and I sipped my sangria as we sat outside listening to music on the radio that was playing low outside.

Sénar looked at me and asked, "What do you need to know ma?"

I was so tipsy, I couldn't decide where to start, I felt like I could float away and not care where I landed. I wanted to taste his drink, so I asked, "Let me have some of yours Sénar?"

He looked at me like I was crazy and answered, "Hell nah, you don't need none of this. You just drink your little Boone's Farm."

He saw my disappointment and gave me some, I snatched it and took a large gulp. It tasted like spiked orange juice; I could taste the liquor content. It was really sweet, but I could taste that It was really strong too. Sénar was halfway through the bottle as we sat on an old couch in the back yard. When he gazed at me again, he asked, "What do you want to know Treasure?"

He took a deep breath and took another swig from his Mad Dog. I looked at him for a moment before asking, "What happened earlier Sénar? Why did we leave in such a rush?"

Sénar's gray eyes grew to almost dark black before he responded, "Your mom may have been looking out for you, but my pops felt challenged. And when Carmel got angry with him my dad switched to psycho Ken; I don't even deal with that dude. He is a stranger to me; I hate him when he's like that. He is ruthless and deadly when he is in a state of rage. Me and my siblings know when my pops switches and we have learned long ago to get out of his way."

I started to worry and asked, "Sénar is my momma going to be ok? We should go back to get her."

Sénar flashed when he asked, "And do what? I can't protect her and you. Hell, I couldn't even protect you from myself, let alone him!"

I wanted to cry but instead I got angry and demanded, "Sénar take me home!"

I wanted to check on my mom. Sénar flashed again before he replied, "No! I don't want to lose you! We are not going back till tomorrow night. We will see the damage then. My dad gave orders and we are going to follow them, or we will all end up dead!"

Sénar was agitated and looked like he was on the verge of snapping. I was afraid to ask any more questions, but I couldn't help but ask, "Well, Sénar where are all of you guys' mommas'?"

Sénar looked like I hit him with an invisible bat as he seemed to crumble before me. He answered, "I don't know!" He became angry as his lie appeared to be eating him alive and he weakly answered truthfully, "Chino's and Cassidy's mom were too weak for my dad. Chino's mom probably died of a broken heart and Cassidy's mom took her own life. Sabrina's mom was found murdered and my mom....... I don't know what happened to her. My dad loved my mom, but she was wild and young. She was the only one he did not violently abuse; I mean he probably did other things to her but not beat her or force her into submission. He wanted her heart she was special to him, but he could not tame her so he had to let her go, so he would not kill her. I loved my mom! She was a beautiful brown girl from Trinidad. She met my dad when he was trying to change his ways and she took advantage of his weakened state. She drove him crazier than he already was. He fell in love with her and she broke his heart then left with the pieces to it. They were married and til this day they still are. So, he would never marry Carmel. My dad is a predator now, he hates women. He thinks they're conniving and poisonous. My mom is the only woman that was able to break my dad's heart, since he could not access hers. I think he resents me because she loved me. I swear he is grooming me, so I never get my heart broken, but he was the first one who broke my heart when he ran my mom away. I pray that he is the last to break my heart. First, I hated my mom and women just like my dad, but I would have left too if I was my mom."

He put his face in his hands and said, "She tried to take me with her and that was the first time he put his hands on her, he nearly killed her. That day he snapped, and he has never been the same since. I never seen my mom again. I swear he only wants them for pleasure or to cause them pain to make himself feel better! Even though he is weak, but no one would ever know by looking at him."

Sénar was devastated after telling me the truth about why Ken is the way that he is. I was so sad, I wanted to hug him, but I couldn't, he looked so fragile at the moment and I didn't want to further injure him with my temporary affection. I was going to be off punishment after this week and didn't want to lead him on. Sénar was uncomfortable in his weakened state because the last time he was in this state his dad nearly beat him to death had my mom not come in. He got up to stretch and took another swig of his drink. He couldn't even look at me, I was starting to worry but he did his best to console me.

He said, "Treasure maybe they are just arguing. I mean, my pops has to care about her, he has been with her longer than any of his other women. She has not treated us badly like the rest of them. She has provided a pretty stable environment for us, like no other situation we have been in prior. So, I prayed for her strength to endure whatever happens Treasure. She is a strong woman and I swear you get it from her because you may not know, but you are pretty strong as well. Chaos breeds resilience if you can learn and grow from it. Besides my Elohim gives strength to endure this crazy thing called life."

I asked, "Who is Elohim Sénar?"

He replied, "What? It's the man upstairs, the Alpha and the Omega, The Great I Am. With His grace and mercy, I am still standing!"

I ignored him, he was drunk and was definitely not a saint, and had the nerve to be talking about God. I just looked at him like he was nuts, his eyes were full of life again. He looked strong and confident like the Sénar I was used to. I picked up his Mad Dog 20/20 and took a big gulp of it, to see if I could gain his level of confidence from his drink.

He took it from me and said, "Nah, you don't need anymore."

He held it up and I tried to get it back from him. I tickled him and he started to giggle when Nevaeh and Louie came out. They saw us playing around and Louie smiled but Nevaeh just stared at us. When Sénar noticed them, he slapped my hand away and said, "Stop it."

He tried to look serious, but he was still smiling. Louie said, "Treasure, you are cheesing for the first time ever."

He smiled genuinely and grabbed Nevaeh to hug her. I was border line drunk, my eyes felt like they were slits and I replied, "Because I'm hungry."

I started to giggle and then Sénar blushed. I wasn't really hungry; I was just being inappropriate. Nevaeh just stared at me and I blew a kiss to Nevaeh, she smacked her lips and said, "You are not cute little girl."

She was sober and appeared agitated when Sénar snatched me up and whispered, "Let me have some dessert."

I was quick to respond, "Hell Yeah!" We quickly went inside. I followed him to his cousin's room. He locked the door and put something in front of it. I quickly removed my pants and panties while he took his shirt off. He said, "Take your shirt off."

I whined because I didn't want to mess my hair up. He said, "Fine." He just raised it instead. He licked all over my stomach and went to work his magic. I was so aroused, I held on to his head and moaned. I covered my mouth with my hands as he continued to pleasure me. He stopped when he felt me explode. He waited for me to stop spasming and then asked, "You good ma?"

I smiled and answered, "Nope, I want a meat voucher." Sénar almost ripped his clothes off before he kissed me. My response, "Eew, stop it." He laughed while pulling me up to bend me over. I had no choice but to grab a pillow and scream into it as I went to a place of ecstasy. We were all over the place as he flipped me over removing the pillow to finish and stare into my eyes. He kissed me but this time I didn't stop him. We both came at the same time and collapsed into one another. We lay there for a minute and got ourselves together. He asked if I wanted to shower and I nodded my head to say yeah. He had everything already prepared for me; it was kind of creepy.

He stared at me before he said, "I would get in there with you but that's being greedy, so hurry up so I can take one too."

I rolled my eyes at him and went to shower. When I got out Sénar went in he handed me a bag for my dirty clothes. He was so meticulous with everything he did. I put my stuff away and went to go sit with everyone. I felt refreshed and relaxed, I was still buzzing quite a bit. I ignored anyone who might be staring at me and looked at the TV. Sénar came in shortly after cheesing and looking refreshed. It was an awkward silence in the room and Cedrick asked, "Sénar, isn't Treasure your sister?"

Daisy happened to hear his question along with everyone else. She waited for Sénar's response but before he could answer Cassidy said, "Her raggedy black ass ain't my sister!"

Sénar laughed and answered, "No, I am her babysitter, her doctor, her masseuse, her coach, her chef and her meat supplier, but her brother I am not."

Louie laughed so hard that he almost fell over and Daisy did not hide her jealousy. Sénar was definitely more buzzed than I ever seen him. He was so comfortable at his aunt's house it was more of his home than me and my mom's home. When I thought about it, Sénar was more like a housekeeper or janitor, he had every key and knew every inch of the house. I was drifting away into my thoughts when Sénar tapped me, saying, "Come on."

He got up and I followed him. We went to the kitchen; he already had the oil on with some fish and potatoes out. The fish just needed to be battered and Sénar quickly cut the potatoes. He smiled at me and reassured me, "We burnt enough calories our last session, so I'm not sweating the potatoes tonight."

I smiled in anticipation of potatoes, but I was feeling bold and asked, "Sénar, what do you like about me so much?"

He rolled his eyes and answered, "Everything."

I smacked my lips and said, "Sénar?"

He laughed and replied, "You are beautiful, I like your personality, your body, your mind, the way you smell, the way-"

I cut him off mid-sentence to ask, "Why? Is there anything you don't like?"

I was so tipsy, I just waited for his answer patiently. Sénar stared at me before he replied, "I am not telling you why and you are going to be mad if I tell you what I don't like Treasure."

I lied, "No I am not Sénar!"

He laughed before he said, "Ok, yeah right. Well, your selfish, hardheaded, and you lie a lot… but you are cute when you do. So, yeah you have a slick ass mouth too that gets you in trouble. Oh, and you-"

I cut him off again to say, "Shut up Sénar! You are selfish, you are hardheaded, you lie a lot, and you are a coochie bandit!"

He corrected, "Pussy bandit, attitude adjuster, meat supplier-"

Again, I had to cut him off and I had an attitude when I said, "Sénar, shut up already!"

He said, "See I told you, you were going to get mad. That's another thing I was going to say before you cut me off, your ass don't listen."

Sénar smiled at me, I was irritated with him and I was hoping he didn't ask what I liked about him. He did ask but he knew what I would say, "Nothing."

He laughed and just made our food. We ate and went to bed in the living room with everyone else. I woke up with Lil' James laying on the couch with me and Sénar as we lay on opposite ends of each other. Sénar made breakfast since his aunt went to church then we all chilled. I tried not to worry about my mom and thought about how Tyrell was probably calling me and wondering why I wasn't answering. I kept having to dodge Cedrick, Sénar saw him but he was patient with him. He made lunch and Cedrick sat next to me while I waited for Sénar to finish cooking. Sénar shook his head when he saw that I was flustered, I thought Sénar would have said something by now.

I finally said, "Why don't you find someone else to talk to like Cassidy or I don't know, somebody else."

He laughed before he answered, "Because I like you, and you are fine as hell."

Sénar was tensing up but he didn't say anything. I got up and replied, "Thanks."

I walked into the kitchen with Sénar. I asked, "Sénar you need help with anything."

He replied, "Yup, cut some potatoes."

He really could use a helping hand, there were lots of potatoes for me to wash and cut. Sénar was quiet and I could not help but ask, "What's wrong with you Sénar?"

He looked at me and then replied, "Nothing Treasure."

I smacked my lips before I said, "There you go, you are lying Sénar."

He snapped at me when he said, "You play too much. If someone is trying to get at you and you are not interested, you need to let it be known. I am not going to run and fight some dude over you, if you haven't let him know you are not interested. He is doing what any dude would do. Don't play games because men already know what they want when they are getting at you and y'all do too."

He was irritated with me, but he was right. Instead of smiling at Cedrick and letting him sit next to me, I could have told him something by now. I started to feel guilty and Sénar looked at me and said, "You are fine as hell though." He laughed and I loosened up a bit.

We finished in the kitchen and everybody ate and one of Sénar's little boy cousins asked, "Are y'all going to live here Sénar?"

He laughed and answered, "Nah, we are going home tonight."

When him and Louie went to the store, I asked, "Latosha, where's Lil' James' daddy?"

She stared at before she answered, "Girl, he ain't shit! He lives with his other baby momma. Girl, just don't be nobody baby momma, be someone's wife. I love my baby, but I want a family, I didn't want to do this by myself."

She picked up Lil' James and went to her room. Cassidy asked, "Where's your daddy Treasure?"

Her cousins laughed I snapped back and replied, "Where's your momma?"

Cassidy was instantly angry and said, "I wish I didn't help your ass that night, I should have let them do whatever their asses wanted to you."

I was shocked at her malice and replied, "Oh you did Cassidy, I just wasn't stupid enough to stay."

She smacked her lips and said, "I hate your ass."

I blew a kiss at her and her cousins rolled their eyes along with Cassidy. Sénar and Louie came back and could feel the tension. Sénar observed the situation around the whole room before he proceeded to roll a blunt out of the cigars they bought. Cedrick of course came and sat next to me. I was highly irritated and thought about my conversation with Sénar. I looked at Cedrick and before he could say anything, I said, "I'm not interested Cedrick. You are wasting your efforts."

He glared at me and then said, "Well, you should have been said something then." Sénar chimed in and said, "Louie had already told you man and now she is telling you, so leave her alone."

Sénar was not asking him he was telling him. Louie snickered and kept rolling his blunt. We smoked and chilled until the sun went down and then we said our goodbyes. I started to get nervous at the thought of going home as we stopped at BoBo's Burgers for something to eat and headed home. We dropped Nevaeh off and before we got to the house, Sénar said, "Y'all go upstairs and go to bed. Don't do anything else."

I rolled my eyes and said, "I am going to check on my mom." Sénar flashed at me when he replied, "Treasure, you are going to take your ass in the room and go to sleep or lay down. I don't give a damn, but you are going to that room with Cassidy and do not come out!"

I huffed and puffed, he didn't care he was adamant, and I knew I needed to listen, but I was worried about my mom. When we walked into the house it was dark and quiet. Sénar carefully closed the door and ushered Cassidy and I up the steps cautiously. Ken bellowed from the kitchen area, "Y'all two go to bed! Come here Sénar and come clean this mess up."

Sénar shooed us and went to where his dad was in the dark. I almost peed on myself when I heard Ken's voice from out of the darkness. I jumped in my bed and pressed my eye lids together and tried to go to sleep. I counted sheep, I cried, I even prayed, I didn't know what to do. I felt sad and overwhelmed all at once. Before I knew it, I was sleep.

My mom appeared fine physically when I saw her, but mentally, she was a mess. She barely came downstairs, and when she did, she wouldn't make eye contact with anyone. One day when Ken wasn't here, I would ask my mom what happened. I just minded my business for now and went to school. The first two days were cool and went quickly. It was already the end of October, and today was Halloween. I had been on punishment for forever; well, it felt like it at least.

Sénar asked, "Do you want to go to a Halloween party?"

I laughed and replied, "I'm still on punishment, remember?"

He replied, "I'll ask my pops; he is in a better mood than he was when we left. Plus, he just doesn't want you with Tyrell."

I smacked my lips with an attitude when I responded, "Oh, but it's ok to be with you?"

He smirked and said, "Yeah, for now, unless he punishes you from me too."

I looked at him like he was crazy, but he was serious. I was disturbed by his little comment, but I didn't say anything. We pulled up to school, and London was waiting for us, except she wasn't looking at Sénar. We pulled up, and I was going to get out, but Sénar instructed me not to.

I looked at him like he was crazy and asked, "Why?"

He smacked his lips and jumped out as London walked to my side of the car. Sénar pulled her back as she yelled for me to get out of the car. I got out anyway, and she tried to come for me. I ignored her, got my backpack, and let Sénar deal with her. She yelled names at me and told me to leave her man alone, but I just kept walking. At lunchtime, Tyrell and Leah did their routine annoying probing. Tyrell asked, "London was fin' to whip your ass this morning, huh?"

I rolled my eyes at him when he asked, "Why? Are you messing with Sénar?"

I snapped at him when I replied, "For the same reason, you scratched me! I just braided his hair. Goodness, what's the big deal."

Leah smiled sadistically and asked, "Does he sit between your legs or on a chair?"

I wisely answered, "He sits on a chair." Leah just laughed as she ate her food, Tyrell eyed me with suspicion. London came and knocked my food onto the floor when I jumped up is when she said, "Keep your hands off, Sénar Treasure!"

I smiled at her and said, "I heard you tell him you liked the braids." I said sarcastically as Leah and Tyrell watched us in our standoff. Sénar came up behind her and got in between us, and I walked away with Tyrell on my heels. Sénar talked to London as Tyrell grabbed me, turning me around to face him.

I yelled, "What?"

Tyrell stared at me and laughed before he said, "Nothing, I'll see you later."

I walked away, not caring what state we were in; I was about to explode. I couldn't stand London, and to have her come at me twice in one day had me on edge. I got to class and sat next to this chubby black boy because I knew he would not decline me sitting there. Leah came in and nicely asked him for his seat for the same reason. I wanted to run out of the classroom, but instead, I said, "Leah, please do not speak to me. I was trying to avoid you."

I glared at her as she pretended to be surprised before she replied, "Damn Treasure, I am not the one trying to beat your ass, that's London. I just wanna know when they break up if you still down to hook Sénar and me up."

I snapped at her and did not bother to lower my voice when I answered, "If Sénar wanted to hook up with you, it would have happened by now. You do it yourself since you are such a pro at it."

She looked at me and smirked when she replied, "Well, Tyrell was tired of your ass anyway. I am just here to console him, but I want Sénar."

She was so bold, she didn't seem to deny her and Tyrell's situation, but she just never flat out said it. I asked, "Are you and Tyrell having sex, Leah?"

She laughed before she said, "Only if you and Sénar are."

She continued to laugh and then did her work. I decided to let her have her fun. I only had a couple of days left on punishment, and I would steal Tyrell back from her because he never belonged to her in the first place. I tried to suppress my emotions in regard to our conversation, but I was running out of mental compartments to stuff emotions into. By the time cheerleading practice came, I was numb to my emotions. I was not present, I was in a trance, and I practiced in a zombie-like state. When I saw Tyrell, I was still numb to emotions.

It wasn't until Sénar grabbed my bag and instructed me to come with him before Tyrell and I could acknowledge the awkwardness between the two of us. Leah called Sénar's name, but he kept walking, and I followed behind him in a hurry. London was already at Sénar's car when we got there, she ran toward me, and Sénar caught her and gave me instructions, "Treasure get in the car and lock the door!"

London fought Sénar wildly as I debated if I would be defiant and whip London's ass instead. Tyrell and Leah came out to witness the commotion. Leah was smiling so big; I could see it as I got into the car. Sénar locked it as London tried to open the door. He shook her and told her to stop, or he would leave her. That was the only thing that calmed her down as she started to cry. Sénar hugged her and told her to chill out. I was being nosey trying to hear their conversation as it was difficult to hear through the closed window and door of Sénar's car. Tyrell watched and shook his head as we made eye contact. I rolled my eyes at him and Leah while I waited for Sénar to deal with his deranged stalker. Sénar said something to London as he got in the car and then drove off like a maniac.

He took deep breaths before he spoke, "Damn Treasure, when all of this is over, I pray it's worth it!"

I don't know exactly what he meant by that, but I didn't want to know at this time. There were lots of Halloween decorations and parties today since it was Halloween. Nevaeh and Cassidy were already going inside when me and Sénar arrived home. Sénar begged, "I know you aren't scared of London, but just go inside just in case she pulls up."

It wasn't but a second before we saw London's car speeding down the street. Sénar was super agitated, and I took my time getting out of the car. We both knew no matter how crazy London was, I was crazier, and I would beat her down if she tried to fight me. I got out a little quicker when I remembered Ken's little speech about not getting into trouble. I left my backpack and hurried into the house. Nevaeh and Cassidy were in the living room sitting on the couch talking when I ran inside and closed the door behind me, locking it. I looked out the window to be nosey. I could see London and Sénar arguing in front of the house as she was trying to come in. I thought to myself how pathetic she was trying to fight me. *What was that going to solve?* Especially for her because she would get her ass whipped and still be second to me. I rolled my eyes and turned around to see Cassidy and Nevaeh behind me, looking out the window as well. I rolled my eyes again at them both and went upstairs with them shaking their heads at me. I didn't care they weren't perfect; they both had their little secrets too. I went upstairs and saw Ken coming downstairs. Sénar came in right on time because if Ken would have seen them arguing outside, I knew he would have been upset.

Sénar tried appearing normal when he said, "Wassup Pops!"

Ken replied, "Hey, Sénar."

He didn't say anything to me, but I didn't care. Sénar grabbed me and asked, "Did you tell London we went to LA?"

I looked at him like he was stupid before I answered, "No, Sénar!"

He quickly responded, "Damn, girl, calm down. I already had to deal with London's crazy ass. Dang, give me a break!"

I smacked my lips and then replied, "No, I did not, Sénar. Why would I do that?"

He shook his head as Nevaeh and Cassidy came up the steps to see Sénar and I talking. Nevaeh had a guilty look on her face, and Cassidy looked irritated with all of us, even Nevaeh. Sénar and I thought the same thing when we saw Nevaeh and Cassidy walk into my room. Sénar was so furious, he went back downstairs. I went into the room cautiously, knowing they were waiting on me, and I was not in the mood. They were both sitting on Cassidy's bed as I went in to grab stuff to take a shower.

Nevaeh said, "That's messed up, Treasure, don't you have a boyfriend named Tyrell?"

I thought how bold she was being she hadn't mentioned Tyrell since she started screwing Louie, and now, she was acting brand new like she wasn't just drooling over Tyrell the day she fell for Louie. She didn't go to our school, so she had no idea Tyrell was most likely messing with Leah.

I ignored her, and Cassidy answered, "He is messing with her little friend Leah, so she is trying to mess up Sénar and London's relationship since hers is all messed up."

Since they had each other to communicate with, I allowed them to have an A and B conversation, and I would C my way out to take a shower. On the way to the shower, Sénar gave me a package and told me to put it on. I examined the package to see that it was a Cleopatra costume.

Before I could say anything, he said, "I'm not dressing up, I don't celebrate this day, but I want to go to this college party. You are a beautiful Black queen already, so it's not really a costume. Plus, I can't wait to see you in it." He bit his bottom lip and eyed me flirtatiously. He winked at me before going to his room. I just thought how crazy Sénar was. Things could be at a high level of chaos and then he could go right back to normal without missing a beat, well most of the time. I showered and put the costume on. It was so pretty it was a silky gold material made like a gown that fitted the upper body and flared out at the bottom. It had an embroidered belt with turquoise stones in it. There was costume jewelry included for the arms and crown. There were two slits up the front of the gown that showed off my chocolate thighs. It was just beautiful, and I must say, it looked really good on me. I twisted my hair and pinned it into a bun to the back. I then put the chain-like crown on my head that had a jewel that hung down onto my forehead. I was ready; all I needed was Coco butter and my gold hoops. I went to my room to see that Nevaeh was crying and Cassidy just listened to her talk.

They both looked at me with envy in their eyes as I sashayed in the room, looking like the beautiful Black queen that I am. I ignored the two of them and put cocoa butter all over me as they watched in unison. I put my gold hoops on and thought about what shoes I would wear. When I turned around Sénar, Nevaeh and Cassidy were staring at me. If I didn't know any better, I would assume they were all thinking the same thing. Sénar had a pair of gold sandals in his hand and grinned at me as he handed them to me. I smiled back at him and put the sandals on while still under observation of Cassidy and Nevaeh. Sénar tried to control himself as I stood up confidently with my assemble now complete. Nevaeh was acting funny, but Cassidy just appeared envious when she cut her eyes at me.

Sénar opened the door for me and exclaimed, "Oh my goodness, Treasure!"

He shivered before he followed behind me, I shook my head. Ken was coming up the stairs and smiled sadistically when he saw me in my costume. His eyes were all over me as he passed by, he told Sénar, "Bring that ass back by twelve."

Sénar replied, "Yes sir," but I could tell he was irritated with Ken's demand. We got in his car and drove to his college friend's party. Everyone was in a costume or the Cal University attire. The girls there were dressed in some beautiful but very provocative costumes. Sénar was grinning as his friend came up to greet us, "What's up, Sénar!" They gave a half hug and handshake to one another.

Sénar asked, "What's up, Mario? Man, you are living it up, huh?"

He smiled at Sénar before he responded, "Yeah my nigg! I love it!"

Mario eyed me then said, "Hey, Treasure."

I smiled and replied, "Hi." I couldn't believe he remembered my name; he graduated with Chino. We followed him to where everyone was drinking, playing games, and dancing. I got several compliments on my costume from both males and females. I drank a couple of drinks and danced on Sénar. I was driving him crazy while he put his hand on my belly and smelled my hair. Sénar didn't drink, but he did smoke with his friends as they talked about football. I only hit the blunt once as I was already buzzing from the drinks I had. We were in a city called San Bernardino. We stayed at the party until about nine o'clock. Sénar drove us up a dark mountain, and when we got to the top, we could see the whole city light up along with the beautiful stars. We got out and sat on Sénar's car while he lit a joint. We smoked and just stared at the lights of the city. Sénar told me to pose for him while he went into his pocket to grab his camera. We had so much fun taking pictures and posing, I forgot I was on punishment.

Sénar sighed, "Well, this is our last week on Treasure Island. Are you going to run back to Tyrell after this? I wish you would leave him alone."

I rolled my eyes at Sénar and said, "Sénar mind your business with London. Let's just enjoy our last Wednesday, please?"

Sénar chuckled then asked, "Oh, it's still hump day?"

Sénar laughed, "Well, let me get some dessert before you run back to his punk ass."

He pulled me to him and caressed my body as he slid his hand up one of the slits of the costume. He kissed me on my neck and smelled my hair before he lifted my costume and worked his magic until I moaned and yelped in pleasure. Then he fed me a full course meal, five stars if I might add. I was smiling like a fat kid eating cake. He took me to Alberto's and asked me what I wanted, although I love Mexican food it was late, so I just asked if I could have some of what he ordered.

He smiled and replied, "Good choice, ma."

We went back to the house, and the first thing I noticed was that Tyrell's car was not there. We went inside; it was just about to be eleven-thirty, which was thirty minutes earlier than Ken's demand. We were going to eat in the living room, but Ken called Sénar into the kitchen. He then told me to get him a beer before I even decided to go to the kitchen. I went to get him a beer as Ken said, something to Sénar. They laughed, but I could tell Sénar was uncomfortable. I gave

Ken his beer, and he eyed me in my costume before Sénar handed me the nachos. I went to the kitchen nook to eat. I was too uncomfortable to eat with Ken at the table in my costume. I ate while Ken and Sénar talked. I didn't wait for them to finish talking. I just ate a couple of nachos and went to bed.

Chapter 9

Thursday morning was awkward as me and Sénar were beyond just bartering. We really enjoyed ourselves, but now reality was starting to set in. I knew London would be waiting to jump on me when we pulled up to school.

I asked, "Sénar, what is London mad about?"

He laughed then replied, "Everything."

I cut my eyes at him, and he said, "To be more specific amongst other things, she is upset because someone told her we went to LA for the weekend."

I smacked my lips, "I didn't tell her. Nevaeh or Cassidy's dumb ass probably told her."

Sénar stared at me then said, "Damn, Cassidy is not that scandalous, to me, at least. It had to be Nevaeh."

I asked, "Why didn't you ask Nevaeh?"

He shrugged his shoulders and said, "That's Louie's girl, I'll let him handle that, and I'll handle London. I already smoothed it over. So just sit pretty."

I rolled my eyes at him, he smirked, "Plus I need my hair braided later."

I smacked my lips and replied, "No, Sénar, she was upset last time about that too, and Tyrell was angry with me too."

Sénar was agitated and responded, "So what! Ditch his ass, and I'll be happy to ditch London."

I rolled my eyes at him and said, "Be realistic, Sénar."

He looked at me, sincerely and replied, "I am being realistic Treasure."

We pulled up to school, and London was patiently waiting on Sénar. She did not appear angry, she looked more remorseful. Sénar grabbed her to kiss her, she melted in his arms and avoided eye contact with me. I just shook my head and went to class, thinking about how he got her to calm down. When lunchtime came, I thought about telling Tyrell the good news about this being my last week of punishment, but I noticed some commotion in the cafeteria. Sénar and Tyrell were having words while Leah and London went back and forth. I sat down and watched everything unfold as I ate a salad for lunch in peace while everyone else argued for once. I just minded my business and went to class after. I sat down, not caring where I sat, knowing if Leah wanted to sit next to me, she would find a way. She came into class and avoided me. I thought to myself, *today must be my lucky day,* as I watched her find a seat far away from me. I could care less, I needed this week to be over, so I could move on with my life, and like Ken said, let Sénar handle his business. Funny how finally, when Sénar opens up to reveal his past to me, it was now time for us to move on to our current victims other than each other. I went to practice totally oblivious to what their commotion was about earlier. I really did not care, I had the rest of today, and tomorrow then I would be free at last. Leah bumped into me and acted like she hadn't noticed me.

I looked at her like she was crazy, prompting her to ask, "What?"

I just rolled my eyes at her and moved away from her. She followed me to say, "You know what Treasure, you are one sneaky lil' bitch."

I frowned my eyebrows at her audacity and decided not to respond to her. She became even more furious with me when she said, "You knew I wanted Sénar and you played so many games, I had to settle for Tyrell while you had all the fun. It's my turn, you just watch."

I laughed in her face, was she implying Tyrell wasn't fun enough? I had to laugh but also wonder if my punishment ending was as good as it sounded. I shook my head and asked, "Leah, there a lot of football players and other boys in the world, and your dumb ass had to choose the two that want me. Sounds like you are a little salty, but maybe you should find someone who likes you and does not belong to someone else!"

She was pissed, but I was right. Leah then said, "Well, maybe you should follow your own advice once you are off punishment."

She smirked at me, and I ignored her because she was on my last nerve. I just focused on my routine and did my best to make it through practice without hitting her upside her head. Sénar came to grab my bag with London attached to his hip and London on her best behavior as we headed for his car. Sénar kissed London and told her he would come over to her house later.

He got in the car and asked, "What do you want to do this weekend?"

I looked at him to answer, "Sénar nothing, we have to get used to things going back to normal. It's been a long punishment for us all, so let's not make it more complicated."

Sénar was quiet; he didn't say anything; he just worked out when we got home and showered. He came down with his hair wild but washed, some grease, and a comb. I hesitated, but I braided his hair for him, I even did them smaller so they would last longer. He was so pleased with his hair; he asked me if he could take me to get some of those tacos we had from the truck. I laughed because he liked them just as much as me and Tyrell did. I told him to get them and bring some back, so we would eat them here at home. He was disappointed but agreed. I needed to ween myself off of Sénar; he was like a drug to me. He was a guilty pleasure of mine, and I just wanted to be cleansed of the filth that I would feel sleeping with both him and Tyrell. Sénar came back with tacos for us to eat. We talked a little before we watched TV and went to bed soon after. Friday was a breeze as I avoided London by not having to practice and went home to get ready for the game. Sénar played his heart out while Tyrell played with envy in his eyes. We won, and Leah and I cheered along with the other girls as our team was undefeated this year, so far. Sénar ran up to me and high fived me as he had three touchdowns and made some important tackles. Sénar took me home as London followed with an attitude. I went in and went to bed without Sénar having to tell me too. Over the weekend, Tyrell avoided my phone calls, so I couldn't even tell him I was off of punishment. I just watched Sénar and London cuddle and make up all weekend.

The weekend went so quickly, and it was my first official day off punishment. I brushed my teeth and washed my face after getting dressed. I hurried to call Tyrell early in the morning he answered, "Hello?"

I quickly said, "Hey, Tyrell. Can I come over?"

He was quiet for a minute before he responded, "Yeah, I guess. You ain't on punishment no more?"

I took a deep breath, so I could answer his stupid question. I replied, "No, Tyrell, I am finally off."

I almost wanted to ask if we were still together, but I didn't want to start an argument. I quickly hung up and headed across the street before Sénar woke up. Tyrell opened the door with no shirt and his basketball shorts on. Which made me instantly aroused as I looked forward to his morning show that I had not seen in what felt like forever. I ran upstairs without him prompting me to; he seemed to hesitate before he followed. Once in his room, I hugged him and tried to kiss him.

He pushed me back, making me angry with him. I asked, "Tyrell, it has been forever, and now you want to push me away?"

He replied, "Oh, now you wanna hug and kiss?"

I was horny and annoyed with his sarcasm. I rolled my eyes at him, letting Treasure number two takeover and pushed him onto his bed. He looked at me like I was crazy and asked, "Treasure, what has gotten into you?"

I took my shirt off, and then my bra, he gazed at my breast before I kissed him passionately. I took my pants off, he was still in shock, looking at me like I was crazy.

He asked, "Treasure, what are you doing?" I pushed him onto the bed and straddled him, kissing him passionately and rubbing my hands all over his shirtless body. I started to pull at his shorts, he slapped my hand away, but I pulled them down anyway rubbing my hand all over his man stick. I felt that I had the upper hand with his member despite his rebuttals. I pulled it out, jumped on him, and rode him like a pro.

He called my name, "Treasure? Treasure? Treasure!"

He pushed me off of him, causing me to land on the floor, wondering why he stopped me before I could climax. He looked scared as we both noticed he made a mess all over his shorts and stomach.

He was in shock when he asked, "Where you learn how to ride like that?" I giggled and replied, "I don't know; I just missed you."

He smiled nervously and then asked, "Well, did you cum at least?"

I thought about my earrings that Sénar gave me and lied, "Yeah, I did."

He grinned at me before he said, "Cool."

I quickly asked, "Can I have my earrings back?"

His smile faded as he went in one of his drawers to hand me my earrings and went to take a shower. As he took a shower, I laughed to myself when I thought, *I would never get my earrings back, especially if I had to depend on Tyrell, making me cum to get them back.* I quickly got dressed and safely tucked my earrings away in my backpack. Tyrell came out with a perplexed look on his face.

He asked, "So we good, huh?"

I looked at him with a dumbfounded expression on my face and replied, "Of course. Tyrell, I am happy to be here, happy to be off punishment, and I just want to move forward."

He was still skeptical when he asked, "You know we have to pick Leah up, right?"

I laughed before I asked, "So, what's new?"

He shook his head as he got dressed. He didn't bother turning away from me as he dressed, so I enjoyed the show as I always wanted to watch him naked. We left, and I prayed I would not see Sénar on my way out. I was so relieved we left before Sénar and Cassidy came out. We pulled up to Leah's house; she appeared happy to see Tyrell until she noticed me in the front seat. I waved at her, and her smile faded as she walked to the back seat. She didn't say anything, and we rode to school in silence. I think everyone was happy that things were almost back to normal. Except for maybe Leah and maybe Sénar, but I couldn't tell with London all over him. It was an awkward day, but Leah's silence was golden. She avoided Tyrell and me the whole day. Sénar still watched my every move while still managing to give London the attention she so desperately needed.

After practice everyone went their separate ways, Leah sat in the back seat where she belonged. When we got back to Tyrell's house, I gave him a hug and a kiss without bothering to ask to go upstairs. I just went home as I saw Sénar pull up. I left the door open for him and went upstairs. I put my backpack down after realizing how heavy it was after not having to ever hold it when Sénar was around. I went back downstairs to watch some TV. Sénar came out of the garage with no shirt on dripping in sweat, but he didn't say anything. He just observed my presence and went upstairs to shower. I swear Treasure number two prompted me to go up there and jump in the shower with him as I shook my head to get rid of my naughty thoughts. I took a deep breath to calm myself and focused on the TV. I couldn't help but think of Sénar and his emotional state after having opened up to me, and the time we've spent together in the last couple of weeks. I started to feel bad when I heard the doorbell ring, and I got up to answer it. Surprise, it was London, she pushed the ajar door open and let herself in. She smirked at me as she walked up the steps to meet Sénar as he waited for her at the top of the stairs. I rolled my eyes at Sénar and closed the door. I went back to the couch to get comfortable and laugh a little at *Martin*, trying to keep my mind occupied with something else. Sénar came down after the sun was going down past the time that we would normally eat. Even Cassidy came down, to check to see if anyone made anything. She went back upstairs, disappointed. I didn't care, I made me a grilled cheese sandwich and went upstairs.

As I was going up, London and Sénar were coming down. Sénar smelled the air and could smell the toast. London rolled her eyes at me, and I rolled my eyes back at her. Sénar shook his head, and I rolled my eyes at him too. I went to my room and laid down. I smelled food, but I was satisfied with my grilled cheese sandwich. The next morning, I boiled an egg and didn't bother making anything else. I just ate it by swallowing it plain, just to have something on my stomach. Tuesday was a replica of Monday as Tyrell allowed me to have my way with him before school and actually took the time to enjoy it. The whole rest of the week went like that, and it was lovely despite a couple of awkward moments. At home, things went pretty smoothly as well, despite a couple of dinner deprived nights.

Finally, Friday was here, and I was impressed by how the week went. Although it was far from perfect, it was better than I would have imagined it to be. Leah left me alone all week and I couldn't be happier. London screwed Sénar every day this week and I screwed Tyrell's brains out every day this week. He was overwhelmed and concerned at why I was so good at it now. I contributed my skills to missing him and reading lots of books. Tyrell declined this morning as he complained about needing his strength for the game. I didn't mind the day went quickly, and before I knew it, I was on the sidelines cheering for both Tyrell and Sénar. They both did pretty swell as they won the game, and we cheered our little hearts out for our undefeated team. Tyrell and Leah were so used to me being on punishment they left without me, and I rode home with my mom and Ken. I went to bed and called Tyrell in the morning to ask him why he left without me, but there was no answer. Despite me being off punishment, Tyrell avoided me the whole weekend.

I was so mad at Tyrell on Monday. I got up and walked to school because I didn't want to deal with Tyrell and Leah this morning. When I arrived at school, everyone seemed to have got there at the same time, ironically, because everyone was a little earlier than usual. I hurried to my class to avoid everyone. When lunchtime came, I ate outside and read a book. Tyrell didn't bother looking for me, but I did see Sénar with his accessory London looking for me. Once Sénar spotted me, I could see him tell London something and saw how upset she got when he walked over to me. I was annoyed already before he got to me.

I asked, "What is it, Sénar?"

He was quiet for a second, he just watched me in my fit before he asked, "Treasure, are you ok?"

I snapped, "I am fine, Sénar! I just want to be left alone."

He shook his head out of frustration and asked, "Why don't you just leave his ass alone, instead of isolating yourself?"

I stood up and looked Sénar in his eyes and asked, "Why Sénar? Your relationship seems to be doing better now, so just worry about yours. I am fine!"

I was taking my frustration out on him, but I knew it wasn't his fault, I just didn't have the courage to deal with Tyrell in that way. Sénar left out of frustration, and I almost felt bad, but I didn't care about anyone's feelings at this time. Tuesday was the same; I isolated myself and ignored everyone. I forced myself to go to practice and avoided Leah's poisonous ass. Tyrell came up to me after practice and grabbed my arm. I looked at him like he was stupid; he kissed me and whispered, "Let's go; I want you to perform for me like you did when you got them earrings back."

I almost forgot about the earrings that were still safely tucked into my backpack. Leah walked up, and Tyrell asked, "You ready to go?"

Leah had an attitude when she asked, "Is she going with us?"

Tyrell hesitated before answering, "Yeah, why?"

Leah smacked her lips and folded her arms when she said, "I'll find a way home."

Tyrell became instantly agitated, he said, "Your ass is going with me, so get your stuff, and let's go."

She was irritated, but she got her stuff while I debated if I wanted to ride with him. Tyrell told us both, "Let's go!" I didn't want to go with him, but I didn't want to make a scene. Maybe I would take the time to talk to him and find out where our relationship was going. We dropped Leah off, but before we left, he got out and talked to her before she went inside, upset. Tyrell got back in the car and said, "So, you call yourself being mad at me?"

I shook my head, no. He looked at me like he wanted to say something but just stayed quiet. We pulled up to his house at the same time as Sénar. I did not want to face Sénar, so I waited until he went inside to get out. Tyrell sensed what I was doing and rushed me out of the car.

He asked, "What? You don't want your other boyfriend to see you over here?"

I didn't answer Tyrell because he just wanted to argue, so he would have a reason to treat me badly. I followed him to his room. He said, "Take your clothes off like you did the other day."

I folded my arms with attitude; he got impatient and said, "Hurry up, Treasure, my mom will be here soon."

I removed my pants, and he didn't wait for me to take my shirt off. He pushed me back and pulled out his eager man stick, and before entering me, he put a condom on. I was barely wet due to his careless attitude. I laid there and let him enter me with his new and improved safety method that sent my coochie into shock. It was a painful and uncomfortable experience. When it was over, he rushed me out, and I went home smelling like a rubber balloon. It was terrible like a fist with a latex glove was shoved up my coochie. I didn't like it at all; I think I would rather not have sex. It really left me irritated and the same for down there. I quickly took a shower to wash the rubber smell away along with the itching sensation. I saw Sénar as I came out, and he was ready to go into shower after me. He didn't say anything; he just walked in the bathroom to shower. It was a miserable feeling to have Sénar ignore me, but I needed to figure out what was happening between me and Tyrell. I could not take all the drama, and the condom situation really had me thinking.

London appeared happy, but deep down, she could tell Sénar was just using her to occupy himself from focusing on me. I spoke too soon as Sénar poked his head in my room while I read a book. He asked, "Treasure how many times you eat bread this week?"

I answered, "I don't know Sénar, I lost count."

Sénar shook his head and said, "Well, if you are going to eat carbs freely, you should work out before or after."

I rolled my eyes at him, he smirked and asked, "What's the attitude for now?"

I snapped back, "I don't have an attitude. I am reading Sénar or trying to rather."

He sighed and closed the door. I just read my book and wondered what type of work out he was talking about. I was still sexually frustrated, even though I had sex with Tyrell every morning last week and today, not having climaxed once. The only thing I accomplished was putting Leah in her place and getting my earrings back. Cassidy came home, threw her stuff on the floor, and went back downstairs without a word to watch TV. I went downstairs when I smelled food and noticed Sénar had his due rag on his head to keep his braids nice and neat. Ken sat at the table while Sénar cooked as I hesitated to go into the kitchen. I was thirsty, so I went to the fridge and got some juice because it had been so long since I had drunk something with sugar in it. The juice was so good; I closed my eyes to savor the taste.

Sénar and Ken watched my every move as I washed my cup and left for the living room.

Before I could leave the kitchen, Ken said, "Get me a beer, Treasure."

I almost snapped, but I remembered Ken was crazy. I reluctantly turned around to get Ken a beer way from the back. He took it from me, and I walked to the living room. My mom came down after Cassidy, and they both went to make plates. Sénar made chicken Alfredo and Garlic bread with no alternative dish for me. I smirked at Sénar before making my plate and skipped the garlic bread out of respect. Everyone ate in uncomfortable silence as I picked the chicken and broccoli out of my Alfredo. I threw most of my noodles away, washed my plate, and went to bed. Tuesday, I knew Tyrell would expect me to come to his house, I just got there later on purpose. He was already dressed and ready to go. We picked Leah up without saying a word to each other. Leah got in the car with an attitude and said, "Hey," to Tyrell, but ignored me. I was fine with it. I just wanted to go to school and get the day over with.

Everything was fine as usual until lunchtime because Tyrell and Leah did one of their hide and seek tricks, being that they were nowhere to be found. I should have just eaten outside like I did yesterday, Sénar watched me as I drifted into my thoughts. I had to snap out of it; I decided I would make under the tree my new spot. I got up and prepared myself to face Leah. I sat down and hoped she avoided me again. She did not; she smiled at me and sat down. I rolled my eyes and doodled on my paper, waiting for the teacher to give instructions.

Leah asked, "Do you and Tyrell use condoms?"

I looked at her with an attitude and asked, "Why?"

I thought about how Tyrell used a condom yesterday and got a little worried. She said, "Just asking, I hope so."

I was agitated now when I asked, "Why, do you guys use condoms?"

She rolled her eyes at me before she answered, "I don't like them, so I would rather he use them with you."

I took a deep breath and thought about how I would be suspended and possibly kicked off the cheerleading team if I beat her to smithereens in class. I ignored her and thought about what she said as she continued her probing, "Does Tyrell go down on you?"

I snapped at her, "Mind your damn business, Leah!"

Everyone looked at me like I was crazy, even the teacher. I felt myself shaking and asked the teacher if I could go use the restroom. Oh, my goodness, I had to leave, or I would have punched Leah in her face. I tried to calm down by taking deep breaths. I realized I had to go back and deal with her, so trusty Treasure number two took over. I went back to class with a smile on my face. Leah had a perplexed look on her face when I returned super calm and collected. She was annoyed by my restored confidence. She did her work, and I did mine. I avoided her as much as I could during practice, and it was noticeable to everyone, even Tyrell.

He was nonchalant about it and told us both, "Let's go."

When we dropped her off, Tyrell asked, "What's up with you and Leah?"

I wanted to punch him in the face for asking such a stupid question, but instead, I just replied, "What do you mean, Tyrell?"

He snapped at me when he asked, "Why are you always playing stupid?"

I snapped back at him, "Well, maybe because I have to deal with your stupid ass!"

He stopped the car so fast; I almost hit the dashboard! Fear took over me as Tyrell grabbed me by my face and roared, "Don't ever talk to me like that again!"

He pushed my face back, and my head hit the interior wall of the car. I wanted to cry, but instead, I became enraged, "Tyrell, don't put your hands on me!"

He got in my face, "I could do what I want because you belong to me!"

He put his car in drive and started to drive towards the house, but then he turned to go towards the taco truck instead. He got out and ordered twelve tacos and gave me six, then said, "There, I know your ass likes food, so here."

He laughed as he drove back to the house. I was at lost for words, I just wanted to go home. When we pulled up to the house, Tyrell said, "I know you don't need all those tacos but eat them all, I don't care, just don't ever talk to me like that again."

He looked at me and waited for a response; I held back my tears as I said, "Thanks, Tyrell. I wanted to tell you I have chores on Wednesday now, so I have to go straight home after practice."

He laughed and said, "Ok, whatever."

He got out, and we went our separate ways without a hug or a kiss. I was so angry with Tyrell; he was becoming mean and more malice toward me; I hated it. I put the tacos on the table in the living room and sat down for a second to gather myself in case Cassidy was up there. I put my head down and tried to think of ways to deal with my overload of emotions as Sénar came in the door.

He called my name, "Treasure?"

I snapped, "What?"

I was overwhelmed when he walked over to me. He asked, "Why do you have so many tacos?"

I couldn't help but laugh hysterically when I answered, "They were a gift."

He raised his eyebrow and asked, "Are you doing ok Treasure?" I know he was trying to help, but I just didn't understand why he cared so much. I lied when I answered, "I am fine, Sénar."

He said, "Yeah, right. You wanna work out?"

I looked at him inquisitively and asked, "How Sénar?"

He smiled sadistically, "However, you want ma."

I rolled my eyes at him and followed him to the garage. He grabbed the gloves down and helped me put mine on then put his on. He told me to hit the bag a couple of times, which felt good as I imagined a couple of people as I pounded on it. Then we sparred for a while until we were sweaty, and I was tired. It felt great, we split the tacos, and I showered. I was way less stressed, so when Cassidy smacked her lips and rolled her eyes at me, she got away with it as I wrote in my diary and ignored her. I was so tired and overwhelmed with emotions; I just went to sleep after. Wednesday was great as I went to Tyrell's house later than usual in the morning to avoid having extra time with him before school. I sat outside during lunch and avoided everyone. Sénar checked on me and went back to the cafeteria. Tyrell and Leah left the cafeteria together, and I ignored them, I was starting to wonder why we were even still together.

After practice, we all rode home in silence. Leah had an attitude with Tyrell and ignored me. Tyrell was agitated, so I avoided saying anything because yesterday was just too much for me. I just wanted to go home. Sénar asked me if I wanted to work out again, and I agreed. When we were done, he asked, "You need a meat voucher?"

He laughed, and it took all my might to say no. I felt guilty about our little bartering because it made me almost except Leah and Tyrell's betrayal. I almost settled for him having dessert when he said, "Nuh-uh, don't even think about it."

It was like he could read my mind. I asked, "Why?"

He quickly answered, "I don't want to do that while you are messing with him."

I said, "Well, we use condoms now."

Sénar looked like he wanted to slap me before he replied, "I really don't want to hear that shit but good because I don't want to use them with you."

I frowned, thinking about the conversation I had with Leah, and with an attitude, I asked, "Well, do you and London use them?"

Sénar answered, "Yup, every time."

I was curious and asked, "Well, why don't we use them?"

He laughed before he countered, "Why, you want to use them?"

I shook my head no, then he replied, "You're so cute. You want some or not?"

I lied, "No, Sénar."

He shrugged his shoulders and helped me out of the gloves. I showered and let the shower head work its magic until I saw flashes of Sénar before reaching my climax. It wasn't as satisfying as the real thing, but it helped tremendously. After, I ate dinner and went to bed. Thursday morning, I tried to give the condom thing with Tyrell another go; it was even worse the second time, but hey, maybe it will get better. That day Leah and Tyrell argued before our math class as I sat outside and finished my lunch. It was exhausting to have some kind of drama every other day. I couldn't wait to get home. I remembered when I could not stand being home, now I could not stand being anywhere else.

Friday was finally here. There was so much tension between everyone. Leah and Tyrell were bumping heads the last couple of days, and Sénar and London were hanging on to threads. Sénar tolerated her, but he was always worried about me. Making sure I was ok, making sure I still worked out, and checking to see if I needed a meat voucher. Sénar was really something else. The day still went quickly, and it was now game time. We cheered our butts off, and the game was great because we won. Although Sénar's game was a little off because he wasn't as enthusiastic. Leah noticed Sénar's lack of drive, and I could see her scheming.

After the game, we all went to a mom and pop pizza place to celebrate the win. Sénar and London were also there since she was his accessory as always. Leah was flirting with some of the other football players agitating Tyrell. He took his frustration out on me when he said, "Well, I am not going home early tonight, so if you want to go home with your brother, you are more than welcomed to."

I knew he just wanted to start an argument, so he could go home with Leah instead. I caught on but still said, "Well, you know I can't go home late, so what do you want me to do, Tyrell?" He glared at me and then shrugged his shoulders, "I don't care what you do. I know what I am going to do and what I am not going to do."

I smacked my lips and watched Leah jump on the back of one of the senior football players. Tyrell grew angrier while she fraternized with all the other athletes. I rolled my eyes and thought about how much trouble I would get into if I went home late on just my second week off punishment. I had to swallow my pride as Tyrell went to retrieve Leah; I went to find Sénar. He was shaking his head at me as I walked up to him. I instantly had an attitude as I had to ask him in front of London. "Sénar?" I said it reluctantly, he looked at me then asked, "What's up Treasure?" London listened attentively as I took a deep breath and asked, "Can I ride with you home?" He had a look of shock on his face, but I knew he was being sarcastic. Before he could answer, London said, "No. Go ask your little boyfriend, we have plans, and besides I am driving, not him."

Sénar rolled his eyes but not where she could see him. I started to walk away, but Sénar said, "Babe, don't be like that. If we don't give her a ride, then she will be on punishment again. Do you really want that babe?" London became agitated and whined when she answered, "No. Whatever, just let her go inside when we get there, so we can have some fun." Sénar agreed and winked at me. London and Sénar walked off to get some pizza, but Sénar turned around to reassure me, he said, "I'll let you know when we are ready ma." I felt so stupid and humiliated that I went to the bathroom to vent. I rinsed my face to bring my temperature down a notch as I was fuming and on the verge of tears. Leah came into the bathroom. She had not said a word to me until today, and she was really buzzing. I tried to leave, but she blocked the door, "Give me Sénar, and I will never bother you and Tyrell again." I laughed in her face before I replied, "Sénar does not belong to me; he belongs to London, and Tyrell belongs to me. You are just a loner." She laughed at me and said, "Well, let's just see who the loner is tonight." She left the bathroom before me. I didn't care; I just didn't want to get in trouble again. I came out and walked over to Tyrell. I could see him whispering into Leah's ear while she giggled. Tyrell was buzzing too, but I was sober and highly irritated. Leah pulled on Tyrell's shirt flirtatiously, and he didn't stop her. Before my anger could reach a dangerous peak, I heard Sénar's voice, "Let's go, Treasure."

I was so angry; I wanted to scream. Tyrell sized Sénar up, and Leah was shocked as she thought she would be able to rub their relationship in my face all night. I turned to leave with Sénar and London without saying anything to Tyrell. Sénar and London walked ahead of me, which helped me conceal my anger. I got in the back of London's car, and Sénar drove us to our house. When we pulled up, I once again swallowed my pride and told them both, "Thank you."

I quickly got out of her car and ran inside to see Ken sitting at the table with my mom. I just ran upstairs to see Cassidy lying in bed talking on her phone. Without saying a word to each other, I got my stuff to take a bath. She saw the tears in my eyes and laughed in my face as I headed to the bathroom. I ran the water for my bath and got in with hopes of drowning my sorrows in there. I was so angry, hurt, sad, and embarrassed. I felt alone again in a house full of people. I grabbed the shower head and straddled it until I saw Sénar's face flash right before I reached a much-needed climax. I laid back until I heard a knock at the door. I sighed because I didn't want to get out, but handy Sénar opened the door and poked his head in.

He asked, "Are you ok, Treasure?"

I lied, "I'm good, Sénar."

He knew I was lying, but he left me alone and didn't pry. I got out to get dressed then went straight to bed with tears in my eyes and a crushed ego.

Over the weekend, Tyrell didn't call me, and I didn't call him. I was tired of him and Leah, I was starting to feel like he just didn't want me with anyone else, but he wanted to be able to do what he wanted. If I questioned him or avoided him, he became aggressive and mean. I still avoided him Monday by walking to school, eating outside, and leaving a little early, so I could walk home. Sénar noticed and asked me so many questions, I lost count. I assured him I was fine; I just needed a break from all the drama.

He said, "You need to leave him alone before he hurts you, Treasure."

Sénar was serious, and he appeared stressed, so it kept me from snapping at him. I just did my best to reassure him when I said, "Sénar, I am fine. I just don't want any drama, ok."

He shook his head and went to go work out, and I avoided him because I knew he was upset with me, I just wasn't exactly sure why. Tuesday, Leah, and Tyrell had so much tension between the two of them; it made it easier for me to avoid Tyrell. Sénar was always checking on me and was growing distant from London. She got on his nerves, and he avoided letting her come over. He was so stressed seeing me in a constant emotional turmoil that I thought no one noticed. Leah noticed Sénar was tired of London as well, so she started to make passes at him. Tyrell noticed and became even more envious of Sénar. Him and Sénar were constantly bumping heads at practice while Leah watched. I know it may sound selfish, but it made it easier to leave and walk home. Sénar came home in a bad mood. Normally he would work out, but he just came and sat on the couch.

He asked, "Treasure, why are you still with Tyrell?"

I was irritated but cautious how I answered, "Why Sénar? Why does it matter to you? Why are you still with London?"

Sénar smirked before he answered, "London doesn't diss me or treat me like shit, and I'm ready to ditch her ass still. So, answer my question." He was frustrated and impatiently waiting on my answer.

I said, "Sénar relax, ok, I will figure out what I am going to do. I love him, and he is not doing anything different than what we were doing, so I am trying to be patient with him."

Sénar was pissed off, "I swear you are both doing this shit just to hurt me."

He left and went to go work out. I went out to the garage and watched him hit the punching bag fiercely until he noticed me behind him. He shook his head at me and threw his gloves and walked out of the garage with me slowly following behind him. Ken was coming from upstairs and noticed Sénar was angry, he asked, "Boy, what's wrong with you?"

Sénar quickly responded, "Nothing Pops, I'm good."

He went upstairs to shower, I softly closed the garage door and quickly tried to bypass Ken when he stopped me. He said, "Come here, Treasure."

I was reluctant, but I turned around and went to him. I answered, "Yes, Ken?" I tried not to have an attitude when he asked, "What's wrong with Sénar?" I shrugged my shoulders and answered, "I don't know Ken."

He knew I was lying and told me, "Get me a beer then. I know you know how to do that." I went to get him a beer, and he met me halfway. Ken said, "You are probably worse than Diamond."

I looked at Ken in a dumbfounded way, and he smirked at me before sitting down at the table. I ran upstairs and knocked on the bathroom door. Sénar opened the door in his towel as the water was still running. He looked at me with fury in his eyes when he asked, "What Treasure?"

I winced at his tone and almost turned away because I just could not take any more drama at this point. But I didn't want him to stay mad at me and then I would have to worry about Ken too.

I was cautious as I asked, "Sénar, why are you so upset when we both have relationships?"

Sénar pulled me in the bathroom with him. My heart rate increased, and I braced myself for what was next. Sénar leaned in close to me as he spoke, "Treasure, London knew how I felt about you before we even got together. So, she knew what she was getting herself into, and she didn't care. Tyrell's ass knew too. Before anyone! I told him how I felt about you and all the things I wanted to do to you. He was my friend at one time Treasure. Yeah, he is with you just to hurt me. He might have some feelings for you because I mean, you are Treasure, but he does not show it."

He was trying not to raise his voice. He looked so frustrated when he said, "Look, I have already told you too much as it is. You don't listen, anyway."

He opened the door to see if he saw anyone and said, "Bye, Treasure, I need to shower."

I eyed him in his towel and left without saying a word. He was so intense; I didn't know what to say. I just waited for him in his room. I didn't want to go in my room, in case Cassidy was in there. When he walked in, he saw me sitting on his bed; he shook his head. "Treasure, girl, you play too much."

I rolled my eyes at him and said, "Sénar when you are mad, you are so cute. I think you need an attitude adjustment."

I took my shirt off, and Sénar grabbed me and kissed me. I kissed him back but then pushed him off; he rolled his eyes at me. I took my pants off as Sénar locked his door. He smiled his famous smile before he tried to kiss me. I stopped him. I said, "I am the attitude adjuster right now." He grinned and put his hands up. I grabbed his towel off of him, and he was ready. I smiled, then bit my bottom lip as I pushed him down and straddled him. He watched me the whole time and squeezed me. I moaned, and he pulled me down to stick his tongue in my mouth before squeezing my butt cheeks while we both exploded. He squeezed me and smelled my hair before he let me go. I laid there on top of him for a second before I sat up and rolled over almost falling on the floor, but Sénar caught me. I looked at him and thought how fine he was with his beautiful dark bronze skin and gray eyes.

The doorbell rang, and we both jumped up. I grabbed my pants, my shirt and put them on while Sénar grabbed some basketball shorts. He quickly opened the door then said, "Run to the bathroom; I'll bring you some stuff."

I quickly ran to the bathroom to see that Ken let London in, and she was coming up the steps as I ran into the bathroom. I quickly turned on the water, thinking about what just happened and giggled. I showered and got out to see a towel with some clothes and then went to my room. Cassidy was talking on the phone when I went to put my stuff away. I went downstairs to see Sénar and London were downstairs watching TV. I tried not to roll my eyes, but sometimes they had a mind of their own. Ken watched me from the kitchen table, so I tried to be on my best behavior. Sénar's attitude adjustment worked; he was in a much better mood and was even nice to London. He didn't want to go upstairs, but he didn't stop her from feeling all over him.

Sénar eventually said, "Babe, I'm tired, and I have to find what I'm going to eat. I'll call you later."

She didn't argue, she just kissed him, and he walked her to the door. Sénar made beef and broccoli with rice. I just ate the beef and broccoli with an avocado and went to bed. I woke up early and walked to school to avoid Tyrell and even Sénar because of our spontaneous attitude adjustment session, which by the way, we both needed. I thought about Tyrell and whether or not Sénar was over-exaggerating about his intentions to hurt him by having me as his girlfriend. I thought that would be absurd, but would it explain some of Tyrell's envy and hatred toward Sénar and vice versa. I dismissed my thoughts as it was too early to be playing inspector gadget. When I got to school, I quickly scurried to my first class and tried to avoid the possibility of running into any drama. I knew I couldn't run away from the truth forever, but today was Wednesday, and I refused to deal with it today. However, tomorrow I would talk to Tyrell and figure out if our relationship was worth fighting for or if it was just an evil plan to destroy Sénar and damage me in the process. When lunchtime came, I had to go to the cafeteria because I didn't bring lunch. I got in line and got a salad with some French fries. My table was empty, so I sat down to avoid going to my new spot and risk my fries being cold. Leah came and sat next to me while Tyrell talked with his boys.

I ignored her existence, but she still spoke, "Treasure, let's be friends again. I can come over, and we can hang out sometimes."

I laughed before I responded, "No thanks, Leah, I will pass, but it was sweet of you to ask." I ate my food and watched London whine about something while Sénar watched me. I wondered what Sénar thinks about when he watches me. Leah was still talking, but I heard nothing that she said because I was watching Sénar and London. Tyrell came and sat next to me. I snapped out of my trance when I heard Tyrell's stupid question, "What are you over here for? Why don't you go kick it with your brother and his girlfriend?" Leah started laughing before I could even respond. I chose my words wisely when I said, "I'd rather not kick it with him and his girlfriend or you and your girlfriend either." Tyrell grew angry and slapped my food on the floor, and some of it got on my clothes. I jumped up and wiped my clothes off and tried to walk away. Tyrell grabbed my arm and squeezed it. I yelped in pain and tried to snatch it away. Sénar was behind Tyrell before I knew it. They started arguing when Tyrell said, "Aye Sénar, mind your damn business and worry about your broad, and I'll worry about mine." Sénar flashed, "Get your fucking hands off her and let her go!" Tyrell let me go and pushed Sénar. I started to run, but I didn't want them to fight and get in trouble. I stood in between them to ask, "Do you guys want to be suspended and not play in the game? Stop acting like little kids!" Leah and London just watched as they both eyed one another. London grabbed Sénar, and he snatched his arm from her. Leah just watched as Tyrell tried to be tough and asked, "What are you gonna do, Sénar? You always worried about mine. I ain't worried about yours?" Sénar was infuriated, but he just smirked,

"She never fully belonged to you, and she never will." When Sénar walked off, I yelled, "Tyrell, you are such an asshole. I don't know why we are even doing this! Why don't you and Leah stop playing games, and you two be together!" He tried to grab me, but I pushed him away and ran to class. I was so angry, I told my cheerleading instructor I needed to leave a little early, and she nodded to indicate it was ok. Leah saw me talking to the instructor. We practiced, and Leah found the opportunity to ask, "Sénar really loves you, huh?"

I looked at Leah like the scum that she was and answered, "Why don't you worry about Tyrell. You will never get Sénar; he is stingy with his bomb D."

She was both shocked and angry because she knew I was telling the truth. I was almost ready to give her Tyrell since he seemed not to be able to choose between the two of us.

I gave my teacher eye contact to verify if it was ok to leave, she nodded her head as to say I can go. I quickly grabbed my belongings and swiftly walked home. I went to my room and threw my backpack on the floor.

My cellphone rang, it was Sénar. He asked, "Where are you Treasure?"

I yelled into the phone, "I am home Sénar!"

He hung up and I cried in my pillow until my phone rang again. I answered it yelling, "What?"

It was Tyrell, he asked, "Why are you yelling at me Treasure! Where are you?"

I was shocked that he was calling me. I replied, "I am sorry, I didn't mean to yell. I am at home Tyrell."

He was quiet and then asked, "Why did you leave? how did you get home?"

I answered, "Tyrell, I walked home. I am just tired of all the drama."

He was quiet again and then asked, "So what are you saying Treasure?"

I saw Sénar in my doorway glaring at me. I rolled my eyes and said, "I don't know Tyrell I-"

He cut me off, "Look, you always play like your innocent. I know your ass is not! Sénar's ass be ready to kill over your ass. So, if he wants you so bad, he is going to have to come through me! I'm not done with you, so you are not done with me!"

Tyrell was so angry, I started to cry and Sénar came in the room. He tried to snatch the phone from me, but I turned away from him. I said, "Tyrell-"

He cut me off again to ask, "Do you love me Treasure?"

I answered, "Yes, Tyrell."

He yelled, "Yes, Tyrell, what?"

I cried, "Yes, Tyrell, I love you!"

Sénar snatched the phone from me and threw it. Sénar yelled, "Treasure what the hell man! Stay away from his ass! You don't listen! This is bigger than just you!"

I went to grab my phone and Tyrell had not hung up yet. I picked the phone up and almost put it to my ear but saw the call abruptly end. I looked at Sénar and he was frantic like he had seen a ghost. He pleaded, "Treasure please leave him alone. End this shit before it gets out of hand. Man, for once just listen to me!"

I was frustrated, I didn't know what to do. I asked, "Why Sénar? Then what? I will be all yours? And then we will live happily ever after?"

I could tell he was hurting but I didn't care, so was I. I was confused and angry that I could not just be happy, either way everything was a mess. Sénar was so angry, he said, "Do whatever you want Treasure. You always do anyways."

He left me in my room on the verge of tears. His attitude adjustment didn't last very long as he was angrier than he was yesterday. He slammed my door as I sat on my bed and contemplated: *how or what I did to deserve such a chaotic complicated life. Was this all my fault?*

Could I have prevented this? Surely it was my fault. I deserved this and I would just deal with it like I dealt with everything else, ignore it. Simple, done deal, and problem solved. I got up to go downstairs when Cassidy opened the door, I knew if I stayed, I would take my frustration out on her. Before I could leave, she asked, "What did you do to Sénar?" I was shocked when I asked, "What do you mean?" She looked at me like she hated me and said, "Maybe you really are that stupid, huh? If you break Sénar's heart my daddy will kill you. Or maybe he will kill your momma first. Then you will be screwed up just like all of us." Cassidy laughed in my face and pulled her phone out. I left and ran downstairs. I looked in the living room; Sénar was not there. I looked in the garage and he was not there. I looked outside and seen his car, so I thought maybe he was in his room. He wasn't in his room either. I was going to go back down to look for him when he walked past me to go to his room, closing the door behind him. When I knocked on his door, he answered it, allowing me to walk in. He smirked before asking, "Did you come in here to adjust my attitude?" My heart started beating rapidly, I was alarmed at how calm he was. His eyes were dark, they were not the pretty gray eyes that admired me. They were dangerously dark while he gazed at me. Afraid, I called his name and he snapped, "What Treasure?" I backed up as he walked closer to me. I quickly asked, "Sénar are you ok?"

He shook his head no before he said, "No. Get out."

I tried to reason with him, but he screamed, "Get out!"

I started to cry as I ran out of his room. Cassidy came out to see what all the commotion was about. Even my mom came out and asked, "What's the problem?" I ran into the bathroom and Sénar went back into his room. My mom knocked on the bathroom door as I rinsed my face quickly to rid of the tears. I patted my face dry and answered the door.

My mom asked, "Treasure what is going on?"

I almost broke down and told my mom everything, but she already looked depressed and broken; I didn't want to further damage her. I answered, "Nothing, everything is fine momma." My mom got angry when she realized I was lying and said, "Treasure, dammit tell me what's going on?"

I snapped, "Nothing momma, I am fine!"

She got her feelings hurt and went back to her room. Sénar and Cassidy both looked at me like they hated me. I ran out of the house, I thought about running to Tyrell's house, but he wasn't even home. I just went for a walk and walked until I was so far from home, I had to force myself to go back. It was getting dark and I was starting to get a little worried about walking at nighttime. I saw a black car coming toward me and sure enough it was Sénar. He pulled over and told me to get in. I folded my arms and he roared, "Get in, Treasure!"

I pouted as I got into his car. Sénar softened his voice when he asked, "What were you thinking? It's about to be dark."

I folded my arms and pressed my lips together to keep from saying something smart. He drove to the taco truck and ordered 25 tacos. We waited while the lady just stared at me; I wish I could read her mind because she always saw me with Tyrell. I looked away in shame and waited for Sénar to come back. He got in and drove us back to the house.

He said, "Treasure, I don't want to see you get hurt. I know I am far from perfect, but I do have your best interest at heart. I know I have been selfish but it's for good reasons. Anyway, as I said you will do what you want anyway. Just don't ever leave like that again, you don't even have your cellphone."

I shook my head and said, "Sénar, you are crazy!"

He smiled my favorite smile before he replied, "Yeah, crazy about your ass!"

We pulled up to the house and went inside. Ken wasn't home and I was thankful, or things could have been much worse. I ate my tacos and went to bed, I was exhausted. The next morning Tyrell called my cellphone early in the morning, but I didn't answer. I waited twenty minutes to call him back while I got dressed to get ready for school. When I called him back, I expected him to have an attitude, but he said, "Treasure are you coming over?"

He asked in a sweet voice that I couldn't resist. I answered, "Yeah, I will be right there."

I walked out to see Sénar, he just rolled his eyes before I left the house to go across the street. Tyrell answered the door fully dressed but we still went back to his room. I sat down on his bed while he just stared at me. He asked, "Treasure, why do I feel like you are ok with the way Sénar feels about you?" I tried to answer without an attitude, "Tyrell I can not control how Sénar feels about me. He could be with any girl he wants Tyrell."

He smirked when he asked, "Even you?" I didn't like where the conversation was going. I answered, "No Tyrell, he can't but he can get Leah for sure. Do you ever ask her why she wants him so bad?" I could tell he was angry when he replied, "Oh yeah? Well, if he can get her, he can have her, but you, nah I will make sure he doesn't get you." I heard the malice in his voice and asked, "Tyrell why is that more important than me or our relationship?" He laughed when he answered, "You wouldn't understand Treasure, you would have to be me to understand. Let's go." Whatever he meant; I didn't like it because it felt wrong in so many ways. We picked Leah up and she was in a good mood. She spoke to both of us when she said, "Hey y'all!" We drove to school in silence only to pull up to the parking lot to see Sénar and London were arguing. Sénar was agitated as he walked off and she followed behind him. I got out of Tyrell's car and tried to go straight to class. Tyrell called me to come back, so I turned back around, and he kissed me. It felt genuine, so I kissed him back.

He said, "Don't leave without me today."

I shook my head in a yes motion then said, "Ok Tyrell."

I went to class and thought about how we would all get through this without killing each other. At lunch time, I went outside to eat and read a book while I ate a salad I made at home. Sénar came to sit with me and I was going to ask him why, but I didn't bother. I just continued to read my book. Sénar laid back and didn't say a word. I looked up from reading to see Tyrell and London talking. I tapped Sénar, he looked at me to ask, "What is it?"

"Look Sénar," I said while looking toward the two of them.

He glanced at London and Tyrell and shrugged his shoulders before he said, "I don't care", then went back to laying down. I had never seen those two talk before, so why now? Tyrell walked to meet Leah as the bell rang and London approached Sénar. She gave me a dirty look as I grabbed my stuff to get ready for class.

Sénar got up and London asked, "Why are you over here Sénar?"

I went to class but heard Sénar's answer, "Because you are getting on my nerves and I didn't want to be mean to you."

As I walked away, I could hear her get angry and ask, "You just wanted to be with her, huh? I should have never gotten with you, I thought you would be over her by now. So, am I not enough?"

He answered, "No."

I turned to see Sénar walk away from her. I wish I didn't hear their conversation; my heart broke for London because she tried to be enough. She overcompensated in every way and she still was not enough. I almost felt the same way with Tyrell. I wish we could be honest with one another but that just didn't seem realistic. In math class Leah was still in a good mood when she asked, "Treasure, are you aware that you are in the middle of a war?"

I looked at her like she was stupid when I asked, "What are you talking about now Leah?"

She laughed before she said, "It must be exhausting to play stupid so often."

I smirked at her then said, "You are the stupid one. You took your bully role to heart and now you are looking just as pathetic."

She laughed, "Ok, Bonquisha, who bones everybody. She even bones her brother."

I looked at her and to avoid punching her, I used my words when I said, "He is my coach, my chef, my doctor, my friend, and my attitude adjuster, but my brother, he is not."

She laughed and said, "Well damn, I'm sure he is because that's what Tyrell is for me, we should trade."

She smirked at me, but I didn't let her phase me. I had already accepted that her and Tyrell were more than buddies and I planned to address it, but she didn't need to know that. We both did our work and met up with Tyrell after school. We left before Sénar and London came out. Tyrell dropped Leah off and we drove home. When we got to Tyrell's house, he appeared agitated when he saw his mom's car in the driveway.

He said, "I wanted to go upstairs but my mom's home." I didn't care, I had no desire to go upstairs with him anyway.

I asked, "Tyrell what is going on? Why are we having all this drama?"

He laughed maliciously then said, "Treasure, I swear you act so dumb sometimes. You know damn well what's going on."

I really did not unless I was really that dumb. I asked, "Why are you with me Tyrell?"

He laughed again then said, "You know you are fine ass hell Treasure. You know you are special to me and you know you are special to Sénar. Hell, I knew there was something about you that drove him crazy, but it's the same thing that makes me not trust you."

I was offended when I asked, "Then why are you with me Tyrell, if you don't trust me?"

He stared at me like he hated me when he answered, "Because I fell in love with you too! And he can't have you! I'd rather we all suffer."

I was confused, "Tyrell you are scaring me. Why can't you just be with me and leave Leah alone, and forget about Sénar?"

Tyrell glared at me before he said, "You are selfish because you know the answer, but you pretend like you don't!"

I started to get angry when I had to defend myself, "No, I don't know the answer but apparently everyone else does. I am tired of not knowing and quite frankly I am starting not to care. You need to choose me or Leah. You can't have us both!"

He yelled, "Then you need to choose between me and Sénar!"

He yelled so loud, I got out of the car. Tyrell's mom opened the front door and demanded Tyrell come inside as I ran across the street. Sénar pulled up but I could see London following him in her car. I ran inside and I tried to appear normal, but I was devastated. I could not sort all this out without feeling overwhelmed. Ken saw how flustered I was and called me into the kitchen. I was about to explode when he demanded me to get him a beer. I had just walked in and was still trying to process the conversation I had with Tyrell. I went to the fridge to grab his beer way from the back. When I realized Ken was walking towards me as I was getting his beer, I quickly gave it to him. He still walked towards me, I closed the fridge and stood up to face him.

He whispered, "Tic toc, your time is almost up."

I was mortified, *what was Ken talking about?* He was so strange lately, I tried to maneuver around him, but he put his hand on my stomach right over my belly button. Ken said, "You are lucky you mean so much to my baby boy because I had big plans for you."

He laughed before I felt the need to run out of the kitchen and straight to my room. Sénar saw me run upstairs, he came to my room and called my name, "Treasure?" I was overwhelmed, I felt like the walls were closing in on me again and I could hear a million voices ripping me to shreds. Sénar grabbed me and called my name again, "Treasure?"

I snapped, "What?"

He looked me in my eyes to assure me, "Treasure, I will do everything in me to protect you, but you have to listen!"

I was on the verge of screaming when Sénar held me close to him and hugged me. He told me, "You are my inspiration from the day I first saw you. Treasure please don't crumble! I need you!"

I looked at him and before I could say anything Ken roared, "Get your ass up! Come here I need to talk to you!"

Sénar squeezed me and smelled my hair before he let me go. I jumped in my bed and went to sleep. I slept later than usual and still felt tired. I looked at the clock to verify how late it was compared to my usual wake up time and then I saw that I had ten missed calls from Tyrell. I called him back, but he didn't answer. I jumped up to get dressed and noticed Sénar and Cassidy were gone. Ken was coming out of the room and asked, "What are you still doin' here?"

I answered truthfully, "I overslept Ken."

He smirked and then said, "Let's go."

He took me to school. I saw Tyrell, Leah, London, and Sénar standing in the front of the school when Ken dropped me off. I was so disoriented; I didn't speak to anyone. I just went straight to class.

At lunch time London approached me, "You are one little sneaky bitch! I hope you get all that's coming to you!"

I ignored her in her psychotic state, she looked like she wanted to kill me, but my glare was far more promising. Sénar came in and refereed the situation, so I could get my food. I was about to snap; everything was unraveling, and I couldn't stop it. Everyone was in a state of fight or flight at lunch, there was so much tension, security and teachers were on high alert. London was talking with her friends and Sénar was talking with his as I got in line. Leah and Tyrell were coming in when I got my food and walked outside.

Tyrell followed me to ask, "Why do you want to eat outside?"

I looked at him before I answered truthfully, "So I don't have to deal with any drama Tyrell. I can just eat and go to class."

He just stared at me then replied, "Well, you didn't seem to mind when Sénar came out to sit with you."

I got an attitude, "Well, maybe he was avoiding the drama too. You and London seemed to get along just fine."

Tyrell became agitated when he replied, "Maybe because the people who are supposed to be with us are so into one another." He said it sarcastically.

I rolled my eyes, "Tyrell, I don't want to argue, ok? You want to sit with me, or do you want to sit with Leah?"

He thought for a second and looked back to see Sénar watching and walked with me to sit down. He said, "You know what? You and Sénar make a cute couple, I guess I'll give you two some space."

I whined, "Tyrell, please stop. I don't want to listen to you be a jerk."

He got angry and walked away. I was finally relieved when he did, I ate my lunch and went to class after. Leah sat next to me, but I pretended to not notice. I did my work and ignored her. With no practice after school I was happy to go straight home. Tyrell's mom was home, so he dropped me off and left probably to go see Leah, but I didn't care. I was happy to be home and Sénar came in shortly after me. He appeared agitated, so he went to the garage to work out. I followed him in to talk to him.

I asked, "Sénar what are we going to do with all the drama?"

Sénar looked at me and replied, "I already told you to leave Tyrell alone. That would solve a lot of drama and London knows if she touches you, I will leave her. If you want me to leave London alone, it's done."

I thought about calling his bluff but then I would have to deal with a single Sénar, and I just wasn't ready for that. Before I left, I asked, "Why are London and Tyrell talking lately?"

He shrugged his shoulders and answered, "I don't know, and I don't care. Maybe they are plotting something."

He said it with a nonchalant attitude, I turned to leave but first Sénar asked, "Can you braid my hair?"

I rolled my eyes before I answered, "I guess but don't take them down. Let me re-braid the braids so the parts will be the same and maybe no one will notice." He shook his head in irritation before he said, "Whatever." I braided his hair and we made dinner together for the first time in a long time. Even Ken observed us in the kitchen and shook his head. I went to bed right after dinner to avoid his demands and Cassidy's face. Friday, Tyrell waited for me to come out as I was later than usual. He complained as we went to pick Leah up, I ignored them both. Tensions were still high today, I made sure to make me a salad, so I didn't have to go to the cafeteria. The day went quickly as I avoided drama every chance I got. I rode with Tyrell and Leah to the game in silence. The game was horrible. Tyrell and Sénar were all over one another to the point where they called a flag on Tyrell because he pushed Sénar on the field and then they got in each other's faces. Their coach pulled them off the field and yelled at them. Sénar threw his helmet down and Tyrell went back onto the field. I knew Ken was watching and was probably angry Sénar got taken off the field. When Tyrell came off Sénar went in. Despite their efforts to keep them apart they still argued on the side lines. To make matters even worse, we lost the game and ruined our undefeated streak. It was an emotional loss; it was obvious that the animosity between Tyrell and Sénar had a lot to do with the loss. The coach yelled at Tyrell and Sénar waited for his turn to be yelled at. Tyrell came toward me and Leah and yelled, "Let's go!"

I didn't want to go with Tyrell, but Ken came by himself and London was all over Sénar as he was being chewed out for his performance. I reluctantly left with Tyrell. He drove like a maniac after he dropped Leah off. On the way home he took his frustration out on me. He yelled, "Your little boyfriend fucked up my play and he probably is fucking you too, huh? He has way too much confidence and the only reason is if he is screwing you, since he didn't deny it." We pulled up to his house and I got out and tried to cross the street to go home.

Tyrell grabbed me and said, "No. Let's go upstairs." I was scared to say no, he was so angry, I answered, "Tyrell ok, but please calm down first. You are really upset." He damn near drug me up the steps. When we got to his room he said, "Take your clothes off!" I said, "No. I don't want to. You are upset, I think I should go home Tyrell." He said, "Nah, give me a kiss." I kissed him even though his tone was scaring me. He kissed me back then bit my lip so hard, I pushed him off me. Somehow even though it hurt, it still aroused me. He saw the glimmer in my eyes and said, "Lie down Treasure. You over here fucking like a pro for them earrings. Talking about you wanna cum all of a sudden. Let me go down on you and make you cum like your girl Leah." I was offended but curious if he was any good at it. I love being licked but I wasn't sure why he chose this time to do it. He rushed me to take my cheerleading shorts off and laid me down. He put his face in between my legs and bit me. I screamed and punched him in the forehead, so hard he released me. I tried to get up and he slapped me so hard across my face, I flew back onto the bed. I quickly got up and tried to leave but he threw me back onto his bed. I was grateful for the little arousal I had early on because it provided slight moisture inside of me to lubricate my walls as Tyrell forced himself inside of me. I tried to push him off, but he wouldn't budge. He just continued to shove himself inside of me as I screamed in agony.

Tyrell roared, "Fuck that! This shit is mine. I am going to show you and him who you belong to!" He bit my neck until I screamed and pried his face away from me. He said, "You are playing with fire now." He exploded inside of me then pushed me down and pulled at my chain until he broke it off of me. I got up and tried to run out, but he snatched me back to say, "Nah, go clean yourself up first!"

He laughed carelessly before he said, "At least if you get pregnant, I'll know it wasn't an accident."

I quickly went to the bathroom and did as he said. I tried to rinse away my tears, but I was in so much pain, I couldn't stop them from falling. I cleaned myself up and put my shorts back on in the bathroom before I tried to run out. He ran behind me to ask, "What, you gonna tell your big brother on me?" I shook my head no and he let me leave. I saw Sénar's car and dreaded going inside. I could hear Ken yelling at Sénar in the kitchen when I came in. They both watched me as I tried to run up the stairs, Ken roared, "Bring your ass over here Treasure!" I couldn't hold my tears back as I walked into the kitchen. Sénar knew Tyrell had done something to me and became instantly angry. Ken saw Sénar's reaction when he noticed the bite mark on my neck and that I had been crying. He yelled, "Sénar get your shit together or I will pack up all our shit and bounce! I worked too hard to train your ass I am not going to watch you mess your future up over some pussy! Hell, you grew up on the shit!"

He snatched me by my shirt before he said, "You probably a little kinky bitch just like yo' momma, huh?"

I couldn't believe he was talking to me like that and he called my mom a bitch.

I answered him, "Maybe I am but I am just not as stupid or weak!"

Ken snatched me up by my neck, picking me up to put me on the counter, and slammed my head against one of the cabinets. He squeezed my throat forcing himself in between my legs and said, "You keep acting like a hoe, I am going to treat you like one and I got next!"

Sénar looked like a scared little boy when he asked, "Pops please, let her go! He did it on pur-" Ken cut Sénar off and said, "Shut the fuck up boy! I don't know why you so sprung on her ass anyway, didn't you already fuck her?" Sénar put his head down and lied to him when he answered, "No."

Ken said, "Yeah right, boy you mean to tell me you haven't got no pussy and you and Tyrell damn near ready to kill each other over her. Risking both of your futures? That shit must be good too. Umph maybe we can do her like we did Daisy or you ain't trying to share with me but you sharing with this lil' nigga? You better give her that act right, before I do it!"

They both noticed I was drained due to the lack of oxygen Ken was restricting from going to my brain with his hand around my neck. He let me go and I fell forward gasping for air as Sénar caught me before I hit the ground. Ken walked out of the kitchen without another word. Whatever screws I had holding me together, may have totally came loose. I was devastated, I had been raped, slapped, bitten, had my chain violently ripped off my neck, belittled, and choked almost to death. I was hanging on to life with short gasps of air, I heard so many voices in my head as I closed my eyes and laid back. I wanted to die; I didn't want to feel any more pain. The physical pain I was feeling I knew would subside, but the pain in my heart, soul, and mind; could never be erased. Sénar held me and gently slapped my face to wake me up.

He begged me to answer him, "Treasure? Treasure? Treasure!"

I responded in a weakened voice, "What?"

He laughed then said, "Knock, knock?"

I cried when I asked, "Who's there?"

He whispered, "Sénar."

I could barely say, "Sénar, who?"

He answered, "Sénar, the one who loves you."

Chapter 10

I woke up hearing Cassidy on the phone with Nevaeh, talking about going to LA with her to see Louie.

She said, "I ain't trying to be here all weekend with Treasure's trifling ass. Her ass is always in trouble and now she is getting Sénar in trouble too. Girl they lost the game last night because Sénar and Tyrell were fighting on the field. My dad is probably going to flip out and I don't want to be here for that shit."

I tried to ignore her as I lay in bed and reality set in. My whole body was sore including my face. I could hear Cassidy rummaging around to get her stuff ready to go to LA with Nevaeh.

She said, "I know you are awake. If something happens to my brother, I will make sure something happens to you!"

I winced at the malice in her voice, but I didn't say a word.

She hissed, "You are such a stupid little bitch."

I couldn't have agreed with her more, I felt stupid. She left as I lied in bed and cried until I heard my door open.

Sénar asked, "Treasure are you awake?"

I just laid there and ignored him. I didn't want to be bothered or hear him tell me he told me so. He came in any way to roll me over to see me, but I hid my face. He shook his head before he said, "Treasure, don't cry I am just here to help you, if you need me too."

I was hurt and angry when I replied, "I am fine! You have done enough Sénar. Go before you get yourself in more trouble!"

Sénar was frustrated but he tried to be patient with me when he said, "Treasure come on, get up."

I snapped at him and said, "No! I don't want to get up! I am going to lay here all day, ok?"

Sénar answered, "Not ok. Get up now, I ran a bath for you, and I want to make sure you are ok."

I was already exhausted, I didn't want to go back and forth with him, and I knew he was not going to give up.

I asked, "What if Ken sees us Sénar?"

He replied, "Let me worry about that, plus he is not here. Come on."

I had pajama pants on that I remembered Sénar helped me put on before going to bed. I could barely walk last night after all the things I had been through. Sénar helped me get up, he picked me up and carried me to the bathroom. He put me down on my feet and I stood up looking him in his eyes. I almost looked away, but his eyes were so pretty. Sénar gazed back at me when he pleaded, "Treasure, you need to listen sometimes. I don't want to lose you."

I didn't want to hear a lecture, so I smacked my lips as he scanned my face and neck. I had the urge to pee and I quickly left his observation to pee. I winced in pain as it burned a little. Sénar looked away in anger and allowed me the privacy to wipe myself. I was not shocked when there was blood on the tissue and soreness. I was scared to look down there because Tyrell had bit me, and it was really painful. I quickly put it in the toilet and flushed so Sénar wouldn't see it. He looked upset and waited for me to remove my clothes. He helped me with my shirt and scanned my body again.

He asked, "Treasure, did he hit you?"

He tried not to sound mad when he asked as he rubbed his hand on the side of my face where Tyrell slapped me. I didn't look him in his eyes when I answered, "No."

He snapped when he said, "Don't lie for him Treasure!"

I winced at his tone as he continued to observe me for damages. He looked at the welts on my neck along with the bruises and fingerprints on my neck. He had to decipher what Tyrell did and what Ken had done.

Sénar said, "Answer me Treasure and how did all these welts get on your neck?" He was getting angrier the more he observed me for injuries. I couldn't look him in the eye, I just looked away in hoped he would just take my silence as my answer. He called my name, "Treasure?"

I snapped back, "What Sénar?"

He demanded, "Answer me Treasure!"

I started to cry when I answered, "I hit him first! He bit my little man in the boat!"

Sénar was confused when he asked, "What?"

He thought about it for a second before he started to remove my pants and then got on his knees to examine my private area. He touched me gently and I still winced in pain. He was so angry when he said, "I am going to kill his ass and it's called a clitoris Treasure!" He shook his head and inspected it like it belonged to him. He said, "And it happens to be my favorite part of your treasure and I would have killed him, if he damaged it. I'm going to get ice for you in a second." He scanned my body one last time and asked, "Is there anything else you want to add to the list of reasons I want to kill his ass?"

I shook my head no because I couldn't imagine telling him the whole story of what Tyrell did to me. The way he stared at me he knew I was lying. I had to look away as the tears stung my eyelids.

He stood up and then threatened, "That's the last time he will ever touch you there or I'll kill both of you!"

He left the bathroom and I took my bra off and got in the water. I didn't say anything because I believed Sénar was crazy enough to do what he said. He left and came back with three small zip lock bags of ice; one for my face, one for my neck, and one for my little man in a boat that Sénar called a clitoris. I was scared to look at it, I never really took a good look at it anyway, but it was swollen and my coochie was sore. I almost thought about putting a piece of ice in there to soothe the burning sensation from the hot water. If I didn't know any better, I would think Tyrell was trying to get me pregnant after his little speech at the end of his terror. I was so hurt and humiliated, I couldn't even think about it without crying. Sénar laid a towel down and laid on the floor. I quietly cried while I tried to relax in the tub as Sénar got comfortable on the floor.

He said, "Treasure, I know I am not perfect, but I try to show you how I feel by my actions. I could tell you all day I love you, but the actions speak louder than words. Tyrell's actions are not love. He might tell you that, but he doesn't love you and even if he does, he rather hurt you to hurt me. He just wants to possess you, so I can't have you."

I thought how Sénar automatically assumed he can have me. What if I said no, I shook my head at the thought; knowing it was not an option.

I asked, "Sénar what makes you think you can have me?"

He laughed and answered, "Treasure, even if you refuse me, I will try forever until you are mine. We are still young, so there is only so much I can offer you, but one day I'll be a grown ass man and I will take care of you. Help you accomplish your goals, feed you, spoil you. I want to spend my life with you. We can have some little Sénars'. We can have a daughter and name her Jewel or Sapphire."

He chuckled while I was quiet and I listening to his fantasy. He asked, "Well, what are you thinking Treasure?"

I truthfully answered, "I don't know."

I was confused and lost for words. Sénar said, "Don't worry about all of that right now. We need to make it out of here alive first."

He laughed but he was serious. He said, "My pops is super mad at me and at you. You need to listen Treasure; I don't know what my dad is capable of until he does it. He is not done yet. I don't know what he will do but I know he is not done. No matter what happens I'll do my best to protect you, but I have to listen to him. Or we will both be in a worse situation. Just don't talk back or challenge him Treasure."

I was angry now because I remembered how Ken spoke to me last night and how he almost killed me. I said, "Sénar your dad needs to leave me alone. He is evil." Sénar didn't disagree, nor did he agree. He just laid there and relaxed while I drifted into my own thoughts. I cried at the thought of Tyrell's actions towards me; I would have never thought he would do that to me. I felt violated, humiliated, damaged and I was on the verge of breaking. I felt my neck and grazed my hand over my chest to feel the empty space where my name should be on my chain. Once again, I was without my chain; the first time was when I lost Tyrell's trust and this time, I lost myself. I started to cry and Sénar got up.

He looked concerned when he said, "Treasure, it's just a necklace. I will get you another one."

I snapped at him, "It's not just a necklace; neither was the one you broke! I lost something both times they were ripped off me."

Sénar got defensive when he said, "Yeah well, I didn't do it violently and I didn't do it to hurt you. I just didn't want to see it because he doesn't deserve you!"

I yelled, "You don't either Sénar! If I can forgive you than I can forgive him!"

Sénar got up to leave because he didn't want to talk anymore and neither did I. I finished taking my bath and got out but there were no clothes, I sighed and thought I would lose my mind if Sénar tried some crazy crap right now. I left the restroom in a towel and went to my room where there was an outfit neatly folded on my bed. I shook my head because Sénar was really something else, I didn't know what to do with him. I was so confused; I didn't know whether to love or hate him. He was everything Tyrell was not, and Tyrell was everything

Sénar wasn't. I did not dream of being with Sénar since I was a little girl. I didn't wait to be in love with him like I did Tyrell. Sénar just knocked down any barriers that were in his way and now I and Tyrell were the only barrier left. My cellphone rang and I knew it was Tyrell, but I wasn't ready to talk to him.

It rang so many times, I just answered, "Hello?" Tyrell was breathing in the phone and said, "Treasure, did you tell your little boyfriend on me?"

I could feel the tears burning my eyelids when I answered, "No, Tyrell. Is that really why you are calling? Is that really all you have to say?" I was so angry and hurt. He responded, "Well, I just needed to know if I am going to have to beat his ass or not."

I yelled, "That's all you care about, huh? You are so selfish Tyrell, I can't-"

He cut me off and said, "No, you are selfish and play to many damn games! Do you belong to me or not? Do you want to be with me?" I was quiet when he yelled, "Treasure!"

I snapped, "What?"

He snapped back, "Don't talk to me like that! You want to be with me or not?"

I yelled, "I don't know anymore!"

He hung up in my face and I cried. All he cared about was himself and his war with Sénar. He didn't care that he had violated me and abused me. He probably thought I deserved it. Maybe I did deserve it, maybe this was all my fault, and this was my karma for being with him and Sénar. I stuffed my phone in the drawer, I didn't want to talk to him anymore. I was still trying to deal with the aftermath of last night. Once again Sénar had to play doctor and I was tired of being his patient. I was just tired; life was too complicated to just be fifteen. How do people make it to be an adult with their sanity, I have no idea, but at this rate I felt like I may not be able to find out. I heard the door slam downstairs and Ken roaring Sénar's name.

I heard Sénar answer, "Yes sir!" Through the door I could hear Ken yelling at Sénar from downstairs. I cracked the door, so I could hear what Ken was saying to Sénar.

Ken yelled, "You better get over her ass! I don't care how much you think you love her! You better find a Treasure look alike if you have too. You can't even keep her from running across the street! She is just like Diamond's ass! I will cut her heart out and give it to you before I watch you throw your life away!" I heard a lot of noise right before Ken called my name. I jumped from the tone in his voice. I hadn't seen him since he choked me, and I was so scared to face him while he was so angry. I slowly and cautiously walked down the steps dreading having to face Ken. I saw Sénar getting up off the floor as I reached the bottom of the stairs. I could tell he was hurting but he hid it from me by looking away.

Ken glared at me when he yelled, "Get over here Treasure!" He put his finger in my face before he said, "Oh, I see Sénar can't tame your little wild ass, but I can!" I didn't talk back or challenge him. It was like he could sense my fear on top of my weakened state and was all over me. My back was against the wall as he continued his tongue lashing, "I'm going to pick you up and drop you off at school every day this week and watch you like a hawk myself for the next two weeks! I'll be your babysitter!" Ken laughed at Sénar and pushed him back down to the ground. He then said, "Get your ass up! If this shit don't work I guess y'all both going to be assed out."

Sénar looked like fire would shoot from his ears as he picked himself up off the ground. He slowly approached me as my back was still against the wall. Sénar glared at me then said, "You don't listen! You are on your own for the next two weeks. I can't protect you from him, if you don't listen. If you're not careful you will end up just like Daisy. Is that what you wanted?"

I was instantly offended, I pushed him away. I tried to run, but he grabbed me from behind and squeezed me. He said, "I am sorry

Treasure!" He rubbed my hair then said, "Just do what he tells you to and don't talk back. Don't have an attitude, stay out of his and Cassidy's way. Don't do anything or offer anything unless he asks for it."

I was scared when I asked, "Sénar is he going to-"

He cut me off and said, "I don't know ma. Like I said he has to dominate everything around him and if you don't want it to be in that way then you need to follow my instructions."

He knew what I was going to ask him, his speech was pressured, and he looked stressed out. Ken yelled Sénar's name as he came down the stairs. Sénar released me and answered, "Yes sir!" Ken roared, "Let's go!" Sénar immediately left my side to leave with Ken out the door. I wanted to run away and never return but I was scared I would end up worse off. I went to my room and cried while I wrote in my diary until I fell asleep. I did not get out of my bed until Monday morning unless it was to use the bathroom.

Monday morning, I brushed my teeth and got dressed then waited downstairs. I did not want to ride with Ken, but I knew he would keep his word. Sénar and Cassidy left for school. Cassidy smirked at me before leaving, and Sénar just shook his head. Ken came down and took me to school. I felt miserable, I skipped dinner Monday, Tuesday too and avoided everyone but Wednesday I was overwhelmed. After school, I stayed in my room until I smelled food. After having skipped dinner in the last few days, I was willing to face reality just to eat dinner. While we all ate dinner, I could not even look anyone in their eyes. I felt fat, stupid, ugly, and everything all the girls called me, I felt I was. Sénar stared at me in discomfort as I struggled to maintain some dignity. I wasn't really sure why Ken insisted on taking me to school. It wasn't until Thursday that I realized Tyrell and I barely spoke, since I ate my lunch outside, and he didn't dare speak to me in front of Ken.

Leah noticed and said, "Damn, Sénar's daddy, is your babysitter now?"

I rolled my eyes at her; I was comfortable not having her speak to me all week. She had a gold chain on her neck that read Leah in cursive, just like mine did but with her own name. Tyrell never gave me mine back; I tried to act like I didn't notice and ignored her question. I was over her nosey self; I just wanted to go home. She waited for an answer, but I never gave her one. I went to my next classes with an attitude and did everything to avoid Leah, Tyrell, and London. After school, the practice was short, but since the boys didn't have practice, Sénar was already gone after my short practice. Tyrell walked up to me before I could escape him and said, "Damn, I have to compete with Ken now too?"

I rolled my eyes at him, he grabbed my arm and asked, "Treasure what's your problem, don't ignore me."

I snapped when I replied, "Tyrell, I got in trouble, remember! You treated me like some whore off the street!"

Everyone was starting to look when he whispered, "Lower your voice!" He was taking advantage of Sénar being gone; he whispered, "Don't ever mention that shit again. Your ass deserved it! And you hit me first!"

I snatched my arm away from him when I said, "You bit-"

Tyrell roared, "I don't want to hear that shit! Leah, let's go!"

I ran out to the parking lot with Tyrell and Leah behind me; Ken was waiting impatiently. Leah waved at Ken, and he waved back but glared at Tyrell before we pulled off. He smirked before he said, "That Leah, sure is friendly. I am sure Tyrell thinks so too." I ignored Ken's remark to avoid making him angry. He smirked at me again and then proceeded to take me home. Sénar was sitting on the couch when we got home but once he saw us walk in the door, he got up to go to the garage to workout. Ken told me to get him a beer and make him a sandwich. I was irritated but I just put my backpack down and did as I was told. There was chicken salad in the fridge, so I used it to make Ken a sandwich. I gave it to him and ran upstairs after.

Before I knew it, the week was over, and I couldn't be happier. They won the game because Tyrell and Sénar avoided each other the entire game. I rode home with my mom and Ken while Leah and Tyrell left together. London followed Sénar home after the game to go celebrate with the team, and I went to sleep.

Saturday morning, Ken came in my room to tell Cassidy to pack her bags for a couple of days. She did not ask questions; she just did as he said, he didn't speak to me. Ken sent Cassidy and Sénar on the train to Northern California to see Chino. He wouldn't let me go even though Sénar asked for me to go, I could tell he was worried. Ken purposely sent them away. My mom was so distant; she didn't even seem to care; she barely spoke to me. I tried to stay in my room as much as possible. My mom made dinner the next few nights, but I barely ate as we all ate in silence. I made sure to go upstairs before my mom. On Tuesday afternoon, the house was quiet, but I still barely wanted to leave my room. I didn't know where Ken was, and I didn't want to see him or do any of his demands. I poked my head out the door to listen for sound or movement. When I didn't hear anything; I snuck down the steps. When I reached the bottom Ken was sitting at the kitchen table. I quickly tried to turn around, so that he didn't see me.

He had already seen me before he said, "Come here, Treasure."

I wanted to run back to my room, but I knew I couldn't. I slowly walked towards Ken and answered, "Yes, Ken?"

He demanded, "Get me a beer, Treasure."

I quickly went to the fridge to get his beer way from the back, by the time I reached it, Ken walked up to me to grab it. He cornered me between the wall and the fridge. He whispered in my ear, "You like being punished, huh?" I quickly tensed up and braced myself for what was next. I closed my eyes as he smelled my hair running his hand down my face, neck, and breast. Before he could reach my coochie, I squeezed out from around him and ran out of the kitchen.

He laughed as I ran out and raced to my room. I was mortified, Ken was much bigger than Tyrell and Sénar, if he wanted me, I would not be able to stop him. My heart raced as I laid down and wished myself faraway until I fell asleep.

When I woke up, I went to use the restroom. I noticed it wasn't as clean as it usually was. There was hair on the sink and brushes, the trash can was full, and there was toothpaste stuck to the sink. After I brushed my teeth and washed my face, I cleaned the sink so there would be no more crusted toothpaste, and then I wiped the counter off. I shook my head, not realizing how much Sénar did around the house. When I went back to the kitchen, there were so many dishes in the sink. Ken came into the kitchen shortly after me, and I quickly tried to leave.

Ken stopped me and said, "Nope, clean this kitchen and then make me some of the tuna you had Sénar make."

I didn't argue with him; I did as I was told. I washed the dishes, dried them, and put them away as Ken watched me. I did not show any fear, but I was obedient without an attitude. I cut the onions and pickles then made the tuna. I made him one sandwich, and he asked, "Do I look like a little boy to you? I need at least two and cut them in half."

I made him another one only because he asked as I remembered Sénar told me not to do anything extra for him unless he asked. I followed Ken's instructions and quickly made the extra sandwich then left the kitchen to watch TV. Ken watched my every move, and it made me uncomfortable, but I did my best to ignore him. He got up after he ate to go upstairs, glaring at me before he went up. He came back down shortly after and left out the front door. I watched TV until my mom came down. Ken had been gone for a couple of hours, so I was way more relaxed now. I walked into the kitchen to greet my mom, but she looked tired and annoyed with me.

She reluctantly said, "Hey, Treasure," without giving me eye contact. I got upset when I asked, "Am I bothering you, mom?"

She snapped at me, "Yes! You are hardheaded! Everyone else has to suffer, not just you!"

She grabbed her wine and went to sit at the table. I was hoping she went back to her dungeon, but she continued her tongue lashing, "Ken is tired of Sénar and your stupid little boyfriend fighting! He is also tired of you coming back looking like a god damn whore, when I swore to him you weren't! You are just like your trifling ass daddy! You make me sick!"

I laughed at her then replied, "I'm sure he treated you better than Ken!"

She got in my face when she said, "Oh, and Tyrell treats you so well, huh?"

She laughed, "Sénar treats you better than him. You better leave Tyrell's ass alone before you get us all killed or before Tyrell kills you first!" My mouth fell open in shock when she spat her words out at me. I almost told her about Sénar, but in her little sick mind, she would probably rather me be screwing Sénar than Tyrell. I responded, "I'll be fine, Momma. I'm glad you seem to care."

She laughed and said, "I don't care anymore. That's why I barely come out of my room. Do whatever; you are the one that will have to deal with the consequences. I am tired of dealing with them for you!"

Before I could say anything, she left back to her room. I was so angry with her; she was like a little kid trying to blame me for her bad choices. It was starting to get dark; Ken had been gone a long time, and I couldn't be happier. I made myself a sandwich and went to bed.

In the morning, I got up to brush my teeth and wash my face before getting dressed. I was coming down the stairs to see Ken open the door with his litter behind him. Sénar was the last to come in, and we locked eyes instantly. Everyone had bags in their hands except Ken. When I saw Chino, I noticed how mature he had gotten, and he looked really great. Sénar saw me as I noticed Chino and rolled his eyes. Cassidy smacked her lips and rolled her eyes too as I came down. Ken walked past me to go upstairs, but he glared at me without speaking. I looked away from him as I reached the bottom of the steps. The silence was awkward, so I acknowledged both Sénar and Chino by saying, "Hey guys." Chino replied, "Hey Treasure," before he went upstairs with his bags with Cassidy going up behind him. Sénar gazed at me and then put his bags down. This was the longest we had ever been apart. Sénar asked, "Are you ok?" I nodded my head, yeah, and couldn't hold back my excitement to see him. I hugged him, trying not to cry as he squeezed me and smelled my hair. He quickly let me go when he saw Ken coming down the stairs.

Ken roared, "Treasure, go get me a beer, and Sénar go put your shit up first! Damn!"

Sénar picked his bags up, "Yes, sir!", he said as I ran to get Ken a beer way from the back. I gave it to him, and he whispered, "You keep playing games, you gonna end up just like Daisy." I quickly left the kitchen and ignored Ken's threat. I bet he wanted to do all those things to me, but I would rather die than to let him. I kept my comment to myself and scurried away into the living room. I didn't want to deal with Cassidy because it was too soon, so I just watched some TV. It wasn't even twenty minutes since Sénar had come back that the doorbell rang. I opened the door to see London looking her best and eager to see Sénar. We rolled our eyes at each other as she let herself in, and her friend she brought for Chino followed behind her. As she passed by, "Hey, Treasure, long time no see," she said with a genuine smile. I smiled back at her, "Hey, Mia." I then looked upstairs and saw that Sénar was waiting for them at the top of the stairway. I rolled my eyes at him then went back to watching TV and ignoring Ken. He eventually went upstairs, which made it easier to relax. It wasn't even an hour, and the doorbell rang again. I got up to answer it, confused as to why it was ringing again. I opened the door to see Louie, Travis, Latosha, and Lil' James. I was surprised, but I was happy to have some company. I greeted everyone and hugged Lil' James as me and Latosha walked over to the couch.

Louie followed and asked, "Sénar is up there, right?"

I answered, "Yeah, but they have company."

Louie asked, "Can you go get him for me?"

I smacked my lips and answered, "No. I don't want to disturb their little party."

Louie insisted, "He doesn't know I was coming down; it's a surprise."

"Girl, go get cho' man!" Latosha said playfully.

I hesitated but went upstairs anyway and knocked on Sénar's door. Chino answered the door with no shirt on and a huge grin on his face. He seemed embarrassed when he saw that it was me and straightened up before he asked, "What's up, Treasure?"

I heard Sénar jump up to come to the door; he asked, "What's up, ma?"

I quickly said, "You have company downstairs."

I turned to walk away but Sénar came out of his room to ask, "Who is down there?"

I looked at him with an attitude, "It's a surprise." I said it sarcastically. Sénar asked, "Why you got an attitude?" I stared at him like he was dumb before I said, "I don't!"

Before I could turn away, I saw London observing our conversation. I went back downstairs, and I told Louie, "I think he is coming."

He snickered and said, "Thanks, Treasure."

When Sénar came down to see that it was his cousins, he got super excited. They hugged and did their handshakes as London came down to observe who was here for Sénar. When Sénar hugged Latosha, Lil' James jumped off my lap and into Sénar's arms. London folded her arms in jealousy. Latosha noticed, "Sénar, who is she?" She asked bluntly. Sénar looked back to see London behind him and reluctantly introduced her as "London," and she corrected him when she said, "I am his girlfriend, London." Sénar tried not to roll his eyes, but he didn't correct her either. He never referred to her as his *girlfriend*, but she always corrected him, and he never corrected her. Chino and Mia came down, and Louie was even more excited to see Chino. It turned into a hug-fest and even Cassidy came in to see what the commotion was downstairs. The doorbell rang again. Then came Ken yelling, "Sénar!" Chino opened the door as Sénar answered to Ken. Sénar responded, "Yes, sir?" Ken asked, "What the hell is going on in here?" Sénar chuckled before he answered, "Oh, Louie, and them came to visit pops."

Ken shook his head and then said, "It looks like a damn party in here. Yo' ass is still making Thanksgiving dinner. I don't care who is here."

Ken and Sénar laughed before Ken went back upstairs. Ken managed to glare at me before returning to his throne. It was the night before Thanksgiving, and there was a whole lot of us. Ken came back downstairs to whisper something to Sénar then gave him some money as him and my mom left out the front door. She waved at everyone before they left. Sénar's smile was so mischievous; I wonder what Ken had told him. Before I knew it some of Sénar's friends came from the college Halloween party that we had went to with drinks in their bags. Everyone seemed to know me but kept asking who London was. All night London had to reassure herself she was his *girlfriend*. Everyone either had a drink or was smoking a blunt in the backyard. I was sitting and talking with Latosha as she noticed one of Sénar's friends that she thought was cute. She told me to hold Lil' James while she made a drink and talked to him. Sénar came in to look for me when Lil' James saw him, he squeezed me and then said, "Mine!" Sénar put his fists up, and Lil' James giggled.

Sénar asked, "What, you a babysitter now too?"

I rolled my eyes at him and replied, "None of these people are here for me, except this little guy." Lil' James squeezed me, and I squeezed him back.

Sénar smiled at us and said, "We gonna have one of those one day."

I smacked my lips and asked, "You mean you and London, right?"

Speaking of the devil, London came behind Sénar and whined when she said, "Sénar?"

He rolled his eyes and snapped, "What London?"

She ignored his attitude and begged, "Come on, babe." She had a drink in her hand. Sénar said, "When Latosha comes back, come hit the blunt Treasure." When Latosha did come back, she had a drink and a grin on her face. I gave her Lil' James and went to hit the blunt. Sénar was happy to see me when I came out; he had a half a blunt saved for me to smoke. I was high after hitting it only three times and tried to go back inside. Sénar complained, wanting me to stay outside with them. London was agitated as she pulled on Sénar's arm to discourage him from focusing on me. Chino noticed and shook his head while he chilled with Mia. The doorbell rang, which gave me an opportunity to escape Sénar. I opened the door to see who it was and almost closed it when I saw Tyrell's face. I took a deep breath and quickly went outside to avoid anyone seeing him. The porch light came on, and Tyrell saw my eyes.

He asked, "Damn y'all having a party? Your eyes are red, are you high?"

I just rolled my eyes and said, "Yes." They were both yes answers, so I didn't bother explaining. Tyrell got upset and had a look of disgust on his face as he asked, "Wow, you get high now?"

I was offended by his facial expression and his stupid question when I responded, "Tyrell, what do you want?"

He instantly got upset when he replied, "You use to be different from all the other girls; now you are just like the rest of them."

I was feeling myself after taking almost a week and a half to gain some self-confidence back. I responded, "Thanks, is that it, Tyrell?"

He flashed, "So what, we are done now?"

I folded my arms and said, "Tyrell, this is not the best time; let's talk another time."

Tyrell snapped, "No. Let's talk now!"

He pulled me by my arm and tried to guide me across the street, but I told him, "Tyrell, I can't go to your house!"

He yelled, "Why?"

I tried to explain to him without him getting upset, but he still pulled me toward his house. I yelled, "I can't go, Tyrell!"

He yelled back, "Oh, so you can have a house full of people, but you can't come across the street to my house?"

I almost gave in and went because he was so adamant when Sénar came out of the house. He looked like he wanted to kill both of us. Tyrell ignored him and tried to force me to go with him, but I knew I definitely could not go now that Sénar had come out. I snatched my arm back from him and said, "Tyrell no, I can't! I'll call you, and we could talk on the phone."

Tyrell was pissed off, so he grabbed me and kissed me. Sénar lost it; he pulled Tyrell and me apart from each other with so much force that he and Tyrell started tussling immediately. Louie and Chino ran out to break them up, Louie grabbed Sénar and Chino grabbed Tyrell. Tyrell pushed Chino, and Chino snapped pushing him back, but before they could fight, Travis ran out to square up with Tyrell. It was obvious that Tyrell was outnumbered, and I was worried for his safety. I screamed, "Just go, Tyrell!" Sénar roared, "Treasure go in the house! Now!"

I started to argue with him, but the look in his eyes sent me to my room crying. I could hear him tell Tyrell not to ever put his hands on me again and never come to our house again. Tyrell laughed in his face, and everyone held Sénar back, telling him to chill. I ran to my room, embarrassed and angry at them both. Sénar came to my room, furious, and slammed the door behind him. I turned away and put my face in my pillow to avoid looking at him.

He called my name, "Treasure!"

I snapped at him, "What?"

He bent down and got into my face. I could smell the alcohol on his breath when he yelled, "You know what!" I pouted and looked away from him.

He grabbed my chin but gently and said, "Stay away from him! If he comes here again, I will beat his ass!"

I yelled back at him, "Well, London's here!"

We heard a knock at the door, and of course, it was London. Sénar was agitated and tried not to be mean to her when he said, "London go back downstairs."

She pouted, making him angry when he demanded, "Go London!" She got upset but went back downstairs. He closed the door and replied, "So what, I told you if you wanted to replace her, I would be ecstatic, but you want to play games! Tyrell already had his chance fair and square! He messed up! Plus, I know he can't please you like me. And he doesn't know how to treat you!"

I was annoyed with him when I asked, "Oh, and you do?"

Sénar almost exploded when he said, "You don't listen! I try to protect you, I try to be here for you, but you keep pushing me away!"

I folded my arms, "Sénar, how about you focus on your *girlfriend*, London," I said it sarcastically. He glared at me, and I glared back at him. He was so frustrated, he turned around and left. I was angry that he could just return to his little girlfriend while I sat here and suffered. The door opened, and Sénar came in, locking the door behind him.

He said, "Take your clothes off." I started to argue with him, but Treasure number two took over.

I removed my pants first, making Sénar drop to his knees and kiss my coochie like he was in love with it. He laid me down, taking my shirt off, leaving my bra on, and proceeded to work his magic. He even did his two-finger hole stunt but just a little more aggressive this time, speeding up my orgasm. Climax was a thing of the past; I grabbed my pillow and screamed into it.

Sénar asked in a seductive voice, "You want A for ass down or B for bent over?" Out of breath, I answered, "B." He immediately flipped me over and did it to me doggy style until I screamed into my pillow again. I felt us explode at the same time. Sénar looked relieved and back to his normal confident, goofy self again.

He said, "Damn Treasure." I shook my head at him because he was really too much. I got stuff to shower, Sénar went to grab boxers, and we went in together to shower. He quickly showered and put back on the same clothes. He left and locked the door behind him as I got out. I didn't want to put the same clothes on, so I put on some pink Puma sweats and a T-shirt. I went outside with everyone, and Sénar was grinning ear to ear. Chino stared at Sénar and then at me while Louie just shook his head. London clung to Sénar like glue as we all smoked and chilled. I was starting to get tired when I noticed Sénar walking London to the door. I went upstairs; where me, Latosha, and Lil' James slept in my bed and Cassidy in hers. I didn't care about anyone else's sleeping arrangements.

In the morning, I was thirsty and went downstairs to get something to drink and noticed Sénar sprawled out on the couch. He looked like he had passed out, he woke up and saw me watching him sleep. He quickly got up to come to me and asked, "You good, ma?"

I looked at him questionably and answered, "Yeah, I'm good, Sénar."

He grabbed me and smelled my hair; I didn't push him off; I just said, "Stop it." The house was still sleeping, so Sénar asked me if I wanted to go to the store with him. He was smiling at me, and I couldn't help but blush. I answered, "Yeah, I guess." I went to get dressed and we went to Walmart. We walked every aisle to grocery shop for Thanksgiving dinner. We even got some hygiene products when Sénar asked, "You gonna get band-aids for your kitty cat?" He chuckled, I ignored him but grabbed some anyway to put them in the basket. My period was all jacked up, I never knew if or when it was coming; it was frustrating, and I would ask the doctor about it on my next appointment. Everything came up to almost 200 dollars, as we were walking out, we saw Tyrell and his mom walking in. They both had a look of disgust on their faces when they saw us. Tyrell made sure to mad dog Sénar and did not even speak to me. I just looked away to avoid getting my feelings hurt. I sat in the car while Sénar loaded the groceries in the trunk.

When he got in on the way back to the house, he said, "I can't stand Tyrell's ass. I don't know what you see in his spoiled ass."

I smacked my lips and said, "I don't know what you see in London's pale skinny ass." He laughed and said, "Damn, you cold-blooded."

I rolled my eyes at him as we pulled up to see London's car parked in front of the house as she waited for Sénar. I smirked at him, and he sighed, then said, "Damn, it's too early for this shit."

I laughed at him as he prepared himself to deal with his stalker. Mia stayed the night, but Sénar made sure to send London home. London came to the car when we got out. Sénar told me to go get Chino and Louie to help him, so I went inside to get the boys. I knocked on Sénar's door and Chino answered with no shirt on; I also couldn't help but notice his morning excitement. Chino hid himself, and I giggled before saying, "Sénar needs y'all to help with the groceries."

I went to my room to see Lil' James and Latosha playing while Cassidy still slept. I gave Latosha stuff to take a shower and took Lil' James with me downstairs to watch TV. Everyone came downstairs while the boys helped Sénar.

Mia said, "Good morning, Treasure."

I smiled at her and replied, "Good morning Mia."

Nevaeh looked at us both strangely. London rolled her eyes at me and greeted her friend, "Hey, girl."

She sat down, cutting her eyes at me and said, "I cannot stand your ugly black ass Treasure."

Lil' James looked at her and then made a funny noise at her. Nevaeh laughed, and Mia just looked shocked at London's disrespect. Latosha came in shortly after and felt the tension in the room as she sat down.

Sénar startled me when he called my name, "Treasure?"

I snapped, "What?"

He stared at me, then said, "Come, help me."

London quickly got up as I handed Lil' James to Latosha to go help Sénar in the kitchen. London said, "Babe, I can help you."

Sénar nicely told her, "Nah, babe Treasure's got it, she knows how I like my potatoes and vegetables cut. I got a lot of stuff to cook, so I don't have time to show anyone how right now. So, just sit pretty."

Nevaeh chimed in, "Oh, you are not going to put a show on for London, Chef Sénar?"

He ignored Nevaeh's question and walked back to the kitchen. Louie called Nevaeh, and she went upstairs as I followed Sénar to the kitchen. Sénar had me cut so many different vegetables, from collard greens to celery, onions, bell peppers, garlic, and potatoes. The boys sat and watched me and Sénar work as a team to tackle both breakfast and thanksgiving dinner. London, Mia, and Nevaeh came to sit at the kitchen nook and observe us as well. London was agitated but she said, "Babe, I didn't even know you be cooking like that."

The boys tried not to laugh as Sénar flexed his muscles and said, "It's Chef Sénar babe, you didn't know, but now you know." He smiled seductively, and she squirmed in her seat. I rolled my eyes as I was annoyed with their conversation, but I kept quiet.

London said, "Well, Treasure is more fitting to help since she looks more like a raggedy slave girl."

Cassidy walked in, and Latosha ran in after little James to also hear London's comment. Everyone impatiently waited on my response. I shrugged my shoulders, "Then that would make Sénar my *Masta!*" I said it seductively, causing Sénar to shiver with excitement.

London jumped up, and Sénar quickly said, "Sit down, babe, you started it."

She sat down while everyone dealt with their emotions separately. London was still mumbling under her breath when Sénar said, "I don't want no drama London, leave her alone, or I am going to send you home."

Sénar handed out plates and made London's plate. She kissed him and quietly apologized. After everyone ate, Sénar and I cleaned the kitchen and finished prepping for dinner. It seemed like it took forever, but it was a process that would be worth it in the end when it was time to eat. When we were done, Sénar chin upped me and said, "Thanks, ma."

I smiled at him before I said, "It's cool." We all smoked and chilled in the living room after. My mom and Ken came home before the food was finish. When my mom came in, she said, "Hello," and waved to everyone before she went upstairs. Ken came into the living room to be nosey and saw almost everyone was booed up, except me.

Ken said, "Come here, Treasure."

Sénar looked uncomfortable as I got up and walked over to Ken. I said, "Yes, Ken."

He said, "Come get me a beer and make me one of them grill cheese sandwiches you made for me when Chef Sénar was gone." He laughed and walked into the kitchen, and I followed. I wanted to say no, but I knew that was not an option. I grabbed him a beer way from the back to give to him before making two grill cheese sandwiches. He watched my every move as I purposely only gave him one sandwich. I went to cut the other one in half and left it on the plate by the stove. Ken eating his sandwich, came into the kitchen and set his empty beer bottle on the counter. He scanned me up and down before he said, "Get me another beer, Treasure." I took a deep breath before turning around and grabbing him another beer way from the back. When I came back up, he was so close to me; I could barely even move. I handed him his beer and squeezed from between him and the fridge door to grab the pan off the stove. Ken raised his eyebrow at me as I headed to the sink to grab the soap and wash the pan. I quickly dried it, before putting it away as Ken glared at me.

I grabbed the extra grilled cheese sandwich and ran into the living room. I gave half to Lil' James and the other half to Sénar as I watched Ken glare at me again before going up the stairs. Sénar tried to keep his composure, but I could tell he was bothered. Even Chino noticed, and just shook his head.

When the food was finally ready, everyone piled into the kitchen happy to eat. Everyone found a seat while Sénar sat on the counter and ate with Louie standing on the side of him. Everyone marveled at how delicious the food was but especially London. She was shocked that Sénar could cook like that, and everyone just stared at her in disbelief. Sénar has never cooked for her before; now, she had another reason to be a stalker. Even my mom seemed to be annoyed with her. She waited for London to finish her praising of Sénar then said, "The greens were amazing Sénar, as was everything else. Hopefully, Treasure learned something." I rolled my eyes, and London seemed offended. Ken shook his head in irritation, and Sénar replied, "She helped Carmel." My mom got up to avoid Ken's glare to say, "Thanks for dinner. Goodnight, everyone." Everybody said goodnight to my mom, except London and Ken. My mom grabbed her wine with a beer for Ken and headed upstairs. We all ate and watched movies after.

The rest of the weekend was eventful and full of laughter despite all the many personalities present. Tyrell called me a couple of times to argue over the weekend. There was a couple of awkward moments, but the most awkward was when I snuck out to meet Tyrell's cousin from Jersey to quickly hug Tyrell before sneaking back in the house, hoping Sénar didn't see me.

When we returned back to school, I walked there and home every day of the week. I managed to avoid drama by eating outside during lunch and avoiding everyone. Sénar would come and check on me with London clinging on to him. On game night, Sénar and Tyrell avoided each other on the field and played hard. They managed to win this game, making everyone happy as the last game was horrible. When the game was over, Tyrell walked up to me at the same time as Sénar.

Tyrell asked, "You coming with me?"

I shook my head no and answered, "No. I am going home, Tyrell. Congrats on the game. Y'all have fun."

He shrugged his shoulders and left with Leah. London asked, "Sénar, we are dropping her off, right?"

Sénar looked at London and answered, "No. We are going home. I don't want to kick it with them anyways, just call me tomorrow."

He kissed her, and she pouted while me and Sénar walked to his car to go home. Over the weekend Tyrell called me to convince me why we weren't spending time together, he said, "My mom is on vacation for the month of December, so since you can't come over maybe we can go to the movies or something."

He acted like everything was all honky dory. He never even apologized for what he did to me. I just pretended to entertain the thought and watched London try to consume as much of Sénar's time as possible. The more me and Tyrell grew apart, the closer me and Sénar became. London hated it; she even brought it up to him in front of me over the weekend. On Wednesday, I sat at the tree and ate my lunch when I saw Tyrell walking up to me to join me. I ate my food and waited to see what he was going to say before I determined how I would feel.

Tyrell stared at me then said, "I miss you, Treasure. Why are you so distant now? I feel like you don't want to try anymore." He sounded sincere, so I loosened up a bit. I replied, "Tyrell, there is a lot of things that have not been addressed, and every time I see you, there is drama or Leah." He sighed as he saw Leah approaching us. He asked, "Will you go out with me this weekend and let me make it up to you?" I looked at his handsome face, and I could see the love in his eyes for me after it had been so long since I had seen it. I didn't want to say, no, but I definitely didn't want to say yes either, so I just replied, "Maybe Tyrell, let's just see what happens."

Leah walked up to say, "What's up, Treasure?" We hadn't spoken in over a week, and I kind of liked it better that way. I didn't bother looking at her when I responded, "Hey," and finished my food. I went to my next class, where Leah found herself sitting next to me. She said, "Looks like Tyrell wants you back. You can have him; I want Sénar."

I was so irritated with her; she was such a bold girl; she had no idea how bad I wanted to slap her. I kept my response short when I replied, "I bet."

She laughed then said, "But you probably trying to keep that bomb D all to yourself, huh? Hell, I would even take Ken's ass if I had the opportunity." She giggled as I told her, "Be careful what you wish for." She smiled and did her work. Knowing her and Ken were both crazy, I wouldn't put it past either of them. I avoided her the rest of the day to prevent having to slap her. After practice, I tried to hurry to gather my things, so I could walk home in peace. London and Sénar were arguing as they were leaving, and Tyrell and Leah were approaching me. I felt like I was being closed in, so I walked faster to try and get through the parking lot, but Tyrell stopped me to ask, "Treasure, you want a ride?" I looked at Leah's smirk on her face and said, "No, I am going to walk." Leah saw Sénar and London arguing as they were approaching us from behind. When they reached us Leah said, "Ooh Treasure, I see you got those pretty earrings on you got from Sénar." I never told her or Tyrell that Sénar gave them to me; she was just trying to start something. Tyrell and London both grew angry instantly. London slapped Sénar, and Tyrell tried to snatch the earrings out of my ear. I pushed London so hard, she fell to the ground for slapping Sénar and Sénar pushed Tyrell for trying to grab my earrings. Triston ran to break Sénar and Tyrell up while London tried to come for me. Sénar broke away and grabbed London.

Sénar yelled, "Get in the car, Treasure!"

Sénar told London, "You put your hands on me, that's one thing, but if you touch her, I'm done with your ass!" She started crying, and Sénar glared at me as I hurried to get into the car.

Tyrell said, "You need to come with me, Treasure!" I still got in the car with Sénar, and he drove off like a maniac.

I immediately said, "Sénar, I didn't tell Leah or Tyrell you gave me these earrings."

He glared at me then said, "I don't care about that; I care how you got them back."

I pouted and said, "I had them for a while."

Sénar smirked at me as I continued, "My first day off punishment, Treasure number two got them back for me." I winked at him, and he looked hurt, but smiled sadistically before he asked, "Did you tell him you learned that on me?" He laughed.

I rolled my eyes and asked, "Did you tell London, you taught me?"

He smirked before he said, "She knows, that's why she hates you so much, and that's why Tyrell hates me so much." I was quiet because he was irritated with me when he said, "Treasure, you got a slick ass mouth. Don't give Tyrell no more chances."

I folded my arms and said, "Sénar, you can not tell me what to do."

He was so frustrated with me that he just ignored me while his phone rung nonstop. He answered his phone and roared, "I'll call you later! And don't bring your ass over here!" He hung his phone up and stormed into the house. Ken was sitting at the table when I came in. I tried to avoid eye contact with him and run up the steps, but Ken called my name. I stopped to take a deep breath before I answered, "Yes, Ken?"

He said, "Come here."

I still had my backpack on. Ken asked, "How was school?"

I shrugged my shoulders and replied, "It was fine, Ken." He looked at me like I was lying and said, "Get me a beer way from the back."

I did as I was told and tried to keep my balance as I reached for his beer way in the back. I quickly got his beer and ran out of the kitchen to my room. Cassidy was already there on her phone, running her mouth. I didn't know who she was talking to until I heard her say, "You should have beat her ass. She is always getting him into trouble. I should tell my daddy."

She eyed me, and I knew she was talking to London, and she was probably telling her what just happened after school. I quickly left before she could say anything to me, but she followed me out the door. I turned around and pleaded, "Cassidy leave me alone, please! This has nothing to do with you!"

Cassidy snarled at me and said, "You are such a poisonous rat. I don't know what Sénar sees in your black ass!"

I slapped her in her mouth, and she pushed me so hard, I tripped and tumbled down the stairs landing on my butt as Sénar turned the corner from working out. He snatched me off the floor with his eyebrow raised in suspicion; I giggled because I knew he was wondering how I ended up on the floor. He looked up the steps and seen Cassidy looking like a madwoman.

He shook his head and went up the steps as Ken asked, "What the hell is going on?" Cassidy waited to see if I would tell on her, but I told Ken that I tripped and then went to watch TV. Sénar came down after he showered and sat on the opposite couch. He had a look of curiosity on his face when he asked, "What the hell happened earlier?"

I ignored his question. He said, "Oh, so you going to act like you didn't hear me?" I totally tuned him out and watched TV. He snatched the controller off the table and turned the channel. I got up to ask, "What are you doing, Sénar? This is a new episode; I want to see it?" I tried to grab the controller from him, and he moved it, so I could not get it. I saw Ken get up, shaking his head as he went up the stairs. Sénar pushed my hand away gently and said, "Your ass is deaf, remember? You can't hear it anyway." He laughed, making me want to slap him like London did earlier. He saw the fury in my eyes, he pulled me to him and then stuck his tongue in my mouth. Instantaneously my coochie started throbbing, my heartbeat accelerated, making me jump up.

I said, "Sénar, stop. Just give me the controller!"

He smirked at me, so I tickled him, making him giggle first before he said, "Stop it before I snatch you up again."

Treasure number two knocked on my mental door, I tried to ignore her, but Sénar looked so good. His gray eyes traveled all over my body, and I saw his man stick grow right before my eyes. I shook my head no and said, "Give me the controller."

Sénar bit his bottom lip and said, "Come get it."

I tried to grab it from him, but he snatched me up and kissed me. He squeezed me and rubbed all over me while kissing me. I didn't stop him, but the doorbell rang right before my anger could turn into passion. I quickly jumped up to answer the door to see London's face when I opened the door. She pushed the door open and stared me down. I glared back at her as she walked past me to Sénar. I closed the door, instantly agitated with her presence. I went back to sit on the couch, but before sitting down, I snatched the controller from Sénar. I grazed his abdomen on purpose, making him jump up. Sénar looked like he wanted to snatch me up in front of London. He kept his eyes on me and acknowledged London by asking, "What are you doing here London?"

She looked remorseful but didn't hide her disdain for me and his fascination of me. She towered over him as he sat on the couch, but eventually, she sat down at his side. She said, "Babe, I love you. I am so sorry about earlier. Let's go upstairs and talk?"

Sénar shook his head no, and without taking his eyes off me, he replied, "Look London, I told you not to come over here because I don't want to talk about that. I am still irritated with you, and I don't want to be mean to you."

She pouted and rubbed all over him and felt his excitement, probably thinking it was because of her. He sighed, and I listened to her beg him to forgive her. She was all over him as we watched an episode of *Girlfriends*. My mom and Ken came down dressed nicely like they were going out and Cassidy left for some skating ring with Nevaeh, so it was just me, London, and Sénar. She was on my last nerve as we sat on the couch watching TV. London was still all over Sénar, and I could tell she was starting to get on his nerves too.

He said, "London chill out damn, you are not even supposed to be here after that crap you pulled earlier."

I was tired of hearing him tell her to stop or chill, and I said, "Damn, go to your room already." Sénar laughed, and London responded, "Why don't you mind your business, little girl."

I rolled my eyes and said, "Well, I am trying to, but your desperate ass is getting on my nerves!"

Sénar's face was so shocked that he was at lost for words, but London, on the other hand, was not. She said, "You're just mad cuz your little boyfriend got a new girlfriend."

She laughed at me, Sénar again was silent, but I was pissed. I wanted to slap her in the mouth; I got up and threw the controller on the table. I walked out of the living room and into the kitchen. I could hear her and Sénar arguing when he told her to leave, and she refused. This was the one time I agreed with Sénar about her leaving. I opened the fridge, and I saw nothing that interested me. I thought about cereal and lost my appetite when I thought about the last time, I almost had cereal and the events that followed after. I left the kitchen and started to go to my room, but something came over me. I returned to the living room, and Sénar stopped talking to look at me. He had lust in his eyes when I sat down next to him, and London looked like I had slapped her already. I smiled before I asked, "Sénar, what are we going to eat?" I folded my arms to wait for him to answer. He smiled his famous smile when he answered, "Whatever you want." For a moment, it felt like just me and Sénar were in the room, before London interrupted, "What the hell is she asking you for?... Sénar?" London jumped up and came for me, but I was ready to snatch her lips off when Sénar stood in between us. Sénar roared, "Look, London, you need to chill or go home!" London was pissed, and she whined, "Sénar let's go upstairs?"

He was annoyed when he said, "Look, just go, and I might come and see you later."

She again whined, "No, I want to stay."

He said, "I'm not about to argue with you; I'll call you later."

She pouted and headed for the door but tried one last time to convince him to let her stay. He nicely told her no. He closed the door, my heart started beating rapidly after realizing he was excited enough to put her out, and we were home alone. Sénar again smiled his famous smile then said, "Let's have dessert first!"

I jumped up to say, "Sénar stop playing!"

He laughed and said, "Nah, you need to stop playing. I just sent London home, so we can play Sénar says."

He was cheesing. I rolled my eyes before I asked, "Sénar, what are we going to eat?"

I crossed my arms, and he smiled before he answered, "Everything is frozen, so I'll thaw something out while you get naked."

I ignored him and kept watching TV. He went to do exactly what he said and returned, expecting me to be naked. I played dumb for a second until he got naked, and we played a game of Sénar says before he cooked dinner. I was peacefully asleep before everyone returned. The rest of the weekend, I went to the movies with Sénar and Cassidy to see the movie *How High*. It was absolutely hilarious because, of course, we were all high as a kite. Cassidy eased up a bit when she found out I only pushed London because she slapped Sénar. That quick she was not fond of London and London would quickly find out. Sénar couldn't take his phone blowing up and went to London's house on Sunday to avoid bringing her around Cassidy or me. Heck, we only had one more week before our two-week winter break. What could possibly go wrong?

Chapter 11

Monday morning, I woke up in a fairly good mood. I knew this was the last week I would have to deal with Leah for a while, so I was excited to not deal with her as often. Tyrell and I talked on the phone, but I avoided being alone with him or spending time with him. We never officially broke up, but we both used his mom's vacation as an excuse for distance. I was feeling lazy this morning, so I went to school with Sénar and Cassidy instead of walking. When we pulled up, I knew immediately it was a mistake. Leah was arguing with Tyrell in the parking lot, and London was waiting impatiently for Sénar to pull up. She was happy to see him and Cassidy, until Cassidy rolled her eyes at her, and I got out of the back seat of Sénar's car. She did not hide her jealousy of me riding with Sénar or disappointment in Cassidy's new attitude. I shrugged my shoulders and went to class. Ignoring London's mouth and pretending I didn't hear Tyrell call my name. I went to my first three classes; dreading going to lunch since I didn't have a lunch packed. That meant I would have to face *drama time* as I thought of it instead of lunchtime. I walked to the cafeteria as quickly as possible to get my food and hurry back outside to my new spot. I got my food and was almost out the door when London bumped into me on her way in. I almost dropped my stuff, but I managed to avoid it. If I would have dropped my stuff, I think I would have had to beat her ass. I brushed it off and kept walking to sit under my tree. As I sat down under the tree to try to avoid people, I saw Sénar come outside with London following him. He didn't come toward me though; he kept walking the opposite way and I could tell London was on his last nerve. Then Tyrell and Leah came out, but Leah looked upset. I just ate my food and hoped they would walk off somewhere too, but I guess I wasn't that lucky. Tyrell came and sat down next to me.

He asked, "What's up, Treasure?"

I smiled at him and responded, "Nothing, just eating my lunch."

He just gazed at me before he asked, "So when are we going to spend some time together?"

I took a deep breath before I answered, "I don't know, Tyrell."

He wasn't happy with my answer and replied, "What do you mean you don't know?"

I finished my food and cleaned up my mess then stood up. He never took his eyes off me as I repeated my answer, "I don't know Tyrell."

He laughed and then responded, "Wow."

I tried to walk off, but he stopped me. He nicely asked, "Can I have a kiss?" I kissed him quickly, but he grabbed me and kissed me passionately. I almost melted into his arms until I saw Sénar and London.

I quickly pushed him off and said, "I have to go."

He got frustrated and asked, "What is your problem?"

I answered, "You, her, everyone. Just leave me alone."

I left and went to my class, Leah avoided me, and I avoided her. At practice, the tensions were high on the field and in cheerleading practice. Everyone was whispering and talking in groups. I was so uncomfortable I asked my coach if I could leave early and she allowed me to go. I grabbed my bag and headed out as swiftly as possible. I power walked home, hoping no one would bother me. I wasn't even in the door before my phone rang. It was Sénar. I answered, "Hello?"

He asked, "Where are you, Treasure?"

I answered, "I am at home."

Ken bellowed, "Treasure come here."

Sénar was quiet on the other end of the phone. I had the phone to my ear and answered, "Yes, Ken?" He stared at me before he said, "Get off the phone." Before I could say anything, Sénar said, "I am on my way," before he hung up. I put the phone away from my ear and waited for his demands.

He asked, "Where is Sénar?"

I answered, "He is on his way, Ken."

He said, "Get me a beer." *I mean, does he just wait for me to walk in to ask me that?* Ugh, I was so angry, but I walked to the fridge and did as he asked. When I came up from getting his beer way from the back, he was already close to me. He said, "You almost ready for me yet?" I tried to squeeze out, but this time he didn't let me. He stopped me by putting his hand on my chest and then pressing me against the wall, he whispered, "I wanna see why you drive him so crazy." He smelled my hair and laughed as he left the kitchen.

Sénar came in, and Ken greeted him, "Wassup boy?"

Sénar said, "Hey, pops!"

Sénar came to the kitchen to check on me; I was flustered when he asked, "Are you ok?" I quickly nodded my head, yeah, and left the kitchen. Sénar grabbed me to say, "Treasure, don't lie to me." I started to tear up a little when he asked, "Why did you leave so quickly?" I answered, "I don't know, I just wanted to avoid drama. I didn't think about Ken." Sénar asked, "What he do?" I was uncomfortable when I answered, "Sénar, I am fine. I'll just wait for you next time, but what about London?" I tried to change the subject, and he just stared at me. I was annoyed with him now because he was quiet, and I had no idea what was going through his mind. I tried to walk away, he stopped me, and I answered, "He just says inappropriate stuff Sénar. And sometimes he gets really close, and I feel trapped…. and he smelled my hair." Sénar winced before he said, "Don't let him smell your hair or get too close. When he asks for a beer, just get it as quickly as possible and close the door then leave. If he gets too close, just get away the best way you know how."

That sounded about right; I just tried to go to my room. He stopped me again to say, "Don't lead my dad or Tyrell on, Treasure. When he comes at you, let him know you don't want it at all. As for Tyrell, If you are done, be done with him."

I was frustrated when I said, "Sénar, you are not my freaking boss or counselor, damn."

He rolled his eyes and replied, "Um ok, but when you don't listen, it always ends up in chaos. Then you drag me into it too!"

I snapped, "No, you drag yourself into it!"

He laughed and asked, "Treasure, so you want me to leave you alone?"

I looked at him with an attitude and replied, "I double-dog dare you too!"

He looked like he wanted to slap me, and I rolled my eyes at him. He smirked before he replied, "Fine, then I triple dog dare you to let me."

I looked at him like he was crazy before I said, "What? You are nuts!"

He laughed to himself before he went to work out. I followed him and asked, "Is that why you do all the stuff you do, so you can throw it in my face?"

He smirked before he answered, "I do it because I want to, and you need me to." I was offended when I yelled, "I don't need you, Sénar!"

He smiled and asked, "Then, you want me?"

He smiled again and waited for me to answer. I left the garage irritated and annoyed with his confidence. I went upstairs to put my backpack down and wrote in my diary. When Cassidy came in, I quickly got up and went downstairs. Sénar was watching TV when I came down, and the first thing I did was look for Ken. I was relieved when I didn't see him but still cautious of Sénar. I sat down and watched what he was watching. It was discovery channel, about all the African tribes and different cultures; it was interesting. When Cassidy came down and sat on the couch, she asked, "Sénar, what are you cooking tonight?"

He looked at her and asked, "Dang Cassidy, I don't know. What do you want?"

She hesitated but smiled before she answered, "Some fried chicken."

He laughed hysterically before he said, "Hell no, I'll make it Thursday cuz I don't have practice. Y'all bout to eat some tacos tonight, or do y'all want enchiladas?"

Me and Cassidy in unison answered, "Enchiladas." Sénar rolled his eyes then said, "Y'all going to let me watch some TV first, damn." He laid back to get comfortable and continued to watched TV. The doorbell rang, and we all looked at each other. Cassidy got up to answer the door, and she quickly came to sit back down. Low and behold, London walked in. Sénar was not thrilled and didn't move from his spot. She came in the living room to sit next to Sénar and whispered in his ear. He said, "Nah, I am about to cook in a minute London." She did her ritual touching and begging as Ken came down and eyed us all in the living room. Cassidy said, "Hi, daddy!" Ken replied, "Hey, Cassidy, come give daddy some sugar." She went to kiss her daddy and came back to sit down; then, Ken called Sénar to the table. Ken was talking to Sénar, but he stared at me the whole time. London took the opportunity to say, "Treasure, you are not on punishment, so don't be riding with my man. You need to be riding with yours or walk. I don't care what you do; just stay away from mine."

I looked at her with an attitude, and Cassidy just stared at the TV, as if to show she was neutral in our dispute. I told her, "I can ride with who I want to London. The only person you need to tell what you expect is Sénar."

When Sénar heard me say his name, he looked back just in time to see London leap toward me and me punch her several times in her face before him and Ken ran in to break us up. As Sénar grabbed London, she hit me in my mouth, sending me into another rage; I punched her square in her eye, almost knocking her out. I tried to rip her to shreds as Ken grabbed me from behind and squeezed me. He tried to smell my hair, but I pulled away from him, and he threw me on the couch. Sénar talked to London as he walked her to the door and Cassidy ran upstairs.

Ken said, "You are feisty, Treasure. Umph, I like feisty."

Sénar slammed the door; he was fuming when he glared at me. I was still on the couch with Ken towering over me when Sénar came into the living room. He was breathing heavy and tried to control his anger knowing Ken was present.

He asked, "Damn Treasure, why you hit her like that? Dang, she gonna have a black eye now. Come help me with these enchiladas!"

Ken just stood there as I jumped up to help Sénar. Ken just watched, but he didn't say a word. I know Sénar was mad, but he minimized his anger in front of Ken to avoid Ken reinforcing his own punishment on me. Ken watched us as we made the enchiladas. I just sucked the blood off my lip and helped Sénar make dinner. Ken got up to get his own beer and took one good look at us before he went upstairs. When Ken left, Sénar snapped, "Treasure, what the hell is wrong with you?" I was still angry too and replied, "She started it, Sénar! She always does! She attacked-"

He shouted, "Stop! You freaking whipped her ass already; you didn't have to give her a black eye!" I got in his face and asked, "How many times have you and Tyrell blacked each other's eye or gave custom made Nike shirts?" He laughed when he thought of the time, he put a Nike shoe print on Tyrell's fresh white T-shirt. I couldn't help but laugh with him when Cassidy and Ken walked in and stared at us like we were crazy. We just made our plates and ate, my mom never came down, and Sénar whispered for me to go upstairs while he cleaned up. I quickly ran upstairs and went to bed without a word to Cassidy.

In the morning, I got up to check my lip, and it wasn't that bad, but it was a little swollen. I got myself together and went downstairs to get some ice for my lip. My mom was sitting where Ken would normally sit. She looked tired but happy.

She said, "Good morning, Treasure."

I was shocked to see her but replied, "Good morning, momma. What are you doing?"

She laughed and said, "Nothing." I took my ice and tried to leave the kitchen when my mom asked, "What happened to your lip, sweetie?"

I thought I would have a tantrum, but I knew it wouldn't work, I was too old for that. I answered, "Um, London hit me, and I hit her back."

She laughed again. I just stared at her; she was almost delirious. She said, "I heard you whupped her ass, good for you!" I laughed and asked, "Momma, what's in that coffee cup?" Sénar came down to get something to drink when he saw my mom; he said, "Good morning Carmel." She gazed at him and smiled before she said, "Good morning, Sénar." He looked at me with ice on my lip and tried not to laugh. My mom asked, "Sénar, you let London hit my baby?"

Sénar smirked at me before he answered, "Carmel, Treasure beat the breaks off London. I think she might need anger management classes."

My mom and Sénar started laughing as I watched them both humor themselves with my situation. Sénar shook his head at both of us and walked out of the kitchen. Cassidy came down, and they left. I looked at my mom again before I said bye, she was still smiling, but she didn't even hear me say goodbye. I decided to walk, it felt like the best thing to do, and I didn't know if London would be waiting there like a stalker with a black eye. If she was, then Sénar could hold her while I made my way to class. When I walked up to the school, I saw Tyrell and Leah talking in the parking lot, and Sénar talking with some of his homeboys. I knew London wasn't coming if she wasn't already there. I laughed when I thought about it being because she had a black eye. Besides, she would normally be attached to Sénar if she was anywhere near. Even Leah noticed as she had her eye on Sénar, Tyrell noticed and flipped out on Leah. I could see her rage when she saw me walking up to witness his tongue lashing. She said, "Why don't you talk to your girlfriend; I see an opportunity I never see." She hurried away in Sénar's direction as I kept walking.

Tyrell called my name, I answered, "What is it, Tyrell? I am going to class."

He caught up to me and then asked, "Damn, you weren't even going to say hi?"

I kept walking and answered, "You were arguing with your new girlfriend."

He smacked his lips and replied, "She is not my girlfriend. I thought you were."

I took a deep breath before I responded, "I did too Tyrell, but it does not feel like it, and I have to go to class."

Before I could turn to leave, he asked, "What happened to your lip?"

I decided to walk away and went to my class without answering his question. I got through my classes but dreading lunchtime. When my last class was over, I debated skipping lunch and just going straight to the tree to read. When I looked, Sénar was already over there. When we caught eye contact, he waved me over to him. I could have jumped for joy, but I just calmly walked to him. Sénar had a sandwich with mayonnaise and mustard packets, some chips, and a soda. I smiled at him and said, "You sure know how to leave me alone, Sénar." He smirked at me then said, "Don't leave without me after practice." I couldn't help but ask, "Where's your accessory, Sénar?" He glared at me before he said, "Very funny Treasure, I should charge you extra for damages that may cause you to put out more often." Sénar winked at me, and I rolled my eyes at him as Leah walked up without Tyrell.

She said, "Hey, Sénar."

Sénar replied, "What's up, Leah."

She tried to start a conversation, but Sénar was already leaving and had his exit line prepared, "See you later, ladies."

Leah tried to hide her disappointment and her need to still get lunch. I could tell she wanted to say something, but she just left to catch up to Sénar, since he was also going to the cafeteria. She didn't waste any time she saw the vacant spot London usually occupied on Sénar's arm and tried to fill it immediately. It was so obvious that everyone was looking for London, but she was nowhere to be found.

After practice, Sénar came to grab my bag when Leah asked, "Sénar, where's London?"

He smirked at her and replied, "Like you really care, Leah."

She smiled and said, "You're right."

Tyrell came and told Leah, "Let's go!"

She rolled her eyes, and they left together. Me and Sénar walked to the car, and when we got in, he said, "Wow. Damn, Leah is a cold piece of work."

I looked at him like he was crazy; he laughed and asked, "What?" I didn't say anything; he just shook his head. We pulled up to the house before we got out, he said, "I have to go check on London and see how she is doing."

I shrugged my shoulders to insinuate I did not care, but just in case he needed to hear it, I said, "I don't care." I really did care because she is the one who started it, but I appeared to be the bad guy. Sénar and I walked in the house, going straight upstairs, then went to our rooms. Cassidy wasn't there, so I lay down in my bed to relax. I figured I would stay up here since Ken was downstairs until I smelled food. I was laying in my bed when my phone rang. It was Tyrell, I almost didn't answer, but I wanted to see what he would say.

I answered, "Hello?"

He asked, "Treasure, why is your lip busted? Every time I turn around, there is something wrong with you."

I sighed before I responded, "Funny that you would say that Tyrell. I didn't think you would notice."

He asked, "What is someone abusing you or something?"

I wanted to ask him if he counted, but I didn't want to argue, so I said, "No, Tyrell, everything is fine."

He asked, "Why do you lie so much?"

Angry now, I answered, "It's none of your business; that's why."

He yelled at me when he said, "Well, you are supposed to be my girl, so it is my business!"

I thought about me and Sénar's conversation and said, "Well, supposed to, is different from me being your girlfriend. I think you made your choice clear, Tyrell."

He was getting angrier, "Leah is not my girl, and you look like you have made your choice as well. I just think London is not happy about it. She probably is the one who busted your lip," he laughed after he said it.

I snapped, "And she paid greatly for it! So, maybe you should be more worried about your little situation since she is the one who chose Sénar." I hung up on him, and he called me back five times before I answered, "What Tyrell!" It was Sénar this time, and he reprimanded me, "Treasure, look at your phone before answering it because this isn't Tyrell's ass!" I felt bad instantly when I said, "Sorry, what is it, Sénar?" He asked, "Where are you at?" I sighed before I answered, "In my room Sénar." He mocked me before telling me he was on his way. We ate leftovers, and I went to bed happy because I was able to avoid Ken the whole day.

Wednesday, London still wasn't back at school. Everyone was starting to notice, and there were so many rumors going around. People that never talked to me were asking me if me and London fought. I was smart enough to make lunch today to avoid the cafeteria. Sénar checked on me, but no one bothered me, and I loved it. Leah came and sat next to me in class. She asked, "What did you do to London?" I looked at her dumbfounded before I asked, "What are you talking about?" She just shook her head before she asked, "You really are a good liar, huh?" I ignored her and did my work. I couldn't decide who I hated more currently, Sabrina, Leah, London, or Cassidy; I think they were pretty much in the order of which I hated them. Even though Sabrina had not been around in a while, my hatred for her still resided in me and was still being kindled somehow. After practice, Tyrell came up to me to say, "I have something I want to give you, I'll bring it tomorrow." He left before Sénar came up to me, Sénar grabbed my bag, and we left. In the car, I asked, "Sénar, how's London?" He raised his eyebrow then asked, "Why Treasure? I thought you didn't care?" I smiled and replied, "I am just asking; I haven't seen her." I tried not to laugh, but he was serious when he said, "You messed her pretty face up, and she got a mean ass slug on her eye. You are cold-blooded Treasure. If she did that to you, I would not ever talk to her again. I know she started it, but you didn't have to do her like that."

I smacked my lips and said, "She had it coming, she is always messing with me. I would have done it a long time ago if I knew I wasn't going to get in trouble."

I smiled at him with my own sadistic smile, and he rolled his eyes before saying, "Treasure, that is not funny. She can't even go to school like that. Shoot, I don't want them thinking I did that to her. It looks like a dude hit her Treasure."

I started to feel bad because she is so pale, so it probably looked worse than I imagined. He smirked then said, "Now I have to go be her doctor." I rolled my eyes at him and noticed Ken's truck was gone. I was so relieved; I didn't care what Sénar did now, I was about to watch *Girlfriends* and chill. I put my bag up and laid down for a second before I went downstairs. Sénar came to my room door and gazed at me before he asked, "You wanna work out?"

I sighed then asked, "What kind of work out, Sénar?"

He laughed before he answered, "Whatever kind you want, ma."

I smirked before I reminded him, "Don't you have to go be a doctor for London?"

He rolled his eyes then replied, "Don't worry about that. I can handle you both."

I was annoyed with him now when I said, "Get out, Sénar!"

He laughed but asked, "What? if you could handle it by yourself, then I would let her go, but you play too much." He was really in his own world and needed a reality check. I said, "Sénar shut up, you really are full of yourself sometimes." He laughed and still asked, "Well, what do you want to do?" I thought about it for a second and then asked, "Are we talking about working out or something else?" Sénar rolled his eyes at me then asked, "Why you play so much?" He pulled me off the bed, and I let myself fall into his arms, he kissed me and smelled my hair. I giggled when I responded, "Stop it, you are such a weirdo." He happily dragged me to his room but playfully and locked his door. Sénar walked towards me slowly, then kissed me. When he was done kissing me, he said, "You are truly my favorite person on so many levels, ma. I wish I could take you away from all of this to keep you safe and all to myself." I just listened because, at the moment, I almost wished he could too, just for a moment. Cassidy knocked on his door, "Sénar! Open the door!" He was annoyed that he was being interrupted and opened his door but not all the way. He asked, "What is it, Cassidy?" She exclaimed, "Have you seen London's face?" He sighed and answered, "Yeah, Cassidy, damn." She yelled, "Treasure's ass is crazy!" Sénar was getting more annoyed with her by the second and said, "Cassidy chill out, why are you so worried about it?" Cassidy snapped back, "Well, why aren't you more worried about it? She better not hit me like that, or I will kill her stupid ass! Hopefully, my daddy takes her stupid ass out!" Sénar snapped at her when he said, "Man, shut your ass up! Don't be saying stupid shit like that! She didn't even do anything to your ass. Look, Cassidy, I am busy." Cassidy smacked her lips then said, "London is in the car outside waiting. She wants to talk to you." He asked, "Cassidy can't you tell her I'll come over to see her later?" Cassidy snapped back, "No!" Sénar sighed before saying, "Ok, well, tell her I will be down there? Please?" She smacked her lips then replied, "Whatever, fine!" He waited until Cassidy went down the steps and turned to me to say, "When you leave go to the bathroom first. Don't mind, Cassidy, but please just avoid her. I'll see you in a bit, just let me handle this real quick." I didn't say anything, I just walked out and into the bathroom like he instructed me to.

I was deep in thought about all the things Cassidy said about me, and I was even more pissed off she would wish something horrible like that on me. Cassidy and her sister have done nothing but harass me from the day they met me. Sénar too, but his harassment just turned into something else after a while, and here I am in the middle of it. She acts as if I infringed on their space. I knew going to my room was not an option, so I went downstairs because I now needed to be entertained to keep from thinking about everything. Cassidy was coming up as I came down with a pure look of disgust on her face. I glared at her, and she sped up the steps; she knew she could end up like London if she kept trying me. I was tired of everyone; they all had their own agendas, and somehow, I was in the center of it all. I sat down on the couch to watch TV while Sénar left with London, and Cassidy went to our room. My mom came down, and I followed her into the kitchen. I sat down at the kitchen nook and watched her. I asked, "Momma, you still love me?" She laughed and answered without looking at me, "Of course I do Treasure. Where is everyone?" She looked at me, and I shrugged my shoulders and said, "I don't know, Momma." I just watched her as she made mashed potatoes, meatloaf, and corn on the cob. I didn't say anything else; I just took her word for it. Ken walked in, he grabbed my mom from behind and smelled her hair then caressed her body. She asked him if he needed anything when he noticed me sitting at the kitchen nook, he glared at me before sitting down. I avoided his eye contact and left to sit back in the living room. When Sénar came back, I went to make a plate before he came into the kitchen, so I could get some mashed potatoes in peace. Cassidy came into the kitchen after Sénar greeted my mom and Ken. Sénar saw I had my plate already with mashed potatoes on it. He smirked at me when Ken asked, "How's London Sénar?" He looked at his plate and said, "She coo' pops." Cassidy chimed in, saying, "No, she is not daddy, her face is messed up! She got a black eye." Sénar rolled his eyes, and Ken said, "As long as they don't think Sénar did that shit, I don't care, but Treasure does need to calm her ass down." My mom asked, "Didn't London hit Treasure first?" Everyone looked at my mom and Ken didn't hide his irritation with her. Sénar answered her question, "Yeah, Carmel, she did hit Treasure first." Ken flashed at them both, "Enough of this conversation because if Treasure keeps putting her hands-on folks, somebody is going to put hands on her eventually." I was done eating after that; I was tired of hearing them talk about me like I wasn't sitting there. I raked the food left on my plate in the trash and went to my room to write in my diary until I fell asleep.

For sure London would be at school today, she wouldn't miss three days in a row. I walked to school early and went to the library to completely skip the whole morning scene. I made it to lunchtime quickly to grab my lunch and was on my way to the tree outside to mind my business. When Tyrell came up to me, he already looked agitated. Tyrell asked, "What did you do to London?" I kept walking, and he followed me outside. I noticed Sénar with his homeboys with London nowhere in sight, watching Tyrell follow me. I ignored his question, so he grabbed my arm. I snapped at him and asked, "What Tyrell?" He said, "Answer me, and don't walk away from me." He squeezed me, prompting me to tell him, I said, "You are hurting me, Tyrell, let me go!" He let me go and demanded me to answer his question. I replied, "Why, Tyrell, it's none of your business!" Leah came out with a smile on her face making Tyrell even more agitated with both of us. Leah said, "Hey, Treasure." I ignored her and tried to walk away, but Tyrell didn't let me. I was frustrated when I answered, "She hit me, so I hit her back! Now, leave me alone!" Leah giggled, and I stormed off to go sit under my tree. The whole school was already talking about it, but Tyrell wanted to hear it from me. Tyrell started to follow me, but Sénar came out, and Leah was all over him that quick. Tyrell almost lost it, I hurried away, so I would not be an outlet for his anger while they all had their little moment of drama. Sénar brushed past them both to get to me; he asked, "Are you ok, Treasure?" I was annoyed, I tried to conceal it, but I was tired of everyone being nosey or putting their two cents in. I answered, "No, but who cares?" Sénar replied, "I care, Treasure." I rolled my eyes at him, but he was being sincere. I ate my food while Sénar watched me, and Tyrell and Leah watched us.

Math class, I was able to avoid Leah, so I didn't have to deal with her until we checked in for a quick rehearsal of our new routine for the last game of the year. Everyone was asking Sénar about London as he and Tyrell and some of the other guys waited until our practice was over. I saw cheerleaders whispering as Leah asked, "Damn Treasure, I heard you messed London up pretty bad." I just ignored Leah because she was next on my list. She continued, "Well, I don't want to fight, I want in. Maybe me, you, and Sénar could have some fun," she said then winked at me. I was disgusted with her; she just does not give up. Tyrell walked up at the same time as Sénar. Tyrell threw my silver and gold-plated name onto the ground in front of me, making a small thud sound when it hit the ground. He said, "You owe me a hundred dollars for that." There was no chain attached to it; I looked at Leah with her new intact chain and became furious. I took a deep breath; I thought I would explode. I was going to pick it up off the floor when Sénar grabbed my bag; he grabbed my silver and gold-plated name off the ground as well. Tyrell and Sénar mad dogged each other as Sénar said, "Let's go, Treasure!" I followed Sénar without another word to Tyrell; I kept my fury inside of me. When we got to the car, Sénar said, "Treasure, you would be better off if you just stop dealing with him completely." I asked, "Don't you have a girlfriend to tend to? Why are you always telling me what to do?" Sénar was agitated with me when he said, "You sure don't have a problem telling me about myself lately, but you let Tyrell dog you every chance he gets!" I wanted to scream, so I let my fury out on him when I said, "This is all your fault, Sénar! If you would have just left me alone, none of this would have happened!" He was quiet for a second and then responded, "Well, I am who I am in this situation, and he is who he is! And I know I am not perfect, but my intentions are not to hurt you! So, believe what you want." We pulled up to the house and saw that Ken's truck was gone, so he dropped me off. I got out and went to my room to cry. I was devastated; I didn't know what to do, how to feel, or what to believe. I thought Tyrell loved me; I thought we had something special. He constantly showed me otherwise in the last couple of months. I blamed Sénar for everything because he was so persistent in getting what he wanted from me that it felt like it was working. Sénar already acquired the keys to my body and my mind, but he wanted the keys to my heart. Hell, I didn't even have the keys to my heart, Tyrell was holding them hostage and I wanted them back. Sénar knew he had them, and that's what kept him from obtaining them. That was the reason he hated Tyrell so much; he just wouldn't admit it. I think deep down inside, we both hoped Tyrell didn't destroy them, and my heart would be locked forever. I had no intention of giving them to anyone ever again anyway. I took a bath and relaxed in the warm water and allowed myself to drift away into my thoughts.

A knock at the door brought me back to my reality when I heard Cassidy's voice say, "Hurry up, I have to use the bathroom!" I got out and quickly got dressed, she brushed past me with an attitude as I went out. I saw Sénar come back from wherever he was, and he did not look happy. I looked away as he passed me by, I felt bad for yelling at him, but I was hurting too. I was tired of being the only one suffering. I went to watch TV and Sénar went to work out. When he was done, he came to the living room and asked, "Can you braid my hair for me?" He was sweating with no shirt on, and he looked so good, I looked away when I answered, "I guess." That was the least I could do for yelling at him earlier.

He took a shower and came back to lay his head on my thigh as I braided his hair. Ken came back as I was braiding Sénar's hair; he just stared at us. Sénar didn't pay him any mind, but I could feel him staring at me. I was on my last couple of braids when the doorbell rang. Ken got up to answer the door; when he let Leah inside, I almost jumped off the couch when I saw Leah walk in. Leah smiled at Ken and greeted him as she spotted us on the couch. I was finishing Sénar's last braid as Leah towered over us, and Ken sat down at the table to watch in amusement. I gave Leah a look that prompted her to say, "Hey, guys." Sénar said, "What's up, Leah." He kept watching TV as I finished his last braid. I was annoyed times a thousand and asked, "What are you doing here, Leah?" Sénar got up to walk to the kitchen, and Leah ignored my question to follow Sénar. She asked, "Can you take me home, Sénar?" He was caught off guard by her question as Ken called my name, "Treasure, come get me a beer." Ken was sitting at the table reading some trucking magazines. I rolled my eyes but made sure Ken didn't see me. I heard Sénar answer her, "Yeah, but we have to go now because I'm about to cook." Leah smiled at Sénar and said, "Well, I want to taste some of that bomb ass food you be making Treasure." Ken smirked at me as I handed him his beer when he noticed my irritation increase. She said it so seductively, I think we all knew she wasn't just talking about food. I couldn't hold my tongue and asked, "Why don't you ask Tyrell to cook for you or Tyrell to take you home?" Leah laughed and replied, "Girl, that's your boyfriend; you know who I want." Ken laughed out loud, and Leah looked at Ken and then smiled flirtatiously. My momma came downstairs to see us all in the middle of an awkward moment. She eyed Leah and asked, "Treasure, what is she doing here?" Before I could answer, Ken said, "Angel baby, give me some sugar and leave them, kids, alone." My mom eyed Leah before Ken grabbed her and kissed her. My mom walked to the fridge to get her wine, and Ken followed her. Ken told Sénar, "Boy make the chicken before you take her home." Sénar replied, "Yes, sir." Leah smiled at us both as she sat down in Ken's chair. Before I could say anything, Sénar said, "Come on Treasure, let's do this, so I can take her home." I kept my mouth closed because I wanted to curse Leah out and send her home with a black eye too. Leah watched us in the kitchen as we whipped together dinner; he fried the chicken while I cut the fries for him to fry and prepared the salad. He even let me cut the tomatoes, making me smile because he told me he trusted me with them. I almost forgot Leah was watching us as she placed her hand under her chin to gaze at us. I could see the jealousy in her eyes as me and Sénar worked together as if she was invisible. She got up to look over Sénar's shoulder, but she knew better with me because I would have added her ass to the salad if she came near me.

Everyone came down when the aroma of the chicken made its way upstairs. Leah quickly got up from Ken's chair when she saw my mom, and the rest of them pile into the kitchen. My mom did not hide her dislike for Leah as she came into the kitchen to make a plate for Ken and herself. Cassidy recognized Leah and reluctantly said, "Hi." She was probably wondering the same thing my mom was wondering about why she was even here in the first place. Sénar gave me a plate and handed one to Leah; I let her make her plate ahead of me since she was so eager. She sat across from Cassidy and on the other side of me while Sénar and my mom sat on the sides of Ken. Before Leah ate, she said, "Cassidy, right?" Cassidy nodded her head, yeah and Leah said, "You're pretty Cassidy, but you are Sénar's sister, so it's not surprising. I am Leah nice to finally meet you." Cassidy eyed her and said, "I know who you are, and thanks." She forced a smile and ate her food. Me and my momma ate in silence as Leah did all the talking as usual. Leah complimented Sénar, "Ooh Sénar; this chicken is the bomb." Sénar said, "I know, but thanks." Ken smirked at Sénar's confidence and the fact that he could sense Sénar's resistance to Leah. My momma was pleased to see he did not take to Leah's desperation. Leah put her attention on my mom and asked, "Mrs. Brady, right?" Leah was being sarcastic, but Ken thought she was hilarious, and my mom did not. My mom looked like she wanted to slap Leah before she responded with pressured speech, "For you, Treasure's mom is fine. Good night everyone," she said as she dismissed Leah. Sénar replied, "Good night Carmel." She smiled, "Goodnight, Sénar. Thanks for the bomb ass chicken," she said it sarcastically, making Sénar chuckle. Ken just looked agitated with her but didn't say anything as she grabbed their drinks and headed to her dungeon. Cassidy threw her plate in the sink and went upstairs. I finished my chicken and salad while Sénar got up and took Leah's plate. He started to clean up as I followed him to the kitchen. Ken said, "Let Treasure do that shit, and you take your little friend home." Sénar looked at me to gauge my emotions and response. He was super annoyed but answered, "Yes, sir." He asked Leah if she was ready, and Leah answered, "Hell yeah." I thought I would shatter the plates when I heard her slogan and excitement at the thought of her being alone with Sénar. I knew she was desperate and waited for the opportunity to be alone with him. Frustrated, I put the food away, and I washed the dishes in a hurry. Ken asked, "Damn Treasure, are you going to beat her up too?" I ignored Ken until I felt him behind me, I left the knife I used for the potatoes last in the sink and said, "Can you give me some space, Ken?" He chuckled as he could sense my nervousness increased. He asked, "Ooh, she might be a little feistier than you, huh? That means she might be kinky too, huh?" Annoyed but also opportunistic, I answered, "I don't know Ken, maybe you can ask Sénar when he comes back. You would have a much better opportunity of finding out with her than me." Ken was agitated with my response and got closer when he whispered, "I know I can find a lot of things you can do with that slick ass, pretty mouth of yours too." I didn't say anything I had already said too much and did not want him to try anything else. I rinsed the knife off until it sparkled and slithered my way from in between Ken and the sink. I walked to the drawer and slowly dried the knife off as Ken watched my every move. When Sénar came back, he came to the kitchen to check on me when Ken said, "That was fast. Why didn't you play a little game of Sénar says with her?" Sénar chuckled and replied, "She is crazy pops, I'll pass." He smirked at Sénar and said, "She likes you more than Treasure's ass does." Me and Sénar both probably wondered to ourselves whether or not that was true. We waited for Ken to leave before Sénar asked, "Are you ok, ma?" I still had the knife in my hand as I drifted into my own thoughts. He called my name, "Treasure?" I snapped, "What?" He looked at me with the knife in my hands and asked, "What are you doing, Treasure?" I answered, "I am putting the dishes away." I asked, "Why didn't you give her that bomb, D?" He smirked and took the knife from me and put it away. He grabbed me from behind, smelling my hair, and squeezing me before we went upstairs to go to bed.

The next day was Friday, game day, and the last game of the year at that. London didn't return to school today either; I even saw some teachers ask Sénar about her. Tyrell ignored me and seemed to be agitated with Leah too because she was all in Sénar's face raving about his chicken. Tyrell watched me but didn't speak to me. Leah made her way over to me and sat down next to me to ask, "What do you guys have planned for the break? Let's hang out?" I looked at her like she was crazy and said, "No, thanks." She looked at me with an attitude then said, "I don't even know why I asked you, I'll just ask Sénar." I ignored her and waited for Sénar, so we could leave. Sénar got ready for the game, and I got ready to cheer; it was exciting. The game was great Sénar played like a beast, scoring three touchdowns and getting several huge tackles. The crowd cheered, "Chef Sénar! Chef Sénar!" We won the game by twenty-two points, and the crowd went bananas. Everyone ran onto the field, while I waited for Sénar on the side lines. When he came toward me, we ran to give each other a high five and then we just grinned at one another. Tyrell was pissed off, and his coach was yelling at him for poor sportsmanship. When he was done getting yelled at, he yelled at Leah, "Let's go!" Leah saw Sénar and I leaving. She ran to Sénar and asked, "Can I ride with you guys." Sénar hesitated but said, "Yeah." I was so irritated with him he should have told her no. Tyrell was so furious, he left by himself in a rage.

Triston walked up to Sénar and asked, "Aye Chef Sénar, come fry some chicken for us at my house!" Sénar laughed and asked me if I wanted to go, I shrugged my shoulders, and as if he was asking her, Leah said, "Hell yeah!" When we got to the car, I sat in the back, and Sénar rolled his eyes at me. He watched me in the rear-view mirror as Leah ran her mouth on the way to Triston's house. Sénar did his thing in the kitchen while we all laughed and talked about the game. I cut potatoes, and his mom had a bag of salad already prepared. We ate Sénar's bomb ass chicken while we had a really good time joking and even had some interesting conversations. It was just a couple of us, so there was no drama except Leah with her over the top personality. Both of our phones were going off, and it was pretty obvious it was the same person. I turned mine off and finished what I was doing. After we chilled at Triston's, we dropped Leah off, but before she got out, she said, "Sénar, I told Treasure we should hang out during the break, so I hope to see you." He nodded then said, "I hear you, Leah, Goodnight." She smiled at him before getting out; she didn't bother saying goodnight to me. I stayed in the back, so Sénar asked, "Why you be trippin' Treasure?" I ignored him, but he said, "You are the one that brought her into the picture. She never did nothing to me, so I don't have a problem with her." I wanted to pop him in the head from the back seat when I said, "Sénar, she is a little snake, and you know that, so why are you playing dumb?" Sénar laughed then said, "Damn Treasure, you mad, huh?" He smirked at me before he continued, "I am not the one who fell for your little trap, but your so-called boyfriend did." He shrugged his shoulders and waited for me to reply. I didn't say anything else to him; he was not going to make me act stupid like I really wanted to. We pulled up to the house and went to bed without another word to each other.

The weekend was great because we went to visit his cousins in LA. We chilled, shopped and played dominoes; it was really fun. During the week Sénar and I went to the parks to run and play basketball, which I enjoyed quite a bit. It kept me energetic and gave me something to do. London only came by once the first week but didn't stay long. Sénar was trying to be good, so we weren't doing anything, but we spent a lot of time together. Ken was driving again, and my mom was starting to come down more. Cassidy and Nevaeh went to LA a lot to visit her cousins and Nevaeh to visit Louie. Christmas and Christmas Eve, everyone just lounged around the house. Sénar made Christmas dinner, and I helped. Ken gave everyone money instead of gifts, and we didn't do all the decorations this year to keep it simple.

The last week before we went back to school, things started to drift back to chaos. Ken was home more and always having side conversations with Sénar; then barking demands whenever he saw me. Cassidy was always snapping at me, and my mom ignored me when Ken was around. Even London's eye was healed enough for her to have an attitude again, but Sénar quickly reminded her not to start, or he would send her home. She was only quiet for a second before she started again. London asked, "Sénar, why do you want to be down here? Let's go to your room." I almost urged him to go, but I kept my mouth shut to avoid an altercation. I just hoped they would hurry along to his room, so I could watch TV in peace. Sénar could sense my irritation as well as London, and it was too soon to have us around one another. I was almost ready to leave when Sénar told London, "Just go home, and I'll call you later." She got upset, but Sénar did not change his mind; he walked her to the door and said goodnight. Sénar eyed me before going to work out. When he was done, he went to take a shower. I waited for him to come down, but when he took longer than usual to come back, I went to knock on his door to be nosey. I heard Sénar say, "Come in." So, I opened the door to see that he was reading. I asked, "What are you reading, Sénar?" He answered, "The word, girl. What do you want?" I looked at him, confused; he sighed before he clarified, "The Bible Treasure." I replied, "Oh, I didn't know you read the Bible." He laughed and said, "It's the most important book you can read." I smirked at him then asked, "Oh, really?" He was serious when he answered, "Yes, really. Treasure as much as you read; you need to read it too sometimes." I just looked at him lying there looking all serious and closed the door. I had to leave before my thoughts reached an unholy level and went to watch TV. About thirty minutes later, Sénar came downstairs. He looked calm and collected when he asked, "What did you want, Treasure?" I looked at him and answered, "Nothing, I was just bored, Sénar." He smiled my favorite smile before he asked, "What do you want to do?" I quickly answered, "I don't know; let's go somewhere." He got his keys, and we left. He took me to Frisbee

Park and tried to teach me how to drive his car. It was a lot of jerking, what he called stalling out. He was patient but complained, "Man, you gonna have me replace my clutch if you don't listen." I saw his concern and tried my best to follow his instructions. I eventually got the hang of it, and we both grinned ear to ear. He said, "I'll ask my pops for his truck, so you can tear his shit up." He laughed and then took me home to make dinner. After we ate, I went to bed and I slept like a baby.

The next day the house was quiet after we ate breakfast. Everyone did their own thing, I watched TV and Sénar came down to the living room. He grabbed the controller but didn't say anything to me. He just laid on the other couch to watch TV with me. He hadn't tried anything in a while, and I was a little curious as to why, but I didn't want to make it obvious. I got up to take the controller and decided to tickle him to get it. He said, "Treasure, stop." I was tickling him because I knew he was ticklish. He laughed uncontrollably and then pushed me off of him. He warned, "Treasure for real man, I told you to stop starting shit. You are going to get your ass in some shit that you can't get out of, if you wake the beast all the way up." I bit my lip and stopped; I laid back on the couch and took heed to his warning. He gazed at me for a while and then got up to make dinner. When I followed him, he giggled a little before he said, "I don't need any help tonight, I'm just making tacos." I washed my hands, then grabbed the cheese, the lettuce, and tomatoes, then set them on the counter. He was cheesing ear to ear as he washed his hands. I asked, "So, are you going to grate the cheese then?" Sénar hated grating cheese, and he had a serious look on his face. He said, "Nah, you know what, you can grate the cheese."

He pulled the ground beef out and seasoned it. He took the cutting board from me and cut the onions for the taco meat. After he rinsed it, he gave it back. He behaved himself so much in the last week; I almost wanted to congratulate him. It was as if he could read my mind, he asked, "Treasure ma, why you play so much?" I smiled at him and asked, "What are you talking about?" He shook his head, and the doorbell rang. I looked at him, and he looked at me. He said, "You answer that it is more than likely for you than me." I hesitated and answered the door. It was Leah; I almost closed the door in her face as Ken pulled up into the driveway. I quickly asked, "What do you want, Leah?" She giggled before she answered, "You already know Treasure, I know he is here. I see his car." Ken walked up to say, "Hey Leah. Damn Treasure, why are you guarding the door? Want to come in, Leah?" She followed Ken into the kitchen where Sénar was. The aroma of Taco meat was in the air, prompting them both to follow the smell. Leah got excited when she saw Sénar in his basketball shorts and tank top on. Ken saw me go back to doing my task before answering the door for Leah's desperate ass. *How did she even know we were home, how did she get here, oh and let me guess she was going to need a ride.* Ken said, "Get me a beer, Treasure." I stopped what I was doing to get Ken a beer; I had some shorts and a tank top on. I noticed Sénar, Ken and Leah were all staring at me when I got up from grabbing him a beer. I gave Ken his beer, and Leah licked her lips and said, "Dang Treasure." Sénar and Ken chuckled as I ignored her inappropriate gesture and comment. I was annoyed and uncomfortable; I hurried with my task as Sénar fried the taco shells. I went to sit at the kitchen nook to avoid Leah and Ken. Leah just giggled while she flirted with both Sénar and Ken. I was annoyed, and I knew if my mom came down, she would rip Leah to shreds. Leah walked into the kitchen with Sénar, she whispered something in his ear, and he raised his eyebrow. Ken had a look of curiosity on his face but didn't say anything, he just read his magazine until Leah asked, "Ken, you want a beer?" He looked at her and answered, "Hell yeah!" She bent over flirtatiously, and Sénar shook his head while he finished his task. Ken smirked at me as she brought him a beer, my mom happened to walk in as she handed it to him. My mom was about to flip out, but Ken got up and sat her on his lap to say, "Angel baby, chill out. Gimme some suga." My momma softened up and kissed Ken before grabbing the beer that Leah brought him and pouring it out in the sink. She headed to the refrigerator to get Ken a beer, her wine, and then got herself a glass. Leah came and sat next to me at the kitchen nook. I wanted to slap her for my mom, but I just rolled my eyes at her as she smiled in my face. When Sénar was done, my mom made a plate for her and Ken. Sénar handed me and Leah a plate, and Cassidy came down to eat. Leah and Cassidy said hi to one another, but it was still awkward tension between everyone. Sénar and Cassidy ate at the table with my mom and Ken. Leah and I ate at the kitchen nook. It was for her protection, well hell everyone's protection in case things got violent. Leah ate her food happily, and I watched her every move. I could not stand her; she was totally reckless and conniving. Leah asked, "Can I spend the night?" I quickly answered, "No." I cringed at the thought of having another unwanted human being in my room with me, and I certainly did not want her to end up in Sénar's room. She whispered, "We could have some fun." She rubbed her hand up my thigh; I jumped up before she could touch my coochie. My mom asked, "Treasure, what's wrong with you?" My heartbeat accelerated as Leah giggled. I answered, "Nothing, momma, I am just done; that's all." Leah smirked as if she caught me in my ability to conjure up a little black lie so quickly. Sénar saw me ready to throw my taco away and snatched it off my plate. He ate it before I could throw it away. My mom took her and Ken's plate to the sink and grabbed Ken a beer before saying goodnight. Ken waited until my mom was gone before he said, "Sénar your friend staying or going home?"

Sénar looked at Ken then at Leah. Clearly, she was not there for me. Leah spoke for herself, "Treasure doesn't want to have any fun, so I guess Sénar can take me home, and we can have fun without her." Leah flicked her tongue at us both, and I couldn't hide my disgust for her or Ken when he laughed at her lascivious behavior. Sénar looked like a deer caught in some headlights as he tried to busy himself with helping me with the kitchen. Ken quickly detoured Sénar when he said, "Why don't you let Treasure have fun doing the dishes, and you take your little friend home?"

Sénar hesitated before he asked Leah, "You ready?"

Leah answered, "Hell yeah!"

I wanted to throw a plate in her mouth, but Sénar grabbed my waist from behind to say, "Chill out, I'll be back ma." Ken was agitated when he saw Sénar reassuring me he would soon return. He quickly told Sénar, "Nah, ain't no need to rush back, boy." Sénar tried to hide his anger, but it was noticeable even to Ken. His glare dared Sénar to try him. He grabbed his keys and went upstairs to grab something before telling Leah, "Come on." She smirked at me, "Goodnight Treasure," she said sarcastically.

I was glad Sénar ran upstairs, giving me a little head start to hurry cleaning, so I was almost done by the time he and Leah left. Ken came on to me so strong as I put the last dish up and tried to run upstairs. He pulled me back by my shorts and slid his hands into the front of my shorts; I could smell the alcohol on his breath. He plunged his fingers inside of me, covering my mouth with his other hand. He whispered, "Ooh, it's hot and tight." He then stuck his fingers in his mouth and said, "Ooh, it's sweet like your momma's umph." He smelled my hair as I squirmed in his captivity. He said, "Maybe Leah can help him get over you, so I can play with you next." I squirmed and tried to talk with his hand over my mouth. He uncovered my mouth just enough to hear me in case I tried to scream. I was praying Sénar would come back, or my plan would work to talk myself out of it. I said, "Ken Sénar is not done with me; he loves me." Ken laughed and replied, "No, he likes pussy, but he really likes yours. That's not the problem now, is it? What about you? You're just like Diamond; you don't love him; you love what he can do. Besides, I taught him all of that, so why not come to the master, he is still a student." I thought about crying but also about why Sénar wasn't back yet. I didn't want to appear weak and encourage Ken to continue his assault, so I thought fast when I said, "I do love Sénar, I am just scared, Ken, that's all. I don't want to break his heart." He chuckled and said, "You don't know what you want, you're confused like every other woman. I swear you are all lying vindictive bags of flesh. I hate you mothafuckas, but I love fucking y'all; that's for sure." Ken was going to cover my mouth again, but I pleaded, "I don't want you, Ken! Please stop!" Ken released me and glared at me with his evil eyes; I almost couldn't believe it worked. He then threatened, "I'll just send Sénar away, since you are such a distraction to him. He would do much better without him having to worry himself with you all the damn time. Then I can have my way with you." I begged, "Please don't send Sénar away, Ken!" I didn't want to cry, but I was desperate if he sent Sénar away, I would be alone in my world of chaos, and surely, I would die from it. Just the thought sent me into a panic. He laughed and left me there to drift into my thoughts of what would happen if he sent Sénar away.

I went to Sénar's room and looked for Leah's number. I searched through his drawers and saw a box of condoms on his dresser. I looked inside; there wasn't that many in there. I was curious, so I inspected the gold wrappers; I noticed an unusual puncture in it. I grabbed an already open one and noticed a few more holes as it was easier to see the holes in the wrapper without the condom inside. I wondered, *why would condoms have holes in it? Wouldn't that defeat the purpose of using them?* I continued to look for Leah's number but couldn't find it. In one of his drawers, I saw pictures of me from yearbooks, and some of me sleeping apparently taken with a camera unbeknownst to me. I also saw a little boy with a pretty dark skin lady with gray eyes like Sénar's. She was beautiful, and she was holding her son in her arms like she was in love with him. The older the little boy got in the pictures, the more I saw Sénar. He had the same gray eyes, but his cheeks were chubby; he was so innocent and happy. I smiled as I looked at the pictures until I heard the front door open and close. I quickly put them back and ran out of the room. I ran the bathwater and went to get the stuff I needed to take a bath. Sénar passed me when he got back, but he wouldn't look at me. I just got my stuff and ignored Cassidy running her mouth on the phone. I took my bath and thought about all the stuff Ken said and did to me. I wanted to scream; I hated him because he was evil. Sénar was fighting his hardest to not be like him, but sometimes I wondered if he was worse and just pretended not to be. I didn't hate Sénar; I just didn't want to love him either. He was so nurturing and affectionate, but he was also selfish and arrogant. I wondered why he took so long and got angry thinking about the reasons why when I heard a knock at the door.

I asked, "Who's there?"

He answered, "Sénar."

I giggled and asked, "Sénar, who?"

He opened the door, he ignored my little joke, and asked, "Are you ok, Treasure?"

I rolled my eyes and hid behind the curtain when I answered, "I'm fine, Sénar. What took you so long?"

He put his face in his hands and said, "I rather not answer that."

I just stared at him while he sat on the floor. He looked at me to ensure I was intact and not lying about being ok. He looked like he was the one that was not ok, but I didn't want to pry. He got up to say, "I just wanted to check on you. Let me know when you are out, so I can take a shower."

I let the water out and stood up naked; I grabbed my towel then said, "I'm out," and then I went to my room. I put my nightclothes on in peace while Cassidy slept and then got in the bed. I thought about the day, and how crazy it was; I just didn't know how much more I could take.

Chapter 12

Sénar was waiting for me to wake up in the morning, he laid by my bed and fell asleep. I woke up and almost stepped on him as I was getting up to use the restroom. Cassidy was still sleeping as I noticed Sénar stretched out on my floor. He looked so peaceful as he slept, but I knew he was not peaceful. He looked very disturbed when he got home last night. I saw his morning excitement through his shorts. I couldn't help but think about all the pleasure I got from his member that appeared to be happy to see me as Sénar still slept. He woke up and saw me staring at him in my thoughts of lust. He quickly sat up and pulled me to his room. He spoke as if he had a secret, "Treasure?" He looked back to make sure no one was awake. He then asked, "Treasure what happened when I left?" I was still trying to forget last night, rather than have to re-live the moment. I sighed before I replied, "Sénar, that is not something I want to wake up talking about." I tried to leave and go to the bathroom, but he stopped me. He appeared angry when he demanded, "Treasure, tell me what happened." The veins were popping out of his neck, and he appeared really upset. I hadn't seen him this mad in a long time; I just couldn't tell if he was mad with me, Ken, or himself. He looked like he was worried about something but didn't want to say it. He asked me again, but this time in a calm voice, he looked me in my eyes and asked, "Treasure what happened?" I looked down before I asked, "Why Sénar, what do you think happened? Why do you care? What do-" Sénar cut me off to say, "Answer my damn question, Treasure!" His voice was alarming, and the scary part was he was careful not to raise the octave to his voice, so it didn't carry out of the room. He impatiently waited for me to answer. I hesitated before I said, "Sénar…" I was scared and nervous because I didn't want him to get mad or blame me for it. I felt pressured when I answered, "He just said inappropriate stuff, and … he grabbed me…and Sénar, I don't know…. he put his fingers inside of me and then put them in his mouth." He winced at the details, and I tried to leave when he stopped me to ask, "Treasure, that's it? He did-" I cut him off and said, "Sénar, that's it, and it was enough, ok? Leave me alone." I stared at him; he appeared sad when he asked, "You would tell me, right?" I glared at him and yelled, "You would know, Sénar!" He asked, "How, Treasure?" I glared back at him and then said, "Because one of us would be dead." I pushed him out of the way and ran to the bathroom. I cried and wondered why he kept asking me, was it because he didn't trust me? Am I doing something to make Ken want to do those things to me? I rinsed my face and opened the door. Sénar was standing there; he looked remorseful. I looked past him and tried to leave the bathroom. He told me to get dressed; he didn't look like he was asking either. I went to get dressed and went downstairs; he was waiting for me. We got in his car and drove off. I asked, "Sénar, where are we going?" He answered, "I don't know." I was worried I couldn't gauge Sénar's emotions, and I started to get nervous. I called his name, "Sénar?" He was in a trance but answered, "What Treasure?" Concerned, I asked, "What's wrong, Sénar?" He shook his head and said, "Nothing, let's just drive for now." We drove towards LA, and we stopped at a restaurant. He asked, "Are you hungry?" We got something to eat and ate in silence. When we got back to the car, I asked, "Sénar, what took you so long?" He didn't want to answer, but he looked at me and said, "I messed up." I waited for him to tell me how, but he took forever. I got impatient and again called his name, "Sénar?" He hesitated, and then said, "I was with Leah last night." I looked at him and said, "Sénar, I was there, remember? You took her home…. Wait, you had sex with Leah Sénar?" He reluctantly said, "Yeah." I almost burst out into tears, but instead, I got furious and yelled, "Sénar! How could you? Why? Take me home, Sénar!" He insisted, "No, Treasure. We need to talk, ma. I can't go back without figuring things out." I was angry with him when I asked, "Sénar talk about what? We have pretty much already talked about the most horrific things I have ever heard and been through. So, there's nothing else really to talk about." I was numb to everything; I didn't even care what happened. Everything was falling apart little by little. He tried to be patient with me until I said, "Ken was right." Sénar almost came to a complete stop on the freeway as he pulled over. My heart was beating against my chest like it would explode. Sénar snapped when he roared, "Right about what Treasure?" I was scared when I answered, "He said that you would get bored of me and give me to him. You guys probably planned my demise, huh?" He smirked and replied, "You have no idea." I looked at him questionably when I asked, "What is that supposed to mean, Sénar?" He ignored my question and got back on the freeway before he asked, "What else did he say, Treasure?" I got myself into this conversation, so I finished it. I continued, "He said that women were conniving, vindictive bags of flesh and-" Sénar appeared to be trying to muffle his laughter when I said, "Sénar that is not funny." He straightened himself up and drove but said, "I know, I am sorry. I just couldn't hold it in; his ass is crazy. What else did he say?" I finished what I was saying, "He said you didn't love me that you just like p u s s y." Sénar stared at me and asked, "Why did you spell it out, Treasure?" I quickly defended myself and answered, "Because I don't like that word Sénar. Look, he said a lot of stuff, ok? All I know is that you are both crazy and I hate Ken. I don't want him touching me, and I don't trust him." Sénar seemed worried when he said, "Well, you shouldn't trust him or hate him. Just stay away from him and stay out of trouble. I will talk with him again, but his ass is trippin' again. He came in my room drunk as hell last night, asking me what happen with Leah. He bragged about how good your p u s s y tasted. I wanted to kill his ass. He said a lot of other shit that I will not disclose, but I just wanted to make sure he didn't hurt you. I knew I shouldn't have messed with Leah, but I was weak, and I didn't think he would take it that far; he knows how I feel about you, and he hates it. He wants me to be cold-hearted like him, but I don't want to hurt women like he does. I want to protect them and keep them from being hurt, not hurt them. I know it doesn't seem that way, but I am trying hard, Treasure." I rolled my eyes at him, and he shook his head as I drifted into my own thoughts.

We pulled up to Louie's house and got out to greet everyone. Latosha and Lil' James were happy to see me, and Sénar's aunt hugged me like I was one of them. Sénar and I walked to the back where everyone was. We sat down and joined their world to escape ours. Latosha asked Sénar and me to babysit Lil' James after only being there twenty minutes.

She asked, "Treasure, can y'all watch Lil' James for me and I'll braid your hair before you go home, please?" I looked at Sénar, and he shrugged his shoulders, Latosha added, "Y'all can sleep in my room, and I'll be back in the morning?" Sénar smacked his lips then asked, "Damn, what you 'bout to go make another one?" She rolled her eyes before she said, "Damn Sénar, shut up!" He retorted, "You shut up! Damn, make sure the nigga gonna take care of it then, at least!" Latosha got her feelings hurt. I felt bad for her and said, "Come on Latosha, don't listen to him; what are you wearing?" I got up and went with her to her room. When we were in there, she said, "Treasure, he is right; my ass don't need to go nowhere. I am just tired of sitting in this damn house all damn day!" I asked, "Well, why don't you go to school or something?" She laughed and said, "I can't stand school. Plus, I have to take these stupid job classes to get my food stamps and cash aid. They make sure your ass don't have time to do anything else."

I thought, *why would you go to classes to get a job when you can just get a job?* I shook my head before I asked, "Why don't you just get back with Lil' James' dad?"

She was annoyed with me when she said, "Treasure, I know you may be sheltered, but don't play stupid. His ass don't want to be with me; he just wanted to fuck, and when I got pregnant, he was on to the next girl. He does have that bomb though, so it was easy for him to move on. Now I am stuck with Lil' James and in this house. I just want to get out, meet some people, or do something." I smiled at her and then offered, "Well, let me help you get ready." She was excited when she asked, "So, you will watch him for me?" I answered, "Yeah, girl go have some fun! Let's find something for you to wear." Everything she had was skimpy or too tight or too short. She looked at me and anticipated my input, but I just stared at her blankly. I tried not to hurt her feelings but asked, "Latosha, you don't have anything else, like I don't know….. not as revealing?" She giggled then said, "You are funny, Treasure, and really beautiful. I can see why Sénar is so crazy about you. You're really lucky because his ass is crazy, but he will love and take care of you if you let him. I wish I had someone to love me like that." I just stared at her and said, "It's complicated, Latosha." She laughed then said, "I bet, you can tell me all about it tomorrow. We will kick Sénar and them out and have a girl's night!" We giggled, and I asked Sénar to take us to the swap meet. I had my own money, and I bought her two outfits that were more appropriate, and she looked great in them. I helped her with her hair and let her borrow my earrings. She was so happy she looked like a lady and not just somebody's baby's momma. Even Sénar smiled when he saw her; he said, "Damn, maybe you will find a man to take care of you instead of some Lil' boy, looking like that." Sénar smirked at her, and Louie giggled. Latosha blushed, "Well, thanks to your precious Treasure, she schooled me on how to be cute without being so revealing," she said it mockingly but then added, "thanks, Treasure!" Sénar looked at me then said, "Damn Treasure." I rolled my eyes and asked, "What?" He just shook his head as Latosha left.

Sénar had Lil' James most of the time, he only gave him to me when he went to smoke, or him and Louie went to the store. Daisy came over, but when she saw me, she didn't stay very long. Even Cedrick came by but didn't dare speak to me. Sénar and I fell asleep in Latosha's room, he wrapped his arms around me, and Lil' James slept in front of me. I was really surprised Sénar didn't try anything; I didn't know whether to be happy or sad. I didn't even bother asking because I didn't really want to know. Sénar had told me enough to last a lifetime; I wasn't sure I could take anymore. Lil' James woke up and crawled over me to slap Sénar. He giggled as Sénar snatched him up, waking me up to laughter and them playing. For a moment, everything felt ok until Sénar's phone rang. He answered, "Wassup pops?" He said, "Yes, sir." I waited to hear bye, but he laughed before he said, "Ok, I'll get it. Nah, we will be back Sunday….. Alright, pops." I was uncomfortable because I have no idea what Ken said, but it didn't sound like he was mad with Ken, to me. Sénar said, "I know what you are probably thinking, but he is my father Treasure. I just wish things weren't so crazy and complicated. Shit, I would rather have had the opportunity Tyrell had, but this is how it happened." I just ignored his reasonings and responded, "I'm hungry." He smiled sadistically and smelled my hair then squeezed me. He said, "I know, let's find something to eat." He grabbed Lil' James, and we left to the kitchen. His auntie was already cooking, so all we had to do was wait with Lil' James. His Auntie said, "Treasure, you sure are pretty. You wake up like that honey? I know you drive them crazy!" She laughed, but I thought, *who is them? And why was it funny?* She put Lil' James food on the counter then said, "Come on, lil' boy." He jumped out of my lap and ran to climb up on the chair to eat. His auntie said, "Y'all help y'all self! I'm gon' sit my tail down." She walked out the kitchen, and we made our plates. Latosha came back around eleven in the morning, and she looked so happy. She had on her second outfit I bought her, and she looked so mature and sexy. Even her momma came in the back and said, "Girl, you sure look like you got some sense today." She had on a nice pair of Capri jeans and a light blue blouse with a short bang covering her forehead. She had a bag with some hair in it and said, "Come on, Treasure." She braided my hair and talked about her night. She told me how different men treated her last night, and how she got some numbers. I smiled, knowing she felt really good, and she added, "Thanks Treasure, I had a great time, and now I know I need a new wardrobe." She laughed then asked, "What about you and Sénar, how was your night?" I answered, "It was cool, we just chilled." She laughed and asked, "Y'all didn't get it in?" I laughed and answered, "No, Latosha." She laughed before she said, "Girl, don't be acting brand new. I know y'all be getting it in!" I sighed then said, "Not lately. I don't know why but I am cool with it. We are not supposed to be doing that anyway." She laughed and replied, "Well, he must be good at it cuz Daisy is sprung on his ass and that Lil' London girl too." I shook my head and laughed before I said, "Yeah, he is." She smiled then said, "Girl, you better get cho' man!" I laughed and corrected her, "He is not my man; he is Sénar." She said, "Whatever." She finished my hair; it was so pretty. It was four braids, but it had little ones going into them. She gave me my earrings back, and I took a shower. When I got dressed, I put one of the outfits I bought for myself on. It was some jeans with pink puma T-shirt and some pink puma shoes.

Sénar looked like he wanted to snatch me up when I came out of the bathroom dressed, with my hair done, and the earrings he gave me shining in my ear. He smiled at me and didn't care who was watching; he grabbed me to squeeze me and smell my hair. He let me go to say, "You look so beautiful!" He gazed at me in awe as Latosha walked in and asked, "She cute, huh?" Sénar laughed before he answered, "Nah, she fine as hell, umph." We got in his car, and he took me to eat, then we smoked and went to the drive-in movies. He was the most relaxed that I had seen him since we left the house. We went back and slept on the couch and woke up with Lil' James lying with us. Before we left Sénar and Louie were talking as he handed Sénar two bags. Louie then asked, "What y'all niggas up too?" Sénar laughed before he answered, "I don't know. You know my pops is crazy, so I need to be ready for whatever." They hugged each other, and Sénar tapped me to say, "Come on, Treasure let's go." I squeezed Lil' James, I said goodbye to everyone else, and we left.

When we got home, Ken was waiting for us at the table. He called Sénar to him, and Sénar gave him one of the bags he got from Louie. I quickly ran upstairs to avoid Ken. Cassidy was on her phone as always and asked, "Why y'all go to LA without me?" I ignored her because it was clear that it was to get away from all of them. I went back downstairs to see that Ken and Sénar were still talking. I started to go back upstairs when Ken called me into the kitchen, he gave me some money and told me to get some school clothes. He tried not to make it obvious that he was aroused by my new look. I took the money and said, "Thanks." I turned to leave without even counting the money he gave me. I just ran upstairs to put it with the rest of my stash of money. I waited until Sénar came up to get me. He came to my door and said, "Come downstairs with me." I followed him downstairs and noticed Ken was gone and couldn't be happier.

The next day at school, I woke up early and walked to school to avoid any drama, especially after all the stuff that took place over the break. I went to my classes and made lunch to avoid the cafeteria. London finally came back to school and had a flock of girls surrounding her to ask questions. She wasn't exactly on Sénar's arm as usual, and it was pretty obvious. Sénar came out, and she walked up to him; he talked to her for a second and came to me after to say, "Wait for me after practice, Treasure." I looked at him and asked, "Why, Sénar?" Leah walked up; she smiled before she said, "Hey, Sénar." She was being flirtatious, but he ignored it and replied, "What's up, Leah." She looked at me to see if I knew about the two of them and their betrayal, but I just ate my food like I knew nothing. Sénar walked off, and Leah followed; I could see London from afar watching Sénar's every move. Tyrell was being himself and flirting with the other cheerleaders. Men were dumb; it seemed like all they cared about was coochie. They never seemed to take the whole person into account, ugh. I just ate and went to class, and Leah made sure to sit next to me in math class. She said, "Hey, Treasure, you should have come with us; we had lots of fun." I was calm and collected when I said, "That's nice Leah. I hope you are happy." I tried to sound as genuine as possible, but she still smirked before she said, "Well, now I see why you be smiling. He really seems to know what he's doing. I know you didn't teach him all that shit, or Tyrell would be up to par too." I laughed at her and said, "Well, aren't you the expert?" She snarled her lips before she spat, "You're Bonquisha, remember? You be boning everybody; you and Ken probably had your own fun, huh?" I was not able to remain calm anymore, I replied, "Leah, you are the snake slithering to everyone's man, not me. So, I suggest you leave me alone before you end up like London." She laughed and turned around to do her work. I was really tired of Leah; she had really crossed the line now. She was meddling, and she had no idea what she was entangled into. I avoided her to the best of my ability until practice was over. Leah came up to me to ask, "So, what y'all want to do after this?" I ignored her and waited for Sénar, but Tyrell walked up and asked Leah if she was ready. She answered, "I'm riding with Sénar and Treasure." Tyrell looked at me, and I shrugged my shoulders before I said, "I know nothing of the sort."

Tyrell smirked at Leah and asked, "So what, Treasure y'all cool now?" I smiled before I said, "Yeah, Tyrell." Leah laughed at him, and he left in a rage. Leah said, "Hell yeah!" Sénar walked up and grabbed my bag before I could pick it up and walked to his car. Me and Leah followed behind Sénar when he noticed her, he asked, "Leah, where's

Tyrell?" She stared at Sénar before she answered, "Treasure told him, she was cool with me riding with y'all." Sénar looked at me in the back seat through the rear-view mirror. I looked away in irritation as I laid my head back, wondering how I ended up in this situation. Sénar dropped Leah off, and she asked, "Damn Sénar, you don't wanna have some more fun?" He laughed and said, "Nah Leah, but I'll let you know when I do want to." She replied, "That's cool." I knew her feelings were hurt, but he did not care. Sénar drove home in silence, and I just kept my eyes closed.

When we got home, Ken was at the table, and he called us both with urgency. We both walked to the kitchen table. Ken dismissed me, by saying, "Treasure get me a beer." He had envelopes on the table and told Sénar to sit down. I handed him his beer and walked away. He and Sénar talked at the table while Ken showed him the different envelopes. Sénar was not as enthusiastic as Ken was, but he listened intently. I just went to my room to lie down. Sénar knocked on the door to ask, "Wanna go to the Winter formal?" I looked at him like he was crazy and answered, "No, that would be awkward." He came in and sat on my bed to explain, "No it won't be. Let's go like this; I take Nevaeh, and you take Louie that way we all go, and it won't be as awkward." I looked at him, and he looked hopeful, I didn't want to mess it up, so I said, "Yeah, I guess." Sénar smiled and was excited when he said, "This is going to be fun!" Before he left, I asked, "Sénar, what about London?" He rolled his eyes and asked, "What about her Treasure?" I was concerned when I asked, "Well, why aren't you going with her?" He looked at me and said, "Look, we are not together anymore. After y'all fought, I was done with her; I just didn't want to leave her like that, but I told her to chill and she didn't listen. That's the one thing I did like about her was that she listened. So, when she let her jealousy jeopardize her ability to listen, she gave the one thing up I liked the most, so I'm done." I studied him for a moment, and he was serious. I said, "Dang, Sénar, that's mean. What about Leah?" He rolled his eyes again and said, "Damn,

Leah is not even relevant, Treasure. I was just really hungry damn. You be playing too much, and I broke up with London, she just had good timing." I looked at him in his eyes and asked, "Well, what about me?" He looked as if I asked him a forbidden question. He asked, "Treasure, what do you want me to say, because obviously, you are looking for an answer, right?" I rolled over and wrote in my diary. He flipped me back over to ask, "Treasure, what do you want me to do?" I ignored him, I closed my eyes and pretended to be asleep. He got frustrated when he said, "Treasure, you really do play too much. I could tell you a million things, and you would hear me, but when I show you, Treasure, you still don't believe me. So, what now?" I said, "Show me again, Sénar, because I can't tell anymore." He shook his head and left me in my room by myself to ponder.

I went through the whole week, ignoring everyone with a face. I barely ate and wanted to be left alone. Sénar gave me my space, and I actually hated it but also appreciated the ability to think without the influence of his nurturing. My mom and Ken appeared to be in love again, and everything seemed perfect for them. Every time I saw Ken, he had some form of paperwork in front of him. I avoided him as much as possible, but he always found ways to utilize me. Sénar worked out and avoided me as well, and for some reason, Ken was less aggressive toward me. I was sexually frustrated, but I just masturbated like three times a day to hold me over.

Friday Leah sat next to me after her and Tyrell disappeared at lunchtime. She said, "Treasure, since Sénar is so stingy with his bomb D, maybe you can slide me Ken's number, or you can give him mine." I looked at her and smiled before I said, "Yeah, why not?" She thought I was being sarcastic, but I was already looking for her number to give to Ken. I said, "Write it down again, Leah, and I'll think about it." I was going to give it to Ken for sure, but I thought about my mom and thought about not giving it to Ken just for a second. Sénar took me home, but he dropped me off when he saw Ken wasn't home. He left and I got dressed in my cheerleading outfit to go to one of their last few games before the season was over. My mom came down and saw me and asked, "Treasure, where is everyone?" Once again, I shrugged my shoulders and said, "I don't know." She said, "Ok, well, I'll see you at the game." Before she went upstairs, she said, "Don't bring that Lil' snake, Leah, over here no more." She went upstairs; then, Ken came home shortly after. When he saw me on the couch, he came and sat down on the opposite couch of me. He said, "Sénar has a lot of offers to play senior football anywhere he wants to ensure he is drafted." He laughed before he asked, "Are you ready to say your goodbyes?" Ken smirked at me before he went upstairs. Sénar came home and appeared to be in a rush as he ran upstairs to get dressed for the game. I just sat on the couch and thought about the possibilities that awaited me in my future, and none of it seemed promising. I tried not to let it get me down as I needed my energy to cheer and deal with Leah's shenanigans.

I drifted into my thoughts anyways. despite warning myself not to. I thought about how Sénar could do it to Leah out of all the girls he could have chosen from, he chose Leah, or she chose him rather. I wanted to slap Sénar just thinking about it when he came down and saw me on the couch. He raised his eyebrow and asked, "Treasure, what are you over there scheming about?" I smacked my lips and rolled my eyes at him before I answered, "None of your business Sénar." He cut his eyes at me before he said, "Whatever, why do you have an attitude?" I didn't answer him, he said, "Treasure come on ma, don't act like that before my game. What's wrong? Talk to me." I glanced at him then toward the door before I said, "Sénar, I am fine. Let's go." He sighed and opened the door for me; he didn't say anything else to me until we got to the school. He said, "Wait for me after the game, ma." I nodded to acknowledge that I heard him.

The game was close; the away team wanted the win just as bad as we did. There were several scouts out tonight in the crowds, along with the local news station. Tyrell played great, he was really aggressive with his plays and avoided any altercations with Sénar. The away team was winning by two points with only four minutes left in the game with the ball in their hands. Sénar was watching the quarterback while in formation, waiting for him to throw the ball. Sénar followed where the ball was thrown and jumped in the air to intercept the throw. When Sénar caught it, he took off like lightning; juking and jiving anyone that came after him. The away team had a huge linebacker try to stop him before the goal line, but Sénar spun around out of his reach for a touchdown. I couldn't help but scream and jump for joy at his awesome play. I could feel the blood rush to my cheeks as I knew he could hear me cheer for him. He smiled my favorite smile and winked at me. I could have melted like the wicked witch in the *Wizard of Oz* before I noticed both Tyrell and Leah eyeing me. I didn't care I cheered and blew a kiss at Sénar, he caught it and put it over his heart. Leah looked like she wanted to get slapped; she rolled her eyes at me and asked, "Isn't Sénar your brother?" I stopped my cheering routine and said, "You know damn well he isn't my brother." She laughed and said, "Right, just like Ken, ain't yo' daddy." I walked away from her to avoid an altercation. My nerves were already thin, and I could not risk an involuntary response with my hand and her face. I stood by some of the other cheerleaders despite their dirty looks and watched the game intently. There were only two minutes left in the game. Sénar made it through the defense line for a two-point conversion, and the ball was back to the away team. Our team didn't let them move the ball at all, the clock ran out, and we won the game by six points. Everyone screamed and ran onto the field to celebrate. The news reporters and scouts greeted the football players to take interviews. After they took pictures of our football team, they even got pictures with us as their cheerleaders; it was a pretty exciting game. I just waited for Sénar as he walked up to me and gave me a high five. We walked to his car, and Leah and Tyrell left together. We just went home, but we stayed outside and talked for a minute. Sénar asked, "How did I do?" I rolled my eyes and replied, "You know you did a good job, Sénar!" He batted his eyelashes when he said, "Yeah, but I want to hear it from you." I smacked my lips and sincerely said, "Sénar, you played really great tonight." He grinned before he said, "Thanks, ma, you did great tonight too!" We both blushed together, making me giggle before I replied, "You are so goofy sometimes." I got ready to get out Sénar stopped me, he stared at me then said, "Treasure?" I looked back at him and stared into his gray eyes before answering, "Yeah, Sénar." He said, "Never stop being you, no matter how crazy life is, strive to be the best you. There is always room for improvement. So, try to always be moving towards a goal in life, so that you will not get complacent with not growing. Don't get so stuck in the past that you jeopardize your future and don't dwell on the future so much, that you are not present to live and learn." I frowned at him and then said, "Sénar, shut up." I got out then closed the door; he came from behind me to squeeze me and smell my hair. I turned around to face him to ask, "Sénar, are you leaving?" He answered, "Not if it's up to me. I would never leave your side if it was up to me. If I had no control of it, I would return or search for you until I found you." I rolled my eyes at him and said, "Yeah, right." I went inside and thought about what Sénar said; he was so deep sometimes. I don't know what I would do if he left; I would truly be alone.

Saturday morning, I smelled food, so I got up and brushed my teeth before going downstairs. Sénar was in the kitchen, making breakfast. He said, "Good morning, ma." I watched him as he finessed the kitchen in his normal cooking attire. He made me a plate and got something to drink for us. He said, "So, winter formal is next week. What are you going to do about your dress?" I shrugged my shoulders and answered, "I don't know, Sénar." He was excited when he offered, "Well, I am going to pick out an outfit today. Do you wanna go?" My mom came down and started to make coffee. I answered, "Sénar, I don't know because I don't want you to see my dress." Sénar laughed and joked, "Dang girl, you act like it's our wedding or something." My mom overheard us talking and asked, "What are y'all two over there talking about?" I was embarrassed, but Sénar answered, "We are talking about the winter formal. Treasure needs a dress." My mom smiled and said, "Oh, Treasure, you want me to take you? It will be fun!" I was a little shocked at her eagerness and responded, "Um, I don't know." Sénar nudged me with his knee, and I quickly changed my answer, "Yeah, Momma, that would be fun." She joked, "You got some money?" Ken came down and grabbed my mom from behind and smelled her hair while caressing her. He asked, "Money for what?" My momma answered Ken, "Treasure needs a dress for the winter formal." Ken fidgeted a bit before he said, "Who are you going with Treasure?" I quickly answered, "Me, Sénar, Louie, and Nevaeh are going, Ken." Sénar ate his food and just remained neutral; Ken smirked before he said, "Oh really, well, you can wash my truck and clean it out, and I'll give you some money for your dress." I was annoyed, but I agreed to do it even though I had my own money, I just didn't want to spend it on a dress.

I put some shorts on and a tank top and went to wash Ken's truck. Tyrell came out and was getting ready to leave when he saw me turning the water hose on. He crossed the street to say, "Damn Treasure, you looking good right now. What are you about to do?" He looked so damn good with his fresh white T-shirt, his dark blue jean shorts, and a pair of signature K Swiss on. I smiled at him before I answered, "I'm washing Ken's truck; I need to buy a dress for the Winter formal. Are you going?" Tyrell answered, "Yeah, I am. Who are you going with?" I was uncomfortable but still answered, "A bunch of us are going together." Tyrell smirked then replied, "I bet." Ken came out, and Tyrell was tense when he said, "There go yo' daddy, I'm out." I turned around to see Ken was standing there, glaring at me. I ignored him and started to wash his truck. Sénar came out to work out, and when he was done, he grabbed the water hose from me to wet me. I ran and tried to avoid getting drenched. I grabbed it back from him and wet him. Ken got up and went inside, but Sénar didn't care who saw us; he kissed me then said, "Damn Treasure." I broke our eye contact and grabbed the towels to dry Ken's truck, and we went inside to change our wet clothes. Before I was even all the way inside, Ken told me to grab him a beer way from the back. I was drenched in water with my clothes plastered to my body. Ken didn't hide his lust as my breasts were enhanced by my plastered shirt and glistening skin. I went to grab him a beer and brought it to him. He took it from me and gave me 300 dollars and said, "Next time, no fraternizing on the job." Sénar shook his head as he went upstairs, and I quickly followed. I grabbed clothes to take a shower, and Sénar came in behind me. I just stared at him because whatever he was going to do, I was down. I was beyond ready for an attitude adjustment. He just gazed at me and bit his lip, then said, "You miss me?" I rolled my eyes; he just had to mess up the moment. I asked, "Sénar, what?" He grabbed me to kiss me passionately, and I melted in his arms. He squeezed me and smelled my hair before he said, "I miss you." I had drifted away already, Treasure number two took over, and I kissed him back. He stopped me to say, "Come to my room first…nah, wait. Never mind." Sénar shook his head and said, "Just take a shower; I have to do something." I was disappointed, but I said, "Fine, get out!" He looked at me like his feelings were hurt, and he replied, "Damn Treasure, why are you so mad?" I was frustrated with him when I said, "Sénar, I am not mad; just go, I need to shower." He left me all hot and bothered; I wanted to scream! I thought, *what was wrong with him? He didn't want me anymore?* I didn't care anyway, I took a shower, but before I got out, I used it for my pleasure to avoid being so gullible next time. I was really going to try to not care about any of this; I was going to focus on school and avoid everyone. Well, after the winter formal that is; I was excited about that, deep down inside. I missed the homecoming because I was on punishment, but everyone else went. I got dressed to go with my mom to pick a dress; Ken was downstairs talking with my mom when I came down. I had on my long jean skirt and a spaghetti strap, so I could undress quickly to try on dresses.

My mom noticed I came down, and she asked, "Ready Treasure?" I nodded my head, yeah, she got up, and Ken smacked her behind. My mom giggled before she kissed him passionately, he squeezed her behind then said, "Get outta here, woman." I watched them interact; it was almost like she forgot I was waiting for her. My mom pulled herself together, then said, "Ok, Ken, we will be back soon." She and I left; we drove in Ken's truck. During the drive my mom said, "I know Ken is a bit much, but he's mine. I don't have to share him. So, I make sure I meet all his needs." I looked at her trying to convince me that Ken was acceptable because he didn't cheat. I asked, "Well, what happened when we all left to LA when you and Ken were arguing?" She looked at me as if I was being nosey and replied, "Treasure, don't worry about it. All I know is you better leave Tyrell alone." I was annoyed when I asked, "Why do you hate Tyrell so much, mom?" She shook her head then she said, "I don't like him. He is a spoiled brat, and he has no respect. I've never liked him with his badass; he killed my damn cat!" I looked at her like she was crazy when I asked, "What cat Momma?" She looked at me before she said, "Exactly, Treasure, I never got a chance to give it to you." I shook my head and looked at her, confused. I asked, "Well, Momma, I don't think, me and Tyrell are together anymore. So, you don't have to worry about him. But what do you see in Ken Momma, he is mean?"

She laughed and then said, "Treasure, he is a man and likes order. There is nothing mean about that. He is a great provider and father. You are too young to understand, but he is the best lover I have ever had, and he's all mine. So, I am good."

I laughed at her in my head as she bragged about Ken being all hers; he was inappropriate with me, so I could only imagine when he was on the road. We pulled into the mall and went to different stores to look at and try on dresses. I finally found a royal blue dress that fit perfectly. When my mom saw it, her eyes lit up when she said, "Oh Treasure, you look, beautiful sweetie! How much is it?" It was clearance and had a price tag of 300.00 at 50% off; we were able to get it for 150.00. We both went home happy as it was a good price and I paid for half, and she paid the other. I got some accessories and shoes, and then we went home. On the way home, my mom said, "Treasure, I love you very much. I know things can be rough sometimes, but remember the poem I wrote you?" I nodded, "Yeah, Momma."

She said, "Never lose sight of that sweetie because we are imperfect creatures, but our creator is not. So, we will always strive throughout our trials and tribulations but pray for strength and endurance. Sometimes we just aren't paying attention to the details because we don't want to deal with the reality, so we create our own to live in. But the reality is that it cannot be escaped Treasure, so we have to make wise choices, so our realities will not consume us like it has me of lately. I just hope you learn from my mistakes and other's mistakes, so you do not have to suffer the same fate or worse."

I was blown away by her exit speech. I mean, I heard some really heavy lines from her and Sénar in the last few days. I just wondered why everyone was so intense lately. I guess I was out of the loop. My mom went upstairs to her reality, and I went to put my dress away. I went downstairs to watch TV and think about what my mom said. I was blown away at some of the stuff she thought and said. Ken came downstairs, and I squirmed on the couch in discomfort. Ken called me into the kitchen. I answered, "Yes, Ken?" I did my best to be obedient to Ken to avoid him punishing me or focusing on me, but it only worked to keep him from being violent with me. He was still inappropriate, just seemed to be less aggressive lately but more strategic rather.

He stared at me and licked his lips before he said, "When are you going to let me play with you next Treasure?"

He rubbed his hand up the split of my skirt, and I moved back before he could get to my coochie. He stood up and towered over me. I tensed up and fought the feeling of fear while he ran his hand down the side of my neck and breast. He whispered, "I might let Sénar stay, if you let me play too."

I quickly said, "No, Ken, take Leah; she wants it. I don't."

Ken laughed and asked, "Oh, yeah?"

He continued to rub his hand down my stomach before he could get to my coochie, I said, "Ken? I left Leah's number in the glove compartment in the left-hand corner." I spoke out of desperation, quickly but clearly.

He sat down. He then eyed me and ran his hand up my skirt again, brushing his hand against my coochie before he said, "Good girl. I guess she can hold me over for now."

I jumped back when the front door opened, and Sénar came in with pizzas. He saw the look on my face and saw the smirk on Ken's face. He rolled his eyes and searched me for emotion, but I just went to grab plates and sat them on the table when Ken said, "Get me a beer, Treasure." I got him a beer way from the back and got a slice of pizza then sat at the kitchen nook. Sénar went to put his clothes he bought away and came back to get pizza. He ate next to me and watched me eat my food before I went to bed. Sénar came to my room, but I was already in my bed, even though it was early. Cassidy was on her phone, so I knew he would not ask me anything in front of her. I just ignored Sénar and listened to Cassidy talk on the phone. She was on the phone with Nevaeh; I heard her say, "I don't know, girl but I am bored. At least you have Louie, shit, I don't have nobody, and I have needs girl. These little boys don't be knowing what they doing. I miss Tony; I am going to call him one day girl, just to see what he is doing. I need some real dick." She giggled, and I squirmed in discomfort, knowing I was feeling like I needed an attitude adjustment myself. I went into dream mode, to try to escape my reality. Even though, my mom just warned me of the dangers of creating our own world to live in, but I needed a trip into my own Lala Land to avoid breaking down and giving into temptation.

In the morning, I woke up to a quiet house. I accomplished eating a bowl of cereal without any hazards or interruptions. Normally Sénar would be up, but I guess he was still sleeping. I watched TV until the house seemed to wake up. Cassidy and Sénar came down at the same time and ate breakfast as I watched TV. Cassidy ate and went back upstairs while Sénar came to watch TV with me.

He asked, "What were you and my pops talking about yesterday?"

I was uncomfortable, but I answered, "He just asked me about the truck and said some inappropriate stuff Sénar."

He shook his head in irritation when he said, "Well, let's go."

I asked, "Where?"

He said, "I don't know; let's just go to the park or something."

Ken came down; he was dressed casually, but almost like he wanted to appear more youthful. He left, and Sénar raised his eyebrow and looked at me to say, "Come on, ma."

He grabbed a basketball before we left to the park. He let me drive for a little bit, and I said, "You know I can't play basketball, right?"

Sénar laughed. "I don't know Treasure you are a pretty fast learner, so don't be so quick to doubt yourself." He smiled at me before we got out to play; he was right; I wasn't so bad this time. We sat down on the grass to rest, and he asked, "What do you wanna be when you grow up, Treasure?"

I shrugged my shoulders and answered, "I don't know, Sénar, alive." We both laughed, but I was being truthful. I continued, "I like to read and write, so what do you think I should do?"

He laughed and answered, "Be a writer or a journalist. You are a fast learner, so computers........ or a wife and a mother." He laughed before he said, "You are beautiful and really smart ma, you could do whatever you want. Just apply yourself."

I rolled my eyes at him and asked, "Why do you always say stuff like that? I am not dumb Sénar, I just don't trust people, and I prefer not to be bothered. I would rather read or write than be around people. I don't know, people are cruel, so I just stay to myself."

He was concerned when he replied, "Right, that makes you a perfect victim. Don't isolate yourself, stay present, Treasure, so you will know what's going on around you. You can't keep ignoring everything, thinking it will go away. You have to learn, grow, and adapt or conquer to move forward in all situations. Ask God to guide and lead you to a plan for your future, so you can survive in this world without having to be of it. The world is cruel and evil, but we all play our roles in it all too. We have to grow daily and reason with him daily. I want to see you grow into the woman I know you are. I want to be the man I know I am supposed to be too, but I know it's hard sometimes." He looked down.

I laughed and asked, "You really love God, huh? You think there really is a God?"

Sénar looked at me even more concerned than before when he said, "Treasure, are you kidding me right now? If there wasn't a God, the planets would smash together like a bunch of marbles. We wouldn't have a soul or spirit; we would merely just be flesh, Treasure. Of course, there is a God, you just have to get to know him personally, and you will feel his love. I promise you that."

I just looked at him and shook my head before I said, "Ok, I'll keep that in mind, Sénar."

He smirked before he replied, "I hope so because you are special to me, and I want you to know the importance of at least getting to know our creator."

I asked, "If I am so special, then how come you don't...never mind." I lost my confidence to ask him.

He said, "Treasure, you mean more to me than just sex. I could have sex with a lot of girls around my age or even older women, but

I have never felt the way I feel about you, about anyone else. What we have is far more than just physical. I want you to be mine, all of you. I want the keys to your heart, mind, and body. So, our souls can intertwine and become one. It's not that I don't want to have sex with you, I think about you all day and that too, but I am teaching myself discipline. If I can abstain from sex with you, I can abstain from a lot of things. Don't worry; my fast is almost up."

He winked at me. I scrunched my eyebrows at him, and he laughed. I said, "Gosh, Sénar; you are so intense."

He wasn't laughing; he was serious. He loosened up a bit and asked, "So, you are taking your braids down before the dance, right?"

I looked at him before I asked, "What? You are crazy, Sénar!"

He smiled sadistically and said, "Crazy about you!" He laughed and then said, "Nah, for real, I want you to wear your own hair. Please?"

I smiled and agreed, "Ok, you think Latosha or my Momma will do it for me."

He replied, "Hell yeah!" I slapped him on the arm, and we headed back to the house. My mom was cooking dinner by herself when we came in.

Sénar asked, "You need any help, Carmel?"

She said, "No thank you, Chef Sénar."

He smiled and went upstairs. I asked, "Momma, what are you making?"

She answered, "Some red beans and a pot roast Treasure."

It smelled so good, I went upstairs to shower, and Sénar took one after me. We both came down to watch my mom finish up. When we got ready to eat, Ken wasn't back yet. My mom asked, "Sénar, where is your Dad?"

Sénar answered, "I don't know; he didn't tell me anything when he left." Sénar ate his food, and his facial expression showed he was pleased with the food. He smiled and said, "Dang Chef Carmel, this is fire fire!" He ate his food quickly and got seconds.

My momma smiled, she seemed worried but said, "Thanks Chef Sénar. That means a lot coming from you because I know you know what you are doing in the kitchen, boy!"

For a minute she was happy but then got sad again. Ken never misses dinner unless he is working. The fact that my momma cooked, I knew she cooked for him because she could give a rat's tail what we ate. She waited a little longer and got frustrated; she put her plate in the sink and said, "Good night, you guys."

My momma went upstairs, I started to feel guilty, and Sénar asked, "What's wrong Treasure?"

I shook my head then answered, "Nothing." I helped him clean up, and we put the food away. We watched a little TV until Ken came home, and my mom came storming down the steps.

She said, "Where the fuck were you, Ken?"

Ken waved my mom out of his face and said, "Don't talk to me like that woman and make me a plate!" My mom didn't crumble or cry; she went to the kitchen to make him a plate and made a lot of noise doing it.

Sénar said, "Go upstairs, Treasure."

I quickly got up and went upstairs. I could hear them arguing and a lot of noise. Cassidy was on her phone and stopped talking when she heard the commotion. She just glared at me and kept talking; I just wrote in my diary until I fell asleep. I got up to get dressed and go to school. Sénar was already down there when I got down, and normally, he is not up this early. He appeared to be washing his hands; the kitchen looked perfect like there was no glass or altercation before we went to bed. I went to school and home; I didn't see my mom most of the day. I just know Ken missed dinner tonight too.

It was Thursday the day before the dance my mom and Ken had been arguing for the last three nights in a row because Ken wasn't home at dinner time. My mom and ken argued every time he came home, and my mom wasn't the quiet, submissive woman she appeared to be normally. She came down and waited for him both nights, and I made sure not to be around too long after Ken arrived. Ken left me alone, so I was happy, but everyone else was on pins and needles. Leah came up to me at lunchtime, she had her nails done, her necklace was glimmering as her name dangled from it, and she had a new cellphone in her hand. Leah laughed at me as I observed her from head to toe.

She grinned before she said, "It was fun being you, but Sénar is stingy with his bomb D. Tyrell, gives it freely. He is much better now too. Thanks to me. But with my new friend, I think I rather be me." London was standing nearby, while Tyrell and Sénar walked towards us from opposite directions.

I told her, "You can have Tyrell, and you will never get Sénar, you would have to be me." I smirked at London and Leah as Tyrell and Sénar walked up. I added, "And I don't care about your new friend, you will probably die wishing you were me, Leah."

She laughed and then asked, "You wish, huh?"

I laughed before I answered, "Hell yeah!" I continued to get my food and walked outside, leaving everyone in there to deal with their own emotions. Sénar followed me out, and we sat down under my favorite tree to eat my food. London followed us outside but watched from afar as she was still a stalker.

Sénar said, "Treasure, that was pretty harsh what you said to Leah." He wasn't being funny; he continued, "Words have power Treasure, and some things are better left unsaid."

I rolled my eyes at him, "You didn't hear what she said, Sénar. Leave me alone she is on my last nerve. I mean, she passed Sabrina's rank a long time ago, Sénar." He shook his head at me, and I ate my food in silence. After practice, I saw London walk up to Sénar; she looked like she was crying. Sénar was frustrated, but he spoke with her before he came to grab my bag. We left, and he seemed to be irritated as we drove home.

I asked, "Sénar, what's wrong?"

He shook his head and said, "Nothing."

I knew he was lying, but I didn't want to pry. He looked at me and asked, "You ready for the dance?"

I smiled and said, "Yeah, Sénar, I'm ready. You are not going to change your mind and go with London or Leah, right?"

He rolled his eyes before he said, "Very funny, Treasure." He smiled sadistically and asked, "Are you going to give me some dessert after?" He bit his bottom lip and waited for my answer.

I rolled my eyes and answered, "No, I thought you were fasting."

He laughed and asked, "Oh, but you heard that part, though?" I got out and laughed at him; he looked annoyed with me, but he didn't say anything. Ken's truck was gone, so I prepared myself to see my momma sitting around, waiting for Ken. At least I could ask her to help me take my hair down if she was sitting around to give her something to do. She was sitting at the table in Ken's chair with a bottle of wine, and she looked miserable. I didn't even speak to her because she looked like she was ready to snap. Sénar saw her, and he almost just went upstairs, but he stopped to ask, "Carmel, are you ok?"

My mom cried when she exclaimed, "No, Sénar, I am not. Does your dad have someone else?"

I wanted to stop listening to the conversation after Sénar answered, "I don't know Carmel; he would be stupid if he does. You're a good woman, don't worry, he will come around. He might have found a new driving gig or something, stay positive."

She laughed and said, "Yeah, right, he wouldn't be asking for money to buy his own truck if he had a new gig."

Sénar said, "Carmel, you need me to do anything?"

She laughed hysterically and said, "No, Sénar, thanks, though."

He left her and came upstairs to check on me and said, "If you need help taking your hair down, you better ask your momma before she gets too bent." I threw a pillow at the door, but I knew he was serious. I changed into something more comfortable and went downstairs to check on my mom. Although I felt bad as I had played a part in her demise, maybe this would be enough for her to leave him, and everything would go back to normal. If only it were that easy. I went downstairs, and my mom was crying as she was swallowing her liquid medicine. She poured her another glass before the glass was even empty.

I asked, "Momma wanna help me take down my hair?"

She looked at me like I was crazy and replied, "Girl, you trust me in your hair? I'll help you just because." She smiled, then got up and took the comb as I cut the braids. She started to take them down as she confided in me. She cried and told me how much she loved Ken and how she would not put up with him cheating. She was at her wit's end because as crazy as Ken was, even with his violent escapades, he never had my mom like this. She didn't hide her despair or her thoughts about Ken's recent behavior. I almost told her what I thought she needed to hear to be done with him when Ken walked in the door. He didn't say anything to my mom or me; he just walked upstairs. My mom threw the comb down and followed him, with no yelling. She just humbly followed behind him. My hair was only halfway down, and I was annoyed that I had to do the rest by myself.

Sénar came in and asked, "Where's Carmel?"

I sighed and answered, "Ken came back." I cleaned up the area and moved to the living room to watch TV while I took my hair down.

Sénar asked, "Are you going to be able to finish by yourself?"

I nodded yeah and then said, "It will just take longer."

He came into the living room with me, "I'll keep you company then." I was actually happy he was here just in case Ken came down. I definitely didn't want to go upstairs and have to take my hair down in front of Cassidy. He saw me taking one braid down at a time.

He got irritated and asked, "Girl, why are you taking them down one at a time?" I looked at him, and he took the comb he turned it on the wide-tooth side and grabbed like five braids and started to comb through them all at once. My eyeballs almost fell out of my head; he laughed. He did it quickly and without any pain. He gave it back and said, "Now you try it." I was ready to let him do it when he said, "My dad would kill me if he saw me taking your hair down." He laughed as Ken came down and looked into the living room.

Sénar sat back to watch TV when Ken called him over to him, "Come here, boy, I know yo ass ain't taking no damn hair down?"

Sénar laughed and said, "Nah pops, what's up."

They talked at the table while I tried Sénar's technique without success. But I did eventually get three of them down at once. They talked the entire time I took my hair down. I was finally done, I was so tired when I got up to clean up my mess. Sénar came and said, "Go to bed, ma, I'll clean it up; we got a big day planned tomorrow." When I looked up at him, he was excited and still energetic. I quickly went upstairs to shower and went to bed.

My mom was in a better mood when we came home early on Friday to get ready for the winter formal. She was waiting on us, so she could help me get ready; she was just as excited as we were. She had a hot comb and flat iron on the stove, and I sat in the chair to let her straighten my hair. I don't know before last night when the last time my mom did my hair, let alone touched me. When she finished, she cut my ends and styled my hair. It was healthy and longer than I expected, she smiled and said, "You go girl, look at all that hair! You look so nice, sweetie; I'll touch it up before you leave. You want me to do your makeup?"

I shrugged and said, "I don't really wanna wear makeup Momma, but I will wear some lip gloss or mascara." She pouted, and I said, "Ok, Momma, you can do my makeup." She ran to get her makeup kit, and I sat there and waited for her to return. She wrapped my hair and put pins to hold it in place. She did my eyebrows with tweezers but said, "You don't need much done to your eyebrows. I guess your dad was good for something because he had some perfect eyebrows." She continued with a little foundation and blush then eyeshadow. I looked in the mirror; it was pretty, but I liked my face better.

I said, "Thanks, Momma." My hair was wrapped, and my face was done up when Sénar and Louie walked in the front door laughing. I said, "Hey, guys." Sénar and Louie both looked at me and said, "Hey, Treasure."

Sénar's eyes were focused on my face, "You look pretty Treasure," he said sarcastically. I rolled my eyes at him, I knew he was serious, but I also knew he didn't like makeup. I went to get dressed, but first, I put cocoa butter all over my body as Nevaeh and Cassidy happen to walk in. Nevaeh was dressed she looked pretty as well; she had a glow about her. She saw me in my bra and panties with the room smelling like Cocoa butter, and she tried to hide her envy. She and Cassidy eyed me as I continued to get dressed. I put my dress on with my gold shoes and was about to put my earrings on when there was a knock at the door.

It was Sénar, he said, "Come here Treasure. I got something for you." I went out into the hallway to see what he had for me. He said, "Turn around," he put a necklace on me, and I went to the bathroom to look in the mirror. I was almost in tears when I saw he had my chain replaced with a gold one and added diamonds throughout my now, gold name on the new chain.

I said, "It's beautiful Sénar, thank you. Why...never mind."

He gave me some diamond studded earrings to match the diamonds in my name. I looked down and tried not to be overwhelmed when he said, "You are worth it, Treasure, besides you're the real treasure. Come finish up, so we can go."

I came back, and Nevaeh and Cassidy noticed my bling bling right away. They tried not to show their jealousy as I let my hair down and finished my assembly. My hair flowed down onto my shoulders as my skin glistened in my beautiful dress. Cassidy wasn't going, so me and

Nevaeh went down together as Sénar and Louie waited at the bottom. Sénar's eyes were all over me; he looked at me in awe. My momma jumped up and down and said, "You look gorgeous, Treasure!" My mom ignored Nevaeh, but Louie quickly embraced her and told her how beautiful she looked. She asked to take a picture of us all, so we all huddled together to take a picture with our best smiles.

Sénar tried to hold himself together in front of Ken and my mom, but he did not fail to let me know I looked beautiful when he said, "Dang Treasure." Ken cleared his throat and said, "Boy don't mess that rental up." He threw Sénar the keys, we left and drove to the dance in a 2002 charger. We smoked and listened to music on the way to the dance at one of the recreational centers in town. Nevaeh didn't smoke, but she did get a contact high as she giggled in the back seat. We had a ball; we danced, we took a billion pictures and joked around all night. Even Nevaeh and I got along and got photobombed by Leah when she came over to our table. She tried to floss her dress and assemble, but Sénar paid her no mind. She got her feelings hurt and went back to Tyrell, but he was already talking to another girl. So, she sat down and entertained herself with her phone. I went to the bathroom, and Nevaeh followed. I used the restroom and waited for Nevaeh while she was throwing up in the bathroom stall. I thought, *what is wrong with her; she didn't drink or smoke, so why was she throwing up?* She was sweating and looked pale when she came out.

I asked, "Are you ok, Nevaeh?"

She shook her head and answered, "I am fine."

We left the dance and went to the teepee hotels, since Nevaeh was old enough to get the rooms. He didn't give us a hard time; he knew it was a dance tonight. We chilled together for a while, and we went our separate ways to our rooms. Nevaeh never stopped staring at Sénar and me as we were unbothered by anyone else. We went back to our room and talked a bit before he asked me to take my makeup off. I was happy to do so when he saw me, he said, "Perfect." I laid in the bed and waited for him to make a move, but he just laid in the bed to watch TV. I was frustrated, and I took my dress off and got in the bed and under the sheets as Sénar watched me the whole time.

He laid in the bed next to me, and I said, "Sénar, you play too much."

He snatched the covers off me and took my panties off and worked his magic. I thought I would pass out from the amount of pleasure I received. I was able to scream and yell as he licked and nibbled on my coochie until I exploded. When he was done, he laid next to me as if he were done. I let Treasure number two take over; I snatched the covers off of him. I looked into his eyes to see the excitement glimmer in his eyes as I got on top of him. I rode him like I did in the summer and passed out into a blissful sleep.

Chapter 13

The next morning Sénar pulled me to him and smelled my hair; I woke up to that and feeling his excitement on my bare behind. I really, for a moment, didn't know whether to jump out the bed or rollover to kiss him. I did neither; I just froze in time and didn't move or speak. Sénar asked, "Treasure, what are you thinking?"

I took my time before I answered, "I don't know, Sénar."

He laughed and said, "You're so cute when you lie."

I sat up and kept the sheet to cover myself; I picked up my underwear and bra off the floor to put them on. He asked, "What are you doing, Treasure?"

I looked back at him, "I am putting my bra and panties on."

He asked, "Are you gonna put your dress back on too?"

I smacked my lips and said, "Sénar, I am just putting something on; why are you asking so many questions?"

He rolled his eyes and replied, "Relax, dang, I won't bite unless you want me too."

I laid back down, pulled the cover-up, and just laid there without saying a word. Sénar shook his head before he asked, "Did you have fun last night?"

Not sure what part he was talking about, I answered, "Yeah, I did."

He smiled then laid back and said, "Me too." He was relaxing with his eyes closed as he lay naked under the covers, only covering his waist but leaving his chest bare. I stared at him and fought the urge to touch him. When he looked me in my eyes with his stunning gray eyes to say, "Come here, ma." I started to shake my head no, but I just went to him instead. He pulled me to him and squeezed me when he said, "Relax ma, it's early; we still have a couple of hours to just chill."

I laid next to him, and we watched TV as we reminisced about the dance until we fell back asleep. I woke up in his arms and to his alarm ringing. It was ten-thirty in the morning as Sénar released me to grab his phone to turn the alarm off. He got up; I tried to avoid looking at his naked body as he walked through the room. He grabbed a bag and started taking out clothes. I could not help but observe his body and all the changes that took place. He was getting taller, and he was more muscular from his dedication to working out.

He looked back at me and asked, "You wanna take a shower with me?"

I tried not to let my excitement show as I got up to take a shower with him. We showered together; I let him have his way with me in the shower before we got out to get dressed. It felt so good, but deep down inside, I still felt guilty like I was falling into something that I was unable to get out of. He had a complete outfit on the table of the hotel room ready for me. I was not shocked but still asked, "Sénar, are you always this prepared?"

He shrugged his shoulders, "I try to be Treasure. Why?"

I shrugged my shoulders too, "I don't know, I just asked."

He smirked, "Well, maybe you should be more prepared." I slapped his arm, and he squeezed me, then smelled my hair before I could put my clothes all the way on. I pushed him off me, "Stop it, Sénar." He released me, and I finished getting dressed. We spent the day with Louie and Nevaeh, going to different places in the mall before going home. Nevaeh couldn't help but stare at Sénar and I with a look of wonder on her face. I just ignored her nosey self and tried to enjoy myself. When we got home, the house was quiet; we put our things away and went to bed. Before I fell asleep, Sénar came to me and kneeled at the side of my bed, "Treasure?" I looked at him and hoped Cassidy was asleep just in case he said something dumb.

He said, "I had a really good time and thanks for going with me. Goodnight, ma." I smiled at him, "I did too, Goodnight, Sénar."

Ken appeared remorseful and stayed home for the next week. He was home for dinner every night and agreed to take my mom with him on his next route. Everything appeared to be getting better. Sénar and I were both working on self-discipline, but it was definitely tempting to just give in to temptation. I was ready for an attitude adjustment already but just waited for Sénar to make a move because I did not have the confidence. London still called Sénar and followed him around at school, despite their relationship status.

Sénar and I were watching TV on the couch after school and practice. He had already worked out and came down after his shower. His phone rang; he answered, "Hello?" He looked agitated when I heard him ask, "About what?" He quickly hung up with a worried look on his face and said, "I'll be back, Treasure." He left in a hurry and was gone for maybe an hour before he came back upset. He didn't even come back to watch TV with me as he went straight upstairs. I didn't want to be a sitting duck for Ken, so I went upstairs too. I started to knock on Sénar's door, but I didn't, I just went to my room. I didn't bother going down for dinner; I just read until I fell asleep.

The next day I went to school and saw everyone in their normal formation; Leah and Tyrell and Sénar and London. I saw London talking to Sénar while he reluctantly listened. I sped my walking up when I heard Tyrell call my name. I just kept walking, but he caught up to me and said, "Treasure?"

I took a deep breath before responding, "Yeah, Tyrell?"

He stared at me before he answered, "I want to talk to you, Treasure."

I sighed and asked, "About what Tyrell?"

He said, "About everything, Treasure. We had something, right? Dang, we need to talk about it, so we can move on."

I looked at him to see if he was sincere; I couldn't tell, he was so handsome and charming enough to be trying to hurt me again. I answered, "Tyrell, we can talk on the phone."

He got upset and said, "Damn Treasure, it's like that? We can't even get together and have a conversation? Wow!"

I answered, "I don't know; I'll let you know Tyrell."

He smirked at me and replied, "Whatever, Treasure."

I wasn't sure I wanted to be alone with him and his temper tantrums. At lunchtime, I stayed to myself; I didn't even eat lunch because I didn't bring one, and I wanted to avoid the cafeteria. I purposely went to my math class early to avoid having to sit next to Leah. I was able to avoid her even at practice as she and Tyrell left right after. I waited for Sénar as I watched London walk beside him, and she appeared to be upset or desperate rather. He grabbed my bag and kept walking, prompting me to follow behind him and avoid eye contact with London to prevent a possible altercation. We drove home in silence, as we pulled up, I noticed Ken's truck in the driveway and dreaded possibly having to deal with him. Sénar asked, "What's wrong, Treasure?" I smacked my lips and said, "Nothing." I got out, walked into the house, and went straight to the kitchen instead of going upstairs, even with Ken sitting at the table. Sénar followed me into the kitchen as Ken nodded, "What's up Sénar?" He responded, "What's up, pops." Watching my every move as I grabbed all the stuff, I wanted to make tuna. I made sure to wash my hands before I started. I opened the cans, cut the pickles and onions, and added the mayo and mustard. I made a sandwich, and Ken said, "Make me some too." I gave him the sandwich I made and asked, "Sénar, do you want one?" He answered, "Yeah, I'll take one." I made him one, and Ken said, "I'll take another one." I was frustrated, but I made him another one, and I brought it to him with a fake smile. I asked Sénar if he wanted another one as I made another sandwich. Sénar answered, "Nah, ma, I'm about to work out, and I don't want any cramps." I bit my sandwich as he waited for me to put everything away and walk out of the kitchen before he went to work out. I ran to my room and saw Cassidy was on the phone.

She eyed me with a look of disgust on her face and said, "Girl, let me call you back; she is here."

She kept her look of disgust consistent on her face as she asked, "So, are you fucking Sénar Treasure?"

I was chewing on a bite of my sandwich in shock at her question. I responded, "What?"

Cassidy stood up when she said, "Don't play stupid Treasure, ugh, you nasty!"

I wanted to force-feed her my sandwich, but instead, I answered, "Why don't you ask Sénar? Why does it matter to you, anyway?"

She laughed and said, "You are such an idiot! You are gonna end up like Daisy's ass, watch! I knew your ass would."

I quickly left the room and ran downstairs to the garage, ignoring Ken sitting at the table. I opened the garage, almost running into Sénar but he caught me before I ran into him and asked, "What's wrong, ma?" I was trying to catch my breath as I answered his question, "Cassidy is tripping, and I can't be in there with her! I want to hit her in her mouth!" Sénar asked, "Treasure what happened?" I folded my arms and answered, "She is accusing me of having sex with you, Sénar!" He laughed at me, instantly irritating me when I said, "That is not funny, Sénar!" He rolled his eyes but tried not to appear agitated when he replied, "Don't listen to her; she been suspected that. Someone probably just confirmed it, so chill out." I was even more annoyed with how he was so nonchalant about it. I almost left when he said, "Nevaeh probably told her something. Just tell her your favorite line; *it's none of your business*." I rolled my eyes at Sénar and said, "Nevaeh is stupid! Why is she always looking sick and throwing up?" Sénar laughed again and replied, "Louie got her pregnant Treasure. So, she probably just being messy because she mad, she is knocked up and not you."

He winked his eye at me. I was kind of shocked because Louie was about to graduate and hadn't even finished school yet, now he was about to be a dad. Nevaeh's dumb ass was out of school already but obviously had nothing better to do. Sénar said, "Well, at least Louie is happy, and it keeps him from going out in the streets doing dumb shit. Plus, he is down to work with me this summer with London's dad."

I looked at Sénar with an attitude when I asked, "I thought you and London broke up, Sénar?"

He smirked at me before he said, "We did Treasure, damn. London's dad likes me and my work ethic, separate from me and London's relationship. He's probably glad we aren't together anymore; trust me, men know each other's intentions most of the time." I shook my head at Sénar and watched him work out to avoid Cassidy until we ate dinner. I went to bed without another word to Cassidy.

Football season was over, and the basketball season had just started, which was a big shift in our schedules. Basketball games were more sporadically scheduled. Though they had a great season for football, there were no championship games for basketball promised to be lined up this year. Sénar was not as enthusiastic about basketball as it showed in his attitude. Ken was constantly asking Sénar about different colleges, and Cassidy was always on her phone. She had turned eighteen at the beginning of the year in January. She didn't even know if she would graduate, but Ken still bought her a car. She didn't have a license or know how to drive, so Sénar took the time to show her in Ken's truck, since he was back on the road again. Sénar even brought me the paperwork I needed to get my drivers permit and told me he would help me get my license when I turned sixteen in March.

My mom barely came down to eat, and I assumed it was because Ken appeared to be back on the road more. London would not give up on Sénar; she called him all day and followed him around at school.

She even popped up at our house one day and begged Sénar to talk to her in his room. London and Sénar went upstairs for what seemed like forever, but when they came back down, she wasn't smiling like normally. She kissed him goodbye, and he kissed her back, but I could see his hesitation. When she left, Sénar came back into the living room, shaking his head. He sat down to watch TV with me, I could tell he was angry, but he tried to hide it.

I asked, "What's wrong, Sénar?"

He shook his head out of frustration and then said, "I don't want to talk about it right now, Treasure."

I looked at him before I asked, "Are condoms supposed to have holes in them?"

He stared at me like I was crazy when he asked, "Why, Treasure?"

I quickly answered, "I'm just asking Sénar."

He looked agitated with my question but still answered, "Condoms are for protection from STD's and pregnancy. Obviously, they have some chance of malfunction, but for the most part, no, they don't' have holes or that would defeat the purpose of wearing one. So, no Treasure they don't, I guess they could break, but why are you asking?"

I shrugged my shoulders before I said, "Well, because yours had holes in them."

He looked at me in confusion when he asked, "What? How do you know?"

He jumped up and ran upstairs to his room as I followed behind him. He grabbed one of the wrappers. He freaked out when he saw the holes in the open ones and checked the ones still in the box and said, "Treasure what the hell? Man, I knew something wasn't right." He seemed to be deep in thought, and then looked at me to ask, "How did you know Treasure?"

I was nervous but answered, "Well, I was looking for something; that's all."

He was pissed when he asked, "You were in my room looking through my stuff? What were you looking for, Treasure?"

He got closer to me, and my heart started to race. I answered, "Um…. Uh, I don't know …the night you were with Leah, I was looking for something when you left, and I saw it."

Sénar tried to be patient with me when he asked, "What were you looking for, Treasure?"

He was so close to me; I could feel the warmth from his body. I answered out of frustration and fear, "I was looking for Leah's number to give to Ken."

He was shocked as I folded my arms in my defense when he asked, "What? Treasure, are you serious?" Sénar almost lost it; he threw the condom box in the trash with the rest of the sabotaged condoms in it. He screamed at me, "Get out!"

I said, "Sénar I-"

He cut me off, "Get out, Treasure!"

I started to cry and ran to my room, closing the door behind me as he was using his phone. I thought he said Leah was irrelevant, then why was he so mad? London probably did it to trap Sénar by trying to get pregnant by him; I was just trying to let him know her plan. *Or was it too late? Was she already pregnant? What if he used them with Leah?* I started to cry until I heard my phone ring. I answered it, and Tyrell was on the other end.

He said, "Hey, Treasure?"

I was trying to hide the fact that I had been crying. He asked, "What are you doing?"

I answered, "Nothing, Tyrell."

He was quiet for a second and then asked, "Well, you wanna come over?"

I thought about my current situation and almost said yes until I could hear Ken roaring in the hallway. I quickly told Tyrell I would call him back, hanging up before he could argue with me about why. I cracked my door open to hear Ken ask, "What? I would beat your ass, but you got an interview with a scout this week! You better buy some more and don't get caught slippin' again, boy!" I heard Ken pause, and seemed to be listening to Sénar, when he responded, "I don't give a damn, you better fuck the shit out of her skinny ass and see if she stays that way! And if that doesn't work, then I guess you fucked up, huh? Don't worry about the other one. I'll take care of her; you just tighten your shit up, boy! You're getting sloppy, and I trained your ass better than that. Get your shit together, or your ass is out of here, boy! I'm not about to watch your stupid ass fuck your life up over some damn pussy, with your stupid ass! Damn, I thought you were smarter than that!"

He pushed Sénar and walked away in a rage; he seemed to sense my presence as he stared at my door, exactly where I was sitting to listen in on their conversation. I froze in position because I didn't want him to see me moving by my door. When he was gone, I jumped up to grab my diary and wrote until I heard Cassidy come in, slamming the door behind her. She glared at me before she put her stuff down. I just looked away without saying a word to her. I continued to write until she finally spoke, "Now I see why no one likes your ass. You are such a sneaky little bitch!"

I looked at her, confused, and almost had my feelings hurt when I responded, "Cassidy, I don't know what you are talking about. What are you talking about now?"

I waited to hear what shenanigans she was mad about now. She just laughed at me before she replied, "Yeah right, you always play stupid, you probably put holes in Sénar's condoms! So, you can get pregnant by him and tried to blame London! You are just mad that she is having Sénar's baby! So, you tried to make that shit up so you can have Sénar and break them up again!"

Who the hell did Cassidy think she was, inspector gadget or something? She had no idea what the heck she was talking about. I was trying to connect the dots myself; she interrupted my thinking when she said, "I hate your sneaky, lying ass!"

I was furious with her accusations, and in my defense, I said, "We don't even use condoms Cassidy, so why would I do such a thing?"

Not even aware that I had just admitted to my secret relationship with Sénar, by disclosing that information to her in my defense, it was already too late to take it back. She looked at me with disgust when she responded, "Ugh, you are so nasty! I hope you get what you deserve, you little bitch!"

I was fed up with her now and ready to beat her face in. I cut my eyes at her as Sénar walked in he heard my response to her wishes for me when I said, "Well, I hope you get whatever you wished on me times ten!" Cassidy jumped on me, hitting me in my mouth when I leaped up to defend myself Sénar pushed me back down onto my bed and grabbed Cassidy, closing the door behind him.

Sénar said, "Stop! What the hell is wrong with y'all? My dad is trippin', and on top of that, he is mad at me already! So, don't give-"

Ken came into our room, giving us all an opportunity to tell him what was going on before having to ask as we were all quiet. He asked," What the hell is going on in here?" Cassidy quickly responded, "I am just tired of her daddy! She gets on my nerves!"

I was trying to control my anger, knowing Ken was already in a bad mood. I answered, "I was minding my own business before she came in here starting stuff! Just leave me alone, Cassidy!"

Ken roared, "Both of y'all need to knock it off before I let y'all fight, and the winner has to deal with me!" He smirked at me as he grabbed Sénar, pushing him out of the room, "I ain't even done with you, Sénar! Bring your ass downstairs!"

Sénar was obedient, despite his reluctance to leave Cassidy and I in the same room together. I looked at Cassidy to say, "If I have to deal with Ken, then I might as well kill your ass Cassidy! So, don't mess with me! Mind your damn business, and I'll mind mine!"

She just gave me an evil eye as she sat down on her bed, without saying a word to me, and pulled out her trusty little phone. I went back to writing to try and calm myself, but I was so angry about so many things that my body felt like it was vibrating again. Listening to her talk about me like a dog on her phone had me wanting to rip her tongue out of her mouth. The more she talked, the more murderous my thoughts got, until I almost snapped. "Treasure?" Sénar called my name.

I snapped back, "What?"

"Come here," Sénar said.

I almost turned my rage onto him but asked, "What do you want, Sénar?"

Cassidy glared at me; I couldn't decide who I wanted to hit more when Sénar sensed my dilemma, he said, "Treasure come here, ma, please?"

Cassidy smacked her lips before she said, "Get out already! Don't act all brand new now! You dog ass bitch!"

I jumped out of my bed, and Sénar grabbed me, pulling me out of the room and preventing me from getting to Cassidy. He closed the door then said, "Treasure calm down, ma. You are trippin, after you already heard what my pops said. Look, just come downstairs with me." I reluctantly followed him down the steps avoiding eye contact with Ken as we headed to the garage. Once we were inside, Sénar closed the door behind him and asked, "What's your problem, Treasure?"

I tried not to yell at him when I answered, "Which one Sénar, there are so many of them!"

He got in my face to say, "Lower your voice, Treasure. Why are you so mad?"

I lied, "I don't know, Sénar!"

He grabbed the gloves off the wall and helped me put them on and asked, "Treasure, talk to me, ma, what's really wrong?"

I let go of some of my fury when I answered him, "Everything is wrong, Sénar! Cassidy accused me of putting holes in your condoms and trying to trap you. And she said London is having your baby? And you guys are back together while Tyrell and I are broken!"

Sénar was upset too, he responded while putting his gloves on, "Well, I never thought London would do anything like that, and I didn't tell Cassidy anything. London probably told her ass. Tyrell is stupid, and he doesn't deserve you anyway, Treasure! He chose Leah's ass over you regardless, and that didn't have nothing to do with me!"

I got in Sénar's face when I said, "You chose Leah over me too, Sénar!"

He was furious, but he smiled sadistically when he said, "She let me call her Treasure from the back. Besides, I only gave her a sample. Only you get the real meal deal! Plus, you aren't no angel Treasure, you threw her ass to the big bad wolf in there, and you didn't even think of Carmel when you did it! You were just being vindictive! You know damn well I don't want to be with Leah. I was just weak and hadn't had none for a while, but I wouldn't touch her again. I just messed up, and with London, what am I supposed to do, Treasure?"

I thought about what Ken told Sénar to do to London and wondered if he would follow Ken's instructions. I swung on Sénar, and he dodged it. He laughed before he said, "Bring it!" I swung on him, and he blocked all the ones to his face, but he let me connect all my body shots. He thought we were having fun, but I was letting all my frustrations out on him, and it felt great. He let me go until I was tired while he occasionally tapped my sides to get me angry enough to keep going. When I was tired and out of breath, he let his guard down, and I punched him in his forehead, but not as hard as I could have. He let his fury with me turn into passion, grabbing me, and kissing me.

He said, "One day, none of these people or problems will keep us apart."

He released me when Ken opened the door to ask, "Sénar, are you cooking boy?"

Sénar answered, "Yeah pops, I'm making fajitas."

Ken said, "Well, hurry yo ass up then!"

Sénar replied, "Yes, sir."

He started taking his gloves off as Ken glared at me before closing the door. I took my gloves off with Sénar's help as I thought about how much I hated Ken; he was my biggest problem, literally, in every aspect. Sénar and I went upstairs and snuck in the bathroom to shower together. We didn't do anything but enjoy the scenery of each other's bodies and then got out. I went to my room to get dressed, purposely giving Cassidy a show as I knew she loved seeing me naked. We were both silent, as I'm pretty sure we both thought about how much we hated one another. I quickly got dressed and went to the kitchen with Sénar. I washed my hands and cut the veggies for Sénar and sat at the kitchen nook while he cooked the meat to avoid Ken's glare. It was Friday night, and it was the Super Bowl weekend as my mom and Cassidy came down just as Sénar was finishing. My mom made Ken a plate and grabbed him a beer after she said hi to everyone. Sénar handed me a plate as Cassidy grabbed one for herself, quickly making her plate before me. I just ignored her stupidity and made my plate. Ken watched us with an agitated look on his face. As soon as everyone was at the table, Ken said, "Me and my angel baby are leaving for the weekend. I'm tired of y'all mothafuckas; I need to get away." Sénar and Cassidy were quiet as I could care less; my mom was the only one amused. I quickly finished my food and went to bed.

In the morning, my mom and Ken were already gone when I woke up. Sénar was making breakfast, while him and Cassidy talked. I was irritated when I saw the two of them talking because I could tell it was about me. They both stopped talking when I came in but had opposite facial expressions. Cassidy was disgusted to see me but Sénar was delighted as I made my way into the kitchen for something to drink. Sénar said, "Good morning ma?"

I rolled my eyes at them but still said, "Hey Sénar."

Cassidy smacked her lips before she said, "Hurry up Sénar, so I can get out of here, ugh."

I wanted to slap Cassidy in her mouth because she was really on my last nerve. Sénar interrupted my deep thoughts about slapping Cassidy clear across her face when he said, "I have to run a few errands today. What are y'all going to do?"

I shrugged my shoulders, I didn't have any plans, I just said, "I don't know."

Cassidy rolled her eyes at me, then answered, "I am going to kick it with Nevaeh today and maybe London later."

Sénar smirked at Cassidy, he knew she was just being messy. He just finished cooking and avoided feeding into her behavior. He served us breakfast, it was pancakes sausage and eggs. Then Sénar said, "Now you too be good little girls and play nice. I have to go; I'll be back later." He didn't even eat; he just cleaned up and went to get dressed. I waited for Cassidy to leave before I took a bath to relax. I was so tired of all the drama and I was sexually frustrated. It had been almost two weeks since me and Sénar did anything. I was mad at him and him at me; I just didn't know what was next. I couldn't take all this information that had my emotions in a whirlwind. I thought about whether or not Tyrell and I were even able to be fixed enough to move forward in our relationship, after we had been through so many different things. I even thought about whether or not I even wanted to work things out with him. He was not the Tyrell I fell in love with anymore. All the love we had, seemed to be replaced with hate, and all the pleasure we had, was now replaced with pain. I still loved him and wished all the things that happened between us that tore us apart, had not happened. *Then would we be happy?* I thought about Sénar and how he came into my world with his sadistic smile to steal my innocence and now was demanding the keys to my heart, in spite of Tyrell holding them hostage. All the confusion Sénar caused me with my sexuality, along with my ability to remain loyal to Tyrell, had me in a confused state. All the pain Sénar caused was mixed with pleasure that I never felt with Tyrell. Nor could I explain my years of forbidden moments in the tub with the flashes of ecstasy that could not be erased from my mind, that had plagued me long before Sénar ever entered my body. Sénar was the epitome of pleasure versus pain, all in one that caused me such confusion.

I didn't know what I wanted anymore, I wanted my cake and to eat it too. Besides, what's the point of having cake if you can't eat it? I wanted Tyrell but I felt like I needed Sénar. *What was I supposed to do now?* With all the drama, I felt so alone while everyone else's world was still somewhat intact, but my world was still being ripped to shreds, in so many ways. I could not take being in my thoughts any longer, I was starting to get angry and think of ways to get revenge on everyone who played a part in tearing my world a part. To help ease my mind, I pulled the shower head towards me and used it to help release some of my pent-up sexual frustration. I was hoping maybe Tyrell's face would bring me to the climax I needed, instead of Sénar's face and actions. I started with pleasant thoughts of Tyrell and tried to think of all the good times we had in the mornings before school together. I became excited when flashes of his chocolate body enticed me and brought pleasure to my body and mind. I tilted my head back and enjoyed the sensations I felt traveling through my body. The more intense the feeling, the hotter I put the water and the faster my thoughts raced. I could feel my passion increase, along with my heart rate, and I could feel my body tense up to prepare for my climax to ripple through me. It wasn't until Sénar's face, body, and actions tore their way into my mind that I reached my climax. I almost ripped the shower head off the wall from the intensity of the convulsions that took over my body as a result. I thought I would drown after feeling like I had suffered a mini stroke at the thoughts of Sénar and all the things he did to my body. Feeling guilty that I could not even climax without thinking of Sénar, I wanted to scream. I quickly got out to get dressed. I looked for my long jean skirt and a cute shirt. I combed my hair into a bun and put the pretty hoops on Sénar bought me. I looked great but felt like crap when I realized everyone else had somebody or somewhere to go but me. I sat on my bed in my feelings when my phone rang, I jumped up to answer it.

Tyrell said, "Hey Treasure?"

A little caught off guard, I replied, "Hey Tyrell."

He asked, "What are you doing?"

I didn't want to seem too eager, so I just said, "Nothing."

He asked, "Well let's go get some tacos and talk."

I thought about my current situation and quickly agreed, since tacos were involved. I knew I wasn't supposed to, but I didn't care, Sénar was probably with London and this might be the opportunity we needed to fix our broken relationship. I said, "Ok Tyrell, but I can't be gone too long."

He said, "Ok, are you ready now?"

I quickly answered, "Yeah."

I went out to meet him and saw his eyes light up when he saw me; or was it my skirt; I couldn't tell. He smiled at me and said, "Hey Treasure, you look really nice."

I smiled at him and said, "Thanks, Tyrell you look great too."

I felt a warm fuzzy feeling inside, which I hadn't felt in a long time with Tyrell as we pulled up to the taco truck. I stayed in the car as the lady serving the tacos was rude and nosey, I knew just by the way she looked at me that she was judging me. Tyrell came back with our tacos and we drove to the park to eat our tacos. He gave me my five and had his normal six. I only ate three and watched him eat his six tacos. Tyrell asked, "Treasure, do you still love me?"

I stared at him blankly before answering, "Yes Tyrell, I still love you. I never stopped loving you. Trusting you maybe but loving you, I never stop loving you Tyrell."

I was being honest; I really loved him and never understood why he started treating me so badly, when all I wanted to do, was love him. He smirked at me and said, "Well maybe we have something in common, but I still don't trust you or Sénar."

I couldn't afford an argument with him and I couldn't tell him the truth about me and Sénar, it would ruin my chance to fix things between us forever. I just did my best to convince him that he could trust me when I said, "Tyrell, I want to be with you not Sénar, but you chose Leah."

Tyrell snapped at me, "Leah and I aren't together Treasure. Don't try to blame all this on me. You know damn well Sénar ass is obsessed with you and you want me to believe there is nothing going on between you two?"

I avoided answering his question and said, "Tyrell look, maybe we should be going home now; I don't want to argue with you. Please."

Tyrell looked at me to ask, "How do I know if you still love me?" I shrugged my shoulders as he gazed at me with his lustful eyes and said, "Give me a kiss." I blushed a little before I reached over to kiss him. He grabbed me passionately, like he missed me. Although our last experience sexually was devastating for me, I couldn't deny the excitement I felt as he kissed and caressed me. He said, "Damn Treasure, I miss you, be mine again." He kissed me and rubbed his hands all over my body, arousing me as he whispered how much he loved me.

I kissed him back, "I missed you too Tyrell."

With lust in his eyes, he said, "Show me Treasure, like you did when you got off punishment the first time."

He grinned ear to ear and almost ripped his door off to get out. I knew I shouldn't. after what he did to me, but I was really horny, and Leah said he was better; so, why not give it a try. Besides Sénar was probably with London anyways and she was having his baby. I got out and got in the back seat with Tyrell. I allowed him to kiss me as he moved his hands up my skirt and pulled my panties down. He was eager as he adjusted his driver seat forward to give us more room. He pulled out his eager member and I couldn't help but smile as Treasure number two took over. He put a condom on, almost detouring some of my excitement, but because Tyrell was so dark and handsome, I could not resist him. I straddled him while we kissed passionately, he squeezed and grabbed my behind while pulling me closer to him. He was more aroused than usual, pulling and grinding me from the bottom; it felt so good my mind started to wander. Pleasure increased as he pulled me down and sucked on my neck. I could feel myself tensing up as I saw flashes of Sénar's face in my mind before Tyrell and I both exploded at the same time.

Tyrell exclaimed, "Wow! Treasure, that was amazing!" I was trying not to blush as that was a compliment and I could not agree with him more. I tried not to think of the fact that I was actually having sex with him and that Sénar's face still flashed before I could reach a climax. Well I couldn't complain that was the first time I ever had one with Tyrell. My phone rang, I pulled myself together as Tyrell removed his condom and got dressed. I looked at my phone and it was Sénar. My heart almost skipped a beat as I got out of Tyrell's car to answer it.

I reluctantly answered, "Hello?"

Sénar asked, "Where are you Treasure?"

I answered, "I just came out for a while."

Sénar was quiet for a second and then asked, "Who are you with Treasure?"

I got nervous and asked, "Why?"

Sénar was angry when he said, "Don't play with me Treasure! Are you with Tyrell?"

I hesitated before I answered, "Yeah."

Tyrell watched me with an annoyed look on his face. Sénar roared into the phone, "Treasure, come home now!"

I quickly hung up and tried not to look frazzled, but Tyrell already sensed who it was when he asked, "Who is that? Sénar?"

I got in the passenger seat to ask, "Why Tyrell?"

He yelled, "Because I want to know!"

I snapped back, "I have to go!"

Tyrell laughed and said, "Oh so, he calls and now you have to run home? Are you fucking him Treasure?"

Thrown aback by his choice words and his tone, I quickly started to regret coming out with him, for many different reasons. I asked, "Are you screwing Leah, Tyrell?"

He smirked at me before he said, "Don't play stupid Treasure, you know we have fun every now and then, but she is not my girl, there's no strings attached. Besides that, do you know that Sénar got London knocked up?"

I rolled my eyes before I said, "Yes Tyrell, I know. Did you know Leah fucked Sénar?"

He became instantly enraged when he asked, "What? How do you know? So, all y'all are fucking Sénar?"

I tried to get out of the car, but he locked the doors and pushed me back against the passenger's seat. He noticed my chain, rubbing his hand across it, "Oh how nice, your little boyfriend fixed it for you and added little jewels because let me guess, you are his treasure?" He asked in a mocking tone. I pushed his hand away making him more upset. I unlocked the door and tried to get out, but Tyrell pulled me back in the car with great force. I didn't feel safe anymore because Tyrell was upset and having one of his tantrums. I quickly thought of what I could say to calm him down, "Tyrell please, we had such a good time, don't mess it up. Please, Tyrell?" I pleaded with him with sincerity as I really did have a good time, prior to his tantrum.

I saw Tyrell soften up a bit as he thought about what I said, then he replied, "We did have fun, huh? Ok but Treasure, let's start over. I want you to be mine again, all mine." I knew I could not do that, but I also knew that this might be my only opportunity to make it home in one piece. So, I responded, "Ok Tyrell, we should be able to, if we really love each other. But can we finish this conversation on the phone? I really have to go." Tyrell tried to hide his anger and frustration when he started the car and my phone rang again. This time, it was a number I had never seen before. I didn't bother answering it but after it stopped ringing, it rang again. I quickly answered, despite Tyrell's agitation and the obvious increase in speed of his driving.

The voice on the other end didn't register in my mind, so I asked, "Who is this?"

He answered, "Markese, what's up shawty?"

I was annoyed and said, "Oh, well hi…. Look, I am busy I have to… can you call me back?"

I quickly hung up when Tyrell looked like he wanted to snatch my phone he said, "Damn Treasure, you sure are popular."

I quickly defended myself, "Tyrell that's just one of Cassidy's friends."

He snapped back, "Oh yeah, like that grown ass dude at the restaurant?"

I started to get uncomfortable again as Tyrell started to have another one of his jealous tantrums. I said, "Tyrell please I don't want to argue. I thought you said you wanted to start over, right?"

He cut his eyes at me as I pleaded with him to calm down. I needed to make it home safely and Tyrell was already driving aggressively. When we pulled up to the house, Sénar was standing at the door waiting for me. Tyrell was instantly angry again as he screeched his breaks. Sénar started to move toward us, Tyrell grabbed the back of my neck and stuck his tongue in my mouth, then said, "Remember you belong to me Treasure!"

I got out as quick as I could to avoid Sénar getting all the way to the car as him and Tyrell locked eyes. I pleaded with Sénar putting my hand on his chest, "Sénar come on let's go inside!"

Sénar moved my hand off his chest and mad dogged Tyrell before he screeched off. Sénar yelled at me when we got inside. He asked, "Treasure, what the hell were you doing with him?"

He appeared hurt and angry as he waited for my answer. I started to cry before I said, "I don't know Sénar. He said he wanted to talk, and I just wanted to see if there was anything left."

Sénar glared at me when he asked, "Well, was there?"

I was frustrated when I yelled, "I don't know Sénar!"

He was frustrated now too when he asked, "How don't you know Treasure? Just leave him alone before he hurts you when he figures out there's nothing left."

I was angry when I corrected him, "I didn't say there was nothing left Sénar." He got upset and asked, "Well, are you going to give him another chance after what he did to you?" I got in Sénar's face when I said, "If I can forgive you, then I can forgive him!"

Sénar was furious when he said, "I never meant to hurt you, Treasure! I hope I get a chance to prove that to you and I hope you give me the same chance you keep giving Tyrell!"

My phone rang and it was Markese again. I answered, "I'm in the middle of something, I have to call you back."

Markese laughed on the other end when he asked, "Damn you a busy girl, aye?"

Annoyed with him, I replied, "I have to go. I told you I would call you back!"

I hung up the phone. Sénar knew it wasn't Tyrell, so he just stared at me before he said, "Whatever Treasure, your ass don't listen anyway!"

He left me standing there as he went to the garage furious with me. I didn't care; he did whatever he wanted; I was going to do what I wanted too. I was tired of being the only one who suffered; I was going to make everyone feel how I felt. I had to deal with pleasure and pain, so I would make sure everyone felt the pain of the wrath that I had brewing in me, for the last five years. I didn't know how but I was going to find a way to free myself from all this turmoil and pain. Thankful Cassidy was not there, I ran to my room and went straight to my bed. I didn't cry; I was tired of crying. I called Markese back, and he answered, "Whats up Shawty, what are you doing?"

I replied, "Nothing."

He asked, "When you going to come kick it again?"

I quickly said, "I can't come over there anymore."

He asked, "Why? Cassidy used to come over all the time."

I said, "Well, Cassidy was not supposed to be over there either. If her brother knew he would have been mad."

Now laughing, he said, "That lil' nigga ain't gonna do shit. Isn't he your brother too? Why was he acting like he was your dude?"

I sighed, then answered, "No and Cassidy isn't my sister either; they just live here."

He laughed before he said, "I hope not because she doesn't seem to like you that much, and he seems to like you, too much."

I thought how strange it was that he noticed that off of meeting Sénar once. Out of curiosity, I asked, "How did you know that?"

He answered, "Because he looked like he wanted to catch a fade with me over talking to you, but he would have got his ass whipped, if he would have stepped to me. I am a grown ass man."

I thought to myself, *right, talking to a young girl on the phone and trying to get me to come over to his house, after having to run for my life the last time.* I just replied, "Well, that won't be necessary because I don't intend to be in that situation again."

He got quiet on the other end but then still offered, "Well, if you want to come by tomorrow, we are having a party. Tell some home girls and come through."

I lied, "Ok, I'll think about it."

I wasn't going anywhere near his house ever again. I got off the phone with him as Cassidy and Nevaeh came into the room. The two of them stared at me like I was a foreign object lying on my bed. I had no patience for the two of them, especially together, so I left to prevent a serious altercation. Their accusing eyes pierced me as I followed my instincts to leave before having to slap either of them.

Sénar was sweaty after working out and appeared to still be agitated when he passed me. I wanted to ask him how long he was going to be mad at me, but I just kept my mouth closed and pretended not to care. I rolled my eyes at him as he glared at me before going to his room. I went to watch TV until the doorbell rang. I saw London's car through the window, I almost left her outside until I saw Sénar at the top of the stairs waiting. So, I went to sit back down, making him answer the door himself.

She was mad when she asked, "Where were you all day, Sénar?"

He sighed before he asked, "Why? I told you I had something to do."

She followed him to the couch while she whined, "Sénar, I haven't heard from you and I feel like you're ignoring me."

He was frustrated with her when he said, "London, I needed to get away for a second, ok? What do you need?"

She blushed batting her eyelashes at him. Sénar got up pulling her off the couch, I watched her desperation turn into excitement. As he went upstairs, and she eagerly followed him. I sat on the couch wondering, *if he wasn't with London did that mean he was with Leah?* I was upset thinking about him possibly being with Leah, despite my own betrayal with Tyrell earlier. I could not stand Leah, London, Cassidy or Nevaeh and my hatred for Sabrina was fueled by all of my hatred for them as well as some unknown force. I sat on the couch and thought of ways to get back at them all, when I heard laughter coming from the stairway. It was Nevaeh and Cassidy coming down the stairs. They both glanced at me as if they had a secret, whispering before Cassidy walked Nevaeh out. When she came back in, she rolled her eyes at me and sat down on the couch.

Cassidy asked, "Where's Sénar?"

I shrugged my shoulders before she said, "Yeah right, you know."

She sneered at me as she got up to go back upstairs. Sénar and London came down after a while. London was smiling and happy as can be while Sénar walked her to the door. She kissed him happily before she left to go home, instantly irritating me. Sénar rolled his eyes at me before going to the kitchen to cook something for us to eat. I could hear him in the kitchen and just by all the noise, I could tell he was still agitated with me. He didn't ask for help or insinuate that he even wanted me around him. Mmmm, I could smell the food cooking. I wanted to go in there to see what it was but really just to see if he was mad at me. I waited a second before going into the kitchen to talk to him but before I could say anything, Cassidy came in to ask, "What are you making Sénar?" He waved Cassidy off, handing her a plate with a burger and fries on it. He handed me my plate and walked to the refrigerator to grab chicken out of the fridge. I was so shocked, he didn't even eat anything, he just handed us our plates and started seasoning chicken wings. Cassidy asked, "What's that for Sénar?"

He was agitated but not with her, so he responded, "I am seasoning some chicken for hot wings tomorrow, so I could watch the game and mind my business." I rolled my eyes at him and Cassidy shook her head at him. After I ate, I went to sleep wondering if I made a mistake leaving with Tyrell after everything we had been through.

In the morning, I stayed in bed. I didn't bother to get up for breakfast. Of course, for different reasons, I didn't want to see Sénar or Cassidy. So, I laid in bed until I heard my phone ring. When I got up to answer it, Tyrell said, "Hey babe, what are you doing?" I hadn't been called that in so long, I almost asked if he dialed the wrong number. I answered, "Nothing, just laying down in my room, chilling Tyrell." I tried to sound unbothered and cool.

He laughed then asked, "Oh yeah? You want to have some more fun?"

What is it with guys and sex, I could not understand why it was so important to every one of them that I had a conversation with? I giggled before I replied, "Tyrell, I can't, but maybe I'll come by tomorrow before school." Since that was the only time, I could slip away without worrying about anyone trying to stop me or punish me for being with him. Besides, that's when we have always had most of our fun anyway, in the past. I figured since he was better at it and Sénar was tripping, I could just have fun with Tyrell and not feel guilty since he was supposed to be my boyfriend anyways. As for Leah, I was going to show her she was just a rebound desperate yamp like Cassidy and Sabrina. I didn't consider myself to be anything like them, although I had some guilt about my choices, I was still confident that I was not a hoe or a fast ass. If it wasn't for Sénar's persistence, me and Tyrell would have been exclusive, well at least I would have only been with him. Leah wouldn't even have had a chance to get so close to me if I hadn't tried to ward Sénar off with her. Without a doubt, I was going to get back at Leah; I just had to figure out how.

Tyrell responded, "Ok, well, me and my dad are going to his friends to watch the Super Bowl. Maybe I'll call you when I get back."

I said goodbye as Cassidy came in on her phone. She sounded really flirtatious when she said, "Yeah, I missed you too. Yeah, I'm down to come over. Ok, let me call her." That was probably her ex-boyfriend Tony because I remembered Markese mentioned they were having a party today. Cassidy hung up to call Nevaeh. She asked, "Hey, come with me to kick it with Tony and them. They are having a Super Bowl party and want us to come." Cassidy looked disappointed and said, "I didn't want to go by myself. Well, will you drop me off then? I will be driving soon, girl and I won't have to ask you…….. Hell no, I don't want to ask her ass to go. Treasure's ass is scary, and that shit was embarrassing." I rolled my eyes at her and her dilemma; she would be crazy to go by herself. Not that I really cared, but a light bulb went off in my head, and I could not resist the opportunity. She said, "Well, let me get ready and see if I could find someone to go with me." She rolled her eyes at me and asked, "You wanna go to the party, Treasure?"

I knew she was desperate to ask me after our last incident there, so I presented my bright new idea. I answered, "No thanks, Cassidy, but maybe you can ask Leah to go with you. I think she is more their type of party girl."

Cassidy smirked at me before saying, "Well, I don't have her number, Treasure!"

She was frustrated with my idea until I said, "I have it, Cassidy, you want it? I'll even give you my number again, Cassidy, just in case you need me again someday." I smirked at her and gave her Leah's number. I didn't have to look for it. I remembered it by heart just for an opportunity like this. I had a little smile of my own as she called Leah, I heard Cassidy say, "Hey Leah? This is Cassidy Sénar's sister," She paused, then said, "Yeah, I just got your number to ask if you wanna go to a Super Bowl party with me?" She paused again and then said, "Ok cool, well me and my friend will pick you up. Let me write down your directions." She giggled and answered, "Nah, she ain't going. Ok, cool, I'll call you when we are on our way." She smirked at me and went to take a shower. I could just hear Leah saying, "Hell yeah!" when Cassidy asked her if she wanted to go to a party, ugh I couldn't stand either of them.

I went downstairs after a while; I was starting to get hungry and wasn't waiting for the game to eat. Sénar was lying down on the couch watching TV as I made my way to the kitchen to find something to eat. I didn't care about carbs; I ate a grilled cheese sandwich. I made two extra ones and cut them in half then put a napkin over them. I got something to drink as Sénar walked into the kitchen. I felt like telling him I was sorry about yesterday, but I just couldn't; I wasn't sure that I was yet. I just rolled my eyes at him and walked out of the kitchen, but still noticed him looking under the napkin. I smirked to myself as I knew he was wondering if I made him some too. He got on my nerves because he had a lot of nerve to be mad at me. I should be mad at him, and he should be apologizing to me for all that he had done to me. I just laid back down on the couch and watched the TV while waiting for the super bowl to start. I was more interested in the commercials and half time than the game. Sénar was coming back in as Cassidy came downstairs dressed.

Sénar asked, "Where are you going, Cassidy?"

He sat on the couch and flipped the channels as she answered, "I'm going to kick it with Nevaeh and some friends to watch the game."

Sénar smirked and asked, "Dressed like that?"

She said, "Sénar, I'm grown and been for a whole month, so I'll be fine. It's just Nevaeh and some friends."

I started to say something, but she pleaded with me with her eyes not to say anything, so I just watched TV. Sénar said, "Pops might be back tonight, so don't come in too late." Cassidy nodded in agreement and quickly left. Sénar looked at me and laid back to watch TV. The game was starting in another 15 minutes or so. I decided to get comfortable while Sénar just stared at me. I smacked my lips and then asked, "What Sénar?" He just rolled his eyes at me and ignored my question. I was frustrated with his attitude, so when I got up to go take a shower, Sénar asked, "Where are you going, Treasure? The game is about to start." I glared at him with an attitude because I had to be leaving for him to speak to me. I dryly replied, "Sénar, I'm going to take a shower and play with myself." He jumped up, grabbing me from behind while smelling my hair, and said, "You play too much Treasure. Umph, I would rather watch that then the game." I wiggled out of his embrace and replied, "I bet." Before I walked off to go take a shower, I could feel Sénar watching me as I walked up the steps. I took a shower, using it to pass time and get some of my frustration out. I wonder if doctors knew how effective having an orgasm or reaching a climax was for a lot of things. Maybe that's why guys were so crazy about sex, I don't know, but I was glad I had a shower head to help me out.

I went back downstairs and avoided eye contact or conversation with Sénar. No one was home and I didn't know what kind of space Sénar was in. We watched the game and witnessed a very shocking win as New England beat the Rams. Sénar was impressed with the game as we ate hot wings and salad with celery sticks. We didn't talk much we just ate and watched TV until his phone rung. I heard him say, "Yeah, I guess." I swear London must have been parked outside when she called, we barely got up to put our plates away before London was ringing the doorbell. I washed my plate and almost left Sénar's in the sink, but I washed it despite my irritation with London being here. I put the food away while London and Sénar headed to his room. I didn't feel like watching TV, so I went to my room to read. I could hear London screaming and moaning. I guess that was Sénar's way of getting back at me and listening to his daddy at the same time.

My phone rang and I answered it, Markese yelled, "Treasure!"

He sounded worried, I asked, "What is it Markese?"

He was quiet for a second and then responded, "Aye, it's Cassidy……. she needs help man!" I listened carefully and asked, "Markese what are you talking about?" He yelled again, "She needs help! Man, I'm going to bring her somewhere and y'all have to come get her! I didn't have shit to do with this, but I can't just let her die! Come get her Treasure!" I almost laid back down and pretend that he never called but I would not be able to look Sénar in his face knowing I let his sister die because of my dislike for her. I quickly got up, slipped on a pair of shoes and despite London's yelling, I opened Sénar's door. I saw London stretched out like a rubber band while Sénar mounted her and appeared to be giving her the time of her life. They both stopped and looked at me like I was crazy.

London yelled, "What the hell! Get out!"

She tried to cover herself as Sénar asked, "What is it Treasure?" He looked like he was in the middle of a very important task.

I almost giggled until I remembered the reason, I came in in the first place. He studied me while I tried to focus again, I said, "Sénar we have to go!"

Sénar stared at me like I was crazy when he asked, "What? Where?"

He started to get himself together, he pulled the condom off and London gawked at us both as I didn't seem to be bothered by his nakedness. I didn't even bother to look at London. She was not much to look at but Sénar on the other hand, he has always been a good piece of eye candy. Sénar searched me for emotion other than my fascination with his body at the moment. He asked, "What's going on Treasure?"

I said, "It's Cassidy, we need to go get her, something happened. I don't know what, but we have to go."

He started to move a lot faster and told London, "Get dressed. I have to go; I'll call you later."

London glared at me as if to tell me to leave but I just stood there until Sénar walked out. He went straight to the bathroom and knowing Sénar, he probably had to wash his hands. I started laughing to myself until I realized the urgency in Markese's message. Sénar came out and asked, "Where are we going and what happened Treasure?"

London was coming out, she asked, "Sénar why can't I go with you? I want to go; she doesn't have to go, Cassidy don't even like her ass."

Sénar was frustrated with her when he said, "London, hell no! Your ass is already starting, and I don't know what is going on. So, go home. I told you I would call you."

My phone rang again, so I answered it and Markese was yelling, "Treasure hurry up! Come to Flores park!"

I hung up when Sénar asked," Who is that? Treasure, what the hell is going on?"

London said, "She probably set her up too!"

Sénar roared, "Go home London!"

Sénar headed for the door and I followed. We got in the car and London went to hers with her feelings hurt. I told Sénar, "She is at Flores park."

Sénar was furious when he asked, "Why the fuck is she there Treasure?"

I started to get nervous and answered, "I don't know! Somebody called me and told me something happened, but they didn't say what. They just said she needed help!"

He drove really fast and I did my best to remain calm as I could feel myself getting scared of the possibilities that awaited us. Sénar looked determined but he still appeared calm until my phone wrung again. I answered it to hear Markese ask, "Are you almost here?"

I said, "Yeah, we are almost there."

Markese said, "I'm leaving, and I don't want to leave her unless you guys are close, I don't want no heat for this shit! I don't have nothing to do with this!"

Sénar roared, "Who is that and what the fuck happened!" Sénar snatched the phone from me and asked, "Who is this? Stay right there or I'm going to find your ass anyway!"

He threw my phone down and opened his glove compartment. He glared at me as he pulled into the park with his high beams on and noticed a car screeching out of the parking lot. Sénar parked and got out to get a good look at the car. He searched for Cassidy, I got out to help him. I saw a blue blanket and ran towards it as I called Sénar's name to follow me. I use the light from my phone and when I saw a foot of a girl, I screamed, "Sénar, I found her!"

She looked unconscious and paler than usual. Sénar touched her and freaked out, he shook her, slapped her face, and then yelled her name, "Cassidy! Cassidy! Cassidy!" He moved the blanket and saw her clothes were ripped and barely on her. He looked like he would explode into anger but instead, despite her exposed breast, he pushed on her chest. He put his hands over her mouth as a shield and blew air into her lungs; I saw her stomach rise. He pumped on her chest vigorously and then gave her another breath. As he pumped on her chest, he gave me instructions, he said, "Pop the hood of my car and put this," he nodded to a brown bag on the ground next to him and then continued, "next to the square battery there is a space. You'll know, just look for the red sleeve. Put it there, close the hood, and dial 911 to ask for an ambulance and tell them where we are." He bent down to give her a breath and started pumping as I went to do as he said. I popped the hood of his car and saw the space he said to put the brown bag. Whatever it was that was in the bag was heavy and needed to be hidden for some reason. I called 911 and the dispatcher answered, "911 what's the emergency?" I tried not to panic and replied, "Um, I'm at Flores park and there's an emergency. There's a girl and she is unconscious and currently having CPR performed. We need an ambulance right away!" Before she could ask any more questions, I hung up and ran back to Sénar and Cassidy. Sénar was still trying to get her to respond. He looked worried as he pumped on her and blew breath into her mouth, one last time. I saw her hand twitch and her stomach rise and fall, then rise again. She was breathing but had short shallow breaths. Sénar noticed too and called her name, "Cassidy? We are here with you! Hey, stay with me please." He gently tapped her face as he called her name. She didn't respond but she was breathing. He held her until the ambulance arrived. I just watched Sénar as he held her in his arms. The EMT responders shined a flashlight to light the path to us and walked over with a gurney. He stood up and let them access Cassidy. Sénar explained, "Her clothing is not intact, and she wasn't breathing when we arrived. I had to do CPR to revive her."

The guy looked at Sénar in a weird way before he said, "Well the police are on their way too, so make sure you let them know all of that. What's the victim's name?"

They got all her information from Sénar and told them what hospital she would be going to, while the other one put her on oxygen and covered her with a blanket. The police pulled up and Sénar tensed up. He quickly said, "Tell them her friend called you from her phone and told you where she was and that's it." They interrogated us and they were really aggressive with Sénar. They searched his car and frisked him over three times. He was trying to remain calm, but they were unnecessarily aggressive with him and questioned us separately. Sénar tried to ask calmly if we could go, so we could check on Cassidy, but he was at his last nerve and the cops knew it.

One of them asked, "How long you been screwing this one? She is a pretty chocolate thing. How about you go, and we keep her."

Sénar's eyes almost turned red immediately when I said, "Sénar please, we have to go."

The cops laughed as Sénar's veins looked like they would pop out of his neck. The cops blew a kiss at me as they walked off. Sénar almost lost it, he yelled at me when he asked, "Who the fuck dropped Cassidy off? And what happened to my sister?" He looked like he wanted to rip me to shreds.

I took a deep breath before I responded, "My friend called me and told me she was in trouble. He said that he was going to drop her off and that he had nothing to do with it."

That wasn't good enough for Sénar, he drove to the hospital where Cassidy was and found a parking spot. He asked me again, "What happened Treasure?" He knew I was leaving out details.

I pouted and nervously told him the part I played in it when I said, "Cassidy asked me if I wanted to go to the guys house that I ran from last time for a party. And I didn't want to go because of what happened last time so she-"

He cut me off and asked, "What? You let her go back there? And by herself?"

He was livid with me and I quickly answered, "No, I was nice enough to give her Leah's number, so she would have some-"

He cut me off again when he asked, "What? You have got to be kidding me! You are cold blooded Treasure. Damn, you really have been doing some vindictive ass shit man! My sister was damn near dead and I don't know if she is alive right now because of your silly little games!" He got out of the car, he was angry and hurt. I was scared to get out and almost stayed in the car until he yelled, "Get out of the damn car! Let's go. My sister better be alive, Treasure. My dad is going to flip either way, but this is beyond my control. I pray to God my sister is alive, Treasure. And I pray we both live after this."

I was silent, I couldn't say anything else. I was starting to feel guilty for not telling Sénar about Cassidy going over there and for sending her with Leah, knowing Leah was a party girl who liked to flirt. He didn't soften his glare at me, he was so angry with me, I was scared of him at the moment. I was quiet and waited by his side to get an update on Cassidy's condition. Sénar just sat there as he seemed to be praying, he had his head down and his eyes closed. He was silent and appeared to be in a calmer state until my phone rang, it was Tyrell, "What happened with Leah and Cassidy?"

I quickly answered, "I don't know! I have to call you back."

Tyrell was angry and said, "No! Tell me what happened!"

I yelled in the phone when I said, "I don't know! I wasn't there! Why don't you asked Leah what happened?" Tyrell hung up in my face.

Sénar looked like he wanted to strangle me, I looked away in shame. The doctor came out and looked at us waiting impatiently to find out Cassidy's condition. He asked us to identify ourselves to ensure we were her family members before providing information to us. He told us her breathing was stabilized and that she had a high amount of drugs in her system and needed her stomach pumped. He told us she had been brutally sexually assaulted and needed some medical attention to stop the bleeding. He mentioned her possibly needing to be psychiatrically evaluated due to the amount of trauma she had suffered. Since she was eighteen, they didn't ask for her parents and allowed us to go in to see her. She was almost back to her normal color and she had her eyes closed as we walked in. I didn't walk all the way over, I stayed by the door. I was pretty sure she didn't want to see me if she opened her eyes. Sénar called Cassidy's name but she didn't respond.

He rubbed her hair and said, "I am going to let you rest, I'll be back tomorrow to check on you. I need to know what happened, so I can take care of it." She moved her fingers as he kissed her on the forehead and told her he would be back. He walked out and I followed behind him without another word. We drove home in silence. I couldn't help but wonder away into my thoughts about what could have happened to her. Sénar looked like he was thinking terrible thoughts as his face looked distorted. I almost started to panic when I saw Ken's truck. Sénar smirked at me when he saw my response to Ken's truck. Tyrell was pulling up across the street at the same time as me and Sénar pulled up. Tyrell was furious as he called my name from across the street. Sénar glared at me, I knew I couldn't talk to Tyrell, so I ran towards the house, but Tyrell ran after me. Sénar grabbed Tyrell, stopping him from coming towards me and they started fighting. Sénar started slamming and choking Tyrell when Tyrell punched Sénar so hard, I thought he would fall but Sénar didn't budge. It looked like he was trying to kill Tyrell when I yelled, "Sénar!" I tried to stop him, but he pushed me back with his other hand.

Sénar told Tyrell, "Since your ass won't stay away, I'll just kill your punk ass!"

Ken came out and called Sénar's name but Sénar didn't respond to Ken calling his name, which alarmed Ken immediately. He ran toward Sénar and punched him in his chest twice. It was the second punch that caused enough impact for Sénar to release Tyrell and fall to the ground. Tyrell jumped up and tried to catch his breath. Despite almost losing his life, Tyrell still asked, "What happened to Leah, Treasure?"

I yelled at him when I answered, "I don't know Tyrell, that's your friend! You need to ask her!"

I ran in the house as Ken gave Tyrell instructions to go home or be finished, as if we were at the end of a Mortal Combat fight. I went in the house with Sénar and Ken on my heels. I wanted to run up the steps, but Ken roared, "Hell nah, what the fuck happened to Cassidy?"

Sénar quickly said, "She went to some party with some grown ass niggas and they did something to her pops, they almost killed her!"

Ken glared at me and asked, "So, what part did you play in it Treasure?"

I got quiet before responding, "Nothing." I waited to see if Sénar would correct me or tell on me, but he didn't, even though I knew he was disappointed in my involvement. Ken and Sénar walked away to talk and I ran upstairs to my room to call Markese. He didn't answer the first time, but I called him back and when he answered, I asked "Markese, I won't tell on you because I know you were just trying to help but please tell me what happened?"

He answered, "Look, I have to go and figure this shit out too. I don't have nothing to do with this shit! All I know is her friend was a little freak. She was getting the guys all riled up and one of them wanted to fuck. She started acting brand new and got into a physical altercation with one of them. She went crazy on him and then she asked me to take her home, but Cassidy didn't want to leave. So, I took her friend home and when I came back, I found Cassidy in the living room passed out. I wrapped her in a blanket and left to call you. That's all I know. This shit is crazy because I ain't tryna sound fucked up, but her friend is scandalous. But they both eighteen, right?"

I smacked my lips and answered, "No, Leah is not even 16 yet."

He said, "What? I have to go!" He hung up in a hurry.

Chapter 14

I woke up in the morning and almost stepped on Sénar when I got up. Although after last night I had no intention to go to Tyrell's house, I wouldn't have been able to go anyway. Sénar jumped up and asked, "Treasure, did you find anything out? My dad is really trippin, and I can't even lie, me too. I just need to know what happened?"

It was hard enough to hide my emotions and thoughts from Sénar as he was way in tune with me despite my reluctance. I just told him what Markese told me, I answered, "He said Leah was being flirtatious and got into it with one of the guys and then he took her home. When he came back, Cassidy was like that."

Sénar looked agitated, and I could tell he was really frustrated with me when he said, "Treasure, I don't think you understand how this could play out. I just pray that we all can move past this, but please know my dad is very upset about this and many other things. I can not stress to you enough to please think before you act. I will do the same because stuff is really about to hit the fan if we don't."

I knew Sénar was sincere in his warning, but I just didn't care at this time, I rolled my eyes at him. He snapped when he said, "Treasure, you are really pushing me to the point that I have been praying to avoid, you have no idea what I am going through and vice versa. The only difference is I opened myself up to you, and now I regret it. You are the only person I have not held a grudge against, but it's getting harder not to. You are becoming vindictive and everything my dad tried to prepare me for with women. The problem is I knew it and still chose to love you. Please Treasure, I know I messed up in the past, but I am trying to make things right, but everything keeps going wrong. Please, Treasure, I need you, don't be a disappointment to me like everyone else. I know we all make mistakes, but please Treasure, things are crazy enough."

I stared into his eyes and felt a twinge of sympathy, but I ignored it. I glared at him and said, "I'm tired of being the victim, Sénar! I want people to feel like I have, so don't try to get me to feel sorry for anyone!"

Treasure number two was speaking for me; I would never say anything like that to Sénar. He recognized it immediately and addressed the situation when he said, "I'm not talking to Treasure number two! I am talking to the Treasure I fell for. The one I love, not the one I created!"

He was distraught, he left me there, and I just sat wondering who I would rather be. *Treasure number one or Treasure number two?* Well, as of lately, I didn't really have a choice. Treasure number two was greedy too, she only showed up for pleasure and showed up to fight my battles for me, but she was still part of me. I went to the bathroom to wash my face and brush my teeth. When I was done; I got dressed in my room. I looked at Cassidy's empty bed and wondered how long it would be that way. I was almost ready to go; I had already decided I would skip Tyrell's house because he was mad at me too. As I left my room, I just prayed I would get to school safely and avoid Tyrell and Leah. When I got downstairs, Sénar was waiting for me. So, my plans for walking were not going to happen, but at least I would make it to school safely. On the way to school, Sénar made it very clear he did not want me riding with Tyrell.

He said, "Do not ride with Tyrell or sneak over to his house in the morning. You ride with me to and from school. Don't talk about what happened to anyone, especially Tyrell. Stay out of trouble, Treasure. Don't give my dad a reason to trip, please."

I just looked at him and tried not to roll my eyes, but I swear it was involuntary sometimes. I just said, "Ok."

He glared at me before he said, "Your ass needs to listen, or you will wish you did."

I frowned at him and then asked, "Is that a threat, Sénar?"

He glared at me and replied, "Nah, it's a promise!"

We pulled up to the school and parked next to Sénar's stalker London. She was standing and waiting patiently for him by where he parks his car. I was glad she didn't park her car over here as she approached us. I got out and grabbed my things. London asked, "Why is she riding with you again, Sénar?"

He didn't answer her, then she asked, "How's Cassidy?"

Sénar said, "London, no more questions, please. I will talk to you about it later."

He closed his door, and I closed mine and walked off, hoping to avoid Tyrell. As if he had radar, I saw him approaching me from afar, but Sénar told London, "I'll see you at lunch London."

He looked at me and said, "Let's go, Treasure."

He walked me to class and detoured Tyrell from coming to me as the bell rung, Sénar said, "If he does make it to you, keep it short and don't let him put his hands on you." I nodded my head in agreement and was thankful that he walked me to class. I didn't want to start my day off being interrogated by Tyrell. I went to my first three classes dreading seeing Tyrell or even worse Leah. I was hoping not to have to deal with either of them. I walked to the cafeteria cautiously. I saw Tyrell and Leah talking, she looked distraught as she appeared to be telling Tyrell what happened, but I couldn't really see any physical damages to her. So, I didn't think whatever she was telling him could be that bad. I hurried to the lunch line to get my food and rushed outside to my tree. I ate my lunch in peace, which I couldn't be happier about. When it was time to go to class, I was one of the first people in class and hoped Leah would find somewhere else to sit. She came in late and had to sit in a seat across the room. She gave me a dirty look, but I just rolled my eyes at her. I purposely sat by the door, so when class was over, I could quickly leave. I avoided Leah at practice as well, but when it was over, her and Tyrell both approached me.

They both asked, "Where's Cassidy?"

Tyrell and Leah both looked like they were impatiently waiting on my answer. I asked, "Why?"

Leah smacked her lips and said, "I am just going to ask Sénar."

Tyrell got an attitude when he said, "Nah, don't ask him shit! Treasure, where is Cassidy?"

Sénar came to grab my bag, "Let's go, Treasure."

Tyrell said, "Aye, we're talking, so you need to wait."

Sénar flashed when he said, "We are leaving, I'm not waiting!"

I quickly followed behind Sénar, but Tyrell grabbed me, and Leah asked, "Sénar, where's Cassidy?"

I snatched my arm from Tyrell, and he said, "You wasn't acting like this Saturday!"

I didn't want him to mention what happened between us, so I just said, "Tyrell, I will call you, ok?"

Sénar smirked at Leah before he answered, "You know more than I do, Leah. She is where she is, and you are here."

He glared at me, and I quickly followed behind him as we walked to his car. I started to wonder where London was; she would normally be stalking him by this time. She was at her car talking with some of her and Cassidy's friends. Sénar became instantly irritated as we walked past them. London called Sénar's name, but he just kept walking as she ran to catch up to him to ask, "What's wrong, babe?"

He answered her with pressured speech, "Nothing London, go finish running your mouth."

London pouted as she knew that's exactly what she was doing. We got in the car and left but we weren't driving in the direction of home, so I figured we were going to see Cassidy. When we got there and checked in the Doctor gave us a rundown of her progress since last night, he said, "Her breathing is stable. She has some stitches that she will need to have checked and removed in about two weeks. She is still heavily sedated from pain meds and the residual narcotics found in her system upon arrival. So, it would be nice to visit but also let her rest, so she can gain back some of her strength. Her father was here earlier and then some other family members, so you guys are her third batch of visitors."

Sénar said, "Thanks, doctor." He was being a little sarcastic but respectful. I knew Sénar didn't care how many visitors she had; he was going to see his sister. She was sleeping, I was reluctant to go in, but Sénar waved me in. I sat down in one of the chairs as Sénar called Cassidy's name gently. She woke up and saw Sénar and smiled at him. He smiled back and kissed her on her forehead.

He said, "I'm here for you, Cassidy. Even though, I should jack you up for going over there."

She managed to say, "Shut up, Sénar."

He got serious when he asked, "What happened?"

She looked around, and she saw me sitting on the chair. She just glared at me, but I didn't say anything. Cassidy asked, "Sénar, why is she here?"

He answered, "She is the one who told me you needed help, Cassidy. Don't worry about all the drama; man tell me what happened and who needs to be dealt with."

Cassidy sighed before she answered, "That girl Leah was dancing and flirting with Slim and his boys. We were all chillin'. I don't know if they put some stuff in our drinks or whatever, but she didn't really drink she just smoked. Slim wanted her to dance for him, so she did. When she was done, Slim wanted her to go to the room with him. When she said no, he got mad and tried to make her. She went crazy and started swinging on him and kicking him. So, Markese took her home, and slim was already mad at me because he thinks I hooked

Nevaeh up with Louie. So, he took it out on me and let his boys too. I couldn't fight all those guys they almost killed me, Sénar. I thought I was dead anyway."

Sénar looked like he wanted to cry; he asked, "Where do they live?"

Cassidy told Sénar where they lived and the names of who was there, she named about ten guys. She even gave him instructions on who she wanted to pay for what they did to her. She didn't mention Markese, but she also didn't pardon him either. She didn't seem mad at Leah, but she did mention she was way too flirtatious and that she riled up the guys before leaving. Sénar looked disgusted with the thought of Leah.

He asked, "You are going to be ok, right?"

She nodded, yeah. She tried not to cry, so she said a catty joke, "Now go before you mess up my high."

Sénar smirked at her then said, "I bet." He lovingly rubbed her hair before he assured her, "I got chu!"

On the drive home, Sénar was silent; he seemed disturbed. I was scared to say anything, so I just drifted away into my own thoughts. I wondered what Sénar was going to do to them or even Ken; he was already asking who was responsible. He even asked me, I was thankful Sénar didn't tell him the role I played, but who knows what they talk about when I'm not around. We pulled up to the house to see Ken's truck. I was nervous, and when Sénar noticed, he said, "Just go upstairs." I nodded my head in agreement and he carried my bag, giving it to me as we reached the door. I tried to run upstairs, but Ken stopped me when he said, "Treasure come here?" I followed behind Sénar as he walked to the table to sit down with his dad. Ken said, "Get me a beer." I went to get Ken a beer and I still had my backpack on. Sénar was telling him about the visit with Cassidy and Ken interrupted him to say, "I already know the story. Treasure make me one of them cheese sandwiches."

I sighed before I asked, "Can I put my backpack away first, Ken?"

Ken glared at me when he said, "Nah, just put it down and do what I said."

I took it off to wash my hands and got the stuff to make his sandwiches. I made four of them, cut them in half, giving him his two sandwiches, and gave Sénar the other ones. I took one of the halves from one of Sénar's sandwiches that I made for him. Before I could eat it and walk away, Ken said, "Treasure, it was so nice of you to give Cassidy Leah's number too."

Sénar shook his head, and I picked my bag up before I said, "Well, I didn't want her to go by herself, Ken."

He smirked at me and told Sénar, "Don't worry, I'll handle it. You just stay your ass out of trouble and focus on something other than pussy, boy."

Sénar rolled his eyes, and Ken said, "Don't play with me Sénar, I will break your ass! Is London still pregnant?"

Sénar shook his head and said, "Yeah, pops."

Ken said, "Well, you focus on that. I already told you what to do about that. So, if you are going to focus on some pussy, focus on that one."

Sénar got up and said, "Yes, sir." Sénar went to work out as I went up the stairs in a hurry. I stayed in my room until I smelled food, I almost didn't go down, but I went anyway when my stomach started to growl. It was just Sénar in the kitchen when I came down, he was making tacos. The cheese was grated and the toppings were already cut.

I asked, "Sénar is your dad mad at me for giving Cassidy Leah's number?"

He stared at me before he answered, "Treasure seriously, I don't know. What I do know is that only you and God knows what your intentions were, but Cassidy would have gone anyway, and he knows that at least."

He gave me a plate as my mom walked in, she looked sad and tired when she asked, "Sénar, how is Cassidy?"

He answered, "She is doing better today. She still has a sense of humor too."

My mom nodded as if to say she understood and said, "Well, that's good. I'm really sorry that happened, Sénar. When she comes home, she might not want to be bothered. She will probably need to rest. So anyway, we will see. What you got going on in here?"

I almost felt invisible until she turned to me to acknowledge me when she said, "Hey, Treasure." I said, "Hey, Momma."

She just looked at me before she said, "When Cassidy comes back, try not to be so mean. She's been through a lot." I just nodded my head in agreement with her, even though I was annoyed with her concern for Cassidy when she never seems to care about all that I had been through as a result of her own decisions. We all ate together without Ken as we all knew he was probably doing his fatherly duty. We ate and went to bed.

The next couple of days were intense. I avoided everyone; I didn't answer my phone when it rang. We made it to Thursday without any incidents, but I guess today was that exception. I made it through my first couple classes and was heading to the cafeteria when Tyrell came from behind me. He grabbed my arm, and I turned to face him. I asked, "What is it, Tyrell?"

He looked frustrated when he asked, "Why have you been ignoring my calls and avoiding me? All that we talked about was a lie?"

I sighed and answered, "Tyrell, the last time I saw you, you seemed to be more concerned with Leah than me!"

He smacked his lips, then said, "Well, that's because she was almost raped by some of Cassidy's friends, and I thought you were there too."

I rolled my eyes at him and said, "Well, I wasn't, and she's no angel. Tyrell knowing her, she probably gave it up to somebody willingly."

He got mad and said, "Well, you're no angel either, shit the way you rode me the last two times your ass probably be giving it up willingly too."

I tried to walk away, but he stopped me to say, "Give me a kiss, Treasure." I hesitated then gave him one as quickly as possible. He laughed before he asked, "What? You don't want your other boyfriend to see?" I walked away as he continued to laugh. I got my food and went outside to see Sénar was sitting under the tree waiting for me. I saw Leah standing over him, talking to him as he laid back listening. I looked around to see if London was somewhere stalking him, and she was but with a group of her friends watching Leah talk to Sénar. She headed over towards them at the same time as me. I rolled my eyes at them both and sat down.

Leah said, "Hey, Treasure."

I sighed before I replied, "Hi, Leah."

I ate my food and dismissed them both. They continued their conversation. Sénar said, "Leah, I'm cool." She smacked her lips in disappointment, "Well, I hope Cassidy gets better and let me know if you change your mind."

London chimed in, "He won't! Now kick rocks, trick!"

Leah said, "Shut up, girl, you are old news!"

Leah walked off and was probably going to find Tyrell to bother now. London looked at me, and I looked at her like she was not supposed to be over here when Sénar said, "London, I need to talk to Treasure, so what do you need?"

She smiled at him before she asked, "Can I come over after school?"

He answered, "No. Cassidy is coming home today, but I'll call you, ok? Maybe I'll come over there."

Annoyed by their conversation, he quickly dismissed her, and she went back to her little friends to run her mouth. Sénar said, "Treasure, Cassidy is coming home today, she is doing much better, but please avoid any kind of confrontation with her."

Offended, I said, "Sénar, Cassidy is always running her mouth and starting stuff. I don't even talk to her; she needs to-"

Sénar cut me off to say, "I don't want to hear it Treasure, ok? Just avoid her, give her some space, and don't bring up what happened. I just don't want my pops trippin' any more than he already is." I just remained quiet until the bell rang. Sénar helped me up and said, "See you at the game."

I went to class and found a seat and hoped Leah would not sit next to me, but she found her way next to me anyway. Leah doesn't waste any time, she said, "Damn, that's messed up what happened to Cassidy. I was cool with just Markese. I didn't want none of them other dudes. It seems like we have the same taste, Treasure." She smirked at me. I ignored her and thought about what she said, ugh she was so annoying. I laughed before I said, "You were right; Tyrell is better now." I smiled at her and did my work. As I waited for the basketball game to start, I warmed up with some of the cheerleaders as they whispered to each other. I ignored them and saw Sénar and Tyrell having words with each other. Neither of them looked like they were being friendly, one of the teammates noticed and got in between the two of them. Sénar walked off first, Tyrell was still talking while his teammate kept him at bay. The game was high tension; Tyrell, and Sénar had words throughout the game and even got a flag from one of the referees. Leah rolled her eyes at me and shook her head. I wish they would stop before one of them gets suspended. Tyrell was usually the aggressor because Sénar knew Ken gave him clear instructions to stay out of trouble. We barely won the game with all the extra tension between Sénar and Tyrell. Their beef with each other always added to the obstacles they had to overcome with the opponent team.

After the game, Tyrell came to me and said, "Come with me, Treasure."

I shook my head no and said, "I can't, Tyrell."

He was angry when he asked, "Why?"

I was nervous, but I just answered, "Because I can't Tyrell."

Leah walked up and asked, "Damn Tyrell, you still fighting over her? Is it because you guys been messing around again?"

She made sure Sénar heard her when she asked. Tyrell replied, "Shut up, Leah, you fucked Sénar?"

Leah smirked at Tyrell as Sénar said, "Let's go, Treasure."

I was leaving with Sénar when Tyrell asked, "I know you fucked Leah Sénar, but what about Treasure?"

Sénar just kept walking. I prayed he didn't answer Tyrell as London met up with Sénar. Tyrell caught up to me to ask, "Treasure, so you going to act like we didn't agree to start over. Well, at least let me beat it up again before you start acting brand new."

Leah added, "Well, she was bragging about it."

Sénar was ready to snap when Tyrell started laughing; I said, "No, Leah, you were the one bragging about Sénar and how he was better than Tyrell. And please, I did all the work the last time with Tyrell, he just got lucky. Just like you, just got lucky with Sénar."

Both of them looked like I had slapped them in their faces. When I got into the car with Sénar, he was extremely agitated, and so was I. We drove home in silence, and I drifted into my thoughts. I just thought about how Sénar was probably tired of me and hated me too, just like Tyrell had started to hate me. I grabbed my bag and headed for the door. I didn't see Ken's truck, so I was happy. I went straight to my room, and Sénar went to the garage. Cassidy was not there yet, and I couldn't be happier. I didn't know how she was going to act, but all I know is, she better leave me alone.

By the time Cassidy came home, it was nighttime, Sénar walked and assisted Cassidy to her bed. He asked her if she needed anything, and she shook her head no, then got into her bed. We both went to bed without a word. In the morning, we had no school because it was an in-service day. I quickly left the room before Cassidy woke up. Sénar was already downstairs watching TV; he told me Louie was coming to visit Cassidy and that he wanted me to help him make breakfast. I was happy he asked me for help; it had been a long time since me and Sénar were in the kitchen together. He tried to be happy and ignore the fact that his sister was brutally raped by several men, but it was difficult for him not to think about it. I cut the potatoes while he went to check on Cassidy. The doorbell rang, so I answered the door for Louie, Latosha, and Lil' James. I smiled at Louie and said hi to them all, and I hugged Lil' James and Latosha as they came in. Sénar came down after checking on Cassidy; his face lit up when he saw his cousins, especially Louie. They hugged for longer than usual and went to the garage while me and Latosha talked on the couch. Latosha asked, "Girl, how is Cassidy?" I shrugged my shoulders and said, "You know she don't like me Latosha. Hell, she probably wishes it was me." She said, "Girl, I know, she is my cousin, and she is something else, but I still love her. I'm going to check on her, watch Lil' James. We got so much to talk about." She went to say hi to Cassidy. I wish I could be a fly on the wall in the garage and in my room to hear their conversations. I played with Lil' James' cute self until Latosha came back down. She smacked her lips and asked, "Who is Leah? She needs her ass beat." I laughed before I answered, "Some lil' desperate slut that's obsessed with Sénar." She rolled her eyes and said, "Sénar ass needs to leave all them little girls alone. He knows he wants to marry your ass." I just looked at her like she was crazy and said, "Latosha, what are you talking about?" She laughed and replied, "Girl, Sénar ass been talking about you forever, he is the one that's obsessed." She laughed, but I didn't think it was funny. She looked at me and asked, "What's wrong, Treasure? Why are you acting like you don't already know?" I stared at her for a moment before I said, "I mean, I know, but how come everybody else knows too?" She whispered, "That's why Ken got with your mom." I looked at her like she was stupid, and she looked like she may have said something she wasn't supposed to. I asked, "Latosha, what are you talking about?" She cleared her throat and asked, "Y'all don't have nothing to drink in here?" I was annoyed with her for the first time when I said, "Yes, Latosha we do. What do you want?" She asked, "Well, don't your Momma drink?" She was really getting on my nerves now, I answered, "Yeah Latosha, but maybe Sénar and Louie can get some because my momma will kill us both, if I let you drink her wine." She said, "I bet shit, having to deal with Ken's crazy ass." She was definitely on one today; I was hoping she would get buzzed and tell me more. Sénar and Louie came in, so Sénar could finish breakfast. When he was done, he went to check on Cassidy, but she didn't want to come down. So, he brought her breakfast to her. When he came back down, him and Louie left while me and Latosha watched TV with Lil' James. My mom came down and noticed Latosha and Lil' James. She came to say hi before she made Ken a plate and went back upstairs.

When Sénar and Louie came back, they had bags of groceries and appeared to be celebrating something. Latosha said, "Louie is so happy. He is about to have a baby, and Louie turns eighteen tomorrow. Hell, that's a big deal where we live because so many niggas never even make it to eighteen. Louie don't even bang no more or do all that dumb shit he was doing before. Ever since he found out Nevaeh is having his baby. He even stopped kicking it with Cedrick because he was a bad influence." She was just full of info today she continued, "Girl, so I met some really nice guy. He is like twenty-six, but he is really nice, and he got a job with his own place. He even knows I have a son, and he is not even trippin'. I have a date with him on Sunday, so Louie better have me back in time. I wonder if he has a big dick."

I laughed at her and said, "Well, if you really like him, don't have sex with him yet."

She looked at me like I was crazy and said, "Girl, please, I am horny. I am going to get me some!" I smacked my lips and schooled her, "Latosha, if you really like him, make him wait and make him work for it. That drives guys crazy trust me." She laughed, then said, "Ok, fine, but it better work. Cuz I was trying to get me some." She pouted when she thought about what I said. She laughed and looked at me to say, "You know what? You are something else, huh?" I rolled my eyes as she asked, "What are you going to do about Sénar?" I didn't know, so I said, "What about him?" She said, "Girl, you be playing.

Do you know Sénar is not going to give up on you until you are his, right?"I rolled my eyes and said, "Latosha, your cousin is crazy, but I am not. I have a boyfriend; it's just complicated." She laughed and asked, "What? You have a boyfriend, and he is still alive?" I thought about the other night and how close Sénar was to killing Tyrell if Ken had not stopped him. I sighed and asked, "Well, what would you do?"

She laughed before she replied, "Girl, surrender already, damn."

I folded my arms defiantly, "No, Latosha. Sénar is just crazy; he will go play professional football somewhere and forget all about me. Plus, he is having a baby too." She was shocked when she asked, "Gurl! You are lying! Sénar got that little skinny girl pregnant? Ugh, I didn't like her; she probably set his ass up. Sénar didn't even seem to like her ass." I laughed because I knew it was true. She just waved her hand and said, "Well, she will be a baby momma, but you will be wifey." I smirked at her, then asked, "Um, how are you so sure?" She smiled and answered, "I know my cousin Treasure, and you are going to be his wife. Just invite Lil' James and me to the wedding." She was freaking me out, so I said, "Latosha, you are funny. Let's see what the boys got."

Ken was gone, but my mom was still home, so we all went to the park to smoke and let Lil' James play. We ate at Mr. Taco and then went home. Sénar bought some pozole home from the restaurant for Cassidy. She didn't eat any of the food Sénar had brought to her, but she did eat the pozole. Sénar checked on Cassidy throughout the day and before we all went to bed. Me and Latosha slept on the couch, so we could talk about juicy stuff. The next morning, we all went to the beach and even got Cassidy to come out. She didn't say much; all she did was lay on her blanket in the sand. Latosha braided her hair and talked with her for a bit before her, and Lil' James went to the water. I went with them into the water; then, we built a sandcastle. The boys smoked and drank while I observed Nevaeh with her little belly bulging in her little two-piece bathing suit. I had my shawl and my own two piece on, which I made sure covered more than the last one being that I was a lot thicker than the last time we were at the beach. I laid there and watch Louie and Sénar celebrate Louie's birthday. Nevaeh was glowing; she actually looked pretty for once to me. She was happy and just gazing at Louie like she loved him. Nevaeh went to sit with Cassidy to check on her. Louie took the opportunity to talk to me while Nevaeh was checking on Cassidy and Sénar was cooking on the grill.

He said, "Hey, Treasure, how are you doing?"

I answered, "I'm good, Louie. Happy 18th birthday, Louie!" He cheesed and popped his invisible collar before he said, "Thanks, Treasure. I know Sénar can't wait till he turns eighteen, so he could snatch your ass up and run away with you!" He laughed, but we both knew he wasn't playing. Cassidy was sleep; she wasn't worried about none of our behinds. We chilled and ate before we all went our separate ways. We had a long day, so sleep was easy when we got home, we all went to bed without any delays.

Sunday morning when I woke up, I laid in bed and didn't want to wake Cassidy, so I just laid there in my thoughts for a moment. I grabbed my phone after having not looked for it, in over a week. I saw all the missed calls, mostly from Tyrell. I saw Markese had called a few times. I listened to the voice mails; most of the ones from Tyrell were of him hanging up, but the two I got from Markese were bone-chilling. The first message, he said, "Treasure let them know I didn't do shit but help Cassidy, man! I don't want no flak from this shit! Man, call me. It's some crazy shit going on, and I don't want no parts of it!" The second one was the one that alarmed me; The message started with Markese asking, "What kind of sick mothafuckas you live with man? This shit is crazy!! What the hell, man, noooooo!" I hung my phone up as Sénar was coming into my room to check on Cassidy. She was awake, he helped her to the bathroom and then left. He just made sure she ate and kept her hygiene up to par, being that she appeared to be very withdrawn. She isolated herself, unless Sénar pushed her to be involved. I went to watch TV after eating some cereal. Ken came home after being gone for the last two days. He didn't speak to me; he just went upstairs without even looking at me. I was fine with that. Sénar came down and made Cassidy something to eat, after asking me if I was hungry and me telling him no. It wasn't long before the doorbell rang, and London pranced her way through the door. Sénar and her didn't stay. They left, and I just lounged all day until I was tired of watching TV. When I went back upstairs, Cassidy was crying in her bed.

I almost felt sorry for her and asked, "Are you ok, Cassidy?"

She snapped at me when she answered, "No, you stupid bitch! This should have been you! Not me!"

I winced at her malice words, and I instantly knew I needed to leave. As I turned to leave, Cassidy attacked me. She hit me at least three times in my face before I hauled off to hit her in her eye, at the same time Sénar opened our door to check on Cassidy. Sénar pushed me onto my bed, "What the hell are you doing, Treasure?" Sénar was furious with me; I got nervous and defended myself when I said, "She attacked me!" Cassidy yelled, "She's lying!" I was so shocked that Cassidy lied like that, so I just got quiet as Sénar glared at me. Ken came in and asked, "What the hell is going on now?" Ken looked tired and frazzled. Sénar was quiet, but Cassidy said, "She attacked me, daddy! She hit me in the eye!" I was so scared, but I did not show it. I let Treasure number two take over when I confessed, "I did hit her Ken, but she attacked me fir-" Before I could finish my sentence, Ken roared, "I am tired of your ass, little girl! I have had it with your ass!" He pushed me against the wall, he had his hand on my chest when he said, "You want me to put my hands on you, then you got it!" He whispered, "You wanna move up higher on my hit list, keep playing with me." Sénar and Cassidy watched Ken threaten me but remained silent. My mom came and saw Ken had me against the wall, and she asked, "What's wrong, Ken?"

He never looked at my mom. He just answered, "I'm tired of Treasure putting her hands on Cassidy. I am about to-"

My mom cut Ken off out of desperation, "Ken, honey, let Treasure sleep in Sénar's room for a couple of days. Cassidy probably just needs her space, please, baby? I will do whatever you want, come on, you need to rest, baby." Ken looked back at my mom he was highly agitated, but he released me and told my mom, "I am fed up with her ass, she is gonna get hurt, if she keeps playing with me woman!" My mom asked, "Sénar, is it ok? She will be ok in there, right? Sénar?" He shrugged his shoulders and answered, "I'll sleep downstairs, Carmel, she can sleep in there." Ken walked out, annoyed with my mom's desperate plea to save me and separate me from Cassidy for a couple of days. My mom summoned me to come out she closed the door to our room and then asked, "Treasure, what is wrong with you? You know she has been through a lot, and you should be able to control yourself!" She put her finger in my face as she continued, "Ken has had it with you! Treasure, please stop getting into trouble, or we will all suffer! And I already told you, I am tired of suffering for you!" She was on the verge of tears as she was pleading with me. She looked at Sénar and asked, "Sénar don't be silly; she can sleep in Chino's old bed. I can trust you, right? I mean, you are always there for her anyway, right?"

He nodded, "Yeah, Carmel." He walked off and went downstairs, my mother cut her eyes at me and threatened, "Treasure if my man leaves me because your ass don't know how to act, your ass might as well go too! Because I don't want to be alone again, and I will make your life a living hell, little girl, like you are trying to make mine!" I laughed at her and said, "Well, I've been living in hell anyway, while you live in your little make-believe heaven!" She slapped me, and Ken came out to see what the commotion was. If he didn't come out, I would have hit my mom back, but the look Ken gave me stopped me dead in my tracks. I ran downstairs right into Sénar's arms; he picked me up and took me to the garage as I cried on his shoulder. He sat down on his bench, where he lifted weights and held me in his arms as he positioned me on his lap. He looked me in my eyes and said, "Treasure, you are doing way too much. Slow down, ma. I know there's a lot going on, but you are making it worse by reacting to everything."

I looked at Sénar in his eyes when I said, "You are always acting like you know everything, Sénar! Giving me instructions on this and instructions on that, but what about you?" He tensed up and answered truthfully, "I know I mess up Treasure, and I never said I was perfect. Every time I open up to you ma, you become more and more vindictive. I hate it, and I'm trying to stop you from self-destructing, that's all Treasure." I glared at him and said, "Right, because I'm the one trying to destroy my life, huh? Everyone around me is just so nice and loving. I am the problem, right? I deserved all this?" Sénar winced at my words but answered, "No, Treasure, but that doesn't mean you have to try and take us all out one by one either!" He tapped my behind to insinuate for me to get up, but I glared at him instead. I then said, "You have no idea!" Sénar smirked at me as both waves of anger and lust-filled him; I could feel his excitement rise beneath me. He squeezed me then said, "You can pick pleasure or pain, but one has to win. Plus, you will need me, no matter how this turns out, and I will be there, no matter how this turns out." He stood up, forcing me to stand with him, he caressed my body while smelling my hair, sending me to a place of ecstasy, immediately. Before I could give in to temptation, he released me and walked out, leaving me to deal with myself and all my emotions. I was so confused and anxious; I didn't bother going back in the house. I grabbed the gloves off the wall, to put them on. I punched the punching bag and drifted away into my thoughts. I thought about everything anyone ever did to me, and the more I thought, the harder I punched. I was in a rage, thinking of everyone and their form of betrayal. My anger increased as each persons' face flashed before me; I hit the punching bag according to my anguish. I had thought of everyone except Sénar, but when his face flashed, I snapped and swung so hard, I heard a thud. Feeling dizzy, I shook my head, and when I looked up, Sénar was getting up off the floor. He looked like he would rip me to shreds when he asked, "What the hell, Treasure! I was calling your name for like five minutes! Why the hell you hit me like that?" I laughed, but it was a chilling laugh that made the hair on the back of my neck stand up. Sénar was wiping the blood off his lip. He had fire in his eyes as I grabbed him and started to kiss him. I was all over him, and as much as he was turned on, he looked worried as well. He called my name, "Treasure?" I ignored him and tried to get to his man stick, he moved my hand and restrained me by turning me around and wrapping his arms around me. He said, "Treasure?" I didn't answer; he called my name, "Treasure?" I snapped, "What?" He laughed before he said, "Calm down. Let it happen naturally. You are upset right now, just chill Treasure." I snapped, "Oh, so now I want to give it to you, you don't want it! I hate you, Sénar!" I tried to wiggle out of his embrace, but I could not. I twisted and turned as he held me until my frustration, and my will to fight was broken. When I was done, he released me and said, "The food is ready, ma." He shook his head and helped me out of my gloves while I glared at him. He looked hurt, but he didn't say anything, he put the gloves on the wall and waited for me to walk out. Everyone was at the table and saw how distraught I was. As I walked in, everyone could tell that I was on the verge of snapping. I rudely brushed past Sénar and into the kitchen with everyone's glare fixated on me. I was ready to kill every last one of them for my own reasons; I glared back at everyone despite being outnumbered. My mom and Ken were already eating with Cassidy at the table. I made my plate with a little food as my appetite was not very big at the moment. I sat at the kitchen nook to avoid having to stare into their faces. Sénar sat at the table with the rest of them.

Ken saw Sénar's lip and asked, "What happened to you, boy?"

Sénar chuckled before he answered, "Nothing pops."

Ken said, "Get me a beer, Treasure."

My mom said, "Ken I-"

He cut her off when he roared, "I didn't ask you!"

Sénar and Cassidy both froze and waited for my response. I was not in the mood, so I said, "My momma can get –"

Ken jumped up and came toward me; he snatched me out of the chair by my neck. My mom jumped up as Ken slammed me against the wall and then said, "You better get me a damn beer, put it on the got damn table, and act like you got some sense before I break your little neck, girl!" Ken pushed my mom out the way as I scurried to the kitchen to get Ken a beer and then ran out of the kitchen to my room. I cried and started to grab my stuff that I needed to take a bath. Cassidy came in behind me and said, "Ooh, I wish he would kill your stupid ass already!"

I grabbed my stuff, my diary and left without responding to Cassidy. I knew her intentions; she wanted Ken to finish me already. I was ready to die if I had to deal with Ken the way I learned to deal with Sénar. I cried and cried until I was tired of crying; I plunged myself into the water and let the water submerge me. I did not intend to come back up; I let my thoughts take me to a place of peace until I felt like I could sleep peacefully forever.

Sénar was frantic as he leaned over me, I could feel the warmth of his lips on mine and the pressure on my chest. I felt the urge to vomit as some fluid started to projectile out of my mouth. I gasped for air as I choked on some of the fluid. I could hear Sénar calling my name and trying to get me to answer him. He gently shook me as I reluctantly responded, "What?" I saw Cassidy standing behind him with a look of disappointment on her face. I was naked, under a towel covering me when I looked down. Images of Cassidy the night at the park flashed before my eyes, but it was me in the blanket; I screamed. Sénar covered my mouth and whispered, "Treasure, please calm down." He rubbed my hair and whispered, "Everything is going to be ok, ma. Shush, just relax, ma." He rocked me until I was calm, and he released my mouth. I felt like I was fading away. I looked into Sénar's eyes, I saw all the pain and worry that plagued him, and I closed my eyes to avoid caring. He picked me up and took me to his room. He laid me on Chino's bed; he didn't say another word to me. He put me under the covers and tucked me in. I was out like a light bulb before I knew it.

Monday in the morning, I woke up in a panic gasping for air and Sénar was at my side. I looked down and saw that I was naked and under the covers. I quickly covered myself and asked, "Why am I naked? And what am I doing in Chino's bed?" I was delirious, I pushed Sénar back and yelled at him when I asked, "Where's my clothes?" He tried to be patient with me, but he first said, "Treasure stop yelling at me. I have all your stuff. I will give it to you. Are you ok to go to school?" I looked at him like he was stupid when I asked, "Why wouldn't I be? What happened?" I was worried, I didn't know what was going on and he was too calm. He still had some worry in his eyes, but he was stable enough to ensure I was ok. I was annoyed and impatient when I said, "Give me my stuff Sénar!" He got my clothes and handed them to me and walked out, so I could get dressed. Cassidy didn't go to school; I honestly don't think she wanted to go back to school anyway. I was not in a good mood, I felt grouchy and tired even though I slept. Sénar waited for me at the door as I came down for us to leave to school.

Sénar started his car and while letting it warm up, he asked, "You don't remember last night?" He had a perplexed look on his face. I replied, "Sénar no, if I did, I wouldn't have asked you what happened!" He winced at my attitude and then said, "Well, you aren't allowed to take baths anymore, that's what happened." He was agitated with me, but I didn't care when I said, "You can't tell me what to do. If I want to take a bath, then I will take a bath!" Sénar got in my face when he said, "Your ass is the crazy one! You could have killed yourself, Treasure!" I screamed, "Then you should have let me! It's my life! If I want to end it, it's none of your business!" He yelled back, "It is my business! I am supposed to protect your ass and you are making it really hard, Treasure! Damn, let me love you! Stop fighting me! Stop fighting yourself! I don't want to lose you, Treasure damn!" I glared at Sénar before I said, "I was never yours to lose in the first place, Sénar!" His eyes filled with rage when he yelled, "Fine! Do whatever you want!" I cut my eyes at him and said, "I will!" We pulled into the school and saw everyone out in the front of the school. Sénar got out of the car and immediately walked over to the crowd to see Leah and London arguing. London saw me and took her rage out on me next; she ran toward me as Sénar tried to stop her. I ignored her until she tried to grab me. I snatched my arm away from her to say, "Leave me alone London! I am not in the mood! I will really hurt you and I don't care if you're pregnant! So, back off!"

Everyone heard me yell at her and looked at me like I was crazy. Everywhere I went people were whispering. My first three classes were always drama free but today people were whispering and giggling in groups. By the time lunch time came everyone was buzzing with rumors and anticipation to watch some drama unfold. Sénar rushed up to me to say, "Treasure, let's go!"

I stared at him and asked, "Where?" He didn't answer my question, he just said, "Come on." I followed him to his car, and he took me to Taco Bell. I ordered a chili cheese burrito with sour cream and It was so good. I still could not help but ask, "Sénar why are we here?" Sénar looked frustrated when he answered, "Look Treasure, there is too much going on man. People are starting stupid ass rumors and stuff. I just need to know that you are ok. I don't want you to react to all the stuff going on. Plus, you have to be careful what you say ma. When you're angry don't speak because foolishness just spews out of your mouth and the damage is already done after. Then people only hear what they want to hear." I was not in a mood for one of his lectures, I just rolled my eyes at him. Sénar had it with me too, he asked, "What do you want Treasure? What would make you happy?" I stared at him, while I searched my heart and mind for the right answer. I started to cry when I answered, "I don't know Sénar! I wanted to live and now I don't. So, I guess nothing or everything." He shook his head before he said, "Ma, I would give you everything, if I had it to give to you and I'm still not sure, it would be enough." He shook his head again and drove back to school, he didn't say another word. I was irritated with him and wanted to slap him silly, just because he always had something smart to say.

We were both irritated with each other when we got back to school and with this being the week of Valentine's Day, everything was even more dramatic with everyone trying to claim their valentines. I could care less about that stupid day or what it meant; it was just another day. I was just ready for this one to be over already. I went to my next class and Leah sat next to me; I was instantly concerned for her safety. I asked, "Leah, can you sit somewhere else?" She replied, "No Treasure, I like you. Why don't you like me? You and Sénar both be playing hard to get. I got Tyrell around my pinky…." she stopped and thought for a second and then said, "maybe I'll get your momma's man, since I can't get Sénar." I tried to back hand her in her mouth, but she moved back quickly. She was fast because she almost got her mouth slapped off her face. She giggled and stood up as the teacher asked," Is there a problem?" Leah laughed and replied, "No, we were just playing. Right, Treasure?" I nodded yeah and avoided eye contact with the teacher to hide my animosity for Leah. She giggled and did her work, while I thought about how much trouble I would get into, if I were to beat her face in.

When class was over the teacher stopped me to ask, "Treasure are you ok?" I wanted to tell him no, but I answered, "I'm fine." He took my word for it and let me go. I went to practice and avoided Leah. I still wanted to finish my assault on her mouth because it was too big.

I wanted to hit her in it, I could care less if she took Ken; it would be a dream come true to have Ken runoff, so he would leave me alone.

After practice London was following Sénar, trying to get him to talk to her but he looked really frustrated. Tyrell came up to me with Leah behind him to ask, "Are you my valentine, Treasure?" I rolled my eyes at him and he said, "Dang Treasure, it's like that now?" He waited for my answer, "Tyrell, I don't want to play your games, ok? Ask Leah she is right behind you." He laughed and said, "Oh, so Sénar is behind you, so you must be his valentines then?" Sénar said, "Let's go Treasure." At this moment, I would rather have Tyrell be mad at me than Sénar. I ignored him and followed Sénar to his car as London followed me. I couldn't help but watch my back because London appeared to be getting too close for my comfort and Leah was probably still mad that I almost slapped her in the mouth earlier. They were both behind me and I could feel myself tense up the closer we got to Sénar's car. I could feel London swing on me and then Leah. I pushed London to the ground and punched Leah in her mouth as we started fighting in the parking Lot. London got up to try to jump in; I pushed her so hard, she tripped falling hard onto the ground. Then Leah pushed me to the ground too and Tyrell grabbed her. Sénar snatched me up off the ground before Leah could kick me in the face, and then he put me in the car. He grabbed London up and said something to her before he got in to drive off. London cried hysterically as she ran to her car. Leah was laughing as Tyrell led her to his car. I was fuming, I knew I should have just beat Leah's ass when I had the chance. Her and London were both some punks because they had to wait until my back was toward them to attack me and then to make matters worse, they tried to jump me, on top of that. I was going to get them back! They were going to pay for what they did to me.

Sénar said, "Treasure, it's over ok, no need to try to get revenge. Man, this shit has to stop!"

I yelled, "Easy for you to say, you are not the one that was jumped!" He acknowledged my feelings before he replied, "Treasure you're right. Trust me Treasure, just lay low man things work themselves out when we just be still. Don't react to everything, it will have a greater impact. Take the power back from them. Use it to restore yourself, Treasure you can barely tell! They couldn't even handle you by themselves. You did way more damage!" I defended myself and asked, "Was I supposed to let them beat me up Sénar?" He laughed before he answered, "No Treasure, you did the right thing by defending yourself. Anyone who saw it knows you were not the aggressor. I know you are probably thinking about all my fights with Tyrell, but I have tried to avoid him. I used to be the aggressor, but I had to learn the hard way and mature or leave. Now, if I ever have to kill his ass, everyone knows that he has been the aggressor lately. I'm done fighting his ass, I'm just not done fighting for you. Look, Just go inside, take a shower, and read. I have some clothes you can wear. You know where to find them. I also have some books in my room but the best one is the word, you might learn somethin'. I'll be right back."

When Sénar pulled up to the house Ken was not there, so I felt somewhat better. I got out without saying anything. I could not believe those heifers tried to jump me. I did exactly what Sénar instructed me to do but I chose to read one of his men magazines instead. He had a lot of them. Some of them, well, a lot of them were explicit pictures of women inside. I saw a lot of different types of women in various positions doing some pretty explicit things. He had one called *Hustler*, I had to put it down because the women were so bodacious, I was blown away. No wonder that's all men thought about; it was not so bad to think about. I laughed to myself as I went through it looking at all the pictures. Sénar came in and saw all the magazines, I had browsed through. I even read some stuff in them and guys were really something else. But this *Hustler* one was something I could not put down again. I giggled to myself as I turned the pages until Sénar said, "Treasure?"

He startled me and I shyly answered, "What, Sénar?"

He smirked at me when he asked, "Out of all the things you could read, you chose that?"

I looked at him like he had some nerve when I asked, "These are yours Sénar? Ooh! You nasty." He laughed and snatched the magazine from me. He stared at me, then said, "Don't be going through my stuff, being nosey." I thought to myself, *it's too late for that*. I knew where everything was, I saw every picture in his drawer, and looked around. There was stuff I wanted to read that I haven't read yet but being in here I might get the opportunity. This was my second day of being temporarily kicked out of my own room for Cassidy's comfort, after having an obviously horrible night, that I can only remember some of. I had one of Sénar's tank tops on and a pair of his smallest basketball shorts rolled up. He had some clothes in his hands and said, "But you need to change really quick."

He bit his bottom lip and just stared at me. I asked, "Why? I like what I have on."

Sénar smiled sadistically before he answered, "Me too, umph but that's why you need to change."

I was confused but I just took the clothes from him and started to undress. I took my shirt off first as Sénar watched while trying to compose himself, he was doing a good job until I took the basketball shorts off and he saw that I had no underwear on. He tried to hold himself together as I purposely took my time pulling my panties up that he brought me in, and then my shorts. When I was done, I asked, "Are you happy Sénar?"

He smirked at me and then pulled me to him before he answered, "One day I pray we will be, when we're together at last!" He was being funny, but he was probably serious, he turned me around and squeezed me while he smelled my hair. He let me go when his phone rung, he answered it and I could hear him say, "Calm down, I'll be there." He sighed before he said, "Damn, I have to go again. Carry on, I'll be back."

I laid back down on Chino's old bed and looked through the magazine. When I was finished, I put them all back. I looked through some of his papers and envelopes. I found a tablet with a bunch of writings in it. Mostly letters to God and a bunch of drawings and quotes. I saw my name scribbled with his last name and a heart with keys missing. Ken opened Sénar's door and asked, "Where is Sénar at?"

I shrugged my shoulders and answered, "I don't know, he said he would be back."

He looked at me reading Sénar's stuff and said, "Put that boy's stuff down. Your ass knows too much already as it is. Bring your ass downstairs!"

He was right, I shouldn't be going through Sénar's stuff, but I couldn't help It, I needed to know more. Why did he want me so badly, when so many girls wanted to be with him? I took my time going downstairs and when I reached the bottom, I tried to go into the living room quickly, but Ken called me into the kitchen. I cautiously walked into the kitchen area as Ken sat in his chair. He said, "Come here." I walked slowly to him with my heartbeat increasing from fear, he pulled me to him. He put his hands on my behind, then put his face in my crotch area and took a deep breath, almost making me run for my life! He had a tight grip on me when he said, "Your sneaky ass then already weeded my girls out but if something happens to my son...... I will strangle your little ass to death and send you out cumming. Trust me, I am good at it." He winked at me before he released me as Sénar came through the front door. Sénar was upset already when he came in and grew even angrier when he saw me with Ken. Sénar went straight to the garage and I ran to Sénar's room to cry in a pillow. *What did I do to deserve this life? Was I going to die and be another statistic?* I was crying uncontrollably when I heard his door open. When I made sure it was him, I looked away from him and put my face back in my pillow. Sénar was still upset but appeared to have calmed down some when he asked, "What were you doing down there?" I had tears in my eyes when I answered, "He was looking for you when he saw me reading something, so he told me to come downstairs." Sénar folded his arms and waited for me to be specific. I carefully continued, "I was going through some of your stuff and he told me that I already knew too much and made me come downstairs." He rolled his eyes and asked, "So, you were being nosey again? Why are you going through my stuff? What are you looking for? What do you want to know Treasure?" He asked so many questions, I lost count and I felt like a little girl at the bleachers, so long ago. I got scared and anxious when I answered, "I don't know Sénar. I just want to know, why me? What is it with you and your dad Sénar?" He shook his head out of frustration when he answered, "Treasure some stuff is just better left alone. I will tell you when the time is right. You need to stop being so damn sneaky and nosey." He was in my face and I was still angry when I said, "Well maybe if I knew, then I would know what to do about it."

Sénar smirked before he said, "You are funny Treasure and cute but don't fool yourself. Just stop giving him reasons to want to hurt your ass." I pushed him back to ask, "Oh, so this is my fault too? It's my fault that Ken wants to screw my brains out and kill me because of you! When you won't leave me alone?" I started to cry but instead I said, "Maybe I should let him! I might like him too!" Sénar almost lost it he grabbed my face and pressed me against the wall when he said, "Don't ever say anything like that again Treasure. I would kill both of you!" He released me and left the room in a rage. I didn't even go down for dinner, I just cried myself to sleep.

In the morning, Sénar was not in his bed when I woke up. I went to the bathroom to get ready for school. I had to go in my room to grab an outfit, I was quiet and quick, but Cassidy still managed to tell me to get out before I could close the door behind me. Once I was dressed, I went downstairs to see Sénar was asleep with a blanket on the couch. I didn't want to wake him; I just didn't want him to be late for school. So, I nudged him and called his name softly, "Sénar."

He sprung up on the couch to ask, "What happen?" I observed him; he was frantic, so I quickly assured him, "Nothing Sénar, I am just waking you up so you can get ready for school." I was worried about him as I watched him struggle to come to his senses. He glared at me before he got up, he went to get dressed. After about ten minutes, he came back down, and we left for school. He didn't speak to me; he was silent the whole ride to school. When we got there, London was waiting on Sénar crying; I could see his irritation level rise. She saw me in the passenger seat, and she ran to my side of the car, I locked the door. London was crying and yelling as she tried to get to me. I could see Tyrell and Leah watching as the scene unfolded. Sénar grabbed London and held her as he summoned me to get out. She yelled, "It's all your fault, Treasure!" I ignored her antics and went to class. I didn't know what London was talking about and I didn't care. Sénar never really wanted to be with her anyway, and that wasn't my fault. I didn't feel the least bit sorry for her.

At lunchtime, I hurried to get my food when London approached me, I was ready to fight. Sénar came and whispered to London as she walked with him. Tyrell and Leah spotted me, but Tyrell came to me without Leah and pretended to be concerned when he asked, "Are you ok, Treasure?" I nodded yeah, even though I was not sure he was being sincere with his concern. Leah walked up, and I got uncomfortable instantly. I was ready to give them both a two-piece combo with a biscuit, if they didn't leave me alone. I didn't trust either of them and started to walk backwards, but I turned around and bumped into Sénar. Even though, he was angry with me, he sensed my need for help and walked me outside, but everyone followed us out, including London. Leah had a smirk on her face, and Tyrell was eyeing Sénar. He could tell Sénar was upset with me, so he tested him.

He asked, "Aye Sénar, you smashed Leah, I heard, but how long you been smashing Treasure?" London and Leah waited to hear Sénar's answer. Sénar was already agitated, but he knew Tyrell's game plan.

He shrugged his shoulders when he asked, "Why are you worried about it?" London got impatient, and Leah smiled her own little evil smile. I ate my food, and Leah asked, "Yeah, Tyrell, why you worried about it? Didn't you just smash Treasure last weekend?" Tyrell flashed on Leah, "Man shut up! You got a couple of new friends yourself!" She giggled, but Sénar was beyond agitated with all of them. Sénar laughed at Tyrell, making him super uptight. Tyrell asked, "Sénar, what's so damn funny, man?" Sénar flashed his famous smile before he said, "You act like I broke Leah's chain or something. Nah, she is not important to me. The one you let slip away, is my real treasure."

Tyrell thought about what Sénar said and became enraged when he asked, "What the hell did you say?"

The bell rang, and Sénar laughed when he said, "Nice chain Tyrell, it looks better on you!"

I almost choked on the last bite of my sandwich as Sénar helped me up off the ground. It was as if Sénar could read my mind when he said, "Some things, are just better left unsaid," he shrugged his shoulders and then walked me to class; I was so angry with him. Tyrell would put two and two together and figure out what Sénar meant, and he would probably never forgive me. I was distraught, and Leah knew better than to sit next to me. To make matters worse, we had a game after school, and I was in no mood to cheer. Also, after Tyrell and Sénar's little standoff they would probably fight during the game if they had to play together, I started to stress. During my last class, the teacher informed me that I was wanted in the office. I sighed because I just knew it was all the drama, and somehow it was always my fault. Sénar was already in the office when I got there; he looked just as confused as me. The secretary told us we had an emergency at home and that we were instructed to head home immediately. My mom and

Ken were waiting for us with Cassidy when we got home. Ken looked upset but more sad than angry. He grabbed Sénar and hugged him and told him something in his ear. Sénar lost it, he started to push Ken off of him and screamed, "Nooooooo!"

Ken held Sénar to keep him from going nuts, my mom and Cassidy were crying. I was the only one who didn't know why Sénar was like a kid having a tantrum. Sénar pulled himself together and asked, "Who did it? What happened?"

Ken put his head down before he answered, "The police shot em Sénar and Lil' James too, he was in his arms." Sénar ran to his room; you could hear a lot of commotion. Everyone was somber and devastated.

I asked my momma, "What happened?"

My mom answered me while sobbing, "The police shot Louie, and they don't think he is going to make it!" Ken looked sick, and his manly stature was dismissed as he went to go check on Sénar. My mom and Cassidy cried as they headed upstairs. I was devastated too. I didn't know where to go, Sénar was still mad at me, Cassidy hated me, and my mom was just as lost as she normally was. I just sat on the couch and cried. *Why? How? Was Lil' James, ok? What about Latosha? Louie was the man of their household what were they going to do? Nevaeh was pregnant, and he wouldn't be here for his baby if he died. Sénar was already going through so much. I couldn't imagine how he was feeling after just getting over what happened to Cassidy.* My thoughts had completely consumed me when Ken had come down to say, "Treasure, go check on him, you're probably the only one that can do any damn thing for his ass!" He was sincere, but he had some animosity in his voice when he gave me instructions to check on Sénar. I was so sad and scared because he probably didn't want to see me either; we weren't exactly on the best terms. He was on the floor with his head down; he looked like a baby in a fetal position. I tried to touch him; he roared, "Don't touch me!" I jumped back, I started to leave him, but I grabbed him anyway. I yelled, "Get up, Sénar! Pray for him! Pray for his soul and his family, Sénar! Don't give up!" He glared at me before he cried, "Leave me alone! This is probably because of what I did to you! I am being punished! I'm sorry! Damn! Please don't take him from me too!" I know he said he wanted to be left alone, but I couldn't leave him like that. I hugged Sénar from behind, I helped him up and led him to his bed; he was weak from all his crying and yelling. He fell back down, putting his face in my stomach and cried uncontrollably. I didn't say anything at first, I just let him vent his pain, and then I told him, "Sénar lie down and be still." His eyes were red, his hair was a mess, and he looked like he wanted to throw another tantrum, but he took his shirt off to dry his face with it. He sat down on his bed, he took his pants off, and left his basketball shorts on. He got in his bed and laid down. I looked at my shirt, and it was wet, so I took it off. I took my pants off and lied next to Sénar, but I kept my bra and panties on. He felt my warmth and could not resist turning over and burying his head in my chest. We both cried ourselves to sleep in each other's arms.

Chapter 15

In the morning, Sénar and I woke up in each other's arms. We quickly pulled ourselves together to recap what happened last night and became emotional all over again. Sénar laid back down and turned over to face the wall. I knew he probably was embarrassed of the vulnerable state he was in last night. I was quiet; I didn't want to make it worse. Sénar said, "You didn't have to do that, Treasure. I would have been fine."

He was quiet for a minute then continued, "Louie was my best friend, if he's gone, I don't know what I will do. In my heart I feel like he is not here anymore, but I don't want to know. I will go out there after school. If you want to go with me, you can go."

He got up to take a good look at me and tried to hide his lust as he went to get ready for school. I thought to myself, *what were we made of that we could go through horrific events and still go to school the next day like nothing happened?* This was confusing because this was not normal, and I was sure of it. Today was Wednesday and Friday was Valentine's Day. We went to school and did our best to remain normal but we both were not able to attend the back to back game due to a family emergency. The coaches respected our ability to make it to school and gave us both a pass to leave. Giving us the opportunity to totally avoid any possible drama after yesterday's events. Sénar and I rolled out to the city with the music blasting. We smoked a blunt and just stayed in our own thoughts while we drove on the freeway. Sénar looked deep in thought and when our song *"Dilemma"* came on with

Nelly and Kelly, we couldn't help but smile at our own thoughts. The closer we got to Louie's house the sadder Sénar appeared. We pulled up to the house and there were a lot of cars in front of the house, Ken's truck was one of them.

Me and Sénar looked at each other and just hung our heads low before we faced reality together. We walked in and everybody just wailed, nobody wanted to talk to Sénar but Latosha came from the back to see what the new commotion was. When she saw us, she broke down crying, she grabbed Sénar and yelled at him, "They took my brother Sénar! He's gone and my lil' baby is in the hospital too. I can't even look at him with all those tubes in him!"

Sénar just held her as she sobbed and crumbled before him. Cassidy was next to her dad and my mom; they looked like they were watching us on a TV show. There was more commotion outside as people were telling Cedrick to leave. Sénar quickly went outside but Ken pulled him back inside.

He roared, "Hell nah, stay your ass in here! Don't go out there!"

Daisy came in with her eyes filled with tears. She grabbed Sénar and they cried together as Ken watched them and my response. She was respectful to me and hugged me before she said, "Hey Treasure, I am so sorry for how I treated you. We never know when life can change, and I am so sorry about Louie, Sénar." He hugged her and told her he would be alright, but I knew he was lying. I had never seen Sénar so sad, not even after what Cassidy had been through. Latosha and I went to her room while everybody stayed up front to comfort each other.

She said, "Treasure, Louie was dead when they took him in the ambulance. The police didn't ask no questions, they just started shooting! We all ran inside scared for our lives; I couldn't even grab my baby!" As I held her in my arms and she cried, I thought about how I had literally hugged more people in this last five minutes than I have hugged in my whole life. It was official; Louie was gone, no more kicking it, and no more lectures on how much Sénar loves me. He would now have a son in this world without him as a father and could be one of Nevaeh's future boyfriend's potential victim or a son. I prayed that she would find a man to love her and Louie's son.

Latosha was distraught and I couldn't help but ask, "How did your date go?"

She forced a smile and answered, "I had a great time and we went back to his place after. We had a ball." I looked at her and waited for more details. She said, "No, we didn't have sex, Treasure. He calls me every day to see how I'm doing and knows what happened to Louie. He is going to help me see if we can sue the police department."

I hugged her again, I could see that she was trying to be optimistic but there was no amount of money that could replace Louie's life and she knew it. She asked me to go with her to see her baby boy. Me and Sénar drove her to the hospital to see Lil' James. Latosha told us what happened when we got there, she explained, "He was shot with the same bullet that went through Louie's heart, it went through Lil' James chest. He had surgery today to have the bullet removed."

The doctor handed the bullet to Latosha and she handed it to Sénar, she then said, "Here Sénar, this is the bullet that killed Louie, they just removed it from Lil' James chest." She was speaking to us, but she was still in a state of shock. Her normal bubbly personality was deflated, and she appeared to be struggling to breathe. Sénar hugged her as she broke down crying, she yelled, "They took my brother from us! What are we going to do Sénar? They almost took my baby too! My baby is gonna be looking for Louie!" She became angry when she said, "They murdered him! He was not doing anything Sénar, he was holding my baby when the police pulled up. They didn't ask questions they jumped out with their guns drawn. We were minding our business when Cedrick ran up to our house, they just started shooting. Louie had to turn to shield little James as we all ran in the house." She was devastated, she appeared vacant, for a moment.

Sénar shook Latosha and then said, "Hey man, stay present! Don't go back to that moment, if you can help it Latosha. Just do your best to be strong for Lil' James, he is going to need you to pull through this. You guys are going to have to work together. I'll be here for you guys and make sure Louie's baby is taken care of. Don't worry we will get through this; we have to. I'll be praying for our strength to endure Latosha because we are going to need it." He pleaded with her and hugged her as she cried on his shoulder. I joined their hug and told her, "I'm so sorry Latosha, you guys are like family to me. I hate to see you hurting like this, but I'll be here too, if you need me. I am going to miss Louie too. I am glad Lil' James is ok, I'll help you love him!"

She giggled a little through her tears and said, "Yeah, he loves you Treasure. You want to see him?" I shook my head yeah as tears escaped my eyelids. We walked in the room to see Lil' James lying down with tubes in his nose and machines hooked to him. He was resting when Latosha said, "Hey my Superman. Can you hear me?"

He wiggled around in the bed until he opened his eyes to see his momma hovering over him. He smiled and looked over to see Sénar. His eyes widened with excitement as he searched for me. When he saw me, he tried to get up, but I stopped him gently, and kissed him on his cheeks. He smiled at me and touched my face. I kissed him again then said, "I love you Lil' James! You're so strong! You really are a Lil' Superman!" He grinned so big, Latosha laughed, "Boy, you are too much!" She kissed him and told him to get some rest. Before we left Sénar kissed Lil' James on his forehead and told him he loved him.

Latosha said, "Thanks y'all, I feel better after seeing my baby smile like that. It truly gives me hope. I'm going to stay here with him, I'll let y'all know everything that's going on."

Sénar nodded in agreement, we both hugged her before we left. Sad or not, we could definitely depend on getting all the details from Latosha. We returned back to Louie's house where everyone was gathered. Sénar gave hugs to all his loved ones and words of encouragement. Sénar was drained but he did his best to be strong and encourage everyone to move forward and to still make Louie proud in his absence. Despite his words of wisdom, I could tell Sénar was deeply wounded by the loss of his cousin or I should say best friend. We left, we were on the road back to the house when I asked, "Sénar are you going to be ok?"

He looked at me and took a deep breath before replying, "Treasure I will be ok, I just don't know when."

I just thought deeply about what he said and put my head back and drifted away into my own thoughts. When we got home Ken and my mom were already there with Cassidy. They were all sitting at the table with sad faces and they all rose when Sénar walked in. They all hugged him one by one and told him they loved him.

Even my mom said, "Sénar you're a strong young man. I know you will get through this; I have seen so much growth in you. I am so sorry about Louie, but I know he looked up to you, so don't let him down."

She hugged him again and started crying as she went upstairs. I followed her up the stairs to give Sénar and his family privacy. I went straight to his room and grabbed stuff to take a shower. By the time I was out, Sénar was in his room on his knees, he appeared to be praying. When he was done, he stared at me before he said, "I swear I am being punished for what I have done to you. When I was about five years old, I went on the ride with my dad. He was doing a delivery to Rialto and I rode with him. We went to the store and I saw something I wanted, and I never asked my dad for anything in the store. Even though he would get it for me, I never would ask. This one day what I saw I wanted more than anything I had ever laid my eyes on."

I was getting impatient and asked, "Well Sénar, what was it?"

He took a deep breath and answered, "You, Treasure. I asked my dad for you and he laughed at me. I had a tantrum so bad that your mom came to you and grabbed you when she heard the commotion." I giggled, and he asked, "Why are you laughing, Treasure?"

I shrugged my shoulders and answered, "I don't know, I could picture you throwing cereal boxes everywhere." I giggled again and he smirked at me before saying, "So, you do remember?" I shrugged my shoulders again and thought about the little boy in the pictures and the little boy I envisioned throwing boxes, and I guess I did remember vaguely. Sénar continued, "Well anyway, your mom was with some dude and she had a baby in her hands. So, my pops said, "Boy, you don't ever ask me for nothing, I'll see what I can do." It took five years for my dad to secure a spot with your mom, she was probably, besides my mom, the most difficult woman he ever pursued. While he was pursuing her, I was praying for the opportunity to pursue you. I wanted you, I dreamed of you every night since that day. He would tell me about Carmel and the things she would say about you or what you were doing, and my dad would tell me. But when my dad told me your name, I knew you were the one for sure. My mom used to tell me to find a woman that I would treasure forever and keep her safe. She told me your woman should be your treasure. So, when my pops told me your name was Treasure, I knew you were the one my mom spoke of, but I was under the influence of my dad. I saw how he did things and thought that was the way to possess women. Then all the horror I saw and the abuse we witnessed just became normal. Everyone was accustomed to chaos and moving forward after. Daisy and her mom's sexual abuse didn't help the situation, but I can't blame them for my actions. I knew what I was doing, I knew what I wanted when I took what I wanted from you and I made that choice on my own recognizance. I was selfish, I wanted what I wanted. I did not care about how it would affect you. I never even felt remorse until recently. I thought just because you enjoyed it, quite a bit if I may add, that it was ok. I failed to protect you from myself, and I am truly sorry, Treasure. I never meant to hurt you.

After what Tyrell did to you, I realized that I was wrong too, but I didn't want to face it. I just made excuses of how it was different, but then what happened to Cassidy made me breakdown and ask for forgiveness for the first time with remorse. I hope you can forgive me one day too, Treasure. I won't ever hurt you that way again or anyone else for that matter." Sénar put his head down and I know it's selfish, but I used this opportunity to ensure my safety from Ken. I said, "Just don't let Ken hurt me that way Sénar." He winced at my response and I could see the fire in his eyes at the thought of Ken hurting me in that way; as I anticipated to see, and I was satisfied with it.

Then I said, "Well great, now that we know how we both got screwed up. Sénar go take a shower and wash your hair, so I can braid it for you."

He stared at me with a perplexed look when he asked, "Treasure is that all you have-"

I cut him off and said, "Sénar, just go take a shower. Chill out Sénar, that's a lot of information…I guess that's what I was looking for when I was going through your stuff. I just never thought I would find it, or hear it, or understand it, ok?"

He saw that I was getting uncomfortable and he backed off, he grabbed his stuff to take a shower. I was overwhelmed with what Sénar told me. *How was I supposed to act? How was I supposed to respond to his confession; it was the most bizarre thing I could have imagined.* I didn't want to disclose my feelings to Sénar, he was already pulling strings I didn't know were attached to him all along. I wanted to run back to my room and away from Sénar but another part of me wanted to cling on to him. I just dismissed my thoughts about Sénar, I needed to make sure Tyrell and I weren't meant to be and Sénar didn't just come along to ruin it with his selfish desires for me. Sénar came in after showering with his hair wild but clean. He didn't put a shirt on, and I wish he would have because now I was fighting my own desires, or *was it Treasure number two's desires?* I couldn't even tell anymore.

He put a shirt on and then pulled himself together before coming towards me. He sighed and tried not to roll his eyes at me while I thought of all the things, I did want him to do to me.

He said, "What are you thinking about Treasure?"

I smacked my lips before I said, "None of your business Sénar." I pulled his hair and turned his head the way I wanted it out of frustration.

Sénar laughed before he said, "Take it easy on me Treasure, dang!" I ignored him and braided his hair as he laid his head on my thigh, I knew he was thinking about Louie. I could feel his pain when he said, "How quick life can change, never ceases to amaze me but I am still thankful to be alive to deal with it." I could feel moisture on my thigh but did nothing to insinuate that I knew he was shedding tears for Louie; I just let him grieve in peace. When I was done, Sénar asked, "What do you want me to do for you?"

I shrugged my shoulders and answered, "I don't know. Sénar, I am fine."

He laughed and then said, "Ok cool. Well, are you hungry?" I was just tired from crying and actually wished he would not have asked but just did what he wanted because I wanted him to; I just didn't want to tell him. I went to take a shower again. When I got out of the shower Sénar was just lying in his bed thinking and I asked, "What are you thinking about Sénar?"

He smirked before he said, "Everything."

I put my stuff away and sat on the side of Chino's old bed to put lotion and coco butter on. Sénar smelled the air and smiled before turning over to face the wall. Sénar said, "You play too much, Treasure!"

I laughed because I knew what I was doing but said, "What Sénar? My skin needs to be properly moisturized."

He laughed and replied, "Oooook, ma I got chu." I am sure we both went to bed disappointed, but I still crawled in the bed with

Sénar when he fell asleep. I smelled his hair and squeezed him before falling asleep with him in my arms.

We woke up in each other's arms, Sénar asked, "What chu doing over here?"

I rolled my eyes and said, "Shut up Sénar, I just wanted to get warm and be there for you like you are for me, sometimes."

He smirked before he said, "Sometimes, my ass!"

He pulled me to him, I could feel his excitement against my behind but when he felt the slightest resistance, he let me go. He said, "Every time you sleep over here, you will feel that, it's natural. When you don't, then you should be worried." He laughed and added, "Shidd, I would be devastated!" He got up and stretched, I tried not to look at it but then he said, "Well, that's all you now, it's always super excited to see you."

He blushed and I just rolled my eyes before I said, "Shut up, Sénar." I shook my head and realized; I didn't have any clothes because they were all in my room.

He said, "I'll pick out an outfit for you, ma."

He left and went to my room to grab some different outfits. He laid them on the bed. He probably put the one that he wanted me to where on top. It was Valentine's Day tomorrow and I totally forgot until Sénar said, "So, you want to do something today?"

I smirked at him before I asked, "Why today and not tomorrow?"

He laughed at me before he said, "Dang Treasure, you are something else, we can do something tomorrow too. It's just that everybody is doing something tomorrow, so I would rather not."

I was offended that he thought I was so stupid. I asked, "Oh, so you can spend it with your baby momma?"

Sénar got angry when he replied, "Your mouth is always getting your ass in trouble. So, use it with caution sometimes. And no Treasure, I will be minding my business tomorrow and you will be too, but with me." Sénar was one sick puppy, he just confessed his plan to possess me like I was some object at the store and told me he was sorry for what he did to me. Now, he was telling me what I could and couldn't do on Valentine's Day. I was annoyed with him, but I didn't want to use his confession against him just yet, plus after tragically losing Louie, we had enough to deal with the next few days.

We got dressed and left for school. On the way, I asked, "How do you know my middle name Sénar?"

He looked at me with his eyebrow raised and asked, "What?"

I shook my head as if to erase my question, then said, "Never mind."

He asked, "Oh, so you were being really nosey, huh?"

I shrugged my shoulders, "Umm, I just asked Sénar."

He rolled his eyes, then said, "Whatever." We pulled into the parking lot of the school. London was crying and had a crazy look in her eyes as she quickly made her way to the car. Sénar said, "Damn, I don't want to deal with this shit. Treasure, stay in the car."

I smacked my lips and said, "No! If she touches me, I am going to beat her ass!"

I tried to get out and Sénar locked the door back, "No! You have done enough, trust me, Treasure. Sit still, I'll be back." Sénar got out and let London cry on his shoulder. She was yelling and trying to open his door to get to me. I just sat there agitated and waited for Sénar's permission to get out. I almost got out anyway but Sénar opened the door and said, "Go ahead Treasure. I'll see you at lunch." He wrapped his arms around her and talk to her as I walked off. I was drained, I didn't want to fight or argue; I just wanted to go to class. Still lots of whispering and laughing, even the teacher addressed it by asking everyone to stop the excessive talking. I ignored everyone in all my classes until I made it to lunch.

Tyrell came to me to ask, "Treasure why y'all leave early yesterday?"

I quickly answered, "There was a family emergency."

I walked to the line for my food, he followed me then mocked me when he asked, "A family emergency, huh? You're part of the Reject Brady Bunch now?"

I smirked and answered, "Yeah, it's Treasure Lee Brady now." Tyrell got upset and came toward me but noticed Sénar behind me.

Tyrell asked, "Oh, so all the starting over and you still loving me was a lie?"

I felt trapped and answered, "Tyrell can we talk later? I had a rough week and I don't want any more drama, please?"

Tyrell was upset that I didn't answer him, he then focused on Sénar when he asked, "Aye Sénar, why you mention breaking chains and shit? Were you trying to tell me something?"

Sénar was annoyed but tried to remain calm when he simply answered, "Aye bro', it's not my fault if you didn't comprehend the message."

Tyrell wanted to hit Sénar so bad but there was security nearby, so he just said, "Treasure, we need to talk without your little bodyguard."

I just nodded ok, but he grabbed me and Sénar took a deep breath. I asked, "Tyrell, let me go, I have to eat before my class."

He asked me for a kiss and I quickly kissed him but when he grabbed me to kiss me passionately, Sénar almost ripped my arm off pulling me away from him. Sénar said, "Let's go!"

Tyrell laughed as we walked away. I yelled at Sénar when I asked, "Why are you grabbing me like that, Sénar?"

He was livid when he answered, "Treasure, leave his ass alone! Before he hurts you!"

I replied, "Says the one who almost ripped my arm off! Sénar, what is wrong with you?"

He was frazzled and appeared deranged for a second. He answered, "He is just trying to trick you, he wants to get you alone again, so he can do whatever he wants to you. Don't trust him! He knows that we have been together, Treasure!"

I was furious when I said, "Yeah, because you told him? I never told him Sénar. He is still my boyfriend, ok? We never broke up and I did tell him we could try to work things out and start over. Why don't you worry about London?"

Sénar was fed up, "Treasure, there is nothing left, it's over between you two! Trust me!"

I snapped when I asked, "Oh, like it's over between us?"

Sénar winced before he answered, "No, I am not done with you, Treasure. It's just beginning, I just don't want to force you to do anything you don't want to do."

I looked at Sénar like he was crazy and said, "Well, you are not doing a very good job. Where is your girlfriend, London?"

The bell rang and he said, "I'll see you at practice, Treasure." He walked off to his class and I went to mine extremely agitated. Leah was late to class, so she wasn't able to sit by me and It was a huge relief. I made it to practice without any drama but when I got to the gymnasium, I could feel the tension between Sénar and Tyrell. I tried to ignore it, but the cheerleaders noticed too. Everyone gawked at me while they all huddled together to whisper and giggle. Leah's dumb ass was with them whispering too. I had enough of all the drama, I was glad when practice was over. I saw London run to Sénar and heard a lot of commotion, I picked my bag up and walked to Sénar's car to wait for him, but Tyrell came running after me. He dragged me to his car by my arm, forcefully. I almost lost my balance with my backpack making me unstable as I tried to keep up with Tyrell and keep from falling. He used his key fab to open the passenger door. He pushed me in the car. When I tried to get out, he slapped me so hard, I was thrown aback. He got in as Sénar and Leah ran out of the gymnasium after us.

He pulled off yelling at me, he asked, "Treasure you were fucking him when I was in Jersey, huh?"

I didn't answer him, so he grabbed me by my neck and demanded, "Answer me!"

I shook my head no, as I cried, he continued to ask me questions, "You were never mine, huh? You and him have been messing around the whole time we were supposed to be together? You are such a liar! Were you lying when you said you loved me? Dammit! Treasure, answer me before I kill your ass!"

He was driving so fast, I screamed, "Tyrell, I'm sorry!"

He tried to choke me, and he lost control of the steering wheel crashing into a pole. The impact jerked us forward, without my seat belt on I hit the windshield. It felt like someone hit me with a brick, I grabbed my head to apply pressure and stop the bleeding. I felt faint but tried to get out when Tyrell grabbed me back to say, "I'm going to get you back for all your lies and games." He was trying to choke the life out of me when Sénar screeched on his brakes before parking in front of the wreck. Sénar came to the passenger side as Tyrell was choking me and broke the glass of the already shatter windshield to unlock the door. He pried Tyrell's hands off of my neck and pulled me out of the car. He saw that I was bleeding, and I barely could breathe after being choked dang near to death. Tyrell came out and kicked Sénar in his back, making him almost dropped me. Sénar carefully laid me down as Leah got out of Sénar's car to witness all the commotion. Sénar and Tyrell fought until the police arrived with their guns drawn, yelling orders at Sénar and Tyrell.

The police officer yelled, "Put your hands up or I'll shoot your black asses!"

I jumped up and said, "No don't shoot them!"

One of the officers pointed his gun at me and said, "Get down on the ground and shut up."

Tyrell put his hands up, but Sénar was defiant, he glared at the police and I begged him to listen to them. One of the officers grabbed Sénar from behind, slamming him on the hood of the car and the other officer grabbed Tyrell and did the same. Sénar struggled as fury filled his eyes, the officer violently pinned Sénar's arm behind his back. Sénar yelled, "Let my arm go! What are you doing?" The officer slammed him down again. I knew Sénar wanted to fight as he struggled to be calm. I yelled, "Sénar, just relax, please!" I saw Leah watching the whole thing take place. The officer checked their pockets, then read the names on their school ID's and drivers licenses. One officer said, "Hey partner! We got our self some million-dollar niggers! These are kids from the varsity football team at the high school over there." He loosened his grip on Sénar's arm and allowed Sénar to stand. The officer laughed and said, "Well, it's you boys' lucky day today." He called for an ambulance and returned their ID's. One officer called for a tow truck for Tyrell's car. Sénar was still fuming when he asked, "Am I free to go?"

The officer said, "Yeah, did you guys exchange information?"

Sénar reluctantly replied, "I didn't have anything to do with the wreck officer."

The officer eyed Sénar before he answered, "Well, you're free to go then."

I got up and ran to Sénar, he grabbed me and secured me behind his seat while Leah told Tyrell she was riding with Sénar home. Tyrell yelled, "I don't give a damn! I will get you back Treasure, you just wait!"

We drove off in silence, Leah sat in the front seat and said, "Dang that was intense, I'm glad you're ok, Sénar. That officer couldn't wait to take you out."

Sénar didn't respond, so she kept talking, "Are you ok Treasure?" I didn't speak to her, I just hoped Ken didn't find out or he would probably keep his promise and kill me for putting Sénar in danger with the police after what happened to Louie. I was in shock everything was crazy, and I couldn't really believe Tyrell was trying to kill me. We dropped Leah off, I swear, everyone wanted me dead or to be destroyed, somehow. I started to feel overwhelmed and I couldn't breathe. I felt like my world was caving in on me again from every angle, the closer we got to the house. I could feel the urge to escape by any means necessary. When Sénar pulled over, I snapped. I tried to get out of the car to run for dear life, and I had no intentions of coming back. Sénar let me get out but he got out too. He came around to my side as I tried to run off, he put his arms around me, and I just crumbled in his arms. I lost the urge to run as he whispered, "I'm here Treasure, I tried to tell you ma. You don't listen!"

I cried and lashed out, "He tried to kill me because of you and whatever you told him!"

Sénar looked guilty but said, "Treasure, I am sorry, but he just wouldn't let up and he was really pushing me to a place that I could not stand! He told me he was going to hurt you and that he didn't want me to have you, so he would rather kill you! He told me this long before he became this way toward you. Damn, you just didn't listen!"

I yelled, "Now what? We just live happily ever after?"

I pushed Sénar off of me and started walking without knowing where to. He followed me and pleaded with me to get in the car. I yelled at him when I asked, "Why? So, your daddy could kill me when he finds out the police could have killed you too!" I started to run but Sénar picked me up and held me.

He promised me, "I won't let him hurt you, I will figure something out Treasure, trust me! I won't tell him what happened, so don't worry. Let's just go home to get cleaned up and then leave."

I just surrendered; there was nowhere for me to run or nowhere for me to hide. I let him walk me back to the car, I was scared and hurting but I didn't want to make things worse by complaining. When we pulled up Ken's truck was gone, giving me a small sense of relief. My head was hurting, I could hear ringing in my ears as I closed my eyes to see if I could block it out, but it just got worse. Sénar called my name, "Treasure? Are you ok? How are you feeling?" I did my best to pull myself together to answer, "I'm fine Sénar." He sat me down on a chair, then got some ice out the freezer. He put the ice into a sandwich bag and then gave it to me, "Here put this on your head. Come on, let's go upstairs." He told me not to lay down while he went to check on Cassidy, but I couldn't fight the urge to lay down. When he came back in, he sat me back up to say, "Don't lay down Treasure, you hit your head on something when you guys crashed, so you could have a concussion and the last thing you need to do is sleep." He checked my eyes and observed my forehead to see the amount of damage that had been done from the impact of the crash. He sighed before he asked, "Damn Treasure, did you have your seatbelt on?"

I pushed him back and yelled, "No! I was trying to stay alive with his hands around my neck Sénar! I didn't exactly have time to put a seat belt on!"

He winced at my anger towards him and said, "Ok, Treasure relax. You wanna go get something to eat?" I wasn't exactly hungry, but I didn't want to stay home and wait for Ken to see what he would do if he found out what happen. We went to get some tacos from the taco truck, but I could only eat two. I was feeling a little queasy as we pulled into the parking lot of the mall.

Sénar asked, "Are you ok?" I nodded my head yeah as we got out. We went to See's Candy and bought two pounds of assorted chocolate, he had one wrapped and left the other plain. He bought something else, but I couldn't see what it was. We left after because he could tell that I wasn't feeling very well. We saw Ken's truck but Sénar didn't seem bothered, he helped me out the car with the stuff he bought from See's Candy in his other hand. As we were going inside, we saw a tow truck coming down the street with Tyrell's wrecked car on the bed of the truck. We quickly headed inside to meet Ken waiting for us at the door, he grabbed Sénar and hugged him.

He seemed scared and worried when he said, "Damn boy, where were you? You had me worried sick! Are you ok?" He searched Sénar for injuries and when he realized Sénar was ok, Ken glared at me. I was already scared and nervous; my stomach still felt queasy when Ken snatched me by my shirt. Ken asked, "Didn't I tell you nothing better happen to my son? I should kill your ass now because if the police would have killed my boy, I would-"

Sénar cut him off to plead with him, "Pops please, it wasn't her fault! Let her go!"

Ken pushed Sénar before he said, "Shut the fuck up boy! She is your problem! Leave her stupid ass alone! Let's just have fun with her like we planned and then get rid of her ass!" Ken laughed when he saw Sénar's face as he smelled my hair and caressed me. Fear gripped me as I vomited all over Ken, it got in his face and all over his clothes. He threw me to the floor and roared, "Get her out of my sight!" Sénar dropped everything in his hands to scoop me up off the floor to carry me to the bathroom. He was frantic when he sat me on the toilet and ran the shower, he tapped my face as he called my name, "Treasure?"

I snapped, "What? You should have just let him kill me Sénar and put us both out of our misery, that was the plan anyway. Right?"

Sénar ignored my question, "Treasure, get in the shower and clean yourself up. I'll be right back to check on you." He left in a hurry as I undressed out of my soiled clothes. I was tired of all of it, just everything, I was ready to give up again. I looked for the stopper to the tub and I could not find it anywhere, I had no choice but to take a shower. I didn't even cry I was beyond tears, I just let the water run on me until it was cold and Sénar came to get me. He looked worried but tried to remain calm when he said, "Treasure come on. Get out."

I got out slowly as I felt dizzy, having to use Sénar to stay stable and keep from falling. He helped me dry off and get dressed. He then took me to his room and helped me lie down on Chino's old bed. He asked, "You want me to read you some of my favorite scriptures that helped me get through so many things in my life?"

I shrugged my shoulders and replied, "Yeah, I guess Sénar."

He was pleased with my answer, he grabbed his bible and said, "Just in case I need to refresh." He grabbed a pillow and propped his head up and laid on the floor next to me as I lied in bed waiting to hear what helped him through his dark moments in his life. He recited, "*Romans 8:28 And we know that all things work together for good to them that love God and are called according to His purpose. Proverbs 3:5 trust in the Lord with all your heart, lean not on your own understanding, in all your ways submit to Him and He will make your paths straight.* One of my favorites, Treasure is *Jeremiah 29:11 for I know the plans I have for you, declares the Lord, plans to prosper you and not harm you, plans to give you hope and a future.* Oh Treasure, there are so many more, you have no idea."

I heard every word he said, yet I did not understand and still asked, "Sénar, how did that help you and what does all of that even mean?"

Sénar smiled at me before he answered, "Well, I don't know everything but what it means to me is, that we belong to an all-seeing and all-knowing creator. Who truly loves us enough to look beyond our faults and through his mercy, He still sees our needs. Even though, we face troubles, He gives us the strength we need to endure and persevere. Some of the worst things that happen to us that are meant to break us, can be the very thing that makes us who we are and who we become. It's our choice to acknowledge Him and He will help mold us into who we are created to be, despite our hardships. We just have to trust Him, no matter what and know that He is who He says that He is. He is the great I Am. The Alpha and Omega. He has helped me correct some of my ways, but as long as we live, there is always room to grow and learn. Despite our shortcomings, Treasure. That is why He sent His son to testify of Him and lead by example. The son learned obedience through the things He suffered, and our Elohim exalted Him despite man's attempt to destroy Him and His testimony of His Father in heaven."

I was tired but felt a little twinge of energy from Sénar's speech when I asked, "Well, do you believe He will help us now, Sénar?" He looked hopeful but he still had some sadness in his eyes when he answered, "It may not be in the way we want but I believe He will make a way, yes. That is what faith is, believing without seeing and trusting without knowing." The only reason I believed Sénar is because I could not deny his growth, in spite his many faults or the strength he has harnessed throughout his tragic life. The skills he acquired through his tragedies, the hope he held onto despite his obstacles, and the love he still had for God after all he had been through, baffled me. I asked, "Sénar, how can you still love God after all that you have been through?" He laughed and answered, "The question you should be asking, is how He can still love us after all that we have done. We are imperfect creatures, Treasure, shaped with inequities and sins. No one is worthy, but He still has mercy on us and knows are heart despite what our mouths confess."

I was getting sleepy and said, "Well, tell Him to help me too."

As I tried to rest, Sénar said, "Tell Him yourself Treasure, I can not acknowledge Him for you. I can just pray that you find the beauty of His love and know He is who wakes us up every morning, until our days on this earth are over." Sénar got up to kiss me on the forehead.

I said, "You never even opened the Bible Sénar, why?" He laughed, then said, "Those scriptures and His promises are written on my heart." I smiled at him before I closed my eyes and I slept like a baby.

Valentine's Day, I woke up to see Sénar lying on the floor next to Chino's bed with his bible opened on his chest. He looked so peaceful as he slept, I just laid there and stared at him. I felt sore all over and had a really bad headache. Sénar woke up and checked to see if I was, only to see me staring at him. He raised his eyebrow and then asked, "What chu looking at Willis?"

I laughed at him and his silly facial expression. I tickled him and he jumped up to say, "Don't start nothing Treasure that you or I can't get out of." He laughed as he got up and yelped in pain as he stretched.

I jumped up to ask, "What's wrong?"

He grimaced when he said, "Nothing, my shoulder is just a little sore, that's all."

He was definitely not being honest, I touched it and he grimaced again in pain. I backed up to observe him. I said, "Sénar, maybe you should have your arm looked at. It doesn't seem to be just a little sore."

He shook his head no and said, "I'm fine Treasure. How are you ma?"

I was sore all over and I had a pounding headache, but I said, "I'm fine."

Sénar searched my eyes, "Maybe we should stay home, Treasure. Everything has been so crazy, and we just need to be still for a while. Trust me we aren't missing anything." He was right, I would rather stay in this room all day than to go to school after what happened yesterday. Ken opened Sénar's door and invited his self in, making me nervous instantly. He grabbed Sénar's shoulder and he tried not to wince in pain. When Ken noticed, he squeezed it until Sénar couldn't take it and jerked his shoulder away from him for protection. Ken snatched him up by his shirt and asked, "What's up with your arm, Sénar?"

He shrugged the other shoulder and said, "I don't know, pops."

Ken was mad when he said, "Don't lie to me, boy!"

I answered, "The police did it, when they forced his arm behind his back."

Ken snarled at me, "Yeah, that's what I heard. So, you weren't going to tell me?"

Sénar looked down when he said, "I will be cool, pops. It's just a little sore, that's all."

Ken yelled, "I told your ass to stop chasing her damn ass, Sénar! What do you want me to do, take y'all both out? I am not going to watch nobody else take you out. If she doesn't want your ass, then forget about her ass. She almost got you killed boy and this ain't the first time either."

I just listen to Ken talk to Sénar as if I was not there in the room with them. I could only imagine, their discreet conversations. I tried to excuse myself when Ken stopped me and asked, "Where do you think you are going?"

I tried to go around his hand as I replied, "I am giving you guys your privacy, Ken."

He shook his head before he said, "Little girl, please, I ain't worried about you. Let's go, boy!"

Sénar asked, "Where are we going, pops?"

Ken replied, "I am taking you to get your arm looked at!"

Sénar didn't argue, he knew his arm was bad and needed to be examined by a professional. He was like a little kid when he said, "Well, Treasure needs to go too, she was the one in the accident not me."

Ken smirked and said, "She is not my concern right now. It's you that has games coming up and scout interviews. Let her momma deal with her!"

My mom came out the room in a good mood, holding the wrapped See's Candy in her hand that we got from the mall yesterday when she asked, "Deal with her, about what?"

Ken gazed at my mom with her bright smile and actually looked like a normal person for a moment, until he had to explain what happen. Ken explained, "Him and Treasure got into some foolishness with Tyrell's ass again. Tyrell wrecked his car with Treasure in it and Sénar's dumb ass, chased them and ended up getting roughed up by the police. Now, he probably a dislocated shoulder, with his stupid ass!"

My mom's smile evaporated as I glared at Ken when I said, "Well, I'm glad your report is so clear, Ken. Momma, it wasn't our fault, Leah started it! She purposely tried to get us all to fight and she jumped me on Monday!" My momma was both shocked and angry when she said, "I told you about both of them Treasure. Tyrell doesn't give a damn about you and Leah's ass is a little snake! Don't let her put her hands on you again and stay the hell away from Tyrell! That boy is no good, I told you that a long time ago! You're lucky he didn't kill your ass like he killed my damn cat!" My mom was mad, her smile was just a memory now and she was holding on to her chocolates as if they were holding her together.

I said, "I'm sorry Momma and Ken I didn't mean to put Sénar in danger. He's the only person who actually cares what happens to me."

Ken was agitated and my mom looked annoyed with me too before Ken said, "Boy let's go!"

I was going to lay back down when my mom whined and asked, "Why can't we just all go together babe? And thank you for the chocolates." She snuggled her face in his chest and he tried not to show his arousal when he said, "Damn, fine let's go!"

Sénar shook his head because Ken had a mini tantrum going down the stairs and complained as his phone rung. Sénar laughed when he said, "Wow. Life is crazy. Why didn't you tell me Tyrell killed your mom's cat? That's cold blooded, and y'all call me crazy." He rolled his eyes at me while I got dressed. I picked jeans and a powder blue shirt, to avoid pink or red. After I washed my face and brushed my teeth, I was coming out and saw that Cassidy looked as if she had rose from the dead. She was pale and her braids that Latosha did at the beach were a mess, but she was dressed. She rolled her eyes at me as she passed me up to go to the bathroom. I went to my room just to make sure my bed and area was intact. When it was, I was relieved. Cassidy came out and started to go downstairs but I stopped her to ask, "Where are you going Cassidy?" She looked at me like I was stupid when she asked, "Why?" I calmly said, "I am just asking, Cassidy." She rolled her eyes at me, then said, "I am going to see Sabrina. Her due date is coming up in a few weeks, Treasure. Even though, you should just mind your damn business! I heard my daddy; your ass always has Sénar in something. My daddy is go-"

I cut her off, to say, "Cassidy, are you going to wear your hair like that?"

She smacked her lips, "Mind your business, Treasure!"

I hissed at her, "Shush, dang, come here." I pulled her toward the bathroom but not aggressively and she still said, "Let me go!" She said it with an attitude as I opened the door and pulled her in the bathroom. Cassidy got scared, she started to scream but I grabbed her mouth, when I remembered how hard she bit me last time, I let her go.

I pleaded with her, "Cassidy! I am just trying to help you."

She said, "Get off of me!"

I shook her before I said, "Cassidy, I haven't done anything to you that you haven't done to me or worse. So, stop it! I am just trying to help you!" Sénar came and saw me with my hands on her and he got angry, but I quickly started to take down Cassidy's braids.

She asked, "How?" She pushed me off her, I moved her hand when I said, "I can't stand your ass but I'm not letting you leave like this."

She stopped resisting and let me take down her hair. Sénar relaxed a bit but still stayed to watch. I got the comb and brush; I kept some of the parts from her hair style and combed the others in. I gave her four corn rows and then took two of them to braid into one braid on each side. She was looking pretty nice with her quick braid style.

From downstairs, Ken roared, "What the hell is going on? Let's go!" I was startled but almost finished. I gave her some lip gloss, but she looked at me with disgust and I said, "You have some nerve! It's brand-new, Cassidy, and your welcome." I waited for her to walk ahead of me before I walked out, she didn't even say thank you. Sénar grabbed me from behind and smelled my hair when he said, "Umph, you don't need meat to be sweet, you just need me." I pushed him off me to say, "Shut up Sénar."

We all left dropping Cassidy off at Sabrina's first before we went to urgent care. It was a quick visit; Sénar's shoulder was only partially dislocated which was better news than It being completely out of socket, but I did hear him scream when they positioned it back in place. Ken was really agitated when Sénar had to wear a sling, but the doctor assured him it would only be a few days but not longer than a week. He also encouraged physical therapy and weight training. Sénar wasn't concerned, he knew he would heal quickly. Sénar loved to lift weights and used everything he went through to become stronger. As for me, I had a concussion, which was no surprise, since my head almost went through Tyrell's windshield. The doctor gave some simple follow up care that Sénar had already provided or was doing when he monitored my sleep.

We left the hospital and my momma whined when she said, "Babe I'm hungry." My mom barely eats now, she had lost a lot of weight, so if she said she was hungry, not even Ken could argue that.

He asked, "What do you want, angel baby?"

My mom said, "I don't know."

Ken got irritated again when he said, "Well, you ain't that hungry then."

My mom pouted and Ken knew he was being mean, so he said, "Fine let's go to Jack in the Box then."

My mom said, "No, Ken."

Ken was acting like a little kid when he asked, "Well, you don't know what you want but you know you don't want Jack in the Box?" My mom reached over, probably grabbing Ken's man stick, making him swerve a bit as he tried to drive. He loosened up a bit, "Stop playing woman, we got kids in the car." My momma giggled, and I just rolled my eyes while Sénar smiled his famous smile. We ate at George's and our waitress was friendly. She asked, "Ooh, are you guys on a double date for Valentine's Day?" Ken and Sénar raised their eyebrow; she was a cute young black girl and she smiled extra big at Sénar. My mom said, "Awe, I never thought about it like that hun'. No, but we are hungry. I want some French toast sweetie." She took my mom's order and then asked Ken what he wanted but he pointed at me. I didn't hesitate to order, I was starving when I said, "I'll have French toast too, but I want to add bacon, sausage and eggs."

Sénar grinned at my order, he knew I was doing too much, but I didn't care. Hell, I almost asked for hash browns too. She took Ken's order for steak and potatoes. When she got to Sénar she was very attentive, she gazed at him as she waited for his order.

Sénar ordered, "I'll take a ribeye steak, medium well, and over medium eggs."

She flirtatiously asked, "What else do you want?"

He looked at me before he said, "Hash browns would be nice, huh Treasure?" He laughed and said, "Thank you."

She blushed since Sénar was the only one that said thank you. Ken shook his head and my momma just smiled at Sénar when she said, "Look at you Sénar, being so polite. Ken, I think you got a Casanova on your hands."

Me and Ken were both annoyed with my mom's fondness of Sénar. When the waitress brought out our food, she winked at Sénar and went to check on her other customers. When we were done eating, she sat the tab on the table. Ken grabbed it and put his card down to pay. When she brought the receipt back, she gave it to Ken to sign and he passed it to Sénar to give back to her. Sénar saw her number was on the top of the extra receipt, he grabbed it off and put ten dollars as a tip. She grinned happily before she walked off. I was instantly annoyed at how women were so desperate at times and guys were so stupid and thought with their man sticks. Ugh, I just wanted to watch TV already and finally forget about all the shenanigans of this week. I don't think it could get worse at this point but with the way things have been going who, knows. We were on our way back home when Ken's phone rung and he answered. My mom was super attentive to his phone call. Ken said, "Damn, I just left the hospital! Well, is it here yet? Then I'll wait, call me when it's born." Ken was agitated but my mom still asked what was going on. Ken didn't hide his irritation and answered, "Sabrina's ass might be going into labor, I hope it's a boy. I don't want to deal with no more women. Shit, y'all the most unstable, confused, needy creatures in the universe!" He was overwhelmed and he was not trying to hide it anymore. He dropped me and my mom off, then told Sénar to get in the front seat. They drove off without telling my mom when they were coming back.

My mom was full and appeared more stable than usual. As we headed inside, she asked, "Who did Leah jump you with, Treasure?" I looked at her surprised she even cared, I didn't hesitate to say, "Leah and London momma." She shook her head when she assumed, "Well, I couldn't tell. They must can't fight because the accident looks like it did more damage. I'm glad you're ok. Why did they do that Treasure?" I tried not to roll my eyes at her when I answered, "I don't know Momma." She cut her eyes at me when she said, "You know why, Treasure. Should you and Sénar be in the same room?"

I was confident with my little black lie when I answered, "We are not doing anything Momma." She rolled her eyes and said, "You better not be." I heard her mumble under her breath, "I rather it be him than Tyrell's ass. That's what her ass gets messing with my baby." As she walked into her room, she turned around before closing her door to ask, "Was that before or after, London had a miscarriage?" My mouth almost hit the floor as I went to Sénar's room ignoring my momma's question. Once in Sénar's room, I realized that I didn't have to be in there, but before I left, I couldn't help but take one more look through Sénar's stuff again. I looked at all his pictures even the ones of me. I gazed at the woman who was probably his mother and how innocent he was, at that time. I searched for his journal again and when I found it, I opened it flipping through the pages, but they were blank all the way until the end. There was a smiley face and a heart with the keys that read pleasure vs pain. With a question that read will the pleasure outweigh the pain, or will the pain outweigh the pleasure? In the end love conquers all. There was a scale with two hearts and one set of keys with a pair missing. Treasure Me Brady is nosey, but she is the love of my life and has the keys to my heart, now and forever. There was a smiley face at the end. I looked up when I heard the front door open, I quickly put it back and ran to my room. Sénar came upstairs, I was so nervous because after reading that, I knew he was aware I had read his journal. He was probably playing a joke on me because he was mad that I read his stuff. I looked for my diary and when it wasn't in my room, I panicked. I was looking everywhere for it when Sénar came and knocked on my door, I didn't say anything. So, he came in and poked his head in to ask, "What are you doing ma?" I was hoping Cassidy didn't have my diary, he saw that I was frantically looking for something. He asked, "What are you looking for Treasure?" I ignored him because I definitely didn't want him to find it, or even know that it was lost. He shook his head and closed the door; he came back to hand me my diary. I was mad instantly when I asked, "Where did you find this Sénar?" He replied, "It was under the mattress of Chino's bed." When he walked away, I tucked it under my mattress. He went to the garage and I followed him. He stared at me before he asked, "What's wrong Treasure?" I glared at him, and despite his injury, he exercised through the pain but just not for as long. He did something he called range of motion to help and just shook his head again before he asked, "Well are you going to glare at me or tell me why you're upset?" I put my hand on my hip before I asked, "Sénar how did you know where my diary was?" He laughed and I got so mad, I wanted to punch him. He jumped up and grabbed me, so I couldn't hit him. He said, "Aye, calm down Treasure. You put it there Sunday night, well I put it there, but it was in the bathroom with your stuff. Calm down, I'm not as nosey as you."

Suspicious, I asked, "So, you didn't read it?"

He shrugged his shoulders before he asked, "Why, should I? Is there some juicy stuff in there?" He laughed, I didn't find it funny at all and said, "Sénar stop, it's not funny! I have personal stuff in there, that is none of your business!" He smirked at me, then asked, "Well, is it about me or Tyrell's punk ass?" I pushed him and tried to leave but he pulled me back to him. He said, "Treasure, I skimmed through a couple of pages, but you have some deep stuff in there. Too deep for me, but don't worry I didn't go all through your stuff like you did my stuff. Besides, there's no fun in that. I would rather find out by you showing me." He smirked at me before he got close to me to ask, "Treasure are you ever going to tell me how you truly feel?"

I crossed my arms before I answered, "No Sénar, I will show you!" I said it in a mocking tone. He looked into my eyes, but I looked away.

He let me go to say, "Fine, go write it in your little diary then."

He pulled me to him and kissed me so passionately, I almost melted into his arms until I realized I was not supposed to be letting him take me there again, so he could leave me all hot and bothered. I pushed him off of me and left the garage. He didn't come after me he just stayed in the garage. I heard his phone ring as I left. He ran out of the garage and ran up the steps pass me. He knocked on my momma and Ken's door. Ken answered the door as I was coming up.

He was naked when he asked, "What boy?"

My mom was hugging him from behind when Sénar said, "Sabrina is going into labor pops!" He sighed before he said, "Shoot, I'll be there later. I am busy with this crazy woman. Y'all go I'll be there." Sénar turned to see me standing there before I went to my room and slammed the door.

He asked, "So, did you like what you saw?"

I rolled my eyes at him and said, "It's not like I haven't seen it before." Sénar pulled me up out of my bed, making me drop my diary. I pushed him off of me and asked, "What's your problem Sénar?" He asked, "What's that supposed to mean?"

I thought about making him angrier, but I could see his eyes change colors the longer he waited for my answer. I said, "Sénar, I told you him and my Momma was naked in the kitchen the day I stayed home from school because my foot had glass in it." I hoped he believed me because I didn't want him mad at me again.

He just glared at me when he said, "I already told you, don't play with me like that when it comes to him. Ever!" He picked my diary up and handed it to me, "Let's go, Treasure." He walked out and I stuck my diary in one of my drawers at the bottom when he wasn't looking. I whined when I asked, "Do I have to go Sénar? She does not even like me and I do not like her."

He quickly answered, "So what, when you have my baby she better be there too."

I said, "You mean London, right?" I forgot my mom mentioned London losing her baby, so I felt bad instantly after asking him that. Sénar ignored my question and waited for me to follow him. I didn't want to go, what if it was an episode of *Maury Povich*, but in real life? I laughed to myself as Sénar opened the door for me he asked, "What's so funny Treasure?"

I didn't realize he noticed, so I shrugged my shoulders and answered, "You are, Sénar."

He smirked before he said, "I bet," then he snickered to himself as well. I folded my arms because now I wondered why he was laughing.

So, I asked, "What's so funny Sénar?"

He rolled his eyes and said, "You are, Treasure."

I smacked my lips as we pulled up to the parking lot of the hospital. We went to the front to get Sabrina's location and headed straight to her room. When we got there, it was just Sabrina and Cassidy in the room. Sénar walked in first, they were both so happy to see him that they both jumped up to hug and kiss him. They were all talking and filled with excitement but when they saw me standing in the doorway, they both stopped talking. For some reason Sabrina was extra nice when she said, "Hey Treasure, it's been a long time. How are you?"

I was shocked by her cordial attitude and responded cordially as well when I said, "I'm fine Sabrina, congratulations on your baby."

She smiled when she said, "Thanks. So, I take it you haven't seen my little bundle of joy. Y'all hurry, go see the baby!"

Sénar was excited and asked, "Did they cut you open? Or did you have it like a G? What did you have Sabrina?"

She said, "Damn Sénar, it was natural. Well somewhat, I did have a lil' help yesterday." She giggled, then said, "Anyway, it's a surprise, so hurry!"

She told us where to go and we left to see her baby. Sénar was so excited because he loved babies and children. He said they were innocent creatures full of light, in a dark world and that he loved to be around them because of their honesty. We walked in the area where the babies were behind a little glass, he was looking for a baby with their last name but when he didn't see one, he had a puzzled look on his face. We could hear laughter from some familiar voices coming down the hall. I was so surprised to see Tyrell and Leah walking down the hall, holding hands and laughing but when they noticed us, they stop laughing. Tyrell had a serious look on his face and then became more annoyed when he noticed me behind Sénar. They walked towards us as they both let each other's hand go. Tyrell asked, "Oh, y'all must be here to see my son?"

Tears filled my eyes when I noticed a little chocolate baby wrapped in a blanket with the plastered name tag that read: Tyrell Carter Jr.. Sénar smirked and laughed to himself. He shook his head before he said, "Congrats man, you must be proud!" Sénar sounded genuine but I knew he was upset, but not as upset as I was. That wasn't even the worst part, the fact that he tried to kill me, just yesterday for my dishonesty and now, I was standing in the hospital staring at a baby that out of all the people in the world, Sabrina and him had made together. No wonder she was so nice and urged us to come see her little secret.

Tears filled my eyes as I said, "Congratulations Tyrell, on your son."

Tyrell glared at me when he asked, "I guess y'all ain't the only one with a little secret, huh? Well, Sénar already knew what was up. Right Sénar?"

I looked back at Sénar in disappointment and he put his hands up before he said, "I told you to leave his grimy ass alone."

Sénar's nonchalant attitude caused me to become instantly angry when I said, "Damn Tyrell, I almost felt bad. I'm glad I got to have my cake and eat it too. We both love dessert and you know Sénar loves chocolate, so I had a ball giving it to him."

Tyrell try to grab me, but I snatched my hand back, "Don't touch me!"

He laughed at me, then said, "You weren't saying that when you rode me in the back of my car like a damn porn star, like you did for them earrings! I shouldn't have given your chain or those earrings back."

I was offended but Sénar came to my rescue when he said, "She learned that on me. I give her tutoring classes when she's being good." Leah giggled as I looked back at Sénar, he shrugged his shoulders and laughed, "Sorry ma, I couldn't help it."

Tyrell shouted, "Man, I don't give a fuck! Sénar, you can have her! I'm done with her ass; I just wish she would have flew out the windshield like the dirty bit-"

Sénar pushed him, "Aye, watch your mouth man!" They both got in each other's face as Ken was coming behind Tyrell and Leah.

Ken laughed before he asked, "What do we have, a little damn reunion going on here?"

Leah laughed, then said, "Hell yeah!"

Ken ignored Leah's enthusiasm, along with the lust in her eyes and spoke directly to Tyrell, "You a busy lil' nigga ain't you? Well you are going to take care of this baby; I'll make sure you don't have any reason not to and if you don't, you are going to have to answer to me!"

Tyrell smacked his lips before he said, "Man, whatever, your old ass ain't goi-"

Ken flinched at Tyrell and he jumped back when Ken said, "Shut your ass up lil' nigga! You don't want this battle, you can't even handle

Sénar, so you definitely can't step to me! I'll break your ass up, in front of your new son and your little girlfriends too." Everyone was silent, Ken looked at their son and said, "If anybody got a problem with what I said, tell them to come see me! Send your punk ass daddy or hell, better yet, you can send your square ass momma too." He dismissed Tyrell, Then asked, "What's up Leah, you cool?"

With a flirty smile, Leah answered, "Hell yeah!" Ken walked off leaving Tyrell scared and infuriated. He flashed on Leah first when he said, "Man, your ass is always flirting! That's a grown ass man, Leah!"

I giggled and Sénar said, "Let's go." I didn't say another word, I walked off with Sénar to leave. We stopped by to say bye to Sabrina and Cassidy. I totally let Treasure number two handle this whole situation because It was beyond me; it didn't even feel real.

Sabrina smiled when she asked, "Did you guys see my son and his daddy down there?"

Sénar answered, "Yeah Sabrina, you real funny. I hope you know what you got yourself into."

She smacked her lips before she said, "Sénar please, you ain't no better with all your drama and messing with Treasure's sneaky ass."

Sénar said, "Whatever Sabrina, it's your life. I'm still gonna be there for my nephew, even though, his daddy is a straight up chump!"

Sabrina said, "I know but please don't have no babies with her, ugh."

I didn't say anything, I was just minding my business when Sabrina said, "Treasure, Tyrell was never yours anyway, so I hope your feelings aren't hurt too bad."

She sounded sincere while Cassidy didn't hesitate to laugh. I smiled at them both and replied, "Well, congratulations on your new edition Sabrina. Wishing you all the best and wishing the both of you a speedy recovery for your p u s s i e s."

I was sincere, as I spelled it out for them too, then walked out when I was satisfied with all of their facial expressions. Sénar said,

"Ouch! Goodnight, love y'all." Sénar caught up to me to say, "Damn Treasure, you are cold, sometimes!"

We drove to San Bernardino to the mountain top where we spent Halloween. We looked at the stars and talked. Sénar said, "Are you ok Treasure?"

I answered, "I am fine." Treasure number two didn't want to talk, she wanted to have some fun to relieve my frustrations. I asked, "Well, what did we come here for Sénar?"

He looked at me before he answered, "To relax and talk. I didn't want to go home yet. Why?" He smiled sadistically, instantly exciting me. I made the first move, I kissed him, and he let me, but he didn't do anything in return.

I was frustrated when I said, "Sénar, you play too much!"

He laughed, then said, "Treasure, this week was crazy as hell. I am still processing it as we speak, and I want to do a lot of things with you and to you but not tonight." I wanted to push him off the hood of his car. He quickly sat up, "Don't even think about it, Treasure. Your ass is nuts! You just want to for all the wrong reasons. So, no." He tried to have a serious face but I knew he was aroused too when he said, "Look Treasure, you have been through a lot this week and you haven't even dealt with that yet, so let's go get something to eat and let's see if you still bout it bout it when we get back to the house."

He laughed and I rolled my eyes at him. Ugh, I could not stand him sometimes. When we got back my mom and Ken were arguing. I could hear Ken say, "Fuck that I'll be damned, if I sit around and watch my daughters get knocked up and ran through while yours is still intact. Then she put Sénar in danger and now his arm is messed up!"

My mom begged Ken, "Babe, don't please, I'll give you the money. I'll do whatever you want Ken, just don't leave me or hurt my baby, please."

Ken demanded, "Get those belts ready!" He came down with no shirt on and saw me and Sénar at the front door. He said, "Well, well,

well, happy Valentine's Day to us all, what a damn surprise! Come here, Sénar. Come talk with me."

I just went to my room and got in the bed. Later, Sénar came in with the chocolate we bought yesterday. We didn't even talk about anything depressing, we just ate chocolate and talked about stuff that got our minds off of all the chaos, until we fell asleep with him lying on the floor beside my bed. We didn't even go anywhere the next day, we just stayed home to rest and watched TV together. Ken was gone the whole weekend. Leaving my mom, a hot mess. She drank excessively and was way more visible while Ken was gone. She would often be sitting in his chair or going over some paperwork while having her a drink. She barely spoke to me unless she was angry about something or was telling me to do something. I never thought I would want to go back to school so soon.

In the next couple of weeks, my mom and Ken fought all the time. It was always chaos when they were around each other. Ken was gone for days at a time now. Cassidy went back and forth to visit Sabrina, after Sénar helped her get her license. Nevaeh was showing and her belly grew since the last time she had come to visit Cassidy. Sénar let me practice driving on his car more, so I would be ready in the next week for my sweet sixteen. Sénar was good. He wasn't inappropriate most of the time, and he wasn't playing basketball because of his shoulder injury, which pissed Ken off even more. It was like he hated me more every day, and my mom was meaner than ever. She would get drunk and get belligerent with Ken, and me when I was around for her to lash out on. She even appeared to be jealous of me and Sénar's relationship. I avoided her as much as possible.

We went to LA to visit Lil' James and Latosha a couple of days before Louie's funeral. She bragged about her new man and how much he loved Lil' James. Everyone that attended the funeral had great things to say about Louie; it was really hard for Sénar to be a Paul bearer; he was so distraught. Cedrick wasn't allowed to attend as a request made by Sénar. When it was over, we just did our best not to think about it and spent our time spoiling Lil' James. Travis and Sénar vowed to spend more time with each other and help raise Louie's baby.

Everything else seemed to be going way more smooth than normal. London backed off after she lost her baby, and I hadn't seen Leah ever since we left the hospital. Tyrell asked me if I knew where she was once or twice, but I ignored him because I didn't care where she was. Besides, his random calls and threatening voicemails, Tyrell left me alone for the most part because Sénar didn't let him get close to me. Even though Sénar and I weren't having sex anymore, we were really close; we did everything together again except that. The shower head needed to be replaced though, after being overused, perhaps.

It was the beginning of March and my birthday was in a couple of days. I was hoping it would be good, since things had calmed down a bit, well, except my mom and Ken. I finished practice, and Sénar was working out. I flipped through the channels and saw a picture of Leah on the news; I was baffled why she would be on the news. I turned up the volume and listened to the story. She was reported missing over a week ago, and they were asking anyone with information to contact the Rialto police department. I jumped up in a panic and started to run to the garage. I opened the door but then changed my mind and I went to go check on my mom instead, after not having seen her for a couple of days. When I opened her door, she was naked and tied to the bed by all fours. I called her name, but she didn't answer. When I called her name again, she woke up.

She was disoriented and appeared extremely drained; she could barely speak when she whispered, "Get out, Treasure."

I could barely hear her, so I asked, "What? Momma?"

She weakly, said, "Go."

Before passing back out as Sénar came to the door and saw my mom, I pulled the blanket over her naked body. Sénar panicked when he said, "Treasure, get out!"

I hurried and tried to untie my mom but couldn't figure out how to undo the straps. Sénar pleaded with me when he said, "Treasure get out befo-"

Ken pushed Sénar back and asked, "Before what?" He closed the door in Sénar's face, alarmed I quickly guarded myself as he walked toward me.

I yelled, "Ken, let my Momma go!"

He chuckled, then asked, "You wanna take her place?"

I shook my head no while walking backwards and then noticed my mom was out cold. She was not even reacting to the situation; I wasn't sure if she was injured or hungover. I tried to move around Ken, but he grabbed me, he smelled my hair while rubbing his hands all over my breast. I started to cry, "Ken, please don't!" He shoved his hand down my pants and plunged his fingers deep inside of me, making me yelp in fear and discomfort. Sénar was banging on the door as Ken sucked on his fingers. I closed my eyes, and with all my might tried to jerk my body away from Ken, which would not have worked, but he released me anyway. I ran to the door, fumbling it as I tried to get out and run for my life. I almost knocked Sénar down as I ran into his arms. He pulled me to him; my heart was racing.

I felt like I was going to pass out when Sénar instructed, "Breathe Treasure, take slow deep breaths and try to relax." I tried to follow his instructions, but I was so scared. I didn't even know if I could trust Sénar anymore.

Sénar seemed to be hurting when he said, "I am sorry, Treasure. He is mad at me because I don't want to play basketball anymore or do his crazy plans. Don't ever go near that room again; I don't care for what. Your mom is a grown-ass woman. That is not the first time her ass has been tied up like that; trust me. I'm not trying to scare you, but it's true, we need to worry about you. He knows you are the best way to get back at me. So, just stay away from him if you can, and I will do my best to protect you, but you have to listen."

I was scared and felt like no matter what, I was the one that was going to suffer. It was always me, I tried to hold my tears back as Sénar hugged me, but I didn't hug him back. I was exhausted after almost having some hope of a normal future. I was reminded that I was in some horrible psycho book or movie that was really just my life. I started to drift away into my thoughts when Sénar called my name, "Treasure?"

I snapped, "What?"

He said, "Come with me."

Sénar grabbed a sports bag, "Pack as many clothes as you can in here. Only your best stuff, no older things. Undergarments and socks."

I got everything I could that he told me to grab and threw it in the bag. I asked, "Where are we going, Sénar?"

He thought about it for a second and answered, "Nowhere yet. But we need to be ready, just in case. Just set it to the side, and if there is ever an emergency, it will already be ready."

Sénar and I left the house. He took me to get something to eat and let me practice driving. My birthday was coming up, and I could either dwell on how sad my life was or move forward and try to prepare for my future, as Sénar had said. I had an appointment for my driver's license test coming up on my birthday and was the one thing I had to looked forward to. I planned to go to summer school again, so I could graduate at the same time as Sénar. Sénar and I became even closer after my last incident with Ken as it scared me and angered Sénar more than any other time. We both fought the urge to be with each other sexually, but I was almost ready to give in and ask why we couldn't anymore. Sénar was being so good, I didn't want to mess up his progress.

The Weekend of my birthday, we went to LA to visit Louie's gravesite. We went to his house after to see Lil' James and to check on everyone else. It was an emotional visit, but we still managed to have fun drinking and reminiscing on all the fun times we had with Louie. Latosha and I talked about her new boyfriend.

Latosha said, "Girl, I am so glad I listened to you, Treasure. Chris is a really good guy, and I don't think things would be going as well if I had slept with him on the first night as I had intended too. Hell, I know more about him than I do about my baby daddy now. I can say we do a lot more talking instead of just using each other for sex. We still haven't done it yet, but I'm glad because if he still around, he must be interested in me and not just sex."

I smiled at her when I realized she might have found her a real man to love her and Lil' James. I had sangria and listened to her while I drank my own inhibitions away. Heck, I asked Sénar for two of them this time. She asked, "What about you and Sénar?"

I took a big swig of my sangria before I answered, "We're cool, Latosha, we are just friends now. We aren't doing anything anymore."

She said, "Don't worry, remember there is more to a real relationship than just sex, Treasure. I wish I knew that sooner. Sénar really loves you, he has just been through a lot and probably is trying to right his wrongs with you."

I thought to myself that it was a little too late for that because the damage had already been done. Latosha told me that Sénar and I could use her room just in case because she was going to her new boyfriend's house. I was almost irritated as I thought she was going to ask me to babysit. Even though I happily held Lil' James in my arms. I felt guilty when she said, "Don't worry, Lil' James is coming with me. Those two are two peas in a pod, and I love it!"

I was happy for her but still felt a twinge of jealousy as I let her and Lil' James get ready, I went to find Sénar. He and Travis were smoking some weed and drinking their Mad Dog 20/20 while Daisy and some of her friends swarmed around them. When I came out, one of her friends was all over Sénar. He was buzzing, so he just let her dance all on him until he saw me come out. He saw me right away, prompting Daisy to look back and tell her friend to stop. I was buzzing too, so I did not hesitate to snatch Sénar away from them. Travis laughed as

I dragged him away from Daisy and her clan. Latosha came to say goodbye and let us hug Lil' James before she left.

She whispered to me and Sénar, "If y'all do get down, wash my sheets, don't be janky!"

Sénar started laughing hysterically when he said, "We got chu, Latosha!" He winked at her. Daisy and her friends were bored once I came out and left shortly after I snatched Sénar out of their trap. Sénar and I went to Latosha's room for the rest of the night. We talked about everything occasionally bursting out into laughter at all the shenanigans we had been through. When we stopped laughing, I looked into Sénar's eyes and realized how much he had grown since I first laid eyes on his dark butterscotch face. With my buzz full in effect and Treasure number two impatiently waiting for an opportunity to experience all the pleasure that abruptly came to a stop; I kissed him. He stopped to gaze at me with my favorite smile, the one that made me feel loved and safe.

He said, "Ok, it's time to go nite nite before we get ourselves in trouble and have to wash in the morning."

He chuckled when he saw my facial expression as I became instantly offended when I asked, "Why Sénar? Why can't we have some fun or work out or have dessert? Hell, I will-"

Sénar cut me off when he said, "Calm down, ma, I just don't want to mess things up. You are not ready to be mine all the way; I want the keys to your heart, Treasure. I want it all or nothing. I'll be patient and keep you safe and love you until we can finally be together."

I didn't want to hear all his poetic justifications of why we couldn't do it. I was going to take it because I just couldn't take it anymore! As if he could read my mind, he got up to request, "Give me access to your heart, Treasure?" He smirked at me as he saw my anger rise as I approached him, he said, "I already have the keys to your kitty cat," He rubbed his hand over my coochie, and that was it. I grabbed him and kissed him passionately and started to remove my clothes.

Sénar was excited but didn't remove any of his clothes, which further agitated me and made me more aggressive. Sénar giggled as I tried to get him to take his clothes off.

Sénar said, "No, means no, Treasure!"

He thought he was so funny until I was fully naked and standing in front of him with a burning desire to feel him inside of me. He gazed at my nakedness, he tried to remain strong, but I grabbed him and kissed him passionately. My nipples were erect, and my coochie was pulsating, I wanted to rip his clothes off. Sénar tried to leave, but I stopped him. I was wearing him down, and him being buzzed didn't help. He did his best to decline, but eventually, he kissed me back, allowing me to take over. I pushed him down on Latosha's bed and mounted him. I thought I would explode before he actually entered me, but I managed to control myself. I rode him until we both exploded and then I fell asleep on top of him.

When we woke up, I could feel his man stick awake before him and realized we were still naked and had not even cleaned ourselves up. He woke up and squeezed me before he said, "Damn Treasure, you wouldn't take no for an answer. You should have taken your ass to sleep." He was not mad, but he appeared disappointed, I just didn't know with who, himself or me. I didn't care, I got what I wanted and would be ok at least for another two weeks. Sénar got dressed and went to his car and came back with clothes for us to change into. We took a shower together and had another moment of pleasure before we got out. Sénar kept his word and washed Latosha's sheets and said, "See, you got us washing and stuff this early in the morning."

We ate breakfast with everyone and talked with everybody before we left. We stopped at the beach after grabbing some food from BoBo's Burgers and then walked the beach with our shoes off. Sénar asked, "Treasure, you ready to take your driver's test this Tuesday?"

I smiled. I was ready, and it was my sweet sixteen, so I was already excited. I answered, "Yes, Sénar; I am ready."

Then he asked, "You ready to be mine?"

Sénar waited impatiently for my answer. I frowned at him when I asked, "Sénar, you have so many options. Why not get a girl who's not so screwed up like me?"

He laughed and said, "Well, you might not be if I didn't screw you up."

He was being nasty, but I still laughed and said, "No, Sénar, your daddy hates me, and I just need to think about what I am going to do with my future."

He was disappointed, but he didn't want to pressure me. I asked, "What do you think happened to Leah Sénar?"

He shrugged his shoulders and answered, "I don't know, I haven't seen her either. You know her ass is crazy, maybe she ran away. Tyrell keeps asking me where she is too, but I haven't seen her since Sabrina's son was born. So, we should be asking Tyrell with his ass being a serial cat killer and after him trying to kill you, Treasure."

I thought about Tyrell and how violent he was when he was jealous but didn't want to think of him as a person Sénar was predicting him to be. We went home and cooked dinner together, but Ken was not there, so my mom came down by herself, she looked sad and lonely. Sénar tried to cheer her up and also remind her of my driving test on Tuesday. She nodded her head in agreement but barely ate before going back upstairs. We cleaned the kitchen and went to bed.

I hadn't seen Ken in so many days and I couldn't be happier. However, my mom was devastated, she barely ate or spoke to me. She dealt with Sénar the same, but she was distant when it came to me. It was my birthday today and I was excited but when Sénar and I pulled up to the school we saw news reporters and police cars. Both Sénar and I were trying to figure out why they would be here so early in the morning; it wasn't like we had a game or anything today. Everyone was whispering and looking at me when I went to class. Before class could start there was a man dressed in slacks and a collared shirt with a pendulum on it that came in and whispered something to the teacher. The teacher pointed to me and he asked me to go with him. I was so nervous, why would he want to talk to me? I followed him to the front office where we were given a room to talk in private. He tried to make me comfortable but that was impossible as I anxiously waited to find out the purpose of our acquaintance.

He asked, "Leah Banks was your friend, right?" I almost passed out from the absurdity of his question. I then realized this would probably not be the best time to express my hatred for her.

I cautiously answered, "We knew each other, but I haven't seen her in a while."

He cleared his throat to ask, "Well, that would be because she was found strangled by a necklace that looks pretty similar to yours but with her name instead."

I almost vomited when he told me that she was dead. I started crying and asked, "Why? Oh my gosh, that's terrible officer. I am sorry to hear that."

He looked skeptical when he asked, "Do you know anyone who would want to harm her?"

I thought of Tyrell and then Ken. I almost took the opportunity to rid of Ken once and for all by telling the detective Ken was a crazy man who probably killed her in the way he threatened to kill me. Instead, I answered, "No," because then I would have to disclose my involvement and didn't want to get into trouble. He let me go after he skeptically took my answer and called the next person. As I was coming out, Tyrell was coming into the front office. We both avoided eye contact with each other as I left back to class. I went through my next classes despite the obvious whispers from everyone. I looked around for Sénar and saw him talking to London. She was crying while his eyes wondered around to search for me. London's tears turned into rage when she noticed me. He said something to her, and she appeared to relax a bit before he left to walk towards me.

He said, "What's up birthday girl?"

I was trying to maintain my composure, but I wanted to cry. He asked, "What's wrong ma?"

I couldn't hold them back anymore, Sénar looked worried, he knew I would never expose my sadness in public, so he shielded me by putting his arm around my shoulder. He instructed, "Breathe in deeply ma and relax. Wait until you finish crying to tell me. Come on let's go to the car and talk." I quickly wiped away my tears and tried to pull myself together. He said, "You, crying in public? I am not sure I want to hear it, but I am here ma." I couldn't help but laugh a little as we walked to his car.

Once we were in the car, I asked, "Did the detectives talk to you?"

He looked at me like I was crazy when he asked, "Why would they want to talk to me, Treasure?"

He was concerned but remained calm. I replied, "Because they called me out of class to talk to me about Leah?"

Sénar looked relieved, he took a deep breath and said, "Girl, you had my heart skip a beat, just for a second." He stopped and raised his eyebrow before asking, "Why would they be asking you anything about Leah?" Sénar was sincere with his curiosity. I started to cry again, and he still had a confused look on his face when he asked, "Why are you crying? What about her, Treasure?"

He was getting impatient now, but he could see the fear in my eyes when I replied, "She's dead, Sénar! They found her strangled by her necklace! What if-"

Sénar cut me off, "Treasure, don't even start spewing nonsense what ifs, ok? Don't worry about what ifs. Don't speak foolishness into existence."

When Sénar said that I had a flashback of what I told Leah when she bragged about her and her, *"new friend". Knowing Ken, he probably killed her the same way he threatened to kill me. What if it was Tyrell? I mean, he was really crazy when he was mad.* I was drifting away into my thoughts. Sénar called my name, "Treasure?" I just stared at him blankly when he asked, "You good, ma?"

I was still trying to ensure myself that I was ok; I was still alive, at least for now and tried not to worry. I answered, "I'll be fine Sénar, I'm just shocked and a little scared, that's all."

He looked concerned but tried to hide it when he said, "Don't be scared. Treasure, I won't let anything happen to you, ma. I am sorry to hear that about Leah. I thought she ran away or something but damn that's crucial." He was only silent for a second before asking, "Well, did you do it?"

I looked at him like he was crazy when I answered, "No, Sénar! Did you?"

As if appalled, he said, "Hell nah, I wouldn't do no shit like that! I'm a lover, not a murderer."

I cut my eyes at him, "Well, you're the cleanup guy, aren't you?"

Sénar was pissed off when he said, "What! I didn't have nothing to do with that shit, Treasure. You are trippin', I didn't even know she was dead! I am obviously not of any interest either. Shit, with your crazy ass, you are way more likely to do that than me." He was irritated with me when he said, "Damn Treasure, I know I messed up, but do you think I would do that?"

I ignored his question when I answered, "It doesn't matter what I think, Sénar. She is dead, and someone killed her. I just don't want to end up like her!"

Sénar was still offended by my accusations but still managed to say, "Well you won't, but don't ever think I would not kill over you because I would be lying if I said that I wouldn't. Just know that I did not kill Leah or have any parts *at all* in her disappearance or murder." He put emphasis on at all as if to insinuate he had no parts in it whatsoever, almost indicating, that I may have.

We got out of the car both offended and wondering what happened to Leah. In my math class there was an empty seat next to me that

Leah would normally occupy. Even though, I absolutely could not stand Leah, I felt bad about her death and hoped that I also could say that I played no parts in it whatsoever. The classroom appeared uncomfortable with the empty seat now after rumors started to spread about what happened to Leah. I just went to my classes and tried not to react to whispers or blank stares from people. After school me and Sénar got permission to leave for my DMV appointment. My mom was dressed and ready when we got home to go to the DMV with us. Sénar and I were both shocked to see my mom was ready. We drove Ken's truck since it was an automatic, but I really wanted to drive the stick instead, so Sénar drove his car in case I wanted to risk it with his car.

My mom asked, "Have you watched the news lately?" I told her no because I didn't even want to talk about, whatever she might be talking about before my driving test. She continued, "Well, I have, and I saw that little fast ass girl is missing. I wonder what happened to her. She probably ran away with some grown ass man, or you know what? She was messing with Tyrell's crazy ass too. He probably killed her lil' tale….."

She just went on and on until I drifted into my own thoughts trying to protect my mind from the horrible thoughts of what ifs. I could hear the lyrics, *"No matter what I do, all I think about is you, even when I'm with my boo…."* Then my mom interrupted the song in my head with, "Treasure?"

Instead of snapping, I said, "Huh?"

She glared at me when she said, "I asked, what do you think happened to her?"

She was agitated when she realized I had tuned her out long ago. I answered dryly, "She is dead Momma." My mom's mouth fell open in shock, but then she just closed her mouth and took in the information. Then she said, "Well better her than you, Tyrell's crazy ass probably killed her. I told you to stay away from that boy……"

I went back to singing the lyrics to my favorite song. I chose to use Sénar's car, since I learned to drive in it. My mom was surprised that I chose the stick shift instead. When this cute light skin boy came out with a clip board, me and my momma smiled while Sénar rolled his eyes. His name just happened to be Tyrell. Sénar immediately asked my mom for the keys and went back to the truck. My mom signed the papers and we went outside for the driving test. Sénar was sitting on Ken's truck playing the song I was humming in my head to tune my momma out. Sénar and I both noticed the driving instructor was impressed with the choice of my car for the test. He was even more impressed when he saw that it was a stick shift. He tried to remain professional, but he couldn't help but say, "Wow! Nice choice, I don't think I have had a girl take a test in a stick before, let alone a mustang. Is this your boyfriend's car?"

He was talking about Sénar as he was sitting on Ken's truck watching our every move. I didn't want to risk failing, so I ensured him he wasn't my boyfriend when I answered, "Nah, he's just my best friend." He smiled and then we both put our seat belts on. My take off in first gear was superb, even the instructor was impressed. I drove like a professional and was sure to follow all the protocols I had studied. When we pulled up to the DMV where I was supposed to park, there was a car parked incorrectly in front of me, so I did my best to park and hoped he didn't dock me for my parking.

He handed me my test and then said, "Sheesh, I was hoping I got to take a point away somewhere or your best friend would think I passed you because you are so beautiful. Anyhoo, it's not. You had some pretty impressive driving skills, whoever taught you should be proud." I blushed when he stapled my permit with the passing drivers test and informed me it would take up to two weeks for my driver's license to come in the mail.

I was so excited; I went inside to take my picture with the biggest smile I had in a long time. When I came out, I was so happy my mom and Sénar knew I passed. My mom hugged me and said, "Congratulations, sweetie, but are you sure he didn't pass you because you're cute? When did you learn how to drive a stick?"

My mom had so much energy, I had to take a closer look at her and make sure she was my momma and not some other human that favored her. With Ken's absence she was more energetic and appeared to be more in tune to what was going on around her. I wasn't sure if I liked it, but it was nice to see that she actually cared.

I said, "Momma, I passed, isn't that what matters?"

She said, "I guess, well happy birthday sweetie!" She almost appeared sad when I got into the car with Sénar.

He said, "Ride with your Momma, Treasure, she could use the company."

I smacked my lips and went to get in the car with my mom. Her eyes lit up as we drove home, she was happy to have someone to talk to. Even though, I tuned her out until we arrived home. When Sénar pulled up he left the car running and waited until I approached him, he snatched the test out of my hand and went over it as I tried to get it back from him. He read through it with a skeptical look on his face. When he looked through the papers, he had a smirk on his face when he asked, "Wow, you put me in the friend zone, Treasure?"

I raised my eyebrow, then asked, "What chu talking about Willis?"

He showed me the note on the back that read: "Your best friend is lucky. I wish I had a best friend as beautiful as you, sincerely, Tyrell." His number was at the bottom and read: "Just in case you need another best friend."

I tried to grab it from him, and he held it high, so I couldn't get to it. He acted like he was going to rip the piece with his number off. My mom walked up to see us and asked what we were doing. Sénar said, "Carmel, she cheated! She was flirting with him and he passed her because she is kinda cute."

My momma laughed at Sénar and observed what was written on the test. She laughed to herself as she ripped the bottom piece with his number off herself and then said, "We don't need any more Tyrells'!"

Sénar was pleased with her actions as I am sure he wanted to do the same. He high fived my mom as he jumped in the back seat of his car. Me and my mom watched him and wondered what he was doing when he said, "Come on ladies, let's celebrate, Treasure's driving!"

My mom was instantly happy and did not hesitate to jump in the passenger seat. I was still a bit shocked and nervous but what the heck, it's my birthday. We had a ball, celebrating my license and birthday, by going to eat and then going to see *All About the Benjamin's*. My mom being an adult, came in handy for both me driving legally and going to see a rated R movie, so I couldn't complain. When we got back Ken was home and when he saw how happy everyone was when we returned, he was instantly agitated. Before we went to bed, I heard Ken arguing with my mom all night, I could barely sleep.

In the morning before school, I came downstairs ready for school but heard voices in the Kitchen. I listened before I went all the way down. I could hear Ken saying he got the money and they could leave after the school year was over. Sénar was quiet but Ken was adamant about leaving.

Ken said, "I picked a school far from here, so I don't have to worry about you running back to Treasure's ass. If I knew she was going to get you sprung like that, I would have never given her the opportunity." Sénar was still silent, so Ken got mad when he asked, "Boy, what's wrong with you? You got a problem?"

Sénar answered, "No, sir!"

Ken asked, "Then why you ain't saying nothing?"

Sénar hesitated before responding, "You are the boss pops. I just don't know why you feel that way about her. She hasn't even done anything to you."

Ken roared, "It's not me I'm worried about! It's you! You let her come between us and you acting like a lil' punk! I worked too hard to raise your ass to be a real man, so no woman would have the power to persuade you. Shit, we all like pussy, but that shit come and go, boy!"

Sénar was respectful when he said, "I hear you pops! I'm not letting her come between us, I'm not doing anything with her dad. She is doing good; she is not messing with no one. Not even me, just leave her alone and I'll do whatever you want pops, please!"

I came down and sat in the living room to wait for Sénar, he was still not dressed yet. He looked stressed out as he got up to go get dressed. Ken glared at me from the table. I looked down because I swear, I was looking into the same person's eyes that killed Leah, although I had no proof. Ken got up and came to the living room, making me really uncomfortable as he approached me, he said, "Happy belated birthday, Treasure. I know I usually give you money for your birthday, but I'll give you something more valuable. You can have yo' momma back and maybe you'll get to keep your life, if my son gets to leave in one piece, since my girls didn't!"

He laughed as Sénar came down. I swear if looks could kill, Ken and I would have dropped dead because Sénar's glare even made Ken uncomfortable as he grabbed Sénar to hug him before he went back upstairs. Sénar was hesitant to hug him back but he did embrace him before we left out the door to school. I am sure he knew it would not be wise not to embrace him back after he had accused me of coming between the two of them. I didn't say anything to Sénar on the way to school because he seemed to be really deep in thought. When we got to school London was waiting for Sénar, even though he swore they weren't together, and he never confirmed her losing her baby to me either. I just knew somethings were better left alone. I didn't react to London's stalker behavior; I just knew she had a good reason to not want to let Sénar go. He was and is maturing so much, I admired his will to self-improve. I did not want to detour him from that, maybe Ken was right. Maybe I was the one who messed Sénar up. I just accepted that he would leave me, and I would be alone again, but I would still have whatever was left of my mom, I guess. Well, at least we had until the end of the school year and maybe he would let Sénar stay for the summer. All I could do was try to stay positive.

One night at dinner, Cassidy announced that she was moving with Sabrina to help her with whom they chose to call Jr. because neither Sénar, nor Cassidy wanted to call her son Tyrell, especially Sénar. We avoided talking about Leah or Sabrina's love child with Tyrell. I was deeply hurt about that but did my best not to express it. I found a compartment to stuff my emotions into, wherever there was room left. I was definitely running out of room, and one day it would probably all come crashing down on me when I least expected it.

Ken had purchased his own truck and was on the road a lot for the next two weeks, on and off. Whenever Ken was home it was turmoil and when he was gone my mom seemed to depend on Sénar for male attention. It was as if she just wanted to be acknowledged by a male, whether it was Ken or not. She even appeared somewhat jealous of me and Sénar's bond. Sénar was distant but he was still attentive to me. He just didn't touch me sexually and fought his desire to be with me. He even complained that I needed to get off birth control because he noticed that I did not have a regular menstrual cycle. He said the birth control was the reason for all my unexplained weight gain, regardless of my cheerleading and healthy eating. He sure was nosey, but I went for my shot anyways and promised him it would be my last. There was no need for it, if I wasn't having sex, I mean it's not like he would let me have a boyfriend.

I was extremely sexually frustrated, so I asked, "Why can you have sex with London Sénar, and I can't have anyone?"

Sénar tried to be patient with me but he was agitated already when he said, "Look, don't worry, I'll be out of your way soon. Then you can do whatever you want, but you should probably stay on birth control then, if that's the case. Oh, and trust and believe, whoever you do get, may not want to still marry you after. So, follow your own advice."

I knew he was talking about the advice I gave Latosha and I also knew he wanted to say more but didn't. I rolled my eyes at him and got out of the car to go to class as London walked up to him. Tyrell happen to be coming towards me, but I was totally oblivious to him as he walked up to me to say, "Sabrina told me Sénar is leaving, how convenient right after Leah turns up dead. Well, I don't know if he had anything to do with it, but umph I can't wait until he leaves, so I can get my revenge too. I wouldn't have hurt Leah, but I would definitely take pleasure in causing you and Sénar the pain you deserve. You know, like yo' momma's cat, you didn't deserve that either!"

I punched Tyrell so hard in his nose, that it started gushing blood everywhere. I panicked and ran to my class in a hurry. When I got to class, I had blood on my fist, and I could feel my body vibrating. When I heard my name, I snapped, "What?"

The teacher responded, "Treasure, do not speak to me in that manner, young lady. You are wanted in the office, again." He said it with an exaggeration on *again*. I reluctantly walked to the office with my heart still racing and feeling like I was on the verge of screaming at the top of my lungs.

The Principal asked, "Treasure, is it true you punched Mr. Carter this morning right before class?"

I answered, "He threatened me, and I believed him, so I hit him."

I kept it short and simple, I didn't want to be responsible for lashing out on him next for asking stupid questions. He shook his head, "You're such a smart young lady Treasure, but you can't seem to stay out of trouble long enough. You will need to sign up for counseling when you return from your three-day suspension. As a result of three consecutive days, you will not be able to participate in cheerleading, per policy."

I nodded my head in agreement to avoid lashing out and saying I didn't care one bit about their stupid cheerleading teams or their policies. I was glad when he released me, until I realized either my mom or Ken would be here to get me. I started to feel queasy as I tried to calm myself down, by breathing in deeply and ignoring the spinning sensation I was feeling. I grabbed my head to try and focus until I heard my name, "Treasure?"

I snapped, "What?"

It was my mom and she was trying to hold herself together as she appeared to be struggling to do so herself. She glared at me, "Don't what me Treasure!"

Everyone looked at us as if we were two crazed peas in a pod as she demanded me to get in the car. When I saw Ken's truck, I was so nervous and hoped he was not in there. I was relieved when he wasn't, I was so happy because I could handle my mom, even if she got violent. Hell, maybe since Ken or Sénar wasn't around, I could show her not to put her hands on me, without any interruption.

She yelled, "I don't have time for this crap Treasure! I was not prepared to come and get you! You are lucky I didn't get pulled over!" She smelled like alcohol and had on pajamas with her hair wrapped. My mom would have never left the house like that sober. She asked, "What happen, Treasure?"

I answered, "Tyrell threatened me Momma, so I hit him."

She was agitated, "Well great, now you're stuck here with me. Why don't you make me a grilled cheese sandwich Treasure?"

I stared at her with my own perplexed look, "Ok Momma, but what makes you want a grilled cheese sandwich?"

She smirked before she asked, "Do you ask Ken that when you make him one?"

I immediately became uncomfortable, but I did as she asked. She poured her another drink and said, "Get me a beer Treasure!" Now, I was really uncomfortable, she was pretty much replacing Ken at this moment. She looked at me when she said, "Yeah, way from the back!" I was alarmed when she reiterated way from the back. She changed her mind all of a sudden and said, "No, I think I want a tuna sandwich, with the onions and pickles that you make so well." I couldn't take it anymore; I was already on the edge and she was really starting to worry me with her behavior. I put the stuff away for the cheese sandwich and got out the stuff to make the tuna instead.

She watched my every move, and if I didn't know any better, I would think Ken was operating inside of her at the moment. I got the same eerie feeling that she wanted something from me, that I wasn't willing to give. She mumbled under her breath, but I couldn't make out what she said. She barked, "Get me another beer!" Startled at her voice, it was deep and aggressive; I hurried to get her a beer way from the back. I thought it's too early to be drinking beer and too early for tuna but what the hell did I know. I guess I needed to feed Ken's little demon that appeared to be working through my momma. I was concerned as I cut the onions and pickles, I refrained from speaking to her until I was completely done with the knife. I mixed the ingredients and made her a sandwich, cutting it in half then I gave it to her. I then washed and put the knife back in the drawer after watching it sparkle like I did every time I put it away. I asked, "Are you ok Momma?"

She yelled, "No!" I quickly left the kitchen and tried to go to my room, but my mom was relentless in her desire to punish me. She surprised me when she said, "You know what! You brought all of this on yourself being hardheaded and mean. Hell, you're the reason Ken is trying to leave me!"

I winced at her accusations. She took a bite of her sandwich and spit it out. She had a look of discuss on her face, "This is horrible, why would you put pickles and onions in tuna?"

I laughed before I answered, "I don't know Momma, it tastes good. You want me to make you a grilled cheese instead?"

She nodded her head yeah, she almost looked like she may have returned to just being my momma and not some deranged, woman version of Ken. I quickly made her a grilled cheese sandwich and instead used a butter knife to cut it in half before handing it to her. She looked like a happy kid while she ate. Once I cleaned up after myself, I looked at the time to see that it was barely turning 9:30am. I started to watch TV, but I wasn't sure staying in my momma's sight was a good idea. She only ate half of her sandwich and glared at me as if hatred seemed to plague her again.

I asked, "Momma, what else do you need me to do?"

She spat, "Why don't you leave instead of Ken? You don't want to be here anyway!"

She was right I hated being here, I hated Ken, and I was starting to hate her too. With Cassidy being gone most of the time, my mom appeared to be my new arch enemy. I quickly headed for the stairway when she followed me, I just sped up my walking. Before I could reach the top, she grabbed my shoulder forcing me to face her. She reeked of alcohol and clenched on to Ken's beer as she spat words of hate to me.

She asked, "You hate Ken so much that you're willing to do whatever it takes to get rid of him, huh?"

I stared at her to see if I was safe to answer but I didn't care. I answered, "Momma, Ken is no angel. He is always inappropriate with me and he hates me enough to threaten my life several times, amongst many other things."

She appeared to get my drift and became enraged when she asked, "Oh, so you aren't just fucking Sénar? You are probably fucking Ken too, huh?"

That was it, I was offended and hurt. I lashed out, "I'm sorry Momma that is what Ken wants not me! It's not my fault, you're not enough for Ken anymore!"

My mom slapped me so hard, I fell back on the steps, after losing my footing. I was so angry, I scooted up the steps to avoid being knocked down again as she approached me. She looked evil as she raised her hand to slap me again, "You're a whore, just like your daddy!"

When her hand struck my face again, I kicked her so hard that she tumbled down the steps. First, the beer bottle in her hand fell and shattered upon impact, then she followed, landing with a heavy thud onto the floor at the bottom of the stairway. I was mortified when I ran to her, "Momma?" She didn't answer. I was so scared, I tried to wake her, but she didn't move. I quickly ran to the kitchen to grab one of the little sharp knives in one of the drawers, and then ran to my room. I grabbed the bag Sénar told me to pack, I stuffed some money in it that I had stashed away but didn't have time to grab much else.

I heard Ken bellow from the top of the stairway as he called my momma's name for the first time that I could ever remember, "Carmel?" I heard him run down the steps urging me to stay put as I waited to hear Ken's next move. My heart was racing because not only was my momma hurt but I didn't know Ken was home. I held the knife tightly in my hand and grabbed my bag. I put my phone in my pocket and waited until everything was quiet. I did not know much about cell phones, but I used the little icon on my phone that popped up with worded text whenever Tyrell wanted to threaten me when he knew I would not answer. I sent Sénar a message: help me. When it was quiet, I quickly left my room, putting the knife in my back pocket and ran down the steps. I stopped at my momma's side to try to wake her but there was nothing. I couldn't leave her like that, so I grabbed my phone to call for help when I felt Ken's arms around me. I attempted to scream but he grabbed my mouth.

I tried to bite him, and he threatened, "If you bite me, I'll break your damn neck, Treasure! Now, be a good girl and take your clothes off and I won't tell anybody what you did to your momma."

He let me go and I shook my head no, then tried to run out the front door. Ken pulled me back by my hair and threw me on the couch. I took the knife out of my pocket to stab him in his chest and shoulder area. Ken slapped me so hard, I flew back, falling against the floor. I frantically looked for my phone as Ken approached me, I begged, "Ken please don't! I am sorry! I don't want to die!"

He laughed and said, "Well, follow instructions and I might let you live."

I desperately nodded my head in agreement to do as he said. He approached me with blood trickling from his superficial wounds, but they didn't faze him. Ken's excitement caused his veins to bulge throughout all his large muscles. He grabbed me, caressed me, and smelled my hair as he removed my shirt. He kissed and rubbed all over my breast, I didn't stop him, I just cried quietly while he had his way with me. He removed my bra and became excited as my bare breast were there for his amusement. I could feel his excitement growing against my coochie. He carried me to the couch and started to remove my pants.

The front door opened, and I could hear Sénar's voice when he said, "Let her go, dad!"

Ken didn't stop, he waved Sénar off, "Boy, shut the fuck up! If you are not going to join, then bounce!"

We both heard a click, prompting Ken to look back at Sénar to see that he had a gun pointed at him.

Sénar yelled, "Treasure, put your clothes back on and grab your stuff now!"

I squirmed from beneath Ken with tears streaking my face because I was crying and distraught. I picked up my bra and shirt up off the floor to put them back on. I saw that my mom had not moved an inch this whole time. I called her name, "Momma?"

Sénar urged me by yelling, "Get your stuff, Treasure!"

Ken said, "Boy, what the fuck are you doing? Put that shit away! All this for some fucking pussy! I'm the one that takes care of your ass, not her! Are you going to turn your back on me for her?"

Sénar shook his head no, then responded, "No dad, I can't let you hurt her too, man! Let me take her somewhere safe, please dad! I'll come back and help you clean this shit up man, just let me take Treasure!"

Ken roared, "She seen too much and knows too much, Sénar! If you don't take her ass out! I will!"

When Ken moved towards us, Sénar put his finger on the trigger, "No dad! Don't come any closer! Treasure, let's go!"

Ken said, "Nah, let me go, you clean this shit up! If this shit comes back on me, I'll take your ass out too! All this, huh, over her ass? Wow, I would never have given you what you wanted if I knew you would turn your back on me, for her!"

Sénar carefully removed his shirt without ever taking his eyes or gun off of Ken. He threw his shirt at him as Ken removed his now bloody shirt. He used it to wipe himself off and put the clean shirt on that Sénar gave him. He left after glaring at me, hopefully for the last time. Sénar waited until Ken left and watched him drive off before he carefully sat the gun down on the floor next to him as he kneeled down to check my mom's pulse. He listened to see if she was breathing. He called her name, but she didn't answer as Sénar's phone rang.

He answered it saying, "No pops, don't come back! Let me handle this!" Sénar was livid, he hung up the phone and yelled, "Carmel!" He gently tapped her face before he searched her body for signs of injury. My mom was awkwardly positioned, so Sénar hesitated to preform CPR. He just blew air into her lungs without tilting her head back like he did with Cassidy. He was careful not to apply pressure anywhere. Tears formed in Sénar's eyes as he called out, "Carmel, wake up for Treasure, please!"

I started crying too when I pleaded, "God please don't take my Momma! I am sorry! Forgive me, please. If you let her stay, I will forgive her and listen to her from now on, I promise!"

Sénar blew air into her mouth over and over until he felt a pulse. He called her name, "Carmel? Carmel, can you hear us?" She didn't respond or move, Sénar looked at me, "She has a slight pulse, just call the ambulance and tell them your mom fell down the stairs."

Sénar didn't ask what happened, he just gave me instructions and I followed them. I called the ambulance while Sénar cleaned up everything. He ran upstairs for something. When he came back down, he had another shirt on, some paperwork in his hand, and a bag. He kneeled down by my mom, I saw him put something under her nose and she appeared to perk up as her breathing became more visible.

He said, "Carmel, hang in there with us, please?" Sénar took our bags to the car and came back inside as we waited by my mom's side until the ambulance got there. When they got there, they asked us questions, Sénar answered them all and remained calm. I was trying to hold myself together as they asked if I was ok, I nodded my head yeah. They took my mom in the ambulance and we followed behind them. We went in to leave information to contact us with her condition before we left. Sénar drove us toward San Bernardino and I felt numb all over. I couldn't believe what just happened. I couldn't even cry anymore, I felt like I had run out of tears.

Sénar called my name, "Treasure?"

I looked at him with sadness in my heart and answered, "Yes Sénar?"

He said, "Treasure, remember chaos can breed contempt or that same chaos can breed resilience. Choose wisely because resilience breeds brilliance, so please, don't let what you have been through, make you vindictive and bitter ma. Life is full of ups and downs, trials and tribulations, but we need to pray for wisdom and the strength to endure. Trust me Treasure, obedience is better than sacrifice. All that we suffer we should learn from and try to prevent it for ourselves and others. It took me a long time to learn that and we have so much more to learn Treasure. I wish we could learn more together. I have already learned so much from you."

I rolled my eyes at Sénar and said, "I have not taught you anything Sénar."

He laughed before he asked, "Are you kidding me? You have taught me more than you know, ma."

I shook my head in disbelief and then said, "Sénar, no I haven't. You're the teacher, remember?"

He shook his head and looked me in my eyes when he said, "Treasure you have taught me how to love and care for someone despite what they could do for me. You have taught me some self-control, over time," he smirked at me, then continued, "you taught me that women may be a lot of things that my pops says, but that is why it is so important for the man to cover, protect, teach, build, love and respect his woman. Not beat them or force them into, submission. I am truly sorry for what I have done and the role I have played in this chaos. Treasure, I never meant to hurt you, I just let my lust alter my task to protect you. I thought you were mine and I wanted you so bad, I was willing to sacrifice everything to possess you. I may have lost a lot, but I don't want to lose you, Treasure. I pray that you give me a chance to show you how I truly feel about you when we are older and wiser to love one another correctly, but if not, I will respect that too."

I wasn't sure I believed him at this moment, but I asked, "So, what now Sénar? I am scared. Do you think your dad killed Leah and all those guys?"

Sénar's eyes grew dark before he replied, "I am not answering that, Treasure."

I was uncomfortable now but still asked, "Well, what am I going to do Sénar? What about my Momma?"

Sénar looked sad for a moment and softened up a bit before he answered, "I am taking you to Job corp. and we have to check in before 1:00pm. As for Carmel, I don't know ma, it didn't look good. Once you are settled in, you can call her and check on her. Keep your phone, I'll pay your bill forever."

I kept my tears from falling but I still asked, "Sénar why did this happen? Are we bad people?"

Sénar's phone rang as we drove into a town called Muscoy, he continued to drive until he pulled into a parking lot of a campus looking facility. He answered it and asked, "What is it?... I am fine, why?.... What? Well, that's what he gets!... Whatever man, I have to go..... None of your business, like I said I am sure she had good reason."

Sénar hung up as I waited for him to answer my question but first, he said, "That was Sabrina, she said you broke Tyrell's nose."

I giggled before I said, "Well, he threatened me, and I believed him, so I hit him."

I shrugged my shoulders, Sénar shook his head and tried not to laugh. Sénar looked me in my eyes while rubbing my hair before he said, "No Treasure, we are not bad people for the most part, we are just imperfect creatures with a perfect God that we can call on, Treasure that looks beyond our faults and sees our needs. That is why we must pray for a new heart and a new mind to work on ourselves daily Treasure. That is one of the most important things you taught me was to place my problems before him and ask him for guidance. You brought me closer to him and he provided me the will and the strength to change or I would have ended up just like my dad. Speaking of my pops, I have to go face him after having pulled a gun on him. If I live after going back to him, I will be obedient to him until I am an adult, I owe him at least that. And two or four years of college maybe?"

He tried to be funny, but I was not in the mood to laugh at the moment. I was still traumatized and devastated that my whole world had been turned upside down and destroyed. Not knowing whether or not I killed my own mother, guilt plagued me as I drifted into my thoughts. He quickly asked, "Will you pray with me Treasure?" I was skeptical then he asked, "Please Treasure?" I looked at Sénar like he was crazy, prompting him to tell me why. He explained, "Please Treasure, it won't take long. I want to go before him together on one accord."

I stared at him in his eyes and knew that I could trust him and agreed to pray with him. Sénar started to pray, "Dear Heavenly Father, who is in the heavens, hollowed be thy name. Me and Treasure come before you to ask that you forgive us for our sins Lord. Provide us with the strength to live a life that is pleasing to you. We are praying for a miracle Heavenly Father, to move past all that we've been through in a way that will bring you glory. May your will be done, Heavenly Father, amen."

I said amen in agreement and started to cry as I thought about Sénar leaving me at some strange place with people I didn't know. I would probably never see him again. We got out of the car as he popped the trunk to his car open, to get my bag. He walked towards me then kissed me on my forehead, my cheeks, then my lips, he hugged me and squeezed me while smelling my hair. I knew he was fighting the urge to cry as I broke down crying on his shoulder, "Please don't leave, Sénar! I'll give you the keys to my heart. I'll give you everything! I'm sorry!"

Sénar broke down when he said, "Treasure, please don't do this to me ma! I'll be back, I promise. I can't take care of you right now; I have to go back and face everything! To protect you!"

I was angry now when I said, "Sénar, if you leave me, don't come back!"

Sénar pulled me close to him and put his hands behind my head, forcing me to look into his eyes when he said, "Treasure, please don't say that, we prayed for a miracle. If it's meant for us to be, Treasure nothing can stop us, if it's God's will. Please take this opportunity to be resilient and have faith! Please? Everything will work it's self out for his glory, it always does!"

I pushed him off me and walked toward the doors of the facility while he picked my bag up with the papers to follow me. I thought about turning around to run out the doors but where would I go? I walked up to the desk and noticed a young girl about my age or so sitting there with bags waiting to be helped. Sénar's face was red as he brought my bags in and handed the lady at the front desk the paperwork. I started to drift away into my thoughts, I was angry that I chose pleasure at the end but was still left defeated by pain. I almost cried, until I noticed the girl staring at me and Sénar. I wanted to ask her what she was looking at but the last thing I needed was another battle after just arriving at what some would call it a second chance at life. The lady read my paperwork to check me in, Sénar handed me an envelope with my name from the DMV. I opened it to see my driver's license inside.

I smiled as Sénar said, "Congratulations, beautiful."

The young girl smiled at me and Sénar as he hugged me. He didn't seem to want to let me go.

As the lady read the paperwork, she laughed to herself, "What a pair." He kissed me on the lips and said, "I am going to miss you ma, but I will see you again, I promise. Goodbye, Treasure, for now."

I cried as I watched him walk out the doors with the keys to my broken heart and leaving me in pain. The lady at the front desk smiled at me, then said, "Treasure, meet your new roommate, Miracle."

Dedications

First, I want to thank my Heavenly Father for everything that He is and for everything that He has done for me. This is also a special dedication to The Original Gospel Gangstaz, especially my cousin Mr. Solo. May your legacy and testimony of Yahshua HaMashiac AKA The Anointed One live on forever through your music. We will see you again!! All glory goes to our Elohim! A living, merciful Elohim who knows our hearts and our desires. It is a special task to gather those who don't know Him and the ones that are unaware of His love for them. May you rest in heavenly places with heavenly duties until we meet again!

ABOUT AUTHOR

My name is Lakeisha King and I am honored to start a new path in my life as an indie author after over 15 years in the medical field. I am a woman of God, a mother, a wife, a friend and many other wonderful things. I am not perfect by far, but I want to encourage those around the world to grow, heal and to make a difference. I started writing this book over 18 years ago and then life happened. Eventually, I just stopped writing and focused solely on my family and career. My career was doing great, but my book was sitting somewhere marinating and collecting dust. Throughout the years I wrote a couple of chapters here and there but then I would just put them away. In the last year I have had the chance to dust them off and use them as a therapeutic method to find the next chapter in my life. No pun intended. Let's just say, "Resilience Breeds Brilliance"~ Lakeisha King AKA Lala Zee

Sneak Peek

And now a sneak peek into my next book within the series of Sénar Says!

Chapter 1

I was with my cousins Louie and Travis playing in the hot sun. We were just some little badass kids playing outside when we saw my dad pull up with my mom yelling at him. My dad got out of the car like he wanted to strangle her, but she wasn't even aware of it since my dad never laid a hand on her. My dad loved her, and that was the only time I ever saw real love in his eyes for a woman. He was a monster to my older brother Chino's mom, Sophia. He dominated her until she just seemed to die of a broken heart. My sister Cassidy's mom was also very unstable because my dad would go back and forth between the two of our moms. My mom could care less what my dad did; she did whatever she wanted and drove my dad crazy. Cassidy's mom, Cassie, was just a babysitter for when my dad wanted to run after mine. Plus, I was bad as hell, so that made Cassie, even more spiteful toward me because she didn't like my mom. She was a white woman with parents that hated my dad. They hated him so much, that they cut her off and stopped providing financial support to her. She had to do whatever she had to do to pay her rent. My dad paid my mom's rent and took care of her but forced Cassie to work. Whatever it was that she did, I was only four, but I saw how my dad treated them. He would always tell me that the man was the boss and women needed to do their womanly duties to know their place. He also said to always keep their basic needs met, or they will run your ass crazy.

My mom was an exception, he was doing his best to tame her, but she was a wild Trinidad woman. She was chocolate brown with a beautiful smile that would melt any monster's heart. My mom was beyond gorgeous; she would often sing me to sleep and tell me love stories before bed. She was so full of life and would tell me she wanted to travel the world. My mom said she was going to take me with her and run away but she promised me not to tell my dad. I loved my mom so much; I never told my dad a word about what my mom said she would do.

One day, she told him she wanted to go to New York to start her dancing career, and my dad flat out told her no. My mom was so upset, she left for two days, and my dad went crazy looking for her. One day she snuck back and tried to take me from Cassidy's mom's house, but she told my dad. He came to Cassie's house and waited outside. He followed us back to our house, allowing my mom to think she had enough time to get the stuff we needed to run away. He came in and grabbed my mom from behind, smelling her hair while he confessed his love for her. She almost gave in until she saw me watching them, and she began to come toward me. My dad allowed her to grab me and kiss me, but he told her she could only leave alive if I stayed. She didn't want to leave me, so they went to their room and left me there to wonder what would happen. I was so bored without my siblings, that I snuck out to Louie's house. Both my mom and dad looked everywhere for me. My mom figured I was with my aunt and tried to sneak me out of there too, but my dad dragged her and me to his car. He hauled us both upstairs; then, he proceeded to torture my mom until I jumped on his back, trying to stop him from hurting her. There was glass and broken furniture flying everywhere while I watched my mom fight for her life.

I was pleading with my dad to stop hurting her, "Dad, please stop, please! Don't kill her, please!"

He hit me so hard, I blacked out and woke up to a world of pain when I realized my mother was gone! I never got to say goodbye or that I loved her because she just left me. My dad appeared broken and tired when I woke up from my involuntary nap. He scowled at me like he hated me before he forced me to clean up the whole house before Chino and Cassidy came home. I had to pick up displaced clothes and broken glass. The anger in me allowed me to use all the strength in my 4-year-old body to rearrange the furniture. My fifth birthday was only a couple of months away, and my mom would not be here to hug and kiss me. I was devastated, but I didn't dare complain, I did what I was told and waited for further instructions from my dad. Cassidy was so spoiled; she didn't hide the fact that her mom was better for not leaving her like my mom had left me. I didn't want to burst her little bubble because she was just a six-year-old princess. She had no idea what kind of monster we had for a dad because he was very strategic with my other two siblings.

He was especially careful around Sabrina because her mom's family would not tolerate her having a black lover either. Sabrina would only see us when my dad ran off with her mom after she would escape her strict family to see him. Cassie was disappointed when my mom left, and my dad still did not settle down with her. She was so depressed and mean to us. She treated us like slaves and talked so badly about black men that she swore we were all garbage to her friends, purposely in front of us. She hated herself more than she hated my dad, but since she did not have the courage to treat him differently, she took it out on Chino and I. Cassidy was unbothered; she had her own room, and me and Chino had to sleep on the floor in the living room. I would just go to Louie's house to get away from the abuse of Cassidy's mom. My auntie had so many kids, me being there wasn't an issue for her. I would watch myself and help Louie with the younger kids. My dad was always paranoid that my mom would come and try to sneak me away, so he was always cautious about my whereabouts.

On my fifth birthday, Louie fell out of a tree and hurt himself pretty bad. I went to get the stuff to tend to him, leaving in a hurry to get back to Louie. My dad must have seen me rushing to get back to Louie. Paranoid about my mother possibly being at my destination, it caused him to frantically look for me after to see where I was going. When he found me, he saw me bandaging Louie up.

He grabbed me viciously and asked, "Boy, what the hell are you doing touching him like that?"

He was angry and scolded me for touching Louie, in what he called a *feminine way*. When really, I was just fixing a gaping wound on Louie's leg and forehead. After that, he was vigilant about where I was and what I was doing because he never saw me running after little girls like the rest of my cousins. I liked girls, I just only saw them as a problem for my dad, so I never desired to acquire those problems. I, for sure, didn't like boys because I wasn't no faggot, I just never saw anyone that I cared to be bothered with. There was a girl named Daisy who lived in the neighborhood. She was way older than me but she was always trying to pull me into a corner to do stuff with me. Daisy was too aggressive and the stuff she wanted to do, was not something that I as a five-year-old should be thinking about. I was so glad that my dad took me on the road with him, and I was like his ace boon coon after that.

It had been a while after I turned five, and my dad was still feeling bad about my mom, so he took me on a run with him to Rialto. We stopped at the store while the workers unloaded his truck. Once in the store, my dad bought some snacks, and I saw a little girl with her

Momma. She was so beautiful; I wanted to take her with me and play with her at home. I pulled on my dad's shirt, and he looked at me with a confused look because he had everything a kid my age could want in his basket, but none of that was what I wanted. This pretty little chocolate girl was something special. She glanced at me, and I went to grab her immediately, but my dad stopped me.

He asked, "Boy, what are you doing? Sénar, you don't ever ask me for nothing, and the one thing you want is not for sale."

He chuckled at me and told me that I could have anything, but that he could not promise me that I could have her. I started to throw a tantrum; I figured if he could not give me my mom back, the least he could do was give me what I wanted. He watched me throw cereal boxes and act a damn fool in the store. The mom scrutinized my dad before shielding her daughter from the flying boxes of cereal. The little girl giggled as she saw me throw a tantrum. I smiled at her because she had no idea, I was going to find my way back to her. I wanted her in an unnatural way and my dad was stuck in an awkward position, but he didn't sweat. He snatched me up and whispered, "I will see what I can do, boy. Shit, at least I know you like girls."

He laughed and almost approached her mom when we saw a man holding a baby walk up to her. My dad stopped his attempt to talk to the mom but didn't hesitate to ask the man for directions. He started a conversation with the man holding the baby while the lady took and secured her daughter. The guy told him his name was Derrick Lee before they exchanged numbers because they appeared to have a lot in common. We left after the truck was unloaded, and my dad said, "Boy, you are nuts like your Momma! But I am going to get her for you, just wait, you will see."

I believed him enough to be loyal to him, so he would keep his promise to me, but my dad seemed to have forgotten about his promise. All he did was work, and spend his time running the streets, terrorizing women. Cassidy's mom was overwhelmed because

Sabrina's mom turned up missing and Cassie had already kept all four of us for the last four days, by herself. She was exhausted and did not hide it. Cassie just let us do whatever we wanted because she could care less about where we were or what we were doing. I used to get a chair and cook on it, so we could all eat. Cassie whipped my ass one time for burning up one of her pots, but she still ate what I cooked. She then sent us to bed after she unleashed her hatred on to all of us. I heard Cassidy crying and went to her Momma's room to see why Cassidy was crying, so hysterically. I saw blood everywhere, while Cassie was holding on to life by threads. She had slit her wrists and was yelling for us to get out while Cassidy begged her to get up. I told Cassidy to get the phone to call 911, but by the time they got there, Cassie was dead.

Cassidy and I were devastated after watching her mom breathe her last breaths. The police were in the apartment and calling social services when my dad came into the apartment. He went ballistic when they told him they were taking us to the police department to wait for social services. There was a cute Black lady there asking for our names and writing down information. Once she saw my dad, she was much nicer than she was before he came in. He noticed and pulled her to the side to speak with her. When the officer asked the lady where we were going, she cleared her throat and answered, "This is their father, he has custody, so there is no need for placement."

My dad smiled as he eyed her to show his appreciation before he summoned us all to take us home. After my brother and sisters went to bed, he told me that he would find someone to help him and not to worry. From then on, we had several women come in and out of our house over the years. I swear the more women he had, the more problems we had. Some were even drug addicts or strippers. They were rude to us and never cared about us, they were only there for one thing, and that was my dad.

The lady named Rose that kept social services from taking us from my dad, started to come by as well. Although, it was years later, she found herself living with us as she went through a hard patch to go to school and raise her daughter Daisy at the same time. They made a pact to help one another, and things seemed cool at first, but it wasn't long before the chaos started to breed when my dad was back to his old ways. My dad's promise to me when I was five, and my siblings was what kept me going. When I felt like I was alone, I would go to my cousin Louie's house and listen to my auntie tell me about God and how good he was. I had no choice but to believe her because she was a single woman with nine kids, and they didn't need for nothing. As a matter of fact, there was no chaos over there, just bomb ass food and a lot of love. I loved them all; they were my home away from home and like my second family. I would always talk to my favorite cousin Louie about the little girl I saw in the store that day and promised him that he would meet her someday. He would laugh at me and tell me I was crazy, but he still believed me. I needed someone to believe me because I was certain. It had been almost four years since I saw her in the store, and it felt like yesterday.

***

It was my ninth birthday when Rose and her daughter moved in officially. Rose had been dealing with my dad on and off for years. My dad was just dealing with her because she would ensure him that he kept us in his custody. She insisted that her daughter could help babysit since she was like seventeen now. My dad was a sick man and had his own intentions in-store, but Rose had hers too. She knew my dad was a hard worker, and she could not stand her own sister, so she would do anything to not live with her. She worked a lot, which gave my dad time to run the streets and leave us at home with Daisy. I hated it because Daisy would bring older guys to our house, and my sisters would be all up in their faces. I would leave because she was so promiscuous, that it made me hate women even more. All the women my dad dealt with were selfish, mean, sex addicts that only seemed to care about what my dad could do for them. He would brag how he could make women cum who never had an orgasm in their lives. He was like a human drug to them and vowed to teach me the real way to pleasure women. One day my dad had a stripper over; he was drunk and high on something. He came into the room to acknowledge us all and called my name, "Sénar, come here. Chino, you too!"

Chino seemed scared, so I said, "I got it pops. What do you need? Chino can keep an eye on Cassidy and Sabrina."

When he led me into his room, the stripper girl was naked. She also appeared to be drunk and high. She said, "Awe, he so cute! Come here, little boy, I will make you a man tonight!"

Although, I knew it was wrong, I didn't want my brother to have to deal with the shenanigans that my dad was about to pull. He said, "Let's play a game of Ken says." He told her to open her mouth, and my dad proceeded to say, "Ken says, suck it until the veins pop."

She proceeded to suck his dick until he came all over her face, I was in a trance when my dad said, "Ken says, Sénar let her do it to you."

I wanted to run out and scream no, but my dad would probably kill me or accuse me of being gay. So, I pretended to be excited as she cleaned herself up to perform the same thing on me. Yeah, I was nine years old when I got head for the first time. It was a mixture of pleasure and pain because I was just there, so nobody else had to be. I knew it was wrong, but my dad was there, so it could not be that bad. She was blowing my mind, literally. It felt so good, I thought I was going to pass out when I came all over her. My dad laughed so loud, that me and her couldn't help but blush before we joined him in laughter. After that, it was all downhill. I would cook and clean when Rose worked while Daisy ran the streets. My dad would take me with him on runs and some of his quick trips to drop his loads. He was crazy, everyone knew not to fuck with him, and the women knew he was good in bed. He often picked up young girls and let them dance or do other sexual things to put money in their pockets. I just went for the ride and sometimes participated willingly, if the girl was super fine, but I just was there to clean up after him when shit didn't go as planned. One day on the road, we rolled back to Rialto, where my dad found a girl who was young and just sitting there. He asked her if she wanted some company and sent her in the truck with me while he went into the bar. The girl was like fifteen, and she was cute. She was a caramel girl with dimples, and she seemed like a sweet girl. She stared at me, and her eyes grew big when she asked, "Sheesh, you are young, what are you doing picking up girls at a truck stop?"

I laughed before I answered, "I am not picking up girls, I am waiting on my pops. What are you doing out here at your age, waiting to get picked up?"

She appeared sad for a moment before she answered, "I was in a foster home, and my foster dad was molesting me. So, I told on him, and they said since I was a teenager, it would be hard to find placement for me. They wanted to put me in a group home, so I ran away. Maybe, I will find someone to take care of me."

I felt so bad for her because even though, my life was crazy, I could not imagine, not having anywhere to go. We had hella snacks and food, so I asked, "Are you hungry?"

She giggled and then asked, "How did you know?"

I smiled at her then replied, "Because women love food!"

She laughed and then turned into a little kid for a second, when she got excited at all the snacks I pulled out. She grabbed what she wanted and eagerly opened a bag of chips. I asked her what her plans were, and she asked, "How old are you?"

I wanted to lie, but I just puffed my chest out before I replied, "I am nine."

Shocked, with her mouth gaping, "What, really? You are way beyond your age."

She started to feel bad, "Well, where's your dad?" She seemed irritated because her reality started to creep into the picture when she said, "Well, this is too good to be true, so I have to prepare myself."

I just stared at her in a confused state. When she noticed, she asked, "What?"

I asked, "What are you talking about?"

My dad came in with a grin on his face when he saw that me and her were talking, but his smile quickly faded when he saw we were just eating. My dad glared at her and then asked, "So, did you have fun and a nice dinner?"

She shook her head yeah, he then said, "Good well, you ready to work?"

She nodded her head, yeah. He took his shirt off, and her eyes grew big before he snatched her up and laid her down. He literally did everything he could do to that little girl, she seemed to enjoy some of it, but I could tell she was wore out. When my dad asked if I wanted some, I replied, "I already got mine pops." I lied, but I knew she was already overwhelmed.

She looked embarrassed but let me know with her eyes that she was thankful for my pass while she gathered her things to leave. Before she left, I told her, "I hope we never see you again. I hope you find someone to protect you and take care of you."

She smiled at me before she said, "Thanks, kiddo." I went to the passenger seat, and my dad asked, "What did y'all do?"

To avoid his question, I just asked, "Pops, why do girls do that?"

He laughed and asked, "Do what?"

I clarified, "Why do they sell their bodies?"

He chuckled before he answered, "Because pussy makes the world go 'round boy. If a woman don't have nothin', she got a pussy and a mouth that someone could use, so they do what they have to do with it. I like pussy and head, so I get mine when I don't want the strings attached. I just don't like to pay for it though because they get off too." He grinned at me before he started to laugh again. He then continued, "The ones I want wrapped around my finger, I strap 'em down and make them cum until they can't take it no more. Then I break 'em down because women will drag your ass to hell and back if you let them. Just get yours and don't fall for their traps. Boy, pussy comes and goes."

I nodded my head in agreement with him before I thought about my mom, I wondered; *what she was doing and if she even thought of me. Was she looking for some man to take care of her? Was she also selling her body to get by? If she was, I would never love another woman again; they were probably really just vindictive bags of flesh.* My dad said, "Well, at least women have something to offer. Niggas ain't shit and they ain't giving up shit, so be careful who you fuck with. Most niggas will listen to your game plan and try to beat you to it, so don't be trusting nobody like that."

My dad schooled me all the time; I was his right-hand man. When he was acting crazy, we knew to avoid him. I would kick it with Louie or read my bible; some of the stories would make me think about life. My auntie would always tell me what scriptures to read when I had questions. I didn't ask my dad about God because he made it very clear, he answered to no one. He hated weakness and when he saw me in an emotional state, he would beat me until I flashed enough to fend for my life. He would literally beat me until I tried to hurt him and then calm me down by putting me in a chokehold. I loved my pops, but he was a cold man. He needed to dominate everything, and anything he could not dominate was a threat. I studied my dad and watched his techniques. I eventually picked up on some of his ways, but I did not like to hurt women, but I did like to make them cum.

My dad saw that I liked to fuck, and he would give me pointers, but then one day, he said, "When you really want to make a woman sprung, you have to know how to eat pussy." He snickered when I turned my nose up at him; he said, "Boy, that shit is where it's at. Women love that shit and food." He laughed, but he was serious. He tapped my shoulder before he said, "I have good news.... remember that little girl at the store?"

My eyes lit up with anticipation when I answered, "Yeah, pops, I sure do, why?"

He grinned again before he bragged, "Well, her mom and I are going out tomorrow. I will be good for her, so I can get us in there."

I smiled at my dad's smoothness. I was so excited; nothing could mess that up for me. My dad would go see the little girl's mom regularly after a while and then talk to her on the phone at night. He would tell me about her daughter, and I would dream about her every night. He told me her name was Treasure, and I instantly fell head over hills for her again. She was already special, but my mom always told me a woman was a man's treasure. I could not wait to see her again. I would sweep her off her feet and love her until she was mine forever. My dad laughed at me when he saw me in my feelings over her and said, "Boy, you get what you want from her and move on. Don't waste precious time trying to win her heart, break her down, and move on. Trust me; you will be better off."

My dad was crazy; I wanted her all for myself; I didn't want to share her. She was mine. I wanted to have her and keep her for a lifetime. While trying to gain the trust of the little girl's mom, Carmel, Rose was starting to get upset. My dad being gone more caused Rose to want to work more to avoid being home with us. When Daisy and my dad started to clash because of all her male company, Rose started to be even more mean to us. She was always yelling and throwing stuff; the only time she was not tripping is when she was getting fucked. My dad couldn't stand Rose's ass, but Daisy started to be really fond of him, and eventually, he started messing with her. He would summon me to eat her out until she came.

He would say, "Let's play Ken says......" making me go down on Daisy while she was strapped down until she came, no matter how long it took. I hated it because she was already aggressive with me, but now, she made me her sex slave. She would force me to do stuff when my dad wasn't around and bribe me. When Rose found out about my dad and Daisy, she didn't say anything; she got back by forcing me to do stuff to her. It was worse than Daisy because she would get off work and not even shower before forcing me to do stuff with her. I was disgusted, washing my hands and face repeatedly to rid of the smell. I swear her stench would be in my nostrils and all over my hands. I hated it; she would force me to do it or threaten me. I wanted to tell, but I knew my dad would blame me for being weak or even kill her as a result. Eventually, she and my dad reached their limits when they almost killed each other. Rose disappeared, and Daisy went to live with her auntie. Daisy didn't have the same authority over me, but she was older and made sure I still met her needs. I never turned her down in fear she would tell on my dad or make herself out to be a victim. Besides, me and Daisy were cool, and girls my age were not ready for what I needed. Me and her had grown people sex, and when we were done, I was a professional at cleaning up after myself. I just didn't go down on her anymore, she would get mad, but I would make it up to her in other ways. I did a lot of shit to her and even partook with my dad sometimes, even after Rose left. She kept me from unleashing my wrath on girls my age. I didn't want to ruin anybody, but I knew what I wanted, and that was Treasure.

Coming soon!!